Charleston was their legacy—
a world of gracious traditions
and shocking secrets,
of careless passion and
painstaking revenge . . .

MARGARET GARDEN TRADD. Not yet sixteen, exquisite child of aging Southern aristocracy, she married the man who could open the door to her dreams— or shut her out of Charleston society forever.

STUART TRADD. He was a scion of Charleston's most revered family, a man without honor. For the sake of one girl, he murdered; for another, he married.

ANSON TRADD. While Stuart caroused, he tried to rebuild the family fortune, all to hide his love for Margaret, his brother's beautiful wife.

GARDEN TRADD. Born in secret shame, raised in the old slave quarters, she would learn to waltz to the genteel rhythms of the Old South even as her true heart beat to the wild dance they would call the "Charleston."

SCHUYLER ("SKY") HARRIS. Unbelievably wealthy, a restless young man of the world, he was reckless—first in his desire for Garden, then for adventure, excitement, escape.

PRINCIPESSA MONTECATINI. Everyone knew she was fabulously rich, but few knew her terrible secret—or just how far she'd go to have her revenge.

ELIZABETH TRADD COOPER. A fierce matriarch, wealthy and independent, she could be a devastating enemy or a powerful friend.

ON LEAVING CHARLESTON

By Alexandra Ripley

SCARLETT: THE SEQUEL TO MARGARET
MITCHELL'S GONE WITH THE WIND*
ON LEAVING CHARLESTON*
CHARLESTON*
WHO'S THAT LADY IN THE PRESIDENT'S BED?
THE TIME RETURNS
NEW ORLEANS LEGACY*

***Published by
WARNER BOOKS**

On Leaving Charleston

ALEXANDRA RIPLEY

WARNER BOOKS

A Time Warner Company

Grateful acknowledgment is made to the following for permission to reprint their copyrighted material:

Lyrics excerpted from "AIN'T WE GOT FUN" by Ray Egan, Gus Kahn and Rich Whiting. Copyright © 1921 (renewed) Warner Bros. Inc. and Gilbert Keyes Music Co. All rights reserved. Used by permission.

WARNER BOOKS EDITION

This Warner Books Edition is published by arrangement with Doubleday, a division of Bantam Doubleday Dell Inc., 666 Fifth Avenue, New York, N.Y. 10103

Cover design by Gregg Gulbronson

Warner Books, Inc.
1271 Avenue of the Americas
New York, N.Y. 10020

W A Time Warner Company

Printed in the United States of America

First Warner Books Printing: September, 1991

10 9 8 7 6 5 4 3

To my best friend,
Patience,
with love

BOOK 1

1900–1902

1

The Reverend Mr. William Barrington's fingers trembled as he adjusted the fresh reversed collar that was an emblem of his calling. Inside his new dark suit he was still Billy Barrington, twenty-two years old, and he was terrified.

"It's only a wedding," he said aloud, but the sound of his voice only made him feel worse. It was quavering. For the hundredth time he wished that his mother had not made him shave off the chin whiskers he had grown at the seminary. For the first time he wished that the bishop hadn't given him his own parish instead of starting his career as assistant to an older minister. It had seemed so wonderful the week before, after his ordination. And his parents had been so proud.

But now here he was, alone in a hired rig, talking to a broken-down horse, afraid to drive on to the house where he was to perform the ceremony. "Dearly beloved . . ." He tried his voice again. A mockingbird answered derisively from the woods that lined the dirt road, and the horse lifted its head. Billy laughed and slapped the reins to start moving again. His moment of terror had passed. The breathtaking beauty of a fresh spring morning was all around him; the woods were starred with dogwood blossoms and fragrant with jessamine. It was the birth of a new season, the first year of a new century, and he was about to consecrate a man and a woman in the beginning of a new life together. What could possibly go wrong, with everything in the world so right?

Billy turned off the road between ivy-covered brick pillars that marked the entrance to Ashley Barony, and his heartbeat quickened. He had been born and raised in the South Carolina red-clay highlands. All his life he had heard about the great plantations of the low country, and now he was entering one. He felt as if he were riding into history, into the glorious Old South that his grandfather had spoken of as a Golden Age.

The carriage drive was badly rutted, its edges long since lost in wild grass that had narrowed it to the minimum space required for a horse and buggy. On both sides the fields were being reclaimed by woods. After a half mile the drive made a slow curve, and Billy saw a group of weather-beaten cabins, their sagging porches bright with flowers growing in cracked china bowls and pitchers. There was no visible human life. He felt a stab of disappointment. You could see the same Negro cabins upcountry.

But then the drive curved again to reveal the Barony. Billy unconsciously pulled on the reins and stopped, spellbound by the scene. Majestic live oaks, their ancient branches hung with Spanish moss, framed an expanse of lawn. On it five sheep grazed, their lambs playing around them. Dozens of peacocks strutted arrogantly, ignoring the antics of the lambs and the placid bulk of the ewes. Overlooking them all, the great house stood, rising from arcs of wide white marble steps, its brick walls softened by time to a warm rose, its soaring columns magnificent despite their flaking paint. Billy breathed softly, enchanted by the past.

The feeling of enchantment deepened when he mounted the steps and entered the house. It was completely silent. The hallway stretched ahead of him to a doorway and a vista of lawn that were the same as the way he had come. Along the shadowy walls, console tables held massed arrangements of white flowers that were hazily reflected in mirrors smoked with age. A heavy sweet scent filled the motionless air. There was an unreality to the duplicated images, the stillness, the quiet. Billy drew in his breath and held it.

"I know. It's awful, isn't it?" The voice came from behind him. Billy started and spun to face the speaker.

"I'm sorry. I didn't mean to scare you. I'm Anson Tradd." The boy held out his hand. "How do you do?"

Billy swallowed. "How do you do," he responded. "I'm William Barrington. The minister." They shook hands.

Anson Tradd smiled, a flash of brightness in the dim hallway. "Let's get away from this smell," he said. "Are you allowed to drink before the wedding or only after? I thought I'd jump the gun; that's why I was so quiet. I didn't want Papa to catch me at the decanter. Come along." He led the way into an enormous dining room. In the center, a long table was covered with a white cloth; on

10

it was a tiered white cake surrounded by white flowers. The curtains were closed, and the ghostly table was the only discernible object in the room.

Anson moved unerringly to a deep shadow that was a sideboard, and Billy heard the chink of glass against glass. Then Anson led the way to the door at the far end of the hallway and the sunlight beyond. "Here's to weddings," he said, placing a glass in Billy's hand.

Billy squinted in the bright light. The boy, he saw, was really a young man, close to his own age. He had been fooled by Anson's short, slight form. Now he looked at the strong jaw, outlined by red-gold muttonchop sideburns, and the metallic dark blue eyes, and he felt like a boy himself in comparison. He lifted his glass to answer the toast. Although he was not used to drinking, he was grateful for the whiskey.

He was also thankful that Anson seemed to have appointed himself his guide. In the next few minutes, without having to ask any questions, Billy learned from his companion's commentary that Anson was the youngest brother of the groom, whose name was Stuart. That there was a middle brother named Koger. That their father liked to be called "Judge" although he had retired from his court years before, when he inherited Ashley Barony. He also discovered that the flowers that offended Anson were gardenias, and that the house was decorated with them in honor of the bride, Margaret Garden. "Some cousin or grandfather or something of hers was the Dr. Garden who brought the first ones back from a trip to South America or someplace, and the smelly thing was named after him. It's so sweet it makes me sick." Billy wanted to say that he liked gardenias, but he decided not to. The bishop had impressed upon him that his parishioners would include descendants of South Carolina's oldest, most prominent families, and that a young clergyman should be tactful. "You have a beautiful view here," he said instead. On this side of the house the lawn was untenanted except for four long tables. It stretched like a green carpet to the banks of a wide brown-green river, the Ashley. On each side of the lawn, tall banks of azaleas were vivid pink and scarlet.

"We were lucky," Anson said. "Sherman's army burned every other plantation house on the Ashley, but my Great-aunt Julia scared 'em off the Barony. Papa says she could have scared Abe Lincoln himself. I hardly remember her, but I can believe it. Anyhow, the Barony still stands. Yankees didn't get it, nor the earthquake neither. The Gardens have the next plantation up the river, and they live in a wing that didn't burn. It's all that's left, and it's pretty ramshackle. That's why the wedding's here instead.''

Billy felt a warm, romantic glow. ''Then your brother and Miss Garden have always been sweethearts.''

Anson's eyes became opaque. ''Not exactly,'' he said. ''We all grew up together, but Margaret's a lot younger than Stuart. He thought she was a pest.'' He shrugged. ''Lord! I'm talking myself dry. How about another shooter?''

'' 'Shooter'?''

''Shot. Bracer. A drop of whiskey.'' Anson was abrupt.

''Oh. No, I don't think so; thanks just the same.''

''You'll excuse me if I go get one? The family will be coming downstairs in a minute.'' Anson darted into the house.

When the family came out onto the veranda, there was no mistaking the kinship of the Tradds. The Judge and his sons all wore their brilliant badge of copper hair. Stuart Tradd was the tallest, a head taller than his father and Anson, several inches taller than Koger. He was clean-shaven, with a deep cleft in his chin. Koger sported a thick mustache, and the Judge still wore the full beard customary in years past. The two ladies with them were paled by the Tradds' colorfulness. Anson introduced Billy to his mother and the bride's mother, then to his father and brothers. There was a flurry of attention and welcome, so intense and rapid that Billy was confused. Then Henrietta Tradd took his arm.

''If you'll be so kind as to come with me, Mr. Barrington, I'd like to be sure the arrangements we've made are all right.'' She took him to the drawing room on the floor above.

Billy had time only for a blurred impression of light streaming through tall windows, of faded brocades and damasks, of haughty faces in gilt-framed portraits while Henrietta Tradd hurried him through the long, high-ceilinged room to the improvised altar at the end. It was a table covered with an exquisitely embroidered cloth. Before it, two petit point-covered prie dieux awaited the bride and groom. ''How lovely,'' Billy said. He felt a second's panic. Everything was so delicate that he was sure he would break something. He looked at the small lady on his arm and found reassurance in the fine lines that bracketed her mouth and the frosting of gray in her hair.

She reminded him of his mother. "I like the flowers very much," he said. Like the hall below, the room was full of gardenias.

Henrietta Tradd smiled. "Thank you," she said. "They're in honor of the bride's family."

"Yes, ma'am, I know. Anson told me all about the name and all. We've been having a nice talk."

Henrietta's eyebrows rose. "Anson? Usually he's quiet as a tomb. You must bring out the best in him, Mr. Barrington. I'm very glad you're here."

Billy felt his cheeks redden and wished again for his whiskers. It was maddening for a grown man to blush. After all, Mistress Tradd was just being polite; it wasn't as if she had meant a personal compliment. He could not think what to say. He was rescued by the hurried entrance of the first guest.

"Henrietta, please forgive my tardiness." Even before Billy was introduced, he recognized her as a Tradd by her hair.

"Elizabeth, this is Mr. Barrington, our new minister at St. Andrews . . . my husband's sister, Mistress Cooper." Billy bowed over the hand offered him.

Elizabeth smiled warmly. "How wonderful that St. Andrews is being reopened," she said, "and how fortunate to have an impressive young rector like you, Mr. Barrington." She encouraged Billy to talk about his plans for restoring and revitalizing the parish, then her bright blue Tradd eyes returned to her sister-in-law. Billy felt dismissed. He stepped back while the ladies talked. Elizabeth Cooper was tall and thin and energetic. Like the men in her family, she eclipsed Henrietta Tradd, and Billy felt an irrational, protective resentment.

"I told the servants to get the Victrola out of the buggy and bring it up," said Elizabeth. "The only recording I could find was the Mendelssohn wedding march. I hope that's all right."

"Is it an organ playing?"

"Organ and orchestra. I guess we can set it behind some ferns to muffle it a little."

Henrietta smiled. "It will be fine," she said. She blinked wetness from her eyes. "Thank you, Elizabeth." Her sister-in-law touched her shoulder briefly. Henrietta turned to Billy. "We're all here, Mr. Barrington. If it's all right with you, we can start in about ten minutes."

*   *   *

13

While Billy was donning his vestments, he puzzled about the oddities of the wedding. The bishop had told him it would be small, just family. But Billy was a Southerner. He knew that families included relatives to the degree of third-cousin-twice-removed. And the room for the ceremony could easily hold two hundred people. It was all very strange. But then, everything had been somehow unreal, ever since he had turned through the Barony's entrance. The deserted cabins, the eerie quiet of the house, the fantastic faded grandeur and beauty of the Barony. Maybe these lowcountry aristocrats really were crazy from their centuries of inbreeding, as the people of the up-country liked to claim. Certainly they were a breed apart. They were warm and welcoming enough—everyone had been very nice to him. But there was a remoteness about them, a distance, an aura of private knowledge and experience that no outsider could share. Whenever they said one thing, he had the feeling that they meant something else, that they were speaking in a code they all understood but could not or would not translate for him. He was offended but attracted, tantalized as by the otherworld music of Sirens.

When the wedding ceremony began, Anson Tradd tended the Victrola behind its baffle of ferns, music filled the empty hollows of the room, and a double file of holiday-dressed blacks moved into the area near the door. There were about forty of them, of all ages. One impossibly old man in a black frock coat looked haughtily at Billy, and he knew that this must be the pastor of the Barony's blacks. These guests were much more festive than the whites; they were enjoying the holiday that the wedding provided.

When the last giggling black child was subdued, the bride entered on her father's arm. Billy Barrington stared. Margaret Garden was beautiful beyond comprehension, beyond reality. Her skin was as white and creamy as the gardenias she carried, and the delicate bones of her small, oval face looked as fragil as their petals. She wore no veil; as she approached the altar, she passed through the thick rectangles of sunlight opposite the windows, and her silver-blond hair became an aureole of brilliance. She was like a fairy princess, a creature of gossamer dreams.

The recording ended before she was halfway down the long room, and Billy looked automatically at Anson Tradd. There should be music, magnificent music for such a bride. What he saw made him ashamed to witness it: Anson was staring at his brother's bride through eyes blazing with pain and consuming love.

The trumpets sounded again as the wedding march resumed. Billy Barrington felt his mouth go dry. The bride was near him now, and he saw that she was barely more than a child, not yet sixteen, and that she was crying. Her hands were trembling; the bouquet she was holding almost fell. Billy noticed with horror that the massed blooms were beginning to brown at the edges and that they were hiding the unmistakable swollen mound of pregnancy in Margaret Garden's young body.

When the ceremony was over the young couple was surrounded, kissed, congratulated by their families as if there were nothing unusual at all in the occasion. Billy came in for his share of handshakes and compliments too, and he forgot his earlier feelings of being excluded. He was part of the conspiracy to acknowledge nothing. Now that he understood the tensions underlying the day, he had nothing but admiration for the clannish self-containment of the Tradds and the Gardens.

"We'll go add my new daughter to the family Bible," the Judge announced, "and then I've got a toast all ready. But if we dawdle, I'll forget it." He offered Margaret his arm, and they moved downstairs to the library. The servants had already gone out to the lawn and were covering the tables there with food for their feast. A fiddler struck up a jaunty tune, and the children began to dance.

Margaret Garden Tradd's smooth cheeks were becoming flushed. There was no trace of tears. She touched her name in the Bible with a tremulous finger and looked at Stuart. Then she smiled for the first time.

A champagne cork popped. Koger poured wine into waiting glasses and passed them around. "Let's hear your toast, Papa," he said, winking at Anson who stood next to him. Billy Barrington stepped closer to the brothers in a clumsy attempt to support Anson. The boy, usually silent, had needed someone to talk to earlier. Perhaps he needed him now.

Judge Tradd lifted his glass. Everyone looked toward him, but he was looking beyond them. "What's the matter with you, Joe?" he said. As heads turned to the doorway behind them, a stocky middle-aged man with an apoplectic red face strode into the room.

"I want to talk to you, Tradd, and to your boy Stuart. Where we can be private. Now."

Elizabeth Cooper put her hand on the man's arm. "Joe—"

He brushed her hand away. "This has nothing to do with you, Lizzie. Keep out of it."

The Judge was scowling. "Listen, Simmons, this is a family celebration. You can't bust in, be rude to my sister and make demands in my house. Whatever you want, it'll have to wait."

"It can't wait." Joe Simmons's voice was an enraged bellow.

The Judge answered him in kind. "It'll damn well have to."

Simmons stepped close to the Judge and grabbed his lapel. "I offered to keep this private between us, Tradd, but if you want it in the open, you can have it that way. Your son is a damned scoundrel. He's gotten my Victoria in trouble and I came to take him back with me to make things right."

Koger whistled softly. "That Stuart," he murmured, "just can't keep his britches buttoned. What do you suppose he's got that we don't, brother?"

Anson hit him in the mouth, then the nose, the eye, the mouth again. Henrietta screamed. The room became a turmoil of people moving, speaking, shouting. Loudest of all was Judge Tradd. He pushed Joe Simmons away with one hand, made a fist of the other and shook it at his sons, bellowing as he did so.

"You boys stop that brawling, goddammit." He returned his attention to the angry man at his side. "And you, Simmons, get out of my house. My son has just been married to this young lady. Even if he wasn't married, he wouldn't give his name to white trash like a daughter of yours."

Joe Simmons let out a bestial howl, so savage that it shocked everyone into immobility. Then, his neck corded from superhuman strain, he lifted the Judge above his head and threw him to the floor. "I'll kill you," he gasped. "Get up." He raised the Judge's body by his shirtfront; the head rolled crazily to one side. The neck was broken. He was dead.

Joe Simmons stepped back and stared without belief at his victim. His big hands opened and closed, helpless to hurt or heal. The air in the room shimmered, soundless, as if everyone had stopped breathing.

Then there was an explosive roar; Simmons seemed to leap into the air before he fell across the Judge's chest. His back was a bloody crater. Margaret Garden Tradd whispered "Stuart" and fainted. Her

16

new husband was standing beside her, a smoking shotgun in his hands. The skirt of her wedding gown was splotched with blood.

"God in heaven," cried Billy Barrington.

The paralysis that had gripped the wedding party was released. Henrietta Tradd fell to her knees and tried to push Simmons's body off her husband. Koger and Anson pulled her away. Mr. and Mrs. Garden knelt by their daughter, calling her name. Elizabeth Cooper strode to Stuart and took the gun away from him. Then she slapped his face so hard that he staggered.

"You murdering swine," she hissed, "you unprincipled, rutting animal. You've killed two men and shamed two women. If it weren't for your mother, I'd turn this gun on you. . . . As it is, I'll clean up your mess. I'll go to Victoria now and arrange for her to go to her cousins in New York." She turned to Billy Barrington.

"Please accept my apologies on behalf of my whole family, Mr. Barrington. I'm sorry you got involved in this. What happened here today was a tragic accident, do you understand?"

Billy tried to say that he did, but Elizabeth was still talking, so he said nothing.

"Mr. Simmons is an old friend of mine and served as my escort for my nephew's wedding," she said. "After the ceremony, the men went hunting. My brother fell from his horse, and Mr. Simmons, in hurrying to help him, dropped his gun. It discharged and killed him. That is what happened. Do you understand?"

Billy shook his head. "I can't say that, Mistress Cooper. There'll be an investigation, and I can't lie to the authorities."

Elizabeth's taut mouth softened. "Dear Mr. Barrington," she said gently. "This is a matter that concerns the Tradds, and the authorities are in Charleston. There will be no investigation. We Charlestonians have our own rules for ourselves. Just remember what I told you. A tragic accident.

"Now, please help Henrietta if you can. She loved my brother very deeply, and she'll need God's comfort in her grief.

"Koger. Anson. Come here. Mr. Barrington will take care of your mother. I want you to hear what you have to say and do."

The following day, Billy Barrington performed the funeral service at Ashley Barony for Judge Stuart Tradd. There were almost three hundred mourners.

Joseph Simmons was buried in the small town of Simmonsville, which he had built and given his name. His funeral was attended by all the workers at the cotton mill there. He was mourned by his daughter Victoria and Elizabeth Tradd Cooper.

In Charleston, the gossip and speculation died down in a few weeks, but the events of that sparkling spring day at Ashley Barony left a legacy of vengeance that would haunt generations yet unborn.

2

Billy Barrington peered at his watch. It was less than a minute later than when he had last looked at it. He snapped the case closed and replaced the watch in its pocket. "There's nothing to worry about," he said aloud. "People are often late."

But he worried nonetheless. The early morning mist had not burned off the way it usually did. It still masked the treetops; wisps clung to the earth and it was impossible to see familiar landmarks. Accidents could happen.

Billy pulled out a handkerchief and wiped his brow. Although the sun was obscured, the July heat was oppressive. He used the handkerchief to polish a nonexistent smudge off the gleaming surface of the baptismal font. He wanted everything to be perfect for the christening of Stuart and Margaret's baby boy.

He thought he heard something, cocked his head to listen. Yes, there it was. The sound of voices. The Tradds were coming. Billy exhaled a long, relieved breath. Hurrying, he lit the candles on the altar, turned and surveyed the small church. Masses of daisies caught the glow of candlelight in their yellow centers, their white petals gleaming. Tall vases of yellow roses stood near the font, perfuming the air. Four elongated cranes, carved from satiny mahogany, stretched their graceful necks to form the cradle for the bowl of baptismal water. Their elegant heads seemed to be moving in the flickering candlelight, as if they were eager for the ceremony to begin.

The sounds were louder now. Billy ran from the church, donning his white vestments. They billowed around him as he blended into the white mist.

The Tradds were coming from the Barony by water, the way the Barony's people had come to the little church for two hundred years. Billy waited on the landing at the creek leading from the river alongside the high ground where St. Andrews stood.

The mist was even thicker on the river. Billy could see nothing. He heard Negro voices singing and the rustle of the water grasses as the tide moved them. Then the barge appeared, as if by magic, materializing from the mist. Its bow was decorated with a wreath of magnolia leaves and blossoms; ropes of plaited ivy garlanded the sides, swagged between bouquets of daisies tied with white silk ribbons. All the passengers were dressed in white; the sunlight, trying to pierce the mist, transformed them into patches of radiance. Billy stood transfixed, enchanted by the sight.

The thud of the barge against the landing brought him back to reality. He held out a hand to Henrietta Tradd to help her step up from the boat. The leg-o'-mutton sleeves of her starched linen shirt-waist fluttered like wings. A wide-meshed white net veil billowed from the brim of her white straw boater hat to a ribbon under her chin. Billy had become accustomed to seeing her in the floor-length black crepe veil of the widow. The change from unrelieved heavy black garments to the sparkling clarity of white linen was like an affirmation of life. "May I say, Mistress Tradd," he stammered, "that you look ex-ex-extremely handsome."

Henrietta smiled. "Thank you, Mr. Barrington, you may indeed. I often think, you know, that the Negroes understand more about life than we do. They always wear white for mourning. I think it would be too sad to surround an innocent baby with darkness, so today we are following the servants' lead." She turned toward the church. "How lovely," she sighed, "the light through the mist. I've always been glad that the builders avoided stained glass."

When everyone was disembarked, they formed an informal procession, Billy leading the way, followed by the Tradds and the Gardens with the baby in the center. The infant was carried by a huge, muscular black woman wearing a towering hat of white silk flowers and feathers. She held her strong arms out at the height of her imposing bust, cradling an enormous lace-covered pillow. On it, the baby slept, his tiny face barely visible inside an embroidered cap. His body was lost in the soft folds of the silk and lace christening gown that Tradd babies had worn for eight generations.

Koger and Anson stood as godfathers for their nephew. When Billy called for the name, Koger's voice rang through the building: "Stuart Ashley Tradd," Anson mumbled unintelligibly.

Baby Stuart woke and cried when the water touched his downy head. Margaret looked as if she were about to cry, too. She started to speak, to apologize or disclaim responsibility, but Henrietta put a hand on her arm to quiet her. "Don't worry, dear," she said calmly. "Babies always cry. It proves they're paying attention."

The ceremony lasted only a few minutes, but it was long enough for the sun to conquer the late-hanging mists. When the little group moved outside, everything was sparkling. The droplets caught in the grass and the leaves of the trees and bushes were glittering, and the dewy Spanish moss looked like cascades of diamonds.

"Oh my," Margaret said, "isn't it lovely?" She pulled her hat from her head, its pins disarranging her piled-up hair, and whirled around, dancing with excitement. Light glinted from her silver-gilt head, shone on her smooth, fresh skin. She glowed with youth and beauty and happiness.

Billy stared at her, conscious of Anson's too-still presence behind him. Then the black woman held up a massive hand. "Stop that foolishness, Miss Margaret. You get yourself all worked up, you going to be sick."

Margaret danced over to her. "Don't spoil my day, Zanzie. You're as grim as a rain cloud in the sunshine. Look how beautiful everything is. And how happy I am. I'm wearing a real frock, not that awful black, and I have a waistline again."

"You ain't but hardly finish with childbirthing. You should be in bed, not prancing around same like a trick pony."

"Pooh on your grumbling, Zanzie. Come meet Mr. Barrington. You love preachers." She pulled on the woman's big arm.

"This is my nurse from home, Mr. Barrington. She raised me from a baby, and now Mama's letting her come to the Barony to raise little Stuart. Isn't that wonderful?"

Billy nodded and said hello. The black woman bobbed briefly in a ponderous curtsy. She had an immense dignity that made Billy feel very young.

The party, now including Billy, returned to the Barony in the barge. Billy was seated next to the Gardens. Jane Garden entertained him with stories about the big black woman, her voice barely above a whisper.

"Zanzibar is really her name," she murmured. "Her mother was a house slave before the War. Sally was her name. Well, Sally was fascinated by the big globe old Mr. Garden had in the library. When she knew she was pregnant, she gave the globe a spin, then stopped it with her finger. Mr. Garden read out the name under her finger, and that was that. We've laughed a lot, thinking of the other things Zanzie might have been called—suppose Sally had happened to hit Russia?

"Anyhow, Margaret couldn't say 'Zanzibar' when she was learning to talk; 'Zanzie' was the best she could do. That's what it's been ever since."

"You're very generous, Mistress Garden, to let Zanzie go to the Barony."

Jane Garden touched the corner of her left eye. A damp spot appeared on her glove. "Not generous, no, Mr. Barrington. It eases my heart to have Zanzie there. Margaret was the blessing of my old age, you know. I was near fifty when she was born. She may be a mother herself now, but to me she's still practically a baby herself. I'm happy to have her nurse there to take care of her. . . .

"I remember when she was a tiny little thing; she used to get the croup every single winter. Zanzie saved that baby's life time and time again. Sitting with her day and night, the croup kettle steaming in the tent we made around the crib, changing the flannels on her little chest.

"And later, when the measles came, and the chicken pox, there would be Zanzie, in the dark room with all the curtains closed to protect Margaret's eyes. She'd sponge her off to cool the fever, then just sit and hold her hands so she couldn't scratch herself and make scars.

"She'd never even let me in the room. I figure she was more Margaret's mother than I was when there was trouble. I feel a lot better having Zanzie with my little girl."

Billy spoke without thinking. "You mean you think there's going to be trouble?"

Jane Garden's faded eyes looked impassively at him from their pouches of wrinkled skin. "There's already been enough for a lifetime, hasn't there? No, Mr. Barrington, I'm not expecting trouble.

But life is full of uncertainties, don't you think? And Mr. Garden is an old man, and I'm an old woman. Zanzie will never be old; she is someone Margaret can count on."

Billy kept his thoughts to himself. He was sure that Mrs. Garden was just a fussy old mother hen. Ahead of them in the barge, Stuart and Margaret were holding hands and whispering together, a picture of happy young marrieds.

Watching them, he felt lonely, and he resolved to write a long letter that evening to Susan Hoyt, back home in Belton. His mother had sometimes mentioned that Susan had asked how he was doing. Billy was, in many ways, innocent about life, but not so innocent that he did not recognize the implications of his mother's casual remark. Susan sort of liked him, and his mother approved of Susan. Yes, he'd do it, he'd write her that very night. Maybe not a long letter, just a note, but he'd certainly write.

3

Before the barge reached the Barony landing, the heat had become heavy on its passengers. The ladies opened their parasols and trailed their fingers in the water to cool off.

"After the breakfast, I'm going to have a swim," Koger announced, "and I'm not going to wait an hour, either. Anybody care to join me?" Billy and Stuart accepted immediately.

"How about you, Anson?"

"Uh, no thanks, Koger. I've got things to do."

"I'll come, Stuart," said Margaret.

"You'd better think that over, Margaret," he said. "Being all boys, we've never bothered with bathing clothes."

Margaret squealed and covered her face with her hand.

"You ain't going in no cold water, Miss Margaret." Zanzie's voice was flat, excluding any chance of argument.

"Thank goodness," Henrietta said into the silence, "we're almost home."

The Barony landing was sheltered by a group of magnolia trees, their heavy leaves forming a thick canopy. The shade was like a cool hand on the party's hot faces. Everyone was instantly refreshed.

"Oh, it smells delicious under here," Margaret cooed. "There must be about a million flowers in these old trees."

"It is nice, isn't it?" Henrietta said. "The deep shade makes the lower branches bloom late, so we have a good long season.

"That reminds me, I want to cut some roses for the table. The mist was so thick, I couldn't see to do it this morning. Margaret, would you like to help?"

"I'll help you, Mama." Anson spoke before Margaret could answer.

"Very well. But first, you and the other boys unload the rest of us. That step seems awful high today. The river must be way down, and no wonder. We haven't had any rain for an age."

The three brothers scrambled up to the landing, followed by Billy. It took all four of them to pull up Zanzie's bulk. The rest of the passengers were easy. Henrietta's step was light and graceful, even with the baby on one arm.

"Let's hurry," Stuart said. "I'm starving. Chloe promised to cook everything I like for my son's christening breakfast." He led the way across the wide lawn.

"I'll get your garden scissors from the shed, Mama," said Anson. "You wait here in the shade."

Billy walked with Mr. and Mrs. Garden, slowing his natural pace to theirs. The old man stabbed at a clump of weed with his cane. "Nobody can keep up a place anymore, even if Sherman didn't burn it. I remember when this lawn was like velvet."

"You're tired, Henry, that's all," Jane Garden said. "When we get to the house, you have a nice toddy first thing."

"Before breakfast? Madam, you're a bad influence on me." Henry Garden chuckled with delight. "I suppose, at that, that it's really well on toward noon. That damn boat may be traditional, but it's a hell of a lot faster to take a good horse and buggy. What time is it, Mr. Barrington?"

Billy reached in his watch pocket, but it was empty. He stopped in his tracks. "I've lost my watch," he said, near despair. "I had it this morning, I know I did."

Jane Garden patted his arm. "It can't have gone far. Probably you left it in the church."

"No, ma'am. I'm sure not. It must have dropped in the boat or on the dock.

"Excuse me, please. I've got to find it. My daddy gave it to me when I graduated from the seminary." Billy took off at a run.

The thick grass made his steps soundless. When he neared the dock, he stopped. Hidden in the deep shadow of the trees, there were two people. A man and a woman. The hem of her white skirt and the bottoms of his white trousers were the only things visible. They were speaking quietly.

I shouldn't intrude, Billy thought. I should turn right around and go back to the house.

But the tide'll be turning. Suppose my watch is on the step. And the boatmen will be moving the barge. Maybe they already have. Or it could be right on the edge of the landing, ready to fall in the water. I've just got to go see.

He started forward.

Then the words being spoken suddenly penetrated his understanding, and he stopped again.

". . . Anson, how could you do this to me?"

"I'm not doing anything to you, Mama. It has nothing to do with you."

"Then, why? If you're not angry with me, why would you want to leave? Is it Stuart? Koger? Did you have an argument?"

Anson groaned. "I told you, Mama, I'm not mad at anybody. I just can't stay here anymore. After Papa died, after the wedding, I told you then that I was going."

Henrietta broke in. "But you agreed not to."

"For a while, Mama. I said I'd stay for a while. That was four months ago. Now I've got to go."

"But, Anson, I don't understand. If you could just give me a reason. Don't you love me anymore?" Henrietta began to cry.

Billy remembered Anson's tortured face at his brother's marriage to the girl he loved; he understood the boy's longing to leave and his inability to give Henrietta a reason.

But Anson was young, not yet twenty. From the wisdom of his greater age, twenty-two, and from a heart that had never been deeply touched, Billy decided that Anson's feeling for Margaret was only

24

puppy love; it would soon be over. In the meantime he had no right to hurt his mother.

I'm eavesdropping, he thought, and he felt the blood rush to his face from shame. Slowly, quietly, he began to back away.

As he did, he heard Anson. "Mama, please stop, Mama. I can't bear to see you so unhappy. Don't cry, please, Mama. I promise I won't go just yet. I'll stay a while longer."

Billy turned and ran for the house.

It was not the Big House, the mansion where the wedding had been held. In May the family always moved to a much smaller, simpler house that stood on a slight hill in a small pine woods on Barony lands. In October they moved back to the Big House. It was the traditional pattern of lowcountry living, developed in colonial days when the early settlers noticed that "swamp fever" attacked only in the months of hot weather and that it did not extend to the areas where the pine forests were thickest.

The Woods House was connected to the Big House carriage drive by a potholed wagon track. The rank wild brambles had been cut back before the move in May, but they had already grown back, and the spiny thorns tore at Billy's trouser bottoms as he ran. He slowed his pace, stepped over onto the ridge between the tracks and walked more safely, wiping his streaming face with his limp handkerchief.

By the time he arrived at the house, he was in control of himself.

He found Stuart Tradd totally out of control, stamping up and down the length of the long, deep porch that fronted the house, bellowing at a cowering old black woman, his face almost as red as his hair, giving an exhibition of the legendary Tradd temper.

Koger was watching with unconcerned interest, smoking a pipe and rocking in a white-painted wooden chair. From the interior of the house came the sounds of Zanzie's deep, rumbling voice making soothing noises that mingled with the crying of Margaret and the baby.

"Where the hell is Mama?" Stuart shouted at Billy. "I can't make any sense out of what this fool woman is saying."

"You're making too much noise to hear her," Koger said clearly.

Stuart spun on him. "When I want your opinion, I'll ask for it," he roared.

Koger made a show of knocking his pipe out against his heel. Then he stood, put the pipe in a pocket and stepped over the porch rail to stroll away into the woods, ostentatiously ignoring his brother's demands that he speak to him.

"Everybody's gone deaf and dumb around here." Stuart shouted.

A soft answer turneth away wrath. Billy reminded himself. "What's the matter, Stuart?" he said softly.

To his gratification, Stuart stopped waving his arms and walking back and forth. He dropped into a chair and put his hands over his face. "That's what I'm trying to find out." he groaned. "There's no meal fixed, none of the servants here except Chloe, and she just babbles some trash about Pansy told her not to light the stove. Mama might make some sense of it, but I can't. Where is she? She'll have to fix things."

Billy remembered Henrietta's desperate tears. It was too much for her to have another crisis to face. "Maybe I can help," he said. "Who is Pansy?"

Stuart's hands fell helplessly onto his knees. "That's what's so crazy. Pansy is just an old crone who lives in the Settlement. She doesn't have anything to do with cooking our breakfast. She doesn't have anything to do with anything. She hasn't done a lick of work in donkey's years. It makes no sense."

Billy persevered. "Where's the Settlement?"

"You know. That bunch of cabins on the drive, halfway to the road."

"I'll go talk to her."

"But I tell you, she's got nothing to do with us."

"I'll go anyhow."

Billy trudged along the drive, his mouth parched. The sunlight seemed to lance through his hat into his head, settling in a dull, hot ache behind his eyes. Dust rose at each step, covering his boots and clothes with a gritty powder. As he rounded the bend, he saw a scurry of movement ahead. People ran into the cabins and the doors closed behind them. When he got closer, everything was quiet and still except for slight twitchings of the drawn curtains at the windows.

There were two rows of cabins, five along the road and four behind them, with a bare-earth area between where chickens scrabbled in the dust and a rusty pump dripped into a tin washpan.

Billy walked over to the pump and pointed at the handle. "I'm awful thirsty," he called out. "Can I have a drink of water?"

There was no answer.

He waited, feeling eyes on him.

4

A door creaked. Billy turned his head slowly in the direction of the sound.

Two children were peering from behind the skirts of the woman who stood in the doorway. The woman thrust one of them forward. "Take a cup to the preacher and pump some water for him," she said.

The little boy scampered across the yard. Billy smiled at him; the child looked back at his mother.

"You, boy, get to pumping," she ordered.

Billy smiled at her. "It's hot out here," he said. "Can I come inside in the shade?"

She drew back into the shadows. "What you want, Mr. Preacher?"

Billy held out a hand to the little boy. He chose his words carefully. "I want some water, and I need some help."

The child gave him the cup. While Billy drank, he looked hopefully at the woman in the door and from one to another of the watching windows in the cabins.

Another door opened, and a dignified black man stepped outside. Billy remembered him from the wedding. It was the minister of the Negro church. "What can I do for you, Reverend?" he said.

Billy walked over to him. "I'd like to talk to Pansy."

The woman in the door gestured quickly, calling her little boy inside. The door closed behind him.

"Pansy, she ain't feel so good, Reverend. She in she bed. Can I do for you?"

Billy shook his head. "I'm afraid not, Reverend." The black man nodded, in appreciation of the title, the recognition of professional parity. Billy continued talking, his voice just loud enough to be heard by all the unseen listeners. He believed that he had made an alliance with the minister; he knew that the minister of a black

27

community was a powerful figure but he sensed that the power of the mysterious Pansy was stronger.

"I have to talk to Pansy herself," Billy said. "I mean no harm. I just want to ask her something."

"You can ask me, Reverend."

"No, Reverend. I have to ask Pansy."

The two representatives of the church stood facing each other in stubborn, un-Christian hostility.

The black man turned and entered his house. I've lost, Billy thought, failed.

There was a cough behind him. He had not heard the young woman's approach. "Come with me," she said.

"You didn't take no sass off that preacher, and no more do I," the old black woman said. "What's your name, mister?"

"Mr. Barrington."

Pansy raised her eyebrows. She was small and shriveled. When she lifted her brows, a ripple ran across her forehead and cheeks as the wrinkles in her skin became more prominent. She could have been any age. Or ageless.

"That too much mouthful for Pansy. I call you Mr. Barry."

"All right," said Billy. "I want to ask you something, Pansy."

She held up her hand. "Not yet," she commanded. "I gots to study on your face for a while. You, girl." She raised her voice. "Give me some light on Mr. Barry face."

The young woman who had served as Billy's escort began to hurry around the room, pulling the curtains open. Then she opened the door.

Billy looked around him as the sunlight poured in. The room was small and made smaller by the size of the furniture in it. In one corner was a tremendous mahogany bed. It had been altered to fit by cutting off the bottom half of its legs and top half of its four posts. Next to it, a massive mahogany chest-on-chest reached from floor to ceiling. Its brass drawer pulls shone like gold. Each was decorated with a bow of bright-colored wool yarn.

On the wall opposite the bed was a rough, plasterlike fireplace. Above it a stuffed peacock hung from the ceiling, its faded feathers still brilliantly iridescent in the sunlight. In front of the fireplace was Pansy's chair, a mammoth, thronelike object upholstered in tattered patchwork. It made her seem even smaller and more wizened.

28

Billy felt crowded and oppressed. He tried to move backward, but he collided at once with more furniture. Pansy covered her mouth with her hand and laughed. The sound was fresh and musical. She laughed like a girl.

"Sit down, Mr. Barry," she said graciously.

Billy looked behind him at the oilcloth-covered table that filled the rest of the room. Four straight chairs were placed around it, their seats under its top. Billy pulled one out, turned it, and sat facing Pansy. There was less than four inches separating their knees.

His action seemed to act as a signal of some sort. While Pansy studied his face, the other inhabitants of the Settlement came in groups to Pansy's house. The first arrivals entered the house, sat on the bed and the floor, leaned against the walls until there was no more room. Then faces filled the windows, and a crush of bodies filled the door.

With the audience in place Pansy was ready. "I know what for you come, Mr. Barry," she said. "That fool Chloe call my name to you, which she didn't noways ought to do. But here you is. Full of question." Pansy laughed again. "Well, sir, I is full of answer."

The cabin vibrated with the laughter of the pressing people in and around it.

Pansy frowned, sending a new shiver of wrinkles across her dark, intense face. "Ain't no call to laugh," she said loudly. Instantly, there was silence.

She leaned toward Billy. "You listen to old Pansy, Mr. Barry. Go away from this place. Ain't nothing to come but misery. You ain't no kin, you can go. Them Tradd, they got a curse on them. Misery there done been, and worse misery coming. This morning, I seen the plat eye."

A moan broke from the throats of the eager listeners. Pansy moaned with them.

Then she straightened in her chair and raised a trembling hand. "This here is Ashley Barony," she said, her voice strong with anger. "It been Ashley land for all time. That river the Ashley River. Ashley earth and Ashley water. There ain't no welcome for no Tradds.

"I is Ashley people; all we colored folks here is Ashley people. Miss Julia Ashley, she was my lady. Ain't I stand by her side when she tell the Yankee soldiers to keep off her land? And ain't they run

29

away. same like rabbits? Miss Julia. she owned me and the daddies and granddaddies of all these folks. We is all Ashleys.

"Not Tradds. This land ain't never feel no good to them. When Miss Julia gone, there ain't nobody left who belong here, 'cept only us black folks. The Judge, he can't noway take care of this land. He been selling a piece here, selling a piece there.

"His boy, now, he do worse than the Judge. The crops ain't growing. We got no rain. The land ain't got no use for this boy.

"Oh, he try to fool the land. Name that baby Ashley. But the land ain't fooled. Don't it know that baby a sin child? Don't it know that baby bring a stranger for he nurse? That the first black woman ever set foot on Ashley land who ain't Ashley.

"The land know who she is. And Pansy know, too. Ain't she the child of that same Sally who run away with the Yankee soldiers? No-good trash, and her child coming to live on Ashley land." Pansy stood up, quivering with indignation.

"I see plat eye, and it ain't no surprise to me. Too much insult to the land, it call to plat eye, and plat eye, he come. He going haunt all them Tradd. He going bring down ruin and tribulation."

Pansy's cracked voice was impassioned, its rhythms mesmerizing. The crowd was swaying now, moaning softly. Billy felt a pressure in his throat and discovered that his body was rocking back and forth. A chill gripped his spine. I've got to stop her, he thought, but Pansy was shouting again and he was helpless.

"I tell these people, I warn them. Plat eye, he done come, I say, he come with the touch of death in he hand." The moaning grew louder. People covered their heads with their arms, drew back from Pansy and her oracles. The doorway became a confused mass of frightened men, women and children trying to escape the words.

"Stop!" Pansy screamed. "Plat eye ain't come for you. He ain't come for no Ashley. He come for Tradd."

"And here's one come to meet him." Henrietta followed her calm voice into the room, passing easily through the recoiling blacks.

"Pansy," she said pleasantly, "you should be ashamed of yourself. You're scaring all these people half to death with your foolishness. And what on earth did you tell Chloe? That plat eye would blow up the stove?"

She looked around the room, her eyes stopping at each face. She spoke to some. "Herklis, we need you up at the house. Chloe's fixing a big feast, and you know you're the only one who can carve

30

a ham . . . Good day, Mungo, you're feeling better, I hope . . . Juno, the beds haven't been made, and there are dead flowers in every single room . . . Susie, you must have grown a mile since I saw you last, and you're getting to be as pretty as your momma . . . Cuffee, I was in the rose garden, and there are some canes that need tying up . . . Minerva, just look at you. You must be carrying twins. I want Dr. Drayton to see you next time he's over . . . How do, Jupiter . . . Hello, Romulus, is that a grown-up tooth I see in your mouth? . . . Cissie, there's wash on the line needs taking in the house . . ." She spoke easily, not hurrying, but demanding their attention and allegiance. She did not look at Billy.

Pansy did not acknowledge Henrietta's presence.

The people in the room were restless; they moved from foot to foot, looking uncertainly at Henrietta, at Pansy, at each other. But the servants did not move to do Henrietta's bidding.

She played her ace. "Preacher Ashley, why don't you come in?"

Billy rode back to the house in the buggy with Henrietta. "You were wonderful," he said humbly. "I couldn't think what to do."

"There was nothing you could have done, Mr. Barrington, though it was sweet of you to try. That was a power struggle between Pansy and me. You see, she wanted her great-granddaughter to be the baby's nurse. When I didn't choose her, Pansy decided to teach me a lesson. If young Pansy couldn't work, nobody would work."

"So all that business about a curse was just an act?"

Henrietta thought a moment. "I truly don't know," she said. "The old, dark superstitions are still with us. Pansy probably did see something, maybe a tree branch, maybe a stray cow or sheep. You remember how misty it was this morning. A moving anything would seem pretty spooky. Maybe she really believed she saw plat eye.

"But I doubt it. She just made a good story out of it." Henrietta pulled up on the reins, stopping in the shade of a tree. "Let's catch our breath before we go back to the house. It'll give the servants time to get everything ready." She had obviously already dismissed the scene in the Settlement from her mind.

But Billy was still curious. "What is 'plat eye,' anyhow?" he asked.

Henrietta patted his hand. "He's the boogeyman, the devil, everything bad you can think of. I've never heard anybody say what he looks like, but I've been scared of him all my life. All colored nurses—and mothers—tell children that if they're not good, plat eye'll get them. When you're little, and you hear the house creak in the night, you just know plat eye is coming. I spent many an hour with the covers pulled up over my head, hiding from him."

"I can see why the preacher doesn't approve of Pansy's stories."

Henrietta chuckled. "Another power struggle," she said. "Pansy knew she was lost the minute he walked in. That made it two against one, whichever way you look at it: Preacher and me against Pansy, or Preacher and the Bible against plat eye. He and Pansy battle all the time for influence over the Settlement people. She generally wins, because he's in love with young Pansy, and she's devoted to her great-grandmother."

"Whew! It's all so complicated. I'll never learn lowcountry ways."

"Of course you will. You're doing fine already." Henrietta paused.

"One good thing about you being from outside," she said with a sudden shyness, "is that people feel like they can talk to you. You're not already set in your mind about things changing or things staying the way they've always been. You've got a sort of a fresh look on our lowcountry ways. A person could tell you things and ask you what you think is the best thing to do."

"I'd be honored if a person shared a confidence with me," Billy said sincerely. "And I'd never discuss it with anybody else."

"I figured you'd feel that way, Mr. Barrington. I think I'll call you Billy if we're going to be such friends. I'm worried about my youngest boy, Anson . . ."

That night, Billy wrote to Susan Hoyt. "This is very old and very pretty and very historic country," he concluded, "very different from home. Maybe you'd like to see it."

He thought a long time, then signed the letter: "Your friend, William Barrington."

5

Susan replied to Billy's letter as soon as she imagined it would not seem too soon. Her expression of interest in the low country was as carefully casual as Billy's suggestion that she should see it. Both of them understood the conventions. The courtship had begun.

Throughout the oppressively hot and sticky summer months the letters went back and forth, growing more revelatory and longer with each exchange. Billy spent less and less time preparing his Sunday sermons; the letters took up most of his evening hours.

He felt a little guilty, he confessed to Henrietta Tradd. They had rapidly developed a curious mutual dependency. Henrietta treated Billy almost like another son sometimes; at other times she poured out her heart to him as her clergyman and asked his advice as if she were the child and he the father. On his side, Billy relied on Henrietta to listen to his problems, and felt protective of her when she admitted to periods of worry and unhappiness.

"Don't be a goose," Henrietta said when Billy told her about his neglect of his duties. "As long as it's summer, you hardly have anybody to preach to anyhow, except us and Margaret's parents."

It was true. The little church of St. Andrews was a peculiar parish. Before the Civil War it had been the place of worship for all the great plantations on the Ashley River. Every Sunday barges had come down the river to unload the large plantation families and their guests, sometimes as many as thirty if there was an important ball or house party.

But all the plantations had been destroyed. The families now lived, for the most part, in Charleston. Some were dispersed even farther. Reopening St. Andrews had been a gesture, a memorial, almost, of the lost era of greatness. In the spring its simple box pews had been filled with the descendants of their former owners. A drive in the country was a pleasant adventure when the air was fresh and cool and deliciously scented with jasmine. In the summer, it was unthinkable. People left their tall, shuttered town houses only to go to the nearby sea islands with their cool ocean breezes and wide sands.

"Yes," Henrietta continued, "everything will pick up in the fall." A happy smile brightened her tired face. "I've been thinking about a little party."

Billy was amazed. Henrietta had, he knew, very strong opinions about the respect owed to her dead husband. She would wear white mourning, but mourning it would be for the full year after the Judge's death. New widows did not even attend parties; it was inconceivable that she would give one.

"Not really a party," Henrietta said. "Just a houseguest. We move back to the Big House on October twenty-fifth every year. Why don't I write to Mistress Hoyt and invite Susan to visit the first weekend in November?"

Susan's train came in to Summerville, the charming little town where Billy, like the Tradds, bought his supplies. He was glad she hadn't chosen the train that went to Charleston. Summerville was more like Belton—small, sleepy, with one main street and a one-track railroad depot. Charleston's big terminal was too noisy, too big, too crowded for a comfortable reunion.

For a moment Billy did not recognize Susan. She looked so grown-up. Then he realized that he must look just as strange to her in his dark clericals. She looked nervous, too, just the way he felt. Suddenly he knew everything was going to be all right.

Susan's reaction to the imposing entrance to the Barony was as awestruck as Billy's had been. "Don't worry," he told her, "you're going to have a wonderful time. The Tradds are awfully nice people."

"They must be very well-to-do."

"Oh, not so very." Billy knew, from Henrietta, that the opposite was the case. The Judge's sister had been quietly subsidizing them for years. When she broke with Stuart on the terrible day of the wedding, he retaliated by forbidding his mother and brothers to have anything to do with her. Henrietta had to return the checks Elizabeth sent her, and the Barony's debts began to mount. The summer's drought had been a disaster for the vegetable crops that were the sole source of income. Stuart had, just that week, sold three hundred acres of land to meet their obligations.

34

Susan gasped when they made the turn in the drive and the Big House appeared. "It's so beautiful, Billy. I've never seen a house like that."

"I told you the low country was different. Look, there's Margaret Tradd come out to meet us."

Susan looked at him with despair in her eyes. "I shouldn't have come, Billy. She's too beautiful to be real. I feel all wrong."

Billy stopped the buggy and turned toward Susan, studying her, learning her familiar plain features. She had a round face, with a small, straight nose and brown eyes. Her mouth was wide and clearly chiseled, the lower lip a bit too full, the upper lip a bit too long. It was the color of a rose. As Billy stared, her cheeks flushed with the same warm, glowing color.

"You look just exactly all right, Susan Hoyt," he said firmly. "You look like a real person. Margaret is more like some kind of doll. Everybody's very patient with her because she's so young, but everybody's going to like you because you're the way you are." He slapped the reins. "Let's get the meetings over with. Then you can relax and enjoy yourself."

"She's a lovely girl," Henrietta whispered to Billy as they moved into the dining room after a predinner sherry in the library. "Are you going to marry her?"

"I don't know about that," Billy mumbled. It was much too soon to think about marriage.

But before dinner was over he had made up his mind.

It was unfortunate that Henrietta had tried so hard to do honor to Billy's girl from home. The dining-room table was sumptuous, gleaming with the treasures in porcelain, silver and crystal that had been the pride of Julia Ashley.

In the center was a delicacy of glass that Julia's father had brought back from Venice, a rosebush with each petal, each leaf veined with the intricate perfection of flowing color that only a great artist could attain. Fresh-cut roses from the garden surrounded the base of the centerpiece and formed an individual bouquet at each place. They were reflected in the deep shimmer of mahogany, for there was no cloth on the table, only squares of lace at each place, lace of cobweb fragility in a design of rose garlands surrounded by fantastic, twining leaves. The napkins were linen, fine enough for an infant's gown, edged with the same lace. They lay across plates as thin as eggshells, decorated with a simple gold band around the rim and the Ashley crest. The wineglasses were also gold-rimmed and so exquisitely blown that they looked as if they were bubbles about to burst. The only weight on the table seemed to be the silver, each piece a heavy, austere fiddle shape with the deep, interior, dull luster of decades of gentle polishing.

Billy, who had been an almost daily dinner guest at the Woods House, suddenly felt clumsy and uncomfortable. Susan sat on the edge of her chair as if she were afraid that she might break it, her hands trembling in her lap.

Herklis entered, bearing a steaming tureen which he placed in front of Henrietta. Juno followed with a stack of warmed bowls in a heavy square of linen. Henrietta lifted the heavy ladle and began to serve. "This is crab bisque, Miss Hoyt," she said. "I do hope you like seafood. If you don't, it's all right. There is some consommé in the kitchen."

Susan, who had never tasted crab, declared that it was a special favorite of hers.

The dinner, each dish one of Chloe's specialties, was an ordeal for the girl. Stuart and Koger vied with each other in the flirtatious compliments they paid her. Susan could think of no responses, and she felt herself blushing. She was also baffled by the strange tastes and forms of the food—pheasant on a bed of rice, tiny green beans with chopped pickled pecans, sweet potatoes as a soufflé.

Billy watched her misery and felt it seep into him as well. Then Margaret, annoyed that Stuart was neglecting her, began to pay him back in kind by flirting outrageously with Anson, who had been silently concentrating on his dinner. She leaned toward him, whispering, and put her hand in his. Anson pulled away from her as if he had been scalded. Billy could read the pain on Anson's face; he looked quickly at Henrietta, but she was, as always, unaware of Anson's agony.

"You're no fun at all, Anson," Margaret said gaily. "Here we are having a party at last, and you're as cross as a bear. We just won't let him come to the next one, will we, Miss Hen?"

Henrietta smiled vaguely. "We'll see when the time comes," she said.

"When will that be, Miss Hen? And who will we have? Now that the summer's finally over, people don't mind going to the country. Shall we have a house party? Oh, with a little ball! Nothing too grand, but definitely dancing. What do you think, Miss Hen? How long would it take to arrange everything? Three weeks? Is that enough time? Or four? That would be better, it'll be Thanksgiving then, and you-all have the deer hunt and barbecue every Thanksgiving. We'll just tell everyone to stay after the barbecue, take a walk in the garden, have a rest, and then it'll be time to dress for the evening and the ball. How wonderful! I'll tell Zanzie to make me the most beautiful gown anybody ever had. What color do you think I should get, Stuart? Blue, maybe. You're kind of partial to blue, aren't you?''

Henrietta spoke before Stuart could answer. "Margaret, you know there can't be any dancing or partying for months yet. We're in mourning. Now that it's getting cool, we'll go back into black.''

"No!'' Margaret cried, "that's no fair. I hate black, and it makes me look awful. You can't be so mean, Miss Hen.''

"It's not a matter of 'mean,' Margaret. It is a question of respect for my husband.'' Her back was stiff and her soft eyes hard.

Margaret was startled by the change in Henrietta. For a minute, she was quiet. Billy and Koger started talking to Susan at the same time, hurrying to fill the awkward silence.

Margaret interrupted them. "I don't see any reason on earth why I should have to wear black and stay cooped up in the country for the Judge. He wasn't my husband.''

"He was my father,'' said Stuart. "Now hush up and behave yourself, Margaret. You're embarrassing Mama.''

Margaret's lovely eyes filled with tears. "Don't take sides against me, Stuart. You've been treating me awful all day.''

"Stuart,'' Henrietta said, "perhaps you and Margaret could discuss all this later, when you're alone.'' She looked at Susan, her face soft again. "Do you come from a large family, Miss Hoyt?''

"Yes, ma'am,'' Susan replied. "I have two brothers and four sisters.'' Her voice was stronger and clearer than it had been. Her respect for Henrietta shone from her face.

Herklis entered with a heavily laden tray. "We got some fine apples from your part of the state this year, Miss Hoyt,'' said Henrietta. "They're always a treat to us. Chloe makes an extra-good cobbler, I think, and it's still warm enough to enjoy a little ice cream.

"Herklis, give Miss Margaret a big dishful. She's particularly fond of apple cobbler.''

Margaret began to sob. "I couldn't eat a mouthful," she wailed. "I can't stand it when everybody acts so hateful." Her sobs mounted in intensity until her entire body was shaking. Then they changed to gasping, racking hiccups which made her head and shoulders jerk in great spasms.

Stuart and Henrietta hurried to her, offering water, a damp handkerchief on the neck, murmuring soothingly.

The door swung wide and Zanzie strode across the floor. She swept Stuart aside and put her arms around Margaret. "Ain't I told you you wasn't to upset yourself?" she crooned. "Poor, sickly little thing, come to your Zanzie."

She cradled Margaret's shaking body against her breast and glared over her head at the others. "I knows what to do for her," she said. "Everybody just leave us alone." She lifted Margaret from her chair and supported her with a strong arm around the waist as they exited. Stuart trailed behind them.

Henrietta sank into her chair and rested her head against its high back. "I am so very sorry, Billy, Miss Hoyt. I'm afraid this has been a ruinous dinner."

Susan quickly spooned up some dessert. "I've never tasted anything in my life as good as this cobbler, Mistress Tradd," she said. "And I've never seen anything as beautiful as your home. Now that I've got through without breaking anything, I can tell you that this dinner was the most elegant thing that's ever happened to me. Would you ask your cook to give me the receipt for the cobbler? And could I please see your rose garden?"

That night Billy asked Susan if she would be his wife. She said "Yes" at once. Susan did not play emotional games.

6

In the end, Anson persuaded Henrietta to give in. "He reminded me," she explained to Billy, "that Margaret is only just turned sixteen. A child that age doesn't wear deep mourning after six months, so Margaret really should be in white with black trim. I guess, being so young himself, he understands better how she feels.

"Of course, there's no question of any balls or formal parties. The Season in town will have to get along without the Tradds this year. But, as Anson said, the Thanksgiving hunt at the Barony was his father's favorite thing in the whole world. We've had it every year since we moved here in '87. If we keep it going, it will be sort of a memorial to the Judge. I won't socialize. Margaret will have to hostess the barbecue. And we won't invite as many people as we usually do. Just the younger ones. Stuart is master of the Barony now. The guests should be his friends . . ."

Her voice trailed off. She looked worried. "Do you think I'm doing wrong, Billy?"

"No, ma'am, I don't."

Henrietta sighed. "I never used to have to decide things. The Judge always knew what to do. I do miss him so." She took a deep breath.

"So, that's settled," she said. "We're having the Thanksgiving hunt. Is there any chance Susan might come? I'd love to have her."

"I wish she would, but I know she won't. She's got so much to do, getting ready for the wedding. January's not that far off."

"I am so happy for you, Billy. She's a wonderful girl. When you write, tell her we'll miss her at Thanksgiving."

Susan delighted them both by saying she'd love to come. The wedding preparations could get along without her for a few days. She arrived on Tuesday and spent Wednesday helping Henrietta oversee the digging of the barbecue pit, setting up the long tables on the lawn, counting and stacking the dozens of plates and napkins, checking the supplies of relishes and sniffing the barbecue sauce that Chloe had bubbling on the back of the stove. Margaret danced around them; she got in everyone's way, but her happiness and excitement were so contagious that no one minded her ineptness.

At nightfall, a cold rain began. "Nobody will come tomorrow if it's like this," Susan said to Billy. "Margaret will have a tantrum, and I'm afraid I'll slap her."

Henrietta bustled past them, shepherding four little black boys carrying canvas and an unwieldy cluster of long sticks. "Don't stand out here in the cold, you two," she cried, "and don't look so glum. We've had rainy weather before. We just put up a tent over the pit so the fire can keep burning, and we put extra tables in the hallway in case we have to eat inside. Go on inside before you catch your death."

The rain stopped shortly before dawn, just as the hunters were arriving. The ladies would come later, in midmorning, in time to greet the men when they came back from the hunt. The beginning of the day was for men only, to tramp through the woods to the stands, to drink whiskey, to curse, to wait, shivering and expectant, for the sight of a buck's points, to load and shoot; to be a hunter, a man.

Billy rode up with a group of four young men he had met on the road. He greeted Stuart, joined the laughing party of hunters that had formed on the lawn, took a glass from the tray that Herklis was passing. The whiskey burned a path down his throat. He did not hunt; he would not kill. But it felt good to be here in the raw, misty air, hearing only deep voices, sharing the rough jokes and comradeship.

"Another shooter, Reverend?"

"No thanks, Koger."

"It's Anson, Billy."

"Sorry. I couldn't see. There's hardly any light yet. How do you fellows see where you're going in the woods?"

Koger loomed near. He slapped Billy heartily on the back. "Hell, Reverend, we've all been hunting in these woods since we were first able to lift a gun. We could find our way blindfolded. Or blind drunk. A couple of times I've done it."

A friend joined them, glass in hand. "More than a couple of times," he said. "More like every time, near as I can remember."

Koger introduced Billy. "Sure you won't come along? All right.

We'll bring you some good venison. Come on, fellows. Time to move."

Billy peered after their shadowy forms as they walked away. The ground mist swirled around their legs to the boot tops. They seemed to be wading in a pale river.

He shivered. The cold was biting. There'll be coffee on the stove, he thought, and headed for the warm kitchen. Susan had promised to get up early and have breakfast with him. It wasn't easy to find time to be alone together on her visits.

Henrietta made sure that everything was ready for the barbecue, then went upstairs to her sitting room before the guests began to arrive. She looked very pale in the uncertain morning light.

Later, Margaret, smiling radiantly, greeted the ladies as they stepped down at the carriage block. Although she had spent her entire life in the country, she knew all the young women who had been invited; her parents had taken her to town for visits since she was small, and little girls in Charleston were always having tea parties or birthdays.

Billy felt conspicuous and out of place in the midst of the excited chatter and feminine squeals. He excused himself and fled into the house to the sanctuary of the upstairs. He tapped at Henrietta's door. "It's Billy. May I join you?"

Henrietta was standing at the window. Baby Stuart was in her arms. "I'm just showing him all the pretty colors," she said. "Don't they look charming, the girls? Like a big bouquet of flowers in their bright frocks. Thank goodness, the sun's come out. We're going to have a perfect day."

Billy joined her at the window. The glass cut off the sounds that had driven him away; he could appreciate the liveliness of the girls, enjoy their smiles and pretty young faces. He looked for Susan, found her, and luxuriated in his own happiness. As soon as the men returned from the hunt, he'd go down to the party and tell her what he was feeling.

"Wet again," said Henrietta. "What a busy life this baby has. I'll be right back, Billy." She left him alone in the quiet room.

Billy stayed at the window, looking at the vista of lawn to the river, daydreaming. When Henrietta returned, she stood next to him, sharing a comfortable silence.

A young hunter broke out of the woods, running. His mouth was stretched wide, shouting. They could not hear his words.

41

"Look," said Billy, "they must be coming. I'd better go down now."

The young man had reached the party on the lawn. The girls clustered around him, then dashed back and forth to one another, waving their hands; the movement was jerky, graceless, nervous.

"Oh, my God," said Henrietta. "There must have been an accident. Hurry." She ran toward the door, her motions stiff and frightened like those of the soundless girls below. Billy raced after her.

Everyone had reached the edge of the woods by the time Henrietta and Billy ran out of the house. The guests were so still now that they seemed to be brightly colored statues. Henrietta and Billy, running, were the only movement in the scene. Their dark-clad bodies were like ominous shadows on the sunstrewn green lawn.

When they were almost to the woods, the crowd in front of them parted, forming an aisle for the procession coming out of the wood. Henrietta looked down the green alley to see her son Anson, his face twisted and wet with tears, walking slowly, leading a horse.

Henrietta cried out. Stuart was sitting atop the horse, staring straight ahead, seeing nothing. His arms held the shoulders and knees of his brother, Koger; the two of them were stained with blood.

"Go away, Mama," Anson shouted. "Billy, take her to the house."

Billy seized Henrietta's arm, but she pulled away with frantic strength. She stumbled to her sons. Anson halted the horse, put himself between his mother and the terrible burden the horse bore. "Go away, Mama," he moaned. "You can't help. Koger's dead."

"No." Henrietta's voice was a whisper. Then she screamed, a piercing, primal cry of anguish. "Koger," she cried. "Koger." She pushed Anson aside and staggered forward. Stuart was like stone, unseeing, unhearing. Henrietta reached up to clasp Koger's limp cold hand. She held it to her cheek, smearing her face with blood, streaking the stain with her tears. "My baby," she sobbed. "Oh, my baby. So cold. Stuart, give me my boy. Let me hold him. Koger, Koger, it's Mama. Let Mama warm you."

Stuart did not move.

"The doctor's given her some laudanum," said Susan. She gently closed the door of Henrietta's room behind her. "You and I will have to manage things, Billy. Stuart's still in shock, Margaret has collapsed, and Anson doesn't even hear you when you talk to him . . . . Billy, this is an awful thing."

"Yes."

"'I mean, worse than you know. Let's go outside; I need some air."

They walked away from the house toward the river, passing the gaily bedecked tables that had been laid for the barbecue. The cooking pigs had been abandoned, and the sweet-sharp, sickly smell of charred pork hung heavy in the air.

"They were talking, Billy, all the guests. When I was seeing them off, I heard them talking to one another. They wonder if it was really an accident. They were talking about the Judge and some other man. Another 'accident.' Billy, do you think it's possible? Could Stuart really have killed his brother? Murdered him?"

"No. I'm sure. It was an accident. Koger left his stand, nobody knows why, and he was mistaken for a buck. But several people fired, and Stuart was one of them. Koger was hit twice, once in the leg and once in the heart. There's no way for Stuart ever to know if he killed his brother or not."

Henrietta looked like a ghost at the funeral of her son. Her face was a pale blur behind her long black veil. She stood between her other two sons, both of them stiff in their black suits. Their blazing red hair seemed to be a shocking blasphemy, too full of life and strength.

The funeral was sparsely attended. Most of the mourners were of Henrietta's generation, mourners for the mother's grief more than for the young man's death.

When the first clod of earth thudded onto the coffin, Margaret screamed. "I can't bear it." She emitted a long, ghastly moan, then fell against Stuart. He put his arm around her, but could not hold her. Her tiny body crumpled to the ground, unconscious. Stuart did not look away from his brother's grave to the bundle at his feet. It was Anson who gathered her up into his arms and carried her away into the house.

Billy continued with the burial service.

At the rear of the Ashley family burial ground, separated from the white mourners, the Barony blacks rocked from side to side in sorrow. Old Pansy was there, her hooded eyes bright. "Tribulations," she muttered. "Ain't I told 'em?"

7

Billy Barrington stretched his arms wide. "Come sit on my lap, Mistress Barrington," he invited. Susan complied. "Ooof," said Billy. Susan tickled his ribs until he begged for mercy, then nestled comfortably on his chest.

"I'm awfully happy, Susan," he rumbled against her ear.

"Me too."

"Do you think we'll ever get tired of being together?"

Susan straightened up. "I don't think so," she said seriously. "After all, we've been married almost five months, and we're not tired yet." The corners of her mouth twitched.

"All right, make fun of me."

Susan hugged him. "You're such a worrywart sometimes, Billy. Over nothing. It's silly."

"But people do. Get tired, I mean. Look at Stuart and Margaret. Haven't you noticed? They don't even talk to each other anymore. They talk to everybody else in the room, but never to each other."

"That has nothing to do with us, Billy. We're nothing at all like Stuart and Margaret. Not in any way."

"I know. I know. You're right. But it bothers me whenever I see them. They were so happy. It wasn't even a year ago that they were obviously so much in love. And now they're miserable. The whole feeling at the Barony is bad. I dread going over there."

"Then why do you go? I don't think you have to go so often, I told you that."

"I just feel that I should. I am their minister, after all, and they've had those two terrible tragedies."

Susan bit her lip, thinking. Then she reached a decision. "Billy," she said, "I'm going to tell you something you aren't going to want to hear. I think you're under some kind of spell with the Tradds; you're not honest with yourself about how you feel. You think about

44

them all the time, you talk about them all the time, you go see them all the time. You're obsessed.''

Billy stood up, pushing Susan away. "I never heard such hogwash in my life," he said. He walked into their tiny kitchen and began to chip pieces off the block of ice in its galvanized tub. Susan followed him.

"I understand how it can happen, Billy, I really do. They're not like us; they're not like anybody else. The Tradds are—extravagant. Everything about them is exaggerated. Their hair is too red, the men are too handsome, their house is too beautiful, the silver too heavy, the china too fine, their lives too dramatic. They're like giants, too much of everything. It's overpowering. And fascinating. Whatever happens to the Tradds is always on a grander scale than whatever happens to other people. It draws ordinary folks in, like a tornado sucking up trees and houses and animals and anything in its way."

Billy kept his back to her.

Susan sighed. "I knew you'd get mad, Billy, but I had to say it. I love you, and I can't stand to see you become one of the Tradds' victims. Besides, to tell the truth, I'm jealous."

Billy turned. "Jealous? Whatever for? Oh, Susan, you're the whole world to me. You must know that."

"Well, I don't."

Billy put his arms around her. "I'll show you, shall I?"

But after they had made love, when they were lying close in each other's arms, he unwittingly broke the spell. "I feel so sorry for Anson," he said. "He'll never get away now. Stuart is doing nothing to run the place, and Anson has to see to the supplies and assigning the jobs and supervising the field hands. He's the youngest and doing all the work on his brother's land."

Susan wanted to cry. He hasn't understood a word I said, she thought. I can't say anymore. I'll just have to keep my peace and pray he breaks free of them. When she was sure that she could control her voice, she spoke. "At least it's a comfort to Miss Hen. She couldn't take losing two of her sons."

"I guess so. It's hard to tell what she's really thinking. She acts just the way she always did, sort of quiet and in control. She used to talk to me a lot, but now she just says everything's going as well as could be expected. I think the baby's the biggest comfort to her. She has him with her a lot."

"She'll probably have him more when the new baby comes—

Billy. don't tell me you didn't know. Margaret runs out of the room to throw up every two minutes, it seems to me."

"I had no idea. I'm only a man, honey. What do I know about those things? I sure am surprised. Seems that she and Stuart have been so distant. He doesn't pay any attention to her at all."

Susan kissed him. "You don't know about a lot of things, darling Billy. I hear a lot when I go to the general store. Stuart Tradd hasn't drawn a sober breath since Koger was killed. He can hardly see straight. But he manages to get to Summerville all right. They say he's lifting every skirt in town. Maybe he thought Margaret was one of his fancy ladies. or somebody else's wife."

Billy was shocked. By the gossip, and even more by Susan's laughing account. "You shouldn't listen to talk like that, Susan. It's not fit for your ears."

"Dearest Billy. You've got so much to learn about women."

Little Margaret Tradd was born in October, on her grandmother's birthday. Henrietta glowed with happiness. "I always longed for a girl." she said, "even when I was loving the boys so much. What a wonderful birthday present. Peggy, we'll call her. She's too tiny for a long name. So little, and so perfect. She's the most beautiful baby in the world."

Indeed Peggy was a beautiful baby. She had inherited the strong Tradd coloring and her mother's delicate features. Her hair grew in soft copper curls, and her bright blue eyes were enormous in her exquisite tiny face. Her hands and feet were miniature perfection, the fingers long and tapered and the arches already high and elegant under the soft rosy flesh.

She was a happy baby, too, content to gurgle and play with her elusive toes and fingers until someone noticed that she was awake, and then gratifyingly ravenous when she was offered her meal. She never vomited and therefore never smelled sour. And she responded to all attentions with such obvious delight that even Little Stuart liked to hover over her cradle, trying to teach her to pat-a-cake.

She seemed to bring joy with her into the gloom and tension of the isolated world at the Barony. "Everything's different now," Billy reported to Susan. "Everything is the way it should be."

Susan had to agree. In spite of her jealousy, she too was falling under the spell of the Tradds and of the world they represented. Peggy was christened on December first, with a celebration at the

Barony. The party marked the end of the secluded period of mourning and the return of the family to the society of the low country. The young Barringtons were swept along by the Tradds into the dazzling round of teas, dinners, balls, and breakfasts that made up the Season. From the middle of December until the middle of January, the old city of Charleston was in full fête. The gaiety and warm welcome were irresistible, even to Susan.

To Margaret, the hectic progression of parties was a dream come true. She was a belle.

If she had not married, she would have attended a few selected parties the year before; then she would have been presented to society in this Season. But because of the tragic deaths in the family, she had not appeared at any party the year before. Her breathtaking beauty, ripened by motherhood, was therefore a new and startling addition to the scene. Married or not, she was surrounded by admirers clamoring for a place on her dance card and begging for the chance to bring her a cup of punch or a piece of cake. Margaret behaved just as if she were a debutante. She flirted, played her beaux off against one another, distributed her smiles and her waltzes like an empress conferring honors. She danced her slippers through and never tired, and she responded to her success by becoming more beautiful than before, glowing with the inner light of triumph.

"I'm so happy," she whispered to Stuart, and she put her head on his shoulder when they drove home each morning as dawn was breaking. He held her close, drawn to her beauty like all the other men they left behind them.

Henrietta was happy too. The disapproving whispers about Margaret's behavior were not important. The renewed closeness of Stuart and his wife was what counted. She did not notice Anson's absence from the house and from the parties in town. He was busy with the Barony, and he had never cared much for dancing.

8

The Season culminated, as always, with the Saint Cecilia Ball, the most cherished of all Charleston's traditions. "I'm so excited I can hardly stand it, Susan," Margaret said. "The Ball is the best part of the whole Season. I've saved my best gown for it, see?"

Susan gasped when Margaret lifted the muslin drape that covered her dress. It was a shimmer of gold and silver beads, sewn in intricate detail on gleaming blue satin. They formed bouquets of silver lilies with gold leaves and gold centers around the skirt. The hem of the skirt and the panels of the train were bordered with gold vines bearing silver leaves. The low-cut bodice was embroidered all over with the spearlike gold leaves of the lilies. Thin silk ropes in gold and silver formed elaborate bows on the tiny puffed sleeves and dangled sparkling tassels over the upper arm.

"What do you think, Susan?"

What Susan was thinking was that the gown must have cost more than Billy's salary for three years, but she couldn't say it aloud. "I'm thinking that it's just as well I'm not going to the Ball," she said. "No one will look at any lady in the room except you."

Margaret ran across the room and hugged her. "I want to be the prettiest one there," she whispered. "I want the others to be green with envy. It's my coming out just as much as if I were a debutante."

Susan returned Margaret's hug. How sad it was. Margaret wanted the one thing she could not have—to be a girl, virginal and courted, with the future still unmapped before her. Her beautiful babies, her husband, her responsibilities had no reality for her. Her world was made up of ball gowns and dance cards and the heavy, engraved square invitations requesting the honor of her company at ten o'clock. Without them she was listless and querulous, an unhappy child.

Susan thought about the baby growing within her womb. Please, God, she prayed silently, give me the wisdom not to indulge my child, no matter how much I love her. Let me teach her what is really important.

That night, just before she drifted off to sleep, Susan sent up a little prayer for Margaret. "She'll be miserable when the parties are over, Lord. Please help her."

Susan need not have worried. For Margaret and Stuart, the parties did not end with the Season. They went into the city nearly every day to visit the great South Carolina, Inter-State and West Indian Exposition that had been built on the grounds of the old Washington Race Course, once the center of Charleston's outdoor social life.

The race course, where plantation owners had wagered fortunes on their own horses against favorites brought over from Ireland, England and France, had never recovered its glories after the Civil War. Even the magnificent carved marble pillars that marked its entrance had had to be sold to New York millionaire August Belmont, to be taken north and used at the race track he was building. It had been a sad day for Charlestonians who remembered the time before the War.

But now the race course was reborn, as parks, a man-made lake, and a series of pavilions with exhibits of new products and inventions that celebrated a new age, an age of progress, the twentieth century. At dusk a master switch was thrown, and the crowds of visitors gasped. Every building, every path, every bridge was outlined with the greatest invention of the age, electric light.

Billy and Susan visited the Exposition several times, but after they had seen each exhibit once, they stayed away. The crowds bothered them. "I guess we're just small-town folks," they admitted cheerfully.

"And I guess I'm just a nineteenth-century lady," Henrietta replied. One visit was enough for her. She was content to stay at the Barony, attending to the myriad details of running the house, and spending happy hours with her grandchildren. She worried about Stuart a little, she confided to Billy, because he was selling more land to pay for the elaborate wardrobes that he and Margaret seemed to require and for the rooms they took at the Charleston Hotel so that they would not have to drive the eight miles home every night.

But there was so much land. And Margaret should guard her strength. She was expecting another baby, even though tight corseting kept her condition a secret.

And Anson could hardly be expected to earn more from the farming than he did. He worked from sunup to sundown as it was, and spent every evening in the plantation office going over the books.

All in all, said Henrietta, life was rich and full of happiness.

Billy and Susan agreed. They were very much homebodies, too, enjoying the lengthening days and the garden they were putting in behind their tiny house, making plans for the future, arguing about names for the baby expected in August.

"We're in a rut, you know," Billy said one evening in April.

Susan looked up from her sewing. "I know," she said. "Isn't it wonderful?"

A week later their world was turned upside down.

9

"Georgia? How can the Bishop of South Carolina send you to Georgia, Billy? That's a whole other state."

"I know it's another state, Susan. I'm not ignorant. I may be a failure, but I'm not ignorant."

Susan hurried to comfort him, to reassure him. It was not his fault that St. Andrews was going to be closed. It was the fault of progress, of the twentieth century, of the Exposition. The Charleston supporters were not driving out to the country on Sunday; they were taking the streetcars to the Exposition.

Henrietta said much the same thing, except that she blamed electricity.

"I'll miss you both," she said. "You must promise to write to me." They promised.

"And you must let me give you a little party before you go. You have more friends here than perhaps you realize." She reclaimed her glasses from Little Stuart, who was trying to put them on the spotted dog asleep on the hearth. "Just let me get my calendar from my desk. When do you have to be in Milledgeville?"

"June the first."

"That gives us more than a month. Good. We'll open up the Woods House a little early and have the party there. It's so much more relaxed. Shall we plan on the twentieth of May? That's a Sunday. You'll have a packed church for your last sermon, Billy. They'll know that I won't give them anything to drink or eat if I don't see them in church before they come here."

Susan chortled. "Let's invite the Bishop."

Henrietta clapped her hands. "Perfect. I'll write to his wife this very afternoon. We'll have such fun."

But it was not to be. While Henrietta was writing to the Bishop's wife, Zanzie interrupted her. "The baby, she mighty poorly, Miz Tradd." Henrietta put down her pen. Both children had been vaccinated three days earlier, and Peggy, usually so placid, had been fretful ever since. Little Stuart complained because he couldn't scratch his arm, but Peggy was too young to tell them what was bothering her.

"Fetch me some warm milk with syrup in it, Zanzie. She hasn't been eating. Maybe she's hungry. I'll just rock her some." Henrietta hurried up the broad stairs to the nursery on the third floor. She heard no sounds of crying, so she tiptoed along the hallway to the room. Perhaps Peggy had fallen asleep.

When she turned into the doorway, Henrietta screamed. Peggy's tiny body was bent into a taut bow, shuddering with convulsions. Henrietta ran to her, snatched her up from her crib. The tiny nightdress was soaked with perspiration, and the strained, rigid form beneath it was terrifyingly hot to the touch. Henrietta held the baby close to her breast, as if the softness of her own body might spread to Peggy's stiff, jerking limbs. "Dear God," Henrietta sobbed, "don't let it be. Please, dear God.

"Hush now, Gramma's angel, everything's going to be all right. Shhh, my precious. Gramma's got you. Gramma will fix." She covered the tiny head with kisses, her tears falling on the coppery curls already damp from the baby's feverish sweat.

Stumbling with haste, she poured cool water into a bowl from the pitcher on the nightstand and dipped a cloth into it. "A nice sponge bath, Peggy. Gramma'll make you feel so much better."

Henrietta placed the baby on the bed and ripped off her nightdress. She began sponging Peggy's head, her neck, her flushed face. The baby's contractions stopped. Henrietta lifted one tiny arm, sponged

51

it, then kissed the small, limp hand. She lifted the other arm and bathed it, more slowly, keeping her attention fixed on it, refusing to look at Peggy's small trunk.

Then she took a deep breath, wrung the cloth in the water again and looked down at the baby. On her abdomen was a faint reddish splotch. Henrietta spread the chubby little legs. There were patches of red on the inner thighs.

Peggy had smallpox. The vaccination meant to protect her from the disease had infected her instead.

Henrietta's tears stopped at once. She needed all her energy to fight for Peggy's life. In the next hour she galvanized all the servants, shouting down from the top of the stairs. She sent a boy for the doctor, issued orders for an immediate move to the Woods House, forced Zanzie to strip to the skin, wash with carbolic soap and burn her clothes. "I'll stay here and nurse the baby. See to it that Mr. Anson and Mr. Stuart and Miss Margaret don't come into this house. Post somebody on the drive and at the doors. Pray God that the infection doesn't spread."

For two weeks Henrietta continued to run the household from a distance. Four times a day, Zanzie came to the lawn and shouted up to the open window of the nursery. She asked her questions about how to handle the needs of the household, reported on the condition of the others; Henrietta issued instructions, gave them a bulletin on Peggy's progress. Everyone at the Woods House was well, Zanzie always said. Peggy was holding her own, Henrietta shouted in turn. Both were lying.

At the Woods House, Zanzie was doing all the housework alone, plus taking care of Margaret, who had collapsed when she heard about Peggy. Two hours later, Margaret cried out for Zanzie. She had begun to miscarry. The doctor, summoned to help the baby, had first to care for the mother. He could not stop the miscarriage, nor the infection that set in afterwards. For days Zanzie sat with Margaret, sponging her feverish body as Henrietta was sponging Peggy's. All the other servants fled, sure that Margaret's fever was the beginning of the pox.

Stuart took his son into the city, to remove him from any danger of infection and to keep him from hearing his mother's agonized moans.

Only Anson remained, to spell Zanzie at Margaret's bedside, feeding her broth, wiping her forehead, holding her hand.

When at last Margaret was out of danger, Zanzie hurried to the Big House. This day, her report would be true.

She heard Peggy crying as she sped across the lawn. "Miz Tradd," she called in a strong, happy voice. "It's Zanzie, Miz Tradd."

There was no answer, only the pitiful mewling sound of a tired baby. Zanzie ran to the house and beat on the great, locked door. Still, there was no answer.

At last she picked up one of the heavy pots planted with rose trees that lined the steps to the veranda. She threw it against a tall window, shattering the panes of wavy old glass, and climbed into the dining room.

Upstairs, she found Peggy thrashing in her crib. Her little mouth was trembling, her huge eyes red from crying. Her hands were tied to the crib railing so that she could not scratch the eruptions of pocks. But nonetheless her face, so exquisitely beautiful such a short time before, was deformed from swelling and from the angry reddish-brown spots that foretold deep scars.

Henrietta Tradd was lying on the floor near the crib, her face covered with pocks, her arms and legs stiff and awkward in death.

Billy Barrington stopped the buggy. "I'm afraid," he said quietly. Susan slipped the glove off her left hand and twined her fingers with his. Wisely, she said nothing.

After several minutes Billy raised her hand to his lips then placed it gently in her lap. He slapped the reins on the horse's back and turned into the Barony drive. The creak of the wheels startled a mockingbird on an overhead branch and he burst into a raucous creaking song.

"It seems like just the other day I was driving this road for the first time," Billy mused aloud. "I thought that a man who lived in a place like this must be the luckiest man in the world. Now I feel more pity for Stuart Tradd than for anyone I have ever known. There has been nothing but tragedy on this beautiful plantation."

Billy and Susan bowed in response to the silently raised hands of the white-clad Negroes as they passed the Settlement. "I wonder if old Pansy will come to the funeral," said Billy. "I wonder if she was right, if the Tradds are cursed."

Susan spoke for the first time. "Don't talk like that," she said sharply. "It's fitting for you to mourn Miss Hen. I mourn her too.

But you can't give in to it, or to foolish fancies. You're a minister, Billy Barrington, and that's what you've got to do. You've got to minister to the needs of this unfortunate family.

"And you can do it. I know you can. You'll be strong, and you'll give them strength. There's nothing to be afraid of. You'll do just fine."

Billy turned to her. Beneath her black veil, her face was pale with grief and an anxiety that belied her words. He took her hand again. "I'll be just fine, honey. Don't you worry."

Henrietta Tradd, who had been loved and respected by so many people, was buried with only her family and the Barony blacks in attendance. People feared the pox too much to set foot on Ashley Barony. Margaret stood between Stuart and Anson, each of them holding her arm to support her. She was like an insubstantial shadow, thin and weakened by illness, covered by a black crepe veil from the top of her black bonnet to the toes of her black boots. At Stuart's left stood Zanzie, also in black, with a black apron over her black dress. She held the two children in her strong arms.

Susan walked to a place at Anson's right. The morning sun came from behind a cloud as she approached the group. It set the brilliant Tradd hair on fire. Susan felt a chill down her spine. It's like they were being struck by lightning, she thought, the two brothers and two innocent babies. They call it down from the skies. What will happen to them?

Billy's clear, firm voice began the awesome, majestic words of the service. Susan's eyes filled with tears. He was a good man, her husband, and she loved him with all her heart. Soon they would be leaving. St. Andrews was already closed, its windows shuttered. Billy had only one duty left to perform there; after Henrietta's burial, they would all go to the churchyard for graveside services for Henry and Jane Garden, dead of smallpox on the same day as Henrietta Tradd.

Billy would, Susan prayed, never again have a day as heartbreaking as this day. But if he did, he would meet it, and he would carry out his duties. He had been here in the low country only a short time, but it had changed him. The Barony, the Tradds had changed him. He had been a boy in a man's suit when he left Belton. Now he was a man.

She looked past her husband's strong shoulders at the ancient live oak whose branches sheltered the moss-covered stones of the Ashley graves. The Spanish moss hanging from the huge gnarled limbs cast moving shadows in the fitful sunlight. Behind it in the distance, she could see the grassy bank that bordered the river. As she gazed at its tranquil, soft beauty, a billow of mist moved on the water and crept up onto the lawn. Susan shivered.

BOOK 2

1902–1913

10

"Jesus Christ, Margaret, it's freezing in here." Stuart poked the fire savagely: a spurt of flame rose, then died down. "Goddammit," Stuart shouted, "this wood is no damn good. Probably green. Or wet. Or both."

Margaret cowered in the corner of the sofa. Stuart's rages were becoming more and more frequent, and increasingly violent. Now he stabbed furiously at the small fire again, then threw the poker across the room. Margaret burst into tears.

"For God's sake, stop that howling," Stuart bellowed. He strode across the room, turned in the doorway. "I'm going out," he said. "Don't fix supper for me. It won't be fit to eat anyhow." He slammed the door as he left.

The vibration jarred the smoking logs in the fireplace. They shifted, sending up a shower of sparks and a tall, bright flame.

Margaret stared woefully at the cheerful sight.

It was November. Outside, a steady cold rain had been falling for three days; the dank oppressiveness seemed to seep into the house through the cracks around the doors and windows. Drafts criss-crossed the rooms and eddied across the floors.

Little Stuart and Peggy had been kept indoors, and their noisy games made the house seem very small.

Which added to Stuart's complaints. Because they were still living in the Woods House. They had not made the traditional transfer to the Big House in early October.

Margaret had had hysterics when Stuart demanded that she organize the move. She became so ill that Zanzie sent for Dr. Drayton from Summerville, and Margaret was sedated for two days. When she got up and rejoined the family for dinner, her eyes were sunken and glazed, and she had a deathlike pallor.

For the first time, Anson intervened in the quarrel between Stuart and his wife. "You're being a brute, Stu. Margaret isn't being stubborn, like you say. She's terrified of the Big House. She thinks it's a death house. Koger was killed when we were there, Papa was killed there before her very eyes, and Mama died there. Margaret's afraid there might still be smallpox in the walls, or maybe haunts. Anyhow, its cruel to ask her to go back there, at least so soon. Maybe next year."

Stuart refused to accept Anson's explanations. "There's nothing bothering Margaret except that she'd have to stir her stumps. She's too lazy to see to the house. She's got six darkies working for her, and I never even get a decent meal on time or a clean shirt to put on. I don't know what she does all day."

Both Anson and Stuart were right. Margaret could not face the move to the Big House for two reasons. She had a superstitious horror of the memories associated with it, and she was incapable of facing the difficulties of directing the maintenance of such a large establishment. She could not even manage the simpler life in the Woods House.

First her mother and then Henrietta had taken care of everything for her. Margaret did not even know what needed to be done to keep a household running; she had no idea of how to do anything, even if she recognized the need for it. When her mother and her mother-in-law both died at the same time, she was left with no one to teach her. She felt like an abandoned child.

She turned to Stuart for comfort, but he was too stunned by Henrietta's death to respond. Instead, he asked for strength and reassurance that life would go on as he had known it, with a warm, loving woman seeing to his needs and wishes. His spoken and unspoken demands added to Margaret's fears.

She turned to Zanzie for the comfort Stuart could not give and for the mothering she wanted so desperately. Zanzie folded Margaret in her strong arms, called her "my baby," encouraged her to cry, built a wall between her and everyone around her.

Zanzie also became a tyrant. She had been an outsider on the Barony ever since she arrived. The Tradd servants had kept themselves to themselves. Now Zanzie would have her revenge. She assumed Margaret's role, issued orders, complained, criticized, threatened.

And the servants retaliated with sabotage. Meals were late, food was burned, laundry was scorched and torn. Dust collected under beds, cobwebs in corners, tarnish on silver and brass, weeds in the unmown lawn. It was war. Undeclared, unacknowledged, and totally disruptive. The very air was discordant, poisoned.

Even Anson was affected. Always quiet and self-effacing, Anson had always looked up to his oldest brother, admired Stuart's daring and his dashing charm. He had even been content to run the farm for Stuart, to do all the work to keep Stuart's inheritance intact. It seemed logical to him. Stuart was too mercurial for the day-in, day-out routine of farming. If anyone were to do it, it would have to be Anson. He had tried to leave, to escape the pain of seeing the girl he loved as his brother's wife, but he had not succeeded. And so he had made his private peace. During the two and a half years since Stuart and Margaret had married, he had learned to live with the pain; time had dulled its edge, even though he loved Margaret even more than he had then. He had expended all his energies and passions on his work, had found his peace in the slow, revolving seasons and the cycle of growth and harvest.

Even when Stuart turned his anger on Margaret, when her suffering tore at Anson's heart, he was able to stay calm and separate, to lose himself in the demands of farming.

But now Stuart trespassed on his world, and Anson exploded.

Anson was on his knees in a field of lettuces when Stuart rode up on horseback. The lettuces were blushed with patches of a pink-white mold. None of the field hands had seen anything like it before. Nor had Anson. He was kneeling to examine the underside of the plants, and he held a handful of earth under his nose to sniff for contagion. Stuart's horse lost its footing in the wet earth and trampled several plants while regaining it.

"Trouble, bro'?" said Stuart.

Anson was very troubled indeed. But he looked up at his brother impassively. "Maybe," he said.

"Doesn't seem worth all the bother just for lettuce," Stuart said. "Only a penny a head or thereabouts. I think maybe I'll plant artichokes or something like that instead. They bring a better price."

Anson leaped to his feet. "You'll plant? When did you ever plant anything?"

"I figure it's time I started. We should be making more money than we do."

Lists of numbers flashed through Anson's memory: his hard-won increases in productivity and income, the cash withdrawals by Stuart to pay for his pleasures, the sales of parcels of land that had been part of the Barony for over two hundred years. He seized Stuart's booted leg and pulled him down from his horse into the mud. "Haven't you done enough damage already? I've been trying my damnedest to save you, with no help and never a thank-you. If you meddle in my business. I'll kill you."

He struggled with Stuart, holding him down, sitting on his chest, smearing his clothes and head with mud. "How do you like it, plantation owner? This is what farming's about. You can't sit up on a horse and farm. You've got to get your hands dirty."

While they wrestled in the mud, the field hands leaned on their hoes and watched the show. "Cain and Abel," commented one.

"You think he goin' kill him?" inquired his neighbor.

"Maybe so."

The struggle between the two brothers was violent, nearly murderous. Without recognizing it themselves, they were fighting about much more than command over the farm. Stuart had ridden out to the field looking for reassurance, for manhood. He had not felt any real responsibility for the Barony until Henrietta died. Anson had taken over his father's role as farm manager, Henrietta had condoned his own extravagances and partying. For Stuart, life had changed very little as long as his mother was alive. Now, nothing was the same. He had taken it for granted that he would always be well fed, well clothed and well liked. But he was none of those. His wife shrank from him, and his home life was completely disrupted. Stuart was afraid.

He was, he realized with a shock, twenty-two years old. A man, not a boy. A man should not be frightened. A man should control his life. He would, he believed, find his manhood in Anson's eyes. Anson had always looked up to him, admired him. Yes, loved him. Stuart had a confused, happy vision of Anson greeting him with joy, of Anson working with him, developing the Barony into something greater than it was, of Anson confirming to him that he was capable of a man's responsibilities, able to control his life.

When Anson turned on him, humiliated him, shamed him, Stuart's hopes were destroyed. Only his fears remained. Anson had betrayed him, and Stuart hated him for it. He wanted to strike, to hurt, to wound Anson physically as much as Anson had wounded him in the invisible depths of his heart.

And Anson wanted, for that instant, to kill Stuart. To punish him for the pain he felt when Stuart took Margaret, for the envy he had always felt of Stuart's easy charm, for the hundreds of times he had waited in vain for Stuart to notice how hard and well he was working, for intruding into the domain where he had found peace. Most of all, he wanted to punish Stuart for not being what he had always believed him to be: confident, powerful, a leader. Anson smelled the sweat of fear on his big brother, and he hated him for it.

They fought until they were too exhausted to fight anymore. Then they lay side by side in the muddy furrows of the field, their chests heaving with the exertion of breathing.

Later they stumbled to the house together, arms around each other's shoulders, mumbling phrases about the fights they had had as boys, pretending that everything was all right. But nothing would be all right ever again. There was no love between them, and no trust. They were enemies, each isolated behind a wall of anger, self-pity and self-justification. They became very careful with each other.

And so the three of them, Stuart, Margaret and Anson, lived together in the Woods House, while the servants' war steadily disintegrated the fabric of their lives, and their individual isolation became more and more burdensome.

They shared a legacy from their childhood: they had all been taught good manners. They held tightly to that single constant. They were very polite. Stuart moved into a separate bedroom, but he was much more dutiful to Margaret than he had been, holding her chair, taking her for rides in the buggy. Anson consulted Stuart about his plans for the next season's crops, and Stuart told him to do whatever he thought best. Margaret smiled constantly and was effusively grateful for all courtesies.

At Christmastime they turned their attention, with relief, toward the children. Stuart took Margaret in to Charleston to shop. She bought Peggy, who was just over a year old, a French doll with a trunkful of the latest Paris fashions. Stuart bought a red saddle for Little Stuart, then found a pony to carry it.

Anson shopped in Summerville, with great success. He bought the latest novelty for his nephew, a stuffed toy called "Teddy Bear" after President Roosevelt. And for Peggy he found another novelty, cookies shaped like animals. They were in a box decorated to look like a circus wagon, and the box had a white string handle so that it could be hung on the Christmas tree.

Peggy and Little Stuart ate the cookies, tried to feed some to Teddy and ignored all their other presents. The adults exclaimed with politely feigned pleasure over the gifts they exchanged, laughed genuinely at the children's attempts to persuade Teddy to eat, and returned to their private loneliness.

It was an unbearable way to live. Something would have to happen to break the tensions that gripped them all.

11

Stuart was the first to find an answer. To pay the expenses of the Season in 1901, he had instructed his lawyer to sell some of the Barony land on the other side of the road that went from Charleston to Summerville. The purchaser's name was Samuel Ruggs.

Sam Ruggs was a hearty, shrewd, red-faced, stout man of thirty. Son of a sharecropper, he had sworn, when he was a boy, that he would never work for another man. When he was eleven he went into business for himself making moonshine whiskey. In spite of frequent arrests, fines and time in jail, Sam slowly gathered a tidy sum in greenbacks. Then he said goodbye to his family, his friends, his customers and the law enforcement officials who knew him so well. He left his Georgia homeland for South Carolina and respectability.

He built a small general store on the land he bought from Stuart Tradd. The location was ideal for his needs: isolated enough for privacy, with thick woods where he could conceal his still. It was close enough to both Charleston and Summerville for his customers to come to him, and the Negro Settlement at the Barony provided legitimate customers for the store's shoddy goods. No sheriff would question his reasons for being there.

The store occupied a single large room. Sam occupied three larger rooms behind it. They were furnished in the best Sears, Roebuck had to offer and were luxuriously overheated. Sam hired a woman from the Settlement to cook and clean for him. She was called Marigold, and she was as cheerful as her name. She spoiled Sam outrageously. When Stuart became Sam's friend, she spoiled him as well.

The contrast to the ill-kept, dissension-ridden household on the plantation was dramatic. Stuart never wanted to go home. It was not merely comfort that lured him to Sam's. Ruggs asked Stuart's advice, consulted him about his plans for expansion, asked him what new things he should add to his stock. He made Stuart feel valuable and important. Soon Stuart was spending almost all of his time at Sam's.

Margaret confided to Anson that she found it nice and peaceful when Stuart was gone. Anson said nothing. It would be dishonorable to agree. But in his heart, he was fiercely glad when Stuart was away. It gave him the opportunity to make Margaret happy. He took her on small outings, short rides in the buggy to her old home, to Summerville, to St. Andrews, now shuttered and still. Margaret's pleasure was so intense that the outings became more frequent and longer. When spring came, they began to go to Charleston, and Margaret was in raptures.

Anson worried about Stuart. They should, he thought, invite him to accompany them. Margaret was, after all, his wife. And there were other reasons, too. Anson had overheard the talk among the workers. Stuart was too intimate, they thought, with Ruggs's acquaintances and with the flashy women who appeared as visitors to the rooms behind the store. The Negroes looked down on Ruggs as "white trash," not good enough for a Tradd to associate with.

While Anson was puzzling about the problem, Sam Ruggs solved it for him. He bought the South Carolina distributorship for one of the new horseless carriages and made Stuart his partner.

"Brother," Stuart shouted at Anson, "you are looking at a revolution. This is the Curved Dash Olds. Ain't she a beauty?" He was perched on the high black leather seat of the automobile. It was black, with red and gold trim on the big wheels and boxlike frame. Shiny brass lanterns were attached front and rear, their bright surfaces glinting in the sunlight as they vibrated to the noisy shaking of the engine. Stuart was wearing goggles and a cap and a wide, happy smile. Anson had not seen him smile like that for years.

The partnership arrangement with Sam was simple. Stuart would drive the Olds around the state, demonstrating it and taking orders. He would use his sales commissions to redeem the note he had given Sam for his half of the dealership.

He took Anson and Margaret for a spin, got some money from Anson, packed a small suitcase and hurried off to tour the state. "Expect me when you see me," he yelled. Then he waved, honked the horn and departed with a fusillade of backfires.

His trips kept him away for weeks at a time, and when he was home he was in high good spirits, spending an evening telling stories about his travels, then rushing away again. Anson and Margaret's adventures were less hectic. They went on pleasure excursions once or twice a week, usually to Charleston. They went to band concerts at White Point Gardens, to the Air Dome, the open-air theater at Hampton Park. They explored the astonishing new store that had opened on King Street, where a glittering array of merchandise was spread on counters and everything cost a nickel or a dime. They took the excursion train to Beaufort and back, with a picnic basket packed full of sandwiches tied with ribbon bows. They took the excursion steamer to the Isle of Palms, where the First Artillery Orchestra played music all afternoon and Professor Waldo E. Lyon, Champion Trick Bicycle Rider, gave free exhibitions every hour on the hour.

"I've never been so happy in my life," Margaret said again and again. Anson held her happiness to his heart like a secret treasure.

When fall came, Margaret begged Anson to ignore the shortening days. It was still plenty warm, she said, for just one more picnic, one more boat ride. He could not bear to deny her. In November she caught a cold that progressed with frightening rapidity into acute pneumonia.

Stuart was away. Stuart was always away. He had missed the children's birthdays, Margaret's, even his own. Anson and Zanzie shared the vigil at Margaret's bedside and the overwhelming relief when the crisis was past.

The illness was short, but Margaret's convalescence lasted for more than six months. Anson took care of her. He tended her with such loving gentleness that even Margaret recognized it as something extraordinary. She had been spoiled and indulged for most of her life, but she had never before experienced anything like Anson's love. Bottled up for years, it poured forth now in response to Margaret's weakness and helplessness. He anticipated her wants before she was aware of them, devised little surprises and treats for

66

her, coaxed her, calmed her, surrounded her with the warmth and comfort of his attentiveness. "Don't leave me, Anson," Margaret begged when his duties called him away.

"I'll be right back," he always promised.

"Always? You'll always come right back? You'll stay with me always?"

Anson promised.

As Margaret regained her strength, they took short walks and drives around the plantation, sharing the beautiful advance of spring into the gardens and woods. The world around them flowered, changed, softened. And they changed with it. Without awareness of what was happening, they slid into a land of make-believe. They lived together in a strange, innocent pretend-marriage, sharing a house but not a bed, exchanging looks but not caresses. They were extremely happy, playing house. It was a fragile world they constructed, successful only as long as it remained self-contained, enclosed in a shimmering bubble of loving deception.

Whenever Stuart came home, Anson and Margaret returned to the real world with a sense of disbelief and alienation. But Stuart's visits were brief, and then they were alone again, enclosed, happy.

They made no effort to deceive anyone. They were, to each other, openly in love. But the emotion was so tender, and Anson protected it so fiercely, that only its innocence was apparent. Not even the servants suspected that anything was changed. Anson was still, as far as they could see, taking care of Miss Margaret while she got well. Zanzie knew that Margaret loved Anson; Margaret confided in her. Zanzie did not concern herself with the morality of Margaret's love. Her baby was happy; that was all that mattered.

Everything seemed to conspire to make their lives satisfying. The skies gave just the right amount of rain and sun, and the farm's crops were better than they had ever been. The servants grew bored with the effort of fighting Zanzie and went back to the routines they had followed before. Dinners were excellent, the house clean, the laundry fresh and crisp. Little Stuart was four, Peggy three. They had their own private child's world and seldom strayed into Anson's and Margaret's. They should have realized the danger of let's pretend. They should have known it was too good, too delicate, too precious to last.

Margaret Garden Tradd was fundamentally a foolish, spoiled child-woman. Although she had put aside her preoccupation with gowns and parties—she had quietly refused all the invitations received for the Season because she could not attend the parties with Anson—she still spent hours going through the box of souvenirs she had saved from the Season of 1901. And she kept Peggy's Paris doll in her room, changing its beautiful clothes at least once a week. She spent hours bathing in scented water, choosing her clothes for the day, trying new ways to arrange her hair. She had no interest in her children, nor in anyone except herself. Even Anson, at first.

It was only when she became Anson's dream-wife that she began to learn what love meant. She began by imitating him, following his lead in the game they were playing. When Anson gave her a little gift, she immediately found something to give him. When he moved her chair out of a draft, she adjusted the curtains to keep the sun out of his eyes.

Then she discovered how good Anson's appreciation made her feel, and she began to try and invent ways to please him without waiting for him to act first. It was not easy, she discovered, to be as thoughtful as Anson was. He had a genius for anticipating her wants, and she had little imagination about his. Still, with time, as she grew to know him she grew at last, after a year together, to understand what would please him. It was her happiness. Anson truly lived for her, drew his pleasure from pleasing her. Margaret was astounded, awestruck. She had never thought that love was like that. She had the grace to feel unworthy of Anson's devotion, and at that moment, thinking only of him, not of herself, Margaret knew for the first time what it felt like to love. She loved Anson.

It was the first adult emotion Margaret had ever known, the first step on the path to growing-up. She was twenty years old.

Margaret was thrilled. She felt that she had discovered the greatest secret in the world. "I have to tell Anson," she thought immediately, eager to share her heart with him. Then she laughed softly. "Silly," she whispered aloud to herself. "Anson already knows." Besides, it was very late. He would be asleep. She thought about Anson, the wonderfulness of Anson, hugging herself with the joy of loving him. She longed to do something for him as testimony of her love. Deep within her something stirred, something new and strange to her, something as old as time.

Margaret took a candle and walked quietly down the hall to Anson's room. She opened the door and closed it behind her without a sound. Holding the candle high, she walked to his bed.

Anson looked young and vulnerable in sleep. Margaret stared lovingly at him. Then she blew out the candle and dropped it on the floor. She dropped her clothes on top of it, then slipped under the bedclothes and nestled close to Anson's warmth.

"Anson," she whispered. "Anson, wake up."

"What?" Anson stirred, felt her next to him, sat bolt upright, wide awake. "Margaret? What is it? What's going on?"

Margaret put her arms around his neck and pulled his mouth down to meet hers in their first kiss. "I love you," she said as their lips touched.

Anson's self-control, perfected by years of application, vanished under Margaret's imploring hands. His tenderness remained, and his uncanny perception of Margaret's desires. He made love to her with patience, gentleness and, when the moment came, with demanding intensity. He was a virgin, and Margaret an experienced married woman. But he led her into sensations and freedom that she had never known existed. The make-believe marriage became eternally real, consummated in body, heart and soul.

The room was darkened when Margaret woke, but she could tell that it must be full daylight outside by the shards of sunlight at the edges of the drawn curtains. "We overslept," she whispered, laughing. She stretched out her arm to nudge Anson.

Her hand fell on a cool, plump pillow.

Margaret sat up. She was in her own room, alone, her clothes neatly folded on a chair. She giggled. Anson must have carried her in after she went to sleep. He needn't have bothered. She was proud of loving him; she didn't care who knew. But, she knew, he was protecting her. Anson always protected her. Margaret felt weak with love for him.

She stumbled in her hurry to get up, to dress, to run and find him. When she took up her hairbrush, she saw the envelope. A love letter, she thought. Oh, perfect Anson. She ripped it open.

"What I did was unforgivable," said the note. "I have betrayed us all. I cannot live so dishonored. I pray your forgiveness. Goodbye."

Margaret could not breathe. She felt as cold as death. Her eyes rolled up in her head, and she crumpled onto the carpet.

12

Margaret's grief was so intense that she wanted to die. He promised, she cried to herself, he promised to stay with me always. And he's gone. She refused to eat, and she could not sleep. She longed for oblivion.

Stuart arrived home three weeks later, on the day the Barony blacks finally abandoned the search for Anson's body. He must have gone into the river, they said, and been carried by the current down to Charleston Harbor, then out to sea. Stuart refused to believe them. He insisted that they cover the woods again, and day after day he rode from one search party to another, urging them on, shouting Anson's name.

"It can't be," he cried aloud. "He can't be gone." When there was nothing left to be done, Stuart stumbled into the house and collapsed onto the floor, exhausted and despairing. He fell into a stuporous sleep.

Margaret woke him. Her face was livid, her eyes burning. She was vibrant with the energy of consuming rage. All the love she had felt for Anson had been transformed into hate by the realization that she was pregnant.

"Let me tell you about your precious little brother, Stuart," she whispered in her husband's ear. "He made a cuckold of you. Then he was too cowardly to face either one of us. That's why he killed himself, because he was a coward."

Margaret believed what she was saying. Memory had blurred, twisted and become a conviction that Anson had deliberately seduced, then abandoned her. Now she poured all her hatred into Stuart's half-heeding ear, telling him what she herself believed. When her words penetrated his consciousness, Stuart moaned, shouted at her, begged her to stop. Margaret sat back on her heels and laughed, her voice cracking.

Stuart staggered to his feet and ran from the house to his automobile and the road that led away from her. He did not return for three months.

He was dirty and bearded and smelled of cheap whiskey, but he was sober and icy calm when he entered the house and spoke to Margaret. "I will acknowledge your bastard as mine," he said, "because I don't want my children to share their mother's disgrace. But I never want to see it, Margaret, and I never want to see you. I will have my things moved to the Big House. Don't ever set foot in it. If you have anything to say to me, put it in writing and send it by one of the servants."

Stuart walked out without looking at his wife. He climbed wearily into his automobile and drove toward the Big House. As he passed between two dusty, unplanted fields, he stopped. His head dropped onto the arm that held the steering wheel. "Anson," he said, and he wept.

Later that day, after he had bathed and shaved and put on fresh clothes, he went to see Sam Ruggs.

Ruggs welcomed him loudly. He had been waiting for Stuart, he said; he had great news. They were both going to be rich.

Stuart responded to Sam's warmth and excitement. For a moment he forgot everything that had happened, and he was carefree when he raised his glass to share Sam's toast to the future.

But Sam's news was not good for Stuart. Sam had obtained the Ford dealership for Charleston, and he wanted Stuart to share it with him. "The Ford's going to outsell the Olds ten to one, I'm sure of it," Sam said. "Maybe a hundred to one."

Stuart put his glass on the table. "I can't do it, Sam. I've got to give up automobiles and see to the plantation. There's nobody but me now. As a matter of fact, I came over to settle up with you for my half of the Olds deal. I've got to sell out."

Sam poured them both another drink. The fact was, he said, that he'd already gotten rid of the Olds business. Sold it to a fellow in Summerville. But Stuart didn't have much more than fifty dollars coming to him. He'd barely made enough commissions to pay for his demonstrator model.

"Sorry, Stuart, but business is business." Sam extended his hand. "Still friends?"

"Sure, Sam, still friends." He took Sam's hand. "Speaking of still, I could use a jug of home brew. I'll drive around back and get it on my way home."

Stuart's Olds was waiting outside. The afternoon sun outlined it with cruel clarity. The bright red and gold trim was chipped, mottled by crusted layers of road dust. One of the brass lanterns, now tarnished, had lost one of its screws. It sagged, ready to fall.

Stuart smiled, made a jaunty salute as he drove away. When he was out of sight of the store, his shoulders slumped.

The records Anson had left included plans for the next year's plantings. Stuart tried his best to follow them, but he knew nothing about farming and everything seemed to go wrong. He came back to the Big House at the end of every day exhausted, discouraged and angry. He found escape in whiskey, usually the cheap, powerful white lightning from Sam Ruggs's still. His evenings followed a regular pattern: sardonic toasts to the portraits of his ancestors on the walls, followed by outbursts of rage against fate, sliding downhill into morose self-pity then into maudlin tears and outcries of "my poor babies." Little Stuart and Peggy were the only ones who had not betrayed him, he was convinced.

Occasionally he went to the Woods House and shouted for one of the servants to bring the children out to him. Then he would frighten them by clasping them in his arms until they began to cry. He pushed them away, then, and hurried off, weeping and muttering that Margaret was trying to turn his children against him.

When Christmas came, Stuart ordered that the children be brought to the Big House for the yearly gift-giving ceremony. Little Stuart was six now, plenty old enough to begin learning what was expected of him, Stuart thought. "After all," he said to the portraits, "I'm killing myself to preserve his inheritance. The plantation will be his one day."

Christmas morning was crisp and sunny, with a slight breeze from the river that stirred the fronds of Spanish moss on the trees and dried the drops of dew on the tall, overgrown bushes of bright red camellias. Stuart felt the weight and comfort of tradition as he stood on the steps that rose to the great columned entry. Just so had he stood with his father, and now his son was standing with him.

The Barony Negroes came forward one by one to receive their gifts, a bottle of wine and new pants and shirt for the men, a length of calico for the women, candy for the children. "Christmas gift," each said, and "Happy Christmas," Stuart replied. Peggy and Little Stuart chorused the reply with him. They handed out the candy and giggled with the black children at the excitement of it all.

After the gifts were distributed, the blacks began to sing. The three Tradds joined in, clapping and stamping their feet in the same joyful rhythm. "Mary Had a Baby," they sang and "Yonder Come the Shepherd to the Manger."

"Come inside," said Stuart to the children, "and see what Papa's got for you." He had bought them dozens of inappropriate, expensive toys.

"Santa Claus brought us a baby sister last night," said Peggy. "Whew, is she ever funny-looking."

Stuart frowned. For a while, he had forgotten. Peggy did not notice the change in her father, and she continued to prattle. "Zanzie says that all white babies look funny, that she'll get better. But she'll have to get a whole lot better before I'll want to play with her. I like my dolls. They don't cry.

"Zanzie says that Mama's papa and mama are smiling from heaven at the baby 'cause Mama named her Garden. I don't think Mama knows that, though. I heard her tell Zanzie she was naming the baby Garden because she wishes that was her name still. What does that mean, Papa?"

13

The baby was fantastically ugly. Her skin had a bluish cast, more intense in the lips and nails. Her long head was grotesque, squeezed by the forceps delivery into a peanut shape. It was completely bald; a large strawberry birthmark covered the back of it. She was making a tiny, plaintive sound, like the mewing of a weak kitten.

Zanzie picked her up and felt her bottom. "She dry. Might be she hungry. I done sent for the wet nurse."

"Tell her to take the baby away with her," Margaret sobbed. "I don't want her in the house. She's cried ever since she was born, and she's ugly as dirt. If I have to look at her and listen to her, I'll go crazy."

Zanzie put the baby in her cradle and hurried to Margaret. "There, now," she soothed, "don't you fret none. Zanzie'll take care of you." She tucked the coverlet around Margaret and rubbed her back until she was asleep.

Then she lifted the baby and tiptoed heavily from the room. She met the nurse on the path to the Settlement. "Here, girl," she said, handing over a big laundry basket. "This here's the baby and all her things. She called Garden. You keep her till I tells you different. Might be a long time."

Reba was the name of Garden's wet nurse. She was tall, as tall as most men, and extremely thin. She had no hips and very small breasts, even when they were full of milk. She looked, at first glance, like a man wearing a dress, because of her figure and her large features. Her jaw was square and powerful-looking; her big, flattened nose spread wide across her face; her forehead was high and prematurely furrowed; her ears were big, with a thick rim of heavy cartilage. She wore her hair in tight braids pinned flat across the crown of her head, adding to the illusion of masculinity. Reba was pure Negro, her blood unadulterated by any taint of Caucasian or Indian ancestry. She was black, as black as rarest ebony, and her gums were blue.

Reba was the wife of Matthew Ashley, the handsomest man in the Settlement, the headman for all the livestock on the plantation, the favorite grandson of Maum' Pansy. He could have had any girl in the parish, and many had tried to marry him. But he had seen Reba in church in her choir robes, singing like one of the heavenly host, swaying to the music with a catlike supple grace, and he never looked at another woman.

Reba and Matthew had two sons, John, who was five, and Luke, who was one. They had lost two children between those two, a boy and a girl, both stillborn. And a third, a little boy, born three weeks before and dead a week after birth. Reba had intended to nurse both her baby and Margaret Tradd's baby. Her small breasts made enough milk to feed four. When her Isaac died, she squeezed her breasts to keep the milk from drying up and waited for the message from the Woods House. Her body craved a tiny body in her arms and a hungry mouth on her nipples.

74

As soon as Zanzie was gone, Reba sat down beside the path and took the swaddled baby from the basket. She held the small form close to her body and rocked from side to side. "Thank you, blessed Jesus," she said again and again.

Then she unbuttoned her sweater and dress. Milk was seeping from her long nipples. "Soon," Reba said, "soon, praise the Lord." She turned back the folds of the blanket to look at the baby.

"No!" she cried. "Not blue. This baby ain't going to die." She put Garden on the ground and kneeled over her. "I ain't going allow it, not this baby too." She cupped Garden's tiny head in one hand and put her mouth over the baby's. Then she blew into it, her other hand on Garden's chest. It hardly moved. Reba inhaled, sucking with her mouth, pulling, demanding. She worked for an endless two minutes, her ears ringing from the tremendous effort.

Then she straightened up and spat a clot of blood-streaked mucus onto the grass. She raised her hands and her head. "Thank you, Lord."

Garden began to cry. Reba watched the frail little chest shudder as the baby screamed and the skin gradually turned pink.

"Now you can eat," she said. She lifted the baby and guided her nuzzling face to the nipple.

The Settlement population ran out into the road when they saw Reba coming. "What you doing home, Reba? Missus don't want you?"

Reba lowered the big basket from the top of her head where she had carried it. "Ain't me," she said. "Missus don't want the baby. She send it to live with me. Ain't nobody want it but me. This here is my baby, sent by the Lord to me on Christmas Day."

People crowded into her house after her. "Matthew," Reba said, "we got us a baby." She lifted the sleeping baby from her nest and offered her to Matthew. He opened the blanket and began to laugh.

"Reba, this here's the ugliest baby I ever saw, including possums." Everyone pushed in for a look, then drew back, exclaiming.

Reba just smiled.

"All white babies is ugly," said one good-hearted neighbor.

"Not so ugly as this." A murmur of assent flowed through the crowd.

"Looks ain't everything," someone offered.

Reba smiled.

After everyone had had a look, Matthew sent them away. He sat down next to Reba and put his arm around her. "Does this baby make you happy, woman?"

"She do."

"Then that's all that counts." Matthew laughed again. "She is sure enough the ugliest thing I ever saw."

Reba laughed with him. "You should have seen her when I got her. I'll tell you all about it."

Garden, who had slept through her introduction to the community, waved her fists and whimpered.

Reba went to her. "Somebody must be hungry. Let me fix this little lady's britches and start her feeding, then I'll tell you while she eats." She reached eagerly for the ugly, unwanted baby.

Garden stayed with Reba for almost ten months. There was trouble in the beginning: Maum' Pansy refused to have Tradd blood in the Settlement. It would bring plat eye down on them. But Matthew persuaded her that Reba needed the baby. "Besides," he said, "the Tradds don't want her, plat eye won't neither." Old Pansy gave in; she couldn't resist Matthew. But she made him paint her door blue, and his, too, to ward off the spirits.

Garden was a constant source of interest in the community. Reba never lacked for visitors, curious to know if the baby's head was getting better. Some meant the shape, others the hair. Day by day, the marks and indentation made by the forceps smoothed out. When Garden was three months old her head had the normal, top-heavy configuration of any baby. But still no hair.

Even Reba began to think that perhaps none would ever grow. She kept little caps on Garden. Garden flailed ineffectually at them with her dimpled hands.

Then, on April Fool's day, Reba felt the first soft fuzz on Garden's scalp. She kept her in a cap, planning to surprise all the critics when the garish birthmark was completely covered.

She couldn't wait that long. The growth was so remarkable that she needed to ask if anyone had ever seen anything like it. What did it mean? Was it dangerous?

Garden's hair was growing in patches. All over her head there were tufts of silken pale gold hairs. But between the tufts, she was still bald.

"Maybe she got mange," said Matthew.

"Huh! Ain't I seen mange in my life? Ain't no sores or nothing, just clean shiny skin."

"We better go see the doctor, the white folks' doctor. No black baby got a head like that."

But Dr. Drayton could not help. "It can't be any disease, Reba. I've never seen such a healthy baby in my life. You've worked wonders. I'll tell you, I didn't expect her to live."

Reba smiled.

"I ain't going worry," she said to Matthew. "When it get long enough, I'll just brush it over the bare places. Until then, she can stay in her cap." She kissed the patchwork little head and deftly slipped the cap on. Matthew watched her, a line between his eyebrows.

"Don't you get too attached, now. Reba, you hear? That baby going be weaned soon, and then she go home. I don't want you to make sadness for yourself."

"I don't believe in early weaning."

"You better start believing."

Reba was startled. Matthew almost never gave her orders. When he did, he meant business. The next day, she asked Chloe to bring a cup for the baby from the Tradd kitchen.

But it was Zanzie who came. Eyes watched through cracks in closed shutters as she walked up to Reba's door, carrying a heavy basket. John hid behind his Reba's skirts, and she held Luke firmly in her arms when she answered Zanzie's knock.

"I bring the baby cup and some things," said Zanzie. Reba let her in.

"Those two fine boys you got, Reba."

Reba nodded.

"I bring some of Mist' Little Stuart clothes he outgrow." Zanzie gestured toward the basket. "And a nice ham for you and a bottle of wine for your man."

"What you want from me, Zanzie?"

Zanzie looked at Reba's stern face. "I see I better talk plain," she said. "I ask you to keep what I say between you and me."

"I can't make no promise."

"Well, I ask you anyhow. It's like this. Chloe, she tell me you fixing to wean the baby. I tell you, if that baby come back in the house too soon, it going do something awful to Miz Tradd. She ain't hardly been herself since she started that baby. I don't know how come, but that poor little creature some kind of poison to she mother. I raise Miss Margaret from when she was littler than Garden she is now. I always knew her heart. But I don't hardly recognize her no more. She full of poison. To the children, to Mist' Stuart, even to me. And it all start with that baby.

"I don't even dare mention Garden name. Chloe or Juno or Herklis say something about how fine she doing, and I make mention to Miss Margaret, and she start to swell up she face and take on and cuss like I never heard no lady cuss. So now I don't say nothing." Zanzie put her hand to her mouth and bit her thumb. Her lips were trembling and her eyes pressed shut.

Reba touched Zanzie's knee. "I get us some coffee," sne said. "John, you take Luke outside and see he don't go in the road."

When Reba brought the coffee from the stove, Zanzie had regained control of herself. "Thank you," she said. She drank. "That mighty fine coffee," she remarked. Reba waited.

Zanzie drained her cup and set it carefully on a table. "What I wants to ask you," she said, "is can you keep Garden till summer end. Maybe by then, Miss Margaret she get well again. If she don't, well, the children they start going to school. They won't need me to look after them. I can watch for Garden without Miss Margaret hardly knowing.

"I don't expect you to work for nothing, Reba. I got some money save for my burial. I can pay you."

"Why don't Miz Tradd pay?"

"She ain't got no money."

"How about the Mister?"

"I scared to ask him. . . . Things is not so good with him and her."

"Everybody know that. Listen to me, Zanzie. I can't tell you yes, and I can't tell you no. I got to ask my husband."

"I understand."

"But I can tell you this. Ain't a soul here in this community but would take that baby sooner than send her back where she ain't wanted. Everybody here care for Garden. If I can't keep her, I'll find somebody who can.

"And we don't want your burial money, neither. We can always find food for another mouth."

Zanzie clasped her hands together in thanksgiving. She bent forward in a sort of obeisance. "God bless you, Reba," she said.

After she was gone, Reba sat quietly, drinking her coffee, her face sad. Suddenly she jumped up and went to the corner where Garden slept in her basket. "She didn't even ask to see you," she told the baby. "She didn't even look around to see where you were." Reba touched Garden's soft cheek, then her mouth. Immediately the sleeping baby began to make sucking noises. "Yes, ma'am," said Reba, "I think you can have dinner early today. I'd like that."

Matthew agreed that Garden had to stay, and he said nothing further about Reba's attachment. But she knew he was right, and she took action. She talked to all the women in the community, and within a week Garden began to be taken from house to house to spend a morning or an afternoon or an evening. She became the Settlement's baby instead of Reba's. Soon she learned the other faces and smiled at them just as she had smiled at Reba's. Reba felt her heart ache when she saw it. Until she discovered she was pregnant. Then she was able to let Garden go.

On the Fourth of July, Little Mose, one of the Settlement children, noticed that Garden was growing more hair. "Look at that," he yelled. "Garden got another batch of hair. It look same like a firecracker."

Sarah, his older sister, took Garden away from him and carried her around to everyone at the church picnic, showing them the discovery. Under the layer of golden silk, filling all the bare patches, there was a thick growth of the characteristic Tradd copper.

Matthew threw Garden up in the air, making her squeal with delight. "Don't you just beat all, baby? You come to us bald, now you is piebald." He kissed her fat neck and passed her back to Sarah.

"Mose," she called. "Come get Garden. It's still your turn to watch her."

Mose obliged. He even let Garden have the rest of his chicken leg to chew.

14

"Independence Day," said Margaret Tradd. She touched the bright red 4 on the calendar and laughed, a sharp harsh sound without joy. There was no independence in her life. She was a prisoner as surely as if she were locked in a dungeon.

She could leave. She could have one of the horses saddled, or she could order the buggy brought around. And then what? Where could she go?

She had friends. At least she called them friends. All the girls she had known from childhood, now grown women. And she had family, those cousins to the third and fourth remove, who had visited her mother when Margaret was young, who had greeted her with soft kisses at the parties in the Season. Would anyone take her in?

For a visit, yes. Any one of them, no matter how remote the connection. Hospitality was easily come by in the South.

But not to an adultress. Perhaps Stuart would say nothing; he had his pride to protect. But he hated her so. And he was almost always drunk. He was capable of broadcasting her shame, from spite or carelessness.

And then all doors would be closed to her. Society could forgive her for her sins with Stuart. There were a number of "premature" babies, born too soon after the wedding, in Charleston society. Everyone knew who they were, labeled them until the day they died and after, but forgave them and their parents.

Adultery, however, was different. Adultery closed all doors. Margaret couldn't take the chance.

Nor could she continue living as she had been. She had been fighting her circumstances, refusing to believe the truth, hysterical, making herself ill. She had to think, to plan, to find a way out. Tears and tantrums would not work anymore.

Nor would smiles and pretty pleadings. Stuart would never take her anyplace ever again, not even to preserve appearances. And he would not give her a penny. He had, he informed her by letter, even notified the merchants in Summerville and Charleston that only he could buy things on account.

She was trapped, isolated, alone. Stuart was her jailer. He would punish her for as long as she lived. Margaret's finger moved across the calendar: 1906. Soon she would be twenty-two. She had many more years to live in her cage. Until she died.

Or Stuart did.

Margaret's heart stopped for an instant. Then, with a painful lurch, it resumed beating, stronger and faster than before. Stuart was drinking constantly. Zanzie had told her so. It would kill him. He would fall from his horse or crash that foolish automobile of his or die from one of those diseases that killed drunks.

Margaret's finger touched her birth date again. Twenty-two wasn't so very old. She picked up her hand mirror and scrutinized her face. Her skin was dry. Tiny lines were forming from her nose to her mouth. Her hair was dull and lank. I've let myself go disgracefully, she thought.

Oatmeal. He has to let me buy oatmeal. And Chloe can make me some rose water. I'll start today making packs for my skin. And milk. And lemons. I have to soften my elbows, put a shine in my hair. I can wait. It can't be long. Then I'll go to the city, I'll see people, I'll dance and I'll be beautiful and admired, and I'll never set foot on this place again.

She ran to her bureau and got her box of souvenirs. She sat in the middle of her bed, spread them around her on the counterpane, remembering her Season.

15

In October Peggy and Little Stuart started school. Although Peggy was still a few days short of five years old, no one objected. The one-room schoolhouse served pupils from the first through seventh grades. There were fifth-graders who were fifteen; why not a first-grader who was five?

The schoolhouse was at Bacon's Bridge, where the road to Summerville crossed the Ashley River. It was almost five miles from the Barony, too far for the children to walk. They rode one of the Barony horses, an aged mare named Judy that had once been part of the smart team that pulled the Judge's carriage. She was placidly obedient to even a small hand on the reins. Stuart and Peggy both had ample space on her bare, bony old back. They considered it a great adventure to have a horse of their own.

In time, the adventure wore off. Judy was just a slow old mare, and school just a place with chalk-filled air and the droning group recitation of McGuffey's Reader and the arithmetic tables. Even the other children in the school, at first such a novelty to the young Tradds, became familiar and predictable.

But by then their routine was established and self-perpetuating. They followed it automatically, not wondering whether there was a different way to do things.

On the Barony, too, an unchanging pattern developed. Somehow Zanzie overlooked her pledge to take Garden back to the Woods House when the older children started school. The little girl stayed in the Settlement, where every house was home to her. She seemed to have been forgotten by her family. Margaret spent her days taking care of her skin and hair. And waiting. Stuart spent his in dissipation.

He had found new friends among the small scratch-farmers who lived along the Summerville road, men who killed themselves truck-farming their forty or fifty acres, being their own field hands. His new friends saw him the way he saw himself, a plantation owner, not a farmer. A gentleman. He developed a habit of dropping in on his friends, drinking with them, talking weather and crops and hunting. It filled his time. That, and the occasional conferences he had with his headmen when he rode his horse to the fields and barns and storehouses, being boss. And the women in Summerville. And the lonely meals in the Big House, followed by the hours of concentrated drinking until he could sleep.

After all the years of drama, a sort of tranquillity had come to Ashley Barony.

The months and years moved on, indistinguishable from one another, like the waters of the wide brown-green river flowing past. Peggy and Stuart advanced from grade to grade, graduated from Judy to horses of their own with saddles and a willingness to gallop.

Every year the crop yield was smaller and poorer than the year before. The factor in Charleston, who contracted for the produce and shipped it North, complained to Stuart but he continued to offer contracts, although at steadily diminishing values. After twenty years, he was loyal to old clients. He also represented Stuart in the annual sale of land required to liquidate debts.

Stuart was a distant, glamorous figure in his children's lives. They loved to go to the Big House. It was like a mysterious, exciting palace to them. Stuart lived in only two of its rooms, the drawing room and the master bedroom. Both were on the second floor. The ground floor was a thrilling, dangerous world of dim, shuttered spaces with frightening dust-sheeted shapes that could be ghosts, dragons or monsters.

Even better was the third floor, with its dusty, cavernous ballroom lined with tall mirrors that reflected a child's image back and forth to infinity. The ballroom was good for running in, and sliding on the wide floor, and making caves and forts from piles of the gilded bamboo chairs that they found there. High over their heads, the crystal chandeliers tinkled secretly in the muslin bags that covered them, whenever the children's games vibrated the stale, enclosed air. Stuart and Peggy were sure that the sound was the magic language of invisible fairies.

Best of all was the attic, its pointed spaces filled with treasure. There were humpbacked trunks by the dozen, locked and tantalizing. Tall wardrobes held strange garments, some disintegrating at a touch. There were heavy metal boxes crammed with papers and albums of funny-looking photographs with names written under them in white ink that flaked off when the pages were turned. Stuart found his name again and again for babies, boys, and men. There were books with colored pictures, stereoscopes with boxes of slides, a Victrola and records, rotting buggy whips and parasols and moldering boots of every size and color. All this, and they had, barely begun to explore.

Peggy and Little Stuart always played in the attic on rainy days if their father allowed it. Sometimes he said yes, sometimes no. They could never know what to expect. They would approach the house carefully. If it were locked or if their father roared at them to go away, they would find something else to do. If he told them to come in, they would still be careful. Sometimes he smelled funny and held them too close and called them "my babies." Other times he made them laugh with stories about himself and his brothers when they were children. Or he made them sit very still on a sofa and listen while he paced up and down telling them about their family, the people whose portraits were on the wall and their grandfather who had been a Judge. He always ended by talking about someone named "Aunt Elizabeth," and then Peggy and Stuart were frightened, because their father got so angry. "Evil," he shouted, "grasping and malicious and evil. She stole the Tradd business and the Tradd house. It should have been ours. She has no right to be so rich when we're so poor." He always went to the table with the decanter on it then and shooed the children away.

That was the signal that they could go up to the attic or the ballroom to play. No matter which mood their father was in, they always got to go explore when he was through with them. They accepted his moods as the price of admission.

As they grew older, they noticed that their father's laughing moods were less and less frequent. Still, they questioned nothing. They were used to thinking of him as the king of the Big House, the palace. And kings were above criticism.

Stuart's opinion of his children was not so generous. He expected something, wanted something from them without knowing what it was. And he never got it.

Peggy was not what he wanted his little girl to be. She wasn't delicate and doll-like, the way a girl ought to be. It wasn't only her scarred face, although he hated to look at it. It was her aggressiveness, her boldness. She acted like a boy.

And Stuart, his son, who should have been a comfort and a companion . . . Stuart was a sissy. There was no getting around it. He winced whenever he saw a string of dead birds or a buck brought back from a hunt. He couldn't ride worth a damn. He couldn't even swim right—kept his head out of the water like the sissy he was.

The only thing that could be said for him was that he knew more about the automobile than any grown man Stuart ever saw. The boy could drive before he was eight years old, and he could do things to the engine that made it sing.

Why couldn't he be that way with a gun and a horse? He was a sore disappointment to him.

Not so to Margaret. One day, while going through her souvenir box, she suddenly realized that ladies, even widow ladies, couldn't go about unescorted. At that moment she became interested in her son.

He was a good-looking boy. It made a pretty picture, the handsome little boy handing his mother down from her carriage, carrying her parcels, handing her her fan, calling for her after she had tea with a friend.

But her son's manners were deplorable. He had learned nothing, stuck out here in the country.

That very evening Margaret began to polish Little Stuart, to turn him into a perfect gentleman by her definition.

She did not tell him what she was doing. He only knew that, for some reason, his mother wanted to be with him and that it had something to do with wonderful times they would have someday.

Margaret was a distant stranger who mustn't be upset, who was very delicate, Zanzie had told him. She was his mother, with all the worshipping implications the word has for a child.

And now she was with him every day, kissing him, enveloping him with the sweet scent that surrounded her, promising mysteries in her soft voice.

Little Stuart concentrated all his efforts on pleasing her, winning her smiles. He kept his hands clean, he practiced bowing for weeks until he got it right, he held her chair and brought her shawl, he learned to speak in a quiet voice and walk with quiet steps.

Peggy, understanding none of it, tried her best to get her mother's attention, too. The only time she succeeded was when she brought a newspaper home from school for a homework project. Margaret begged Peggy to give it to her, kissed her repeatedly when she thanked her, then hurried to her room and closed the door so that Peggy could not follow.

Papers came rarely to the Barony. Stuart had no interest in them, and he would not give Margaret the money to buy them. Whenever a newspaper came her way, Margaret savored every page. She read slowly, deliberately looking at every word and illustration, restraining herself from looking ahead to the pages she most wanted to see.

These were the women's pages, with advertisements and society news. They were Margaret's only link with the life she longed for.

Now she saw that hats were bigger, wider in the brim and in the crown. Ostrich plumes were the thing, not egret feathers. She pictured herself in the model featured in the Kerrison's Department Store ad. "The Gainsborough," it was called. She would, she knew, look beautiful in it.

Kerrison's also showed a gown it called "the Merveilleuse." Margaret found it shocking. It was so narrow, it looked as if there couldn't possibly be more than one petticoat beneath it. And the waist was peculiar, halfway up to the bosom, where no real waist ever was. She was relieved to see that the other frocks looked the way they should, with a nice S curve which emphasized a woman's attributes. If she had a decent corset. Margaret's were all very worn. Zanzie had had to patch them.

There was a half page devoted to a reception Mr. and Mrs. Jenkins Wragg had given to honor Mrs. Wragg's parents on their golden wedding anniversary. Why, that's Caroline Wentworth, Margaret thought. I didn't think she'd ever catch a husband, much less somebody as handsome as Jenkins Wragg. . . . He was the one who nearly went into conniptions because I wouldn't give him two waltzes. Which ball was that? I believe I was wearing my blue gown with the velvet bows on the shoulder, because he said something about wishing he was a bow and not a beau. He spelled it, and I laughed fit to kill. That makes it the Tenneys' ball. Or the Marshalls' . . . Margaret ran for her souvenir box.

She had Zanzie bring her supper up on a tray. It took her until an hour past her usual bedtime to go over the names of all the guests at the reception that the newspaper mentioned and match them with her memories.

She folded the paper carefully and put it in her souvenir box.

Then she went to bed. It won't be long, she thought. Then I'll be there, with everybody. She drifted near sleep, thinking of blue bows and an ostrich-feather fan. Her lovely mouth was curved in a smile. "Not long," she heard herself murmur aloud. "I can wait." And then she was asleep.

16

In 1912, Garden came home to live with the family. She was six, and it was time for her to start school. She could be overlooked no longer.

Reba spoke to Zanzie, and Zanzie spoke to Margaret, and Margaret spoke to Peggy and Little Stuart. "You'll have to take your little sister to school and bring her home," Margaret said.

Little Stuart and Peggy rebelled. They would not, they said. Everyone would laugh at them. They had not been unconscious of Garden's existence the way Margaret had managed to be. When they rode home from school, she was always among the group of Settlement children who waved and danced with excitement at the sight of the horses going past.

They had wondered why their sister was put in with the pickaninnies and had guessed, from Zanzie's reaction when they asked her, that there was something different about Garden. Zanzie had even gone so far as to say that their mother was upset about Garden and that they should not bother Margaret by talking about her. Peggy and Stuart had decided that Garden must be half-witted. "That's why her hair's so funny," Peggy declared. "There's something wrong with the inside of her head."

"Must be," Stuart agreed. "She's a simpleton."

"We're not taking a simpleton to school," he said to Margaret. She turned to Zanzie for help. Zanzie beat Stuart with a leather strap until he submitted. Peggy gave in at the sight of Stuart's welts and the promise of the same for her.

The next day Chloe brought Garden into the living room after breakfast. Garden was very excited. Reba had told her about school, started teaching her her numbers and letters; Matthew had given her rides all summer on old Judy, and she felt comfortable on horseback. She was ready and eager to be a "big schoolgirl."

Garden had known nothing but happiness for most of her short life. Everyone in the Settlement loved her, and she loved everyone in return. She had been disciplined, with swats on her chubby bottom and stinging lashes from a young tree switch on her legs. But she had never known criticism. Or cruelty.

She ran to Stuart and Peggy immediately, jabbering about their horses and Judy and her lessons with Matthew. "You ain't got no need to put me up behind you," she said. "I can ride my own self, same like you, excepting only more slow."

Stuart and Peggy were horrified.

"Mama," Stuart said, "she talks like a nigger."

"And looks like one, too." After playing outdoors all summer, Garden was freckled and tanned a deep brown, and her bare feet were as tough as leather. Her strange, marmalade-streaked hair was so thick that Chloe had braided it in four plaits, tied with yarn because she had no ribbons.

Garden looked confused. She knew they were talking about her, were displeased with her, but she did not understand why. She looked to Chloe for help, but Chloe just shook her head slightly and put her finger to her lips. Silently Garden looked at the three faces, at the three pairs of eyes of her family. They were all cold.

"Stuart," said Margaret, her soft voice steely, "I have told you a hundred times that no gentleman ever says 'nigger.' And your sister does not look like a colored person. A ragamuffin, maybe. That can be fixed. . . . And she'll learn to talk right in school.

"Chloe, tell Zanzie to give Garden a bath and a haircut and see what she can find in Miss Peggy's hand-me-downs to fit her."

Chloe led Garden from the room. In the kitchen, Garden started to talk again. "What for did she say to bath me, Chloe? Ain't I just had a bath after supper last night? What did I do wrong?"

Chloe held her close to her warm, soft bosom. "Nothing, child," she said. "You ain't never done wrong in your whole sweet life. Only wrong there is been done to you."

"What you mean, Chloe?"

"Never you mind, baby. Chloe just talking to hear herself talk. You just do what you're told and keep your own counsel."

"You mean, be quiet?"

"That the best way. Now we gots to find that Zanzie. I'll give her some storebought soap to make bubbles in your bath."

"I done what little I could," Chloe reported to Reba and the others that night, "but that poor baby, she going to have a hard row to hoe."

It was hard, but Garden hoed it. She kept her mouth shut unless someone asked her a direct question, and then she answered it as briefly as possible. She did what she was told to do, and did it immediately. She listened and watched and learned. She was a good observer and a quick study; soon she was speaking exactly like the other children at school, except that the musical cadence of the Gullah dialect that she had learned from the Barony blacks left an indelible imprint on her pronunciation, making it distinctively pleasing to hear.

She suffered stoically when she was teased about her hair. Zanzie had cut it, using a bowl over her head for a guideline, then trimming bangs across her forehead. The result was disastrous. Garden's hair was very strange. It was as if she had a double supply, a full head of blond hair and another of red. The individual strands were terribly fine and had no hint of curl in them, but the number of hairs, doubled, made a thick, unmanageable mass. Uncontrolled by braiding, it flew around Garden's head at her slightest motion or the merest touch of breeze in the air. It made her look wild and ridiculous.

She also looked absurd in Peggy's clothes. She wore the dresses Peggy had worn at her age, but they flapped loosely on her. Not only was Peggy's frame bigger, with larger bones and wider shoulders, but also Garden had begun losing weight as soon as her days at the Settlement ended. She could not swallow her food when she ate at the table with her brother and sister. She tried, sometimes succeeded, and then vomited. Chloe fixed her special treats and gave them to her in the kitchen, but Garden had trouble eating more than a few mouthfuls. Matthew found the only way to get nourishment into her. Before and after school, she went to the barn when the cows were being milked and had the concoction known as "syllabub-under-the-cow." Crouching next to the legs of the big, warm animal, Garden held a blue china pitcher containing powdered sugar and vanilla extract. Matthew's expert hands directed streams of warm milk into the pitcher until the sweet foamy liquid poured over the top. The whole process was special—the warmth of the lantern-lit barn, the steamy, acrid animal odors, the skill of Matthew's fingers, and bubbling sweetness drunk from the lip of the pitcher. The syllabub nourished Garden's heart and her body.

But she continued to lose weight. By the time school ended in June, she was, according to Reba, nothing but skin and bones. "We going feed you up, missy," Reba promised. "All summer, you going be here with your friends. You'll find your appetite again. You skinnier than Reba. That won't do."

Garden hugged her violently. She felt that she was home again, although she had learned that it was not really true. Her home was the Woods House, no matter how unwelcome she felt there. And her family was Stuart and Peggy and Mama, not Reba and Matthew and John and Luke and Tyrone and the new baby, Flora. Still, while summer lasted, she could be with her friends. They would not miss her, her family.

Even when school started again, and that seemed a long, long time away, things wouldn't be so bad. She had made some friends, and next year the girls were going to learn to knit, and she was going to be an angel in the Christmas play and sing a carol. Best of all, she'd have a running horse instead of tired old Judy. Peggy and Stuart were graduating. They wouldn't be going to school anymore.

17

"Stuart, you take off your graduation suit and hang it up carefully. Lord knows, you have few enough clothes, and you'll wear suits all the time in high school."

Stuart gaped. "High school? But Mama, I thought I was done with school."

"You're done with children's school. Next year you'll go to high school in Summerville."

"Why, Mama? I'm not all that good at school. Let Peggy go. She likes books."

"Peggy is a girl. She doesn't need high school. You do."

"What for?"

"To get ahead in the world. To make something of yourself. A man needs an education."

"Papa never went to high school."

Margaret raised her eyebrows. "So you don't think you have to. You want to grow up to be just as irresponsible as he is, to let everybody down the way he does you. He didn't even come to your graduation, and Peggy said he had promised."

"He didn't exactly promise, Mama. I was there when Peggy asked him. He said he'd see what he could do."

Margaret shrugged her shoulders. "Typical," she said. "I don't know why I'm even bothering to talk about him. You go hang up your suit. Carefully."

Stuart trampled noisily upstairs.

"Sometimes a fellow gets tired of being told what to do," he muttered. "I'm going to be thirteen years old next month; I'm not a baby. Papa said he'd get me some long pants for my birthday, too, and then I'll never wear this old knickerbocker suit again, no matter what anybody says."

While he was hanging up his jacket, he heard his mother calling him. Her voice sounded funny. He put the jacket on again, grumbling, and stomped heavily down the stairs. Margaret was lying back in a chair, her face drained of color. Zanzie was fanning her and glaring at the black man standing uncomfortably in the doorway.

"What's the matter?" Stuart cried.

The black man shifted his weight and looked at the boy. "I didn't mean to bother your momma, but I gots to know. It's your papa. He just put he hand to he heart and keel over. I gots to know whereabouts we should carry the body."

BOOK 3

1913–1917

18

Margaret had always thought that Stuart was rich. She couldn't believe what the lawyer was telling her. "Two hundred and eight dollars? That's all the money I get?"

Logan Henry, the Tradd family lawyer, was not shocked by the undisguised greed of Stuart Tradd's widow. His firm handled many estates. Widows, in his experience, were always eager to take hold of their late husbands' money. And they usually thought there was not enough of it. Logan Henry was a confirmed bachelor.

"There are, of course, substantial assets in the form of real property. Your son is heir to them. Until his majority, our firm are designated trustees. I am the member in actual charge of the estate, and I assure you that the best interests of the boy will be my primary and continuing concern."

"You mean he left everything to Little Stuart? Only two hundred dollars to me? How am I supposed to live?"

"Mistress Tradd, I beg of you, don't upset yourself. The properties generate income which should be sufficient for the needs of your children and yourself. When your son comes of age, I am confident that he will recognize his responsibilities to his sisters and his mother."

"Don't talk lawyer talk to me, Mr. Henry. What can this place do with no one to run it? Stuart's only twelve years old. He can't boss a plantation. We won't have any income at all."

"I have already instituted inquiries for an experienced farm manager. Additionally, the town house generates a small return above expenses."

Margaret was thunderstruck. Mr. Henry's soothing voice was only a hum in her ear as he continued to utter reassurances about her future.

I never knew there was a town house, she was thinking. If Stuart wasn't dead, I could kill him. All these years, all these eternal, miserable years, I could have been in town all the time. He never told me.

"Where is the house, Mr. Henry?" she said, agitated by a sudden fear. "Is it in Charleston?"

"Why, of course." Mr. Henry was himself a Charlestonian. To him, it was inconceivable that anyone would consider owning a house in any other town.

To his horror Margaret leaped from her chair, swooped down upon him and kissed his wrinkled cheek. Her own cheeks were pink, her eyes bright, her face alight with happiness.

"When can I see it, Mr. Henry? I want to move right away."

Henry did his utmost to dissuade her. The house was little better than a tenement, he told her. Its once-grand rooms were now flats, with a family in each room. The neighborhood was run-down, even unsafe.

Margaret did not listen to a word he said. "When can I see it?" she asked him repeatedly. Finally Henry agreed to arrange a viewing the following Monday afternoon. He was confident that she would abandon her absurd idea when she saw the house.

He was very nearly right. Margaret wrote him a letter the day after his visit to the Barony. She did not wish to live in the house; she wanted him to buy or rent a house for her in the old, downtown area of Charleston, the small triangle of the city below Broad Street.

Logan Henry had brought a newspaper when he called on Margaret. It contained a carefully composed obituary of Stuart Tradd, and Mr. Henry believed it was something she would want to show the children.

The newspaper also had a story on the society page about Margaret's old friend Caroline Wentworth, now Mrs. Jenkins Wragg. Described as "one of the city's most celebrated hostesses," Mrs. Wragg was interviewed about the duties and responsibilities of her busy life. One of her comments was, "I never go uptown except to shop on King Street. Everyone lives below Broad, so there's no need."

The townhouse the Tradds owned was on Charlotte Street. Margaret located it on a map of the city in the Big House library. It was fourteen blocks above Broad.

Logan Henry replied at once to her letter. "Out of the question" was his response.

Margaret decided that she would have more luck persuading him in person. She wrote that she would see him on Monday as planned.

Mr. Henry knew at once what she had in mind. He stayed late at his office, composing a document that would forestall any tearful pleadings from Margaret. He sent a clerk from his office to deliver it into Margaret's hand on Friday.

It was a simplified balance sheet of the estate's income and expenses. Even Margaret, who had never had any experience with money, could understand the figures and Mr. Henry's concluding statement.

The Barony was mortgaged for more than its market value. The income from the crops, if the farming was well managed, would be just sufficient to pay the interest on the loan, the workers' salaries, the cost of seed and fertilizer, and land taxes. Mr. Henry hoped to find a manager who would agree to work for whatever profit he could earn by increased yields under his management.

The tenement on Charlotte Street was fully rented. The income from the rents was thirty-eight dollars a month after property taxes were paid. The gas and water bills for the building amounted to an average of four dollars a month.

If Margaret stayed at the Barony, she would have few expenses. The plantation produced its own food, had its own wells and wood for its fires.

If she moved to the city, to Charlotte Street, she would lose the little income she had when she evicted the tenants before moving into the house. She would also have to buy food and fuel.

"I feel safe in assuming, therefore," Mr. Henry concluded, "that you will agree that your only recourse is to remain in your beautiful home at Ashley Barony, continuing to afford your children the benefits of its healthful atmosphere and your son the opportunity to learn to maintain, and, in time, expand the fruitful exploitation of its rich fields.

"I beg to remain, Madam, your most obedient servant."

" 'Obedient,' my foot," Margaret stormed. She would not, could not stay at the Barony. It was only the thought of someday moving to town that had kept her going all these years. There has to be a way, she thought. There just has to. Maybe she could appeal to Stuart's rich Aunt Elizabeth. Margaret composed several notes in her mind. Then she realized that it would do no good. Elizabeth must have seen the obituary. She hadn't even sent flowers to the funeral.

Mr. Henry's letter had also said that he would be in his office on Monday if she wanted to keep their appointment. Perhaps she would be interested in seeing the property on Charlotte Street as a matter of information about the estate. She should in no way feel obligated, however, and he did not recommend that she take the arduous journey from the plantation.

Margaret decided that she did not want to see her lawyer on Monday or any other day as long as she lived.

She stayed in her room for three days with the windows darkened and the door locked. Her mind raced in erratic, plunging hypotheses, all ending with a crash at the solid wall of her lack of money. She was still in prison.

When Stuart finishes high school, she thought, he'll be able to get a job, earn some money. Then we'll have enough to live on in town, if we rent just a tiny little house.

But I can't wait four more years. I can't. It would kill me. I thought the waiting was over. I was so happy. I can't go back to waiting again. I'll be twenty-nine this year. I'm old. I can't wait any longer.

The thought of the town house drove her half mad. The rents couldn't have meant that much to Stuart. He must have spent them, and more, on whiskey. He managed to find money for anything he wanted, all right. He could easily have let them live in Charleston. Even if it was the wrong part of town, at least it was town. She became obsessed with the house. It was hers and yet not hers. There, in the city, but not to be touched. She had never known such frustration.

In the end, she decided that she had to see it. Mr. Henry said that it was practically falling down, had not been repaired or painted for over forty years. If she saw it, saw how disgusting it was, maybe then she could stop wanting it.

The next day, Stuart drove her to town in the buggy. He wanted to use his father's car. It was, after all, his now, an idea that thrilled him and made him feel guilty because it thrilled him.

Margaret refused absolutely. Stuart did not argue. Margaret was frightening-looking, dark circles around sunken eyes, skin drawn too tight, hollows in her cheeks. She had barely slept for a week.

Stuart believed that his mother's condition was due to grief for his father. He didn't deserve it, he thought. He was awful to her, called her terrible names to Peggy and me. He should have treated her nice, like a gentleman. I will. I'll be nice to her. I'll make her happy. I'll make her pretty again. He handed her into the buggy the way she had taught him to, and fetched her parasol from the house.

Margaret did not speak as they rode the long miles to the city. Her face was pale beneath her long crepe veil. In the lap of her black wool dress, her black-gloved hands twisted restlessly. She had not opened her parasol. Stuart glanced anxiously at her from time to time and remained silent, too.

They clattered over the wooden bridge that crossed the Ashley River and stopped at the elaborately decorated Victorian house where the tolltaker lived. Margaret spoke then. "Ask him how we get to Charlotte Street."

"Straight on," the man answered, "till you come to a paved road with streetcar tracks on it. That's Meeting Street. Turn right and stay on it for about, let's see, about eight blocks. On your left there'll be a green with the Presbyterian Church at the back end of it. That's Charlotte Street."

The road from the bridge led them through an area of ramshackle slums. Margaret felt increasingly depressed.

When she had come to the city before, with her parents and later with Stuart and Anson, she had never noticed the neighborhood. She had been just passing through, confidently anticipating the pleasures that lay ahead. Now there was nothing to look forward to. For the rest of her life.

When they turned onto Meeting Street, her spirits picked up. The brick paving and shining steel trolley tracks were city, definitely city.

Stuart was so excited that he was all but hopping in his seat. As they proceeded down Meeting Street, automobiles passed them, going the other way. One, two, three, four, and not one of them a Model T. He could recognize the Cadillac; he had seen one once at Ruggs's store. The other three cars were new to him. The city was a wonderful place if its streets were full of autos.

There was a long, shiny black car approaching, traveling, Stuart would bet, over forty miles an hour. He stood up for a better look.

"Stuart!" Margaret jerked his sleeve. "Do you want to kill us? Sit down. You're going to miss our turn; there's the green."

"Hispano-Suiza. Mama, I think that was a Hispano-Suiza. I've seen pictures, but I never thought I would see a real one."

"Our turn, Stuart. Pay attention."

The lawn in front of the church was a brilliant green. A mower had left ribbonlike tracks down its long length. The church building was imposing, a columned stone mass.

Margaret threw back her veil to get a better look. "It's beautiful. Look, Stuart, how handsome. So this is Charlotte Street. What a humbug that old lawyer is." She clapped her hands with joy.

It was short-lived. Once past the church, there were two blocks of Charlotte Street, two blocks lined with magnificent mansions in states of advanced decay. The last house in the second block was set back deep in a yard shadowed by huge trees. Margaret could see only a glimpse of its tall columns and high roof. All the other houses sat close to the street. She could see them only too well. Several had lost all their shutters; all had lost some. The walls of the two frame houses were leprous; the only paint left on them was in discolored patches on the mottled gray of their rotting, weathered wood. Most of the houses were brick, their proud walls largely intact, their trim and fittings ruined, like once-beautiful women in dirty, decayed finery. It was a street of ghosts.

As they drove back and forth along the short street, heads appeared at windows and doors, eyes stared curiously at the unaccustomed sight of a horse and buggy. "Look at that boy's red hair," they heard a child say, then a slap and a wail and "hush" in an adult voice.

"Maybe we should ask one of these people which house it is, Mama."

"Certainly not. We don't talk to those kind of people. Run quick into that store on the corner there and ask. And hurry back . . . Remember, it's called the Ashley house; your grandpapa's Aunt Julia used to live there . . . Hurry back."

Stuart wished he could dawdle in the store. Its shelves were even more crowded than Ruggs's, and the friendly owner was Italian, the first foreigner Stuart had ever seen.

But he hurried back to his mother.

They sat in the buggy for a long time, staring at the Ashley house. It was brick, with white marble steps, chipped and stained but still majestic. The steps were double, two semicircles rising to meet on a high marble stoop ten feet above. They had once had black, intricate, lacelike wrought-iron rails. The iron was rusted now, sections gone, replaced by unpainted wooden planks.

A tall iron fence separated the house from the sidewalk; its rusty spearlike uprights were intact but there were large open squares, once the frame for delicate designs in iron tracery. These were clearly used for entrance to the grounds; the gate, a masterpiece of workmanship, was rusted shut, its heavy bolt immovable.

From the walls of the house to the fence, there was a courtyard of black and white marble squares. They were uneven, most of them broken. Dandelions made a defiant show of color in the cracks.

The front of the staircase, in the center, had an arched gateway, the gate again of wrought iron, scrolled and red with rust. It sagged on its hinges, half open.

Refuse was scattered all over the courtyard, papers, broken glass, tin cans rusting new stains on the cracked marble paving. At the top of the stairs a great carved door stood ajar. The glass in the fanlight above it was broken, the jagged holes stuffed with rags.

"It sure is big," said Stuart. It was. It was a mansion, three stories tall from the top of the staircase, with a slate-covered hipped roof and dormer windows. It was sternly symmetrical. Four big windows were evenly placed on each side of the entrance and repeated on the two floors above, with wider arched windows above the doorway.

"It's bigger than the Barony Big House," whispered Margaret. If only she could have lived here, she was sure she would have been the happiest woman in the world.

"Let's go peek through the windows," she whispered. The impulse was childish. She did not even know what she hoped to see. Such squalor that she would be revolted, perhaps. Or perhaps beauty to match the exterior, to feed her angry misery. Stuart was delighted. He was feeling very bored sitting silently in the buggy. He jumped down, tied the reins to the hitching post and handed Margaret down via the carriage block in front of the unusable gate.

He ran ahead, stepped nimbly through the opening in the fence and plucked some dandelions. He presented them to Margaret through the fence, bowing with a flourish.

"Thank you, Stuart. Now come on. This was a foolish idea. I can't climb through a hole in a fence. It's common."

"Oh, come on, Mama. It's not hard. I'll help you. Let's see inside. It's empty."

"Empty? It can't be. Mr. Henry wouldn't lie."

"I could see when I got the flowers. It's empty."

Margaret gave him her hand. With Stuart's help, she clambered awkwardly through the fence. It couldn't be, but suppose it was. Empty. They would move at once.

Stuart led her to the gate beneath the stairs. "See, Mama, you can see all the way through to the back. There's light from the back door to the front. And it's empty."

Margaret began to cry. "Oh, Stuart, that's the basement. Of course nobody lives in the basement." Just for a moment she had thought perhaps Stuart was right, that the house could be hers. Now her hopes were dashed again.

Above her head someone came out of the house. Margaret darted into the basement so that she wouldn't be seen.

A smell of stale urine and decomposed animal flesh made her gag. "Stuart, Stuart, where are you?" She fumbled in her purse for her smelling salts.

Stuart came quickly from the shadows at her left. "Stinks, don't it?" he said cheerfully. "Almost as bad as when the skunk died under the schoolhouse. Boy, Mama, this place is huge. There's a room over there goes on and on."

Margaret covered her mouth and nose with her handkerchief. She wondered if the person on the stairs was gone. Then she noticed that Stuart was right: the place was huge. The hallway was as wide as a room. It led to another arched gate at the back of the house, a long distance. The floor, Margaret saw, was a marble checkerboard, like the courtyard, but undamaged.

She lowered her hand, the handkerchief crumpled in her fist. "Show me that room," she said.

The basement mirrored the house arrangement, its thick brick walls the foundation for the weight of the plastered ones above. The wide hall crisscrossed the house, creating a big, empty square in the center beneath the staircase that began on the main floor overhead. Doorways opened on two sides of the four tremendous rooms at the corners. Each was twenty-four feet square.

There were no windows in the front of the house, but each room had four windows, high in the wall on the side. The rear rooms also had two full-length arched windows overlooking a jungle of weeds that had once been a garden. The windows were all boarded up, but light streamed in through cracks between the boards, illuminating the trash and piles of rags on the floor.

"Somebody's been living here and not paying rent," said Marga-

ret crossly. Then she whirled around in a circle, her arms held wide.
"If they can, we can. Stuart, we're going to move to town."

"Mama! You can't mean it."

"Oh yes I can."

"But it's so dirty, and so low. I'm afraid of bumping my head."
The ceilings were no more than seven feet high, approximately half
the height of the ones at the Barony. They seemed even lower
because of the tremendous spaces of the rooms and hallway. The
great house above seemed to be pressing down on them.

Margaret waved her hand impatiently. "They're just fine. You
won't be full grown for years yet. By then, something will happen.
We won't stay here long. But we're going to move to town. I've set
my mind to it."

"Stop at that store again," Margaret said as Stuart helped her into
the buggy, "and ask him how we get to King Street. I want to see
the shop windows."

They were only a few blocks away. They went back to Meeting
Street and turned left. As they did, they heard music. A band was
playing. "Quick, Stuart, let's go see."

After only one block, they saw it. To their right, there was an
enormous crenellated building. It looked like a castle in one of the
picture books Stuart had had when he was small. In front of it there
was a tremendous green. Crowds of people were standing around its
edge, watching uniformed young men march to the music of the
uniformed band in the center.

From the buggy, they could see over the heads of the crowd.
Margaret clasped Stuart's arm, and laughed. It was thrilling. The
music, the precision of the march, the bright gold of the band
instruments, the braid on the uniforms, the rows of buttons on the
proud young chests of the marchers. "It's the Citadel," she shouted
above the noise, "the military college. I remember it now. They
parade like this all the time."

Stuart was overwhelmed. He had never seen anything so exciting.
"Oh, yes, Mama," he yelled, "let's move to the city."

They watched the parade until the cadets had all followed the
band through the sally port into their barracks. Then they drove
down King Street. Margaret looked at shops, Stuart looked at the
automobiles parked in front of them. They were both supremely
happy.

The shops ended suddenly. Ahead of them, King Street was lined with houses. Margaret looked at the sign on the corner. They were crossing Broad Street.

South of Broad, she thought. I wonder where Caroline Wentworth lives. She turned from side to side, studying the houses. At the end of King Street, she directed Stuart to turn, then again, then again, back and forth through the part of town where "everyone lives."

Paint was peeling there, too, and there was trash in the streets. Margaret felt very pleased.

They stopped at the very end of the peninsula at White Point Gardens. Stuart watered the horse in the trough there, then tied him to a hitching post. He and Margaret had a drink at the artesian fountain nearby and walked slowly along the oystershell path to the promenade on the other side of the park. They passed a circular white and green bandstand.

"There's music here, too, on Sunday afternoons," Margaret said. It was the only time she spoke for over an hour. Her head and heart were too full for conversation.

So also were Stuart's. He was overstimulated; too much had happened in too short a time. He did not even notice the palm trees and flowering shrubs that were the pride of the gardens.

They strolled along the esplanade overlooking Charleston's broad harbor, relishing the crowds of people walking, as they were, without haste, enjoying the breeze from the water. So many people. It was the city.

"It's getting late, Mama," Stuart said when they had walked the length of the promontory. "We'd best go back."

Margaret nodded. "But let's not hurry. I don't want this day to end too fast. I've been waiting for it a long time."

It ended perfectly. They went back the way they had come, on King Street. As they passed the first block of stores, the electric lights came on. They were overhead, in arcs of brilliance above the darkening street, and in the store windows, filled with colorful temptations. It was magic.

And soon it would be theirs. They were moving to town.

19

That summer the Barony's fields were neglected and choked with weeds. But on Charlotte Street, a metamorphosis was taking place.

Like all great plantations, Ashley Barony had been, before the War, a self-sufficient empire unto itself. There were workshops for carpentry, cabinetmaking, metalwork, weaving, pottery-making, candlemaking and tanning, with gluemaking as a by-product. The craftsmen were highly valued and respected, as they deserved to be. Many of them were artists.

In the fifty years since that time, the Barony had gone from empire to farm, and the artists were dead. But their traditions lingered. There was still a blacksmith to shoe the horses and mules and to repair broken tools. There was a carpenter to mend the roof or plane a swollen door or repair a broken table leg. And there were many strong men and women to clean, scrub, paint, carry heavy loads.

Peggy, who liked to read, called the Charlotte Street house the Augean stables.

"What on earth are you talking about, Peggy?" said Margaret. "The stables are back in the garden, with a whole wall fallen down."

"Never mind, Mama. I think it's wonderful. You know what I'd do if I was you?"

"No, what?"

Peggy barely waited to be asked. Waving her arms, talking a blue streak, she pushed and pulled her mother from room to room, suggesting alterations, furniture, decoration.

And her ideas were very good. Peggy was vastly more inventive than her brother and mother, and her eclectic reading had included studies of color and the mathematics of volume and proportion. She also had a fantastically retentive mind; she remembered every curtain, rug, chair, table and bed at both the Big House and the Woods House.

Margaret had ideas of her own. She brushed off Peggy's suggestions. But later, when she began to see that she was making disastrous mistakes, she asked Peggy to tell her again what she thought would work.

"You made a mess, huh, Mama? I knew you would." Peggy had not developed tact with her taste. She ignored Margaret's invitation to collaborate, and grabbed command.

"Your sister is so aggressive, Stuart, not like a girl at all," Margaret sighed. "I wish she wasn't so pushy and bold."

But before long she was glad to call on Peggy's assertiveness.

Even with the labor provided without direct cost to Margaret, there were still expenses. For materials, for the occasional purchases at Canzonieri's corner store, for things that Margaret could not remember buying, which seemed vitally necessary at the time they were bought. Margaret's money seemed to evaporate.

I know, she thought, feeling very clever. I'll sell all that old china and silver and stuff Miss Julia set such store on. We never use it anyhow.

But, she discovered, her husband had had the same idea. The locked storage room was bare.

The furniture, then, Margaret decided. We've got ten times more than we will ever use. Having found a solution to her problem, she did not know what to do next.

It was Peggy who came up with the obvious answer. "It's all real old, isn't it? We'll sell it to that antique store we saw on King Street."

Margaret quailed at the thought of asking the storekeeper if he would buy it. "You'll have to do it, Stuart. It's business; men always handle business. And you're the man of the family."

"I'll go with him," Peggy insisted. "I'm the only one who remembers everything."

George Benjamin was reading Spinoza when the door to his store opened. It rang a bell in the comfortable back room where he was resting. Mr. Benjamin muttered a curse. He thought he had locked the door. It was summer, and there was never any worthwhile business in the summer. Rich Northerners passed through Charleston in November on their way to Florida and in March on their way back. No one traveled in the summer. He could have closed his store

106

altogether, and would have, too, if it had not been his refuge from the chaos of his home, with four children and his wife's card parties.

Mr. Benjamin put on his shoes and limped to the front. He had a bunion, aggravated by the hot weather. He did not feel friendly to whatever stranger was interrupting his scholarly peace. He was scowling when he parted the curtain that served as door to the shop.

He saw two children.

"None of your pranks," he shouted. "Go away."

The little girl drew herself up as tall as she could be. She was all in black, from her boots to the ribbon on her wide black straw boater. Black ribbon also tied her long, carroty braids.

"Good afternoon, sir," she said loudly. "I am Miss Tradd, and this gentleman is my brother Mr. Tradd. We have a business proposal which you'd be smart to listen to. We are bereaved, as you see, and bereaved people don't play pranks."

"I didn't know what to do, Dorothy," he told his wife when he went home. "Of course, the name Tradd made me pay attention. And when the little girl said 'Ashley Barony,' my acquisitiveness was boundless.

"But they were just children, red hair and freckles. Knickers and pigtails. It wouldn't be right to take advantage of them, I thought."

Mr. Benjamin laughed hugely. "I should have counted the fillings in my teeth. That little girl sold me furniture, sight unseen, for prices higher than I've ever charged the greenest tourist. Then she did me the 'favor of taking that big round table off my hands.' She sent a wagon for it before I had time to take off my shoes.

"I've never enjoyed an afternoon so much in my entire life."

The table was placed in the center of the apartment where the wide halls crossed. It was a huge circle of white marble, eight feet in diameter, set on a walnut pedestal base. The wood looked black in the shadow of the marble top. When Margaret saw it on the black-and-white marble floor, she capitulated. Peggy could make all the decisions about arranging the apartment from then on.

The workers had thought Margaret was a hard taskmaster. When Peggy took over, they realized they had been fortunate before.

On September the fourteenth, the house was ready for them to move in.

20

Garden wore her new dress to say her goodbyes at the Settlement. It was gray cotton, with a round white collar and white cuffs on the long sleeves. Deep pleats fell from the square yoke and were held in neat folds by a black belt around her hips. She had black stockings and boots with buttons up the side. It was the proper mourning attire for a child her age. And it was suitable to wear to a city school. Garden was careful with it; Zanzie had warned her that it had to last her a long time.

Her little face was puffy. She had cried all night. But she was all cried out now, and did not break down. All the adults and older children matched Garden's dignity. It was a solemn, sad occasion. After she shook hands or hugged everyone, Reba told her there was one more person she had to see.

"Maum' Pansy want to tell you goodbye." Reba's voice was hushed. In all the seven years Garden had been virtually living in the Settlement, Old Pansy had never allowed her in the house. Pansy, now bedridden, was still the matriarch, the ruler of the Barony blacks. Garden's visit was a command performance.

She understood that it was a very important occasion. Maum' Pansy was a legendary, powerful mystery to her, and now the mystery was to be revealed. Garden felt very grown-up. She mounted the step of Pansy's cabin alone and opened the blue door.

The light from the door reached only halfway across the room, and the windows were shuttered. Garden squeezed her eyes tight, then opened them, adjusting to the sudden darkness.

An oil lamp burned on a table by the great bed. It lit the white bed linen, the big white pillows and the white hair of the shrunken old woman sitting up against them. She was wearing a white cotton nightdress, with a string of small brilliant blue beads around her neck.

Garden curtsied.

"Come here, child." Old Pansy's voice was cracked but still strong. She held out a clawlike hand. The skin was ashen with age.

Garden walked to her. She took Pansy's old hand in her young one.

"It do my old heart good that you is leaving this place, child. This ain't no place for no Tradd. I know your heart sick, but you mind old Pansy."

With her other hand, Pansy made the sign of the evil eye. "You 'scape the curse.

"Lift up that light and let me see you. I done hear you all these years. Laughing and singing. I always want to see you."

Garden obeyed.

Pansy cackled. "Your head half angel and half devil. You a funny-looking young one for true. Put back that light."

Garden set it carefully on the table.

"Sing a song," the old woman commanded. "Sing about the flood and old Norah."

Garden took a breath. She was frightened by Maum' Pansy, her dry clutching hand, her strange words. She was afraid she would sing as cracked as Pansy talked. But she had to try.

> "Who build the ark?
> Norah
> Who build the ark?
> Norah build the ark.
> And the animal come in
> Two by two . . ."

Garden stopped. Maum' Pansy was asleep, she thought.

The hooded old eyes cracked. "That's right," the old voice croaked. "That's enough." Pansy released Garden's hand. "Scrabble under my pillow. I got a present for you. Then I wants to rest my eye."

Garden reached gingerly to the edge of the pillow, then under it, then deeper.

The old woman weighed nothing at all, she felt. It was scary. Her fingers touched some warm feathers. With all the courage she could gather, Garden closed her hand around the object and drew it out.

It was a white cotton string about two feet long, knotted in the center to hold a blue bead like Pansy's, a small bone and a cluster of small black-and-white feathers from a wild turkey.

"Protect you," Pansy mumbled. "Goodbye," Her toothless mouth dropped open, and she began to snore.

Garden ran to the bright day outside.

Reba did not need to ask what had happened inside; she had listened at the window. She took Garden by the shoulders and held her firmly while she spoke. "That a strong gift Maum' Pansy give you, Garden. She took one of her own bead to make it. She must have a powerful caring for you. Don't you never lose that nor treat it careless. You is honored more than you got sense to understand." She caught the little girl to her, then released her.

"Time for you to go, baby."

"Will you come see me, Reba?"

"No, sugar. I can't do that."

"But I'm going to miss you so much."

"You always be in Reba heart, Garden. Remember that. They's people here going love you all your days . . . . run on now. You'll be late."

Garden cried hopeless tears as she said goodbye again to everyone. She returned to the house by memory, her eyesight blurred.

There were more ceremonious farewells to go through at the Big House, but Garden did not have to participate. She sat in the wagon with Zanzie and the parcels and baskets of food they were taking to town.

Margaret and Stuart walked along the line of servants saying a few words to each. Then to Jack Tremaine, the manager Mr. Henry had hired for the plantation.

Stuart helped Margaret and Peggy into the buggy, climbed up himself, and they were off. The servants waved and cheered, joined by the field hands. Peggy and Stuart cheered with them, and Margaret opened her parasol with a gay flourish.

It was a festive occasion for all of them. The house servants were happy to see the last of Zanzie. There would be no intruder at Sam Ruggs's big house where they were all going to work. And they would have fancy uniforms plus twice their former salaries.

The field hands looked forward to breaking Tremaine in to their ways.

And Tremaine was counting the hours until his wife and children joined him in their new home at the Woods House.

There was one more leave-taking, unanticipated by anyone. At the bottom of the drive, Sam Ruggs ran out of the store to stop them.

He swept his hat off his head and bowed to Margaret. "My best wishes, ma'am," he said, "and here's a little trifle for your trip to the city." He presented her with a satin-covered box of chocolates.

Margaret inclined her head slightly, but did not speak. Peggy reached across her and grabbed the candy. "Thank you, Mr. Ruggs."

Ruggs walked around to Stuart's side of the buggy. "So long, boy. Now don't you forget what I told you. Your father was my friend, and if I can ever do anything for his family, it'll be my pleasure." He held out his hand for Stuart to shake.

Stuart grasped it. Sam winked. Stuart grinned. He managed to pocket the five-dollar gold piece without Peggy or his mother noticing.

"Such brass," Margaret huffed when they drove off. "As if I'd speak to that horrible man . . . And look at that monstrosity of a house. Common as dirt."

Sam's new home was a columned, white-painted brick house that looked more like a city hall than a residence.

Margaret forgot her indignation as soon as the house was out of sight. Before they were halfway to town, she was sharing the sticky chocolates with Stuart and Peggy.

They pulled up in front of their new home, and Margaret felt a clutch of terror. She had been totally preoccupied with the process of getting to the city. Now she was here: a new life was beginning, and she had no idea what to expect. The future was a great unknown, and frightening.

"Come on, Mama, let's go in. Everyone's staring." Stuart was waiting to help her alight. Peggy jumped onto the sidewalk and opened the freshly painted, free-swinging gate to the courtyard. The wagon lumbered up the street, bringing the last load.

Margaret stepped down onto the carriage block. There was nothing else to do.

111

21

Margaret always referred to the basement apartment as her "house on Charlotte Street." The tenant-filled spaces above did not exist for her. The basement was clean and comfortable; the Barony workmen and Peggy had done a good job.

They had erected walls dividing the rooms to the right of the hall. Now there were four long rectangular bedrooms. Stuart's at the front of the house, Margaret's next to it, opening onto the cross hallway. Peggy was opposite her mother, with a small bed for Garden in the corner of the room, and Zanzie had the back bedroom, with closest access to the enormous kitchen. It occupied the original square space in the back left corner of the apartment. The sitting room had the front square.

Fireplaces had been opened in the mammoth chimneys. In the sitting room and kitchen, they were located in the center of the outside walls. The partition of the bedrooms made the grates very small, cramped into interior corners.

The brick walls were whitewashed, the floors in the bedrooms and sitting room covered with faded jewellike Persian rugs from the Barony, ruthlessly cut down to fit. The kitchen floor was brick, painted green.

Peggy had selected the furnishings that were the least worn. The result was a mix of chairs, tables and sofas from both the Big House and the Woods House. Louis XIV and Regency fauteuils mingled with wicker rockers and needlepoint-covered wing chairs. The windows in every room were hung with the white muslin curtains from the Woods House; they were too small for draperies.

Margaret insisted on bringing the portrait of herself and her mother, painted when she was five. She could see that it was not a very good painting; her mother looked rather cross-eyed. Still, it was the only family portrait she owned. All the Garden family paintings had been lost when the plantation house burned.

Peggy added the portraits from the Barony. The Ashleys were a handsome family, and her own ancestors. The result was that the hallway became a sort of gallery. It did not invite dawdling; faces stared from every wall, largely imperious and disapproving. The exception was the earliest colonial Ashley, a rakish satin-and-lace-clad cavalier with a challenging small smile turning up one corner of his mouth. Peggy gave him the place of honor. When the front door was opened, light from outside made his eyes glimmer.

The front door was now solid, with a heavy lock. The wrought-iron gate to the basement had been repaired and painted. It, too, had a lock. Any caller could be examined in safety behind its barrier after the inner door was opened. There were doors on the rooms, too, and a double door and gate onto the backyard.

The Barony gardener had cleared the weeds and the trash. The outlines of the old brick paths and patterned flower beds could now be seen. So could two privies at the rear. Margaret told the gardener to stop work. The Tradds would never go into the yard.

For their sanitary needs, they would use slop jars, pitchers and basins to clean their hands and faces, and a hip bath for bathing. These had served them fine at the Barony; there was no need to change now. They had plenty of water from a pump outside the back door.

Upstairs the house was fitted with gas lighting and heating, but the basement had never been piped. The Tradds did not even notice the lack. They had always used oil or kerosene lamps; candles for parties, in the days when there had been parties. With ice delivered by a daily wagon and Margaret's long-desired newspaper brought by a boy before breakfast, they had a sense of luxury they had never known on the great plantation.

There was no sense of being cramped, crowded into only six low-ceilinged rooms, because they spent so little time in the house. The whole family breakfasted at eight, then set out to explore the wonders of the city. They returned for dinner at three, but were out again before four. The days were still long. Often they did not get home until almost eight, footsore, hungry and happy.

The buggy had gone back to the Barony. There was no place on Charlotte Street for them to keep a horse. Or, Margaret insisted, the decrepit Olds. So they walked and rode the electric streetcars.

They were like four children on an adventure. Stuart was a willing escort, feeling very adult in the long-pants suit he bought with the gold piece Sam Ruggs had given him. Margaret was at her best, laughing, undaunted by rain or crowds or fatigue. The city was exciting to her, and she enjoyed everything in it. Even her children.

Garden had never been in the city until the day they moved. She was thrilled by the activity, the crowds, the lights, the colors, the variety of sights and sounds and experiences. Most of all, she was dazzled by her mother. Margaret had never smiled at her; now she smiled all the time, laughed, talked to her, asked if she was having a good time. Garden was bewitched. She fell in love with her radiant, beautiful mother.

Peggy and Stuart were also enchanted. This Margaret was a new person, a playmate. They wanted the games to last forever.

No one, not even Garden, missed the Barony.

The start of school meant the end of their pleasure-filled days. Margaret was more disappointed than the children. "But we'll still have weekends," she cried. "We can plan all week long what we want to do, then we'll do it."

They all tried, but the carefree excitement was no longer there. Each of them had private worries that got in the way.

Stuart and Peggy discovered that the school at Bacon's Bridge had ill prepared them for the demands of high school. They were assigned extra lessons at recess and as homework to make up for the deficiencies of their background. There was nothing to be done to make up for the seven years that the other students had already spent together. Peggy and Stuart were outsiders, country bumpkins, figures of fun.

They did not even have each other. Stuart escorted his sister to Memminger High School for girls, on St. Philip Street, then backtracked up Meeting Street to the High School of Charleston, for boys. At the end of the school day he called for her and escorted her home. They could not even share their problems with their work. Boys were required to study Latin and Greek; it was not offered to girls.

Garden was in the second grade. She had no trouble catching up with the schoolwork; alphabet and numbers were the same, and she had learned hers well. All her problems were social.

Zanzie walked her to the neighborhood grammar school and came for her at two, when classes were over. She was the only child in her grade who had a black maid; most walked to and from school alone or with older brothers or sisters.

Also, her mother had given strict instructions. "Do not look to right or left," Margaret told them. "Just look straight ahead and don't speak to anybody on the street. The people who live in this part of town are trash, and we have to show them that we want nothing to do with them." Zanzie had already repulsed the friendly overtures of several women who called to welcome the new residents. "And, Garden," Margaret added, "you must keep your distance from the children in your class. I don't want you to have anything to do with them. They're not your kind."

Garden did not understand what her mother meant, but she knew it was serious by the urgent tone of her voice.

"Can't I talk to anybody?" she asked.

"Don't be difficult, Garden. Of course you'll have to be polite. Just don't let them be too friendly."

That presented no problem. No one wanted to be friendly. Garden's mourning dresses, Zanzie's perpetual frown and her new-school timidity kept Garden isolated and unhappy for weeks. When, at last, a little girl named Marjorie asked her if she wanted to play jacks with her, Garden was overjoyed. Soon she had several friends, secrets to be kept from Zanzie and her mother. She paid a high price for them in her shame about her disloyalty to her mother's wishes, but they made the hours at school happy.

She needed that happiness. There was little at home. By November, even the forced gaiety of the weekends was abandoned. Margaret was worried about money; she had no spirit for play.

The furniture had brought such a lot, it seemed to her at the time. And she had done almost no shopping. She was, after all, in mourning and would be in black for three years. She had needed stockings, and a new corset, and her shoes had been practically worn out. But those few things weren't what Margaret called shopping. Shopping was frocks and hats and pretty little things like muffs or lacy handkerchiefs.

Of course, the children had needed things too. They were all growing so fast, and they were so hard on things. Peggy's stockings already had darns; Garden's were beyond darning. Zanzie patched the knees.

Margaret felt desperate. Canzonieri, the corner storekeeper, had actually made a public scene, shouting at Zanzie through the locked iron gate, demanding to see Margaret, threatening the police if he wasn't paid.

Zanzie had always believed that Margaret should have everything she wanted. But now even Zanzie grumbled about the consequences of the move to the city. Mr. Tremaine sent food from the Barony every week and cut logs every month. According to Zanzie, the chickens were never fat enough, the ham never lean enough, and the wood was always green. "You ought to go back to the country," she said daily.

That was the one thing Margaret vowed she'd never do. We'll have to be more careful, she decided. No more carfares. Stuart and Peggy can walk to school . . . Zanzie can cut Stuart's hair. The barber is a thief, charging fifteen cents for a little boy . . . We don't have to use so much sugar, either. Or flour. Or milk. We can make do with the food we get from the Barony. The only thing we'll have to buy is salt . . . and lamp oil . . . and soap . . . and . . . and . . . Margaret buried her face in her hands. There were so many things, and they all cost so much.

I don't care, she thought. I don't care if we have to burn pitch pine to see by. I'm not going back to the country. Not ever.

Stuart and Peggy complained loudly about the sudden strictures on spending. Garden tried to bring back the happy, affectionate mother of the first weeks in town. She colored pictures in school and brought them home to Margaret; she offered to sing for her; she got up before anyone else and brought in the newspaper, silently creeping in to Margaret's room to lay it on the floor by her bed.

Margaret remained cold, frowning, adamant. She had neither money nor affection to dispense. As the weeks passed, she slid back into her old patterns of daydreaming escape. The newspaper was her lifeline. She pored over advertisements and society happenings, envisioning herself in the clothes at the parties. When Stuart finished school and had a job . . . When they moved south of Broad . . .

Even Zanzie had to admit that the city was better in the winter. The low-ceilinged basement was warmer than either house on the plantation. But when the heavy, humid days began in mid-May, the apartment was oppressive. By June the brick walls were sweating, and the carpets felt spongy with moisture. Worst of all, the smells came back. There was a miasma of decay and old wine and cooking. The air was soul, fetid, rank. Beneath the odors that could be recognized, there was something worse. It invaded the nostrils and clung, nauseating and inescapable, a peculiar foul, sweet, sickening smell. It was the stench of poverty.

Margaret retreated. "We're going to the Barony," she announced. And she broke into hysterical sobs.

22

Life on the Barony wasn't the same, of course. They were in the Big House, which had almost no furniture, and they had only Zanzie for help. The enormous, echoing rooms showed the decades of neglect. The silk-covered walls were discolored and peeling, and the silk brocade window hangings were shredding from rot. It looked as derelict as the Charlotte Street mansion.

But fresh air, cooled by the acres of weedy lawn, filled the tall spaces at night, and the folding interior window blinds held it inside during the day.

There were other compensations, too.

Margaret found riches in the attic, a wardrobe of Miss Julia Ashley's clothes. Miss Julia had never bought anything but the best, and for the last thirty years of her life she never wore anything but black. Some of the clothes were forty years old and still intact. All the gowns had yards and yards of fabric in the skirts; Miss Julia had resisted the changes in style. She always wore hoop skirts.

"Let the cobwebs stay, Zanzie," Margaret shrieked down the stairs. "You're going to spend the summer sewing."

Peggy spent the summer reading. The Barony library was well stocked. The Ashleys had been educated, cultivated men and women, none more so than Miss Julia. In addition to the classics and the "complete works of" all the great novelists, essayists, playwrights and poets, there was a case with volumes bound in green leather bearing Julia Ashley's monogram. They were works by women, some of them inflammatory in their independence. Miss Julia had added marginal notes in her spiky handwriting, their content even more inflammatory. Peggy began to teach herself French. Julia's notes, in French, were thickest in the books written in that language.

While Peggy was trying to learn French, Stuart was learning to spit tobacco. Sam Ruggs gave him a job in his store, and he was taken into the fraternity of the area's small farmers who used the front porch for their social club. Stuart had to turn over the money he made to Margaret, but he didn't mind. He would gladly have worked for free, just to be there in the long twilight, listening to the tall tales and coarse jokes. It made him feel like a man.

And Garden was back in her real home with the people who loved her. She had the Settlement.

In September they returned to Charlotte Street and their city lives. For the next three years they spent summers at the plantation and the rest of the year on Charlotte Street.

Life was easier. Stuart had a job after school in Sam Ruggs's Ford dealership. He gave potential buyers their demonstration rides. "Why, mister," Sam would laugh, "this car's so simple even a kid can handle it." Stuart was miserable because he wasn't growing very fast, but Sam made him feel a little better by assuring him that his looks made him the best salesman in the business. "And the best mechanic, too," Sam always added. "I swear, boy, there ain't nothing you can't do with a automobile." Stuart's happiest hours were spent in a coverall, wrench in hand, chaw in cheek, showing his stuff to the older mechanics and talking learnedly about integral water jackets, detachable cylinder heads and planetary transmissions.

His salary took the whole family out for Sunday afternoon excursions and visits to the ice-cream parlor; it bought important trifles like toilet water and ribbons; and it made it possible to have special treats. On major occasions Stuart escorted his ladies to the Academy of Music to see stage plays with famous stars like Minnie Maddern Fiske and Evelyn Nesbit or to the Princess Theater to see motion pictures.

He also removed a quarter from his pay envelope before he gave it to Margaret and went every Wednesday night to the vaudeville at the Victoria Theater with Jimmy Fisher, the head mechanic. Margaret believed he was in a study club at school. His grades were abysmal.

There were terrible scenes. Margaret emerged from her dream world in a fury. Everything depended on Stuart. He had to graduate.

118

He had to get a good job. She railed at him, shamed him, screamed that he was just like his father, no-good, lazy, inconsiderate. Then she blamed all his faults on the company he was keeping, "that white trash Ruggs," and threatened to make him quit his job at the Ford place and spend his time studying.

Stuart was shrewd enough to believe that his mother's threats were empty. They needed the money he made, and when he delivered his nine dollars and twenty-five cents every two weeks she was always very happy. But the accusations that he was like his father upset him profoundly. He remembered the way Margaret had been, so sad and forlorn, neglected, ignored. He had vowed then that he would make it up to her, and he still felt it his duty.

But he really hated school, and he could not understand the work no matter how hard he tried. He promised to do better, he hoped vaguely for a miracle, and he spent more time with Jimmy Fisher, lying to cover his absences from home.

"Don't feel so bad," Jimmy said. "Your trouble is, boy, you're hagridden. A mother and two sisters and a big black witch. You never get a chance to be a man. If it takes bending the truth a little, well, that ain't no crime. Women'll drive a man to a lot worse than that."

When Margaret was fighting with Stuart, Peggy always tried to join in. Peggy thrived on loud, passionate arguments. She was, in her high school years, a tall, ungainly girl, bigger than her brother and most of the girls in her class. Her hands and feet were her only claim to beauty. Her pockmarked face was further blemished by angry red adolescent pimples, and her hair seemed to demonstrate the passionate rage in her heart. It was fiery red, the legacy of the Tradds, and wiry, with tight, springing curls. She wore it in the style of the day, pulled back from her face and tied with a big bow at the nape of her neck. It was an unmanageable, unattractive mass.

Peggy was passionate about causes. She tried fasting, emulating Gandhi, who was in the news. And she was taken to the principal's office for marching up and down the school's corridors with a sign demanding the vote for women. Emmeline Pankhurst and her daughter were her heroines. She signed her tests and homework "Suffragette. Peggy Tradd."

All authority infuriated her, but she bowed to it at school. She wanted to learn even more than she wanted to fight.

At home, authority meant Margaret, and her mother was the most infuriating of all. It was almost impossible to get her attention; Stuart was the only one who could do that. And when Margaret did notice her, it was always in the wrong way. She assumed Peggy's fast was a diet and complimented her on doing something about her figure. She dismissed the suffragettes as women who couldn't find a husband and "not ladies."

Peggy's only audience was Garden. In their room after bedtime, Peggy would pour forth all her anger and frustration. "Do you know that there are people begging for a crust of bread in India, and the English just walk right by them and let them starve? And they force-feed Mrs. Pankhurst, just jam this awful old rubber tube down her throat, and pour mush in it. It makes me sick just to think about it.

"You say, well, that's the English. You think that's all the answer you need, don't you? Well, you're wrong!"

Garden, who had said nothing and had no idea what Peggy was talking about, shook her head violently, agreeing that what she had not said was wrong.

"Wrong," Peggy emphasized. "Because right here in this country, things are just as bad. When the suffragettes paraded in Washington, they sent the U.S. Cavalry to break up the parade. Rode them down under the horses' hooves. And do you know who sent them? Politicians. That's who. They don't care what's right and what's wrong. Do you know, Garden, that people are killing people all over Europe? The Huns sticking bayonets in babies' stomachs, but does anybody care? Oh, no. It's not our business, the politicians say.

"Well, if murdering innocent people isn't our business, what is? Somebody's got to care about what's right. And nobody does. Even the teachers at school, they don't care. Let Europe worry about Europe, that's what they say. And those dumb girls in my class, they don't hardly even know what Europe is. They think the news is what Irene Castle is doing, what kind of shoes Irene Castle wears. They're all shocked because Irene Castle cut off her hair. They don't have time to be shocked by millions and millions of people getting killed every single day.

"I tell you, Garden, it makes me so mad I could spit."

Garden was wholeheartedly sympathetic to Peggy's distress. "Me too," she said. She raised the window next to her bed and spit explosively.

Peggy was diverted from her oratory. "Gosh, Garden, I never knew you could spit like that. It must have gone clear to the house next door."

Garden grinned. "I can spit better than anybody. John, Reba's oldest boy, was the best spitter in the Settlement, and he taught me, but now I can spit better than him. Want me to teach you?"

Margaret would quite possibly have fainted if she could have seen her daughters practicing the art of spitting. The news stories that angered Peggy so much were alarming to Margaret. Women parading in the streets of Washington, a lovely person like Mrs. Castle bobbing her hair. It was all part and parcel of a terrible change in the world. Theda Bara was the biggest star in the moving pictures, and she was obviously immoral. Margaret nodded vigorously when she read an outraged editorial in the *News and Courier*. "The Trouble With the Tango" was its title. It expressed all of Margaret's worries. The world was losing all its standards. Fashionable was becoming a synonym for lewd.

Margaret's mother had given her a simple, proud philosophy to live by. "You're a lady, Margaret, and nobody can ever take that away from you. We may have lost things, but we still have our traditions and our breeding. As long as you live up to them, act like the lady you are, everyone will recognize and respect you."

Mrs. Garden had intended a wealth of meaning in the words "traditions," "breeding" and "lady." It encompassed courage, selflessness, consideration, a genuine, cultivated *noblesse oblige*. Margaret, too young to recognize her own ignorance, believed she understood her mother. She interpreted the words to mean that by birth she was better than most people and that if she was feminine in her appearance and behavior, she would be treated like royalty.

To a large extent, Margaret's system was successful for her. The romantic traditions of chivalry were still prevalent and powerful in the South. No one, except her husband, had ever acted or spoken roughly in Margaret's presence. Men, even if they weren't gentlemen, automatically stepped aside to let her pass, and vehicles stopped to allow her to cross the street. In shops she was served while women, as opposed to ladies, had to wait. Being a lady was Margaret's career. The rushing changes in twentieth-century culture were threatening everything she lived by.

She was reassured when she saw her children leave for school each day. Stuart held the door for his sisters as he had been taught.

And the girls, with their drab frocks and clean-scrubbed faces, were obviously proper, well-brought-up children of good family. There was nothing modern or suggestive about them.

Margaret congratulated herself. Despite their hard times, the shame of living on Charlotte Street, the isolation from their own kind of people, she had taught her children proper standards. When they moved below Broad, everyone would notice, would compliment her. Stuart would be a credit to her. And Peggy and Garden. She had to admit that they were unattractive. Ugly, even, if the truth be told. Peggy so scarred and husky, Garden so scrawny, with her bug eyes and striped hair. But they would be ladies, and that was the only thing that really mattered.

Margaret had no inkling of the mutiny that was brewing.

23

"You just give Mama this for me." Stuart thrust a wrinkled envelope into Peggy's hand. He tried to hurry away, but she caught his sleeve.

"Not so fast, brother. If I'm going to take a chance on Mama killing me, at least you can say thank you." Peggy laughed, but her eyes were swimming.

"Sure, sure. Thanks, Peggy. You're a brick." Stuart pulled away.

"Stuart!" Peggy threw her arms around him and hugged him. Her hat fell off, and she released Stuart to run after it. "Be careful, hear?" she called back.

"Sure. See you." Peggy did not see Stuart blinking as he walked away. His back was straight, his pace eager. It was April 7, 1917. The United States had declared war on Germany the previous day. Stuart was going to enlist.

Margaret folded his note carefully after she read it. Then she went to her room. She returned wearing hat and gloves. She did not speak a word to Peggy before she left the house.

She marched to the corner store, entered and walked to the counter. Mr. Canzonieri gaped at her. She had, to his certain knowledge, never left her home alone before, and she had never crossed the threshold of his store.

Margaret spoke before he gathered his wits enough to address her. "I believe you have a telephone," she said. "I would like to use it."

The following day two Army officers delivered Stuart to his mother. The governor of South Carolina had responded at once to the demands of a determined mother bearing the illustrious Tradd name.

Stuart was angry and humiliated. Margaret let him suffer her silent disapproval until Peggy got home from school. Then she sat them on the sofa and paced up and down while she addressed them.

"I can see now that I have been wrong in the way I treated you two children. I trusted you, and you conspired to deceive me. From now on, I'll have to be more careful.

"Stuart, tomorrow morning I will go with you when you escort Peggy to school. Then I will go with you to your school to have a word with your principal.

"I assume you told that Ruggs person you were leaving. I assume you had more consideration for him than for your mother. So you won't have to let him know that you are not going to set foot in his automobile place or his store ever again. Because you aren't."

Stuart burst out in protests. Margaret burst out in tears. "See how he treats me," she sobbed. Peggy couldn't think of anything to say. "Stuart," Margaret cried, "you're going to break my heart, just like your father."

"Aw, Mama, don't. I'm sorry." Stuart jumped up and put his arms around his mother.

"So they're all huggy-weepy, and I'm sent to my room," Peggy complained to Garden. "And all I did was deliver the note, for heaven's sake. It's not fair."

"Want to spit?" Garden offered.

"No, I'm too mad."

Julian Cartwright looked approvingly at the lady in the chair opposite his desk. She looked delicate and demure and very pretty in her mauve silk dress and little tricorne hat. Her white-gloved hands were folded in her lap, and her tiny black boots wore immaculate side-buttoned white high-tops. They were barely visible, Mr. Cartwright noted with pleasure. The new fashion for skirts inches above the ankle was, he thought, deplorable. Yes, Mistress Tradd was a charming little lady. It was hard to believe that she could have a son as old, or as oafish, as Stuart.

"This is indeed an honor, ma'am," said the principal. "I'll be happy to do anything I can for you." It was Mr. Cartwright's standard statement to mothers of his students. Usually they wanted him to listen and agree to an account of their sons' virtues which offset their poor performance.

Margaret Tradd had something else in mind. "I want you to find employment for Stuart," she said. "Something suitable for a gentleman, of course. He can begin at once, working after school. When he graduates, of course, he can begin at once on a full-day schedule."

Mr. Cartwright was at a loss for words. It was extremely unlikely that Stuart Tradd would receive a diploma at all. The High School of Charleston had very high standards. Stuart would have been asked to leave long before except for the special pleading of his guardian, Logan Henry. Mr. Henry and Mr. Cartwright were old friends.

That's it, thought the principal. I did Logan a favor; now it's his turn. "I'll begin inquiries immediately, Mistress Tradd," he said smoothly. "Perhaps we won't even have to wait for the graduation ceremonies. They are in some ways a mere formality, as I'm sure you are aware."

Margaret thanked him prettily. "If I could just bother you for one more thing?" she added.

"Of course, ma'am."

"I'll have to borrow my son for a little while to see me home. If you'd just have him called out of class. I could hardly go on the street alone, you understand."

Mr. Cartwright did not understand. His wife went out alone all the time. But he sent for Stuart all the same.

That evening he told his wife about his encounter with Margaret.

"The Tradds?" said Mary Cartwright. "I haven't heard that name in ages. I thought they were all dead. Wasn't there something fishy about it? They were all out hunting or something."

Her husband corrected her memory. Logan Henry had corrected his when he talked to him.

"Well, that explains everything, then," said Mary. "The poor woman's been in mourning practically all her life. She was wearing mauve? That's second mourning. She'll be in pink in another year if she wants to. But maybe not; she must be really devoted, if she stayed shut away all those years. So old-fashioned. Nowadays everyone understands that life must go on. Personally, I don't think it's healthy to grieve like that. Maybe I should write her a little note or something and ask if I could call. She should be out in the world."

Mary Cartwright was not the only person preparing to take a hand in the Tradds' future. A few blocks away Logan Henry was having a whiskey and water with Andrew Anson, president of the Carolina Fidelity Bank.

"Tradd? Of course the name rings a bell, Logan. My mother nearly married Pinckney Tradd, but he was killed in the earthquake. Lord yes, I remember the Tradds. That red hair and wild streak. Who is this boy? . . . Stuart. Yes, that'll be the grandson of the Stuart I knew. He was one of Wade Hampton's boys when they turned out the Reconstruction rascals. Hampton made him a judge. . . . Lord, what a long time ago it all was. I used to play with Lizzie. She was three or four years older than me. That makes her almost sixty now; you'd never know it, would you? Elizabeth Cooper, you know, ran the phosphate company."

"I know, Andrew. We could reminisce all night. But the point now before us is this boy who has nothing to recommend him but his grandfather's association with Wade Hampton. Can you find him work at the bank?"

"Of course I can. You said he tried to enlist, didn't you? That's a Tradd all right. What is he, sixteen?"

"Seventeen in July."

"That's plenty old enough to learn and young enough not to think he already knows everything there is to know. I'll do it."

"You're an excellent fellow, Andrew. There's one other thing. He's the family's sole support. I'll want you to pay him more than he's worth. The plantation is starting to show a handsome profit. I'll renegotiate the contract with the manager and give you an extra ten dollars a week to put in the boy's pay envelope."

"Why don't you give it to him?"

"Because he's still under age. I'd have to give it to his mother, that dreadful woman."

Andrew laughed. "Logan, you do love your widow clients, don't you? All right. I'll conspire with you, but I hope it's not against the law."

The following week Stuart escorted his mother to King Street, where she supervised the purchase of a new suit for him, and to Tradd Street, where she looked at a small house and signed the rental agreement on the spot.

"We'll get the wagons and the men in from the Barony and move over the weekend. Isn't it wonderful, Stuart? You can walk to work in no time at all when you start on Monday."

The bank, like most Charleston banks, was on Broad Street. Tradd Street was a block south of Broad.

BOOK 4

1918–1923

24

UNCLE SAM WANTS YOU.

Stuart walked in front of the poster on the wall of the lobby. He didn't even cringe anymore. He was too miserable. He hated banking, he hated having to take his mother to all those parties, he hated having to dance with all those girls who were taller than he was, he hated all the people who told him how much he looked like his father. Or his grandfather. There sure were a lot of old people in Charleston.

"Good morning, Stuart."

"Good morning, Mr. Anson."

"One of our clients will be making a special deposit this morning, Stuart. Mr. Walker will need your help." Andrew Anson winked.

Stuart nodded glumly. He had thought the special deposits were funny at first. Now all they meant to him was that he'd mess up his clothes and his mother would give him another lecture. The crates were always full of splinters; some of them had cobwebs all over them.

The special deposits were wine and liquor. The drys had already won in Columbia, the South Carolina capital, and they were obviously winning in Washington. The Eighteenth Amendment was being ratified all over the country. In September it became the law of the land that no whiskey could be manufactured. Soon it would be law that none could be imported. Who could say that the legislators wouldn't pass a law saying that none could be owned?

Andrew Anson built an addition to the bank, a large room with storage racks from floor to ceiling. The word spread quickly that safety deposit bins were available, and many of the bank's clients hurried to reserve space for the supplies they had at home or the cases they had ordered from their spirit merchants.

Stuart thought wistfully about the still in the woods behind Ruggs's store. Sam Ruggs had let him go out there sometimes and feed the fire. He remembered the sharp-sweet smell of the mash and the plopping sound the flies made. They'd dip too low over the open filled Mason jars, get drunk from the fumes and fall in. Some of the men who operated the still would make bets about how many flies would drown in the next ten minutes.

He'd be willing to bet plenty that Sam's business was going to pick up with Prohibition coming in. It would probably do even better than the Ford agency. Stuart yearned for some honest grease on his hands and the feel of an engine under his sensitive fingers.

"Mr. Tradd? I need your help out back."

"Yes, sir, Mr. Walker. I'm on my way." His feet dragged. I hate this place, he thought. Even more than I hated school. At least you get vacations from school. Last summer I didn't even get out of the city. Peggy and Garden got to stay at the Barony all summer, and what did I get? The bank all day and listening to Mama talk all night. Why couldn't she have let me stay in town alone at least? Then I could have seen some of my friends. Oh, no, she had to stay too. To have tea parties with all her lady friends and to make me move the furniture in that hot, nasty little house.

"Mr. Tradd!"

"Yes, sir, Mr. Walker, I'm hurrying."

Across the floor, Andrew Anson sighed. Stuart had to stay. Andrew had given his word. He just wished that he could find something the boy could do without fouling it up. And that the boy wouldn't look so gloomy.

Margaret was thinking much the same thing. What was wrong with her children? She honestly could not understand why they did not seem to be happy. Perversely blessed by single-mindedness and lack of imagination, Margaret truly believed that her lifelong goal was the only ambition anyone could have. Now it was attained. They were in the city; they were part of society. Why on earth did Stuart and Peggy resist going to the parties? Why had Garden turned so glum? She was finally in a school where she would make little friends, where the other girls were from her own kind of people. Had she invited one child home to play? She had not. She didn't even want to play herself, only to mope. Zanzie complained daily about having her underfoot . . . Zanzie. Even Zanzie had changed. The children got on her nerves a lot more. Of course, she was getting on. Margaret wondered idly how old Zanzie must be. You could never tell with colored people. She felt a sudden chill grip her spine.

Goose jumped over my grave, she thought. It stopped her thinking about age. Margaret was thirty-three now. On her birthday, she had thought about it a great deal. It had been a time of tears, of looking closely in the mirror, of facing unpleasant surprises. They had been in the Tradd Street house for several months by then, and Margaret was securely established in the round of calls paid and calls received that marked the days of every Charleston matron. The tray on the hall table had been piled high with cards in the first weeks, as news spread that the Tradds were living in town. Margaret had been hard pressed to return the calls. She had drunk gallons of tea, talked herself hoarse. And learned a great deal about the one subject that interested her, Charleston society.

She now knew that she need not be escorted everywhere, that ladies shopped and went calling, and even walked for exercise, alone. She knew a hundred tidbits of gossip. She knew that she need not have been ashamed of Charlotte Street; the secluded house down the street from the Ashley house was the home of the Wilsons, prominent in the social world. She knew that everyone was poor, and that even if they weren't they lived as if they were; respectable people had lost everything in the War. She knew that she and her children were welcomed, back home where they belonged. And she knew that she was a matron, not a girl. The days of the dance card were gone forever; fifteen seasons had come and gone since she filled her box of souvenirs, and there were no over-thirty belles. It didn't do to think about it or a lady might cry.

That would ruin her eyes and give her wrinkles and then no one would ever want to dance with her. Margaret was rescued by her inconsistencies: she could be simultaneously shrewdly realistic and blind to unpalatable truths.

She sat up in bed and rang for Zanzie. "Build a fire in here, Zanzie, and hand me a shawl. I'll just stay in bed until it's warm enough to get dressed. Hand me the newspaper, too. Peggy grabbed it this morning before I finished with it. She thinks she's the only person in this house who can read."

Peggy was, at that moment, reading a pamphlet about the life of Susan B. Anthony. At the same time, she was scrubbing the big soup pot in the scullery of the Red Cross canteen. All of Charleston's young ladies worked at the canteen; it was their contribution to the war effort. Peggy would rather have been a volunteer nurse, but that work was reserved for older ladies. Girls did canteen. The pretty ones served the servicemen. Less decorative faces worked in the kitchen. Peggy had proved herself a poor cook; she washed dishes.

She wiped her soapy hands on her apron and turned a page. Before she started to read it, she put her two arms about the enormous pot and lifted it.

"Let me help you with that, ma'am," said a male voice behind her.

Peggy heaved the pot over to pour out the wash water. "I don't need any help," she said. "Women can do things just as well as men." She lowered the pot into the rinse water with a far-reaching splash. "There," she said triumphantly.

"That's fine. But it seems to me, if a person is going to do something, it should be done right, man or woman."

Peggy turned to face the stranger. "Who says I didn't do it right?"

"I say." He was a Citadel cadet in dress uniform complete with white gloves, gold braid on his sleeves and hat, a wine-colored sash and a glittering, tassel-hung saber. "That pot wasn't clean."

"What?" Peggy plunged her hands into the water. Her fingers felt a crust of dried soup under the rim of the pot. "All right," she grumbled. "Thank you very much, Mr. Inspector General. I can take care of it now." She returned the pot to the soap-filled water, drenching the front of her uniform, and grabbed the scrub brush.

The cadet picked up her pamphlet.

"Put that down!" Peggy waved the brush menacingly. The cadet dropped the booklet.

"Sorry. I just wondered if it was Gogol."

Peggy lowered the brush. "What do you mean?" she said.

"You called me 'Inspector General.' That's the name of a play by a Russian writer named Gogol. When I came in, I saw you were reading something. I just wondered if maybe . . ."

"I know who Gogol is." Peggy was truculent. And amazed. She had never met anyone else who knew.

"My name is Bob Thurston."

"I'm Peggy Tradd."

"Oh, I see, like Tradd Street."

"Yes, I guess so." Peggy felt her accustomed tongue-tied state come over her. She couldn't talk to boys. That was why she hated being dragged to the parties her mother loved so much. They made her clumsy; she stepped on her dance partner's feet. She knew her face was scarred, that she wasn't pretty. She couldn't do what she was supposed to do, smile and coo and say flirtatious, flattering things. This was the longest conversation she had ever had with a boy . . . except for Stuart, and the boys in the Bacon's Bridge school who always treated her like one of them.

Peggy realized that her frock was wet and soapy, that she had splashed Bob Thurston too. There were dark wet splotches on his uniform. She looked at his magnificent, marred splendor, then at his face. He was, she recognized suddenly, as handsome as a moving-picture star, as Francis X. Bushman—no, he was too old; as Douglas Fairbanks. She wished the floor would open and swallow her. She fell to scrubbing with an energy that threw water in all directions. Bob Thurston jumped back.

"Excuse me, Miss Tradd. I'm looking for Miss Emily Pringle. Can you tell me where to find her?"

Peggy kept her eyes on her work. "Out front," she muttered. "Handing out doughnuts."

She heard his steps, then his pause. "Well, goodbye," he said.

Peggy looked up. "Goodbye," she said. Bob Thurston saluted smartly and walked through the door.

"I'm sorry I was rude," Peggy whispered.

Then she threw the scrub brush on the floor. "No, I'm not," she said to it. "He's just Emily Pringle's type. Handsome is as handsome does. He'd no right to be such a smart aleck about the pot. Let him wash it himself if he cares so much about getting it clean." She rinsed the pot and slammed it on the counter. "And let him keep his hands off my book." She concentrated intensely on the life of Susan B. Anthony until the next wagon of dirty dishes came in.

Emily Pringle was pushing it. "Ooh, Peggy," she squealed, "isn't that Bob Thurston the handsomest thing you ever saw in your life? I'm so excited I could just die. His roommate was my escort for the tea dance this afternoon but he flunked a test or something so he's confined. Bob Thurston is going to take me. I can hardly stand it.

"He said you told him where to find me. What did he say, Peggy? Did he talk about me? Did he look interested?"

Peggy started unloading the dishes. "He just asked me where you were, that's all. He didn't say anything at all."

"Gosh, Peggy, you're no fun at all. How did he look? When he said my name, did he look any special way?"

"He looked like somebody who didn't know which way to go."

Emily sighed. "I had such hopes," she said. "After all, he said 'your interesting friend Miss Tradd told me where to find you.' He might have said something about me to you."

Peggy smiled. "Sorry, Emily," she said warmly, "he really didn't. I'd tell you if he did."

Peggy burst into the house when she went home after her shift. "I've been washing dishes until my skin's about to come off," she announced. "Is dinner ready? I'm starving.

"I guess I'd better wash my hair," she said, buttering her bread with extreme precision. "You're probably going to make me go to that horrid old tea dance, aren't you, Mama?"

25

"What's happened to the Tradd girl?" said the Red Cross canteen supervisor. "She's become so agreeable."

"She must have a beau," her assistant replied. "There's nothing that makes a girl so agreeable as a beau."

Peggy had talked with Bob Thurston every day for three days after their first meeting. Not for very long. They met at the tea dances that were the opening flurries of activity before the Season got underway. Bob correctly danced with the hostess and with the guest of honor before asking Peggy to dance. Then he danced with each of the debutantes. "That's what I'm here for," he explained to Peggy. "With so many Charleston men away at the war, dancing partners are hard to find. The hostesses call the commandant and order the number of cadets they need. It's understood that our duty is to dance."

Peggy thought at once that he was dancing with her as a duty, too. But then she noticed that he didn't dance with any other non-debutantes. She wouldn't be presented until the following year when she would be seventeen, the proper age for coming out.

The whole tradition of making a debut, which she had scorned as a kind of exclusive white slavery, now seemed to Peggy to be a very good idea. How else would people meet people?

It seemed less good when the Citadel closed for Christmas vacation and Bob Thurston went home. She was meeting, Peggy complained, all the same boring people over and over again at every party. "And they think I'm boring too," she said accurately.

But then she received a letter at breakfast the day before Christmas. "I'll be returning to Charleston on January second," Bob Thurston wrote. "May I call on you?"

Peggy startled everyone in the family by suddenly hugging her sister, who was sitting next to her. "Happy birthday, Garden. Happy, happy, happy birthday."

She ran all the way to the Western Union office on Broad Street and sent a telegram. "Letter received stop Do call stop I will be home all day stop." Halfway down the block, she turned and ran back to add "Merry Christmas." It put her over ten words, but she didn't care.

Bob Thurston was a serious young man. When he told Peggy that she had not washed the soup pot clean, he was not trying to start a conversation with a young lady, he was calling attention to a dereliction of duty. Duty and responsibility were the guiding principles of his life.

He came from an interesting family. Bob's father, Walter, was originally from Wisconsin. He had visited South Carolina in 1886 to learn about the Farmers Alliance, a populist political movement led by Benjamin Tillman. Walter Thurston was a lifelong friend and supporter of Robert La Follette, the progressive Wisconsin Republican who was then a member of the House of Representatives.

Walter reported favorably to his friend on the goals of the movement and the organization of granges. He also reported that he would not be returning to Wisconsin. He had met a certain Miss Betty Easter in the small tobacco town of Mullins, South Carolina.

Miss Easter agreed to be his bride, but only if he stayed in Mullins. She was the eldest of five children and mother surrogate for

135

her brothers and sisters. Her mother had died when the youngest was born. Betty Easter could not move to Wisconsin; she took her responsibilities seriously.

Walter Thurston became a partner in the Easter Tobacco Warehouse and, two years later, sole proprietor when Mr. Easter died. He and his wife raised and educated her brother and three sisters and their own three sons. Bob was the youngest, Robert La Follette Thurston his full name. Walter never lost touch with his friend or his friend's ideals.

"So you see, I'm half Yankee," Bob told Peggy, "and half socialist in most people's minds."

"Socialist!" Peggy echoed. "Me too! Kerensky was obviously the leader to make everything right for all those peasants, not that horrible Lenin person." She continued at length, growing more and more excited, with her ill-informed view of the revolution that was going on in Russia.

Bob listened with full attention. When Peggy ran out of steam, he explained carefully the true meaning of socialism, of communism and of revolution.

"Oh, all right then," Peggy said. "I'm not really a socialist, if that's what it means. But somebody had to do something for the peasants. Do you know, the winters are so terrible that they eat the bark off the trees?"

Bob smiled. "You care so much, don't you?"

"Yes, I do. I can't stand it when things are all wrong, when some people push other people around." She was not smiling.

But she smiled radiantly later that evening when she learned that Bob shared her enthusiasm for the poetry of Emily Dickinson.

Bob called on Peggy every Saturday evening. On Sunday afternoons they went for walks. They talked. They talked about books, about politics and, more and more, about themselves.

"Peggy has a beau," Margaret told her friends. "I can hardly credit it. She's as brash and noisy as ever, and this good-looking, much older boy seems to like it. There's just no accounting for tastes."

The reasons were simple enough. They shared a love of learning, a concern for humanity, and an earlier life of being almost outcasts in their own age group. Peggy's greed for knowledge had cut her off from other girls preoccupied with pursuits more appropriate for young Southern ladies. Bob's populist leanings had made him suspect in the rigidly structured man's world of boss-tenant, white-black, Democrat-heathen.

Peggy and Bob were loners, and lonely. They fit together like two halves of a puzzle. After a few weeks of sharing ideas, Peggy forgot that Bob looked like a movie star. Bob had never noticed that Peggy was not beautiful.

Margaret found life almost as satisfying as Peggy did in those first months of 1918. She, too, did volunteer work for the Red Cross. In her case it was rolling bandages. She met two afternoons a week with other ladies in the basement of the Masonic Lodge building and chattered happily about nothing at all while she worked. The smocks and head scarves provided by the Red Cross kept them all free of the lint the bandages produced and made them look, someone said, like angels of mercy.

She was also involved with activities at St. Michael's church. Margaret had not bothered to go to church once St. Andrews closed, nor had she ever arranged for her children to go to Sunday school or confirmation classes. On Charlotte Street she had kept the same routine as had grown up on the Barony. They had grace before meals, and the children were taught "Now I lay me down to sleep." On Sundays they slept late and then went out for amusement. But when they moved downtown, Margaret was reminded that she was a practicing Episcopalian. Everyone went to church. She learned that the Tradds had a family pew in St. Michael's. She and the children now occupied it every week.

Every Thursday she joined the group of ladies organized to pack the donations of clothing and blankets for the Belgians.

That left only two weekday afternoons free, one to pay calls and one to receive them. Margaret complained merrily that she was so busy that she couldn't call her life her own.

Her only problem was that prices were rising so, especially for necessities that were in short supply because of the war. "Stuart," she said, "you'll have been at the bank a year this spring. Tell Mr. Anson you should have a raise."

"Mama, I couldn't do that."

"Very well, then, I'll tell him."

Stuart convinced her that he would take care of it. It was man's work. A week later, the money in his pay envelope was doubled.

Margaret kissed him and told all the ladies she knew how well her son was doing.

"Of course he wanted to join the Army," she added quickly. "But they wouldn't take him. He was too young. He still is." A number of her friends had sons on their way to France.

26

The house Margaret rented was almost identical to hundreds of others in the city. It was a unique architectural plan that had evolved in response to the geography and climate of the old town, was seen in no other place and had become known to architects worldwide as the Charleston single house.

It sat with its shoulder to the street, entrance on the side, reached by a brickpaved walkway. Because of the near-tropical summers, it had high ceilings and was only a single room wide. Each floor had two rooms, one on each side of the central hall into which one entered. Built this way, each room had windows on three sides for cross ventilation. And the houses were very tall to accommodate the required numbers of rooms.

Most Charleston single houses had piazzas, long porches on their south or west walls to shade those windows and to catch the prevailing afternoon breeze that came across the waters of the harbor.

Margaret's did not. It was on a lot too small for their addition, crowded in between two other old houses, equally small, that dated from the time when Charleston was a walled city. In that colonial era Charlestonians were more concerned with defending themselves against raids by Indians and Spanish troops than with ameliorating the summer heat. They huddled together for protection and comfort and built their high, graceful houses along the four original streets within the walls.

One of them was Tradd Street, named to honor the first male child born to one of the brave adventurers who came to build a new life in a new world. Margaret Tradd did not know why Tradd Street had its name. She knew only that it pleased her to say that she was Mistress Tradd of Tradd Street.

If she had known that the house she lived in was one of the oldest in the city, it would have pleased her to say that too. However, the house gave her quite enough pleasure without needing to know. The ground floor contained the library—attractive, Margaret thought, with the rich, colorful bindings of the books Peggy brought from the Barony—and the dining room, terribly cramped because of the huge marble-topped table. The kitchen was behind the dining room in a frame addition.

On the second floor, as in all old Charleston houses, was a drawing room and a bedroom. The drawing room was Margaret's pride. Here she answered and wrote invitations, studied the newspaper with unfailing pleasure, and entertained at teatime under the amused eyes of the colonial Ashley. The bedroom was Stuart's. In spite of the extra stairs, Margaret preferred to have her room on the third floor.

There was a bathroom there, with water piped from the big cistern on the roof that captured and held the rain. It was squeezed into the space on the landing between Margaret's room and the one shared by Garden and Peggy. For all the Tradds, it was a great luxury. For Zanzie, it was a lifesaver. She was getting too old to haul water and empty night jars. She did not find the gas light as wonderful as the family did, and the gas stove in the kitchen was a constant source of terror to her. But she was wholeheartedly in favor of the plumbing.

Stuart applauded the plumbing, too. The waste pipe was his route from his bedroom to the street after he had supposedly gone to bed.

It had not taken him long to find it. Less than a week after he began his job at the bank, he surprised Jimmy Fisher, finding him at the Victoria just before the vaudeville show started.

Stuart used the exit with increasing frequency as his loathing of the bank grew. It did not take long for Jimmy Fisher to introduce Stuart to his circle of friends and to pleasures more sophisticated than a vaudeville show. Stuart began drinking and smoking, and he lost his virginity. Soon he was leading a double life.

Stuart knew he was not doing a good job at the bank. To his shame, he knew that he should have been fired, that only Andrew Anson's good nature was keeping him employed. He couldn't do anything right, Stuart thought, just as his father used to tell him. Jimmy Fisher told him differently. But Jimmy wanted him to break the law. Stuart said no. Again and again.

Until Margaret told him to ask for a raise.

That night Stuart said yes. And on the following Sunday Stuart met Jimmy at the Pavilion on the Isle of Palms.

"There she is, buddy," said Jimmy. "What do you think of her?"

Stuart could not speak. Sitting on the hard-packed sand of low tide was the legend he had never dreamed he would see. Long, low, luxurious, powerful, blindingly bright in the sun. A Rolls-Royce Silver Ghost.

Jimmy slapped him on the back. "Go ahead. See what she can do. You won't believe it. There are some goggles on the front seat."

Stuart walked across the sand in a trance. He had read about the Ghost, seen photographs of it, but he was not prepared for the magnificent reality. He walked all around the car, his outspread hands held close to the gleaming body, not touching, reverent. Then he stepped up into it and lowered himself carefully into the leather seat. He touched the car then, feeling the gearshift, leaning his head close to the gearbox as he shifted, his sensitive fingers absorbing the smooth, silent meshing. When he pressed the starter, the engine turned over at once. Stuart held his head up, face toward the sun. He experienced the action of the motor; it became part of the beating of his heart.

"He's hooked," said Jimmy aloud. "And he hasn't even let her out yet. Wait till he tops a hundred."

Sam Ruggs stepped out of the shadows. "With a good driver, that machine will leave anything on wheels ten miles behind it in two minutes. With that boy driving it, it might take off and fly. I never saw anybody who could handle an automobile like him. He made a Model T hum like a Bearcat. Lord only knows what he can do with a Ghost."

South Carolina had already adopted Prohibition, a year before the Eighteenth Amendment became law. Sam Ruggs was going into the import business. The production at his still turned a respectable profit, as it always had. Now he was going to go after the carriage trade. The Rolls-Royce had a custom-built body. Four cases of the

140

finest Europe had to offer could be concealed under its seats. And the last male to bear the finest name Charleston had to offer would deliver it in style. In the dark of the night. In a Ghost. Sam laughed mightily at the joke of it all.

27

"I'm forever blowing bubbles," sang the tenor. The gramophone Stuart had bought sat on a table in the library; Margaret did not want it in her drawing room, or even near it in Stuart's room. Peggy loved being custodian. Every week she took all the records from their paper envelopes and dusted them. And she turned the crank carefully to wind it, not with her customary excessive vigor.

They had records of all the good songs, the newest ones like "I'm Forever Blowing Bubbles" and "I'm Always Chasing Rainbows" and the older ones, "Over There," "Oh, Johnny," "For Me and My Gal," "Till the Clouds Roll By," "Roses of Picardy," "Pack Up Your Troubles," and "When You Wore a Tulip." Stuart had even arranged for an account at Seigling's Music House. Peggy was planning to get the whole set of records of Enrico Caruso to play for Bob when he called on Saturday.

"Come in," she called in answer to a tap on the door. She expected it to be Garden. Garden always came in to hear the gramophone if she was home when Peggy played it.

The door opened, and Bob Thurston walked in. "The commandant declared a holiday this afternoon," he said. "There's good news from France. Foch is named general of all the Allied Armies."

"Is that good?"

"Very good. He beat the Germans at the Marne in '14 with an army of taxicabs. Just think what he'll do with an army of American soldiers."

The record was over. Peggy took it off. "What would you like to hear? Would you like something to drink? Eat?"

"Nothing, thanks. Not to hear or drink or eat. I want to talk to you about something. How about going for a walk? It's a nice day."

"I'll get my hat."

They walked down Meeting Street to White Point Gardens and the esplanade along the harbor. Bob took Peggy's arm as they crossed from the gardens to the railed sidewalk. "Seems funny to have an asphalt road here," he said. "When I first came to the Citadel, it was all cobbled. Automobiles are changing the world."

"That's what my brother says. He's crazy for motors."

"I know." Stuart had talked about nothing else when he met Bob.

They walked slowly. Sea gulls swooped above the sparkling water. Behind them the high-pitched calls of little children at play in the gardens blurred into almost music. A breeze rustled the stiff fronds of the palm trees that lined the street, and tiny waves slapped the sea wall. Peggy realized that the sounds were new to her. She had walked here with Bob a dozen times, but this was the first time they had walked in silence.

She stopped. "What do you want to talk about, Bob? It must be important or it wouldn't take you so long to get to it."

Bob looked down at her. Her hat was askew, the hair beneath it coming loose from its ribbon and coiling into wild red tangles. Her frock was rumpled, with a smudge of ink on one cuff. "I love you, Peggy," he said.

"Bob!" Peggy threw her arms around him, knocking her hat to the side of her head. Bob pulled her arms down to her side.

"We're in public, Peggy."

"I don't care. I don't care if we're on the front page of the newspaper." She pushed her hat back onto the top of her head and smiled radiantly from under the bent brim. "I love you, too."

"I want you to meet my family. They want to meet you, too. I've written so much about you."

"I can't wait. I hope it will be soon."

"It will. My parents and my brothers will be coming for graduation. I want you to come to the ceremony with them and then have dinner with us at their hotel.

"And then, dear Peggy, I have to leave at once for Camp Jackson. I get my commission when I graduate."

"No! Bob, you told me yourself that you came to the Citadel to

142

learn to be an engineer, to build things. You're not a soldier. You don't even believe in the war."

"I don't believe in any war. But we're in it, and I have a duty to my country."

"Duty! That's a man's word. It's dumb. Getting killed is dumb."

"Peggy, stop it. You know you believe in responsibility, in duty. Just as I do. There's so much that's wrong in the world, and we all have a responsibility to try and make it better."

"Not this way. Not by dying."

"But I'm not going to die."

Peggy shook her head. "Yes, you will. I know you will. And if you do, I'll kill myself."

Bob laughed. "That's my Peggy. You know, I love your extravagances. I love the way you feel things a thousand times stronger than anybody else in the world.

"You're so young, Peggy. You keep me from being so old before my time. I love everything about you, Peggy Tradd. There, now. Did you hear me? Have you calmed down?"

"I heard you, Bob. You were saying goodbye, weren't you? You've made up your mind."

"Yes, I have."

"Then why? Why tell me you love me just when you're going to go away?" Peggy turned away from him. She hunched her shoulders and dropped her chin down on her chest, making her back a wall between them.

Bob put his hand on her shoulder.

"You're in my heart, Peggy. You're part of my life, the best part. I hate to leave you. But I have to. Help me. I need you to help me."

Peggy lifted her head, turned it, kissed his hand. "I'll do anything you tell me, Bob. Tell me how to help."

"Turn around and try to smile . . . Good girl. You have the prettiest smile there ever was, even when it's a little wobbly.

"Now give me your hand. Both hands. Now tell me again that you love me. As I love you."

"I love you, Robert Thurston."

"And you'll marry me when I come back and follow me to the ends of the earth, living in huts full of spiders while I build dams."

"I'll marry you and kill all the spiders in the jungle so they won't bother you while you're building your dam."

Bob squeezed her hands. "You know," he said, "I believe you

143

could. Peggy, I think I'm going to kiss you right here on the boulevard for everyone to see."

"Then quit talking and do it. I've been kissing my pillow all this time pretending it was you. I want to know what it's really like."

Caroline Wragg nearly ran her Cadillac into a palm tree. "Did you see that?" she gasped. "That was Margaret Tradd's girl, I'm sure of it."

Her mother craned her neck. "Isn't it sad, Caroline? This new century is changing all the rules. I wish I'd been born fifty years later."

28

Garden went to the Barony alone that summer. Margaret arranged for her to stay with the Tremaines at the Woods House.

"I don't hardly know them, Mama," Garden complained. "Can't Peggy go with me, like last year? We did fine with Cissie taking care of us."

"Peggy doesn't want to be bothered with you, and neither do I. We've got our Red Cross work to do."

"Then let me stay by myself with Cissie."

"Nonsense. You're only twelve years old. It's settled. Stuart will drive you out on Sunday."

"In the new car?" The Tradd ladies were all impressed by Stuart's Rolls-Royce. They were too naïve to wonder how he could afford it. Cars had always been Stuart's special interest, not theirs.

"Of course in the new car," said Margaret impatiently. "Go on and leave me alone."

Margaret closed the shutters in her room and stretched out on the bed, a damp cloth over her eyes. What a trial children were. She shifted, her body searching for the coolness of a different place. It was so hot already, and June wasn't even half over. Maybe she should go to the country too. No, she couldn't. She had to roll bandages, pack boxes for Belgium. Being in society had its responsibilities.

Hot tears rolled from her covered eyes. Margaret shook with choked, small sobs. She wasn't in society. Not really. Not the way she wanted to be. She had been fooled by the piles of cards on the tray in the hall those first weeks after the move to Tradd Street, by the effusive welcome at St. Michael's, by the invitations to work on committees at the Red Cross, at the church, at the Confederate Home. She had believed that she was at the center of the only world that mattered, the exclusive, tight circle of Charleston society.

She had been so wrong. The circle was really a series of circles, ring within ring. She was on committees, but not the committee that sent the invitations to join the lesser committees. She was invited to big receptions, but not to small suppers. She was only on the edge. Why, when the vestry decided to reupholster the prayer stools, her opinion had not even been solicited. It was the Judge's sister, Elizabeth Cooper, who had chosen to recover the ones in the Tradd pew with tapestry instead of velvet. And she never even went to church.

Well, she'd show them. She did not know how; she did not even know who she meant by "them." But she'd do something. Even after she drifted into sleep, her hands were knotted into fists.

"This used to be your old room, didn't it, Garden?" Harriet Tremaine's voice was anxious to please.

"Yes, ma'am." It looked much smaller than Garden remembered.

"I'm afraid there's a stain on the rug," said Mrs. Tremaine nervously. "My little boy Billy has been using this room, and he dropped a bottle of ink. I think it's terrible the way the school makes children do writing in ink. They aren't old enough to understand what a mess it can make." She rattled on, apologizing and excusing every flaw she feared Garden might notice in the house.

Garden was confused. Why was Mrs. Tremaine telling her all this? It's not my house, she thought. Then she understood. It wasn't Mrs. Tremaine's house even more than it wasn't hers. It belonged to the Barony, and the Barony belonged to her family. Mr. Tremaine worked for them. They could tell him to go away forever if he did anything wrong. Or if his wife did. It struck Garden as very sad.

It also struck her that it was going to be a very long vacation, living with somebody as nervous as Mrs. Tremaine. She took a wild chance. "Say, Mrs. Tremaine, I'd like to ask you an awful big favor."

"Anything, Garden, anything I can do."

It wasn't hard to persuade her.

"I'll run over to the Settlement, then, Mrs. Tremaine. I'll arrange for Cissie to come do for me, and I'll send a boy to take my grip up to the Big House."

"Lord have mercy, who this big grown up buckra lady come to call?" Reba squeezed Garden in a wiry hug, shouting to everyone to come see.

"Sit yourself down, honey, and let Reba get some refreshment. What you like? Coffee-milk, some nice lemonade?"

"Coffee-milk, please. And fried bread. And some bacon."

"Child, you don't get no food to eat in Charleston?"

"Not like here, Reba." Garden felt the changelessness of Reba and her kitchen settle around her. "It's so good to be back." Heads peeked around the door and over the windowsills. "Hey, Tyrone," Garden yelled, "hey, Mose, hey, Sarah, hey, Flora, hey, Cudjo, hey, Juno, Minerva, Daniel, Abednego. Come on in out of the hot. I want to see everybody."

It was all the same, and yet it was different. Garden couldn't tell why, until Tyrone called her "Miss Garden."

"Reba," Garden said, "what's wrong? Why is Tyrone acting so strange, why is everybody skittering around looking sideways at me?"

"Honey, you done growed up."

"No! No, I haven't. I'm just the same. You watch. Tonight for supper, I'm going to go out to the cowshed and have syllabub-under-the-cow. Where's my blue pitcher?"

Reba put her hand on Garden's head. "It too late for syllabub, honey. All kind of too late. That blue pitcher been bust and throw away two-three year gone. And Matthew, he ain't here. He join the Army."

"Oh. Is he all right?"

"Fine, mighty fine. And send me money every two week. Your Reba getting to be a rich woman."

"Oh, good. Is anybody else gone? Where's Luke? John?"

"They left to catch some fish right after church. They be back directly. Ain't nobody gone in the Army save only Matthew and Cuffee. Otherwise, people gone to the Navy Yard. Men and women both. Cissie, she work in the laundry there making more money than Matthew and Cuffee all two together."

"Oh-oh. I was going to look for Cissie." Garden told Reba about her escape from the Woods House.

Reba laughed. "What you need with Cissie when you got Reba? I ain't got no man at home, I can come take care of you. I just bring Columbia with me."

"Did you have another baby, Reba?"

"Sure I did. What you think, Matthew going off and leave me with nothing to occupy my mind? I got a beautiful little girl."

Garden tried desperately to hold back time that summer. And time mocked her at every turn. Her old frocks were still hanging in her wardrobe, but they were too short and too tight. She was taller, and her body was changing. It frightened her and made her angry. She tried pulling out the hairs that were growing on her pubis, but it hurt too much. So she refused to look at them, or at her breasts, and she locked her mind against the disturbing sensations when she pulled on her clothes and fabric rubbed across her nipples.

She clutched childhood with a frenzied grasp. And it slipped inexorably through her fingers. The evenings at the Settlement were as they always had been. People sat on porches and steps, singing, talking, laughing softly at the antics of the children; then, as the darkening sky cooled the earth, singing with increasing power, adding the percussion of clapping hands, sticks drummed on a step or a wooden pail; mounting in intensity, in joy, excitement, until the dancing began. First one, then two, then five, then nine dancers leaped up, and with shouts and clapping and laughter from dancers and watchers they released their emotions in a wild, flailing rhythm of drumming feet and flashing, outflung arms and legs. Garden sang and she danced, as she had for years when she was a backdoor child and every Sunday meant a picnic and a celebration.

But something was happening now that was different. The clapping and the singing seemed to enter her blood, to take control of her arms and legs and twisting shoulders and hips. It left her exhilarated and restless instead of tiring her into contented sleep.

Reba watched and felt the sorrow of endings. Her baby, the ugly little blue baby she had sucked away from death, baby no more, innocence lost, knowing it not.

Stuart turned off the big electric lamps, and the road ahead was instantly lost in blackness. It did not matter. He could feel the road through all his senses. The surface of it came to him by the vibrations of the seat under him and the wheel in his hands, turning as the softly inflated tires adjusted for changes in grade, for remembered ruts and holes. He felt the presence of tree limbs overhead and knew he was in the grove of live oaks immediately before the road turned in a long, easy curve. He smelled water and slowed for the bridge ahead. Past it, he had three straight miles ahead of him. He closed his eyes then, to feel the darkness more, and gave the Ghost full throttle.

The rushing excitement was over too soon. It always was. But it was what Stuart lived for. These runs were always made on a night when there was no moon or when heavy clouds blotted out even the stars. The precaution was not really necessary, but Stuart insisted. He needed the danger and the demand on all his skill and knowledge.

He turned into the Barony drive and shifted down. Silence was what counted now. The Settlement was asleep, but the dogs might be roused. The Rolls-Royce earned its appellation; the big machine moved almost without sound. It ghosted.

Stuart's destination was one of the most beautiful spots on the plantation, the cypress swamp. The cypress were unearthly-looking trees. They grew straight from the still water of the pond, their gray-bark trunks soaring to great heights before they branched, their bases swollen with the gnarled, sinewy growths known as knees. They were like distorted dreams of trees. Or nightmares. And they were doubly dreamlike because of the mirror reflection of the pond. The cypress stained the water to a deep black, as if night had been liquefied. There was no spring in the pond, no tide. It was always still unless rain was falling.

And stillness surrounded it, a hush, uncanny, almost palpable. The swamp was breathtakingly beautiful. Or terrifying. The Barony blacks never went near it, convinced that it was the home of an evil spirit or an alligator of monstrous size and age. The Tremaines feared it, reacting to the unnaturalness of black water and landless trees. Even poachers avoided it, claiming that there was no game to be had.

It was the perfect place to keep something that had to remain undiscovered. It was where Sam Ruggs hid his smuggled whiskey.

The swamp held no fears for him. He thought it was "kind of handsome." And for an hour on Sunday, when every inhabitant of the Barony was away at church, he was free to drive in and unload his trucks.

There was a road from the Barony drive to the swamp, overgrown with scrub bushes but easily cleared to be usable without being too clean. Ten men working on three Sundays had done it. A pile of dead brush masked the point where the road entered the woods. The pile was not hard to move and replace.

Of all Sam Ruggs's enterprises, the cache at the cypress swamp pleased him most. It was beautifully simple. Hardly anyone living was old enough to remember when the wood of the cypress trees had been used to make shingles, buckets, even boats, when axes rang around the swamp for days at a time and oxen pulled wagons along the fine road with its base of logs and surface of hard-packed earth. Sometimes Sam wished he could have seen Ashley Barony when it was the finest plantation on the river.

But, he reminded himself, it was better for Sam Ruggs's purposes now. He had a gold mine at the swamp. And a foolproof system. Because of Stuart Tradd. It was his land. He could keep any damn thing he wanted on it. The only danger was getting it on and off about once a month. Bribes got it to Summerville, good planning and lookouts got it to the Barony. Stuart took care of the risky transport into the city and the customers. But who could wonder about a young plantation owner, especially with a name like Tradd, driving the road as often as he pleased? It was his place.

Stuart loaded the compartments under the seats and drove out to the swamp road. Using a dark lantern, he put the concealing brush pile back in place. He smiled and blew out the lantern. Now he could drive.

He closed his eyes to adjust to the darkness and to hone his senses. A breeze stirred his hair. Damn, he thought, if the clouds blow away, there's a half-moon.

He moved quickly along the drive, racing the breeze to pass the Settlement in the dark. If the dogs woke, he'd be gone before anyone could open a shutter.

He thought he'd made it. The moon gleamed for only a moment before the clouds closed over it again, and the dogs made only a dreaming, whimpering noise.

But there was one unshuttered window, left open for air to lungs that could no longer pump more than wisps of breath. Old Pansy's hands fumbled for her blue beads, and she moaned.

"Plat eye."

29

Sarah woke Reba and Garden before dawn. "Maum' Pansy, she dying. She want to see Garden before she go."

Garden found her necklace and put it on. Old Pansy always looked for it when she saw Garden. This summer, she had asked for her often. Sometimes by the time Garden came in the old woman's mind had taken her far back in her life. Then when she heard Garden's buckra voice she thought Garden was Julia Ashley, and she talked about people long dead and routines on the plantation that no one could understand, so different had been the life when Pansy was young. Garden would murmur "yes, yes" to everything Pansy said until the ancient eyes closed in sleep.

Other times Pansy was fully in command of herself and everyone around her. She would, on occasion, tell her story about driving away the Yankees. Or she would demand one of her favorite songs and waggle a finger to set the tempo. Once Garden had burned her arm on Reba's stove, and was rushed to Pansy's cabin. Pansy "used." She held Garden's arm close to her face and whispered to the long red wound. Garden bent her head close, but she could not hear what Pansy was saying. The whispering grew even softer as the old woman tired, but she continued, her lips barely moving, while the pain, then the burn, faded away.

Garden was fascinated by the ancient mummylike figure in the big bed. She loved to listen to Old Pansy, sing to her. The only times she wanted to get away were when Pansy held her hand and fretted about the curse on the Barony, pleading with Garden to run away. Garden didn't know what to do or say. She could only wait until Pansy, exhausted by her emotions, collapsed into unconsciousness.

Pansy's cabin was ablaze with light. The entire population of the Settlement was there; they passed one by one into the cabin and bowed to the matriarch and to her great-granddaughter Young Pansy who had been sent for at her home next to the church. Her husband, Preacher Ashley, stood in a corner, tears on his cheeks, sorrowing for the death of his longtime antagonist.

Garden and Reba paid their respects. Old Pansy whispered to Young Pansy. "She say don't go," Young Pansy interpreted. "She want Miss Julia to stay with her." Reba sat Garden in a chair at the big table. She sat next to her, stroking the distraught girl's arm. Swaying and stroking in a slow, soothing rhythm, Reba began to sing.

"I going to rest from all my labor . . ."

The people outside took up the refrain of the spiritual, singing, ". . . when I dead."

Reba led, and they followed.

> "I going to rest from all my labor,
>> When I dead.
> In the morning, oh Lord
> My soul so happy now
>> Oh, Lord, Lord, Lord, when I dead.
>
> Going to rally with the angel Gabriel
>> When I dead.
> Going to rally with the angel Gabriel
>> When I dead
> In the morning, oh Lord
> My soul so happy now
>> Oh, Lord, Lord, Lord, when I dead.
>
> Sister Pansy going where the dew can't wet um
>> When she dead.
> Sister Pansy going where the dew can't wet um
>> When she dead

In the morning, oh Lord
My soul so happy now
  Oh Lord, Lord, Lord, when I dead.

Going to walk and talk with Jesus
  When I dead
Going to walk and talk with Jesus
  When I dead
In the morning, oh Lord
My soul so happy now
  Oh Lord, Lord, Lord, when I dead."

"She going," said Sarah. "The morning done come."

The lamplight in the cabin had become pale. Outside the sky was pale gold with newborn sunlight. It shimmered in the disheveled tangle of Garden's red and gold hair, silhouetting her where she sat before an open window. Maum' Pansy shuddered and jerked, suddenly sitting up. She seized Young Pansy's shoulder with one birdlike hand. Her old, powerful laughter filled the room. She pointed at Garden. "Thank you, Lord," she said clearly, "a pennyworth o' candle."

Then she was gone.

Garden sang for Maum' Pansy one final time. Dressed in white like all the other mourners, she stood by the grave before it was closed. Her face was stained with tears and she was shaking, but her rich, low voice was firm. She held a bunch of field flowers in her trembling hands, dropping them one by one onto the casket, singing the song that the old woman had loved best.

I look to the east and I look to the west
And I see the chariot a-coming
Four gray horses all in the lead
To land you on the other side o' Jordan.

Moses in the bullrushes fast asleep
Playing possum in the two-bushel basket
Every hair on he head a pennyworth o' candle
To light you on the other side o' Jordan.

30

Margaret and Peggy arrived home at almost the same time. The shuttered house felt like an oasis after the thick heat in the streets. "Gummy," Charlestonians called their humid August weather.

Peggy threw her hat on a chair and mopped her face and neck with a crumpled handkerchief. "I've got wonderful news," she puffed.

Margaret was already sitting in the corner of the sofa, her feet up on a pillow, cooling herself with a palmetto fan sprinkled with cologne. "So do I. Sit down, Peggy."

Peggy was too excited to sit down. She strode back and forth across the small drawing room, endangering the delicate Sheraton table that stood in the center of the floor. "I've just come from the College of Charleston," she said. "They're taking women this year, and they'll let me be one of them."

Margaret lifted her chin and fanned close to her damp throat. "Don't be silly, Peggy. You're coming out this year. I've just come from Edith Anson's. She didn't want to do it, but I made her give me a good date for your party. And I got the South Carolina Hall. You'll have a reception before the Montague girls' ball. It's the best night of the whole Season."

"Mama, you never listen to me. I don't want to make some dumb old debut. Besides, you've said a hundred times that we don't have the money. I can get a scholarship to the college."

Margaret waved Peggy's words away with her fan.

Peggy put her hands on her hips, prepared for battle. Stuart's arrival headed off the confrontation. He too had news, but it was the reverse of wonderful.

"There's Spanish influenza in town. Almost forty people went to Roper Hospital today. One of them was Mr. Walker. He just keeled over in the bank."

*   *   *

Peggy's battle with her mother came a few days later, but it had a different subject. Margaret was fleeing the plague, as people called it. Peggy refused to go with her to the Barony. The Red Cross was accepting volunteers of any age to help nurse the victims. "I'm strong as an ox, Mama. It's my duty to help where I can." She would not be budged.

Stuart could not go. The bank had to continue business as usual. He went to work, as did most men, wearing a gauze mask and crossing the street to avoid contact with anyone whose gait was unsteady or who was coughing. There was seldom occasion for the maneuver, however. The streets were virtually deserted.

Margaret wore a mask, too, for the drive to the country. She also carried an orange pomander to hold to her nose. People were trying anything they could think of to ward off the mounting, terrifying epidemic.

As the great silver automobile sped along the Barony drive, Stuart and Margaret saw a bizarre, brightly colored apparition ahead. It was Garden carrying her clean clothes from the Settlement, where Sarah had washed and ironed them, to the Big House. The laundry was in a big basket, which she balanced on her head as she walked, scuffling the dust on the drive with her bare feet. The black women always carried things that way; Garden had learned the trick of balancing the load when she was eight, but no one in the family had ever seen her do it before.

Margaret let out a little scream of horror. "Look at her," she cried to Stuart. "What a disgrace. Stop the car and make her get in."

Stuart honked. Garden turned quickly, disturbing the basket not at all, and waved, smiling widely. Margaret moaned. Garden was wearing a makeshift garment because none of her clothes fit. It was a loose, calf-length shift made of bright-patterned flour sacks. Her thick braids were tied with shoelaces. Her face and arms were a solid mass of freckles, and her bare legs were crisscrossed with bramble scratches in various stages of healing.

"Garden! What's happened to you?" said Margaret.

"Isn't it something? I've grown four inches since June."

Stuart could not hold his laughter in any longer. He disguised it by a false cough, which terrified Margaret. She grabbed her mask and pomander. Garden looked bewildered.

*   *   *

The influenza epidemic ended in November, as mysteriously as it had begun. It left one half million Americans dead. It did not touch the Tradd family. Margaret was so terrified of contagion, even in the isolation of the Barony's acres, that she put the Big House in quarantine. No one was allowed to come in; Reba and Garden were not allowed to go out. Nothing came into the house except canned goods that Sam Ruggs delivered to the kitchen door. Even they were dipped into a kettle of boiling water in the yard before they were allowed inside.

The period of confinement was the longest three months of Garden Tradd's young life. And a turning point from which there was no return.

As enormous as the Big House was, it seemed that there was no place Garden could play without disturbing her mother. The empty rooms and bare floors magnified every sound. The attic was her sanctuary. Crammed as it was with trunks and boxes and wardrobes, it swallowed the noise Garden made with her games and songs. Like Peggy and Stuart years before, Garden found the attic a storehouse of delight, of make-believe.

One afternoon she found a box of books that Stuart and Peggy had not bothered to explore. They were collections of sermons. Garden took them out and used them to build a chair. The two at the bottom of the box, she decided, would do fine for a footstool. But when she lifted them, one fell open. It was hollowed out, a secret hiding place.

Inside, wrapped in a piece of embroidered silk, was a shiny brass key. It was engraved all over with a design of stars and moons. Garden was thrilled. What did the key unlock?

"Where is that child?" Margaret scowled at Reba. "It's bad enough to eat this awful food; at least I don't have to eat it cold." She threw her napkin on the table. "Put my plate in the oven, Reba. I'm going to find Garden, and after I whip her good, I'll come back and eat. Leave Garden's plate; she'll have hers cold. And stand up to eat it."

It took her ten minutes to go through all the rooms, calling angrily. She was furious when she stomped up the attic stairs and threw open the door.

A creation of another age met her eyes. In the dimming late-day light from the small attic windows, she thought she was seeing ghosts. Then the vision spoke, with her daughter's voice. "Don't be mad, Mama. I was just playing I was this lady." She held out her hand, showing a miniature portrait in a pearl-rimmed frame.

Margaret spoke very slowly and carefully. "I'm not mad. Stay very, very still. Don't move." She stared unbelievingly at Garden.

Her head was encased in a tall white wig, its stiff curls topped with a bright blue-and-silver beaded butterfly. Under the wig her face was chalk-white, painted with a thick paste. Her cheeks and lips were brightly rouged, a wide blue line circled her eyes, and she wore a crescent moon in black velvet, a beauty patch, on her soft chin. Another, a star, was on her breast, also stark white. She was wearing a gown of satin the color of a summer sky, with full ruffles of pleated silver lace edging the deep décolletage and elbow-length sleeves. The skirts spread around her in rich folds, embroidered in silver thread in a pattern of butterflies. A silver lace petticoat showed at the hem. She was breathtakingly beautiful; her long slim throat and tender, swelling young breasts looked heartbreakingly vulnerable, but the proud carriage of straight young back and uplifted head balancing the heavy wig were regal and womanly and ageless as Eve.

"Where did you find these things, Garden?"

Released by Margaret's question, Garden held up a mildewed book. "Oh, Mama, it was so exciting. I found a key in this secret book, and I went from trunk to trunk looking for the one it would unlock." She reached down to touch the open lid, and the gown slipped from her shoulder. She caught it to her body quickly. "It doesn't really fit. I couldn't hook it up." She turned to show Margaret the open back. "This lady must have been tiny."

"Don't worry," Margaret said, "it's all a matter of the right corset." Her voice was strange, distant. Margaret was still bemused. Garden, a beauty. She had seen no signs of it. How could she have been so blind? Not just a beauty. A great beauty. With such a gift, anything was possible.

"Oh, gosh, it's getting dark. I must be late for supper. I'm sorry, Mama. I was having such a good time."

"That's all right, Garden. Take the wig and the gown off. Carefully.

They must be very old. Then come downstairs. I'll go tell Reba to warm up your supper."

"May I keep the lady's picture, Mama?"

"Of course. Bring it with you. I want to look at it in the light."

31

Stuart came for them in the middle of November. "It's over," he said. "You can come home." He was astonished to find his mother in such good spirits after her long exile from the city. He was shocked to find her paying so much attention to Garden. She was playful, affectionate, caressing, interested, admiring. Garden was euphoric. Her eyes followed her mother everywhere, shining with love and gratitude.

Stuart was glad to get them off the Barony. He had to get back to business.

"Reba, Reba, I'm going to miss you." Garden held on to Reba as if she'd never let go. Reba hugged her for a long time.

"Honey, is you got your beads Maum' Pansy leave you?"

"Yes. Of course I do. And my other string necklace too. Why?"

"Nothing. Just hold fast to them, that's all. I'll watch out for your other thing." Old Pansy had instructed Preacher Ashley about her last wishes. The furniture that Julia Ashley had given Pansy was to go to Garden, together with her cherished beads.

"Stuart won't wait for me to go to the Settlement and tell everybody goodbye. You'll tell them for me?"

"Sure, honey."

"I love you, Reba."

"I know that. And Reba love her baby."

Garden waved from the back of the car as long as she could see Reba. She waved again as they passed the Settlement. Back at the Big House, Reba wept and held Columbia to her breast to feed. "I done lost my buckra baby, little girl. She grown and gone." The baby sucked hungrily, and Reba began to hum, rocking, no longer crying.

Margaret questioned Stuart eagerly about what had happened in town in her absence. Who died, she wanted to know, were there any marriages, what had happened about paving Tradd Street?

"You mean you didn't get your newspaper, Mama? I thought you couldn't live without your newspaper."

Margaret lifted her chin. "Don't be fresh, Stuart. I couldn't risk getting a paper; it might have been contaminated."

"Good God, Mama. Then you don't even know about the war. It's over. The Armistice was signed last week. People were dancing in the streets."

"That's nice. Maybe they'll stop that stupid sugar rationing."

If Margaret was unimpressed by the end of the World War, Peggy was ecstatic enough for them all. Bob Thurston had written. He would be home as soon as possible, probably within a few months.

Peggy was generous in her happiness. She no longer cared greatly about college or about her debut. She'd do whatever her mother wanted.

"Garden can stand in the receiving line with us at your reception. It will be good practice for her. Now, you'll be in white, of course, so she'll have to wear a color . . ." Margaret threw herself happily into a frenzy of shopping, invitation lists, caterers, flowers, dressmakers and schedules. Peggy's party would be held on December twenty-third.

Garden showed everybody at school where she had burned herself and told how Pansy had talked it out. She showed her necklaces and told about plat eye. The other girls shivered deliciously at the spookiness of it all, and Garden was welcomed into the group that had closed her out the preceding year. With new friends and her mother's attention, she was so happy she was able to forget that she was growing up.

The Season was exceptionally festive that year, celebrating the end of war and deliverance from the epidemic. For the Tradds, it was the first time they had all been happy together since the first giddy weeks after they moved to the city.

Stuart enjoyed the parties. He no longer felt inadequate because he was not in the Army, and the recklessness of his secret life gave him confidence in his manliness. He had a slightly dashing air about him, which impressed the debutantes and dazzled the predebutantes. The Silver Ghost made him the envy of all the other men, of every age. Stuart whistled when he tied his white tie, and escorted the ladies assigned to him with a flourish.

Peggy floated through the round of parties, the hurried change of clothes between them, the polite attention to the conversation of the escorts assigned to her, the long periods of sitting on the sidelines, an acknowledged wallflower.

Garden found it all terribly grown-up and exciting: the stacks of invitations, the wilted bouquets, the dresses waiting to be put on, the boxful of long white gloves, the toilet water, face powder and curling iron on her mother's dressing table. Most of all, she was practically feverish at the prospect of going to Peggy's party in a long dress. And at Margaret's promise that she would have all this herself one day. All this and more.

Margaret was in her element, and she knew it. She was genuinely charming and gracious, and impressed many people who had thought her unpleasant before.

She saw, or fancied she saw, pity in the eyes of the other mothers. Peggy was decidedly not a success. Margaret laughed secretly. In four years she'd show them, she'd show everyone. Garden would have the most brilliant Season, make the most brilliant marriage Charleston had ever known. Margaret sat demurely with the chaperones and studied the beaux. Which of them was good enough? Or would it be one of the young men still overseas?

Peggy's debut was not dazzling. It was not meant to be. A reception was dignified and placed no great strain on the debutante. Peggy could not have carried off a ball, or even a tea dance. She had no small talk, no coquettishness, and she was a poor dancer. The reception consisted mostly of a protracted period of receiving, as the guests arrived and moved slowly past Peggy and her family, talking with each one. There was only a short period before the same thing happened in reverse, as the guests thanked the family and said goodbye. The earlier arrivals ate and drank and talked while later guests continued to pass down the line and join them. After the interim period, the early ones began their departure and the later had time to eat and drink before they left.

Stuart watched it all from his place between Peggy and Garden in the receiving line. He saw the men slipping out onto the big porch at the front of the Hall, and he knew that they were adding something from their flasks to the punch. Damn Prohibition, he thought. This is a party. There should be champagne, not rotgut whiskey on the sly.

Hell, this is my sister's debut. Everybody should celebrate. There aren't any policemen here. There's going to be champagne. He ducked out of the line and down the wide stairs, nodding to the guests in a line on them waiting to enter.

The Silver Ghost roared up Meeting Street, heading for the Ashley River Bridge. At the tollhouse, Stuart realized that he had no cash.

"I'll make a deal with you," he offered the bridgekeeper. "I'll pay with a drink of good whiskey." He pulled out his flask, silver like the magnificent car. He was a handsome sight in his dress suit, shirtfront gleaming in the moonlight, teeth flashing in a confident grin, leaning back against the fine soft leather of the seat.

He offered the flask, watched the tolltaker's surprise at the quality of the liquor. "Nothing but the best," Stuart said. "Tonight's my sister's party." He had a drink as a salute to Peggy.

"Tell you what," he laughed. "You hold on to that. We'll finish it off when I get back. I won't be long."

The Rolls-Royce devoured the miles. Stuart drove expertly, loving the speed, exhilarated at the knowledge that he would burst into Peggy's party with four cases of champagne. That'll be a present she won't forget. Good old Peggy.

At the usual place, he stopped the car and turned off the headlights. A cloud covered the moon, as if Stuart had turned it off, too. Stuart chuckled. Everything was working perfectly. He shifted, enjoying the feel of it, and let out the clutch. His heart started to race as the familiar thrill began. Hurry, he told himself; get back before they start to leave. The Silver Ghost sped, a blur of power.

The car crashed through the railing of the bridge and dived through a bank of fog into the deep, rushing stream. Stuart was thrown across it into the woods that crowned its bank. His neck was broken on impact.

"Where is your brother?" said Margaret through her teeth. Her face was fixed in a smile. "So happy you could come. Thank you, I'm glad you enjoyed it. . . I'm going to take a strap to him, no matter how big he is . . . Why, how nice of you to say so. I do

160

agree, this is the best Season ever . . . Thank you, Mary. See you later at the ball . . . Running out like that. There's no excuse for it . . . Yes, Mr. Mitchell, we all miss the Judge. He would have so loved to see his granddaughter all grown up . . . Thank you . . . Thank you . . . So happy to see you . . . So glad you could come . . .''

32

Logan Henry was so angry that he was indiscreet. "That idiot woman," he told Andrew Anson, "is determined to undo all the good I've done for her."

Andrew poured his friend a drink and settled into his chair to listen. What he heard made him sit up straight. The "idiot woman" was Margaret Tradd. She was her son's heir, and she had instructed Mr. Henry to sell Ashley Barony, even though it was making a respectable profit. The only prospective buyer was Sam Ruggs, and he had offered barely enough to pay off the mortgage. Nonetheless, Margaret seemed disposed to take it.

It was Andrew's turn to startle Mr. Henry. The bank had a client, he said, who would be interested in buying. No, he wouldn't give any names, but there was plenty of money to top Ruggs's offer.

Logan Henry chuckled. "I expect that'll make Ruggs a little less stingy," he said.

He had no idea how openhanded Sam Ruggs could be. Sam needed the cypress swamp for his business. The bidding went on for weeks, with Sam topping the bank's offer and being topped in turn by Andrew Anson's mysterious client. By the time Sam realized that he was bidding out of stubbornness and not logic, the figure was grossly inflated. Andrew's client bought the Barony for more than ten times its value.

Charleston buzzed with speculation and gossip. Who was the

buyer? And just how much had Margaret Tradd really been paid? Neither Mr. Anson nor Mr. Henry would answer any questions.

"Are we rich, Mama?" asked Garden. "Some girls at school said we're very rich."

"It's vulgar to talk about money, Garden."

"Can't I know?"

"Well, yes. But you must never, never, never talk about it. The truth is, we're not really rich, but we got a lot of money for the Barony."

"What will you do with it, Mama? Will you go to the mountains in the summer? Wentworth Wragg's mama always does, and everybody says they're rich."

"As a matter of fact, Garden, you and I both are going to the mountains this summer. I'm investing the money."

"What's that mean?"

"You're going to have every advantage, Garden. You're going to make me proud of you." Margaret's eyes filled. "You're all I have left."

Garden knelt by Margaret's chair and took her in her arms. "I'll try, Mama, I'll try. I'll try to make you happy." Over Margaret's shoulder she saw the cluster of framed photographs on Margaret's desk. Stuart smiling from behind the wheel of the Rolls-Royce, and Peggy smiling at Bob in their wedding picture. The wedding had been austere and hurried. The Tradds were in mourning, and Bob was being sent to Europe in the Corps of Engineers. Peggy barely had time to get her shots completed before their boat sailed.

Garden and Margaret had only each other now.

From the moment her mother told her they were going to the mountains, Garden's excitement grew with every hour that passed. The only travel she had known was the ride between Charleston and the Barony.

Early on the morning of June 22 a taxicab came to the house to take her, her mother and Zanzie to the train station. Garden could hardly sit still. She had never been in a taxicab. Or a train station.

The huge locomotive was like a dragon, chuffing great billows of smoke up, up, up to the roof, as high as a sky, above the huge shed. Smoke also spumed around the great wheels. Garden walked through a hissing spurt of it, her legs skittering in an ecstasy of terror. She knew the dragon was tamed. For that matter, she knew the dragon was not a dragon. But the sense of adventure and the peril of the unknown made everything seem like something from the pages of a storybook.

A young man with a notebook and pencil scurried back and forth along the platform, trying to speak to everyone, to ask their names. The annual exodus to the mountains was always an important story on the society page. The departure of the *Carolina Special* was covered every morning all summer. Margaret Tradd smiled secretly behind the discreet black veil that covered her face.

Two of the train's five coaches were filled with Charlestonians. They did not occupy all the seats, but they were in full possession. There was another coach for other passengers, some of them inhabitants of Charleston who did not belong to the select population of "real" Charlestonians. The fourth and fifth coaches were for Negroes. One of them was unofficially reserved for the Charlestonians' maids and nursemaids, known as "dahs," and children, under their dahs' watchful eyes.

There was a half hour's pandemonium as children and toys were bustled aboard and lunch hampers were handed up through the open windows. The conductor shouted "All aboard," steam hissed in deafening blasts, bells rang, goodbyes were shouted, and the *Carolina Special* clanked out of the station twenty minutes behind schedule. Seasoned travelers knew that it would stop at every town and village on the long diagonal across the state on its way to North Carolina, and that it would lose another five or ten minutes at each stop. They called the train the *Carolina Creeper*, but it was said with affection. The holiday began the moment they arrived at the station, and the long, soot-laden ride was an integral part of it.

The long trip was tedious, but Garden did not think so. The trestle bridges made her heart pound as the coach swayed from side to side over the water on the invisible rails. She waved at children in the yards of cabins, at men driving wagons on the dusty roads that paralleled the track, at the people in the stations where the train stopped with a hiss, filling the length of the Main Street. The names of the towns were as exotic to her as the names on the globe at school. She read the advertisements on barns and watched the hypnotic, silvery scallops of the telegraph wires between the poles that rushed by the window to the hurrying clackety-clack of the wheels.

163

An elderly lady sitting in the center of the car in regal isolation was the first to open her wicker hamper. It was the signal for dinner. All through the car, young men handed down hampers and baskets for seated ladies, and soon laps and empty seats were covered with yard-square napkins.

Garden was too excited to eat. The hills were beginning. Garden had never left the low country before. She had never seen a hill. She was fascinated. Then, hours later, the train rounded a long curve and the mountains were visible in the distance. Garden caught her breath. The hills, thrilling as they were, had not prepared her for the mountains. No one had told her they were so high.

The train pulled in to the little station in Hendersonville, North Carolina, with a tired sigh of escaping steam. The graveled yard around the station was filled with vehicles, automobiles, buggies, and shiny green horse-drawn buses in a neat row, parked with their rear doors facing the station platform. Each bus had the name of a hotel lettered above the door.

"Where are we going, Mama?"

"The Lodge, Garden, at Flat Rock." There were numerous popular resorts in the towns around Hendersonville. Flat Rock was known as "the little Charleston of the mountains." Garden started to run toward their bus, but Margaret grabbed her arm. "First you say 'goodbye and have a nice vacation' to everybody from the train."

"But I don't know everybody."

"That doesn't matter. Soon you will." Margaret pushed Garden gently toward the crowd and looked around for Zanzie.

The summer at Flat Rock was a period of constant surprises and delights for Garden. The Lodge was a long, low building with unpeeled log walls on the exterior and plain pine paneling for the interior partitions. It was surrounded by a deep porch with chairs and tables made of bent twigs. There were organized excursions and picnics, square dances on Saturday nights, with instructors for the novices, rides along steep mountain trails on surefooted, bored ponies, and guided nature walks on the paths through the huge mountain laurel to waterfalls and railed lookouts. The sun was warm in the daytime, and at night the Lodge provided hot-water bottles to tuck under the bedcovers; two blankets were needed in the chill night air, because everyone slept with open windows. The resinous air was a tonic and a soporific. Garden woke every morning when the rising sun woke the birds outside her window, feeling more energy than she had ever known before.

There were three other girls at the Lodge who were near her age. When they were not on one of the planned outings, they spent their energies riding the level road from Flat Rock to Hendersonville on bicycles supplied by the Lodge, or wading in the icy stream that crossed the hotel's grounds. During the crashing thunderstorms they sat under the porch, watching the jagged lightning bolts strike the thick woods on the mountains around and below them. Garden often thought the mountains were heaven on earth.

But paradise had a price. Margaret began the polishing of Garden the evening they arrived at Flat Rock. Their trunks had been sent ahead and were waiting in their room. Zanzie arranged to use one of the irons in the laundry room in the servants' wing, then came up to help Margaret unpack. Garden oohed and aahed when new frocks were brought out for her. She lost her jubilation when Margaret showed her the wide-brimmed hat that she was to wear outdoors and the stacks of white cotton stockings and gloves.

"We've got to get started right now getting rid of your horrible freckles, Garden. You must not let any sunlight touch your skin anyplace ever again."

The buttermilk poultices on her face began the next day, an hour after dinner daily while she soaked her hands in a basin of buttermilk. Before bed, Zanzie scrubbed her all over with a paste of salt and lemon juice and then scrubbed her again with white soap in her bath.

After a week, Margaret began to work on Garden's "awful hair." Garden's hair had always been a problem. First because of the lack of it, then because of the overabundance. The Dutch bob Zanzie tried when Garden entered first grade had made it worse than ever. After that she had cut only part of it, lifting the top layer and trimming a swath to the scalp underneath. But Garden's hair was not only preternaturally thick, it was also unnaturally fast-growing. Within a few weeks, stubby new growth bulked the hair and stuck out through the top layer. Zanzie gave up then. At twelve, Garden had braids as thick as her arms; they hung to her waist.

Margaret had brought the miniature that Garden found in the attic. She studied it closely. The eighteenth-century gown and cosmetic set had not been worth saving, but the portrait was a guide to the incredible beauty Garden had had in the costume. The wig, Margaret decided, had been the most startling change. The tall white headdress was what had to be re-created out of Garden's marmalade-striped gold and copper mop of hair. Every third or fourth day Margaret tried a new experiment.

Lemon juice paled the gold and gave it a jewellike shine, but it only brightened the red and made it more prominent.

The pomades available at the Hendersonville drugstore dulled both red and gold and made Garden look dirty.

Washing the hair, then wrapping Garden's head in tight bandages while it dried, made no apparent difference except to make Garden ill with headaches.

"If only we could get rid of the red, the gold would be no problem," Margaret said. "You do have the worst-looking hair in the world, Garden." Margaret tried plucking the red hairs out. Garden bore the pain stoically. She didn't want to have the worst-looking hair in the world, nor did she want to make her mother unhappy by complaining.

Her bravery was wasted. There were too many red hairs, and they were too concentrated. If they were removed, Garden would have dozens of little bald spots.

Another trip to Hendersonville, to the barber, gave a near-solution. Margaret bought two pairs of thinning scissors, a special tool with sharp overlapping teeth on the blades, and learned how to use them. Then she and Zanzie went to work. Now, after her bedtime scrubs, Garden sat near a lamp. Margaret and Zanzie brushed her hair, separated out a streak of red, twisted it into a tight rope and made four or five cuts from top to bottom with the thinning shears. When the twisted strand was released and brushed, individual hairs of various lengths floated to the floor. They worked every night until their arms were tired. By the end of the vacation, they could see progress. Garden's braids were smaller by a third, and the blond hair clearly predominated.

"When you're old enough, Garden," said her mother, "you'll be able to wear your hair up. It will be lovely. We'll keep working on it to get rid of the nasty red part. You've seen how it's done. I want you to thin it for at least a half hour a day. That should keep up with the new growth."

Margaret was pleased with what she had accomplished, though not satisfied. Garden was ashamed of her appearance and grateful to her mother for trying so hard to make her presentable.

She was also grateful for the trip. In spite of the hat and gloves and stockings, in spite of the treatments for her freckles and the experiments on her hair, she enjoyed herself enormously. And she had, for the first time in her life, her mother's full attention. Garden missed Peggy, but not often. She cried sometimes when she thought of Stuart. But having her mother with her, and making her mother happy, was all the comfort she needed for the loss of her brother and sister.

And Margaret was undoubtedly happy. She was subdued, somewhat retiring, as a mother mourning her son should be. And she did genuinely grieve for Stuart. But her single-mindedness had a new focus now, the shaping of Garden. And she had a new daydream, the success of Garden. Together, they occupied almost all her time, making the past fade rapidly. The time that was not occupied by Garden was filled in the way most gratifying to Margaret. She was being courted.

33

Margaret Tradd was a foolish woman, but that did not make her a fool. She knew that the rumors of her sudden wealth were responsible for the interest Caroline Wragg suddenly showed in her. Caroline was gushy with remembrances of their childhood friendship and saccharine with condolences for Margaret's "tragic bereavements." She was as phony as her laughter. She was also, Margaret remembered, one of the city's "leading hostesses." The inner circle was wooing her.

Margaret responded warmly. The two mothers, in turn, encouraged the friendship between their daughters, Garden and Wentworth.

The two girls needed no encouragement. They admired each other from the first. Wentworth could ride a bicycle with no hands; Garden could spit.

"Mama," Garden said happily, "I'm so glad I got to know Wentworth. She's my best friend in all the world."

167

"That's good. Wentworth can be useful to you. Next year you'll be going to private school, to Ashley Hall. Wentworth already goes there; she'll introduce you to everybody."

"Ashley Hall?" Garden's heart sank. Wentworth had moaned about how hard the classes were. Then she bounced back. Wentworth had also said that they did wonderful things there. There were tennis lessons. And a swimming pool!

Classes began on the first Monday in October. On the afternoon before, there was a reception and tour for the new girls. Parents could not attend. Margaret fussed with Garden's hair and clothes so much, Garden knew that there was something exceedingly important about the occasion. She was already nervous at the prospect of walking into a roomful of strangers. Her mother's agitation made her so upset that she felt sick to her stomach. Fear was added to her nervousness. Garden did not know what it was to be sick; she had never had so much as a cold in her entire life. The unknown sensation of cramps and nausea made her think she was dying.

Margaret brushed off her complaints. "Don't be irritating, Garden. You've already had your time of the month. Hurry up and put on your hat. Zanzie's waiting to take you."

The trolley car was crowded, and Garden had to stand. The motion of the car made her feel worse for the first few blocks, then the problem of keeping her balance occupied her full attention and her pains disappeared.

She and Zanzie alit from the trolley opposite the school. "Zanzie, look," Garden cried, "it's like a park." Ashley Hall was housed in a magnificent Georgian mansion with expansive lawns and plantings. The main house was set well back from the street, almost hidden from view by an ancient, spreading, moss-hung live oak. A wrought-iron fence separated the grounds from the sidewalk. It had two gates, a small one that opened onto a walkway and a generous double gate to a carriage drive that curved gracefully between wide lawns to meet the path in front of the house. On the lawn between the path and the drive stood an iron deer, his head raised proudly and his blank eyes staring disdainfully at passersby.

"Do you suppose I can touch the deer, Zanzie?"

"I suppose you going be late if you don't hurry. I'll wait for you here."

Garden hunched her shoulders, remembered that her mother told her not to do that and tried to relax. She turned the brass knob on the gate, opened it and marched in. She slowed when she neared the house. It was impressive. Everything about it seemed to be reaching up. A deep porch topped a glassed-in conservatory at ground level. Two pairs of towering Ionic columns stretched up from the porch to support a tall triangular pediment. It was pierced with a tremendous Gothic window, its apex pointing to the peak of the pediment. Smaller pointed windows flanked the center one.

Garden stared, swallowed, then walked between the clusters of potted palms in the conservatory, up two stairs and into the entrance hall.

"Oh," she gasped. Ahead of her was a staircase. It was floating in midair, turning in a spiral of upward motion.

"Good morning," said someone at Garden's right. Garden looked, saw a lady smiling at her.

"Oh, please," said Garden, "how do those steps stay up? It looks like magic."

The lady nodded. "It does, doesn't it? In a way it is. Nobody today can build stairs like that. This house is a hundred years old."

"Aren't you afraid they'll fall down?"

"No. Think for a minute. If they haven't fallen in a hundred years, why would they decide to fall now?" She touched Garden's arm. "You'll see how strong they are. Go on up; the reception is in the drawing room to your left at the top of the stairs."

Garden smiled shyly. She liked the lady's brisk voice and her kindness. She wished she could stay with her instead of facing the strangers upstairs. "My name's Garden," she said.

"I thought it might be. My name is Miss Emerson, Garden. I'm your English teacher. Now, you're the last to arrive, so you must go upstairs. Everyone is waiting for you. This is what you do. At the door to the drawing room, there's a pretty lady with dark red hair. That's Miss Mary McBee; she's the headmistress of Ashley Hall. You walk up to her and say, 'How do you do, Miss McBee? My name is Garden Tradd.' She'll shake your hand and take you in to meet the others."

"Yes, ma'am. But my mother told me to curtsy."

"Miss Mary doesn't believe in young ladies curtsying. Little girls curtsy, but Ashley Hall girls are not children; they're young women. Off with you now."

*   *   *

Miss McBee shook Garden's hand firmly. She was pleased to feel Garden's grasp become more substantial in response to hers. Garden looked at the headmistress. She saw an attractive woman with beautiful auburn hair softly puffed around her face into a loose coil at the nape of her neck. She felt the vitality that suffused Miss McBee. It was in the atmosphere that surrounded her and in the touch of her hand on Garden's.

Miss McBee saw a pale, anxious young girl with a desperate eagerness to please.

"You're going to like Ashley Hall," she said, "and we're all going to like you, Garden."

"Thank you, Miss McBee," said Garden, with all her heart.

She met the other girls in her class, the teachers, Miss McBee's sister, Miss Estelle; she had a glass of milk and some cookies; and she hurried, with the other girls, in Miss McBee's wake on a tour of the grounds and the other buildings. Then she said goodbye, shaking hands again, and Zanzie took her home.

When her mother asked her to tell everything about her morning, Garden's mind was a blurred tangle of impressions. She remembered the staircase, the iron deer, a fountain, lots of flowers and brick paths and big rooms with desks and one girl had a big bandage on her arm and they were going to have to speak French and there was a little house made out of shells. "And, Mama, Miss McBee is wonderful."

•

Mary Vardrine McBee was a Southerner, from Tennessee, and she was a rarity for a young woman in the Victorian age; she had received an excellent education, including a bachelor of arts degree from Smith College and a master's from Columbia University. As a young lady from the South, she was very nearly unique.

Mary McBee was dynamic, and she was an idealist. She recognized the luck she had had, she deplored the waste of female minds for lack of equal luck, and she determined to do something about it. She could not really change the world, but she would change the lives of as many Southern girls as she could.

She bought the house on Rutledge Avenue, collected a group of teachers with the same crusader dedication and opened Ashley Hall in 1909 with a student population of forty-five. Fourteen of them were boarding students, sent from towns where there was no good

170

school for girls by parents who believed in the near-radical idea of education for women. Three years later, an Ashley Hall graduate went to Smith.

Most Ashley Hall graduates got married; that was the pattern, and Miss McBee recognized it from the beginning. She knew that the most successful girls' schools were the "finishing" schools that polished young ladies into successful candidates in the marriage market. Ashley Hall taught drawing, music, elocution, and deportment; there were classes in riding, in dance, in fashionable sports like tennis.

The students were finished. And while they were acquiring the accomplishments that finishing implied, they were also given an education that surpassed that available in many colleges and universities. Even if they didn't know enough to want it.

Margaret Tradd wanted Garden to go to Ashley Hall because it was exclusive, because Caroline Wragg's daughter went there. Garden wanted to go because it would make her mother happy and because there was a swimming pool. The most important influence in Garden's development came about by accident. And by the dedication of an energetic young woman from Tennessee. Miss McBee was wonderful.

34

"Bonjour, mesdemoiselles. Je m'appelle Mademoiselle Bongrand."

Garden looked at the other girls in the class. All but one looked as bewildered as she felt. That one said, *"Bonjour, mademoiselle. Je m'appelle Millicent Woodruff."*

Nine young faces gaped at Millicent Woodruff.

"Très bien, Millicent," said Mlle. Bongrand. "Now, girls, we are suddenly in the middle of our first lesson. I said 'Good morning, my name is Mademoiselle Bongrand.' And Millicent said, 'Good morning. My name is Millicent Woodruff.' We are all going to say 'good

morning,' and then say our names. Now watch the way my mouth looks when I say '*bonjour*,' and then, when I lift my finger, say it together with me. Ready? All right . . . *Bonjour*. . .''

Before first period was over, Garden knew the names of all the girls in her grade.

Millicent Woodruff was a boarder from Philadelphia. She had been taking French since first grade.

Virginia Anderson was also a boarder. She was from Virginia, so her name was easy to remember. She was very tall.

Charlotte Guignard was from Charleston. Garden had seen her in church, so she wasn't really a complete stranger.

Rebecca Wilson was a day student too. She had beautiful dark braids, not too thick, that she could sit on.

Louisa Ferncliff was a boarder from Georgia. She started crying when she had to repeat her turn twice. She looked like a crybaby, all pink and dimply.

Betsy Walker was the smartest girl in the class. She got everything right the first time. She was from Charleston. Garden thought maybe she had seen her on the train coming back from the mountains.

Lynn Palmer and Roseanne Madison were both from Aiken, South Carolina. They were roommates and they were even dressed alike in middy blouses and pleated skirts.

Julia Chalmers was in the seat next to Garden. She was a day girl, and she wanted to be friends. She passed Garden a note, but Mademoiselle took it away before Garden got to read it.

When the bell rang, Mademoiselle told them to go directly across the hall to their English class. "Before long," she said, "we'll be having our lessons all in French. *Au revoir, mes élèves*.'' The nine new French students shuddered. Millie Woodruff sailed past them into the other classroom, looking superior.

Miss Emerson said good morning, and Garden sighed happily. She had her first crush.

The day students were dismissed at two o'clock so that they could be home in time for Charleston's traditional three o'clock dinner. Zanzie had to pull Garden's braids to get her attention when they reached their stop. Garden was in a daze, intoxicated by the impact of all that had happened in one short day.

"Look, Mama, look at all my books. We get all new books, and they're ours, we can keep them. There are bells that ring, and we all get up and go to a different room. Sometimes we go upstairs and sometimes we go downstairs. I saw Wentworth going up when I was going down, and she asked me to sit with her in chapel. That's what they call a kind of meeting in the middle of the day, with prayers and a hymn and announcements. Wentworth says sometimes they have people come to talk, and sometimes there are even movies.''

"Garden you talk so much you make my head ache. Go wash your hands for dinner. Don't change your frock. We have to go to the dressmaker right after we eat.''

"But I have homework to do, Mama. In Latin. Do you know about Latin, Mama? I learned today all about the Romans and about how many of our words were Latin once. I'll bet you can't guess why we say A.M. and P.M. when we tell time. Can you, Mama, can you guess?''

"I can guess that dinner's getting cold. Hurry up. We have a lot to do before the stores close. Don't you remember anything? Dancing school starts Friday, and we haven't found any shoes yet.''

That night Garden wrote to Peggy.

"Bonjour Peggy,

"I'm learning to speak French, just like you. Will you please send me a picture of where you and Bob and the Army are in France. I'll show it to my French teacher. Her name is Mamed—no, cross that out—Mademosel Bongran, and she is very nice, but she is stric, too. She took a note a girl gave me I never even got to read it. I am liking Ashley Hall. We have to do a lot of homework and I have to do mine. Love,

"Your sister Garden

"P.S. I have a new dress for dancing school and shoes with buckles on them. They pinch my toes but Mama says never mind.''

Charleston had long ago developed a process for the social maturation of its young people. No one thought of it in such scientific terms; they simply did what was always done and let things work as they always had.

For girls and boys both, it began with Friday night dancing school when they were thirteen. There was a lady to teach them to dance, and they also learned from the example of the fourteen-year-olds, who were experienced in the mores of the class. After dancing school, the parents took over. Fifteen was the year for private parties and informal dances in the home. For girls, there was the added attraction of the Citadel cadets. They were in college, they were grown-up; the girls felt very sophisticated to be meeting older men of eighteen and nineteen.

The parents knew that these "older men" had to be in their barracks by midnight, were not allowed to drink or smoke, and usually had girlfriends in their hometowns. There was no danger, and the girls were, without knowing it, learning skills they would need. They were meeting strangers, with whom they had to be interesting talkers, interested listeners, and more grown-up.

The following year these skills got their first tests. The girls became pre-debutantes, participants in the Season. Theirs was a carefully limited participation; they were invited to tea dances and, usually, one ball. Their escorts were carefully chosen from among the young men they already knew from dancing school and parties, so that they would feel comfortable and be at their best. But they were thrown in with all Charleston's bachelors, with whom they could try out their social skills and, if they were perceptive, identify their weaknesses and use this opportunity to try and improve.

The ball was always a special occasion. A girl had her first ball gown, her first pair of long white gloves, her first late-night homecoming, her first glass of champagne. It was a thrilling preview of what was in store for her the next year, when she would be a debutante, the center of attention for her Season.

Being presented was a formal acknowledgment that a young lady was ready for marriage. During her Season, a girl was seen by all the eligible men. If she was successful, she was courted by one or by several, and during the year before the next Season, she was married. Thus the process achieved its aim, with pleasurable, progressive steps along the way.

On the first Friday in October, Garden climbed the wide steps of South Carolina Hall to begin. Wentworth Wragg was by her side. The Wraggs lived on Church Street, around the corner from the Tradds, and Jenkins Wragg had offered to escort Garden along with Wentworth. They had only a few blocks to walk; as Caroline Wragg had told the newspaper reporter years before, everything south of Broad was within easy walking distance.

"All right, ladies," said Mr. Wragg when they arrived. "I'll be back for you at nine sharp. Don't break too many hearts, now."

"Not too many, Papa," Wentworth giggled.

Garden took Wentworth's hand. "Don't be nervous, Garden,"

she said, "nobody's going to bite you, not even Miss Ellis. Wait till you see her teeth."

But Garden was nervous. Her mother had talked all week about how important it was for her to learn to be a good dancer. "You have to float, Garden. People have to say that dancing with you is like holding a feather in their arms." Margaret had also bemoaned the problem of Garden's hair. "Straight as a stick and so ugly. We'll have to do something." The night before, Garden had slept on knobs all over her head. They were fat little sausages made when Margaret rolled her hair up on rags. Her hair was straight again before she got to school. When she got home from school, Margaret grabbed her and rolled her hair again, spraying it with toilet water this time to set it. It stayed in the rags until Garden was all dressed and ready for dancing school. Then Margaret pinched each sausage with hot curling tongs. Garden had a cluster of fat curls held at the nape of her neck by a wide black velvet bow.

She felt them uncurling when she and Wentworth were climbing the stairs. Wentworth's hair, she noticed, was also in a bow, just like hers. But Wentworth's hair waved on either side of her part, and shining brown waves with red highlights cascaded down her back from the bow.

The girls went into the cloakroom at the stair landing to leave their coats. "Darn," Wentworth exploded, "Rebecca Wilson is already here. That's her red cape."

"Why 'darn'? I'm glad she's here. I know her from school."

"Pooh, Garden, you'll know everybody from school—all the girls, I mean. No, I said darn because I thought maybe her brother would bring her. I was going to listen on the stairs."

"Does he come to dancing school?"

"Maine? Gosh, no. He's old, all grown up. And so handsome I could die. I'm in love with him."

Garden was impressed. "Does Rebecca know?"

"Of course not, and I'll kill you if you tell her or anybody. Cross your heart and hope to die you won't tell."

Garden crossed her heart. "Hope to die," she said.

"Then let's go. Don't worry. This is my second year, and I know: everything will be all right."

Garden nodded and smiled. But her hands were sweating inside her new kid gloves. Suppose the water runs out the top, she thought. She pulled her long sleeves down to cover the edge of the gloves.

"You look fine, Garden, quit fidgeting. Come on." Wentworth pulled her toward the stairs.

Garden shrugged and set her foot on the path to womanhood.

Miss Ellis had long yellow teeth, with thin lips that would not meet over them. An old-fashioned tall boned collar did not quite hide her stringy neck; it reached to the bottom of the jet drops that hung from her pendulous earlobes. Miss Ellis was no beauty; she was a caricature of an old maid, she knew it, and she was bitter. She earned a precarious living teaching Charleston's privileged children to dance the waltz and, after pressure from the parents, the fox trot. She was invaluable, because her sour coldness intimidated the boys and averted rebellion.

Miss Ellis carried a baton with which she set the tempo for the pianist, Mrs. Mayes. Miss Ellis intimidated Mrs. Mayes even more than she did the children. All of them were convinced that Miss Ellis would not hesitate to hit anyone who made a mistake.

"New students step forward," Miss Ellis ordered. Garden looked appealingly at Wentworth and obeyed. "Form a line, girls." Garden moved closer to Julia Chalmers. Wentworth was right. Every day girl in her class was here. "Now boys. Forward and form a line." The boys lined up facing the five girls. They looked apprehensively at one another.

"How was it?" said Margaret eagerly when Garden walked into the drawing room. "Oh, Garden, your hair. How awful. Tell me, was your frock the prettiest one? Who did you dance with? Did you dance with anybody twice?"

"It was all right. Mr. Wragg said how pretty my frock was. We learned the box step for the waltz. The older girls and boys know how to reverse."

"Well, who did you dance with? Do you have a beau yet?"

Garden shrugged.

"Stop that twitching, Garden. You look like you've got palsy. Answer my question."

"I danced mostly with Tommy Hazlehurst. Miss Ellis tells people who to dance with."

"I see. That won't last; once you know the steps, the boys will ask the girls. Then you'll dance with them all. You'll be the first one they'll ask."

176

Garden looked down at her painful new shoes. "I don't think Miss Ellis would allow that, Mama," she mumbled. She couldn't bear to tell her mother that she was the clumsiest dancer of them all. Miss Ellis had assigned Tommy Hazlehurst because he was the biggest boy in class. "Maybe you will be able to keep Miss Tradd from tripping over her own feet," she said loudly in front of the whole group.

Garden honestly could not understand why she had so much trouble. She loved dancing; she had danced as long as she could remember, in the Settlement at the Barony. She danced, she knew, as well as anybody there. And she had been one of the best square dancers at the Lodge. But, try as hard as she could, she could not float like a feather. I'll have to try harder, she vowed. She went to her room to buttermilk her face and hands before bedtime.

35

I'll have to try harder, Garden thought when she failed the first algebra test. And Latin test. And English composition assignment.

When Mlle. Bongrand handed back the French tests and Garden saw the big red D on her paper, she despaired. French was the only subject she had thought she was doing well in. This was only her second week in school, and she was already a failure. She stumbled across to her next class.

"Garden," Miss Emerson said. "Will you please stay and talk with me after class instead of going to study hall?"

She's going to tell me I've flunked out, Garden said to herself. "Yes, ma'am," she said aloud.

The staff had discussed Garden for a long time at the meeting they always held early in the school year to evaluate the new students. Each of the teachers contributed an example of Garden's work and an appraisal of her. The consensus was not optimistic about her academic future. Everyone commented on her eagerness to please. "That poor child," said Miss Mitchum, the algebra teacher. "She clutches her pencil so hard I'm surprised it doesn't break. I half expect to see blood-sweat on her homework papers."

Mlle. Bongrand shook her head. "I simply do not comprehend. She has an excellent ear and a good memory. Her oral work is the best in the class. But she cannot write the simplest exercise."

"She does have a good memory," the history teacher said, "and she works hard. She has the kings of England down pat, but she doesn't understand why they disliked the kings of France."

Everyone looked at Miss Emerson. "Me again?" she said.

"It's your own fault, Verity. You're the one they all get a crush on. It must be the way you read Browning to them."

"Drivel. We won't get to Browning for two more years. It's just my accent. They find me so exotic." Miss Emerson was from New England; her consonants were never blurred. "All right, I'll take her on." Ashley Hall recognized that not all girls had equal intellectual gifts. It refused to accept that any girl could not be educated. A student in difficulty was identified early and given special help by the teacher best suited to her needs.

Garden stood next to Miss Emerson's desk as the other girls filed out of the classroom. She looked so miserable that Verity Emerson wanted to hug her. But babying was not the way to help her. "Garden, I know you're having trouble with your schoolwork," Miss Emerson said in her crisp voice. "You can do much better."

"I'll try harder, Miss Emerson."

"Trying is not doing, Garden. You must do better."

Garden hung her head.

"I know that you can do it. I'm going to show you how. I want you to stay for the afternoon period every day until we solve your problem. Do you know how the afternoon period works?"

"Yes, ma'am. I'm supposed to start music lessons in the afternoon next week."

"Garden if you're unable to keep up with your regular work, it makes no sense to add music."

"My mother wants me to take it."

"I see," Miss Emerson said. And she did. Margaret Tradd was not the first mother to want an accomplished daughter. Miss Emerson thought for a moment. "Garden, I'm going to write your mother

178

a note. I'll tell her that we believe it would be better for the school if you had your music training in singing instead of piano. You'll enjoy the Glee Club. And I'll tell her that I want you to stay for a special project with me in the afternoon. We don't need to talk about grades just yet."

"Oh, Miss Emerson." Garden looked up, idolatry in her eyes.

"I have a class coming in any minute now." Miss Emerson did not respond to worship. "You go to study hall; here's a permission slip for you to be late. It allows you to go to the library first. I want you to take out a book called *Pilgrim's Progress*. You and I will read it together."

And I'll probably need the encouragement more than you, Miss Emerson said silently to Garden's departing back. She has wonderful posture, that child. Miss Emerson made a note to have Garden take the deportment class. She'd be the best one in it. The Glee Club idea seemed to please her. Miss McBee, from the front of the auditorium, had noticed that Garden, in the last row, had an unusually pleasant voice. Miss McBee noticed everything.

Day students who took part in afternoon program had a choice of going home for dinner and returning at three or of staying at school and eating dinner with the boarders and staff. Miss Emerson suggested the latter in her note to Margaret Tradd, adding that the additional fee was regarded as of negligible importance by most parents. "Recognizing as they do," Miss Emerson wrote, "the value of the experience in formal dining for a young lady's future career in society."

As she expected, Mrs. Tradd instructed her daughter to stay for dinner at school every day. Mlle. Bongrand agreed to let Garden sit at the French table, where all conversation was in French. She predicted, accurately, that Garden would soon equal or surpass the other girls. "Let her see that she has strengths, and she'll have more confidence about improving her weaknesses," she said with assurance.

Miss Emerson was in agreement with Mlle. Bongrand in principle. But in practice, she had to deal with the weaknesses. "Garden," she said firmly the first afternoon, "there is one thing you must learn at once. All of us can do better than we think we can. We defeat ourselves. It is not circumstance, nor other people, nor malign fate that defeats us. We do it to ourselves. Unless we make up our minds that we will not be defeated."

179

She looked at Garden's adoring, uncomprehending expression and sighed inaudibly. "You'll understand what I mean in time. Now, let's begin . . ."

Just before Thanksgiving, report cards were sent out. "I know I got one D, Mama," said Garden dolefully, "but all the rest are C's. And I'm sure I'll do better."

"It isn't important, for heaven's sake," Margaret said. "Don't make such an ugly face. Girls who are too smart just scare off men. If you have to do better at something, do better at fading those freckles. Are you doing your buttermilk every night?"

"Yes, Mama."

"You'd better do it in the morning too, then."

"I go over my homework in the morning."

"You can do that on the streetcar. The outside of your head is what people see, not the inside. You work on your skin."

In spite of her mother's obstructiveness, Garden's schoolwork improved steadily. She had to work hard but she was willing to, and she gradually learned how to study to best effect. Even her Latin grades went up to the C level, and in French she began to get B's.

Mrs. Ladson, who directed the Glee Club, was delighted with Garden. Most of the strong voices were soprano; Garden had a true contralto range, with a richness in the lower register that added warmth to the chorus.

Her speaking voice was equally strong and full of color. Miss Oakman, who taught declamation, gave Miss Emerson some of the credit. "She tries to pronounce words the way you do, Verity. It makes her so much more distinct."

But in the spring, Miss Oakman made a discovery that Garden had a talent all her own. The girls progressed from reciting poems and speeches to acting out scenes from plays. "Garden is shy about declaiming in front of the class, but in a play she becomes a different girl altogether. She's a natural-born actress."

Miss Oakman had no idea how true her opinion of Garden was. Nor did the other teachers, although they were all extremely perceptive. Garden had been acting for most or her life.

"Keep quiet and watch what other people do," Reba had advised Garden when she entered first grade. Garden did what Reba told her; she watched and then did what the other children did. At home, with her family for the first time, she had watched Peggy and Stuart to learn how to behave in her new situation. Less than a year later they moved to the city, and she had to adjust to two different school and home environments before she had become fully at home in the earlier ones. Garden became a chameleon. She took on the coloration of her surroundings, assuming the patterns of behavior and attitude of the people around her, adapting in response to them in order to please, to be accepted, to fit in, to be like them. It never occurred to her that they might not be right.

Miss Oakman's elocution class was not the only one that expanded its activities in the spring. The art class left the classroom altogether for outdoor sketching on the school grounds. One afternoon a week, Mr. Christie, the art instructor, took a group of boarding students on walking and sketching excursions in the city. Miss Emerson put Garden in the group. Her schoolwork had improved enough to give her another afternoon free of tutoring.

Mr. Christie, like others before him, had found Charleston by accident and fallen in love with it. He was on his way from New Jersey to Florida when his car developed engine trouble.

To kill time while the mechanic was working, he decided to have a look at Fort Sumter. The only thing Herbert Christie knew about Charleston was that the first shots of the Civil War were fired there. The mechanic gave him directions to the Battery, the promenade by White Point Gardens. "You get a pretty good look from there," he said, "but it ain't much to see."

Long before Mr. Christie reached the Battery, he had decided to cancel the rest of his trip. He sent a telegram to Palm Beach, to the man who had commissioned a portrait of his wife. Herbert Christie was just beginning to make a name for himself as a portrait painter. He abandoned it without a second thought. No face in the world could be as exciting to him as the beauty of the walls and houses of old Charleston.

"Look at that, you Philistines," he roared at the girls trailing behind him. He threw out his arms, gesturing wildly, standing on a tilted carriage block on Church Street. "Can't you see? Are you blind?"

Garden saw Wentworth Wragg's house. Mrs. Wragg was in the garden having tea with Julia Chalmers's mother. Garden wondered if they were having brownies; the Wraggs's cook made the best brownies of anybody in the world.

Several of the older girls saw Mr. Christie being artistic. They swooned inwardly. He was just the way an artist should be, they agreed, with a lock of hair falling across his forehead, and long, long eyelashes.

Some of the girls were jolted by Mr. Christie's passion into making a real effort to look around them. They saw a narrow cobblestoned street shadowed by the interlaced branches of the trees that grew on either side. House fronts and walls rose from the sidewalks, making cliffs of brick and stucco in shades of weathered pink and buff and ocher. The only break in the cliffs was an open gate near them. Through it they glimpsed a brick-walled garden with azaleas in every gradation of pink along the wall; a luxuriant wisteria vine climbed the wall and stretched across its top, dripping heavy purple panicles and casting a scent so sweetly strong that it reached them in the street.

One of the girls saw the pattern of light and shadow on the walls, the pattern of the wrought-iron balcony on one of the houses, so airy-light that it might have been only another shadow. Her breath caught in her throat at the austere lines of the buildings, the splendor of their simplicity, the contrast between the severe purity of line and the soft, worn pastel colors. A ragged triangle of stucco had fallen from the nearest house at the corner of a tall shuttered window. It exposed the beautiful pattern and texture of old brick. She felt her eyes sting, and she turned away from the group, lest anyone ask her what was wrong.

Mr. Christie observed, understood and was satisfied. "Now, ladies," he said, "we will walk on. Follow me. Today we will breathe some salt air and watch the flight of gulls."

"Mr. Christie is funny," Garden told her mother after a later art outing. "He calls us by our last names with no Miss in front. 'Tradd, you swine,' he calls me."

Margaret stiffened. "That's not very nice."

"Oh it's just a joke. He says that Charleston is a pearl, and I don't appreciate it, like the Bible, you know. Mr. Christie just loves Charleston, and he knows all about it. Today he showed us a house with flowers carved into the gateposts. He said it was the Garden house and the flowers were gardenias. Is that Garden like me, like you before you married Papa?"

Margaret nodded. "It belonged to us before the Yankees came.

By rights, we should be living there now instead of those awful Carson people. They're not even from Charleston. He's in trade.''

"What's 'in trade' mean, Mama?"

Margaret wasn't listening. "My papa," she said, "told me that the ballroom in that house had the finest floor in Charleston. It gave with the dancers and then lifted so that it was like waltzing on air. It's just not fair that we don't live in our own house. Next year, you could have the best parties of any girl in your crowd."

"Are we going to have parties? I'd like to have a birthday party like Betsy Walker's. We played card games instead of dumb baby games like musical chairs."

"Don't be such a ninny, Garden. Next year you'll have real parties with dancing, you know that."

Garden was puzzled, and horrified. Her dancing was not improving. Do you mean I have more dancing, besides dancing school?"

Margaret covered her eyes with her hand. "Lord, why did you burden me with this child?" she groaned. She dropped her hand. "You . . . will . . . be . . . fifteen . . . next . . . year," she said slowly, speaking to an idiot. "When you're fifteen, you're through with dancing school."

Garden was more confused than ever. Dancing school was always two years; all her classmates at Ashley Hall would be going for another year.

"Don't look so dim, Garden. You are older than the other girls in your school class because you're a year behind, that's all. You'll just be with Wentworth's class when you come out. It doesn't make any real difference."

It made a difference to Garden. That night, she cried herself to sleep for the first time in many years.

The next day Wentworth cheered her up. "Lucky duck," she congratulated Garden, "you'll get away from Miss Ellis. Having our own parties will be so much fun. This summer we'll make lists and lists of who we like and who we don't. And I'll help you practice dancing, Garden." Wentworth Wragg had a generous heart.

36

The summer at Flat Rock was so exactly like the year before that time seemed almost to have reversed itself. Garden and Wentworth were inseparable, Margaret and Caroline Wragg were approving.

Margaret looked at Garden with satisfaction. Her freckles were virtually gone, her skin was a beautiful, creamy white without blemish. Her carriage was perfect, an easy elegance gained from all the baskets she had carried on her head in the Settlement. She had superlative good health; it showed in her clear eyes and perfect teeth and in the rich rose that flushed her cheeks and lips when she had been exercising or when she was excited.

She was fourteen now, and her body was losing its sturdy look; her waist was well defined and her hips and breasts developing. Margaret observed her carefully, relieved to note that Garden was still young for her age. She did not want her to bloom too early. The beauty was there, but not noticeable as yet. Margaret chose loose-fitting frocks and tight-fitting shoes for her daughter and kept her hair in tight braids, looped double and tied with big bows behind her small, flat ears.

For the first party that fall, Margaret crossed the braids over the top of Garden's head. She looked like a girl queen with a rich coronet of red and yellow gold. "How pretty, Mama," Garden said. "I look so grown-up." She was not nervous about the party. It was at Wentworth's house, which she knew well, and Wentworth had practiced with her all summer. She now danced quite decently. She smiled and turned her head from side to side to admire herself in the mirror. "May I have my ears bored, Mama? Wentworth had her ears bored, and she's wearing earrings to the party."

Yes, Margaret thought, earrings would call attention to the perfect, small ears and the long, slender, satiny white throat. But not yet. Not until the right moment.

"You're too young for earrings, Garden, and so is Wentworth. I don't know what her mother's thinking of." Margaret started to take Garden's hair down, then changed her mind. She was chaperoning the party tonight with Caroline Wragg. She'd like to see the effect Garden made on the Citadel cadets. The dress was just right, a high neck with a round lace collar, deep pleats front and back, a satin sash around the dropped waist. Nothing grown-up about it, nothing to draw the eye. Only the regal head and soft, lovely face, still a girl's face, not a woman's. Yes, it should be interesting to see the reactions.

"How charming you look, Garden." Mrs. Wragg kissed the air near Garden's cheek.

"Thank you, Miss Caroline. Thank you for inviting me."

"Margaret." Kisses from both ladies. "You've certainly taught that child beautiful manners. Give your cloaks to Rosalie. Run on upstairs, Garden, everybody's in the drawing room. . . . Isn't this fun, Margaret? I feel like a girl one minute and as old as Miss Ellis the next. The girls all look so sweet and the boys are all flustered. There's only Lucy Anson left to come, then we can go up."

The party was a nightmare for Garden. When she walked into the drawing room, she froze. Wentworth and her two classmates, Alice Mikell and Marion Leslie, were talking and laughing with great animation to four Citadel cadets. In one corner of the room three Charleston boys were talking loudly about the deer one of them had shot. Two of the boys were strangers to Garden; they looked very old. One of them was even smoking a cigarette. The third was Tommy Hazlehurst, but Garden could not catch his eye.

Wentworth did not see her, either. Alice glanced at her, then looked away. All three girls were wearing frocks with waistlines. Garden could tell that they had on corsets because their waists were so small and they looked so grown-up. All the happy anticipation drained out of her, leaving her empty and frightened. She stayed that way all evening, clumsy, tongue-tied, miserable.

Tommy tried to rescue her. "You're dancing as bad as the beginning of dancing school," he said with misplaced honesty. "Come on, Garden, one-two-three-four, one-two-three-four. You can

185

do it. Just make believe we're at South Carolina Hall and Miss Ellis is waving her teeth at us. . . . Golly, Garden, that was a joke. When a fellow makes a joke, you're supposed to laugh.''

"I can't. I can't laugh, and I can't dance, and I wish I was dead." Miss Ellis's menacing baton had never frightened her as much as the look of icy disapproval on her mother's face.

"Garden," said Margaret when they arrived home, "I don't think I ask too much of you. I give you every advantage, I do without all little luxuries so that you can have everything a girl could want, and I ask nothing in return except a little effort on your part. Just a little effort, that's all. I was humiliated in front of my best friend tonight. There we were, in her home, and you made absolutely no effort to take part in the party. You stood around like a stick, making everybody uncomfortable. What do you have to say for yourself?''

"Nothing, Mama.''

" 'Nothing' is what you said all night. I've never seen such a disgraceful performance.''

"I'm sorry, Mama. I'll do better, I promise.''

"Well, see that you do. I'm disgusted with you. Go to bed. I don't want to talk to you anymore.''

The next day was Sunday. Garden knelt in the Tradd pew and respectfully asked God to help her learn to ''be good at parties.'' She also thanked Him for having school start on Monday.

Garden's second year at Ashley Hall was less happy than the first. Miss Emerson was no longer tutoring her. "You did very well last year," she said. "I know you can do very well this year too, Garden. On your own." And she did not belong to a group the way she had before. Academically she was still with Charlotte and Betsy and Rebecca and Julia, but they were still in dancing school; Garden did not know what they were talking about when they gossiped about what had happened over the weekend. Socially, she was allied with Wentworth and her friends, but she had no classes with them. At the Saturday night parties she could not share their jokes about events at school. She had to try harder than ever to fit in, and she was less successful.

But there was Glee Club and Drama Club, and she still had dinner at school with boarders from all grades at the French table. She adapted to her semi-isolation in the classroom and at the parties by becoming quieter and more involved in school activities. Without her realizing it, the atmosphere and spirit of Ashley Hall became a part of her. The orderly but flexible routine of bells and duties, the respect for the individual, the value and pleasure of self-discipline, the enthusiasm for learning, the appreciation of beauty and harmony were instilled in her by the example of the teachers and the entire staff from Miss McBee to Turps, the janitor. Garden did not know why she felt her unhappiness lift when she looked at the noble main building, but she felt it. If she was despondent, she would stand in the hallway and look at the magic perfection of the flying staircase. It always made her feel better. As the weeks passed, every path, every lawn, every tree and shrub and flower gave Garden comfort and strength. "I love Ashley Hall," all the students said enthusiastically. Garden said it too, with exactly the same intonation. But for her, it meant something more profound than she knew.

The outward pattern of Garden's life changed very little. She worked diligently at her studies, conscientiously bleached her skin and thinned her red hair, accepted her mother's choices of clothes and how to wear her braids, attended all the Saturday night parties and pretended to enjoy them. And, after a time, there were happy developments in her life.

She was invited to join the choir at St. Michael's, and every Sunday became a joyful occasion. Tommy Hazlehurst appointed himself her official admirer, and Saturday nights ceased being a trial. Garden was comfortable with Tommy. He was in love, hopelessly, with Wentworth and needed a friend to talk to about his misery. Soon he was escorting Garden to every party, the word was out that she had a beau, and she did not have to try and flirt with the other boys.

Even her mother was pleased. Tommy Hazlehurst was far from being the future Margaret had in mind for Garden, but he was nice-looking, well-mannered and from a good family. And he was proof that Garden was attractive. He was just right for a beginning. Margaret showed her affectionate side again, and Garden basked in her mother's approval.

And when the powerful lush Southern spring came with its intoxicating mixture of scent and color and warm whispering breezes that touched the skin like a caress, Garden subdued the disturbing, inchoate, unnamed uneasiness that tried to invade her body and her mind. She liked things as they were. She didn't want anything to change.

While every hour that passed took childhood away from her, bringing her exquisite, fragile womanliness closer to perfection.

187

37

That summer Garden fell in love. His name was Julian Gilbert, and he was from Alabama. He was over six feet tall, with dark hair and eyes so brown they were almost black. He wore white linen suits that never seemed to wrinkle and a soft string tie in a small drooping bow. His accent was like honey, and he bowed to ladies with the flourish of a courtier. He was the essence of every romantic cliché: tall, dark, handsome, dashing and gallant.

And he was married. He and his bride were spending their honeymoon at the Lodge. Her name was Annabelle; when Julian said it, it sounded like music heard through a cloud. She was tall too, and willowy, with a heart-shaped face framed by a halo of blond curly hair that she wore in loose ringlets. She dressed always in white dotted swiss and she wore wildflowers in her hair and at her belt. Julian picked them from the mountain meadow and brought them to her, kneeling to present them.

Garden watched them with wide, star-struck eyes. Her mother said they were common. Caroline Wragg said they were sweet, just like Mary Pickford and Douglas Fairbanks.

Wentworth conceded to Garden, in secret, that Julian Gilbert was almost as handsome as Maine Wilson. The two girls bicycled to Hendersonville for Eskimo Pies and ate them at the drugstore soda fountain, languishing and comparing their anguished one-sided loves. In the evenings they sang "Some Day I'll Find You" and let tears roll down their cheeks in the darkness.

Wentworth made Garden cross her heart, then whispered her deepest secret. "I let one of the cadets kiss me."

Garden was awed. "Weren't you afraid you'd get caught?"

"Terrified. I think that was the best part. We were all out on Lucy Anson's piazza, remember? That last party when it was so hot. There's a big shadowy place there at the back where the honeysuckle vine is. He kind of nudged me in it. I knew what he was up to. It was Fred, the one who always tries to dance too close."

"What did you do?"

"I let him nudge, silly. And then I turned my face up, and he did it."

"Right on the mouth?"

"Yes. We didn't bump noses or anything. You could tell he's done a lot of kissing."

"But Wentworth, you don't even love him. Why did you do it?" Garden had gooseflesh at the thought.

"Garden, look, I'm going to be sixteen in August. I just couldn't bear to have anybody call me sweet sixteen and never been kissed."

"What was it like, Wentworth? Did you feel dizzy?"

Wentworth considered. "No, I didn't feel all swoony or anything. But it was exciting. It's not like anything else at all."

That fall when the parties started again, Garden stopped Tommy Hazlehurst when he was walking her home from the Mikells'. They were in the shadow of a huge oleander. "Tommy," she quavered, "will you please kiss me?"

"What? Are you crazy, Garden?"

"Please, Tommy, I'm going to be sixteen in December, and I've just got to be kissed before then."

Tommy did the gentlemanly thing. He bobbed his head, depositing a hurried peck on Garden's pursed lips. "Okay?"

"Yes, thanks, Tommy." Garden tried to feel daring and reckless, but she couldn't manage it. Kissing wasn't much, she thought.

Garden was now in her third year at Ashley Hall. She felt as much a part of it as the rocks in the fern-edged grotto near the main house. She was elected vice-president of the Drama Club and was invited to join the Verre d'Eau, the organization that raised money and did volunteer work for Charleston's poor children.

Garden reported the honors to her mother and received the perfunctory response she had learned to expect. Margaret wanted to know everything her daughter was doing at school, but she wasn't interested in it.

The most interesting news at Ashley Hall Garden failed to mention to her mother. Millie Woodruff and two other boarders arrived in the fall with bobbed hair. Millie also had a copy of a scandalous book called *This Side of Paradise*. It went from hand to hand until its pages were limp, and everyone whispered about the petting parties and girls drinking and smoking in the novel. Most girls were sure it was all a lie, but Millie swore that she personally knew somebody who knew a girl in Philadelphia who was just like that.

As Christmas approached, Garden concentrated on two big occasions in the last week of school. The Glee Club was presenting a concert for the school and the parents; she was singing a solo, a French version of "Twixt Ox and Ass." And the Verre d'Eau was, as always, helping to trim "Miss McBee's tree" with presents for poor children. Garden tried not to think about the vacation period. This year she would be a pre-debutante.

Her mother did not let her forget. Garden had to fight Margaret over the relative importance of Glee Club rehearsals and fittings at the dressmaker. It was the first time she had defied her mother, and it made her feel heavy with guilt, but she did fight and she won.

She tried to atone by pretending enthusiasm when Margaret talked about the Season. "A proper ball, Garden, you can't imagine how exciting and wonderful it is. The tea dances are great fun, naturally, but your first ball is the most glorious thing in your life. Except *the* Ball, of course, the Saint Cecilia. But that's next year. This year, there's no question, the ball will be the best thing that's ever happened to you." Margaret brought out her treasured box of souvenirs and turned over the yellowed, foxed invitations and faded dance cards one by one, telling Garden all the details of every event.

Fresh cream-colored invitations began to arrive the first week in December. Margaret met Garden at the door when she got home from school and barely allowed her to take off her coat before sitting her down at Margaret's desk to write her acceptances.

But on December tenth Garden found her mother pacing back and forth in her drawing room in a rage. "How dare she," Margaret demanded of Garden, "how dare she invite you to that house?" She waved the cardboard square in Garden's face.

"Who, Mama? What house?"

"Mistress Elizabeth Cooper, that's who. That awful woman." Garden took the invitation from her mother.

"It's a tea dance for Lucy Anson," Garden said.

Margaret glared at her. "I can read, thank you very much, Garden. What I cannot do is understand how that horrible old woman could have such nerve."

Garden tried to be helpful. "I know about this party, Mama. Lucy told me I was being invited. She and her mother addressed the invitations themselves. The lady who's giving it probably didn't know I was on the list."

Margaret stopped raging, but she was still upset. It was not until breakfast the next day that Garden dared ask her about the invitation. "Am I going to Lucy's tea dance, Mama? She might say something about it at school."

"Yes, you are. There aren't so many invitations that you can afford to turn one down. Why is Lucy coming out this Season anyhow? I thought she was in your year."

"Didn't you hear? Lucy's engaged. She's already seventeen, you know. She lost a year when she had scarlet fever."

"Why didn't I hear about it? Who's she marrying?"

"It's sort of a secret, Mama. Don't tell I told. They aren't announcing it until after the Season. The wedding's not till June, after Lucy graduates. Wentworth says she heard that Lucy's papa doesn't want her to marry so young."

"Who, Garden, who? Who is Lucy marrying?"

"Oh, Peter Smith. I never even met him. He's a lot older. They have a house next door to the Ansons on Sullivan's Island, and Lucy's known him forever."

Margaret relaxed. Peter Smith was not one of the men she had in mind for Garden. He was acceptable enough, but not a stunning catch.

Garden recognized that her mother was pleased about something. Now, she thought, was a good time to ask. "Mama," she said in a by-the-way tone of voice, "who is the lady who's giving the party for Lucy?"

Her mother bristled, but only slightly. "She's an aunt of yours, Garden. She was your grandfather's sister."

"She must be very old."

"I'm sure she is. I met her when I was young, but I hardly remember her. Your father had a terrible argument with her, and after that none of us ever spoke to her or mentioned her name."

Garden waited hopefully for more.

"I can't remember all the details. Your papa told me once, but I forgot. She cheated him out of a lot of money and out of the Tradd family house. That's where she lives, you know; that's where you're going for Lucy's dance. That's the Tradd house. We should have it, not Elizabeth Cooper.''

"She must be an awful lady.''

"Terrible. I'm surprised she's giving a party for Lucy, even though I do think I heard somewhere that she's her godmother. Or something. The Tradds and Ansons are all cousins.''

"Lucy's my cousin?''

"Somewhere. I don't keep track. In Charleston, everybody is everybody else's cousin.''

"I'm going to be late. 'Bye, Mama.''

"Don't forget to come home early.''

"I know, I know. I've got a fitting.''

Margaret had a gown to be fitted, too. She was going to the ball also. It was scheduled for Christmas Eve, which was Garden's sixteenth birthday and the day after Margaret's three-year deep mourning period ended. She could now wear gray, mauve or a combination of black and white. She would have loved a white gown with black lace trim, but white was reserved for the debutante whom the ball honored. Gray, Margaret decided, was really too old-lady. Thirty-seven was not that old. Mauve was not exactly becoming, but if she had a slight décolletage of silver lace, it would relieve the purpleness of it.

And in truth, she was more concerned with Garden's appearance than her own. Garden must be noticed, admired, perhaps even rushed. But not too much. She must look young, not yet ready to entertain suitors. Margaret would not allow anything to cheat her out of Garden's successes in her own Season. There would be no early engagements for her daughter; she intended to have, through Garden, everything that she should have had herself, that she would have had if she had not been tricked into an early marriage. Garden would burst onto the scene in her full beauty when she made her debut, she would be the belle of the Season, dozens of bouquets would arrive every morning from her beaux, she would be courted, perhaps fought over, perhaps even cause attempts at suicide.

She chose a pattern for Garden's gown that was practically a middy blouse and skirt in cut. Puffed sleeves, a bateau neck, dropped waist and accordion-pleated skirt. It was made up in pale blue silk with a small ruching of ivory lace at the neck and pink rosebuds embroidered on the bodice and sleeves. The sash was a wide pink satin ribbon, and her dancing slippers were pink satin with a low French heel. She would wear pink roses in her hair and carry a nosegay of rosebuds surrounded by lace and blue ribbon.

"Mama, this feels so strange," Garden said.

"Hush up, Garden. Breathe in and hold it while Mrs. Harvey laces you tighter." The corset made Garden's waist the desired hand-span size and brought her firm young breasts into prominence. Margaret nodded acceptance to the fitter. The gown would hide everything the corset revealed, but when a man put his arm around Garden to dance, he would feel the tiny waist and be able to imagine the rest.

Garden was already wearing a light corset under her everyday frocks. It would be adequate for the tea dances. The older bachelors only attended them when a close relation was being honored; this year, none were.

38

Margaret did not recognize the voice on the telephone. It told her that her daughter had been knocked down by an automobile. She was in the Emergency Room at Roper Hospital.

Margaret screamed.

"Don't worry, Mrs. Tradd," the voice soothed. "Her injuries are not serious, only a broken ankle."

"I'll be right there," said Margaret. She hung up the phone and screamed again. Garden would miss her pre-debutante Season. "Zanzie," she called, "fix me a cup of tea. I feel just terrible."

"I feel just fine," Garden told everyone at the tea dance on December 19. And she did. Her terrors about the Season were laid to rest. All she had to do was sit in the big wheeled chair and watch the dancing. People stopped to ask how she was, she said she was fine, then they left. She enjoyed the music, real music with four instruments, not just a piano. And she was enthralled by the spectacle of Charleston at its most gay. Her mother had predicted that she would love the Season. She was right. Garden looked forward to the rest of her schedule: another tea dance on the twentieth, then the ball on the twenty-fourth, and the tea dance for Lucy Anson on the twenty-eighth.

Margaret sat next to her daughter at the ball. She was satisfied with Garden's restricted success. All four of the bachelors that interested Margaret came up to offer sympathy. Two of them were visibly impressed when Garden smiled and spoke in her throaty, womanlike voice. Next year, Margaret thought, will be a triumph.

She tried, at the last minute, to persuade Garden not to go to Lucy Anson's tea dance, but Garden wanted very much to go. She was enjoying the Season from her chair, and it was the last party she could attend.

"I'm not nervous about meeting Mrs. Cooper," Garden said. "She can't bite me."

In fact, she was curious about her great-aunt the ogress, and about the house she lived in. It was Elizabeth Cooper who was nervous about the meeting.

Lucy Anson gave her godmother the list of guests for her party as soon as all the acceptances were received. Elizabeth Cooper did not bother to look at it until the day after Christmas, when the holiday rush was over. She knew that forty-five people had been invited, that probably they had all accepted. Now, two days before the tea dance, she had only to refresh her memory with the names so that she could greet people easily when they came down the receiving line. It was so easy to confuse older and younger brothers or sisters, and nothing upset a seventeen-year-old boy more than being called by the name of his fourteen-year-old brother.

She was having a cup of tea while her eyes skimmed the list. She dropped it in her lap when she came to Garden's name. "Oh, Lord," she whispered. She mopped up the liquid in her lap with jerky, inadequate motions. She was deeply disturbed.

I should have done something, she thought. I've been a wicked old woman. This child is my brother's granddaughter, and I've never laid eyes on her. There were other children, too. I should have

194

done something, made some effort. There's no excuse for my behavior. She covered her eyes with her hands and bowed her head.

In truth, there were reasons for Elizabeth's neglect. Her nephew, Garden's father, had been a seducer and a murderer, and Elizabeth's response, her outrage and disgust, had been extreme but justifiable. And she, too, had the Tradd temper. Once she swore to have nothing to do with Stuart, her anger and grief fed her resolve. She would not allow anyone to mention the Barony Tradds in her presence.

When Stuart died, in 1913, she did not know it. She was in seclusion, hiding from the world, unable to face life, almost destroyed by the death of her only son, Tradd, the previous year, in the senseless sinking of the *Titanic*.

She put her world back together slowly, determination overcoming despair, but for a long, long time she saw no one except her closest friends and her daughter and grandchildren. Someone told her then that her brother's son had died, but the information made no impression. The Barony and everyone on it seemed very far away. She did not really think about the family until she learned that young Stuart was working at Andrew Anson's bank. Andrew assured her that the family was doing well, and Elizabeth seized on his guarantee to look out for them. It gave her an excuse to leave old wounds closed and to concentrate on the rebuilding of her own life.

She went to Europe not long after, and she heard nothing about young Stuart's accident. When she returned, the gossip was that Margaret had come into a fortune, that she was furiously social climbing and that Garden, the only child left at home, was safely settled in a routine of Ashley Hall, dancing school and St. Michael's choir.

She had not seen any of the Barony Tradds for twenty years. It was easiest to leave things that way.

Easiest, she thought now, but wrong. I was, and I am, a wicked old woman. I wish the wretched little girl wasn't coming to Lucy's party. I don't want to know her. I don't like feeling guilty.

When Garden was wheeled down the receiving line, Elizabeth acted perfectly composed, but she was not.

She must have known who I was, Garden was thinking, and she didn't even bat an eye. She was nice enough, though. "Thank you," she said to her escort, "yes, this corner is fine. I'll have a good view." She smiled and waved to people greeting her. Then the dancing began.

This party was different. People did not leave the floor to talk to her. Garden in her chair was a fixture, not a novelty.

Garden shrugged. Oh, well. Being a wallflower was nothing new to her.

Across the room Elizabeth Cooper put her hand to her heart. So many years ago, so many, she'd had an older brother. Pinckney. He was all that was wonderful, and she adored him. He had a habit that she had forgotten. When troubles weighed him down, he used to shake them off, shrugging. Just like that child. The movement of the shoulders was identical, and the composed expression on the face, masking who could tell what kind of worry. The face, too, now that she really looked. The nose was Pinckney's nose, the chin had a hint of the cleft in his. Those eyes were Tradd eyes, too. They'd be Pinckney's eyes if they were laughing.

Elizabeth walked around the edge of the crowded floor and took the chair next to Garden's. "Hello."

"Hello." Garden looked apprehensive.

Why, she's frightened, thought Elizabeth. That's absurd. I mean her no harm. "Did you know, Garden, that I am your great-aunt?"

"Yes, ma'am."

"It would please me if you called me 'Aunt Elizabeth.' How old are you, Garden?"

"I was sixteen last week."

"I'm sixty-two. But I remember being sixteen. It was horrible. It seemed to me that everyone but me was already grown up and afraid of nothing. Do you know what I mean?"

"Oh yes, ma'am."

"I was wrong, of course. They were all afraid, just like me. I learned that later. You will, too. I have a sort of tea party every Wednesday afternoon from three o'clock until five. You're welcome to come."

"Thank you, ma'am."

Elizabeth rose and walked purposefully to the stairs. What a scared little rabbit, she said to herself. And what a liar I am. When I was sixteen, I wasn't afraid of anything on earth. She went up to her bedroom and lifted a box down from a shelf.

Downstairs, Wentworth was in the chair she had vacated. "Your aunt? Garden, you never said Mrs. Cooper was your aunt."

"Great-aunt."

"Same difference. Garden! Do you know what that means? You're Maine Wilson's cousin. She's his grandmother. He and Rebecca are over here all the time. They just love her. Is she wonderful? I only know her a how-do-you-do worth."

Garden was trying to decide whether she thought her great-aunt was wonderful or not so that she could answer Wentworth. But then she saw her coming back, and Wentworth disappeared.

Elizabeth placed a square box on Garden's lap. "This is a birthday present," she said. She untied the wide blue satin ribbon and removed it. "Go ahead, see what it is."

"Thank you . . . Aunt Elizabeth."

"You're welcome. But you'd better see that the box isn't empty before you do too much thanking."

The box was not empty. Garden took out the gift; it was a delicate porcelain figurine, a ballerina, atop a circular box enameled in white with garlands of flowers.

"Wind it up," Elizabeth ordered. "It's a music box—Andrew! Tell the musicians to stop playing for a while." Mr. Anson, distinguished bank president though he was, scurried to do Elizabeth's bidding.

The music box was a marvel. Everyone crowded together to watch the ballerina dance. Her arms and legs were jointed; they moved in intricate tiny gestures and pirouettes to "The Waltz of the Flowers." The music was richer than that of any music box any of them had ever heard, a melody rather than a tinkle. It increased in volume, the ballerina twirled on one toe, then suddenly her leg broke and she fell. A gasp from the crowd almost drowned out the happy music.

Garden wanted to look at her great-aunt. She wanted to tell her that she liked her present even if it was broken, that the box was pretty; the music a favorite of hers. Before she could gather courage to speak, the music ended, the box whirred, and the ballerina stood up and bowed from the waist.

Garden laughed. Everyone laughed, Elizabeth more than anyone. Garden's eyes tipped up at the corner when she laughed. Light danced in them. They were the eyes of Pinckney Tradd.

"I brought that back from Paris," Elizabeth said. "I love the French; they are so mischievous."

"Play it again, Garden," said Lucy Anson. "Yes . . . wind it up

. . . I thought it was broken . . . I've never seen . . . heard of . . . thought I'd die . . ." people clamored.

Garden turned the little gold key, intent on what she was doing, her eyes still laughing. Elizabeth smiled. "Here," she said. She tied the ribbon in a bow around Garden's injured foot. "Happy birthday."

Garden laughed again. "Thank you, Aunt Elizabeth." She looked at Elizabeth, her expression earnest and shy. "Thank you. I never had an aunt before. I'm awfully happy that you're mine now."

Elizabeth was taken aback. "Dear child," she murmured, a catch in her throat. "Bless you." She kissed her fingers and touched them to Garden's soft cheek. The music box began to play. While all eyes were on the ballerina, Elizabeth left the room. She needed a moment to herself.

Margaret was not happy about Garden's admiration for her great-aunt, but she neither said nor did anything to discourage it. Elizabeth Cooper was a powerful figure in Charleston; Margaret did not care to fight her.

The estrangement between Elizabeth and her brother's family had been a fascinating scandal when it began, but that was long past. The young people at Lucy's party did not realize that they had witnessed a reconciliation. If they thought about anything other than the wonders of the music box, they thought it was peculiar that Garden had never known her aunt before. Peculiar, but not especially interesting.

Andrew Anson and his wife Edith found it very interesting indeed. So did everyone they told. The story was the favorite gossip in town for over a week.

Then there was news that took precedence over everything else. After almost three years, the mysterious purchaser of Ashley Barony had finally come to live at the plantation. A private train, a whole train, came to Summerville with one car full of luggage, one car carrying two limousines, a refrigerated car packed with crates of who-knows-what, two Pullmans of servants, men and women and all of them white, a car that was nothing but a kitchen, and three cars with real bedrooms and bathrooms, three of each in each car, for the fancy-looking ladies and gentlemen in the house party. Best of all was the car with the gilded woodwork around the big windows and the big coat of arms on the side. It was tremendous, at least half again the size of any regular car. It had a living room, dining room, bedroom and bath with a tub. That was the owner's own separate, private car. The coat of arms was foreign. The Barony belonged to a princess.

Charleston was proud, some said excessively proud, of its old families and close-knit society. But it was not immune to the glamour of royalty. Ladies who would not bother to cross the street to meet the President of the United States—if anyone ever asked them—were in a ferment of frustration. No one could think how to meet the princess. No one even knew what she was princess of.

Edith Anson dropped her bombshell on the tea table at the February meeting of the Carolina Art Association. "Andrew and I have been invited to Ashley Barony for dinner. Andrew is the princess's banker in Charleston."

When the hubbub died down, she convinced everyone that she knew no more than that. "Andrew thinks I'm a nitwit to be so curious. He hasn't told me a thing. But we're going for dinner on Saturday. Saturday night. The princess doesn't eat dinner until nine o'clock.

"On Sunday, I'll be at home all day after church. I'm inviting everybody to come over any time."

39

Margaret Tradd was one of the first callers at the Ansons' big house on South Battery. "What has she done to the Barony?" she asked.

"No, no, Margaret, that can wait," said Caroline Wragg. "What is she like, Edith? Does she wear a tiara?"

Edith Anson poured tea, prolonging the suspense. "The Barony is all fixed up; it looks like a museum," she said. "And she looks like a movie star. She smokes! With a long cigarette holder, black, and diamonds around the part where the cigarettes go."

The tea cooled in their cups while Edith Anson's guests drank in her report of her dinner with the princess.

"She's an Italian princess, which is pronounced preenchee-pess-a. Actually, she's American, from New York, but she married an Italian prince. The Principessa Montecatini. I asked Andrew why the bank had an Italian prince on its board of directors, and you'll never believe what he told me—he's not the director, she is."

"A *lady* in business?"

Edith leaned forward. "Hardly a lady," she said in a low voice. "The prince is her third husband. She was divorced two times."

Her audience was speechless. Divorce was a scandal so immense that they could not conceive of actually meeting a person who had been divorced. Two divorces were beyond imagination.

Edith went on, building a tower of incredible, titillating information. The Principessa was wearing a dinner dress of yellow crushed velvet beaded in black jet flowers down the front and around the hem and the train, yes, it had a train. But that wasn't all. In the front, the hem was halfway up to her knees, at least four inches higher than any hem any one of them had ever seen.

And her hair was yellow. Not blond, mind you, it was yellow, the same color as her dress. One of the houseguests told Edith that the Principessa had her own hair bleached until it was pure white. Her private French hairdresser tinted it a different color every day to match what she was wearing. Furthermore, her hair was shingled. There was hardly any at all in the back. In the front it was in bangs and came to sort of a point in front of her ears. And the earrings, the jewels! Chandeliers, positively chandeliers of diamonds hung from her ears, practically to her shoulders. She had diamond rings on both hands; one was almost as big as a pigeon's egg. Diamond bracelets, too, four or maybe five on each arm. And her arms were completely bare. Her dress had no sleeves at all.

The houseguests had almost as many jewels as the Principessa, but they weren't as big. All of them had bobbed hair, one was shingled, and every single one of them was wearing lipstick and rouge. Yes, the Principessa wore makeup, too. She even had paint on her eyes, a black line all around and beads of mascara on her eyelashes.

Yes, Edith said, she'd have to say the Principessa was beautiful. Shocking, but definitely beautiful. She couldn't say how old she was, certainly older than she looked, maybe thirty, maybe even forty. Who could tell, with all the makeup and dyed hair and the diamonds?

The men? Yes, the men were all very elegant, in full-dress dinner clothes, not tuxedo jackets. But Edith had hardly looked at the men, she was too fascinated by the women. Andrew said they were a bunch of popinjays. No, the prince wasn't there.

After hearing about the Principessa, Edith's guests were almost too glutted to listen to her description of the house. It was all done in English antiques, mostly Chippendale; everything was polished to perfection, the upholstery was all fresh. There were huge flower arrangements everywhere, porcelain and gold and silver bibelots on all the tables and chests. And silver bell pushes on the tables next to chairs and sofas. The Principessa had put electricity in the Barony! There were silk-shaded lamps all over the place, and electrified coach lamps at the entrance. She had put in plumbing, too. Edith had gone to a powder room downstairs after dinner. The basin was carved blue marble, and the taps were gold dolphins. The water closet was like a chair, blue wood with gilt trim. It had a thronelike caned back and a caned seat you lifted to find the necessaries. "For a minute, I thought there was no toilet at all, just a chair. I nearly panicked, after all that wine."

There had been plenty of it, champagne before dinner, then three different wines with dinner and brandy afterward for the men. The women drank creme de menthe. Prohibition meant as little at the Barony as it did in Charleston. Less, even. The women drank as much as the men.

Menu? Edith couldn't really tell. She was so busy trying not to stare at the footmen that she hardly saw what was on her plate. Yes, footmen. One behind each chair, in livery, knee breeches and all.

Besides that, she couldn't recognize anything she was eating. The Principessa had a French chef, and all the food had sauce on it. It was all delicious, but foreign. The only thing she could put a label on was the crêpes suzette for dessert. The chef came out himself to flame them in a silver skillet over a silver alcohol burner. Whatever they had eaten, it was a feast.

Edith's guests sighed. She had given them a feast. There was enough to talk about for weeks.

"We just got here," said a recent arrival, "when you were in the gold bathroom, Edith. Tell about the Princess. What's she like?"

Edith poured tea for everyone who had come in after the first group, while the early crowd gathered themselves together to leave.

"When can we meet her, Edith?" said Caroline Wragg. "Can you invite her in to town? I wonder what color her hair will be?"

Mrs. Anson shook her head. "I'm afraid she's already gone. They were all in a twitter about leaving. Some friend of theirs has just bought a yacht, and they're all going to Palm Beach for its christening. As far as I could tell, they travel all the time."

While Edith Anson's guests were luxuriating in gossip about the immorality of the Northern rich, the daughters of two of the ladies were investigating depravity in the desert.

"Hurry up," Wentworth said to Garden. "We'll miss the streetcar." Wentworth closed the street door behind her.

"Why are you coming out, Wentworth? I thought I was invited for dinner to your house."

"Shhh. Don't talk so loud. Papa thinks I'm leaving to go to dinner at your house. Come on, we can't be late."

"Where are we going?"

Wentworth shook the pocket of her coat. A heavy jingling noise made Garden blink. "You sure sound rich. But what can you buy on Sunday? All the stores are closed." She was talking to Wentworth's back. "Slow down, Wentworth."

Wentworth walked faster. "No, you hurry up. I've been saving up for weeks. I'm treating, Garden. We're going to the picture show."

Garden's speed tripled. Her ankle was healed, and, although she claimed it was still too weak for her to dance on, she could move as quickly as anyone else when necessary.

A movie was worth running for. The girls were allowed only one a month, and that one chosen by their parents. Garden did not even have to ask where they were going while their mothers were busy at Mrs. Anson's. *The Sheik* was playing at the Victoria.

"Ooh, Garden, wasn't he wonderful? I thought I was going to faint, I really did."

"Do you think people really kiss like that? How can they hold their breath so long?"

"Garden, sometimes I wonder about you. They were doing a lot more than kissing. He had his way with her."

"Wentworth! Do you know what that means?"

Wentworth was thoughtful. "No, I don't," she admitted. "Mama said she would tell me when I was old enough."

"My mama said that boys only want one thing. I asked her what one thing, and she just said that if anybody tried to touch me I should slap his face."

"It drives me nuts."

"Me too. I hate the way grown-ups all have secrets and never tell us anything."

Wentworth giggled. "Well, whatever it is, Rudolph Valentino sure wanted it. And he got it, too." She sighed dramatically. "Masterful, that's what he is. I'd love to be pushed around like that. I'd love to marry a masterful man."

"You're crazy He'd hurt your arm or bloody your nose. I want to marry a man like Mr. Gilbert in the mountains, who'd bring me flowers and kneel at my feet."

"I'll bet Maine Wilson is masterful when he wants to be. Garden, when are you going to take me to tea?"

"Gosh, Wentworth, I'm too busy to go have tea with Aunt Elizabeth. I went once as a thank-you for the music box; I don't have time to go again for a while. Besides, Maine's not going to be there. He goes to work, not to his grandmother's tea parties."

"He does so go. Rebecca told me. He goes to Mrs. Cooper's any time he can get away from the office. You promised, Garden, you promised you'd take me."

"Okay. I'll have to ask her if it's all right for me to bring a friend."

"I know that. You go next Wednesday and ask her, and then the Wednesday after that we'll both go."

On Wednesday, Garden presented herself at the street door of the Tradd house on Meeting Street, calling card ready in her gloved hand. The short black man who answered her ring recognized her from her previous visit. He lowered the small silver tray he was holding to his side. "Keep your card, honey," he said. "You is family." Garden followed him along the piazza to the house's front door. He held it open for her.

"Thank you, Joshua," she said, sailing in. She was a little disappointed that she hadn't been allowed to put her card on the tray. In Charleston, young ladies had their own calling cards made when they reached sixteen. On her previous visit Joshua had borne it in to Mrs. Cooper with a flourish, and Garden felt very grown-up. Still, it was nice to be remembered and welcomed by Joshua.

Elizabeth smiled at Garden and motioned her into the room. She introduced her to the handful of people there. "Sit here, Miss

203

Tradd," said one of the gentlemen, pulling up a chair next to his. Garden obeyed, awestruck. She knew the gentleman by sight. He had spoken to the girls at Ashley Hall about the Poetry Society and its magazine, and he had read them some of his poetry. His name was DuBose Heyward.

Garden sipped her tea and helped herself generously from the plates of little sandwiches and cookies passed by a uniformed maid. She listened to the easy, amused conversation of the adults, impressed by how comfortable they all were with Mr. Heyward, a real poet whom Miss McBee had introduced as "an important writer."

Later, her Aunt Elizabeth said, "DuBose is a delightful young man, and I believe he is a fine poet. I don't have any real ear for poetry myself, so I can't say. I do have an ear for people, though, and he never strikes a false note. You'll have to learn, Garden, not to be impressed or influenced by labels. It's the person that counts, not whether he's famous or important in the world's opinion."

"Yes, ma'am," said Garden. But she was still impressed. And she was impressed that her great-aunt was on such familiar terms with "an important writer." She was a little afraid to ask if she could bring a friend to call. But she had promised. And she was fiercely loyal to Wentworth.

Elizabeth agreed at once. "By all means," she said. "I'd be happy to meet your best friend." She chuckled. "I don't suppose this could be the same Wentworth Wragg that Rebecca teases her brother about?"

Garden admitted that Wentworth thought a lot of Maine. "Well, Lord knows," Elizabeth said, "that boy's head doesn't need to swell any bigger than it is already, but Wentworth has my blessing if she wants to join the crowd of girls after him. Even though he is my grandson, I think he's the most attractive bachelor in Charleston. Do you know him, Garden?"

"I met him at the ball, that's all."

"I think you'd like him. I'll tell him to be here next week. Mind you, I can't promise he will be. Once in a great while, he actually does some work."

Garden stopped in at Wentworth's on her way home to report the success of her mission.

Wentworth screamed and hugged her. "Oh, I'm going to die, I can't wait a whole week." She twirled around the room and fell onto a sofa in a mock faint. "Wait till you meet him, Garden. He's the most wonderful man in the whole world."

40

Maine Wilson was twenty-four on February 15, 1922. He did not relish his grandmother's telling him, on his birthday, that she expected him to appear for tea on the following Wednesday and to be attentive to two girls who were not even "out" yet. But Elizabeth had just given him a handsome bank check and some pearl studs, and he did, in fact, love and admire his grandmother very much. On Wednesday he appeared at three on the dot.

Garden and Wentworth arrived shortly after. Joshua took their cards with a solemnity that lifted Garden's heart.

But when they were shown in to the drawing room, her heart quickly sank. Wentworth, her friend Wentworth, the accomplished flirt, giggler, chatterer, was struck dumb in the presence of her hero. It was up to Garden to cover her friend's discomfiture. She could not talk only to her great-aunt and ignore the presence of her cousin. She had to do what was the most difficult thing in the world, after dancing. She had to make conversation with a man.

Maine made it as easy as possible for her. "It's a terrible thing," he said, "to have cousins you don't even know. You have a sister, don't you, Garden? I'd like to meet her, too. Where is she these days?"

Garden's eyes glowed. "You'll be able to soon. I got a letter today. Peggy will be home in just a few weeks. Her husband's in the Army Corps of Engineers, and he's being sent to Texas. He has a month's leave after they get back before he has to be there."

Maine, with some help from his grandmother, asked exactly the right questions about Peggy and her life in France. Garden had only to repeat what Peggy had said in her letters. Peggy's letters were, like Peggy, opinionated and outspoken. What Garden had to say was genuinely interesting. Before she realized what was happening, she was part of a lively three-way conversation.

She remembered to keep her eye on the clock, however, and to observe the proper limit of twenty minutes for a call. Then she corralled Wentworth and nudged her through her leave-taking. After that, she got Wentworth home and stayed with her through her orgy of self-recrimination and tears. "How could I have been such a stick, Garden? I wanted to be so charming and attractive, and I just froze. It was so important to me, it made me panic."

Garden patted Wentworth's sagging shoulder. "I know," she said. "I know just how you felt. I always feel that way." Privately, she could not understand why Wentworth would care so much about Maine. He was all-right-looking, Garden thought. But except for his brown hair and brown eyes, she couldn't see why Wentworth said Valentino and Douglas Fairbanks both looked to her remarkably like Maine Wilson.

"You're a thoroughly satisfactory grandson sometimes, Maine," Elizabeth said after the girls left. "You may switch to the decanter if you like."

Maine grinned and poured himself a drink. "I actually enjoyed myself. Think of a cousin of mine getting mixed up in a riot over the Sacco-Vanzetti thing. Do you think this Peggy was actually carrying a placard?"

"From Garden's account of her, I see no reason to doubt it. She sounds a most unusual young woman. I'm looking forward to meeting her." Elizabeth gestured; Main poured her a glass of sherry. "Now," she said, "I want to talk about Garden. I'm taking an interest in her. I've asked a few people, and I've learned that her abysmal mother is pushing her and that it's made her so nervous that she's a social disaster."

"Come on, Grandmother. Not with that face. The girl's a tearing beauty."

"And doesn't know it, thank God. But that's beside the point. What matters is that ordinarily she's as gauche as the Wragg child was today. Garden probably said more to you this afternoon than she has said altogether to anything in pants in her entire life. I want you to help her, Maine."

"Oh, no, I'm not going to run a kindergarten. There are plenty of girls who are more my type."

"Like your Southern Carmen at the cigar factory, I suppose." Maine's jaw dropped. His grandmother smiled. "I hear things, dear boy; old ladies always know more of what's going on than anyone else. But this old lady doesn't talk, so stop catching flies. Close your mouth and listen to me.

"I'm not asking you to pay court to your little cousin. Just keep an eye on her. Her father and her brother are both dead; you're the closest male relative she's got. She'll be coming out next Season, and I'm afraid that ten months isn't long enough for her to grow up before she's thrown to the lions."

Maine made a fierce growling sound. Elizabeth was not amused. "Okay, Grandmother," he said, "I'll be good. I'll watch out for your lost lamb."

A lost lamb, Mr. Christie thought, looking at Garden. All that beauty so forlorn. For the first time in many years, he wanted to do a portrait. His fingers longed for a brush, found a piece of charcoal. With quick, sure lines he began to sketch Garden's face.

She was sitting on a camp stool, her drawing pad on her lap, one of a row of ten girls with identical stools and pads. They nearly blocked the sidewalk outside St. Michael's. Today's art outing was concentrating on the arabesques of wrought iron that were one of Charleston's wonders. After walking and looking at balconies, fences, stair rails and gates, the students were resting and working at the same time. They were drawing the tall gates that led to the old graveyard.

The gates were a masterpiece of scrolls and swirls, classic urns in tracery above four-part curling shapes like the fans of a peacock's tail. They were extremely difficult to draw. Garden was concentrating with all her might. Her hat had slipped, unnoticed, to the back of her head, exposing the pure curve of her forehead. Her chin was raised when she looked up at the tall gates. The line of her throat made Mr. Christie draw in his breath. He worked quickly, turning page after page for a fresh attempt, trying to capture the mysterious blend of happiness and sorrow, youth and timelessness, determination and helplessness. If he could just catch it, he would have the essence of the eternal myth of Sleeping Beauty, woman submerged in the untouched fragility of girlhood, life stirring but not yet felt under the domination of innocence, the pain and glory of passion only hinted at in the sorrows and joys and loneliness of the unawakened, perfect face and the slender, vulnerable neck.

Mr. Christie cursed silently and turned another page. All his skillfulness was inadequate, but he was so close. Just one more try, then just one more.

Garden erased a mistake. She had erased the same spot so often that she tore a hole in the paper. She sighed a small sigh and turned to a fresh page. This time she'd start with the urns instead of the fans. Maybe they'd be easier.

"Hey, Garden, that's very good." Garden's pencil made a startled jagged line across the page.

"Look what you made me do," she wailed. Then she realized who had spoken over her shoulder. "How do you do, Maine," she said politely.

"Say, I'm sorry, Garden, I really am." Maine ignored the flutter of excitement among the other girls. He was all too accustomed to causing a flutter. Garden introduced him to Mr. Christie; Maine learned that the afternoon outing was near its end and arranged to walk Garden home; he wondered why the art teacher looked as if he would like to kill him, but he dismissed the thought. "How about a detour to the ice-cream parlor?" he suggested to his young cousin.

Maine watched indulgently as Garden dug in to a strawberry sundae. He often wondered where his skinny little sister Rebecca put the quantities of sweets she ate. Garden was exactly like her, except that she wasn't skinny. Garden interrupted her dedicated attack on the sundae only to ask Maine questions about Elizabeth.

He was delighted to talk about his grandmother. "She's really something," he said. "She was a little girl during the War. When Sherman burned Columbia, she managed to get through the flames all by herself; she had gotten lost from her mother. She lived through Reconstruction, too, when people were practically starving to death. But I've never once heard her go on the way people do about how all Yankees are devils. She never talks about any of it. I wouldn't know anything except that I used to ask her to tell me stories."

Garden captured a wayward piece of strawberry and ate it. "Tell some more, please, Maine." Her spoon moved steadily from the trumpet-shaped glass to her mouth.

"The biggest thing about Grandmother, I think, is the business of never complaining. She's had a lot of hard luck. Her husband died very young in an accident, and she had to bring up my mama and her brother all by herself. She actually worked, just like a man. Her brother—not your grandfather but another one—was killed in the earthquake. He had a phosphate company, and he left it to her so that she could provide for her children. She ran it, and she was a good businessman, too. Turned it into one of the biggest in South Carolina. She sold it after her son was killed."

Garden lowered her spoon. "How sad. Poor Aunt Elizabeth. How did he die?"

"He went down on the *Titanic*. He was on his way home after years and years in Europe. I remember it; I was fourteen. Grandmother never broke down in front of Rebecca or me, but her eyes were always red, and she seemed to have trouble hearing what people were saying to her."

Garden thought about her mother. She had lost a husband, too, and a son. And she had never broken down in front of Peggy and her. She must have suffered silently, just like Aunt Elizabeth. Garden resolved to try harder to make up to her mother for her suffering.

"Anyhow," Maine continued, "Grandmother sold the phosphate company. She knew I would go into Papa's firm; there wasn't anybody to keep the company for. And she wanted to go to Europe, to see the places her son had been."

"Where was he?"

"All over, but longest in Paris. He was an artist. By the time Grandmother was ready to go, though, the Great War was starting. She didn't get to Paris until 1919. She looked all over for anybody who knew him. She wanted to buy some of his paintings. But she never found anything."

Tears rolled down Garden's cheeks and fell into the melting ice cream. "I wish I could do something for her."

Maine handed her a handkerchief. "I know just what you mean. It's hard to think of anything, though. She's so independent. Do you know, when she went to Europe, she wouldn't hire a guide. She had a bunch of books, and she spoke a little French. She said that was plenty. And it was, too, for her. Hey, I've got an idea. Why don't you give Grandmother the picture you were drawing today? Sign your name on it. That was her son's name, Tradd."

"I don't think it's the same thing as having one of his pictures, Maine."

"Of course not. But she'll know why you gave it to her, that it was because you wish you could do something. I'll bet she'll like it.

Do you want me to give her it for you?" Garden nodded. "Okay, hand it over when we get to your house. I'll walk you home."

"She's a nice little girl," Maine reported to his grandmother when he delivered the labored drawing of St. Michael's gates.

Elizabeth looked at him carefully. No, he meant exactly what he said; he thought of Garden as a child. Elizabeth was relieved. Maine would do Garden a world of good as a big brother. As a suitor, he had a dangerous reputation of being a heartbreaker.

Margaret Tradd regarded Maine's kindnesses to Garden in quite a different light. He was one of the four bachelors she had in mind for Garden.

41

At the end of March, Peggy came home. It was like a whirlwind entering the house. Three years in France had changed her very little outwardly. She wore her mop of wiry red hair in an untidy bun on the top of her head, her eager pockmarked face was devoid of any powder or other artifice, her clothes were serviceable and bare of ornamentation. She was noisy, enthusiastic, argumentative. And she was very happy.

Margaret had no longing for grandchildren, but she dutifully asked Peggy about hopes for a baby. "Bob and I decided not to have children for at least five more years," Peggy replied. "After all, I'm only twenty. We've got plenty of time."

Margaret commented that children were not a matter of choice.

"Don't be a ninny, Mama, of course they are. At least as far as not having them. Naturally I use a contraceptive."

"Shh," Margaret whispered. "Garden might hear you."

"Good grief, Mama, why shouldn't Garden hear me? Surely she must know about birth control. After all that Margaret Sanger suffered to get the right to publish her papers after the conference last year. If I heard about it in France, every woman in America must know what she's done."

Margaret looked blank. Peggy launched into a polemic about a woman's right to control over her body, striding across the room and waving her arms. It was just like old times. Margaret wondered how she could survive the three weeks until Bob came down from Mullins to take Peggy to Texas. Garden, listening from upstairs, wondered how soon she could ask Peggy to explain to her what she was talking about.

Peggy did not wait to be asked. That night, she sat on the side of Garden's bed and told her about sex. She was matter-of-fact about the act of intercourse, drawing pictures on a page of Garden's school notebook and showing her her genital area in a mirror. She was lyrical about the experience of making love. Her voice and face softened, and her blue eyes deepened in color. "It's wonderful, Garden," she said, "when a man and a woman love each other."

Then she became brisk Peggy again. "And there's no reason why they should have to worry about unwanted children every time they go to bed. Now this is what a diaphragm looks like . . ." Peggy drew in the notebook again, explaining the process of fertilization and the means of preventing it.

Garden asked her about babies, if you wanted to have one. Peggy drew and talked some more. Garden remembered Reba's swollen abdomen when she was pregnant, and she nodded in agreement until Peggy told her about birth. Then she looked in the mirror again. "I don't believe it," she said.

"Believe it, Garden. I worked as a nurse's aide with the refugees, and I helped deliver babies. It's a miracle what the body does. Everything about it is a miracle. I'm going to have at least six when the time comes."

Garden could barely contain herself until the next morning when she met Wentworth to go to school. "I know what the one thing is," she announced. "I have pictures and everything."

Garden had only one revelation to offer Peggy in exchange for the mysteries Peggy had unveiled. She told her about their Great-aunt Elizabeth. "She never stole anything from Papa at all, but I didn't say so to Mama, and you mustn't either, Peggy. She'd never believe us; Papa told her different."

"Ran a company all alone? I want to meet her," Peggy said.

211

Elizabeth Cooper became her newest enthusiasm. Elizabeth liked Peggy at once, but Peggy's energetic admiration was exhausting. "I've tried to tell her that I never was a feminist, I was just a survivor," Elizabeth told DuBose Heyward. "But she wants to see me as a crusader. She tires me out, visiting every day. The girl has an excellent mind, DuBose. Please let the Poetry Society take her off my hands."

Two days later, Peggy was happily typing for the magazine. A week later, she was badgering shoppers on King Street for contributions to the Society.

When Bob arrived, she was ecstatic. The look on her face when she presented him to Elizabeth almost brought tears to her great-aunt's eyes. "I do wish we didn't have to go to Texas," Peggy told her husband. "I'm having such a marvelous time in Charleston."

Bob nodded. "You'll have a good time in Texas, too, Peggy. There's work to be done everywhere."

"Peggy's Bob is a fine young man," Elizabeth told her friends. "And she's a fine young woman. She aged me at least ten years, but I'm delighted to know her."

Garden missed Peggy when she left. She also missed the stir and excitement that Peggy took away with her. Margaret made things worse by talking to Garden about Peggy; she made comparisons between the two daughters, always in Garden's favor. Pleased as she was to have her mother's approval, Garden hated to hear her speak unfavorably about Peggy. Garden's loyalties were intense, and Margaret was forcing her to choose between her loyalty to Peggy and her loyalty to her mother. She wished fervently that Margaret would talk about something else.

Until Margaret did. The new subject was Maine Wilson. Garden listened, in despair, while her mother crowed about Maine's "attentions" and speculated about his suitability as a husband. Garden knew that her mother was destroying the ease she had felt when she was with Maine.

As it happened, she did not run into Maine in the next month. She was busy at school every day, preparing for exams and rehearsing her role in the Shakespearian play for the commencement ceremonies.

Then school was over. She applauded her friends as they walked up to receive their diplomas from Miss McBee. Next year she, too, would have a long white dress and an armful of long-stemmed red roses. She felt very grown-up.

Two days later, she cradled an arm bouquet of yellow roses and walked in step with Wentworth up the aisle of St. Michael's. They were two of Lucy Anson's ten bridesmaids.

And then it was time to leave for Flat Rock. Garden climbed into the train with the relaxed expectation that this summer would be just the same as all the earlier ones.

But it was not possible. No matter how much Garden tried to hold time still, she was growing up. She was nearing the official recognition of her change of status, her debut into the adult world. Everyone around her seemed to talk of nothing else.

Wentworth and her mother Caroline brought pattern books and fabric swatches with them. So did Margaret Tradd. The rivalry between the mothers was submerged in endless talking and planning about party frocks, ball gowns, gloves, hats, and slippers. Worse, Wentworth was just as interested as they were. She preferred looking at fashion magazines to bicycling with Garden to the drugstore in Hendersonville to sneak looks at *True Story* or *Photoplay*.

"What's wrong with you, Garden?" Wentworth said impatiently. "Don't tell me you don't like pretty clothes."

"What's wrong with *you*? You sound like a mother or something. I thought we were best friends."

"I did too, until you stole Maine Wilson from me."

Garden was aghast at the injustice of Wentworth's accusation. She was also angry. But the isolation of the Lodge and the pattern of intimacy imposed by the summer routine were stronger than Garden's anger or Wentworth's jealousy. After a few days, they were again inseparable. Garden joined in the discussions of fashion, and Wentworth rediscovered the pleasures of bicycling and swimming.

The excitement of the wardrobe plans infected Garden before long. She had never really understood the magnitude of the step from young girl to young lady. Sometime in July she looked at the list Margaret had made. It was very impressive:

> 6 ballgowns
> 1 ballgown—St. Cecilia
> 6 luncheon frocks and hats
> 5 dance dresses
> 2 long gowns for receptions

4 tea frocks and hats
1 evening cloak
1 dress coat (day) and hat
4 pr. dress shoes
12 pr. dancing slippers
1 dz. pr. long white gloves
1 dz. pr. short white gloves
1 fur wrap
6 evening bags
4 day purses
3 dz. embroidered handkerchiefs
1 dz. corset covers
1 dz. envelope chemises
2 dz. bloomers
1 dz. camisoles
6 bandeaus
6 underskirts
6 petticoats
3 day corsets
4 evening corsets
2 dz. white silk hose
1 dz. black silk hose

The Season lasted for twelve days. During that time, there would be four balls given by the debutantes' families, the Bachelors' Ball and the New Year's Eve Ball at the Yacht Club. In addition there were five tea dances, two formal receptions, six luncheons, two teas and five breakfasts following balls. These were given by friends or relatives to honor one or more of the girls who were coming out. When all the frenzy was over, when everyone had had time to catch her breath, came the Saint Cecilia.

"Mama!" Garden shrieked. "Are all the things on this list for me?"

"Of course. My list is much simpler."

"But, Mama, that's a different dress for every single party. I know Wentworth's not going to have that. She was grumbling about only two ball gowns."

"Well, Wentworth is Wentworth, and you are you. You are going to have the most gowns and the most beautiful gowns any girl has ever had. I do wish you had already finished school like the other girls. It's going to take every minute of the day to get ready."

It took every minute of the day and many minutes of the night, beginning the moment they arrived back home on October first.

Garden's schoolwork, in this her final year, was also very demanding.
She was perpetually hurrying, busier than she had ever known it was
possible to be. She had to snatch bites of food while she was being
fitted or while she was reading. The rustle of silks and the shining
fall of satin became part of her restless dreams, in a kaleidoscope of
color and sound and the heavy perfumed scent of the dressmakers'
back-room studios. She was so rushed that she had little time to
think of the purpose of all the preparations. When she did, the
familiar tight nervousness stiffened her limbs and her body. But she
pushed it away. Surely everything would be different now. She was
grown-up. Her new clothes were proof of it.

42

Ashley Hall dismissed the students at noon on the day vacation
began. Garden ran out the door without even putting on her coat and
hat. The Season made no allowances for debutantes who were still in
school. The first party, a tea dance, was that afternoon.

Her mother was waiting for her in a taxicab. No young lady could
ride alone in one, and Zanzie was complaining about being
overworked. "Hurry," said Margaret. She had the door open.

The taxi sped down Rutledge Avenue, honking at intersections.
Nothing could have conveyed Margaret's sense of urgency as effec-
tively as the wild ride. She despised automobiles, constantly deplored the paving of so many of Charleston's streets. To Garden, the
race was exhilarating. Normally the houses passed the windows of
the trolley at a leisurely rate; now they were almost a blur.

Their dinner was ready. Three hours early. Garden ate ravenously;
her mother had put her on a diet, and she was always hungry.
Margaret picked at her food. She was too excited to eat. Her cheeks
were pink, her eyes bright. She gleamed with happiness. In the next
two weeks she would see all her plans, all her dreams, come to
fruition.

"Now for your bath," she said when Garden was done. "Then I have a surprise for you."

"Another one, Mama? You're spoiling me." For weeks Margaret had been producing surprises: a string of pearls, ear boring and pearl bobs, fans, a powder case, perfume, hair combs, ribbons. It was as if every day were Christmas.

The surprise this day was really surprising. It was a man. After her bath, Garden rubbed glycerine and rose water into her skin as her mother had taught her. Then she put on the things laid out in her bedroom: a day corset, lightly boned and laced from just under the breast to the top of the leg; white silk stockings with leaf-shaped clocks over the ankle; an embroidered cotton corset cover with wide lace straps; white cotton bloomers with lace inserts and ruffle; a white batiste underskirt with a wide lace hem. She had never owned anything so delicate. All her underthings had always been plain white muslin. Garden put on her old, scuffed house slippers and plaid wool wrapper, hating to cover her finery, and went looking for her mother. She wanted to thank her. She loved being a debutante.

She must be in the dress room, Garden said to herself. She ran down the stairs humming. The bedroom opposite the drawing room was the repository for all the new clothes Margaret had bought for Garden and herself. Racks from the dressmaker's studio stood along two walls, hung with sheet-draped gowns and dresses. The bed was turned parallel to a third wall, its surface covered with stacks of gloves, hose, handkerchiefs, underthings, treed shoes and tissue-wrapped evening and day bags. All the hats were on chairs placed beside the wall. It was bad luck to put a hat on the bed.

The fourth wall had a cloth-covered table with a mirror hanging above it. Near it was a tall pier glass. When Garden entered the room, she saw that the table was covered with bottles and boxes and jars and an array of combs and brushes. That must be the surprise, she thought. It had been bare when she left for school. She looked around for her mother, but Margaret wasn't there.

Then she heard her voice in the drawing room. "Garden?"

"I'm in here, Mama."

Margaret came across the hall. "Here's the surprise I promised," she said. "This is Mr. Angelo."

Garden ducked behind the pier glass. "Mamma," she cried. "I'm not dressed."

Margaret laughed. "Don't worry. Mr. Angelo is used to ladies in

216

their dressing gowns. He's a hairdresser. I've engaged him for the whole Season to do your hair. Sit down at the table and let's begin."

Garden nodded nervously at the rotund, smiling man behind her mother. He bowed, gestured her to the chair next to the table, and flexed his fingers. He was wearing a smock over his suit. It had pockets all over the front, at least a dozen pockets. They bulged with the implements of his art. Mr. Angelo was only recently arrived in Charleston from Rome. He was reputed to be a near-magician.

He walked all around Garden, looking at her tangle of striped hair, muttering to himself in a Trastevere dialect. Then he made a sudden lunge and grabbed her hair with both hands. Garden looked at her mother, frightened. Margaret was frowning with concentration.

Mr. Angelo kneaded Garden's hair, talking to himself all the time. He separated a lock and pulled it straight up, squinted at it, sniffed it, rolled it between his fingers and dropped it into the mass of hair on her shoulders. It was a scene from grand opera.

"*Si Signora*," he sighed. "Angelo can do it." He took two hairbrushes from the table and began to work. Despite the daily operation with the thinning scissors, Garden's hair was still extremely thick and heavily streaked with red. It hung down her back, absolutely without wave or curl, almost to her waist. It was, Margaret said frequently, hopeless.

Mr. Angelo approached it as if it were a wild animal that he had to tame. He cajoled, stroked, murmured, commanded, all in liquid Italian. Strand by strand, he separated the polished gold from the fiery copper, twisting, pinning, pomading, snipping, turning, weaving. He labored for more than two hours.

Then he stepped back and clapped his hands. "Bravo," he said to himself, applauding his artistry. "*Ecco, signora*," he said to Margaret. He presented the hand mirror to Garden with a flourish and turned her chair so that she was, for the first time, facing the looking glass.

She did not recognize herself. Her hair was a shining mass of molten gold, flowing smoothly away from her face into a gleaming, intricate double Psyche knot that covered the back of her head from the crown to the nape of her neck. There was no visible trace of red.

Margaret's face appeared in the mirror next to Garden's. "I knew it," she said. "I was sure it would work if someone just knew how to do it. There you are, Garden, just as I wanted you to be." She congratulated Mr. Angelo and saw him to the door, reconfirming the schedule for the following day. Garden stared at the stranger in the looking glass.

Margaret returned quickly. "Don't touch anything," she said. "You just sit very still while I finish you up." She cocked her head to one side and looked at the metamorphosis of her daughter for a long, satisfied moment. Then she walked rapidly to the bed and picked up a thin silk scarf.

She held it above Garden's head, released it, watched it settle gently over her hair. "Good," she said, "now close your eyes and take down your wrapper. I'm going to powder your shoulders and neck."

For the next hour Garden obeyed her mother's orders. She closed her eyes, opened them, closed them, moved her arms, her hands, her chin, her mouth. Margaret powdered Garden's skin, buffed it, pinched it, rubbed it, scented it. She darkened her eyelashes, applied glycerine to her eyelids and lips to make them shine, shaped her nails and rubbed them until they were a warm pink.

Then she lifted the silk gently from Garden's head and, like Mr. Angelo, she stepped back to admire her creation. Garden was breathtaking.

Margaret uncovered the dress she had selected for the first party, for Garden's first entrance. It was shell-pink, the color of her nails and her lips. "Stand up," Margaret said. "I'll hold it for you to step in." She settled the dress on her daughter's soft shoulders and fastened the tiny pearl buttons that closed the back. "Let me look at you," she said.

The dress fell fashionably straight from Garden's shoulders to her ankles. Margaret deplored the style, remembering the tight waists of her dresses when she was Garden's age. Still, the dressmaker had done a wonderful job, copying an illustration from *Vogue*. The neck was wide, with a soft cowl that bared Garden's delicate collar bones and the elegant curve from neck to shoulder. The bodice was covered with white lace sewn onto the silk georgette of the dress. The lace ended just below the bust line; it molded the gentle swelling of Garden's breasts. Margaret tied the simple ribbon sash around Garden's waist, loosely, as the styles dictated, but tightly enough to indicate the narrow shape beneath the delicate silk. "Turn," she said.

Garden turned. The lace-edged cape sleeves fluttered on her arms;

they were bare from the elbow. And the skirt swirled around her elegant thin ankles.

Margaret giggled. "You're still in your house slippers."

Garden looked down at her feet. She laughed. It was her first natural action for hours, and it felt good.

Margaret put a pair of white kidskin dancing slippers on the floor near Garden's feet. "Rest your hand on my shoulder and step into them. You must not sit down or you'll wrinkle your dress."

She put pearl dots on Garden's ears and another dab of perfume behind them. "There," she said "you're ready. Your fur cape is in the drawing room with your gloves and your bag. There's a vial of perfume in the bag. Put a drop behind each ear and on each wrist after an hour or so."

They heard Zanzie answering the door knocker. Margaret dropped her voice to a whisper. "Who's calling for you? Alex Wentworth, isn't it?"

"Yes," Garden whispered.

"Well, you watch the clock over there next to the window. Keep him waiting for exactly fourteen minutes. I'll talk to him in the drawing room." She chose a scarf of weightless white silk from the selection on the bed. "I'll tuck this in your bag," she whispered. "If he has an open car, be sure you cover your head. There he is. I have to go. Remember, fourteen minutes exactly. And don't sit down."

Alex Wentworth goggled when Garden entered the drawing room. He presented her with a bouquet of Pink Perfection camellias. When Garden smiled, he swallowed audibly. Margaret's face was impassive. She handed him the light squirrel cape and watched him settle it on Garden's scented shoulders. A sheen of perspiration appeared on his forehead. Margaret gave Garden her gloves and bag. "Have a wonderful time," she said. "I know you will."

When the street door closed behind them, Margaret slipped off her shoes and sank onto the sofa. Pink Perfection, she thought. How perfect. She was tired, but she didn't mind all the effort. It was worth it. She remembered the look on the Wentworth boy's face and chuckled. Oh, yes, it was definitely worth it. Garden was going to be the belle of the century.

43

The tea dance was being given in honor of Marion Leslie by her grandmother. She had opened the ballroom on the third floor of her big house on South Battery and taken down the sign that usually hung on the iron gate. "Guests" the sign read. The Leslies had managed to keep their handsome house in the family ever since the Civil War by renting out the extra bedrooms to transients.

Garden left her wrap in the ground-floor sitting room set aside for ladies' cloaks and began to mount the stairs. Halfway to the second floor she had to draw to one side to avoid being knocked down by two young men who were making a hurried, laughing exit.

The men could almost have been twins. Both were dark-haired and deeply tanned, nearly six feet in height and chunky in build. They had the particular gloss that only a great deal of money can produce. Their evening clothes were made of exceptionally fine materials, with the easy, flawless fit of custom tailoring. Their white shirts and ties were blindingly white, their patent dancing pumps gleaming. They moved with the grace of athletes and the assurance of those to whom the world had never denied anything.

Outside on the sidewalk, they leaned against the Leslies' fence and laughed uproariously. "By God," said one, "when you said we were going to check out the natives, I didn't know how serious you were. I feel like an anthropologist. No, more like a paleontologist. What a bunch of fossils."

"You said it. And the place as dry as the Sahara. But did you see the peach on the stairs? Maybe we left too soon, Mark."

"The candy-coated blonde? I didn't get a good look, just the pinkness of it all."

"She had a face like Helen of Troy. Oh, hell, come on. I heard there were some great speaks near the docks."

* * *

"What time is it, Tommy?"

Tommy Hazlehurst consulted his watch. "Eight-thirty."

"There's something I have to do. Will you excuse me for a minute?"

"Sure, Garden. I'll wait for you at the top of the stairs."

Garden walked down the two long flights of stairs as she had been taught at Ashley Hall, head erect, not looking at her feet, not touching the banister. In the cloakroom, she found her evening bag and applied perfume, as her mother had instructed. Then, disobeying her mother's orders, she sat down.

"Can I get you anything, Miss Garden?" Marion's old dah was the attendant for the evening.

"No thank you, Susie. I just need a little rest for a minute."

Susie clucked and chuckled. "You girls all going wear yourselves out with all that dancing."

Garden tried to smile. It's all the same, she was thinking. Nothing's changed. I still can't dance. I still can't talk. Mama has fixed up my outside, but inside I'm no different. I wish I could die.

She straightened her shoulders. The fragile butterfly sleeves fluttered. "Nice to see you, Susie," she said. Then she climbed the stairs, her head high, not looking at her feet or touching the banister. She would dance with Tommy, listen to him worry about Wentworth's indifference to him. No one would cut in, Garden knew. She had been tried and found wanting. It only took a little while for every man there to cut in and dance with every girl. They did not cut in a second time on Garden's partner.

Alex Wentworth would dance the last dance with her and take her home. Until then, either she allowed Tommy to be stuck or she sat and talked to the chaperones while she watched the other girls flirting with the succession of men who whirled them around the floor.

The following day, Margaret was admiring Mr. Angelo's deft manipulation of Garden's hair when the phone rang in the drawing room. "Excuse me," she said. "I'll just be a minute."

She was gone considerably longer. When she returned, Mr. Angelo was finished. Preparing Garden for a luncheon was easy. Her hat would cover everything except the two blond poufs Mr. Angelo had created on her cheeks.

"What time this evening, *signora*?"

"Let's see." Margaret consulted the invitations pinned to the mantel. "Reception, then ball. You'd better be here by five, Mr. Angelo. I'll be going to these parties, too, and I'll want you to arrange my hair."

As soon as the hairdresser left, Margaret shook her finger at Garden. "You are a naughty girl," she said. Garden was stricken. Then she saw that her mother was smiling.

"Why is that, Mama?"

"You didn't tell me who was at the dance. It's the biggest news in town, and I must be the last person to hear it."

Garden shook her head. "I don't know who you're talking about."

"Don't move your head like that, Garden. You'll mess up your hair.

"I mean the Principessa's son, of course. He just got to town yesterday and called Andrew Anson for some money. Of course, Edith got him put on the list right away. What's he like, Garden? Why didn't you mention him?"

"I don't remember him."

"Well, Annie did say that he left early. I can't believe you wouldn't have noticed him. Or that he wouldn't have noticed you. It's not important, really. He's on the list. He'll be around. It will be fun for you to add him to your beaux; the other girls' mothers will gnash their teeth. But, after all, he's not from Charleston. He's not for you. You'll have your pick, and you'll pick Bill Lawrence or Rhett Campbell or Maine Wilson or Ashby Radcliffe. They are the ones who count."

Garden stared at her mother. This was the first she had heard of Margaret's grandiose plan. The enormity of Margaret's ambition left Garden speechless.

Margaret did not notice Garden's silence. She was occupied with a new thought. Schuyler, she thought, Schuyler Harris. It even sounds rich. If his mother is a princess, does that make him a prince, or is it only if his father's a prince?

Since the days at Miss Ellis's dancing school, Garden had dreaded the moment when her mother would learn that she was not successful, not popular like the other girls. That evening the moment arrived. During the reception for Alice Mikell, Margaret edged up to her daughter and hissed in her ear, "Say something. Don't just stand there. Make an effort."

At the ball that followed, Margaret glared at Garden even while she smiled and talked to the other mothers.

That night she scourged Garden with every verbal whip at her command. There were many. Her sacrifices for Garden, her attention to Garden, the luxuries she had provided, Garden's education, her clothes, the vacations in Flat Rock, the expensive dancing school, the incredible cost of Mr. Angelo's services.

"Not one single thought have I had," Margaret shouted, "that wasn't for you, Garden Tradd. Not one little second have I given to thinking about me or my happiness. Everything has been for you. How can you betray me like this?" She threw herself on the rug and wept loudly.

Garden's beautiful golden head drooped. She had no answer. Her mother had been angry before, she had wept before. But never like this. Never in the midst of all the evidence of her goodness, surrounded by the racks of clothes, the profusion of elegant accessories.

"I can't help it, Mama," Garden said. Her usually warm, low voice had no color, no resonance. It was as wooden as her heart. "I do the best I can, but it's no use. It never will be."

On December twenty-third, Elizabeth Cooper gave a tea dance for Garden, as she had done for her godchild Lucy Anson the year before, and as she would do for her granddaughter Rebecca Wilson the following year. Joshua got some cousins to come move the furniture and roll up the carpets.

Elizabeth left Joshua in charge. She wanted to have a rest before she dressed. Spending three hours with that tedious woman, her label for Margaret, would be exhausting. Perhaps it wouldn't be three hours. It was all arranged that Garden was to leave early, at seven. People with any decency wouldn't stay after the guest of honor was gone. What was she thinking? That tedious woman hardly fit into the category of people with decency. Elizabeth had found it necessary to be very severe with her about Garden's commitment to the choir rehearsal. The girl was singing a solo at the Christmas Eve service. Elizabeth was sure that Margaret had no respect for Christmas, although she went to church every Sunday. Not only tedious, but a hypocrite, too. Elizabeth snorted into her pillow, then fell into a deep, short sleep.

*   *   *

223

"I'm going to sneak out now, Aunt Elizabeth. Thank you for the lovely party." Garden kissed her great-aunt's cheek. The party had certainly been the best so far. As guest of honor, she profited from the social rule that decreed that she never be left unattended or unamused. Her mother must have been satisfied for once. Garden had had at least four cut-ins per dance.

She waved goodbye to her mother, smiled at Wentworth, dancing with Maine, and dashed for the door. Joshua was posted there, ready with her cape.

Before he could open the door for her, someone pushed it from the other side. Schuyler Harris walked in. He handed Joshua his coat and cane without looking at him. His eyes were on Garden.

"Hello," he said. "Are you leaving just as I arrive? Last time I saw you, it was exactly the reverse. Please don't go. I only came to meet you."

Garden smiled automatically. One always smiled at arriving guests, no matter what foolishness they talked. "May I introduce myself?" he said. "I'm Sky Harris."

Garden was reaching her hand for her cape when she suddenly realized who the stranger was. She stopped, hand outstretched. "Oh, I know who you are. You live at the Barony. I wish I could talk to you, I have so many questions. But I really have to go. I'm afraid I'll be late."

Sky took her hand in his. "Won't he wait for you? I would."

Garden had a mental picture of the choir director, an irascible former colonel with an egg-bald head. She laughed. "I'm going to choir practice," she said. She pulled her hand away, took her cape from Joshua and put it around her shoulders before Sky could help her. "I really am sorry. Goodbye, Mr. Harris."

Sky followed her onto the piazza. "Can I go with you?"

Garden heard St. Michael's bells ringing the hour. "No," she said. She was late, and this man was making her later. She picked up her skirts and started to run.

"Will you be at the ball?" Sky yelled.

"Yes," Garden answered. Her feet moved faster.

Schuyler Harris stood in front of the Tradd house, one foot on the doorstep, watching the most beautiful girl he had ever seen in his life. "My God," he said, laughing at himself. "I feel like I'm in the third act of Cinderella. Why didn't she leave a slipper behind?" His friend Mark had ragged him unmercifully when he said he was driving into Charleston. But he had to do it; he had to see if the girl was as exquisite as he had thought after that brief glimpse of her on the stairs. Well, he had seen. She was even more lovely than he remembered. And her voice. Not shrill and grating like most young women's. Sky laughed again. He was quite sure that he knew no girl who would leave a party to go to choir practice.

Well, he guessed he'd have to go to the damn ball. Mark would never let him live it down.

44

"Do you want Mr. Angelo to fix your hair first, Mama?" Garden was flushed from her bath, ready to be dressed. She was also very hungry; she had gotten home from practice and gone immediately to bathe.

"I'm not going to the ball," said Margaret. "I cannot bear to see you destroying all my hopes."

Garden sat down at the dressing table. She knew that her hair would take forever. Mr. Angelo outdid himself readying her for a ball. No tea-dance Psyche knots. He created a crown of coils and braids with ribbons and flowers wound through them. Garden submitted herself to the long process.

It was almost eleven before her mother announced that she was finished. Maine was her escort; he had been reading one of Peggy's books in the library for an hour.

Garden's gown was blue velvet, a blue so deep that it was almost black. It made her white skin look even paler, and it cast blue shadows in the hollows under her collar bones, in the separation between her high white breasts, which showed ever so slightly above the square-cut high décolletage. Her blue eyes looked almost as dark as the velvet. Under them, bluish shadows of fatigue showed through her powder.

"You look beautiful, Garden," Maine said when she finally

225

appeared in the doorway. It was the first time anyone had ever told her she was beautiful. She did not believe him. There had been too many years' reminders about her horrible freckled skin and hideous hair.

"Thank you, Maine." Garden knew that she should say he looked handsome, and she believed he did. But the words stuck in her throat. This wasn't her friend and cousin Maine. This was one of the most eligible bachelors that her mother wanted her to enchant.

Maine offered her a bouquet of red roses. "I hope you'll carry these."

Garden looked at him. He wasn't mocking her, she was sure. He didn't know. It was the custom in Charleston for admirers to send bouquets to a debutante in the morning. She could choose from among them, or she could accept the offering of her escort. Messages and manipulations could be achieved by her choice. Everyone looked to see what she was carrying when she arrived at that evening's ball.

Garden had received no bouquets at all. "They're lovely," she said to Maine. "Thank you."

The receiving line was beginning to dissolve when Garden and Maine arrived. The ball had started at ten. Garden hurried; she knew that they were shockingly late. She shook the hands of the parents, the debutante, her brothers, her sister, murmuring apologies to each one. The last hand she shook did not let hers go. "You should be sorry to be late," said Sky Harris. "I've been waiting for you forever."

Garden looked back at the line. "Oh, I'm no relation," said Sky. "I just added myself to the end of the line when I saw you coming. I didn't want anyone else to get the first dance." He put his arm around her waist and spun her into the midst of the dancing couples. Garden was too startled to object. Or to freeze.

Almost at once, Maine cut in. "I am this lady's escort," he said. "The first dance is mine."

He took Garden's hand from Sky's clasp and put his hand on her waist. "Who is that character, Garden?" Maine danced a step. Garden felt her old trouble come over her. She couldn't follow his step.

But then a white-gloved finger tapped Maine's shoulder. "May I?" said Sky's friend Mark. Maine stepped back and bowed. Mark took Garden in his arms, turned a half turn and delivered her to Sky.

226

He held her hand and laughed at her. "You might as well give up," he said. "I brought Mark with me to take you back from anyone who cuts in on us. I intend to keep you to myself all night."

Garden did not know what to say or do. She felt herself blushing; it made her blush all the more. Sky watched the color in her cheeks with fascination. The girls he knew did not blush.

Couples brushed past them. They were an obstruction, standing still in the middle of the floor. "People are looking at us," Garden said.

"Let them look . . . Oh, all right, Garden. We'll dance. You see, I know your name. I asked all about you. I know I'm living in your house. It's a super house. Do you miss it?" He slid his hand down her back to her waist and drew her to him.

Garden did not even know she was dancing. She wanted to know all about the Barony. Was the Settlement still there? Sam Ruggs's store? The attic with its treasures? The walled garden? The strawberry thicket? The big fig tree with the wide limb that made such a good seat?

Before Sky could answer, Tommy Hazlehurst cut in. Then Mark again, with the half-turn into Sky's outstretched arms. Garden felt dizzy. "Now, about the plantation," said Sky.

Maine cut in. Then Mark. Garden was in Sky's arms again. He walked her to the edge of the floor. "This isn't working out," he said. "We'll have to sit out if we're going to get acquainted."

"May I have this dance, Garden?" Ashby Radcliffe bowed and held out his hand. The Charleston men did not like a rich Yankee and his friend moving in and playing tricks on them. Without having to say a word, all Maine's friends were ready to protect his lady and his honor. Garden had been assigned to him for the ball, not to this outsider.

Mark headed for Ashby and Garden to cut in, but Maine got there first. He took Garden to a chair. "This spectacle has got to stop, Garden," he said.

"I can't help it, Maine. What should I do?" Garden didn't know whether to laugh or cry. The one time in her life she was rushed, and it was a disaster.

"Who are these fellows? Maybe we should throw them out."

"No, Maine, don't do that. Mr. Harris is the son of the lady at the Barony. He's trying to tell me what it's like now, but people keep cutting in. Why don't you just let me talk to him for a while?"

"Nobody's going to leave you alone with him now, Garden. It's gone too far. I'm afraid things might get really ugly. Now listen, you go powder your nose. I'll talk to your Yankee friend, make him see reason. He can call on you sometime and tell you all about the Barony."

Garden got up. She started to walk to the door. Sky started after her, but Maine intercepted him. She heard him introducing himself in a cold, overly polite voice. Garden forced herself to walk slowly, normally.

The ball was being held in the South Carolina Hall, scene of her weekly misery at dancing school. Garden walked down the short flight of steps to the broad landing and turned into the cloakroom. She remembered all the times she had come here to flee from unhappiness because no one wanted to dance with her. Now she had to run because someone wanted to dance with her too much. She started to laugh, a dangerous, shaky laugh at the edge of hysterics.

"Garden!" It was Wentworth. "What's going on? I've never seen anything like it. Is Maine going to whip him or what? What's he saying to you? Is it dirty?"

Garden tried to explain, but Wentworth wouldn't listen. "Pooh on the plantation. This Sky person has evil designs on you. He wants *one thing*, and Maine's going to save you from him. Maybe they'll fight a duel. It's the most exciting thing I ever heard of."

"Oh, Wentworth, don't be such a goose. It'll all die down. He'll never call on me, I'll never find out if Reba and Matthew and their children are all right or anything."

"Garden, you're such a spoilsport. Come on, let's go back up. I'll walk with you; I want to hear what they say."

Maine had a white line around his compressed lips. He had seldom been so angry in his entire life. He was sure that Sky Harris and his friend were laughing at him, at all of them. But he was Garden's escort and her only male relative. However he might feel about what he had to do, he must protect her from scandal.

Garden could not keep herself from looking over Maine's shoulder. "They've gone," said Maine.

"Oh," said Garden. "I see."

Wentworth sighed her disappointment.

"No, you don't see," said Maine. "The only way they'd agree to leave was if I gave my word to a compromise. We'll stay at the ball

228

for another half hour or so, until the talk dies down. Then we'll leave. I'm going to take you out to the Barony."

"In the middle of the night?"

"You started this, Garden, all this business about how much you miss the plantation, what's it like now and all. If I didn't take you, he was going to. It wouldn't do. There's no chaperone there. His mother isn't with him. Better go tonight than to have him knocking at your door tomorrow or staying here and causing more trouble."

"I'm sorry, Maine."

Maine's face softened. She was just a kid, after all. How could she know anything about men like Harris? "We'll have to find a lady to go with us. Do you want to call your mother?"

"I'll go." Wentworth stepped to Garden's side. "Garden's my best friend."

Maine looked patient. "Wentworth, you have an escort. Maybe he doesn't want to leave early."

"Come on, Maine. I'm with Billy Fisher, and he's drunk as a billy goat. You know how he is. You might be saving my life if you take me with you."

"Is Billy driving his car?"

"Yes, he is. I'll probably end up wrapped around a tree. Garden, tell him. Make Maine let me go with you."

Garden looked at Wentworth's imploring eyes. Please, she was saying, please let me ride in Maine's car, ride with Maine, be with Maine. It's my big chance.

"Wentworth's my best friend, Maine."

Maine's lips whitened again. How did it happen that he became the keeper for the entire kindergarten class? "All right," he said. "Both of you, act natural. I'll talk to Bill when it's time to go." He signaled a friend with his eyes. The man came over and danced away with Wentworth. Maine held out his arm to Garden, to escort her onto the floor.

Garden stumbled. Oh, Lord, thought Maine, I forgot that she can't dance. This is the longest night in history.

Mark and Sky were racing across the Ashley River Bridge in Sky's Stutz Bearcat. "Why in God's name did you do such a dumb thing?" demanded Mark.

Sky flipped his cigarette into the river. "I just didn't like Robert E. Lee pushing me around." He imitated Maine's accent: " 'Suh, heah in Chawstun we show moah respeck foah owah layadies.' I wanted to see him dance to my tune.''

"But why make such a fuss in the first place? I grant you, the little deb is gorgeous, but she's like Ivory soap, Sky. For God's sake, she was wearing a corset. Underneath it, she's probably just as stiff as she is in it.''

Sky threw his head back and shouted with laughter. "You don't know the half of it, buddy. She sings in the church choir!''

Mark laughed until he choked.

45

Garden sat in a tapestry-covered wing chair, her head high and her back straight. She smiled unconvincingly at Wentworth. "My sister Peggy used to spend hours and hours in this room, reading every book on the shelves,'' she said. Her voice was flat, but at least it was under control. What she felt like doing was screaming, weeping, anything but making conversation. She had never been so unhappy.

The Barony had shocked her. Everything looked false, unreal. The electric lanterns at the front gates, the big red-and-gold coat of arms on the gates, the bright white-painted houses where the Settlement used to be, the paved drive and the immaculately maintained, richly furnished, brightly lit house. This wasn't the Barony. Even after her mother sold it, Garden always felt that her home was there. Someone else might live in it, but it was still in her heart. Now it was gone, there was no more home.

Instead there was this: she and Wentworth sitting in two big chairs on one side of the library while everyone else was on the opposite side, clustered around the bar. They were all drinking and laughing. Probably laughing at us, Garden thought. Even Maine. He had changed the minute he met the girls. Sky hadn't said that he had a girlfriend with him, and that Mark had one too. Why had they come to the ball, if they had girls with them? It was obvious why they hadn't brought the girls to the ball. They wore paint on their faces, and they smoked, and Garden suspected that they did not have anything on under their dresses except camiknickers. They were loud, too, and they made jokes she didn't understand and rolled their eyes.

Maine understood the jokes all right. He looked embarrassed at first, but then one of the girls actually sat on his lap and whispered something in his ear, and they had been whispering to each other ever since.

She and Wentworth had tried not to notice. They had talked to Sky and Mark and the other girl, the one named Bunny. Mitzi was the one after Maine. They had funny names, Wentworth remarked when she and Garden went to the ladies' room. That was after they had been talking for what seemed an eternity.

When they came back, everyone was around the bar. "What are we going to do?" said Wentworth.

"We'll have to wait for Maine to drive us home. We'll just sit and talk to each other."

"Garden," Maine called, "you and Wentworth come on over here. We're opening champagne."

Wentworth stood up. "Sit down," Garden said. "We don't want to get mixed up in *that*." Mitzi and Bunny were draped across Maine and Mark. Mark had his hand on Bunny's thigh. Sky was laughing and pouring champagne. To well-brought-up young ladies, it was a picture of everything that was sinful.

"Maine said for me to come, Garden. Maybe he means it. Maybe this is my chance." Wentworth tossed her head and pretended to smile. "I just love champagne," she cried, running across the room.

I'm going to cry, Garden thought, I can't hold it back any longer. I'm going to cry, and if they see me I'll die from shame. She jumped up and ran from the room, from the house.

"Garden!" Maine pushed Mitzi away and ran after his cousin. He stopped on the drive, peering into the black night beyond the light from the house.

Sky came up behind him. "Don't worry, Wilson. She knows this place like the back of her hand. She's probably in the garden, or up that fig tree she kept talking about. She'll be back soon." It couldn't be soon enough for him. He was bored with his little joke, bored

231

with these Charleston stiffs, most of all bored with Garden Tradd. It was a crime to put a face like that on a wooden doll. Because that's what she was. A prissy, lifeless wooden doll. There was no life to her. The sooner they all left, the better. He didn't much like Mitzi making so much of old Robert E. Lee here, either. He hadn't brought her all the way from New York to let some local hero get his hands up her dress.

"Come on, Wilson," said Sky. "The champagne's going flat."

Garden ran by instinct along the drive. Its hard surface was strange to her feet; so were her slippers. She had run this way every day of every summer for most of her childhood, but her feet had been bare and the rutted earth soft beneath them.

The Settlement dogs barked when she neared the first house. Garden slowed to a walk. They wouldn't bite someone walking. Then she realized that these were not the dogs that she knew, that knew her. She had been away for four years. She was a stranger. She began to cry.

The cabins were gone. In their place were four houses. Garden stood on the drive, sobbing. She did not know the houses, she didn't know who lived in them. Maybe all her friends were gone. Maine had deserted her, and Wentworth. If Reba was gone, and Matthew, and Chloe, Herklis, Juno, all of them gone, she would have nobody to care, nobody to help her.

A light went on in one of the houses, and a window was raised. "Who's that out there?"

"Matthew! Matthew, it's Garden. Oh, Matthew, I'm so happy to hear you. Let me in. Open the door. Reba, Reba, it's Garden. I need you."

"You all right now, honey?"

Garden nodded. The paroxysm of tears was over, and the hiccuping account of her woes that followed it. Reba had held her, stroked her shoulders and back, moaned soft sympathy. Garden felt empty and relieved.

Reba tapped Garden's wrist with a bony finger. "Now you listen to Reba, child. Ain't nobody never found no good in running away. People do you dirt, you stand there and take it. You laugh in they face. Then they stop. You run, they run after, throwing more dirt on you. You always was Reba's brave little girl. I never see you run away. And I ain't ready to see that now. You hear me?"

Garden nodded.

Reba pulled her to her feet. She smoothed her gown, marveling at the soft richness of the velvet. "Too pretty," she crooned, "my grown-up girl look too pretty." She clucked in dismay over the soiled hem and Garden's battered slippers. "Ain't I done tell you a million times you gots to take care of thing? Here." She unfastened Garden's belt and rearranged it, buckling it around her hips with folds of skirt over it so that the hem was raised above Garden's ankles. "We just heist this some, keep hem clean."

She wrapped her strong arms around Garden and held her close for a moment. "Now, you go," she said when she released her. "And you don't pay no never mind to them people. Ain't this your plantation? What do them trash Yankee folks know about how to do on Ashley Barony? Ain't for you to cry, honey. You gets mad."

Garden stiffened her jaw. Reba clapped her hands. "That's Reba's girl now."

Garden heard the sound of the gramophone when she entered the house. "In the morning/in the evening/Ain't we got fun?" Through the music she heard the voices of Bunny and Mitzi. "Come on, Wentworth. You can do better than that. Do the Black Bottom, not the waltz."

She went into the library unnoticed. Mark was holding Wentworth around the waist, shaking her and laughing, his legs and his body against hers. Wentworth was trying to follow his steps but failing miserably. She was pale; she had a desperate, fixed smile.

"Stop," Garden said loudly. She would not let them torture her friend. Everyone looked at her. "If you're going to come down here and dance, you should learn to dance the way we do in Charleston." She threw her arms wide and moved her feet in the wild, primitive motions of the Settlement blacks. "There," she shouted, to Reba, to Little Mose, to Sarah, to Cuffee, to Maum' Pansy. The beat of the music became her pulse, and she surrendered to it, a child again, free of constrictions, free to be happy. She shook her head from side to side as she danced, defying the careful postures of deportment classes and the artifices of Mr. Angelo and her mother. Ribbons, combs, flowers, hairpins fell to the floor around her to be trampled by her twisting, flying feet. Her hair tumbled over her shoulders and down her back, springing free into an unruly torrent of gold streaked with flame. She was primitive, pagan, a cyclone of unleashed movement and passion. "In the meantime/and between time . . ." Garden was a dervish, unrestrained, a fury of black silk legs and ivory white arms and whipping, burning hair.

The record ended, in a clicking scratch, scratch, scratch. Garden lowered her arms, her feet stopped and she stood, panting. Then her two hands pushed the hair back from her forehead into the fire-striped mane framing her pale face. Splotches of crimson stained her cheeks, and her blue eyes blazed defiantly.

"My God," breathed Maine.

Sky Harris strode across the litter of ribbons and crushed flowers. "Magnificent," he said. He caught her to him and kissed her, pressing his mouth painfully against hers, trying to open her lips.

Garden twisted, broke his embrace. She pulled her arm back, swung it with all her strength. The slap sounded like a pistol shot and sent Sky staggering, the mark of her hand on his cheek.

"Maine," Garden commanded, "take us home."

46

"Wake up, Garden. It's almost eleven o'clock." Margaret's cheerful voice penetrated the delicious deep sleep Garden was enjoying. It was the best sleep she had had in weeks. She opened her eyes reluctantly. "Here, dear, put this on. It's a birthday present." Margaret was holding up a peignoir, a delight of fine cotton and heavy cotton lace with wide blue satin ribbon ties. "That old wrapper can go in the trash." Margaret was beaming, a different woman from the dour creature of the evening before. "Come on," she urged, "wash your face and come downstairs. Zanzie's getting your breakfast. No diets on birthdays. She's fixing shrimp and hominy and buttermilk biscuits."

Garden climbed out of bed quickly. She brushed her hair and tied

234

it back with a ribbon, then gave her face and teeth a quick scrub. I'm going to have a bowl of butter, she decided. She could hear her mother downstairs chatting gaily on the telephone. What a nice birthday present, having her mother in a good mood. So, too, was the peignoir. It had yards and yards of the silky cotton gathered into a lace yoke. When Garden put it on, it billowed around her like a cloud. Her house slippers were too awful, she thought, to wear with such a robe. Besides, it was her birthday. She scampered down the stairs barefoot, the full back of the peignoir floating up the stairs behind her.

Margaret intercepted her in the hall outside the drawing room. "Come see." She pulled Garden by the hand into the sun-filled room. There were flowers everywhere, vases of roses on every table, in every color, and open boxes with green florist paper cradling bouquets of roses, of camellias, of violets.

"Look," said Margaret, "this one is from Maine, this from Tommy, this from Ashby, this . . . this . . . this." There were nine in all, tokens of the possessiveness of Charleston's bachelors, reminders that a young lady need not look outside to strangers. Garden did not wonder about the motives. The bouquets were there, that was enough. She felt, for the first time, the intoxication of success, the heady thrill of being a belle. She pirouetted around the room, touching the flowers with hesitant, gentle fingers, inhaling their scent.

"Oh, Mama, it's wonderful."

"There are more down in the library and the dining room. All those roses. I declare, there can't be a rose left in South Carolina. There were sixteen boxes full. The prince sent them."

What prince? Garden started to say. Then she understood who her mother meant. Her fingers moved involuntarily to her lips, remembering, and she felt a strange chill, then a stranger warmth.

"Come on," Margaret said, "your breakfast will get cold. There are presents on the table." She was exceedingly pleased with her daughter.

Garden gobbled a big plateful of steaming white hominy with yellow swirls of butter and delicate pink shrimp yellowed by the butter in which they had been sautéed. While she ate, she read the long letter Peggy had sent with her present, a book on pioneer women.

"Peggy says she and Bob are working weekends on an Indian reservation," said Garden. "They're happy as clams." She passed the letter to her mother and buttered the pile of biscuits Zanzie brought in.

"Now," she said happily, looking at the brightly wrapped boxes in front of her. She opened the one from Wentworth first. "Look, Mama, what a pretty bottle. It's toilet water." She removed the stopper and sniffed, then gave it to Margaret for her approval.

There was a knock at the door. "More flowers, I'll bet," said Margaret. Zanzie puffed theatrically as she trudged through the dining room.

"Oooh, how pretty," said Garden. "Look, Mama, from Aunt Elizabeth. It's a locket. Does it have a picture, do you think?" She felt along the edge of the chased gold oval for an opening.

"You can't go in there," they heard Zanzie say. Schuyler Harris rushed into the room. He stopped inside the door, looking at Garden with her long, pagan hair down over the virginal white peignoir.

Before she or Margaret could speak, he strode to Garden's side and knelt by her chair. "These made me think of you," he said; he opened his cupped hands and dropped three sprays of flowers into her lap. They were japonicas the size of saucers, with nearly transparent white petals streaked with crimson. They were fragile, perfect, beautiful and bold.

Garden gazed at her lapful of flowers. Her heart felt squeezed. "Oh, Sky," she whispered, "thank you."

"Young man," said Margaret sternly. Sky rose to his feet and bowed.

"Please forgive me, Mrs. Tradd. I'm in love, and it makes me impetuous. My name is Schuyler Harris." He lifted Margaret's hand from the table, bowed again and kissed it. "Am I forgiven?" He smiled winningly at Margaret.

"Well, I don't know . . . I never heard of such a thing . . . not ready to entertain . . ."

"Good," Sky said. "May I have one of those biscuits?" He pulled out the chair at Garden's right and sat down. "Thank you, my angel. Do you happen to have any coffee?"

"You can have my milk."

"Milk. I might have guessed. No, my darling, I'm not a milk drinker. It suits you, you drink it." His eyes feasted on the contrasts of Garden, her milk-drinking innocence and the maenad dancing of the night before, her little-girl lace and blue ribbons tangled with her vital, provocative hair.

She blushed and looked away. Her hand trembled as she reached across him to the remaining gift.

"What's this? You can't open Christmas presents the day before. Santa Claus will give you a black mark in his book."

Garden made a triumphant face. "Smarty boots. Today's my birthday. Would you like another biscuit?"

Margaret rang for Zanzie. She knew that she should send Schuyler Harris packing, but his self-assurance had defeated her the moment he walked through the door. The only thing to do, she supposed, was to act as if Garden were properly dressed and Sky Harris were a normal guest. "More biscuits, Zanzie," she said, "and a pot of coffee, please."

"Your birthday," Sky exclaimed. "What a gyp timing for you. But it's fine for me. I brought you a Christmas present. Now it's a birthday present, and I can watch you open it." He took a thin rectangular package from his breast pocket. "Happy birthday, Garden."

Margaret recognized the wrapping. It was from James Allen, the jeweler. It would have to be refused, of course. A young lady could accept nothing so valuable. But it wouldn't hurt to see what it was before Garden refused it.

The dazzle of the bracelet made her speechless. It was an inch-wide lattice of diamonds with sapphire flowers where the lattice bands crossed.

"Let me put it on you," said Sky. "Give me your hand." Garden looked helplessly at Margaret.

"She cannot accept it, of course, Mr. Harris," Margaret said.

"But it suits Garden, Mrs. Tradd. I want her to have it. We don't have to tell anybody where it came from."

Garden put her hand in his. "I've never seen anything so pretty, Sky, but you know I can't take it. I thank you just the same, though. Just as much as if I could." She was radiant. Sky's clasp tightened on her hand.

"Suppose I dropped it down the chimney tomorrow?"

Garden shook her head, smiling.

"Left it on the doorstep in a basket?"

Garden laughed. "No." She took her hand away and pushed back her chair. "I have to go now."

"Choir practice?"

"How did you know?"

"It figures. When do you sing?"

"Tonight at the midnight service."

"I'll be there."

The midnight service on Christmas Eve was always crowded. Sky wondered whether he should stand in the back. He had not been in church in years, but he recognized the privacy of the old-fashioned box pews. They were for families who owned them, not for strangers. Luckily, Andrew Anson saw him in the crowd and invited him to join them. Sky was seated by the aisle; when the organ signaled the beginning of the processional, the congregation stood. Sky turned to watch for Garden.

She was in the center of the two-by-two procession, on the side nearest Sky. Her head was lifted, her throat vibrating, her face lit with the joy of singing and the majestic music of the anthem. The choir robes were simple white starched surplices over long black robes. They were unornamented, severely beautiful, with an air of the cloister. Garden looked as pure and serene as a nun. She did not see Sky until she was next to the Anson pew. Then she smiled with surprised delight, a smile innocent of guile or artifice, a smile of honest happiness. Sky's heart turned over.

Heaven help me, thought Sky. I think I really am in love. With her freshness and directness, not just her beauty. And with her innocence. I know what lies within, I saw it, the passion and the wildness, but she does not. I've never known anyone like her. There isn't anyone like her.

When Garden sang, Sky recognized the intriguing contrasts of her nature again. Her voice soared clean and rejoicing. "*Adeste fidelis . . .*" And yet it had a low, throbbing quality that hinted at secrets told in husky whispers.

Sky glanced around him at the congregation. They were placidly enjoying the lovely youthful voice. They have no idea what she's like, he thought. I'm the only person who knows.

But he was wrong. Maine Wilson had witnessed the transformation of his little cousin when she danced at the Barony. And he heard the mystery in her voice from his place between his mother and his sister in the Wilson family pew. It thrilled him.

238

47

Christmas Day was a time for family and friends. There were no organized parties. Sky, with permission from Margaret, called on Garden after breakfast. He brought an acceptable gift, candy, but he brought twenty pounds of it. Garden laughed, Margaret was nonplussed, and Zanzie bore it off to the kitchen to begin eating right away.

Sky did not observe the proper limited duration for a call. At three o'clock he was still sitting comfortably in the drawing room, talking easily about his efforts at mountain climbing in the Alps, the Rockies and the Pyrenees. "I'd like to try the Himalayas," he said, "but I'm really not that good at it. And it takes so long to get there, not like Europe."

Margaret could hear a crescendo of pots and pans rattling in the kitchen. In desperation, she invited Sky to have dinner with them.

Margaret and Garden watched with admiration when Sky carved the turkey with the precision of a surgeon. He watched with incredulity while Garden ate everything on her plate: turkey, dressing, rice and gravy, candied sweet potatoes, creamed onions, spinach, cranberry sauce and watermelon pickle.

Margaret chattered. "Yes, we have rice every single day in one form or another, with gravy or tomato sauce or in a pilau or fried rice cakes or a rice ring with a filling. Charleston was built by rice, you know, Mr. Harris. The best rice in the world was grown right here. That's why the store rice is all called Carolina rice. It's really grown in Texas or someplace now . . . Ashley Barony was a rice plantation. All along the river, those marshes were once rice fields. Garden's grandfather, the Judge, used to tell stories about when he was a boy, working on the gates that let the water in from the river.

239

That was when his aunt lived on the plantation. Miss Julia Ashley she was; the Ashleys were among the earliest settlers in Charleston of course.

"Now our plantation, the Garden plantation, was right next to the Barony. My papa remembered when our plantation was all rice, too. Before the War, naturally, when we had our slaves and our natural rights. My mama said there were twenty slaves just to keep the gardens. She would make a little joke about it. 'Twenty slaves to keep the little ''G'' gardens,' she would say.

"The gardens were the pride of the family. We had practically miles of gardenia bushes. That's because the flower was named after our family."

Sky made a skillful pretense of being interested and impressed. Margaret decided that she liked him very much, even though he was a Yankee.

After dinner Garden announced that she had promised to call on her Aunt Elizabeth. Margaret declined to accompany her. Sky accepted with deceptive alacrity. The idea of being charming to another Southern genteel poor lady was far from pleasing. On the other hand, he would get to drive Garden to her aunt's house and perhaps they could take a lengthy detour.

They walked to Elizabeth's. "It's just around the corner," Garden said. Sky resigned himself to an hour's boredom.

The moment he saw Elizabeth Cooper, he rearranged his thinking. This lady might be many things, but she would never be boring. She was tall for a woman, almost as tall as he was, and she was impressive. Not because of her looks. She was thin, she had deep lines on her face, and her hair looked like rusty corrugated iron. It was heavily sprinkled with gray. Another woman who looked like Elizabeth Cooper might have been ugly. She was enormously handsome. It derived from the intelligence that showed in her bright blue eyes and from the sense of strength about her. Sky knew immediately that Elizabeth Cooper had lived her life without excuses and that she had little patience for weakness in others. Her gaze was warily friendly. He would have to prove himself if he wanted her approval, or even her toleration. For some reason, it seemed very important to him to win over Elizabeth Cooper. Her opinion, her good opinion, would be a valuable thing to gain.

"How do you do, Mr. Harris," she said.

Sky felt as if he should tell her the condition of his mind, his heart and his soul.

Garden kissed her great-aunt and showed her the old locket she was wearing. "I love my birthday present," she said. "Thank you so much."

Elizabeth nodded. "I'm pleased that you like it, dear. Sit down, both of you." She tugged a bellpull near the door, then took a chair near theirs. Sky observed that her back never touched the back of the chair.

"Did you get the locket open, Garden? Good. The portrait in there is of my brother Pinckney. You remind me of him; that's why I wanted you to have the locket." Joshua entered, pushing a tea cart. It held all the equipment for tea, plus a decanter and siphon and glasses. "It has been my observation," said Elizabeth, "that remarkably few gentlemen really like tea. Make yourself a drink, Mr. Harris. Garden, I'll ask you to prepare the tea."

Sky watched Garden, fascinated by the ritual she was performing. She poured scalding water from the huge silver samovar into a rosebud-patterned porcelain teapot. Holding it in both hands, she moved it in circles in front of her to swirl the water while she looked at her great-aunt and listened to her story. Elizabeth was talking about her brother. He sounded like a hero from Scott, thought Sky skeptically. Garden lifted the samovar's lid and poured the water from the pot back into it. She opened the silver tea caddy and dipped three spoonfuls of tea from it to the teapot, then tipped the samovar's kettle over the teapot and returned it to its cradle.

Garden half-filled her aunt's cup, pouring through a pierced silver spoon. Then she added hot water from the samovar.

"Two lumps, please," said Elizabeth. She held out her hand for her tea.

"This must be boring for you, Mr. Harris, all this family history. That's one of the perils of visiting elderly ladies. We talk about the past or our friends who just died. You young people must find us very odd." She put her cup on the tea tray. "Garden, who's the oldest person you ever knew?"

"Maum' Pansy at the Barony. She was so old she had been a slave."

"Good gracious. I remember Pansy. She must have been a hundred."

"At least. She was so proud of it." Garden told about Pansy, the

241

plat eye, her burn, and the songs she used to sing for her. At the same time, she deftly dumped the dregs from the teacups into the silver slop bowl, rinsed them with hot water from the samovar, emptied the water on top of the dregs, and refilled the cups with tea, water and sugar for Elizabeth, milk for herself. Sky was entranced by Garden's graceful motions and enthralled by her account of mysteries that he could hardly believe. He realized what an intruder he was on Ashley Barony and in the South, and for a moment he envied these Charlestonians with their interlocked generations of blacks and whites.

"Sing us the baby Moses song, Garden. I've always liked that one." Elizabeth hummed softly as Garden sang. She sang the words in the full richness of the Gullah dialect. Sky did not understand a single word.

"That was charming," said Elizabeth. "I hope you'll stay and sing carols with us. My daughter and her husband and my grandchildren are coming for carols and supper. We could use your voice, Garden. I'm afraid we all sound like frogs. But I'm confident God doesn't mind. Do you sing, Mr. Harris?"

"Nothing special, Mrs. Cooper, but I don't think God minds." Elizabeth laughed. Sky felt rewarded.

A moment later the Wilsons arrived. Sky was not pleased to see Maine. His displeasure turned to something more like hate when he saw the way Maine looked at Garden. After all the greetings and introductions, Garden took her place near the piano. Rebecca Wilson played. Maine moved close to Garden, and somehow there was no room for Sky. Elizabeth cleared her throat, and when Sky looked at her, she beckoned him to her side.

The carol singing made up in noise for what it lacked in musicality. Elizabeth spoke under its cover. "I rather like you, Schuyler Harris," she said, "but I have no reason to trust you. Garden's mother is a ninny; she won't protect her, so it's up to me. She may get a broken heart one day, but I don't want it to be too soon. No matter how beautiful she is, or how much she excites you, Garden is still fresh from the egg. If you do not have what we Victorians refer to as serious intentions, I want you to go away before she falls in love with you. If you don't, if you deliberately play with her affections for your amusement, I will have your heart cut out, and I'll feed it to my dogs."

Sky looked at her with admiration. "I'll bet you would, too." He leaned forward and kissed Elizabeth's cheek. "Don't worry, Aunt Elizabeth," he said, "my intentions are so serious they scare me."

Sky had realized when he met Elizabeth that Garden could not be taken lightly, that there was a structure of family and tradition and honor that surrounded her, supported her, placed her in a different world from the sophisticated, independent, free-thinking girls he was used to.

He learned, when he saw Maine Wilson touch Garden's arm, that he could not tolerate any other man's possession of her. He wanted her for his own; he wanted her with a dimension of desire he had never before experienced; he wanted to teach her all the pleasures of living, of love. He wanted to marry her.

Maine said something to Garden; she threw her head back and laughed. He looked at her with eyes that held longing and desire. Elizabeth chuckled. "Good luck, Mr. Schuyler Harris," she said. "In this part of the world, they could be described as kissin' cousins."

The following day Elizabeth telephoned Andrew Anson. "Tell me about this Harris boy, Andrew," she ordered.

Andrew temporized. "Now, Miss Elizabeth, you know a banker can't divulge private information about one of his clients . . ."

Elizabeth cut him short. "Hogwash, Andrew. You and Edith are sponsoring this young man, arranging to have him invited places. I want to know who's coming into my house. Don't make me pry it out of you. Speak up."

Andrew Anson spoke up. Schuyler Harris, he said, was the son of the Principessa Montecatini, who was one of the directors of the bank. No, he was not the son of the prince. His father was the princess's first husband, a man of good family in New York. His name was also Schuyler Harris, but he was dead, so the boy was no longer called Schuyler junior. He had been raised by his mother, had gone to the best schools, had never been in any trouble that Andrew knew of, and was perfectly acceptable in polite society.

Elizabeth was not satisfied. "What about his mother, Andrew? I heard she was divorced."

Mr. Anson cleared his throat. "Well, yes, she is, Miss Elizabeth. But she's from New York. They don't think the same way about things up there. She's a very prominent socialite up North."

"You are a great ninny sometimes, Andrew. I'm not concerned with what people do up North. Thank you, anyhow. Goodbye."

Elizabeth stared at the telephone after she hung up. She didn't like the sound of what Andrew Anson had told her. How could a young man from New York be trusted with an innocent like Garden? If he took divorce for granted, he would never understand Charleston standards.

She told herself that she was being a busybody. The Harris boy wouldn't be in town long enough to cause any trouble. The Yankee plantation people never stayed long. And Garden would be back in school in a few weeks. There was nothing to worry about.

48

The next week was like a dream to Garden. On the morning of her birthday, everything had changed for her. The array of bouquets, Sky's bracelet, the flowers he dropped in her lap. She felt desirable, grown-up, as if she had become a different person, as if she had only had to wait until she was seventeen for everything that was wrong in her life to correct itself.

Because she believed it, it was true. Her clumsiness vanished; she could dance like a feather. Her tongue came untied; she could not gush or flirt, but she was not afraid to talk, to ask questions, to listen, to laugh, to express appreciation or admiration.

Maine's interest in her awakened the interest of other men. Sky's determined attentions brought their interest to the boiling point. Suddenly, Garden was a belle. Bouquets cluttered the drawing room, poems appeared in boxes of candy delivered to the house, she was rushed at dances, surrounded by beaux at receptions. Her mother was ecstatic. Garden became more beautiful than ever.

It drove Sky mad. He hardly had a chance for four consecutive words with her. She was assigned an escort for every dance, reception, ball, breakfast, and she had no time that was not filled by the

Season. He attended everything, danced with her as much as he could, brought her punch, if three other men did not beat him to it.

Sky had had plenty of experience at winning hearts, but none of his methods would work. He could not take Garden to dinner or to the theater; he could not give her jewelry; his flowers were lost in the quantities she received from other men.

In desperation he went to Andrew Anson for advice. "I'm a fish out of water, Mr. Anson. I need help."

Mr. Anson touched the tips of his fingers together. "Mr. Harris," he said gravely, "this young lady is a cousin of mine . . ."

"She's a cousin of everybody's," Sky shouted. "You're all each other's cousins here. I don't know what the hell anybody's talking about half the time. That's just the trouble. I'm an outsider, and you all let me know it, in the politest, most infuriating way possible."

"Do you want to be an insider?"

"No, Mr. Anson. I've got better sense than that. I know I never would be, not if I lived here for a hundred years. I want Garden, that's all. I want to get to know her and have her get to know me. I want to make her love me."

"And . . . ?"

"Yes, and marry me." Andrew's hands dropped to a comfortable rest on his desk. His duty was done. But Sky's anguish touched him to compassion.

"I'll tell you, Mr. Harris, as a Charlestonian, I believe the best thing for Garden would be to stay here, to marry her own kind, to be part of the life and the tradition we have here. We believe we've got the closest thing to the Garden of Eden. That's what you're up against.

"What you've got going for you is that you're an outsider. That makes you forbidden fruit, and you know what happened to Adam and Eve. The other thing that makes you appealing is, to be coarse, a lot of money. You do have money of your own?"

"Yes. My grandfather Harris left me some."

"Forgive a banker's question, Mr. Harris. How much?" Andrew Anson whistled when Sky told him. "Well, Mr. Harris, that makes you very different from anybody in Charleston. We all say that money doesn't matter; some of us even believe it. But all of us have to put food on the table and shoes on our children's feet. Use your money, man."

"It does me no good. How many flowers and chocolates can a girl take?"

Andrew Anson shook his head. "Think, man. Look for the weak link. Who has the most influence over the girl? Her mother. She's ambitious for Garden, and her ambitions don't look beyond Charleston because that's all she knows. Dangle some dazzle in front of her eyes; tell her you'll wrap Garden in ermine, deck her with diamonds."

"Do you think it will work?"

"It's worth a try."

After Sky left, Mr. Anson looked out the window for a long time. I hope I did the right thing, he said to himself. Margaret Tradd won't wait for that bait to hit the water before she jumps.

The next day was December thirty-first. Sky thought of taking a case of champagne to Garden's mother and following Mr. Anson's advice. But the idea was repugnant. Garden was too precious to be bought.

That night, at the Yacht Club Ball, he watched the clock and the competition. At one minute to twelve, he cut in on Garden's dancing partner. Garden smiled, held up her hands to touch his shoulder and his hand. But Sky caught both her hands in his. "I have something to tell you, Garden," he said seriously. "In all my life, I've always gotten everything I wanted. I want you more than I've ever wanted anything else. And I intend to have you."

Horns tooted in raucous disharmony to signal the New Year. Sky released Garden's hands and held her face in his. He leaned close to her and whispered in her ear. "I love you, Garden Tradd. I'm going to marry you." Then he moved, brought his lips slowly to meet hers and held her in a long, gentle kiss until he felt her tremble. He put his arms around her then and held her tight, his eyes closed, his ears deaf to the din that surrounded them.

"Mama, I'm engaged. I'm so happy, Mama."

"But Garden, the Season's not over yet. The Ball's not for two weeks. Don't rush things. You don't need to choose for months yet." Margaret was pleading.

"I don't have to choose, Mama. I know. I love Sky, and he's asked me to marry him."

"The Yankee? No, Garden, it won't do."

"I've already said yes, Mama. I love him and nobody else. He's coming to call tomorrow to talk to you."

"I won't give my permission."

Garden giggled. "Yes you will, Mama. Sky is very forceful."

Sky called on Elizabeth Cooper before he went to see Margaret. "I care about your approval," he told her bluntly. "I respect you."

"You have my blessing," Elizabeth said. "You'll have to earn my approval."

Sky drove from Elizabeth's house to King Street. The jewelers had not been pleased to be telephoned early in the morning on New Year's Day, but when they heard what Sky wanted, they all agreed to meet him. So did the florist.

"Delivery boy," Sky called out when Zanzie opened the door. "Happy New Year, Zanzie," he said more quietly. He presented her with a box of candy. A fifty-dollar gold piece was tied in the box's ribbon. Sky gestured to the florist and his son, and they followed him up the stairs to the drawing room. "Set it down on the table," he said.

He looked at Garden with his heart in his eyes, but he walked to where Margaret was sitting on her sofa. "Happy New Year, Miss Margaret."

"Thank you." Her voice was cold.

Sky stepped to one side, allowing Margaret a clear view of the table in the center of the room. A rosebush in full bloom was on the table. The roses were recognizable blush pink damask roses; their sweet perfume was familiar.

"Garden," said Sky, "come here, my love. I want you to pick a rose. You should probably ask your mother to help you. Don't worry, all the thorns have been removed."

Garden ran to his side. "I like it just the way it is. Thank you." She went up on tiptoe and kissed his cheek.

"Thank you," he said. "You're blushing. Am I the first man you've kissed this year?"

"Sky!" Garden tried to look disapproving.

Margaret did not have to try.

Sky led Garden to the roses. "I think a girl should have some say-so about what kind of engagement ring she wants."

Garden let out a small scream. Then she turned to Margaret. "Mama, come look. Every rose has a jewel in it."

Margaret was there in an instant.

247

The pale petals surrounded centers that were round, square, rectangular, blue, red, green, and all colors collected in clear prisms. "I didn't know which you would like best," said Sky.

Margaret was dumbfounded. "There's not a store in Charleston with this many jewels," she marveled.

"I know," Sky agreed. "I had to go to all of them."

Margaret was taking the rings out and looking at them. Garden looked at Sky. "You never do things the way other people do," she said. "I think you must be the cleverest person in the whole world."

"I must be, if I'm clever enough to catch you." He led her into the hall and kissed her, out of Margaret's sight. She did not notice that they were gone until they returned.

"I can't decide between this one and this one," Margaret said. A big round diamond was on her right hand, a square one on her left.

49

The wedding was set for eight o'clock on the evening of February seventeenth. "As I said to Garden," Margaret told everyone, "she has a complete trousseau already, with all her things for her debut, and if we waited any longer we'd run right into Lent. There was plenty of time to have the invitations done, and the dressmaker was more than happy to have the gown to do. Once the Season is over, the poor woman practically sits on her hands for months.

"Elizabeth Cooper insisted that Garden wear the Tradd family veil, and that meant that her gown had to be simple anyway. The Princess sent her a darling little pearl tiara to wear with it. She was in Europe when Schuyler tracked her down, by long-distance telephone, mind you. She's thrilled, naturally. Princess or no, she understands what it means to marry into an old Charleston family. Two, really. Garden Tradd. Two names that mean something, even in Europe.

"Schuyler understands it too. He's the luckiest man in the world, he says. They'll visit in Charleston a lot. Of course there is the Barony, but that does belong to his mother. Schuyler said he thought there should be a place for them that felt more like theirs. So he bought the Garden house, the one that was my family's, and he's counting on me to fix it up. They won't be on the spot to watch out for things, and I'm glad to do it for them. He's bought it in my name."

"The Yankee paid a pretty price for the little Tradd girl," said a gentleman at the Yacht Club bar. Maine Wilson hit him in the mouth. The members close by grabbed their glasses. Even in Charleston, even at the Yacht Club, the supply of good whiskey was unreliable.

The Principessa put Andrew Anson in charge of arrangements for the rehearsal dinner and the overflow of New York wedding guests. The Barony could only accommodate fourteen. Andrew immediately put his wife in charge.

"Couldn't you kill Andrew, Edith? All that work."

"No, I love doing it. I've always dreamed of buying anything I wanted without asking the price. I do wish that decorator she sent would stop hitting his fist on his forehead and yelling 'Save me from provincials,' but I'm having a good time otherwise. And I've got all my friends renting rooms for the guests at prices that would make your hair stand on end. Nora Leslie will be able to paint the house and get a new roof."

"Where is the rehearsal party going to be?"

"Dinner, my dear, not party. Remember, Yankees eat at night. I took the whole Villa Margherita. Schuyler and his ushers will be staying in the guest rooms, and the party will take all the public rooms."

The Villa Margherita was a curiosity in Charleston. It had been built as a private house in a style that was neither typical of Charleston nor typical of Italian villas, but it was handsome, with its tall Corinthian columns and balustraded terraces, and everyone was used to it. Inside there was a covered atrium, with a marble reflecting pool in the center and a double colonnade of white marble. Four tremendous rooms surrounded it. The Principessa's decorator pronounced it an adequate setting.

On Friday night it was a fantasy from the Arabian nights. The ceiling of the atrium was covered with striped silk. Hangings of the same silk stretched from ceiling to floor, looped and swagged with thick gilt ropes and tassels at the doors. A smaller tent of the same silk was set up above a stage erected in one of the public rooms for a string ensemble.

The stripes' colors were magenta, pink, gold, green, cobalt and vermilion. In the rooms around the atrium, round tables for six were covered in floor-length silk cloths in the different colors. The chairs were gilt Louis XV with striped silk seat cushions. Linen napkins in assorted colors were folded like flowers. They centered gold-bordered white place plates. Gold-bordered place cards perched in the folded linen petals. The wineglasses were made of iridescent gold-colored crystal.

Except on the tables for the bridal party. These tables were rectangular, four of them, one on each side of the pool. The goblets and plates on the tables were gold, the tablecloths emerald green velvet.

All the tables held gilt candelabra with emerald-colored scented candles. Colored candles molded in the shape of water lilies floated in the pool.

When Edith Anson told her husband what the decorator was doing, he refused to go to the dinner. "I know it will give me heartburn," he said. When they arrived, she gave him a tour of all the rooms, ending in the atrium. Andrew Anson looked at the glittering rank of goblets. "Nothing succeeds like excess," he commented.

"Isn't it awful, though," agreed Edith. "Who would have thought that a person could decorate a party in Charleston at the start of spring and not use a single solitary fresh flower?"

The Principessa's gown was gold lamé, her hair metallic gold, her jewels an astonishment of emeralds set in diamonds. Receiving lines were a bore, she said, so there was none. She stood in a corner of the atrium with a background of striped silk curtains and talked to her friends while the guests arrived.

Sky joined her for a moment, kissing her on both cheeks in approved Continental fashion. "Vicki, you really are a princess," he said. "You've pulled out all the stops on this one."

The Principessa shrugged one shoulder. "Darling Sky, you made it plain that you were determined to have this marriage. What could I do? It would be dreary to be a bad sport."

"That you never are, Vicki. I'm going to go find Garden." He cleared a path through the Principessa's entourage.

Garden was near the entrance, greeting people as they arrived. Sky watched her face for several minutes; he loved to look at her. When Elizabeth Cooper came in, he went to stand by Garden. He admired her great-aunt, although he had a strong suspicion that Elizabeth did not approve of him. She had not seemed very pleased when Garden took him to her house to tell her about their engagement. Still, she did offer the Tradd family's wedding veil. Maybe he was being oversensitive.

"Aunt Elizabeth," he said, "I'm so glad to see you." He kissed her cheek. Then Garden's. "Have you ever seen such a beautiful bride?"

"Never," said Elizabeth. Garden was alight with happiness. "I wish you both all the joy in the world."

Garden hugged her great-aunt. "We already have it, Aunt Elizabeth. Isn't it wonderful?"

"Yes, my dear." Elizabeth smiled and moved on into the room; other guests were arriving. When she was out of the way, she turned to look at Garden and Sky. His evident love for Garden told her that she was a fool to worry about the marriage, and she relaxed.

Dear heaven, she thought, what gaudy taste these Yankees have. It's better than a circus. She looked at the decorations and at the clothes of the New York guests and began to enjoy herself thoroughly. Edith Anson had promised everyone a show, and she had not been wrong. Elizabeth circulated through all the rooms, speaking briefly to the people she knew, her sharp eyes taking in every detail of her surroundings, the gowns and the jewels of the strange women. They certainly make us look dowdy, she admitted cheerfully to herself.

A woman hurried through the doorway from the atrium and almost collided with her. "Sorry," she said.

Elizabeth caught her arm to steady her. "Not at all," she murmured automatically. "I was in the way." Then her hold on the woman's arm tightened. "Wait," she said. She looked closely at the woman's face turned in profile.

The woman swiveled to face her. "My God," she said.

"I can't believe my eyes. Am I right? Are you Joe's girl? Victoria Simmons?" It hardly seemed possible that this glittering, rouged woman was the clinging, weeping girl Elizabeth had put on the train after her father's funeral. But the chin, the nose, the ears were the same. Elizabeth had to ask.

"How clever of you, Elizabeth. Yes, I am. It is all right to call you by your first name, isn't it? I'm a little old to say 'Miss Elizabeth.' "

Elizabeth smiled. "My dear, you may call me anything you like. I am so very happy to see you. Tell me how you are. You look well. And beautiful."

"I'm well. How are you?" Victoria Simmons's tone did not have the warmth of Elizabeth's. Her eyes were cold.

Elizabeth's smile faded when she looked into them. "Victoria," she said, "I wrote to you and to your guardians so often in that terrible time after your father was killed. I wanted to know how you were, that you were all right. There was never an answer."

Victoria raised her plucked eyebrows. "You were curious about the little bastard Tradd, I suppose. It was no problem, Elizabeth. I had a convenient miscarriage. It's marvelous what a cooperative doctor can do."

Elizabeth recoiled. "How awful for you," she said.

"Don't be ridiculous." Victoria was smiling now. "There's nothing to an abortion. You sleep through the whole thing. I had forgotten all about it until you reminded me."

Elizabeth looked at Victoria sadly. This woman looked like someone who could forget. She was so brittle—her voice, her masklike painted face, her artificially bright hair, her talonlike fingernails. She was as hard as the glittering jewels she wore.

"That's very generous of you, Victoria," Elizabeth said, with an effort to match the woman's unemotional tone. "And coming down to the wedding is generous, too." She supposed that Victoria was a close friend of the Principessa.

Victoria laughed. "Elizabeth, darling, I wouldn't dream of missing it. I'm the mother of the groom." She smiled, eyes glinting. "You're thinking incest, aren't you? So Southern. Well, don't fret, darling. There really was an abortion. You can look at Schuyler's birth certificate. I would have had to be pregnant for twenty months for him to be a Tradd. Sweet little Garden isn't marrying her brother."

Elizabeth was shocked into immobility. Victoria removed Elizabeth's hand from her arm. "Don't gape like that," she said. "Really, Elizabeth, you must try to be just a little bit less provincial. I'm disappointed in you. . . . Now I must run. I have friends waiting for me."

Elizabeth watched Vicki's golden form disappear into the crowd. Then she pulled herself out of her semitrance and pushed her way past the clusters of partying people until she found Margaret.

She grabbed Margaret's wrist. "Excuse us," she said to the man Margaret was talking to, and she hurried Margaret out onto the rear terrace.

"You've got to stop this wedding," Elizabeth said frantically.

Margaret tried to back away from her. "I think you've lost your mind, Mistress Cooper. What on earth are you talking about?"

Elizabeth took her by the shoulders and shook her. "Margaret, listen to me. There must be no wedding. Do you know who that boy's mother is? It's Victoria Simmons, Joe Simmons's daughter.

"Dear heaven, Margaret, don't you understand? Your husband ruined her life. He got her pregnant, he abandoned her, and he murdered her father. What do you suppose she feels about her son marrying the daughter of Stuart Tradd?"

Margaret put her hands on Elizabeth's chest and pushed her away. "How dare you manhandle me like that? And how dare you meddle in my daughter's life? I know all about Vicki and Stuart. She and I had a nice little talk yesterday. Mother to mother. She wants her son to be happy just like I want Garden to be happy. We agreed that it was best for the children to know nothing about it.

"Good Lord, that was a million years ago. There's no point digging up old skeletons. All Vicki wants is to pretend it never happened, and I think she's absolutely right."

Elizabeth wanted to slap her. "Margaret, don't be a fool. It's impossible to forget a thing like that, to pretend it never happened."

"But that's what we're going to do, Elizabeth. Including you. You've never liked Schuyler, I know that. You're just looking for some way to justify yourself. Well, I won't have it. He loves Garden, and she's crazy about him. They're getting married tomorrow, and nobody's going to stop it. If Vicki can be big enough to put the past behind her, you have no right to cause trouble."

Elizabeth was in despair. Maybe Margaret was right. It was true that she had distrusted Sky from the beginning. And that the Principessa seemed unfeeling enough to have no emotions at all, not even hate. But Garden was so vulnerable, so young, so helpless.

"She's not your daughter, Elizabeth, she's mine," said Margaret.

"You didn't even know she was alive until last year. You can't ignore a child all her life and then try to interfere."

Elizabeth was beaten.

The next evening St. Michael's Church was filled. Even the galleries were crowded. Outside, police waved traffic away to a detour. Meeting Street was clogged with spectators, reporters, photographers. The Cinderella wedding of the beautiful, aristocratic debutante to one of the richest young men in America was news in every world capital.

Inside the church, tall white tapers cast a warm light on the masses of gardenias at the altar and on the deep windowsills. St. Michael's bells chimed the hour. At the last stroke, the organ music rose and filled the church. Everyone stood.

The bridesmaids walked up the long aisle in slow lockstep, followed by Wentworth Wragg, maid of honor, and Peggy Thurston, matron of honor. There was a pause. Necks craned. Then a collective sigh made the candle flames dance. Garden, on the arm of her cousin Maine, moved like a goddess past the ribboned doors of the old box pews. Her golden hair glimmered through her veil. Her face was dreamy, the wide blue eyes shining. Behind her flowed twelve yards of cobweb-fine lace, the cherished veil that Tradd brides had worn for six generations.

In the Tradd family pew, tears rolled down the face of Elizabeth Cooper. Everyone cried at weddings.

BOOK 5

1923–1931

50

A limousine took Garden and Sky from the wedding reception to the docks on East Bay Street. When Garden saw their destination, she wiggled with excitement. "What a wonderful surprise, Sky. I've always wanted to go on the boat to New York. When the windows were open, I could hear them whistling and tooting, and I used to wonder what it was like to be on one."

Sky kissed her. "Angel," he said. He led her up a rope-railed gangplank to the deck. A mate blew a bos'n's pipe, and a man in uniform saluted.

"Welcome aboard, sir."

"Thank you, captain. Mrs. Harris and I are looking forward to the trip." Garden felt an exciting, strange quiver at the sound of "Mrs. Harris." She squeezed Sky's arm. He moved it close to his body, pressing her hand in a secret embrace.

"This way, darling," he said. Suddenly he lifted her in his arms. "One threshold's as good as another." He carried her into a large room and sank into a soft armchair, with Garden on his lap.

"Sky, someone will see us."

"Let them. I want to kiss the bride. It's the custom at weddings." Garden put her arms around his neck and closed her eyes.

When she opened them again, she looked around guiltily. They were in what looked like a living room, with sofas and chairs, tables with lamps, tables with ashtrays and cigarette boxes, curtains at the windows and small Persian rugs on the floor. There was no one there but the two of them.

"Where are all the other passengers, Sky?"

"There are no other passengers. This isn't the Clyde Lines, darling, this is a yacht."

Garden was visibly amazed. "It looks like a steamship."

"Not quite, pet. But it's plenty big enough for two. And the

257

crew, of course. Would you like to look around?" Garden nodded vigorously. Then she put her hand up to her eyes. A bright light had been turned on outside the window opposite them.

Sky jumped up, nearly dropping her on the floor. "Bastard," he said. There was the sound of shouting and running feet on deck. Sky ran out.

When he came back, he threw the bolt on the door and closed the curtains on all the windows. "What's the matter, Sky?"

"Damn photographer. I thought we'd given them the slip, leaving by the back way. It's okay. We destroyed his camera and we'll cast off any minute . . . Sorry, darling. They'll be tired of us by the time we come back, and they'll leave us alone. How about that tour now?"

Garden stood up. She was glad that no one had a picture of her sitting on Sky's lap, but she felt sorry for the man who lost his camera. She also felt a little bit sorry that the reporters would be tired of them. The hubbub outside St. Michael's had been very exciting. She had felt like a movie star.

The yacht's main deck was made up of the living room, which Sky told her was called the saloon, a dining room, service pantry, two guest cabins with bathrooms and a master bedroom, dressing room and bath. This last was like a room in a French country house. The walls were upholstered in blue-and-white toile de Jouy; the same print covered the carved armchairs, the windows and the bed. The bed was a four-poster unlike any Garden had ever seen. Its top was of carved wood, part of the ceiling, upholstered on the inside and hung with curtains of the toile. The bedspread was neatly folded on a luggage rack, and the covers were turned back in two neat triangles.

Sky put his arm around Garden's waist. "Would you like to have something to eat before we turn in? You didn't have anything at the reception." His voice was tremulous.

Garden looked up at him. "No," she said. "I want you to make love to me. I've been wanting you to for a long time."

Sky stared at her. His mouth began to twitch. Then he pulled her close to his chest and laughed, burying his face in her hair. "Garden, you're always surprising me. I never know what you're going to say or do."

Garden waited until he stopped laughing. "I'm not being funny," she said. She stepped away so that she could look into his eyes. "I

258

love you, Sky, and I want to love you in every way. Isn't that the way it should be?''

Sky matched her grave seriousness. "Yes, that's exactly the way it should be.''

He led her to a chair. "I want to make love to you this instant, my darling, but I'm not going to. You sit down while I open the champagne. We'll have a glass while we talk. I think there are some things I should tell you.''

Garden watched him at the silver cooler; he twisted the wires on the bottle with a practiced hand. "I know everything you're going to tell me," she said. "Peggy told me all about it. She drew pictures for me and showed me myself in a mirror, and she said it hurt at first but it was wonderful.''

Champagne spurted all over the rug, and the cork hit a wall. "I don't mind the hurt, if that's what's worrying you, Sky. I won't cry.''

He took her in his arms and rocked back and forth, torn between laughter at her childlike pride in her knowledge and melting tenderness for her trust and courage. "I adore you, Garden Harris.''

She smiled against his chest. "I like that. Say it again. It's the first time I've heard my new name.''

"Garden Harris. Beloved bride of Schuyler Harris, the happiest man in the world.'' Beneath their feet, the deck vibrated. The yacht was moving. "Our wedding trip has begun, Mrs. Harris.'' He picked her up and carried her to the bed.

He undressed her gently, astonished by the underclothes she wore. They were all cotton, tucked and embroidered and trimmed with lace like an infant's baptismal gown. When she was nude, he removed her ivory hairpins one by one, so carefully that her hair was undisturbed until he pulled out the final one. Then the heavy gold knot unfolded, spilling onto the pillow and revealing the hidden tongues of flame. He nearly lost his herculean self-control when Garden changed before his eyes into the incredibly beautiful pagan of the wild dance at Ashley Barony. He stroked her hair, almost surprised that the red streaks did not burn his fingertips, then wound it around his hands and arms, and brought it down over her white throat and shoulders and breasts. Garden whimpered softly. Tremors ran through her body. She looked at him with wonder darkening her eyes.

He kissed her eyes closed, kept touching them with his lips while he touched her veiled breasts and caressed her belly and the sweeping curve of her waist. Her breathing was rapid, as was his. He felt her pulse leaping in her throat, counted it with the sensitive end of his tongue while he shed his clothes.

Then he took her in his arms and lay beside her, holding her trembling form next to his, learning her body, letting her discover a man's. Garden's hands felt the strong muscles in his shoulders and arms, explored the sinews in his back, and moved on his face and neck with urgent fingers as delicate as swansdown.

"Now, my darling?" he whispered.

"Oh, yes."

Both cried out at the pain of penetration, then held each other tightly, experiencing a mystic union of shared wonder. He withdrew gently and kissed her lips. They were salty from her tears. His fingers touched her wet eyelashes. Garden caught his hand and held it. She moved her head, kissed his salty fingers. "I promised not to cry, but I have to. I'm so terribly happy. I never dreamed . . . how could I know . . ."

"Shhh," he said. "I know, I know, my own love, I feel like it too. See, I'm crying with you."

51

Sky woke before Garden did. He raised himself on one elbow and looked at her, astounded by the power of his love for her. He had known many women, enjoyed them, even loved a few of them for a while. But nothing had prepared him for the complex emotions he now felt. He wanted a new word, a word never used by any other man, to express what he meant. Love was not adequate. But he could find no other.

"I love you," he said when Garden's eyes opened.

She was distressed when she saw the blood on the sheets. "I'll wash those spots and put them back," she said.

Sky stopped her. "The stewards change the linen every day

anyhow, don't worry about it." And, he thought privately, Vicki's probably expecting a report.

They had to breakfast inside. A cold wind was whipping the deck with spume from the white-capped waves. Garden exclaimed over the low rail around the table that kept their plates from sliding off when the ship rolled. "What a good idea. Did you think of it, Sky?"

Sky said he thought it had been around since the Vikings, if not earlier.

Garden held her plate in place with her left hand while she ate her bacon and eggs and toast. Sky attempted nothing more ambitious than coffee. He was a good sailor, but he did not have Garden's imperturbable stomach.

"What fun this is," Garden said. "Do you use your yacht much?"

"It's not mine, it's Vicki's. I don't like to own things."

"It always sounds so strange to hear you call your mother by her first name. Do you call the prince by his first name, too?"

"The prince?" Sky looked blank for a moment. Then he laughed shortly. "Oh, him. No, dear Giorgio's been out of the picture for a long time. Vicki divorced him years and years ago."

Garden did not show the shock she felt. Sky spoke so lightly about divorce. She put it out of her mind and concentrated on important matters. "About your mother, what should I call her?"

"Vicki, I suppose."

"That sounds so disrespectful. Maybe I should say Miss Vicki."

"No, my angel, that sounds too Southern. Vicki doesn't think much of Southerners."

Garden nodded. "I got that feeling. I reckon that's why she doesn't like me."

Sky covered her hand with his. "That's not so, Garden. She doesn't dislike you. What makes you say that?"

"Nothing special. Just a feeling I got. She didn't look very happy at the wedding."

Sky grinned. "Is that all? That's because she was in a fever to get going. The British have found the tomb of one of the pharaohs, and Vicki was itching to get to Egypt and see it."

"Egypt? That's so far away."

"Not for Vicki. She likes to be where things are happening, no matter where that might be. She's got enough guts and energy for a dozen normal people."

"You think a lot of her, don't you?"

261

"Everybody does. She's really extraordinary."

Garden decided that she was silly to be afraid of Sky's mother. But she was. Until his next words explained everything to her. "You mustn't be upset, darling, if Vicki seems abrupt. It's because she's always in a hurry. And also because she's not accustomed to girls. I'm the only child she's got, and I've always gone my own way. She's told me a hundred times she wished she had a daughter instead of me so that she could feel like a mother."

They cruised the Florida keys for two weeks and the Bahamas for six. They kept away from busy ports, anchoring off deserted beaches and taking the launch or swimming to them, usually by moonlight so that Garden would not be burned by the sun. They needed nothing outside themselves. Day by day Garden came nearer to her latent explosive nature, until at last she became the woman Sky had seen in her when she danced. She threw off all constrictions and became urgent, giving and taking love with pagan freedom. But she remained demure and somewhat shy with the captain and the stewards and even with the ladies' maid who was part of the crew. There was a private Garden who was Sky's own, and a public Garden for the world to see.

The play on words was their special joke. They were giddy with happiness and thought themselves very witty. When they reached New York, their car was stopped by a parade. They did not know what was being celebrated, and they decided that the parade was in their honor. It made it easier to wait for their car to cross Fifth Avenue and it seemed a reasonable thing to say. Brass bands and flags flying were appropriate salutes to the miracle of their love.

52

"Just across Eighty-second, cabby," said Sky. Garden was swivel-ing her head from side to side, trying to see everything. The yacht had moored in the Hudson River, and she had marveled at the huge buildings on Riverside Drive. They were apartment buildings, Sky said, with elevators in them just like the one in Kerrison's Depart-ment Store in Charleston. Driving east, they passed long rows of dark houses which she learned were called brownstones, and then went through Central Park, where they stopped until the parade passed. Now they were on Fifth Avenue. Garden saw more automo-biles in a few blocks than there were in the whole city of Charleston, she was sure. Different kinds of automobiles, too. There were very few black Model T's.

The cab turned to enter a semicircular drive, and Garden bent her head to look up through the window. The building was immense, but not as high as the apartment buildings on Riverside Drive. She hoped that the Principessa's flat was on the top floor and that there was an elevator.

They stopped under a porte cochère, and a man in uniform came down the wide steps to open the door of the taxi. As Garden stepped out, three men ran across the street from Central Park. "Goddammit," Sky muttered. He took her arm and rushed her up the steps. "Reporters," he explained. "Don't look back, they may have cameras."

The immense double doors opened when they reached the fifth and top step, and they ran inside. They were in an enormous lobby. Its floor was green marble, almost covered by a carpet with a design of green dragons on a gold background. In the center of the lobby there was a big round table that reminded Garden of the one Peggy had gotten at the antique store, except that the pedestal of this one was made up of four carved dragons.

At the far end of the lobby a wide staircase curved up in a semicircle. It had elaborate wrought-iron balusters and white marble steps with a carpet of green up the center. Garden heard the splashing of water and stretched her neck to see the fountain that filled the inner curve of the staircase. It, too, was shaped like a dragon. Spouting water instead of breathing fire. She thought everything very fine and sophisticated, but she was disappointed that there were only stairs.

Sky picked up a packet of mail from the table. He broke off a cluster of white flowers from the arrangement in the center of the table. "Here, angel, have a sniff. It's really springtime."

The perfume of the flowers filled the big lobby, but Garden sniffed anyhow. Up close, the sweetness was intensified so that she felt weak. "It's wonderful," she said, "what are they?"

Sky put his arm around her shoulders. "Lilacs, my little magnolia blossom. Yankee flowers. Come on, let's go up. Do you want to take the elevator?"

"Oh, yes! Where is it? I didn't see one."

"You have to know where to look." Sky swung her to the left and she saw a man in an elegant black swallowtail coat holding a door open. She wondered if he lived in one of the apartments or if he was some kind of manager. Sky did not offer any explanations, nor did he introduce her. Garden smiled slightly when she walked past him, and he bowed his head briefly.

The elevator was smaller than Kerrison's and much fancier. Its interior was of quilted green leather. Bronze wall lamps with white pleated shades were on one wall. Between them there was a carved crystal vase full of lilac in a bronze holder.

The elevator shuddered and stopped. "They were supposed to fix that," said Sky. "It's perfectly safe; don't worry." Garden wasn't worried; she was a little sad that they hadn't gone higher.

Sky opened the door. Garden stepped out into a hallway. A shower of rice pelted down on her head and shoulders, excited voices screamed, "Surprise!"

"I'll be damned," said Sky. "Duck, darling." He caught Garden's hand and ran, pulling her behind him, through the shower of white pellets into a big room thronged with people.

They mobbed the newlyweds with kisses from the women and slaps on the back from the men for Sky, and handshakes and an occasional cheek pressed to cheek for Garden. It seemed to her that they were all talking very loudly and all at the same time. She smiled and said "thank you" to everyone, supposing that they were congratulating them or welcoming them or both. She was bewildered and lost. Some faces looked almost familiar; probably they had been at the wedding but Sky had had a list of two hundred guests, and there had been no time to get to know anyone. Sky knew everyone here, and he was obviously delighted to see them all. He seemed to have forgotten her.

But he had not. When the pandemonium of greetings was over, Sky waved away the press of people surrounding them. "Give us some air," he said, "or this party will turn into a wake for the young Harrises, dead of asphyxiation." He put his arm around Garden. "Come on, sweetheart, take off your hat and stay awhile. I'll find you a chair."

He settled her in the corner of a sofa, then sat next to her, his arm over the back, hand touching her shoulder lightly. Garden put her handbag on a table next to her with her gloves on top. Then she lifted her hat off and placed it with them.

"There!" said a woman's voice. "Didn't I tell you? She's half redhead." Garden recognized Mitzi, Sky's guest at the Barony. She looked around and picked out Mark's face, then Bunny's. She felt better now that she knew some names. But she was unhappy about her hair. She knew the red was ugly; her mother had told her so for years. And it was definitely showing. The maid on the yacht did not have the skill of Mr. Angelo; she had fixed Garden's hair in a crown of braids that morning before she left the yacht.

Garden smiled uncertainly at Mitzi.

Mark spoke up. "Yes, sir, Garden's got wild hair, and she's a wild dancer. Do the Charleston dance for us, Garden."

"Yes, Garden, come on. I want to learn it," said Bunny.

"Oh, no, I couldn't possibly."

"Sure you can. Come on, Garden. Somebody put some music on," Mark ordered. "Something good and hot."

Other voices joined in, urging, begging. Garden looked at Sky. He'd have to stop them; they were his friends.

He was smiling, pride and pleasure in his eyes. "Go on, darling, put the Yankees in their place."

"Sky, I can't. I don't know these people."

"They're all friends, angel. It's all right. And I like to show off my bride."

Garden stood up. Her knees felt shaky. Everyone applauded, and she looked desperately at Sky. He nodded encouragement. "That's my girl," he said. "Do me proud." From the corner, music blared into the room. It was a jazz band playing "Twelfth Street Rag." Garden moved one foot, then the other. She threw her arms out for balance and danced. The beat of the music was infectious, but her motions were stiff. She was afraid that she was making a fool of herself, that everyone would laugh at her. A man and then a girl and then another girl stood up and tried to copy her steps. They weren't laughing, they were seriously trying to learn. They really like it, Garden thought. She smiled at them, exaggerating the movement of her feet, the swing of her legs and arms so that it would be easier to reproduce.

"Swell . . . terrific . . . sensational . . . great . . . me too . . . let me try . . ." All over the room, people were attempting to dance as Garden was dancing.

When the record ended, there were cries of "start it again" and "roll up the damn rug" and "teach me" and "do it again, Garden." They like me, Garden thought, and her nervousness evaporated. She was the center of attention, she was making Sky proud. She looked at him. He was standing, too. "I get the first lesson," he said. "I'm married to the teacher."

Garden danced until her feet were numb. After everyone mastered the basic four-beat step, she showed them how to turn and to kick. The record played over and over, the enthusiasm and admiration was loud and never-ending. Garden responded, relaxed, rejoiced. Her cautious, shy restraint vanished, and she gave herself over to the music and the dance and the exhilaration of her body's movement.

"That's enough," Sky shouted.

Garden stopped. She felt the blood racing through her veins, touched her hot cheeks with her fingers, and her damp temples. Her braids had fallen to her shoulders and were coming undone. "My goodness," she panted, "I'm a mess."

"No, no, dance some more," said a girl near to her. Her feet were still dancing.

"Let Garden catch her breath," Sky said. His voice was near anger. "Sit down, darling, and let me get you a drink." He guided Garden to the sofa. She sank gratefully into the deep cushions. She hadn't realized it, but she was tired.

"Thank you, Sky."

"Here, Garden." He gave her a handkerchief and the handful of hairpins he had picked up from the floor. "What would you like? Champagne? Or milk?"

"Milk, please." Sky kissed the top of her head.

"Coming right up," he said.

Sky ran down the stairs to get Garden's milk himself. He needed to get away from the hubbub in the living room. Something strange had happened to him when Garden was dancing. He felt proud of her, pleased that his friends were impressed, smug that the world could see what an exciting girl he had married.

Until her hair started to come down. Then he felt as if everyone in the room was intruding on the most intimate part of his life, his marriage, his love for Garden. Her long red and gold hair, streaming free and wild, was something no other man should ever see. It was his, for him alone. Before they made love, Garden loosed her hair from its braids or coiled bun, and the sight of it tumbling down over her pale, glowing skin was a sensual stimulus that took his breath away. He would not share his wife, not even with the eyes of another man, not his private Garden.

He ran back up with Garden's milk. The crowd of his friends were engrossed in a new star. Vicki had arrived while Sky was in the kitchen.

"My dears," she was saying, "Egypt is simply too marvelous. Every hotel is swarming with sinister, swarthy, bearded men in white draperies who hiss at you from behind the potted palms. They all claim to have stolen trinkets from the treasures of the tomb, and they'll sell them to you at a ridiculously low price because their grandmothers are dying. Or their camels."

"Did you buy anything, Principessa?"

"Darling! Everything was appallingly bogus. No, for once in my life I resisted temptation. At least in the hotel lobby. I got the ambassador to introduce me to a reliable antiquarian. He was a robber too, it goes without saying, but at least his things were authentic."

Vicki rummaged in the camel's saddlebag she was using as a purse. "Ah, here they are. These are scarabs, my dears." She opened the neck of a draw-string leather pouch and poured a hundred carved colored stones onto the table in front of her. "They are dung beetles, isn't that delicious? Actually, of course, these are

267

quartz and faience and cabochon whatevers. But they are all guaranteed antique and sacred. I think they'll make wonderful summer jewelry."

She fished in the bag again. "This is the only thing I found that was really beautiful. I bought it for my new daughter. Schuyler, here, put this on Garden."

It was a collar of gold and lapis lazuli beads, strung on fine gold wire. It covered Garden from shoulder to shoulder, dipping to her breastbone in the front and below her scapula in the back.

"It's beautiful," Garden said. "I don't know how to thank you . . . Vicki."

"Darling, don't even think of it. I was sure your eyes were just the color of lapis, and they are. I simply adore being right. It's so gratifying to have a daughter at last. Can you imagine Sky wearing a necklace like that?"

Sky obligingly put it on, to great catcalling.

Vicki invited everyone to stay for cocktails and informal dinner. About two dozen people did. The day stretched into a very late evening. Garden watched and listened and learned a great deal.

The house was not an apartment building. It was Vicki's New York home. She also had houses in London, Paris, Palm Beach and Southampton. As well as Ashley Barony.

Sky's friends were familiar with most of Vicki's houses. They had all been Sky's guests in one or more of the houses at one time or another. They all seemed to have known each other forever. Garden wondered if she would ever learn who was who, who was married and who was not, who of the married was the husband or wife of whom.

She was tired, and her head began to ache. But everything was all right. Sky was by her side. He refused to be parted from her, even at the dinner table, and he held her hand the whole time he was talking to his friends.

"Don't worry, darling," he whispered at one point. "In no time at all, you'll feel right at home."

53

Garden's acclimation began with a shock the next morning. She woke up and did not recognize where she was. She had never seen the shadowy bedroom before. Nor the nightdress she was wearing, the slippers on the floor by the bed, the robe stretched across a chair at the foot of it. And she was all alone.

What happened, what was she doing in this strange room, where was Sky? She put on the robe and timidly opened the door by the bed. It led her to a room with eight doors on each wall. Garden felt as if she were lost in a nightmare.

She tried the door nearest her. It opened onto an empty closet. The next and the next and the next were the same. She ran frantically to another wall of doors and pulled them open, disclosing inner walls of drawers. "Oh, no," she cried. She fled back to the bedroom.

There was another door on the other side of the bed. Garden turned the knob and pushed frantically but it did not move. She began to cry. She turned, searching for some way out, and the door opened silently. Inward.

She wiped her cheeks with the back of her hand. How silly you are, she said to herself. She poked her head around the open door and found a wide corridor. It had doors on both sides.

"Sky?" she called in a tiny voice. "Sky?"

Sky kissed the tears from her face and eyes. "What a foolish little thing you are," he said. "You should have rung for a maid and sent her to find me. Nobody could hear you calling. It's lucky I got impatient and came to wake you up or you'd still be lying here bawling like a baby."

"I didn't know where I was."

"Poor darling."

"Or where you were."

"Well, I'm right here now. Everything's all right."

The explanation was simple enough, Sky said. "You were so sound asleep last night that I just carried you into your room and tucked you in. Your night things were laid out, and I thought they were from your luggage. You must remember, darling, that on the yacht you somehow never got around to wearing a nightdress."

"But why do I have my own room? Why don't we have a room together?"

"Because everybody has to have a private bedroom, sweetheart. We may go to bed at different times. We always wake up at different times. Besides, it's more romantic if I visit you with lustful intentions than if we start getting used to bumping bodies in our sleep.

"You can, of course, visit me, too. My bedroom is right across the hall. That would be very nice."

Garden supposed he must be right. After all, her mother and father had had separate houses. "Will you help me find my clothes? That dressing room is nothing but empty closets. And I'd like to wash my face."

"Follow me." Sky opened all the closets and left them open. Garden's clothes were hanging behind three of the doors and in drawers behind one. Two of the doors opened to reveal a dressing table. Her combs and brushes were on it, with atomizers of perfume and a stack of handkerchiefs.

The final door was directly opposite the one that led to the bedroom. It opened into a gleaming rose marble bathroom.

"I'll order your breakfast while you tidy up," Sky said. "Do you want it in bed or at the table?"

"Makes no difference."

"Okay. See you in a minute. I'll be in your room."

When Garden returned to the bedroom, the curtains were open and it was bright with sunlight. She forgot all her fears. Sky was sitting at a table set in front of a wide window of french doors. He got up and pulled out the chair opposite him for Garden. The table was covered with a pink linen cloth. Pink-flowered china filled half the space. Sky had only a cup and saucer in front of him.

Garden sat down. She pressed her nose to the window. "Look, Sky, there's a balcony, a big one. We could have breakfast out there."

270

"When it gets warmer, we will. It's not really spring yet in New York."

Garden was looking past the balcony at the walled garden below. She was surprised to see it in the middle of New York. Somehow she had thought that the only grass in the city was in Central Park. "I'm so glad there's a garden," she said.

"I'm glad there's a Garden," said Sky, touching her hand.

Garden giggled. She looked up through the window. "I'm glad there's a . . ." she looked back at her husband ". . . Sky!" she said emphatically.

"Silly."

"You started it." They held hands and looked at each other, exchanging unspoken declarations.

"Your breakfast will get cold," Sky said softly.

"I'm not hungry. I'd rather hold hands with you."

Sky released her hand. "You won't say that in about an hour, when your stomach starts to growl. Eat up, darling. We have a busy day."

Garden lifted the domed covers, discovering an omelet, grilled trout, grilled tomato, and an assortment of hot breads. "Yum," she said. "Won't you have some?"

"No thanks, dear. I've already eaten. You can pass the coffeepot, though."

Garden poured coffee into his cup. She liked doing wifely things. "What are we doing on our busy day?"

"Some sightseeing, lunch with the Pattersons, cocktails at Mark's, dinner with somebody, I don't remember who, then the theater, and after that we'll see what turns up."

Before Garden could ask him to identify the Pattersons, there was a quiet knock at the door. "Come in," Sky said.

A stout middle-aged woman entered, sketched a curtsy and walked over to stand near the table. She had gray hair pulled tightly into a knot on top of her head and a plain, severe face with a prominent nose between small brown eyes. Her white shirtwaist fairly crackled with starch. She wore a plain black skirt to her ankles, black stockings and pumps with a buttoned strap, and a tiny black taffeta apron. "Good morning," she said. "I am Corinne, Madam's maid."

"Good morning," said Garden. She did not know what to say next. Corinne stood silently, her hands folded over her apron.

271

"Good morning, Corinne," said Sky. "Mrs. Harris will ring when she's ready to dress."

"Very good, sir. Madam." Corinne left as efficiently as she had come.

Garden looked blankly at Sky. "Do I have a maid just for me? I'm not that messy. Zanzie always said I was much neater than Mama and Peggy."

"She's a lady's maid, darling, not a chambermaid. By the looks of her, she knows exactly what to do; you won't have to train her. Just let her do her job.

"But don't let her do your hair. She might do you the way she does herself. I asked Laurie Patterson who was the best in town, and she promised to send someone. If he's not good enough, we'll get somebody who is."

During the next half hour Garden met Miss Trager, her social secretary, and Mr. François, her hairdresser. Sky told Miss Trager to consult him about which invitations to accept. "Until you learn who we like and who we don't, darling." And he told Mr. François that Mrs. Harris wanted her hair arranged so that it appeared to be all blond. "Explain to him what your man in Charleston did, Garden." Then he left. "Miss Trager will find me when you're ready to go out. I'll have Corinne sent up," Sky said from the doorway.

Garden put herself in the hands of the experts. It was not so very different from the Season and her wedding, except that the maid and secretary had taken her mother's role and Mr. François was much faster than Mr. Angelo.

At eleven she met Sky in the sitting room that adjoined her bedroom. She was wearing her best blue silk frock. Sky winked at her. "Prettiest girl in town," he said.

Corinne cleared her throat. "Madam needs some blue shoes and stockings," she said.

"We'll see to it." Sky took Garden's hat and coat from the maid. "And, Corinne, yesterday evening someone laid out the wrong night things for Mrs. Harris. Dispose of them." Sky remembered where the satin gown and robe had come from. Mitzi had left them one weekend.

"Very good, sir," said Corinne impassively. She would have done it anyhow. Before Garden saw her room again, Corinne intended to give it a thorough going-over. In cases like this there were always overlooked hairpins. lipsticks. and perfumes. if not more intimate accessories.

Sky led Garden on an abbreviated tour of the house. Their quarters consisted of the living room. where the welcome-home party had taken place. Sky's bedroom. study. dressing room and bath. and Garden's sitting room. bedroom. dressing room, bath plus a bedroom and bath for her maid. Vicki's rooms. he told her, were on the same floor in another wing. And some guest rooms. No need to look at them now.

But she might like to see the ballroom. It occupied the center section of the second floor. He opened the door and touched a switch. Six crystal chandeliers burst into dazzling refracted light. They were reflected in mirrors on all four walls.

"This was Vicki's Versailles period." Sky said. He turned off the chandeliers and walked across the vast width of the room to open the gold brocade curtains at one of the windows. "That's better." he said. "Come over here. You can see the leaves starting to come out in the park."

"Another balcony. What a wonderful house. Sky. It's like a castle."

Sky laughed. "Where else should a princess live? When I was a kid. I used to drop balloons filled with water on the people on the sidewalk." He opened the french doors. "Ummmmm. It smells like spring."

Garden sniffed. It smelled more like gasoline to her. All those motorcars on the street. She walked out onto the balcony to look up and down the busy avenue.

"Garden! Hi. Garden!" Someone was calling from across the street. She smiled and waved.

Sky jerked her back inside.

"There's somebody who knows me. Sky."

"They all know you. Garden. It's some damn reporter. Don't encourage them." Sky slammed the doors and drew the curtains, shutting out the sunshine.

Garden tried to see his face in the abrupt gloom. He sounded angry. "I'm sorry," she said. "I thought it was one of your friends."

"Never mind. Just remember not to do it again."

The rest of the tour was rapid. Sky's anger, if there had been any, was gone; Garden giggled at his sardonic commentary on the first floor. "These are the reception rooms," he said, sliding wide doors apart. "Also known as the halls of the dragons." Garden blinked at the walls. They were hung with brilliant Chinese ceremonial kimonos and magnificent screens with Chinese landscapes and figures. Red carpets with gold dragons covered the floors. The furniture was unlike any Garden had ever seen, black polished wood with fantastic carving.

"This was all done when Vicki discovered mah-jongg," said Sky. Garden shook her head. "It's a game, darling. I can't believe it hasn't gotten to Charleston yet. Everybody in the world seems to be crazy about it. I'll teach you right away. We all play."

He led her to a smaller room, also Chinese, with four baize-covered tables. "This is the mah-jongg room. These are the mah-jongg costumes." Sky opened a closet and showed her the rack of embroidered silk kimonos in all the colors of the rainbow. "Everybody picks one to wear while we're playing."

Sky looked at his watch. "We'd better get a move on. The rest is just regular stuff. The dining room you've seen. There's a breakfast room, a library, and the billiard room, the bar, also Chinese, and the dressing rooms for guests. Got it?"

"I will. If the dragons don't eat me."

Sky laughed. "I know what you mean. They take some getting used to. But they may all be sphinxes next month. Vicki's high on Egypt right now. She's always doing over some house or other. I think she supports one or two decorators in every city in the civilized world."

"My room is awfully pretty. The sitting room, too."

"That was when Vicki was nuts about Elsie de Wolfe. I think she did a crackerjack job, and I told Vicki to leave my part of the house alone after that."

Garden was happy to hear that Sky could tell his mother to leave things alone. She'd hate to wake up one morning in a mummy case. She put her arms into the coat the butler was holding for her.

"Thank you, Jennings," she said with a smile. Jennings, Sky had told her, was the real boss of the house. He could do anything, get anything, get rid of anything. All one had to do was ask. Garden wished she could ask him to make her feel less country-come-to-town. But she thought was probably beyond even Jennings's ability.

54

Garden recognized Laurie Patterson the instant she saw her. Laurie was a small, dark, energetic young woman with seal-slick shingled hair and a wide, brightly painted mouth that was her most noticeable and attractive feature. She had learned the steps of her Charleston dance faster than anyone, Garden remembered, and she had seemed to be having more fun than anyone else at the party. Garden smiled eagerly when she and Sky joined the other couple at their table.

"My dear!" Laurie shrieked, at a carefully restrained volume, "that blue, with your eyes, is absolutely smashing. Isn't it, David? I'm so jealous I could die. I'd give my right arm for eyes like yours."

David's quiet rumbling voice was the exact opposite of his wife's staccato vivacity. "You're making Garden blush, Laurie," he said, making Garden redden even more. "But I do have to say that you're right, as usual. A right arm would be a bargain price for eyes like Garden's. Trust old Sky here to find such a gorgeous wife."

Garden and Sky reveled in the compliments, each of them pleased by the praise of the other. David poured a martini from the "water" pitcher into Sky's goblet.

"How do you like Mr. François, Garden?" asked Laurie. "Antoine was furious when I practically kidnapped his right-hand man, but I told him he'd just have to lump it."

"He's very nice," said Garden.

"Unless you really like him a lot, you don't have to keep him, you know. New York is teeming with hairdressers."

Garden looked at Sky. "You like the way my hair looks, don't you, Sky?"

"Very much, darling. But what Laurie says is true. If you don't like this man, there are plenty more. I want you to be happy."

"I like him fine, I really do."

Sky raised his goblet to Laurie. "Another stroke of genius, Laurie. I don't know how you do it. Compliments." He took a hefty swallow.

"And compliments to you too, David. Best mineral water in Manhattan. You two are the tops."

"I'll drink to that," said Laurie. She clinked her glass against Sky's and sipped her martini.

Garden looked around her, fascinated by the subdued hum of so many voices and the controlled busyness of waiters and busboys. People in Charleston did not go to public places to eat. She had never been in a restaurant, except for the ice-cream and soda parlor drugstore on King Street near the movie house.

Sky gave her a menu, and she lost herself in the dilemma of choosing from the dozens of foods offered. "Shall I order for you, darling?"

"No, no, I want to pick. I'll just be a minute."

Sky told the waiter to come back in a few minutes. David refilled the glasses. "What have you two been doing on Garden's first day in New York?" asked Laurie.

"Sightseeing. We went down to the end of the island and back up again, looking at everything. The Woolworth Building, the Waldorf, Grand Central, all the big things I could think of. The tallest building in Charleston is about twelve stories, and it's the only one. Garden was suitably flabbergasted. We really should have had lunch at the Plaza. She told me this morning that there's only one hotel in Charleston, and she's never been in it."

"Are you talking about Charleston?"

"Hello, again, Mrs. Harris. Happy to have you join us." Sky took her hand in his. "I was just telling about our sightseeing tour. What I didn't say was that you really were more impressed by the department stores than anything else."

"They're so big."

"So is the Public Library, my love, but you didn't ask to stop the car for a longer look at it."

Laurie made a grotesque face at Sky. "Stop being nasty, you brute. What does a mere man know about anything as important as Lord and Taylor?"

"Guilty, guilty," laughed Sky. "This mere man knows damn all. I wanted to ask you, Laurie, if you'd take Garden around some. You know all about what places are best. Would you show Garden and have her accounts opened, and all that female rigamarole?"

"I'd love to. I adore going to all the shops. You never know what irresistible new thing might have just come in. We'll have such fun, Garden."

Laurie and David touched knees under the table, celebrating. They were a hardworking team, and they had just scored a major success. The Pattersons were not related to the multimillionaire family of that name. They never said they were, but they never denied it. It was important for people to assume that they were very rich, because it was important that they be friends with the very rich, and they knew that the rich only felt safe and comfortable with each other. In fact, David and Laurie were so deep in debt that they survived only by a perpetual nerve-racking juggling act of kited checks, money borrowed from one lender to pay off another, long weekends as houseguests when their grocer and butcher would extend no further credit, and David's dangerous, dishonest manipulation of funds in his clients' accounts. David was a stockbroker.

Laurie brought in as much income as David did. She, too, was a broker, but her activities were all underground. She made it her business to know every supplier of goods and services to the rich in New York, and she had built a reputation as the person to call if you were looking for anything difficult or unusual. Laurie always knew where you could find it. Many times, Laurie had an arrangement with the dressmaker or decorator or orchestra or caterer; her commissions were a necessary part of the Pattersons' survival system.

Garden should be an unwitting gold mine. Even more important in the long run, Garden's gratitude would soften Sky up. David had been waiting for just the right moment to suggest that Sky take his investments away from the Principessa's brokers and let David handle them. An account like that, with normal activity, would give David and Laurie an income big enough to live the way they were living. And to pay off all their obligations, especially the risky holes in other clients' portfolios. The Pattersons did not like being dishonest, they did not even admit that they were; they were, by their lights, just doing what was necessary as an investment in the future.

David scrawled his name on the lunch check. He always kept his account up to date at one restaurant so that he could entertain clients. For some reason, the very rich never thought of paying for anything.

"Say, David, what say we send the girls off to bankrupt us while you and I play a little squash? We're only a couple of blocks from the club."

"Why not?" There were some letters David had to write, but they'd have to wait. He figured that every man at the Racquet Club was a potential client.

"Fine." Sky checked the time. "Why don't you ladies pick us up at five. Will that give you enough time?"

Laurie shook her head. "Not even close. But we can get started." She touched her cheek to David's, blew a kiss to Sky, smiled at Martin, Sky's chauffeur, and climbed into the waiting Daimler.

Sky tilted Garden's chin up so that he could see her face under the deep brim of her hat. "All right, my love?"

"Of course." She echoed Laurie, "We'll have such fun." Sky handed her into the limousine. Martin closed the door and walked around to the driver's seat while Garden watched Sky and David disappear around the corner. Poor little thing, thought Laurie.

"Where shall we go first?" she said gaily.

"This is awfully nice of you, Laurie. I hate to put you to so much trouble."

"Nonsense, Garden; I love shopping, I absolutely adore it, and there's a limit to what one person can buy for herself."

"Well, I do need some blue shoes and stockings for this dress."

"Perfect. I know the most wonderful little bootmaker. You'll simply adore him." Laurie picked up the speaking tube. "Madison and Fifty-first, Martin, just past the southwest corner." She opened the console built in to the panel in front of them and took a cigarette from the malachite box in the recess. "I have to hand it to Sky's mother," she said, "she does greens so well."

Garden thought of the deep-green uniforms of the maids she had glimpsed in the house, the same green knee breeches on the footmen who served dinner, the green uniform that Martin wore, the rich green color of the car. It was the first time she had put it all together. "Thank goodness the upholstery is gray," she said. "Green makes me look like I'm dead."

Laurie trilled a giggle. "You are a stitch, Garden." Privately she thought, you'd better get used to green, little girl. It's the color of money.

*　　*　　*

278

The bootmaker took measurements of Garden's feet and promised to have the forms carved by the next day. Then he brought out samples of leathers in various textures and colors and a notebook of suggested designs.

"But I need them now," she said to Laurie.

"And we'll get you some," Laurie promised, "but they'll only be for the time being. Ready-made shoes never fit quite properly; people can tell the difference from across the room, and your feet tell you the difference with every step you take. Look how red your toes are, Garden. That's because of poor fit. Your feet will be ruined before you're twenty . . . Shall I suggest what you should have?"

"Would you? Thank you, Laurie. I don't know anything about what people wear in New York."

"I'd be glad to, darling." Laurie leafed rapidly through the sketches and samples, selecting only four simple styles. "If these are satisfactory, Mrs. Harris will think about some others," she said. "We want them absolutely posthaste. Send them to the house as they're done."

"He's wonderful for basics," said Laurie when they were back in the car. "When we have time, we'll go to a fabulous atelier where this absolutely insane genius designs incredible evening slippers. And naturally you'll want English shoes for walking . . . Martin, we'd like to go to Lord and Taylor, please."

Laurie put the speaking tube on its hook. She shifted in her seat to look intently at Garden. "You're scared, aren't you? You don't have to tell me, I can imagine. New York's a different world. I want to say something dreadfully personal to you, Garden. I hope you won't be offended.

"Sky is crazy about you; right now he thinks you are absolutely perfect. But the truth is, he won't think so forever if you don't make some changes. He's used to a certain way of living and a certain kind of people who live the same way. One of these days he'll notice that you don't look the way his friends look or act the way his friends act, and he won't think you're perfect, he'll think you're a drag. Do you understand what I mean?"

Garden twisted her hands. "Yes," she said, "I've been worrying about it ever since we got here yesterday. I'm trying, but there's so much to learn."

"I like you, Garden. I'd like to help you."

"I'm awfully grateful, Laurie."

"Don't mention it, kiddo. Look. Here we are at Lord and Taylor. Follow me. I know this place better than my own living room."

Laurie settled Garden in a comfortable chair in the shoe department, told the salesman she wanted to see everything in her size in blue, then whispered in Garden's ear, "I have to visit the powder room. I'll be back in a minute."

Outside the door to the ladies' room, she stepped into a phone booth.

"Miss Pierce, this is Laurie Patterson. May I speak to the Principessa? . . . Hello. Yes, I'm with her now . . . Yes, it will be easy. It'll take some time, but there's no problem . . . Thank you, Principessa. Goodbye."

Laurie rested her cheek on the door of the booth. "How the hell did I ever sink so low?" she asked the silent telephone.

55

Laurie stopped in at the business offices after she repaired her makeup in the ladies' room. When she went back to the shoe department, she was accompanied by a gentleman in striped trousers and a pearl-gray frock coat.

She found Garden in the same state of confusion the restaurant menu had caused. "Laurie," she said, "I never knew there were so many different kinds of shoes. I can't decide which ones I like the best." Laurie surveyed the scene before her. Garden's cheeks were glowing pink. She was so fresh and beautiful that people were unable to stop staring at her. The salesman had been joined by two others. All three men looked as if they would cheerfully lie down and let Garden walk over them in the shoes that lay all around her on the floor. Her naïve excitement had won the hearts of all the blasé New Yorkers in the entire area. Laurie felt her own heart melting. It was so simple to please this lovely girl, and she was so appreciative.

"There must be three or four you like best, Garden," she said. "Tell me which ones they are."

She turned to the gentleman at her side. "Please send down for stockings and handbags," Laurie murmured. Then she sat down next to Garden. "Try them on, and walk out to the middle so I can see."

After an hour Garden and Laurie left, accompanied by a pageboy with six boxes tied together and the gentleman from the accounts department. As they walked across the main floor to the exit, Garden suddenly stopped. "I'm sorry," she said when Laurie bumped into her. "I just saw something I'd like to buy." She looked at their escort with a shy smile. "May I please have one more thing, Mr. Anders? I can get it instead of one pair of shoes."

Mr. Anders assured her that she could have anything she wanted. Garden thanked him warmly. "It's that book," she said. "The one about the Himalayas."

"For Sky?" asked Laurie. Garden nodded. "Then we'll have it gift-wrapped," said Laurie. "Mr. Anders, you'll have it brought to Mrs. Harris's car, won't you?" She ushered Garden past the curious customers in the book section.

At the door leading to Fifth Avenue, Laurie grabbed Garden's arm. "Smile!" she ordered.

Garden smiled at the doorman who opened the heavy entrance door for them. Lights flashed on the sidewalk. "Now run," said Laurie urgently, hurrying Garden into the Daimler and pulling the shade.

I've done my good deed for Lord & Taylor, Laurie thought. That picture will be in at least three newspapers tomorrow. And I don't even get a discount here. She added up the fees she would earn from the newspapers and decided that she had done almost as well.

"Racquet Club, Martin," she said when the chauffeur was in his seat.

"What a wonderful store," said Garden. "Everybody is so nice. I want to go back and look at everything on every floor."

"And so you shall, dear. All the other ones, too. We have a lot to do."

Sky climbed into the car on his hands and knees on the floor of the back seat. "Kick me," he moaned. "I'm a terrible, unworthy person." David swung his foot back.

"Not you, Patterson. You should let me kick you for that last shot. I never saw it coming; damn ball nearly got me in the head."

"No, I'm talking to my beautiful wife. I forgot our anniversary. We were married for two full months yesterday, and I did nothing. No fireworks, no blanket of roses, no small tokens of my regard. I'm a swine." Sky got up onto the jump seat opposite Garden. "Can you ever forgive me?" he declaimed, his hand over his heart.

David took the other jump seat, and Martin closed the door. "Please forgive him, Garden," said David. "He's been carrying on like this for the past hour. I was ashamed to be seen with him."

Garden slipped her hand out of her glove. She touched Sky's temple where the skin was still damp from his after-exercise shower. She would have forgiven him if he had plunged a knife into her breast. Sky covered her hand with his, brought it down to his lips. "I am besotted with this lady," he said through her fingers.

Laurie felt her eyes sting. She forced a convincing laugh. "You should be, Sky Harris," she said. "While you were playing boyish games and forgetting your anniversary, your wife was searching high and low at Lord and Taylor for a gift for you."

"Garden." Sky grabbed her in a bear hug.

"Sky, we're in public." Garden tried, not very hard, to extricate herself.

"David," Laurie said loudly, "do you ever get the feeling you're in the way? I'm feeling very bulky right now."

The speaking tube whistled and Martin's distorted voice said, "Excuse me, Mr. Harris. My schedule indicates Mr. Mark Stevenson's address at five o'clock. Will you be wanting to go there now?"

Sky released Garden. "Christ!" he said. "I forgot all about Mark's party. It's after five now. Are you and Laurie going, David?"

"We were supposed to, but I forgot too. It'll be over by the time we change."

"Damn. Mark's so touchy, too. I've got to go. I'll tell you what. We'll drop you two, dash home and change and pick you up in forty minutes. Then up to Mark's, with a bottle of something good and profuse apologies . . . Martin, can you hear me? Full horsepower to Mr. Patterson's.

"I want to take Garden to the theater tonight, and we won't have time for dinner. Would you like to join us in eating all Mark's canapés and then a show and supper afterward?"

David shook his head. "We really can't, Sky. I've got a pile of

282

paperwork to do. I think we'll even bypass Mark's. He won't miss us the way he would you. Maybe we can do Broadway another night."

"You're on. In that case, I'll change our itinerary . . . Martin, take us home, then Mr. Patterson. Then back to the house to pick us up."

The big car swerved at the next corner. Garden was dizzy with the hectic planning and changing and racing through the thick traffic. New York was like the circus she had been to once. So much going on that she didn't know where she should be looking.

Soon Garden understood that the circus was never going to stop. Every day and every night were packed, with so much to do that she and Sky seemed always to be late wherever they went. There was always a cocktail party at someone's place or a dinner or a planned rendezvous at the Plaza for tea dancing or at Madison Square Garden for the fights or at Texas Guinan's speakeasy to watch her rob the butter-and-egg men.

And there was the theater. Garden never tired of it. The big round table in the entry was supplied every day with four orchestra tickets to every show on Broadway, plus concerts, the opera and any special event going on in New York. They saw Jeanne Eagels in *Rain*, and Garden was shocked. They saw Will Rogers in *The Ziegfeld Follies*, and everyone sang "Oh, Mr. Gallagher/Yes, Mr. Shean" in the speaks for days. Because there was always everyone. They were always part of a group, Sky's friends and his friends' friends, at parties and in the frenetic mass moves from one place to another, forever discovering a new restaurant, a new speakeasy, a new band, a new singer, a new game. They rode the subways and the Staten Island ferry, taking a band from a jazz spot and their own champagne and glasses. They went to Greenwich Village and Harlem, to the Brooklyn Bridge and Grant's Tomb. They came home when the stars faded and went to bed when the sun came up. And then at last they were alone and together, and the world did not exist outside the circle of their arms around each other. Garden's sleep was sweet then, her head on Sky's chest, her heart beating with his. And in her sleep, she felt his kiss when he tucked the covers around her and left her bed.

She always woke with a lingering smile on her lips. It turned into a giggle when she reached for the nightdress laid out for her the previous evening. After she had it on, she pressed the bell on the table by her bed, then curled into the warm nest of pillows and eiderdown to doze until the maid brought her breakfast.

"Bridget," Sky called all the maids, and all the footmen "Harold." There were too many, he said, to learn their names. Garden thought it was outrageous, but not when Sky did it. Everything Sky did was right when he did it. She learned that the chambermaid for her room was named Esther.

While Garden drank her juice, Esther opened the curtains and commented on the weather.

And the day began, as busy as the night before and the night to come. Daytime was learning time, learning to be what Mrs. Schuyler Harris should be. Garden learned to play mah-jongg and to practice the Coué ritual. She learned to tango and do the Black Bottom and the Bunny Hug. She learned the difference between the East Side and the West Side, the location of the Avenues, Broadway, Chinatown, and the Village, which she learned not to call Greenwich Village.

She learned that the hours had to be used with care, because there were never enough of them. Her personal letters were sent in with her breakfast, the envelopes slit for easy opening. They were in one deep pocket at the side of the white wicker tray. The *Herald* was in the other. She scanned the headlines and the social pages while she ate breakfast. It was important to know what everyone would be talking about that evening.

She read her letters, if she had any, while she drank her coffee. Her mother wrote often—long, detailed letters about the furnishings she had found for the Garden house on East Battery. Wentworth wrote letters that Garden relished, full of gossip and news about the girls she knew in Charleston. Peggy wrote an almost unreadable note every few weeks to say that she was too busy to write.

Garden saved the best for last. Underneath her letters there was always a note from Sky. Sometimes it was a page covered with X's, sometimes a heart with their initials in it, sometimes a scrawled "I love you, Private." Often the note was wrapped around a present. Once it was a box from Cartier containing "an acceptable gift for a lady," a single peppermint. More often, it was a box from Cartier or Tiffany with a bracelet or ring or earrings or necklace or brooch. Sky loved the color and dazzle of jewels. He loved to see her wear them, and he loved to choose them for her. His taste was excellent, but opulent. Garden felt as if she would never be grown-up enough to wear the big stones without self-consciousness. She was not yet accustomed to the fiery square diamond on her left hand. She loved to turn it in the sunlight from the window and watch the dancing flashes of blue, pink, green, yellow.

When she had finished her breakfast she rang for Corinne, and while her bath was being prepared she sat at her dressing table staring at herself, repeating "Every day, in every way, I'm growing better and better," concentrating, willing herself to believe it. She was trying, trying very hard.

After her bath Garden put on the underthings Corinne had laid out, then her clothes as Corinne held them out to her. She sat at the dressing table again, Corinne covered her shoulders with an embroidered cotton "combing-out" cape, and Mr. François came in, followed by Miss Trager. While he fixed her hair, Garden dictated responses to her letters, and Miss Trager told her what her schedule was for the day.

With every week that passed, it became more crowded. Twice a week a manicurist came in to do her nails while Mr. François worked. Once a week Garden went to Elizabeth Arden for a facial and a pedicure and, every other week, removal of the hairs on her legs and under her arms. Garden hated it. A pink-smocked technician spread warm melted wax on her, and when it had hardened stripped it off with sharp jerks, pulling out the embedded hairs from Garden's skin. "It gets easier in time," the Principessa said when she advised the treatment for Garden, "and it only stings for a second." Garden humiliated herself by screaming loudly every time.

She didn't blame the Principessa. Vicki, she knew, went through the same thing herself. Garden saw her mother-in-law two or three times a week, always for a short time. They were both so busy. Vicki always asked if Garden was happy, was there anything she wanted, did she need any help with anything. "Schuyler will do anything on earth for you, sweetheart, but he's only a man. Don't expect him to tell you what you need to know. Ask me."

It was Vicki who made sure that Garden went to a gynecologist to have a new diaphragm fitted, Vicki who told her that no man wanted a frumpy wife. "You really should just give everything you own to the Salvation Army, darling. Start from scratch. I don't want to depress you by criticizing, lamb, but frankly you depress me by looking so dreadfully Southern. You mustn't be an embarrassment to Schuyler. After all, there are dozens of girls around who'd simply adore to take him away from you."

With Laurie Patterson's help, Garden did what Vicki advised. She went out virtually every day in the Daimler, called for Laurie, and then shopped with a determination that left Laurie breathless. She attended fashion shows, studied *Vogue* and *Vanity Fair*, went to department stores and boutiques, bootmakers, dressmakers, hatmakers. She discarded her corset and learned to endure the pain of binding her breasts to achieve the right silhouette. The closets in her dressing room filled up with frocks with the shorter, mid-calf skirts and longer, hipline waists. For evening, they were sleeveless and extravagant with beading. Her evening slippers were fantasies designed by Laurie's "genius" bootmaker. He called them "Charleston slippers" and would make them for no one but Garden. Every night, at parties, dances, nightclubs, Garden danced the Charleston dance. Their friends demanded it. Garden ordered the fragile beaded silk slippers by the dozen. She destroyed a pair every night.

The servants at the house sold them to souvenir hunters for more than Garden paid for them. They sold her discarded silk stockings, too, and the perfumes and lipsticks she tried and did not like. Garden remained the darling of the press. It was an era of fads and frivolity. The transformation of Cinderella into the bright star of New York's café society was a story that never palled for the working-girl and housewife readers of the tabloids. They believed in the fairy tale, in the happy ever after.

And so did Garden. Her life was almost as much a dream to her as it was to the millions who read about it.

Everything that touched her was soft and luxurious: the silk sheets on her bed, changed every day so that no wrinkle might irritate her skin; the deep pile of the rugs to cushion her steps; the pillowlike upholstery of the Daimler; the scented, oiled water of her bath; the fluffy warmed towels to wrap herself in; the smooth satin of her underclothes and the caressing lightness of her maribou dressing gown.

Her hungers and thirsts were satisfied at the touch of a bell, never more than hand's reach away. Her rooms were always immaculate, always filled with flowers, always supplied with bowls of candies and fruits and boxes of biscuits and nuts.

She could buy anything that caught her fancy, and she did not have to carry it, unpack it or put it away.

She was surrounded by people who told her she was beautiful, admired her every accomplishment, applauded her dancing and found her every word charming because of her accent. She was the pet of her circle of friends and the idol of the public.

And she was only seventeen years old.

56

On June seventeenth, Sky and Garden celebrated their four months' anniversary with a dinner party at the house. Laurie had helped Garden plan it. Miss Trager and Jennings took care of the rest.

The theme of the party was four. The ballroom was arranged like a nightclub, with tables for four and a four-piece dance band. There were four courses, each with four items of food, four kinds of wine, four tiny vases of flowers on the table, four candlesticks, four wrapped favors at each place to be opened one with each course.

The invitations bore special instructions: men were to wear four-in-hand ties, the ladies four rings on each hand and four bracelets on each arm.

The climax of the evening came at 4 A.M. when Jennings opened the door for a group of four trumpeters who blew a fanfare for four footmen bearing a long table, which they set down in the center of the floor. On the table was a cake four feet long, made in the shape of an airplane. It was covered in green frosting, with the number four on its wings made from yellow candies. Garden threw her arms around Sky. "Happy anniversary, darling," she cried, and kissed him four times. She was wildly excited. At last she had surprised him, given him a present all on her own. The cake was a replica of the airplane she had bought him. She had earned the money by giving her endorsement for a new brand of cold cream. The advertisements would be in all the magazines in the fall.

"Here," she said happily, handing him a key ring. It had a four-leaf clover charm on it and four keys. "You said you wanted to learn to fly this summer. The plane is in a hangar on Long Island."

Sky whirled her in a circle with her feet off the ground. "We'll fly to the moon," he shouted. He was as excited as a child with his first big toy. The gift from Garden was thrilling in a way that buying the plane for himself would never have been.

He lowered her to her feet and returned the four kisses. "I'm afraid I'm a dud in the imagination department, angel," he said. He took four boxes from his pockets and put them on the table. Garden opened them to the exclamations of all the women. They contained four bracelets of diamonds, sapphires, rubies, and emeralds. Each bracelet was a band of one kind of jewel, each stone four carats cut in a square.

"What will they find to do when they've been married a year?" muttered one of the men to his wife.

"Three hundred and sixty-five pearls, of course," she replied. "That's the luckiest little dancing doll in the world."

The party was a celebration for Garden and Sky and also a farewell party. People would be leaving the city soon for the summer in Europe, Newport, Cape Cod, the Adirondacks or Long Island. They would not all be together again until October when, everyone assured Garden, New York was at its best.

Vicki had already gone to the house in Southampton. Sky and Garden would join her in two days.

They had one more big evening in the city. The following night, Mark hosted a dinner for a small group, only twelve, and the opening night of *George White's Scandals*, the new Gershwin show.

Garden had read about opening nights, but she had not been to one. Sky wanted to know that a show was a hit before he went.

The first night was everything that Garden expected, and more. Mounted police kept the crowds back while limousines pulled up and top-hatted men and elaborately dressed women crossed the narrow sidewalk to the doors of the Globe Theater. Garden saw Lon Chaney and Lillian Gish, and for a moment she thought she saw Rudolph Valentino. Photographers were everywhere, on the street, the sidewalk, even in the lobby. Unaware of what she was doing, Garden smiled without rest and opened her cape enough to reveal the gown she was wearing.

After the show, their group went to the Brewery Restaurant for supper. The Brewery was regarded more highly as a speakeasy than as a restaurant, but its German sausages and fried potatoes were considered very clever and witty for after the theater. They went with the atmosphere of the neighborhood, the tenements, the cluster of artists' one-room flats across the street, and the abandoned brewery next door. The East River was darkly mysterious, the alleys between the tenements thrillingly menacing. It was exotic, which the restless, novelty-hungry young New Yorkers admired; the simple food was exotic to them, too.

It was only one o'clock when they left the Brewery. Too early to go home, particularly on their last night in town. They argued amicably about what to do next. Someone shouted at them from an open tenement window to shut up; from another window they heard a man whistling "Way Down Yonder in New Orleans."

"Harlem," said Mark and Sky at the same time.

They had been to Harlem before, and Garden had not liked it. The black people there were different from the ones she had grown up with on the Barony; they were more black, in some way that she could not define, and they made her feel like an outsider, an unwelcome outsider, in spite of their big smiles and deep bows.

She said nothing to Sky about her dislike. Anything Sky wanted to do was what she wanted to do. And maybe she was wrong before. She had been tired when they went there; that might have made her imagine things.

"Let's go to the Cotton Club," said Mark. He was riding with Sky and Garden. The others were following in three more cars.

"I like Small's Paradise better than the Cotton Club," Sky said.

"Okay, okay. It's your wheels."

"Hell, it's your party. We'll go to the Cotton Club."

"No, no, Small's."

"How about both? It's early."

Garden suppressed a sigh.

They arrived at Small's Paradise after three. By then, Garden had a headache. It looked hardly different to her from the Cotton Club—the same audience of formally dressed whites, staff of formally dressed blacks. The headwaiter signaled, and a dozen waiters scurried to move tables together to make one big one for their party. The music was loud, and the air was thick with smoke.

The headwaiter bowed and led them on a weaving path between occupied tables to their places. A spotlight went on, focused on the curtains through which the next entertainer would come. The edge of the beam illuminated a waiter near the stage. Garden stopped in her tracks. Then she darted across the room, bumping into people in her haste, mumbling apologies. For an instant, the spotlight touched her gold head and was refracted by her diamonds. Then it moved on to the singer on stage.

"Where did Garden go?" shouted Sky above the sound of the music.

"Probably the ladies' loo, Sky," said Laurie. "Give the girl some privacy."

A few minutes later Garden slipped into the empty chair next to Sky. She put her head close to his so that he could hear her. "Guess who I just saw, Sky? John Ashley, Reba's oldest boy. You know, from the Barony. He's a waiter here."

"Garden, you shouldn't be friendly with the help. You'll get him fired."

"That's what John said. So I left. But it was wonderful to see him. He's one of my best friends. He taught me to spit."

Sky's laughter was louder than the music. He put his arm around Garden and hugged her. "You are the most unpredictably talented girl in the world," he said.

When the singer finished, the lights went on and the band started to play for dancing. "Come on, angel," said Sky, "save the spitting for another time. Show these tourists some Charleston dancing." He led her to the small square in front of the stage, set aside for a dance floor.

Garden looked around for John Ashley. He was on the far side of the room, by the bar. She smiled, and he smiled back. Then she began to dance, remembering the times when they were both children, dancing in the packed-earth yard between the ramshackle houses in the Settlement. Her body moved with the unselfconscious abandon of a child, responding to the music and the joyful freedom of the dance. Her jewels flashed, and her carefully styled hair gleamed, and the sequins on her expensive gown glittered in the dim light. But her happiness outshone them all. She was Reba's girl again, dancing for the pure pleasure of it.

One by one, the other dancers drew back and stopped dancing so that they could watch Garden. Sky stood to one side, pleased by the admiration he heard all around. Garden was unaware of any of them. The rhythm of the music was in her veins, and she had forgotten where she was.

When the music stopped, she looked around, surprised. Her face and shoulders and arms were shining with perspiration, but she was not even breathing heavily. She did not feel that she had made any effort. The music had carried her. The music and the memory.

The bandleader started to clap. The musicians, and then the waiters and bartenders joined in. John Ashley nodded his head and grinned, clapping with the rest of them. He knew, although Garden did not, that no white woman or man had ever before been applauded in a Harlem nightclub this way. He was proud of his momma's ugly little blue baby.

57

Life in Southampton was very different. Vicki's house there was a rambling, shingled barn of a place, the product of random additions by various owners over the years.

"Darlings," she cried when Sky and Garden arrived, "what do you think of my little tomb?"

"King Tut's revenge." Sky said under his breath. The living room was Egyptian, from the frescoes of hippopotamus hunts on the walls to the gilded animal-paw feet of the low divans and tables. Vicki's hair was coal-black, cut in straight bangs over the forehead and in a straight line from earlobe to earlobe. She was wearing a floating caftan and sandals made of strips of red and black leather.

"Darling Principessa," said Sky, "you are, as always, without equal." He kissed her on each cheek and introduced his guests, Margot and Russell Hamill.

"Darling," Vicki said, "I've known the Hamills for ages." She kissed Russell and Margot, then Garden. "Come along, you must be exhausted from that dreary trip from town. We're having cocktails on the porch." She led them through a confusion of rooms.

Garden stepped onto the porch and sighed with pleasure. It reminded her of the Lodge at Flat Rock, with rocking chairs and lounge chairs and a look of lazy, long twilights. The furniture was wicker, not bark, and it had cushions covered in a print of sphinxes and hieroglyphs, but that did not alter the clear impression of summer living without clock or calendar.

"I love your house, Vicki," Garden said. The sentiment was heartfelt. Until this moment, she had not recognized the exhaustion that had been building in her. Now she understood why all their friends said that one had to get out of town in the summer.

There were several dozen people on the porch, most of them new to Garden, many of them obviously old friends of Margot and Russell Hamill. Garden was not really surprised. Margot and Russell were at least ten years older than Sky; he had invited them to visit because Russell was going to teach him to fly.

That's good, Garden thought. I'll be able just to rest. It will be quiet as the Lodge, but with a sea breeze.

The vacation turned out to be considerably more complicated. Corinne was with them, and Mr. François, who was given a suite of rooms and the responsibility of all the lady guests' hair. There were still manicures and facials twice a week, and there was a party at someone's house or the club every evening. And of course they dressed for dinner every night, even though they were served by maids in bright yellow cotton uniforms instead of footmen in livery.

They worked as hard as ever to have fun. Perhaps harder. Because Sky was up early every day, after a late night. He and Russell used every hour of sunlight for flying.

And while he was away, Garden worked at her education.

She didn't call it that; to her it seemed that she was simply making friends with Margot. But the older woman was teaching her about the world she lived in. Margot loved to gossip.

She knew all about Vicki's friends, who came and went in bewildering combinations. Margot explained the marriages, the divorces, the affairs, the sexual preferences of them all. Garden didn't believe her at first. She thought Margot was trying to be funny. Garden had never heard of adultery or homosexuality or promiscuity.

But it was all around her, and she began to realize that Margot was telling the truth. She began to see things she had been blind to. before and to catch jokes that had gone over her head. The dinner-table conversations and undercurrents of eye contact were like daily lessons in sophistication. Vicki and her friends were amusingly malicious, often about names that made Garden's eyes widen. Dukes and duchesses, Vanderbilts and Mellons, even the Prince of Wales were subjects for gossip. At parties, she saw everyone through the eyes of the group at Vicki's. Slowly, she stopped being shocked.

Until Margot's gossip moved closer to her own life. Vicki, Margot said casually one day, was less discriminating than she used to be. The current interior decorator looked as if he had no stamina at all.

Garden didn't know what she was talking about.

Margot explained gigolos.

"I don't believe you," Garden blurted.

Margot laughed. "Honestly, Garden, you're so green you deserve your name," she said. "Everybody knows about Vicki. Her family arranged the marriage to Sky's father, and after five years, she ran off with a would-be actor. She was crushingly bored with being the proper Mrs. Harris, Gramercy Park hostess and heir-producer. The scandal gave poor old Harris a heart attack even before the divorce was final, and she promptly married number two. Nobody can remember his name. He was a flop as an actor and as a husband, in spite of all the plays Vicki backed and all her youthful charms. So she paid him off and got a divorce.

"Then she bought herself the title. The prince had a falling-down palazzo and a lot of relatives to support, but Vicki didn't find out about them until after the honeymoon. He cost her enough to pay the national debt of Italy. And the divorce—the price was astronomical. After that, no more husbands.

"Now she buys lovers she can fire when she gets tired of them. And she has the princely coat of arms on all her linen. Why not? She can afford it."

Margot looked at Garden's tear-filled eyes. "Grow up, sweetie," she said kindly. "You're in the big wide world now."

"That's so sad, Margot. Poor Vicki. Maybe she'll meet a nice man and . . ." Garden was stopped by Margot's raucous laughter.

Later, when they were having cocktails on the porch before dinner, Garden caught herself looking at Tony, the decorator who was translating the house into Egyptian. Her speculations about his relationship with Vicki embarrassed and upset her.

I shouldn't listen to Margot, she thought. I'm as bad as she is.

That night she talked to Sky about it. She repeated everything Margot had told her, except about Vicki. "I don't want to believe her, Sky, but she seems so sure. Is it all true?"

Sky kissed the top of her head. "Poor baby, you're shocked, aren't you? Don't let it bother you. That's just the way things are."

Garden stared up at him, pleading for reassurance. Sky held her close. "For other people, darling," he said. "That's the way things are for ordinary people. Not for us. We're special."

For the next week, Garden avoided Margot. She didn't want to learn any more about life. She buried her head in books on flying. She did want to learn about what Sky was doing. He was having the time of his life, he said, and he was the luckiest man alive to have a wife who would think to get him an airplane for a present. His wife, his marriage, his happiness. They were all special.

58

The books were boring, and Margot was not. Garden rejoined her on the porch for lemonade and conversation. Margot smiled and told her funny stories about Mrs. Keppel and King Edward.

"Of course, poor Edward had the most appalling mother complex," she said, "but nobody knew what it was in those days." Like everyone in her circle, Margot talked breezily about Freud.

Garden looked blank. Margot recommenced her role as teacher. Sexual inhibitions, she explained, were the root of all illnesses, physical and mental. The rules society imposed on people were unnatural, impossible to follow without repressing basic instincts that were the healthiest part of the mind. That's why people had inferiority complexes and asthma, bitten fingernails and homicidal mania.

Garden listened and learned. And every night nestled in Sky's arms hearing about his adventures in the airplane, happy that they were different, were adjusted, were special.

*　　*　　*

By the start of August, the house party was breaking up. "Beach life is so boring" was heard on all sides. Vicki declared that what Southampton needed was a casino.

"In France, there's always a casino. Beaches demand baccarat." She organized a group to go to Deauville. Margot and Russell were invited to Ireland for the horse show and yearling sales. Sky could fly as well as he could now, Russell said, so there was no need to stay.

Sky complained that the thunderstorms in the afternoon made it impossible to make any distance flights. "I think I'll head for the plains," he said. "I'd like to see the barnstormers in action anyhow."

Garden's heart sank. She had been up with Sky several times, and she told everyone how thrilling it was. But flying terrified her. She felt exposed and vulnerable, and she was convinced that the wind would tear her out of the open cockpit and drop her, screaming, spiraling, to the patchwork earth below. "What a lark, darling," she said brightly. "When shall we leave?"

"You can't come on this trip, Garden. There'll only be men and dusty fields to land in and half the time only some shack of a hangar to sleep in."

She was so relieved that she barely realized it meant that she and Sky would be apart.

Until the day he left. She rode to the field with him, although Sky protested that his 5 A.M. departure made it absurd for her to even think of getting up. He was vibrant with enthusiasm for the adventure of heading west without knowing what might be in store. Garden waved and smiled valiantly while the little green plane bounced down the sere brown grass of the airstrip and took off. Sky circled and buzzed the field, leaning over the cockpit to blow her a kiss. In his leather helmet and goggles, he did not look like Sky at all.

Garden cried for the entire drive back to the house. Smith kept his head rigidly facing front. She wiped her eyes and blew her nose before she went in. It was now seven-thirty, and some early riser might see her.

Vicki met her at the door with a cup of coffee. "Poor precious," she said. "I was afraid you'd be blue. Here, drink this. It'll perk you up."

Garden took a swallow. It warmed her and felt sharp in her nose.

295

"There's a tot of brandy in it," said Vicki. "It will do you good."

Garden started to remind Vicki that she never drank anything except a sip of champagne when there were toasts, but she didn't want to appear ungrateful. And the warmth was comforting. She didn't know how she could bear the feeling of emptiness without Sky.

She sobbed; Vicki patted her shoulder with a scarabed hand. "Why don't you come along to Deauville, Garden? It's terribly amusing. I can book your passage in half a minute."

"Thank you, Vicki, but I really can't. I want to be here when Sky gets back. Whenever."

"More fool you, sweetie. What you should do is dash off for a good time and collect some admirers. It would do Schuyler good to be a little jealous. Imagine the crust of him, heading for the wild blue yonder the week before your six months' wedding anniversary."

Garden wept harder than ever. She put her head in the Principessa's lap and abandoned herself to her misery. She could not see the small, satisfied smile on Vicki's face.

Two days later, Garden was alone. After she finished her morning Coué, she spoke firmly to herself in the mirror. "You are not going to mope. There is plenty to do." She walked briskly to her desk and made a list. "Learn to drive. Read. Write letters." She was trying to think of something else when a knock on the door saved her from having to add anything to the list.

"Good morning, Mrs. Harris. I'm Mrs. Hoffmann, the housekeeper. I have today's menus for your approval."

Garden looked blank.

"The Princess is gone, Mrs. Harris."

"Oh. Yes. Of course. Well, let me think." She had never wondered how the meals got on the table; they had just been there. She held out her hand for the loose-leaf notebook Mrs. Hoffmann was holding.

"Wednesday, August 8, 1923," read the top of the page. Then:

LUNCH
Cream of Watercress Soup
Toast Fingers
Cold Salmon, Sauce Verte

Endives Vinaigrette
Popovers
Peach Compote
Macaroons

DINNER
Pâté de Foie Gras Truffé
Toast Triangles
Medallion of Beef, Bordelaise
Pommes de Terre Soufflées
Petits Pois
Lettuce Salad
Cheeses: Gruyère, Camembert, Edam,
Bel Paese, Gorgonzola
Assorted Breads
Strawberries, Crème Fraîche

Romanée-Conti 1913

Garden studied the page for almost a minute. "You know what I'd like?" she said. "I'd like a hot dog and a hot fudge sundae."

"I beg your pardon, Mrs. Harris?"

"Oh, nothing. I was just talking to myself. This looks fine, Mrs. Hoffmann."

"Thank you, Mrs. Harris. The Princess always tells me to keep the meals light out here. I know you're used to better in the city. Would you just initial the page, please."

Garden put a neat G.T.H. in the corner and returned the book to the housekeeper. After Mrs. Hoffmann left, she picked up her list of things to do. "Run house," she added. She blotted the page with a firm touch. It felt good to be busy.

Sky telephoned that night when Garden was having her solitary dinner. He had gotten all the way to Ohio. "I don't know the name of the town," he shouted over the static of the bad connection. "Hell, I don't even know if there is a town. I met up with some guys, and they showed me how to sling a blanket-hammock under the wing of the plane. How are you, darling?"

"Oh, I'm just peachy. I played mah-jongg at the club all afternoon, and there's a party at the Wellfleets' tonight. Tomorrow I'm going to make Smith start teaching me to drive. I'm very busy."

"Good girl. I'm starting lessons tomorrow too. One of these fellows is a stunt pilot."

"Sky, don't! I'll be scared to death."

His laughter crackled with static. "Don't be silly, angel. Don't you know I'm the best cloud jockey in America? I just need the guy to show me the ropes. There's nothing to worry about."

"But I do. Worry, I mean."

"Well, don't. You just have a good time."

"Okay."

"All right, then, sweetheart. So long."

"Sky! Sky!"

"Yes?"

"I miss you, darling."

"I miss you, too, angel face. You take care of yourself."

Garden held the telephone earpiece for a long time before she hung up. He doesn't miss me one single little bit, she said to herself. Then, I will not mope.

She went back to the table and finished eating. Then she fixed her makeup, and Smith drove her to the party.

Elliott and Francine Wellfleet were Vicki's friends, but there were six or seven of the fringe friends from Sky's age group there. Garden circulated easily, parrying jokes about being deserted for the farmers' daughters of the Midwest and the sex appeal of the airplane. "It's enough to give me an inferiority complex," she said with a make-believe pout, and, "Well, we all know about dreams of flying." When Elliott Wellfleet put his arm around her waist and asked if she wasn't lonely in that big house, she was able to smile, despite his familiarity. "When I start getting lonely, Elliott," she said, "believe me, you'll be the first one I'll tell." She moved his hand from her hip and joined a group that was talking about the new President.

"Harding's stroke was just the kind of damn fool thing you could expect from him. The man was a clumsy jackass at everything he did. Coolidge may be a cold fish, but at least he gets things done. Remember the police strike?"

Garden drifted away. Politics was boring.

A few days later she telephoned Wentworth Wragg at Flat Rock. "Please come visit," she said. "I'd love to see you. The porch here

298

makes me think a lot about the Lodge and you and all the good times we had."

Wentworth's train arrived at Pennsylvania Station in New York at four-thirty in the afternoon. Garden took the train in from Southampton that morning. She wanted to be on the platform to meet her friend herself.

"Garden, you look so elegant."

"Wentworth, you look just wonderful."

Privately, Garden saw Wentworth as rather frumpy, with her ankle-length skirt and face clean of cosmetics. Wentworth thought Garden looked fast. She had on flesh-colored stockings, a thing no lady would wear, and her dress had short sleeves.

"The heat is awful in the city. We'll leave first thing in the morning." Garden started up the platform to the stairs.

"Hey, Garden, what about my bags? Shouldn't I get one of those redcaps?"

"Martin's got them."

The chauffeur took her baggage check, touched the visor of his cap. "Thank you, miss. I'll take care of everything."

Wentworth hurried to where Garden was waiting. The platform was crowded with people, elbowing, shouting for redcaps, counting their bags, perspiring and irritable because of the heat.

"This must be New York, all right," Wentworth said cheerfully.

"Say, Garden, this really is the life," she said when they were in the back of the big limousine. "I could get used to this kind of treatment in about half a minute."

Garden giggled. She had really not thought of what her life would look like to Wentworth. To her, it had become commonplace to be driven by Martin. "Wait till you see the rest, Wentworth. It's a fairy tale come true."

Wentworth was loud in her admiration of everything. Sometimes vocally loud, sometimes with silent oh's of her lips and raised eyebrows. Her enthusiastic amazement did not stop for hours. "Gosh, Garden, you mean you have all these rooms . . . a marble bathtub . . . all these clothes . . . shoes . . . hats . . . a man to fix your hair . . . breakfast in bed every day . . . a real butler . . . a lady's maid . . . parties all the time . . . *all that jewelry?*"

Miss Trager accompanied them back to Southampton. Partly because, with the Principessa's secretary in Deauville, there was no one to manage the mail, but mostly because Garden was enjoying the exhibition of her sophisticated life to Wentworth. If Wentworth happened to be in her room in the morning, Garden always made a change in the menu. At parties, she called everyone she knew "darling" exactly like Vicki. She wore her diamond bracelets every night, whether they were going out or not.

But for the most part, she was still the Garden of the summers at Flat Rock, giggling, playing games and eating forbidden treats. She had ordered some bicycles so they could ride into Southampton village for Eskimo Pies. But they never used them.

The bright yellow roadster was in the driveway in front of the house when they arrived from the station. It had a foot-wide blue velvet ribbon around it, with a bow in the center of the hood. "What is it, Smith?" Garden cried.

Vicki's chauffeur smiled. "It's an anniversary present, Mrs. Harris, a Duesenberg with a six-cylinder engine. Mr. Harris said I was to teach you to drive it."

Garden hugged Wentworth. "You'll teach Miss Wragg, too, Smith."

The driving lessons, and later the driving, took up most of Garden's and Wentworth's daylight hours. The two of them agreed that Garden was the luckiest girl in the world.

"I can't complain," Wentworth said. "Ashby Radcliffe took me out a lot last spring, and he came up to Flat Rock for a week in July. I guess he'll ask me to marry him when I go home."

"Do you love him, Wentworth?"

"Sort of. I miss him when I don't see him. But . . . cross your heart you won't tell?"

Garden crossed her heart and begged lightning to strike her if she said a word.

"I'm still crazy about Maine Wilson. I shouldn't even be your friend anymore. He's carrying a real torch for you."

"For me? He's my cousin."

"Only second. That doesn't count. I'd wait for him to get over it if I thought he'd look at me. But, let's face it, Garden, I threw myself at his head, and it did no good at all. He'll never want me, and I'll always want him. That's just the way it is."

"Wentworth, that's so sad. I'm going to cry."

"Don't. I've done enough crying for both of us and a dozen

besides. I like Ashby a lot, we'll be happy. You'll be in my wedding, won't you?''

"I'll kill you if you don't ask me."

"Sky's coming home, Sky's coming home." Garden put the telephone on its hook and ran onto the porch shouting.

"Wonderful. When? Will I get to see the plane?"

"Sunday. And no, you won't get to see it. Thank goodness, he gave it to some friend he made in Nebraska. I hated that thing. He's coming home on the train. I can stop fretting about him getting killed."

"Shoot, Garden, my train leaves on Saturday. I'm sorry to miss him."

"You can't go, that's all. We'll have a wonderful party. I'll tell Miss Trager to hire a brass band to meet the train, and we'll just keep on going."

"I can't stay. Do you realize how long I've been here? It's the end of September."

"But, Wentworth, now it's time to go back to the city. There'll be the theater, and all the speaks, and everybody will be back from everywhere. October's the best time of all in New York."

"The best time for funerals if I stay. Mama is losing patience."

In the end, Garden capitulated. Maybe it was all for the best, she thought. It was fun having Wentworth visit at the beach, but she really wouldn't fit in in the city. Nice as she was, she was still kind of country-come-to-town.

59

Garden nearly bit Mr. François's head off. "You missed a place." She threw the hand mirror down on the dressing table. "There's a streak of red showing in the back. My husband hates it when you can see any red. I don't have all day, Mr. François. I'm meeting his train."

301

Mr. François showed her that it was only a trick of the lighting. Her thick coils of hair were a uniform gold to the observer.

"I'm sorry," Garden said. "Everything's been going wrong, and I'm upset."

Going wrong just when she most wanted everything to be perfect. The day before, after she put Wentworth on the train, she had gone out to buy an especially pretty new outfit to meet Sky in. The clothes this year were different, she discovered, very different. Hats had hardly any brim at all, and skirts were over an inch shorter. Nothing that she had in her closets would do. Maybe some frocks could be hemmed, but certainly not the evening dresses with all the beading. It would ruin the patterns. She'd have to go through it all again, all the shopping, all the fittings. Worst of all, she hadn't found a dress good enough for meeting Sky. She looked dowdy, she just knew it.

My God, Sky said to himself, I'd forgotten how beautiful she is. How could I have forgotten? He enveloped Garden in a close embrace, and the image of the sun-tanned, jodhpur-clad girl in Nebraska faded from his mind.

She had been exciting. Different. A pilot herself and an exhibition wingwalker. He had really hated to leave her; he'd given her the plane and a diamond necklace to remember him by, sworn that he never would forget her.

But she was part of that other world, the world of spins and Immelmanns and moonshine whiskey and flying. And he was tired of that world. It was fun, totally absorbing until he was good at it. Then it became, all at once, confining and screamingly boring. Just the way mountain climbing had. And polo. And sailing. And tennis. Sky's interests were intense, and then over.

"Is Martin here?" Sky said close to Garden's ear.

"Yes."

"Let him bring my luggage. We'll take a taxi. I want to make love to you so bad I can't wait."

He had forgotten how good it was. Better than whatever her name was, better than anyone else ever. Sky wrapped Garden's breasts in her magic hair and began to love her all over again.

The Principessa came back from Paris with a young lover who had no profession other than his charm. She was displeased. Her son was honeymooning with his wife in her house.

"The magazine will be out next week," Miss Trager told her. "I checked on it myself."

"Garden, what the hell is this?" Sky threw the November issue of *Vogue* across the room onto her bed.

"Sky, you spilled my coffee."

"I don't give a good goddamn about your coffee." He picked up her breakfast tray and threw it on the floor.

Garden burrowed into her pillows, frightened by his anger. "What is it, Sky? What's wrong?"

"You. Your picture in this magazine. Selling cosmetics."

"Oh. Let me see. I'd almost forgotten." Garden sat up and started leafing through the pages. "This is how I bought your present, Sky. The plane. They paid me five thousand dollars to take my picture." She smiled radiantly, confident that now he would understand and approve.

His face was a portrait of disgust. "Who the hell do you think you are, Garden? A showgirl from the Ziegfeld Follies? You do not sell your face for money. It's as whorish as selling your body for money. Don't I give you enough? Do you want for anything? Jesus, I thought you were great to get me the goddamned plane. To order it. Have it delivered. I never thought you would insult me by paying for it. And certainly not this way. I'm ashamed of you."

Tears streaked Garden's cheeks. "I didn't think," she whimpered. "I'm sorry, Sky. I'm sorry."

"You sure are."

He slammed the door behind him.

Miss Trager left the sitting room quietly to go make her report.

Laurie Patterson called that afternoon. "I haven't seen you in an absolute age, Garden. I've called, but your secretary is such a dragon, she always tells me you're busy."

"I was, sort of."

"Can you make room in your schedule for an old friend? Henri Bendel has some hats in the window that I've just got to get a close look at. What about lunch at the Plaza tomorrow and then a little spree?"

"Thank you, Laurie. I'd like that."

"Twelve-thirty, then. Palm Court."

* * *

Garden walked unseeing through the soaring marble lobby of the hotel. The first time she saw it, she had stopped to look in awestruck wonder at the magnificence of it. Every other time, she had slowed her steps a little to appreciate the elegant space and the feeling of luxury it gave. Now it was only a passage to the restaurant.

The headwaiter unhooked the velvet rope across the entrance and bowed. "Good afternoon, Mrs. Harris." Garden had been known by name at every public place in New York ever since the first photographs of her wedding appeared in the newspapers.

"I'm meeting Mrs. Patterson," she said. Her voice was flat.

"Of course. Permit me." He led her to the table where Laurie was waiting.

"Champagne," Laurie said, "to celebrate seeing you again—Sweetie, what's the matter? You look like your best friend died."

"I'm so miserable, Laurie. Sky and I had our first fight."

"Poor baby. Have a drink, it'll make you feel better, even if it is in a coffee cup. You should have seen the look the waiter gave me when I pulled out my flask. Go on, Garden, drink it. Then tell me all about it."

"Is that all? Garden, don't be a silly. That will be forgotten as soon as the next issue comes out."

"The photographers are after me again, too. They were waiting when I came out of the house."

"Darling, they'll go away. Some new story will be all the rage in a week. Besides, Sky isn't really worried about the picture. He's upset because you did something on your own. It hurt that stupid male pride all men have. He'll get over it in no time."

"Laurie, I don't know how to say it—"

"Go on, darling. You can tell me."

"Last night, Sky didn't . . . I mean, I waited, the way I always do. I thought we'd sort of kiss and make up, you know. But he never came to my room."

"Darling, that happens. Married people don't make love every night. That's stolen weekend stuff, not marriage."

"But it's the first time, Laurie. Since we've been married. Except for when he went out west. It's the first time."

"Listen to me, Garden. It may be the first, but it certainly won't be the last. It happens. It happens to everybody after they've been married a while. Believe me, it's more comfortable. It doesn't mean that you don't love each other. It's just—well, it's the way marriages are.

"Now let's order something to eat. Then we'll go over to Bendel's. There is nothing on earth as good as a new hat for picking up the spirits. You'll see. What you absolutely must not do is droop. When Sky gets over his little temper tantrum, he's going to be looking for a pretty, happy, smiling little wife."

"Try this one, Garden. The blue lining will be sensational with your eyes."

Garden took the hat from Laurie's hands. "It doesn't fit. None of them fit. I've tried on ten hats, and they're all too small."

The saleslady whisked the hat away. "Madame is trying the cloches. They do not allow for so much hair. Now, we have this one. The crown is roomy, for long hair. And the blue feather will be lovely with the eyes."

Laurie waved her hands. "Horrible," she said. "It's absolutely horrible. It's—old hat. Garden, darling, you've simply got to bob your hair."

"Laurie, I couldn't."

"Of course you could. And should. You'll feel like a different person. Aren't you sick to death of depending on François? With a bob, all you do is run a comb through it and—poof—ten seconds, and you're ready to go."

"But you don't understand. I have these hideous streaks of red in it. Mr. François hides them underneath."

"Is that all? My dear, I know a man who can do things with bleach that would make Raphael weep with envy. I'll call him this instant and tell him that he must take you at once. Get them to wrap up that divine number with the blue lining. You'll be wearing it this afternoon."

"Shake your head, madame."

Garden shook her head. The smooth golden cap of hair swung from side to side, then slid back into place. Bangs skimmed her eyebrows, and heavy wings of hair folded themselves just under her earlobes. She held the hand mirror to look at the shingled back. It was like a series of shining steps. "I feel so funny," she said, "so light."

"It's called light-headed," cracked Laurie. "You look absolutely smashing. Didn't I tell you Demetrios was an artist? I don't know

305

why people flock to the French, when the Greeks were the ones who invented art.''

Demetrios accepted the compliment with an inclination of his curly head. "You understand, Mrs. Harris, that you must be diligent about the trim, the color, and especially the thinning. Never in my life have I seen such thick hair.''

"It's not thick now. And not striped. And not heavy. I love it. Make me a regular appointment for every Friday. You won't believe how fast it grows.''

"Here, Garden, put on your hat.''

"Oh, Laurie, do I have to? I'm so pleased with my hair. Sky always despised the red. He was the one who insisted on Mr. François so it could be hidden. He'll be so surprised.''

Laurie held out the hat. "Put this on. You'll look adorable.''

Garden did not look adorable. She looked stunning. Like a model. Or a movie star. Or the most beautiful showgirl from the Ziegfeld Follies.

"This is Judas Iscariot, Principessa,'' said Laurie into the telephone. "Send the pieces of silver. Your daughter-in-law is now no different from any other well-groomed, well-dressed, excessively rich, young New York society girl.''

60

On October twenty-ninth, a new show opened on Broadway. It was an all-black musical revue called *Runnin' Wild*, and it took New York by storm. The song *Runnin' Wild* was an instant hit, as was another song, and the dance that it accompanied. The song was "Charleston," the dance the Charleston.

It was the dance that Garden did—less wild, more polished for the Broadway stage—but it was the same. Her friends all felt as if they were vastly superior to the hordes who were doing the Charleston now.

They had learned it from Garden months before the rest of New York. She was the group's pet, their star. They loved to wait until everyone in a nightclub was doing the Charleston. Then they would bang on the tables and begin to shout. "Garden, Garden, Garden. Do the *real* Charleston."

And because Sky was watching, because Sky always nodded encouragement, Garden would dance. She danced with a furious abandon, born of despair, giving herself to the beat of the music for the momentary oblivion it gave back.

And sometimes, sometimes it excited Sky, and when they got home in the pink morning light, he would follow her into her room and make love to her on her pink silk sheets.

So that next time, Garden danced even more frenetically, hoping that everything would be the way it had been, that Sky would be the way he used to be.

It did not happen.

There were no more fights, no shouting, no harsh words. Sky was charming, conversational, attentive to her comforts. He treated her with the same practical consideration he extended to all the women he knew. The same.

Garden tried tears, pleading, even writing notes and leaving them on his pillow. Just tell me what's wrong, she begged, so I can try to make it better.

And Sky answered that nothing was wrong, that he was busy . . . or tired . . . or he didn't answer at all.

Runnin' wild. It seemed to Garden that the mad pace she had set last spring was only a crawl compared to her life now. There were more parties, more escapades, more nightclubs, more speakeasies, more search for excitement, for something new, more rushing from place to place than ever before. She was tired all the time.

And sad. But she couldn't let it show, especially to Sky. She had to win him back. With smiles, with laughter, with dancing.

"You've got to be gay, darling," Laurie said. "Drink some champagne, it will make you bubble."

"You've got to be chic, darling," said the Principessa. "The sweet little small-town girl is charming for a very short time."

"You've got to show you don't care," said Margot, "or you become an embarrassment."

The woman's name was Alexa McGuire. She was a thin redhead

from California. She had come to New York after her divorce to "get away from all that goddamn sunshine." She cursed, drank, chain-smoked and did nothing without consulting her astrologer. "Sky." she said when she met him. "what a superbly suggestive name. What's your sign . . . Sky?"

Sky's birthday was November eighteenth, he said.

"Scorpio. Magnificent. Scorpios are so sublimely sensitive."

Margot hissed over Garden's shoulder. "Snakes are so sensationally sinuous. Watch her wiggle her tail."

Sky did not come home on his birthday. Garden had planned a dinner, just the two of them, in front of the fire in the living room.

The next day she found an astrologer in the Village who charged her a thousand dollars to draw up her chart. "You have a bad configuration," the woman said. "You are unhappy. But Venus will enter your sign in a good aspect after three weeks, and all will be well."

"Hooey," said Laurie when Garden told her what she had done. Garden agreed with her. The astrologer had not been very convincing. Still, it gave her something to be hopeful about. While she was being massaged, peeled, pedicured, bleached and fitted for frocks, gowns, hats, coats, furs.

Alexa was always attired in something new, something startling, something shiny; and furs. Furs against which she rubbed her face, eyes closed, lips parted, growling a rasping purr; furs which she shed from her shoulders into Sky's waiting hands; furs which she slid down her arm and dragged behind her as she walked. Garden bought scarves, stoles, jackets, capes, coats in seal, mink, leopard, fox, caracul, ermine, chinchilla.

The astrologer's three weeks were up on December tenth. When Garden came home from shopping at five, it was already dark.

She was dressed à la Russe in a fitted red coat with a full, swinging skirt and elaborate black braid frog closures. Black Persian lamb trimmed the hem and made up the wide collar and cuffs. She wore black suede boots with red tassels and a deep shovel hat of black lamb. Her nose and cheeks were pink, her eyes bright. Melting snow spotted her coat and glistened on her hat.

Sky was in the living room, in a chair by the fire. Garden did not see him until she had taken off her outdoor things and crossed to the fireplace. "Oh, Sky," she exclaimed. "Do you know what? It's snowing. I've never seen snow before. It's so exciting, the air's full of it, and the ground is getting all white. I couldn't bear to sit in the car. I walked home, just letting it fall on me and catching it in my hands." She rubbed them together near the flames.

Sky smiled indulgently. Her enthusiasm was charming, her pink nose adorable. "Sit down," he said. "Let me take off your boots. Your feet must be frozen."

Garden tumbled into a deep armchair, still chattering. "Do you suppose it will just snow and snow and keep on snowing? The hedges in the park are already white on top. Everything would be white and sparkly. They're playing Christmas carols on the streets. I passed a Salvation Army band. People were all crowded around, singing. I stopped for a while and sang, too. 'O Little Town of Bethlehem.' It was lovely."

Sky rubbed her feet between his hands. They were like ice. "You'd better have a hot bath or you'll catch cold. How far did you walk?"

"Oh, I don't know. From St. Patrick's. I crossed over and came through the park when I got to the Plaza."

"That's two miles, Garden."

"I don't care. It was wonderful. Do you think it will keep snowing until Christmas? It'll be just like Currier and Ives. Do you think I could learn to skate?"

"You can learn to skate, but not this year. We're going to the South of France."

"Oh, no! And miss the snow?"

"We can take a trip to Switzerland. You'll see more snow than you ever dreamed existed. You'll love the South of France. The Mediterranean is like nothing else in the world. The water is an incredible blue, a lot of blues. It's changeable, like your eyes are sometimes."

"My eyes?"

"Yes. The blue in your eyes changes. Sometimes it's darker, sometimes it's lighter. And when you wear green, they become the color of the Mediterranean. You'll have to wear a lot of green over there."

Garden felt cozy and loved. "Mlle. Bongrand told us about the South of France. You know, she was my French teacher at Ashley Hall. 'The Azure Coast,' she called it. Isn't that a lovely name? I

309

always wanted to see it. She made it sound so beautiful. When are we going?"

"The day after Christmas."

Garden's half-closed eyes flew wide open. "But we can't. Wentworth's wedding is January third. I'm a bridesmaid, Sky, don't you remember?"

"No, I don't. You didn't tell me."

"Yes, I did. It was right after you came home from Nebraska. Wentworth had been visiting at Southampton, and she called about a week after she went back to Charleston."

"Well, I don't remember. It doesn't matter anyhow. Just write her and say you can't make it."

"I can't do that. I promised. Besides, Wentworth is my best friend. She was in our wedding, and I want to be in hers."

Sky put Garden's feet on the floor. He moved to the chair opposite hers. "Okay, then," he said. "You go to Charleston. You can come over to Monte Carlo after the wedding." He picked up the evening paper and began reading.

Garden's feet felt cold. She tucked them up under her body. "Aren't you coming to Charleston?"

"I already told you. I'm sailing the day after Christmas." His voice came from behind the newspaper.

"Why can't we both go in January? It's only a week later."

"Because my horoscope says that the early days of Capricorn are the best time to begin a new venture."

"For Lord's sake, Sky. Are you really doing that horoscope junk?"

Sky put down the paper. "It's not junk, Garden. That's ignorance talking. Astrology is a science, pure mathematics. It's been proven for centuries. In spite of all the efforts of the churches and governments and other powerful groups, it still exists. It can't be stamped out. because it's there, it's real. You can't destroy the universe and all its workings."

Garden had seen that fired-up look on his face before, when he first got interested in flying. She felt a surge of hopefulness. If it was just astrology, the way it had been just flying . . .

"Is Alexa going to the South of France too?"

"Of course. She's going partners with me."

"In what?"

"The venture. We're going to break the bank at Monte Carlo. It makes such sense, don't you see? The roulette wheel, or the dice, or the cards, they're all numbers. Mathematics. Astrology is all numbers, too, in its measurements and calculations. All we have to do is chart the numbers and find the relationships and then—,–pow!—we'll be able to forecast what numbers are going to come up. It's all science."

61

Garden arrived in Charleston on December thirtieth. She came alone. Corinne was packing her things for France, and Miss Trager was organizing the delivery of the last-minute warm-weather clothes that were not yet finished as well as the change-of-address announcements and travel arrangements.

Garden took a regular compartment in the regular train and took her meals in the diner. Vicki had offered her private car, but Garden declined. She thought it would be fun the other way, she said.

Several people in the diner recognized her. One asked for her autograph. The most recent photographs had been in the newspapers only two days earlier. There was an entire page devoted to the send-off party on the *Paris*, the French Line's modern new ship, for Sky's sailing. Garden was pictured on the dock, on the gangplank and a half dozen times on the grand staircase to the giant steamer's foyer. The page's headline was "Modern. Classy. *Paris* Chic." There was also a photo of Alexa McGuire in a leopard cape with a leopard cub in her arms. The cub's name, the tabloid reported, was Zodiac.

Margaret Tradd was at the station to meet her daughter. "Garden," she cried. "Garden, you look so different." She kissed Garden's cheek.

"I've cut my hair."

"I knew that. I've seen pictures. What I mean is, you look so grown-up."

"Well, Mama, what do you expect? I was eighteen last week. Thank you again for the earrings. They're lovely."

Garden gestured. The sleeping-car porter, two redcaps and the station master hurried forward. She spoke briefly, accepted an envelope from the stationmaster, and put folded bills in various hands. Then she took her mother's arm.

"Come on. I can't wait to see the house. Don't worry, my bags will be delivered." They walked through the cavernous station; heads turned to look at Garden. She was wearing a gray fox coat that fastened with a gray satin bow on the left hip. She moved with an assurance that announced that she was someone to watch.

"The taxicabs are at this end, Garden."

"I've hired a car. I'm so used to having one now. If you like it, I'll leave it with you. It's really easy to learn to drive."

The car was a gray Packard phaeton. "I know it looks big, Mama, but you wouldn't have traffic problems with it. Everybody would get out of your way." Garden got in behind the wheel, opened the envelope and took out the key.

That's it, thought Margaret. That's how she's changed. She's used to giving other people orders. She's used to being rich. Margaret got into the car without a word. When they arrived at the house, she showed her daughter around, anxious for her approval.

The house was on East Battery, one of the row of great houses overlooking the Cooper River near its meeting with the wide harbor. It had a handsome anomaly, with piazzas that stretched across the front of it as well as the side, and a five-sided bay on the front that rose from the granite-block walls of the tall ground-level basement to the pointed-cap roof four floors above. The bay extension contained a delightful, airy circular staircase to a wide hallway along the north wall. From it opened the usual rooms of a great Charleston single house.

The woodwork on the windows, doors, cornices and mantels was exquisite, Adam in its grace and lightness, but particular in its design. The gardenia made subtle appearances in every decorative element. Even the bronze knobs on the doors were incised with the symmetrical petal pattern of the flower. In the center of each ceiling, a flat plaster rosette of gardenia design surrounded the base of the chandelier. In the drawing room, the medallion was an entire wreath of gardenias with interwoven vines of ivy.

312

The furniture had the unmistakable patina of wood that has been cared for during more than a hundred years of use. Some of it Garden remembered from the house on Tradd Street. Much of it was new to her. So were the curtains, carpets and upholstery. It did not, however, have the stamp of newness. The colors were soft, the patterns discreet.

"It's beautiful," she said sincerely. "Much more handsome than the Barony or any of the Principessa's other houses."

Margaret flushed like a girl. "I'm still working on it," she said eagerly. "I'm trying to track down things that belonged to the Gardens before the War. I get letters from antique dealers all through the northern states. That's where everything went, naturally."

Garden looked at the roguish Ashley cavalier above the drawing-room mantel. He seemed to be thinking the same sardonic thoughts she was about Margaret's gullibility and the honesty of antique dealers. "That's a wonderful idea," she said.

She found it strange to be in Charleston again, a bewildering blend of the familiar and the unexpected. She had dinner with her mother, reminding herself not to think of it as lunch, then went for a walk along the Battery. It gave her heart a lift that was both happy and sad, she didn't know why. The day was warm, typical of Charleston at the end of the year, and she needed only the light wool jacket to her suit. The tide was low, and she inhaled the rank, sulfurous odor of the marsh mud with a feeling of homecoming. Visitors always wrinkled their noses in disgust at the smell of pluff mud. Garden, like all Charlestonians, thought it smelled just the way low tide should smell.

There was a breeze that white-capped the waters of the harbor and made her lips taste of salt. Gulls swooped and cried their raucous cries. At the park, White Point Gardens, little children played games and climbed on the cannons, relics of Charleston's wars, while their dahs sat on green-planked benches and talked in sharp, singing Gullah. Garden walked through the park, crunching the oyster shells of the path under her feet, swinging a long beard of Spanish moss as she passed under a great live oak. She stopped at the perpetually bubbling artesian fountain and drank the warm mineral water with a half-dreamy feeling that she had never been away, that it was a year ago, two years, ten. Everything was as it had always been.

Except that she saw it so clearly. She had never looked before, or listened, or tasted. The children had been there, and the dahs, the

313

sounds of play and warm black voices, the metallic ever-spouting water. She had never noticed them. Now she saw the colors of the children's sweaters, the funny, unsteady, lurching walk of a little boy in pursuit of a squirrel, the comfortable sleeping child pillowed on the white apron of his dah's soft breast. There was so much happiness in the small park, such a wealth of love.

Garden smiled as she passed by the benches, exchanging "good afternoons" with the black women. She stood for a moment beneath a palm tree, listening to the rattle of its spearlike leaves. Then she crossed South Battery and walked up Church Street.

She thought of Mr. Christie when he was trying so hard to make the art students see what they were looking at. I see, Mr. Christie, she said silently, I see it now. A black man came along, pushing a weathered wooden cart with squeaking wooden wheels, singing a song of his own making about the fine edge he could sharpen on knives. "How do?" said Garden.

"Pretty fine, Missus," he said, incorporating the words in his song.

Garden walked to Tradd Street. On the corner a turbaned black woman was sitting on a canvas stool, half dozing in the slanting rays of the sun. She waved a palmetto fan lazily above the small table at her side. Garden stopped, and the waving became more vigorous. "Shoo, fly," the woman said.

"Have you got any groundnut cakes, Mauma?"

"Sho' I do, honey. Fresh made this morning." She took a wrinkled brown paper sack from the pocket of her calico skirt.

Garden pointed to two of the candies. She felt her mouth watering. Groundnut cakes had always had the lure of forbidden fruit; Zanzie and her mother did not allow them. Twice only had Garden dared to buy one, and she had been terrified for days that she would be found out.

She ducked in a recessed doorway, took one out of the bag and bit into it. Her eyes watered from the pleasure of it. Ground peanuts, honey and orange peel combined to create an ambrosia of salt, sweet, tart. She ate the second cake too, savoring the candy and the sin of eating on the street. Then she walked on to the house she still thought of as her home in Charleston.

It looked extremely small. Garden walked past it at first without recognizing it. She didn't remember its being so little. Or dilapidated. Surely that corner had not been like that, bricks missing like gapped teeth in an old crone's mouth. And that paint, had it always been dirty and peeling? She was standing in a shadow. The chill of the winter afternoon cut through her clothes.

She walked briskly to the end of Tradd Street, past the dock where she had boarded the yacht on leaving Charleston, along East Bay Street to East Battery and the mansion where her mother now lived.

"Wentworth has been calling every ten minutes," said Margaret. "The ringing kept me from getting my nap."

"Sorry. I'll call her in a minute." Garden took off her gloves and her hat. The right glove was sticky; a crumb of groundnut was stuck to it. Garden picked it off and put it on her tongue. "I can't remember, Mama. Is my room at the front of the house or the back?"

"The back. Over the garden."

"I'd rather sleep at the front. I want to hear the shrimp man and the vegetable man in the morning."

"Whatever for, Garden? They'll just wake you up."

"We don't have street callers in New York. I want to hear them."

"All right, if that's what you want. I'll tell Zanzie to move your things."

The phone rang before Garden could say thank you.

Garden drove to Wentworth's house and parked near the corner where she had bought the candies. On the way she stopped on the Battery and threw the gloves, the evidence of her crime, in the water. No point in having Zanzie accuse her; she'd have to confess that she had done it and that, furthermore, she was not sorry at all. The gloves didn't matter. She had plenty more just like them.

She made the proper fuss over Wentworth's wedding presents and trousseau. She had sent a lace-trimmed silk gown and peignoir to the bridal shower and a silver punch set as the gift from Mr. and Mrs. Schuyler Harris. They were glaringly prominent amid Wentworth's other things. "Lord, Wentworth, I'm embarrassed to be so splashy," Garden apologized. "But there's no way to pretend that I'm not rich now, and I figured you'd understand."

Wentworth was not embarrassed. "I love them, and I sure never would have got them any other way. When I have a baby, I'm going

315

to wash him in the punch bowl. A silver spoon in the mouth is nothing to compare with a silver bathtub."

They ate supper with Wentworth's parents. It was an elaborate meal for a Charleston supper, and the Wraggs made sure that the conversation never flagged. Of course, Garden thought. Wentworth told them all about New York and Southampton. They must think I expect a Harold or an Elsie to hand me my food. She knew that Mr. and Mrs. Wragg would never feel natural with her again. Or probably anybody else in Charleston. The sooner I leave, the better for us all, she thought with sorrow and resentment. I haven't changed a bit. They're the ones who are different.

62

"Swimp, swimp, raw swimp. Get your swimp he-ah."

The cry woke Garden just as the sun was rising. Her hand felt automatically for the bell on the bedside table. There was none. Dammit, she thought, two flights down for coffee, and I'll have to talk to Zanzie while I drink it. She turned over and went back to sleep. The vegetable seller woke her next. This time she went to the window and opened the curtains to listen. Across the railings of the piazza she could see the river, the waters flat and glassy in the early morning stillness. The green-gray water looked like pewter. The sky was the same. The sun had not been up long enough to clear off the winter overcast. A white gull flapped across the gray sky and dived at the gray water, scooping up a silver fish. Then all was still again except for the now-distant song of the vegetable man. It was very peaceful.

Across the rooftops, St. Michael's bells chimed. "Dick Whittington, bring back my cat," sang Garden softly with them. Then again. It was the half hour. Half after what, I wonder, she thought. "Half after coffee time," she said aloud.

She put on her cashmere dressing gown and slippers and ran down to the kitchen. "Good morning, Zanzie," she sang.

316

"What you doing up? It ain't but half past eight."

"I'm sniffing for coffee, that's what I'm doing, and I smell some."

"You done got mighty brassy since you turn Yankee," Zanzie grumbled.

Garden drove out to the Barony in the morning to see Reba and Matthew and the rest of her friends at the Settlement. Reba admired her haircut and her dress and was fascinated by the solution to Garden's bi-color hair. "And all that time, I was bleaching clothes and never knew you could bleach people." Garden told them about John, urged them to go visit him. "Maybe so," Matthew said. That meant they never would, Garden knew.

When she got back to town, Garden went, on a whim, to Ashley Hall. She'd love to see Mlle. Bongrand, tell her that she was going to the Côte d'Azur. A maid came to the door of the Main House conservatory. "Nobody's to home," she said. "This here is vacation." Garden felt like a fool. Of course nobody would be there.

"You're new here, aren't you?" she said. "I'm an old girl. Garden Tradd. I don't live in Charleston any more, and I just wanted to see my old school. May I come in?"

The maid admitted her reluctantly. Garden walked up to the hall, felt the rising spirits the spiraling stairs had always given her. "I didn't realize how much I loved this place," she said softly.

"Yes, ma'am, but I gots my floors to do."

"I understand. Thank you for letting me in." Garden walked down the drive, conscious of her posture, re-creating deportment class. How they had all laughed when she showed them the way she could carry a basket of laundry on her head. She'd have to remember that. In New York, it would be a great party game. One she would win, too.

"Garden, my dear, I'm so glad you could come." Elizabeth Cooper kissed her. "Sit down and tell me about the big city. Can you stay for dinner? I should have asked you on the telephone, but I was so delighted to hear from you, I wasn't thinking."

"I should have called earlier; I didn't know what my schedule would be until I got here and talked to Wentworth. I'll have to go home for dinner."

317

"Of course. We'll just have tea." Elizabeth tugged the bellpull. "Now let me hear all about you."

They talked comfortably for about an hour, speaking with affectionate dishonesty. Elizabeth did not say that she thought Garden was becoming brittle or that her laugh was shrill; Garden did not say that her great-aunt was annoying her with her questions. Can't you see that I don't want to talk about my life? she wanted to shout. Can't you see that I'm trying to pretend that nothing has changed?

That night Garden went to the Yacht Club New Year's Eve Ball with Wentworth and Ashby. They're all going to stare anyhow, she thought, I might as well give them their nickel's worth. She was angry because she couldn't find anything. Zanzie had unpacked her suitcases and put things away. She pulled out drawers and pawed through her underthings, trying to match camisole to underskirt, and shoved her dresses around in the wardrobe, uncertain of what to wear or where her slippers were or what Corinne had packed. When she finished dressing, the room was a wreck and she had a headache.

But she looked like a queen. Her white gown was beaded all over in a honeycomb pattern of silver paillettes. It rose almost to her knees in front and dipped to the floor in the back in a masterpiece of seaming to produce a trumpet flare from below the hip. Her slippers were beaded all over in silver. Her shoulders and throat were powdered and buffed, her face rouged and her eyes lined with blue. Her lips were bright pink.

Garden looked at herself in the mirror. "Very Cinderella," she said. She felt again the way she used to before a dance in Charleston: frightened and tongue-tied, clumsy and stiff. "Come on, Garden," she said to the mirror, "you're the darling of the best speakeasies in New York. You've sold more cold cream than Pola Negri. What are you afraid of?"

She opened her jewel case, pulled out drawers, unsnapped suede pockets. Then she put on her birthday present from Sky, a necklace with honeycombs of diamonds, and lozenge-shaped diamond clips in her hair above her ears. She pulled on a fresh pair of long white gloves, fumbled with the buttons at the wrist, hated herself for not bringing Corinne. A wide diamond bracelet on one wrist, two narrower ones on the other. Sky's Christmas present.

She found her evening bag in the desk, then realized that it was empty. No handkerchiefs, no powder case, comb, lipstick, perfume. She wanted to scream. Never again would she travel without a maid.

Never again would she come home and feel that nobody wanted her.

Margaret was waiting up when Garden came home at one-thirty. "How was the dance?" she said eagerly. "I don't have to ask if you were the prettiest one there."

"It was horrible, like Charleston dances always are. The men all talked about how many ducks and bucks they shot, and the girls all said, 'Oh, really? How wonderful.' " She dropped her floor-length white fox cape into one chair and her glittering self into another. She had been the belle, undisputed. And she had been genuinely bored. She missed the crackling, fast-paced, competitive humor of New York conversation, the puns, innuendos, gossip. She missed the good dance bands playing the latest songs, the professional singers, the blue spotlights and popping champagne corks. She held out her arms. "Would you please undo these bracelets, Mama? I can't work the clasps with gloves on."

When the bracelets were off, Garden peeled her gloves down and dropped them on the table. The clips followed. They fell on a huge leather-covered book. "What are you reading there, Mama? I don't see how you can lift it."

"I thought you might want to look at it." Margaret carefully moved Garden's things and turned back the book's cover. The newspaper announcement of Garden's coming out party was pasted in the center of the first page.

"It's your scrapbook," said Margaret proudly. "The *News and Courier* gets everything that's in any paper anywhere for me."

Garden leaned forward, turning the pages and reading. She had never seen the results of all the cameras thrust at her when she went out. She was stunned by the volume and fascinated by the pictorial change from pale, nervous young girl to polished, poised young woman. "Is that really me?" she said with delight.

Margaret nodded proudly. "I haven't had a chance to paste this one in yet. It's a whole page."

They were the pictures from the sailing. Garden looked at them, smiling. Until she came to the one of Alexa. Next to her, Garden thought, I look like what I am, a small-town hick dressed up in big-town clothes. "I'm tired," she said. "I think I'll go to bed."

"Garden, you're leaving your jewelry."

"Leave it. It's not important. My secretary probably picked them out."

The wedding rehearsal was the next afternoon, with a tea afterward at the Radcliffes' house. Garden dressed very carefully. I'm going to look as frumpy as I possibly can, she promised herself. This is Wentworth's time to star. She was sorry now that she had had her own dressmaker do the dress she would wear as a bridesmaid. It was from the pattern and fabric Wentworth specified, but somehow it would look New Yorky, Garden was sure. She put on a plain blue dress. Too cool. She removed the striped silk belt and tie. Too funereal. She added a wide gold necklace. Too rich. She took it off. Then she took the nail scissors from her manicure case. She cut across the yoke of a silk dressing gown that had a lace collar, stuffed it inside the neck of the dress and smoothed the collar. Almost. She rifled the jewel case, hoping against hope. It was there. The antique locket that Elizabeth had given her. Perfect. There was nothing she could do about her blue lizard T-strap pumps, but probably no one would notice. No makeup except a little powder. No other jewelry except her wedding and engagement rings. Wentworth would wonder if she didn't wear those. She packed a blue handbag, grabbed gloves and car keys and ran down the stairs.

"Garden, you don't have a hat."

"I have a lace handkerchief for my head, Mama. All the girls wear them." And my hats are all too damned fashionable.

The wedding party was gathered under Saint Michael's portico. Garden parked her car across the street in front of the post office. When she stopped, four black women came hurrying up to the car, vying with each other to hold bunches of flowers closest to her. These flower sellers were a regular part of the Charleston scene, the post office their prized post. Garden waved them away. "What do you take me for, a Yankee?" Her Gullah dialect was strong.

The women laughed and exclaimed and backed away. Garden laughed with them. It was a beautiful, sunny day, the baskets of flowers by the post office wall were bright masses of color, her best friend was getting married, and she would be on her way back to New York, then to France, day after tomorrow. She felt good. She

320

walked with them to the place where their stools and baskets were and began to bargain fiercely.

A few minutes later, with the flower sellers' claps and laughter accompanying her, Garden crossed Meeting Street with all the flowers in one basket and that basket balanced on her head. "Bouquets for the bridesmaids," she called.

It was much later when she realized how lucky it was that no photographer had been there.

63

The *France* was smaller and older than the *Paris*, but it had an elegance that the modern, geometric-design decorations of the newer ship could not even approach. Gilt boiserie, brocades and damasks, murals of Fragonard-like pastoral scenes abounded. It was Louis XIV from stem to stern and had a nickname that summed it up exactly. It was known as the "Château of the Atlantic."

It was festooned with flags, its funnels already smoking when Garden boarded. Cameras clicked constantly, recording the scene.

Miss Trager preceded Garden, carrying a portfolio with travel documents and special instructions, neatly typed, to be delivered by the chief steward to all crew members who would have any contact with Mrs. Harris.

Garden followed her, ignoring the photographers, the other passengers on the ship's decks, and the people on the pier who were waving goodbye to friends when they were not staring at Garden. It was January 6, and it was cold. Garden was wrapped in sable, the deep collar turned up to form a hood, her gloved hands tucked in their opposite sleeves. The coat was pinned closed at the neckline with a diamond sunburst brooch.

Corinne was heavy-laden with more furs over her arms and a square leather case clasped in both hands.

"Snatch that, and you could buy Brazil," said one reporter. "That's the lady's jewel case."

His friend whistled. "My wife's clothes wouldn't fill that case. How many diamonds can a woman use?"

"As many as she can get, junior. Shut up and count the luggage. Three, four, six steamer trunks."

"I make it sixteen suitcases."

"Close enough."

"Wait a minute. What are those?"

"Hatboxes. Call it fifty, and let's blow. It's starting to sleet."

Garden had a pale blue-and-gold bedroom, a gold-and-white sitting room, and a green-and-gold small sitting room for Miss Trager's office during the six-day crossing. Miss Trager's stateroom was on a different deck, Corinne's in second class.

"I'll be on deck, Corinne," she said. "I want to see the Statue of Liberty. When I come back, I'll want a bath and a glass of champagne."

"But, madame. How do I locate the bootlegger?"

"This is a French ship. They never heard of Prohibition."

Garden had read the folders provided by Miss Trager with close attention. Secretly, she was very excited at the idea of crossing an ocean. And she was happy to be back in her pampered life where someone knew where to find whatever she needed.

Miss Trager found her on deck. She shouted above the deep hoots of the tugs' horns. "The Captain has invited you to sit at his table, Mrs. Harris."

"No. I want a large, single table. By myself. Not even you, Miss Trager. And I want second sitting."

The first-class dining room of the *France* was two stories high, with a domed ceiling soaring above the open center. Elaborate iron rails edged the balconylike second level surrounding the oval. The balconies and dome were supported by paneled columns with gilded bas-relief Corinthian capitals. The second level was entered directly from the ship's central foyer. The lower level was reached by a magnificent wide staircase designed for grand entrances.

Garden Harris's arrival for dinner was the essence of the grand entrance. She was opulently gowned and jeweled, with a small ermine wrap for her shoulders, but most of the women in first class were equally richly dressed. She was extraordinarily beautiful, but so were several of the women. What made heads turn when Garden entered was her proud carriage, her effortless descent without looking down, and her taking her seat at a table that would hold six comfortably and had a place setting for one.

The table had already excited speculation. Royalty was the only logical explanation. Garden was an astonishment.

She had not intended to invite attention. She really wanted to be by herself on the crossing. Now that the trip to Charleston was over, she had nothing to distract her from the awful dilemma that she had to face. How was she going to get her husband back? She was miserable, and she had to think, to plan. She couldn't stand the prospect of making conversation with a group of strangers for six days. Nor did she want to be crowded at a tiny table. The cuisine of the French Line was famous, and Garden liked to eat, especially when she was unhappy. She intended to eat well at every meal, and she wanted room for breads and relishes, sauces and bowls of butter. Therefore, she had wanted a big table.

Now that she had it, and so conspicuously, too, she determined to see it through. She even enjoyed the attention, although she gave no sign of noticing it. Let them gawp. And talk. Let Sky Harris hear about it. His wife could make everyone look at her without cheap tricks like leopard cubs.

The seas were smooth for the North Atlantic in winter, but rough enough to distress many travelers. Garden was not bothered at all. The heavy clouds meant that she could be on deck as much as she liked without fear of sunburn. She bundled up in her warm hooded coat and walked the Promenade Deck for twenty minutes at a time. Then she stretched out in her deck chair with a blanket over her legs and spent twenty minutes working at her chief project. She was learning to smoke. All the women in their group smoked. Alexa smoked constantly. Garden puffed and coughed for twenty minutes, then walked for twenty minutes while the cold wind cleared her lungs.

"I have been watching you." The man was tall and menacing. His tweed coat had a full-cut body and a cape across the shoulders. Both were blown by the wind into flapping shapes that came too close to Garden's face. Her legs were imprisoned by the blanket

323

tucked around them; she couldn't walk away. She looked for a deck steward, but there were none in sight.

"Go away," she said.

The man bent his knees and stooped by her chair. "My child, I am not offering to rape you," he said. "I would like to give you a helpful hint about smoking. I've seen you every day, and you're not making much progress."

He had a nice face. Deep wrinkles around the eyes and windburned skin. And he wasn't laughing, as far as she could tell.

"Are you a doctor?"

"As a matter of fact, I am. Francis Faber, M.D. Would you like to have my card?"

"No, thank you. Are you a chest doctor?"

"Alas, no. I'm a brain doctor, a psychiatrist. Does your chest hurt?"

"I can't stop coughing. I wondered if maybe I have a deformed chest."

"I seriously doubt it. You're not taking in enough air with the smoke."

Dr. Faber took one of Garden's cigarettes and demonstrated. After a while, they walked together. Then they went into the bar and smoked some more. With a bottle of champagne. He was wearing plus fours and a heavy turtleneck sweater. His shoulders were very broad.

"I thought all psychiatrists wore beards," Garden said. She was smoking rather well.

"We don't have to follow Freud's face, just his mind," said Dr. Faber.

They talked about Freud.

The steward asked if they cared for more champagne. The doctor said no. "It's almost time to change for lunch. May I escort you to your cabin?"

"I know where it is, Dr. Faber."

"I beg your pardon. I'm afraid I'm very old-fashioned."

Garden sighed. "No, I'm very rude. I don't know why I was so snippy. I apologize." She giggled suddenly. "You probably know why I was rude. You're a psychiatrist."

"You weren't rude at all, Mrs. Harris. A bit defensive, perhaps, but I can understand that. A strange man speaks to you without being introduced . . . It's not what a lady is accustomed to."

"What does 'defensive' mean?"

64

The next day, Francis Faber was already flapping around the Promenade Deck when Garden went out for a walk. He doffed his cap. "Good morning, pupil."

Garden fell into step with him. "I must have bored you with all those questions yesterday. I'm sorry.

Faber laughed. "You cannot conceive of the luxury it was to talk so much. In my profession, the only thing I do is listen to other people. Please, I beg of you, ask all the questions you like."

There was only one question that mattered to Garden: how do I make my husband love me again? She couldn't ask that. And, she suspected, Faber couldn't answer it.

"How did you become a psychiatrist?" she asked instead.

The story Faber told lasted through walking, smoking, bouillon, more walking and lunch served on trays in the deserted bar with champagne and cigarettes. It was a story of poverty, hard work, scholarships, dedication and ultimately service to the suffering.

"Such a long time," Garden said when the story was ended. "It took you such a long time before you were a doctor." She was astounded that anyone could work so hard for so long without giving up.

"Yes, it was a long time. I was over forty when I received my final degree. Now I am fifty, and I'm going to Vienna to start learning all over again."

Fifty. He could be her father. "What will you do in Vienna?" she asked politely. She almost added "sir."

That afternoon, Faber suggested that they have dinner together. "I have my meal alone on the balcony," he said, "and I look down and see you alone at your table. It seems a shame, when we could be enjoying a meal together. I could light your cigarette instead of the four waiters who collide trying to be the first one there."

Garden considered it; it would be pleasant. But, "No," she said, "it would give people the wrong idea. You know what they say about what goes on on shipboard."

"Very prudent. Yes, it makes me sad, but I agree. However, there is no reason not to meet in the nightclub after dinner for a brandy and a dance. The orchestra is quite good."

They were. Garden had heard the music on the way to her suite after dinner. "I'd like that," she said.

"What a good dancer you are, Dr. Faber."

"What a good flatterer you are, Mrs. Harris. I know only one thing, the box step. I'm hopeless with anything more modern than the fox-trot."

Garden thought of Miss Ellis and her dancing school days.

"Why are you smiling such a charming, misty smile?" said Faber quietly.

Garden told him about Miss Ellis and about her abysmal failure as a dancer.

"I can't believe it." They were dancing perfectly together, bodies moving in flawless coordination to the easy beat of "Who's Sorry Now?"

"It's true. And it got worse. Do you know, I was hit by a car, and when I saw it coming, the only thing I could think was 'thank goodness, now I won't have to go to that tea dance.' "

"My poor child." He pulled her closer to him to execute a smooth spin. When it was done, he kept her close.

Garden did not notice. She was occupied with a new thought. "If it's true that there are no accidents—psychologically speaking, I mean—then do you suppose I stepped into the street on purpose?"

"Accidentally on purpose?"

"Yes. I wonder. Good grief, I might have been killed. How stupid." She saw that Faber's wide shoulder was very close to her cheek. I'd like to rest my head on it, she thought, and close my eyes and dance all night. The music was so good, the sway of their bodies, the feel of a strong arm around her waist. She came to with a start. What on earth was she thinking? Her foot stumbled against Faber's.

"I'm sorry," he said. "Did I crush your toe?"

"No, not at all. It was my fault. I must go now."

"Must you? I did hurt your foot, didn't I?"

"No, no, I promise you, you didn't. I'm just ready to leave."

"Of course." He escorted her to their table. While Garden gathered her bag and gloves, Faber picked up her cape. He followed her to the exit and laid it across her shoulders.

"Please allow me to see you home," he said. "I want to be sure you're not limping." He offered his arm.

Garden tucked her hand in his elbow.

"Shall we go by the deck? The fresh air will make you sleep soundly." He did not wait for her assent, but led her to the door onto the deck. An attendant opened it on their approach.

"At last," Faber said, "it's clearing. We'll have our first blue skies tomorrow." There was no moon; the stars were as bright and as close as lanterns held overboard from the top deck.

"How beautiful," said Garden.

"You've never seen the stars at sea? Come, have a good look." They walked past the lighted windows to the bow of the ship. It looked as if they were moving ahead into the star-strewn heavens.

Then the stars were blotted out by Faber's shoulders and his head as he embraced her and pressed his mouth to hers. His lips moved against hers, and his strong warm hand moved under her cape to her neck, down her back, pressing her to him, to the base of her spine, pressing her against him, pressing himself against her.

A warmth filled Garden's heart; a tingling filled her arms and legs. Her hands traveled up his sides to his shoulders and around his neck, and she returned his kiss with all the hunger in her love-starved heart.

Her cape fell away. Faber's lips moved to her throat and down to her shoulder.

"Oh, my God," Garden cried. She twisted in his arms. "What am I doing? Let me go."

Faber lifted his head, loosened his arms, caught her wrist in his fingers. "Don't be frightened," he said soothingly. "Trust me. It's the most natural thing in the world for a man and a woman to want each other, take each other."

"I love Sky. Only Sky. I want him."

"And so you should, my dear. And at this moment, you want me. It takes nothing away from your Sky. He is not here. I am. We can enjoy each other."

"No. I don't believe that. It's wrong." Garden wrenched her arm free and ran across the deck. Faber picked up her cape, started to follow her, then stopped. He tucked the wrap under his arm, took out a cigarette and lighted it in his cupped hands. The flaring match illuminated his smile.

"So fashionable," he murmured, "to spout their misconceptions of Freud. And so frightened when they meet them head on." He flipped the match overboard. "A pity, though. She must be extraordinary in bed, this one."

Garden did not leave her staterooms for the rest of the voyage. Her meals were sent in, and her champagne and cigarettes.

She had been caught off guard, she told herself, Dr. Faber had taken advantage of her. She had had—what was it called?—transference to him.

But she knew that, for a moment, she had felt something that she had never felt before. Faber's kiss was different from Sky's kiss, and it was thrilling. Dangerous. Exciting. New.

She had never thought that one man's kiss was unlike another's. Or that she could tolerate the touch of anyone but Sky. Or that there could be any desire without first being in love.

Now the thoughts invaded her mind day and night.

65

The baroque opulence of the *France* had prepared Garden perfectly for the Principessa's Paris house. Great Paris mansions, she had learned, were called, in French, *hôtels particuliers*. Vicki's house was roughly the size of a small hotel. Like the *France*, it was decorated in style Louis XIV, with an exuberance of gilt, marble and murals.

The colors of the *hôtel* were plum and gray, for livery, uniforms, letter paper. Instead of the green and gray of New York or the yellow and white of Southampton. The butler was an English-speaking Frenchman, named Bercy. The chauffeur was Maupin. The automobile was a gray Delâge with plum upholstery. The life was the same.

A maid showed Garden to her rooms. Her bedroom even had a balcony overlooking the garden, like her room in New York.

But this was Paris. Garden looked through the books on the shelves in her sitting room, confident that a guide to the city would be there. Sky was coming up to meet her; she'd like to have some suggestions of things to do together before they left for Monte Carlo. Maybe they could have dinner out. No matter how good Vicki's chef was, it wasn't the same as the restaurant in the Eiffel Tower. Or Maxim's.

She was looking at an illustration of the curious device used to press duck when Alexa came in.

"Darling Garden, how divine to see you. Do be an angel and get a Marie to bring up some domestic champagne." Alexa sank gracefully into a chair.

Garden was looking at the door.

"Sky didn't come, Garden. He's working dreadfully hard, and I was coming up anyhow, so he asked me to bring you back."

Garden was too stricken to speak. Alexa rattled on.

"Dear boy, he's really wearing himself to a frazzle. The system just won't come right. One kink after another. But he doesn't let it get him down. He's a bucket of laughs all the time. I stole the joke about the domestic wines from him. Imported in New York is domestic here. Get it?

"And, for God's sake, get some right now. Ring the goddam bell in the goddam gold cupid's belly button. I've never seen anything as obscene as this house in my life."

Garden's hand found the bell push concealed in the table leg beside her chair. When the maid entered, she ordered champagne.

"But, my dear, you speak French, how smashing. I, of course, do not speak a word. I find there's always someone around to translate . . . I wish that Marie would hurry. I do think it's too funny, the way Sky names the servants. At the hotel, he calls all the waiters and bellboys and desk clerks Maurice. The croupiers are Henri."

When the maid returned, she was accompanied by Bercy. He opened the champagne, poured two glasses and put the bottle in the silver urn cooler. "Will there be anything else, madame?"

"No, Bercy, thank you." He bowed out. "What is your name?" Garden asked the maid.

"Véronique, madame."

"Very well, Véronique. We shall serve ourselves. You may go."

Alexa walked over to the table with the champagne. She carried a glass to Garden, drained hers and refilled it.

"This isn't easy," she said. Bringing the bottle with her, she pulled a chair close to Garden's and sat down, leaning forward. "Listen, kid. I'm not as cold-blooded as I look. I don't like to see people suffer. I told Sky I had to come up to see about some clothes, but I really came to head you off. Don't come to Monte Carlo, Garden. Stay in Paris. Go home. Your husband is in love with me. Everybody knows it. They'll laugh at you. Why go through all that pain?"

Garden looked intently at the bubbles rising slowly in her glass. "Are the Paris clothes really that different?" she said.

"Are you crazy, Garden? Didn't you hear what I said?"

"I heard you. I'm thinking about what you said. I just wondered, since you mentioned seeing about clothes, what was worth traveling all the way from Monte Carlo for."

"If you must know, Chanel's winter collection was all Russian. And Monte Carlo is simply crawling with Russians. I thought it would be amusing to get a few things before the spring collection makes them out of date."

"Démodé."

"What?"

"Démodé. It means out of fashion. And I'm betting that's what you are, Alexa. I know how long it takes for fittings. Sky would never have let you go away for days if he was really in love with you. I think you're trying to bluff me."

"You're wrong. But it shows there's no sense trying to be nice." Alexa poured more champagne. She raised her glass to Garden. "No hard feelings, I hope. I've got nothing against you personally."

Garden leafed through the guidebook. "I think I'll go see the Eiffel Tower this afternoon. Would you like to come?"

"Ah . . ."

"And the Louvre."

"No, thanks, kid. I have some shopping to do. See you at five or so."

As soon as Alexa left, Garden turned back through the guidebook. *"Train Bleu,"* it said, "the luxurious mode of travel to the Côte

330

d'Azur. The train connects Paris directly to the beaches and casinos of Cannes, Nice, and Monte Carlo. Meals are prepared under the supervision . . ." She read quickly through the long paragraph. Then she ran across the room and opened the door to her bedroom. "Pack all those things again, Corinne. We're leaving in a half hour. Find Miss Trager. I need reservations at once."

Garden found Sky at a table in the sitting room of his suite in the Hôtel de Paris. Papers with calculations scrawled on them were spread all over the table and the floor around the table.

"What a surprise," he said. "I thought it would take days for Alexa to turn Russian."

"Maybe it will. I came on without her." She hovered in the doorway, waiting to see if her gamble would pay off.

"Well, come on. Don't you have a hug and a kiss for your poor, hardworking husband?"

Garden ran to him.

Their lovemaking was tempestuous and totally fulfilling. "My darling, my own darling love," Sky mumbled into her shoulder, "you are wonderful."

I've won, Garden exulted silently. She cradled Sky's head close with her hands, feeling the familiar, beloved contours of his skull. He was bewitched by that astrology mumbo jumbo, but now he's over it and Alexa with it. She'd forgive him before he even asked.

They spent the afternoon driving along the Corniche, the winding road on the mountains that overhung the narrow strip of land along the sea. The views were breathtaking. "This must be the most beautiful place in the world," Garden said again and again. Above and below them, gleaming pale villas clung to the mountains, surrounded by steep terraced gardens bright with flowers, soft with the blurred gray-green of olive trees. Ancient towns stepped up and down the crags, their only streets a series of twists and steps so narrow that the stone walls of their houses seemed to lean together overhead. The road turned and wound, sometimes in a steep bend with nothing between them and the mountainside below. As it turned, the sea vanished, then reappeared, freshly surprising the eye by the rich, incomparable purity and power of its color. Garden was terrified and enchanted. "The Azure Coast," she cried triumphantly. "I'm really here."

They stopped at an inn that perched precariously on the edge of a cliff and drank a wine that was made there from the grapes that grew on terraced slivers of earth behind the inn. They sat in a stone courtyard with their backs warmed by the sun. The wine was tangy—pink, not red, with an edge of effervescence. An occasional leisurely bubble rose from the bottom of the heavy goblets. The proprietor brought them bread and cheese. Garden was completely happy.

"I wonder what the inn is like. Why don't we stay here instead of at the hotel?"

"It's probably full of fleas. Besides, the hotel is only a step from the casino. I wouldn't relish this road at night."

"You're still gambling?"

"Darling, that's what Monte Carlo is for . . . When did you start smoking, Garden?"

"On the ship. Everybody seems to enjoy it so much, I thought I'd try."

"We'll go to Cartier tomorrow and get you a holder or two."

"Wait a few weeks. You can give them to me for our anniversary."

Sky put his arm across her shoulders. "That's right," he said with a smile. "We're an old married couple. A whole year."

Alexa gave an anniversary party for them at the flat she had taken in a house in Nice. She had returned from Paris the day after Garden's arrival and found her suitcases neatly packed by Corinne.

"You were right," she said to Garden. "I was bluffing. I could feel my time running out, and I figured I had nothing to lose by trying to keep you away."

"No hard feelings, I hope," Garden said.

Alexa laughed. "You do remember things, don't you? No, kid, no hard feelings."

She found a flat that afternoon, a lover that evening. He was a Russian, with a name Alexa could not pronounce. She called him Peter the Great.

The party was held on the stone terrace outside the flat's living room. Candles in hurricane shades lined the stone balustrade and filled the center of a long table that held bowls of caviar and bottles of champagne and vodka.

"We're very Slavic these days," Alexa said. "I wish I had gone to Chanel when I had the chance." She spread caviar on a piece of toast and sprinkled it with chopped onion from another bowl. "Peter's going to make a speech. Isn't he divine? I don't understand a word he says."

Peter made an eloquent salute to the anniversary in flawless French. He was holding a small glass filled with vodka. At the end of his toast, he put the mouth of the glass to his lips, threw back his head as he twisted his wrist, then flung the glass onto the floor with enough force to break it.

Alexa led the applause. She imitated the quick movement of the wrist and threw her glass down, too. A little bit of vodka glistened on her chin. "I did it wrong. Show me how, Peter." She filled a new glass for him and for herself.

In a half hour the floor glittered with broken glass, and almost everyone at the party was drunk. The guests included several of the old crowd from New York: Mark, Sky's cousin Ann and her husband. Two of Vicki's friends were also there, Alice and Leo Phillips. In addition there were about a dozen men and women Sky had met since he arrived in Monte Carlo. They were English, French, Swiss, Polish, all speaking a combination of their own tongue and French.

When the vodka glasses were all gone, they started on the champagne flutes. Peter clapped approvingly at each crash, including his own.

Garden held her hands over her ears; this was an anniversary party no one would ever forget. The three loops of pearls around her neck gleamed in the candlelight. Three hundred and sixty-five matched pearls.

66

As the months went by, more and more Americans swelled the group of Sky and Garden's friends. The word was out in New York, Chicago, San Francisco, and all points in between: the dollar bought a lot of francs, and there was no Prohibition in France.

People came, and people left; the group did not have the stability of their crowd in New York. Some stayed a week, some a month. Some discovered that the Riviera, for all its flowers and palm trees, was cold in the winter, and they left almost at once for Greece or Italy. Sky and Garden remained. He was too absorbed in his theories about astrological control of the roulette wheel to be away for more than a few days at a time. "I know I'm close," he said at least once every ten days. "I've figured out why the last one didn't work, and I've fixed it. This calculation is the one. This will do it."

And so Monte Carlo was home. "Why don't we get a villa?" Garden suggested, but Sky said it was too much trouble. The hotel supplied them with everything they needed. They rearranged their living quarters. A two-room suite was converted to a double living room. Garden bought a Victrola and records, four mah-jongg sets and some cigarette boxes for the tables. Miss Trager made arrangements with the hotel for a bartender and waiter every afternoon. And every afternoon, the rooms were full. People they knew, friends of people they knew, friends of the friends. "Look up the Harrises," someone would say when Monte Carlo was mentioned. "Just mention my name."

"We're running a speakeasy," Garden complained. Sky said they were lucky to have so many friends. He enjoyed the busyness of it all.

The cocktail hour lasted until eight for Sky and Garden. Then they left the click, click of mah-jongg tiles and the hubbub of voices and went down to the restaurant for dinner. Usually four or five of their guests went with them. Others went to their own hotels or to restaurants or simply stayed at the party, making a meal from the endless supply of hors d'oeuvres and drink.

After dinner they went to the casino, and Sky followed his plan for the day at the roulette table. Afterward they went out, looking for fun to erase the sour taste of another error in his calculations.

Up and down the coast they went, in one, two, three or more cars, following Sky's lead on the road that he now knew so well. Slow drivers got lost, careless ones had accidents. The fearless and skillful became infected with Sky's love of speed and risk. He led them to nightclubs, workmen's zinc-countered bars, the dance floors at hotel boîtes, other casinos. There were many places where they were not welcome, a few where they were not admitted. Sky was known everywhere. Known as a lavish spender and generous tipper. And as the man who liked to break things. Peter the Great had initiated him into it at the anniversary party. Sky liked to watch the shock change to fun, the fun grow to riot.

He always paid for the damage, and then some. And he took Garden home to the hotel at daylight, his spirit almost cleansed of the rage and frustration that the failure at the roulette table had spawned.

Garden hated their lives. She hated the roulette table. She hated the roaring through the night in the open Mercedes. She hated the noisy nightclubs and their drunk "friends" pawing her on the dance floor. She hated the disgust on the workmen's faces when the group burst into their bar in white tie with silk hats and fur-wrapped, diamond-trimmed women. She hated the tension she felt until the sound of shattering glass broke the tension and filled her with shame. Most of all, she hated the glassy look of Sky's eyes and the angry, mechanical way he made love to her without ever saying her name.

She drank too much and smoked too much and ate too much. She despised herself because she couldn't make Sky stop, and she loved him all the more because she believed he needed her to save him from destroying himself, as he destroyed the glasses, china, tables and chairs of the places they went. He wept sometimes when they were making love, and Garden's heart broke for him.

So she made herself beautiful, and she laughed, and she did the Charleston amid the wreckage, and she sent postcards to her mother and her Aunt Elizabeth and her friends in Charleston with pictures of the flower market at Nice and the zoo at the palace of Monaco and the palm trees against the blue beauty of the Mediterranean. "Too wonderful for words. Love, Garden."

At the end of the summer, Vicki arrived. "I'm looking for a villa," she announced. "The Riviera is getting to be *the* summer place now. Southampton will be a ghost town before long." She had an architect with her, a middle-aged man with a pot belly, a bulbous nose to match, and no conversation.

"The Principessa means business," said Sky. "She'll want Cap d'Antibes, of course." That sleepy little promontory was being talked about a lot on the Riviera, thanks to Cole Porter, who had first spent a summer there a few years back. An American couple, friends of his, were remodeling a house there now and intended to live year round. In the meantime they were at the hotel with a succession of guests, many of them members of the Diaghilev group that was so chic in Paris.

Garden and Sky joined Vicki for lunch at the hotel. "There they are," Vicki whispered when they were almost through dessert. "There, just being seated by the window." Garden had never heard Vicki sound so excited. She turned her head to look at the handsome man and attractive woman.

"Who are they?" she whispered.

Vicki was staring openly. "Scott and Zelda Fitzgerald," she said. Garden turned for another look.

Driving back to Monte Carlo, Sky chuckled. "Pity any artists or writers in France. I think my dear mother is getting ready for some lion hunting."

"Sky?"

"What, darling?"

"Do you think I'm as pretty as Zelda Fitzgerald?"

"Ten times prettier. Pass me the bubbly, will you?" Garden took another long swig from the champagne bottle and gave it to Sky to finish before it got warm. That night, she danced more wildly than ever, while their friends threw glasses to break around her feet like exploding bombs.

All except Sky. He was using his glass to drink a toast to the melting black eyes of an Italian girl who had recently been incorporated into the group with her American protector.

She was replaced by a Danish girl, and the bar in the party room stocked aquavit. The aquavit vanished and Calvados appeared, for a French girl from Normandy. Sky moved from the roulette table to the one in the Salle Privée dedicated to baccarat, with colored ivory plaques for stakes in the thousands instead of the round chips to represent hundreds.

Garden was adored by a succession of would-be Oscar Wilde Englishmen, who wrote poetry celebrating her beauty and liked to borrow her more extravagant fur coats when the nights became chill. They clutched the dashboard of the car Sky bought her, a twin of his, while Garden drove on the all-night chases after pleasure and after her husband's white car ahead of them.

One night when Garden left the party early, the poet with her saw her to her suite and followed her into the sitting room. Garden fell into a chair; he knelt on the floor beside it. He recited a poem he had written for her. Then he wept, his head resting against her knee, and begged her to help him be a man like other men. Garden lowered the straps over her shoulders to expose her breasts. The poet reached out a quivering hand to brush the female roundness of her. Garden seized it, pressed it hard against the stiff nipple and cried out. The poet jerked away as if he had been burned; he scrabbled from the room on hands and knees, so frantic to get away that he did not stop to get to his feet. Garden's tears poured from her closed eyes, down her agonized face, fell onto her hands kneading her breasts, and collected in little pools between the fingers.

67

"I'm sick of the Riviera. Let's go to Paris."

"I am too. Let's go home, Sky."

"Home? Where's that? New York? Practically everybody we know in New York is in Paris."

"Let's go to Charleston, to the Barony."

"You've got to be kidding. What would we do, watch the mold grow on us? No, Paris is where the action is. That's where we belong."

"When do you want to leave?"

"Today, tonight, right now."

Garden lit a cigarette. They were having dinner. Alone, for a change. Unfortunately, on the rare occasions that they were alone, they always seemed to end up arguing. "We can go on Friday," she said, in what she hoped was a conciliatory tone. "Our second anniversary party is Thursday night."

Sky concentrated on his entrecôte.

"Is that all right, Sky?"

"Sure."

*   *   *

Paris was a tonic. For over a year they had been living under the high, blue, brilliant sky of the Côte d'Azur. They arrived in a gray Paris, with low gray clouds dripping cold, relentless rain. The streets were crowded with automobiles, all tooting their horns, and with pedestrians under umbrellas held at a forward tilt like weapons. They defied the traffic, jumped out of the way of splashing wheels, shook fists or shouted at drivers who did not make way for them.

"By God," said Sky, "I had forgotten how great a city is."

Vicki welcomed them to the house with open arms that swept them up the great staircase and into the ballroom. It was now a studio, reeking of turpentine, for five painters, all hard at work. "It's a competition," Vicki explained. "They're all doing portraits of me—Cubist, of course—and I'll buy the one I like the best. I'll just introduce you around, and then I have to take my pose again." The painters were uniformly young and virile-looking, Garden noted as she moved from easel to easel in Vicki's wake. It neither shocked nor interested her that Vicki seemed to be buying sex in quantity these days. After the stories about some of the Riviera's inhabitants, Vicki was tamely straightforward in her pleasures. She was looking flamboyantly healthy, her hair a vigorous auburn bound by a scarf that crossed her forehead, tied on one side and streamed down over her shoulder into the chiffon panels of her chrome yellow dress. "You look marvelous, Vicki," Garden said.

"You, my dear child, look a fright," Vicki rejoined. "Sky, you must send Garden out at once to get some decent clothes."

"Not at once, dear mother of mine. At once we are going out to meet some people for lunch."

Garden shook her head. "Not 'we,' darling, you. I'm going to have a bath and a nap. I didn't sleep a wink on the train."

"It shows," said Vicki with a flashing smile. "Bring your friends back for dinner, Schuyler. I'm having a few people in. Then we'll all go up to Montparnasse and be bohemian."

Corinne shook Garden gently at six. "You told me to wake you, madame. Ought I order coffee?" Garden stretched, groaned. She didn't want to get up, get dressed, pretend to be having a good time. She knew who was in town. Mark, with his latest, Mimi, with hers, Laurie and David Patterson. She had seen them all at one time or another in Monte Carlo. She didn't want to see them again. Not them, not anybody. Not now.

"I'm so tired." she said aloud.

"The coffee, madame?"

"No; Corinne. Get me some champagne. I'll have another bath, scalding, and drink it while I soak. Then lay out the white beaded gown with the trumpet skirt."

"It has the stain on the hem, Mrs. Harris. It would not come out."

"Oh, hell. Well, the blue then, the one with the ostrich on the shoulders."

"You threw that away, madame."

"So I did. I don't care. Anything will do. You find something."

Corinne found a pink silk with an over-all embroidery of rose petals. It was in perfect condition because Garden had never worn it. She couldn't imagine why she had ever bought it. When she was dressed, she was more tired and despondent than before she had rested.

"Darlings," she caroled, "how scrumptious to see you!" She kissed the air near the cheeks of all her New York friends, shook hands or extended hers to be kissed when she met Vicki's group, burbled about how divine it was to be in Paris, made a good show of being a happy, sophisticated, lively young woman. It was an act that she had polished to a fine gloss in Monte Carlo. Sometimes, if she got enough attention and enough champagne, it was almost real.

She was seated at dinner between two of Vicki's guests, both bankers from New York. No wonder, Garden thought, that the competing artists were nowhere to be seen. The bankers talked across her about world finances and politics. She hid her yawns behind her napkin.

"But it's true." The woman on the other side of one of the bankers was loudly vehement. "I just came up from Rome, and the train did run on time. I think Mussolini is just what Italy needed."

"Martha," the banker said impatiently, "there are more important things than timetables."

"Not when you have to make a connection there aren't. Two years ago I was simply left high and dry in Milan, of all awful places. Nobody goes to Milan."

"Nobody goes to Milan," Vicki mimicked after Martha, the bankers, their wives and Martha's husband were gone. "Forgive me, everyone, for those drearies. I couldn't get out of inviting them.

Now. let's get ready to have some fun." She opened a drawer and removed a tray. It held a dozen bowls of white powder. "I couldn't have these on the table or Martha would have used hers as a salt cellar."

"What is it?" Garden asked Mark.

"Knowing Vicki. I'd say it's cocaine. and probably the best grade there is. Have you ever had any, Garden?"

"No. I've heard of it. but we stuck with champagne."

"But my dear. there's no hangover with coke, and it doesn't rot your liver like liquor. It's great stuff. I'd use it all the time if I could afford it." Vicki passed the tray. Mark took a bowl and held it in his hand. "There must be two ounces here. Vicki, you're not a princess, you're a queen."

He showed Garden how to close one nostril. hold the minute spoonful of powder to the other and sniff. "Whew," he said. "That's great."

Garden was reluctant. There was something repulsive about Mark's loud sniffing, about putting anything in one's nose. "Go on. Garden," he said. "Don't be such a prude. Believe me, you'll love it."

Garden lifted the spoon. held her other nostril closed. "Like this?" Mark nodded. She closed her eyes and inhaled the powder.

"Ayee!" She screamed, held her hands over her face. She must have done something wrong. Her nose, behind her nose. up to her eyes. she was frozen. numb. dead.

But. all of a sudden. the rest of her was more alive than she could ever remember being. She felt elated and calm at the same time, afraid of nothing, full of energy. in control of her body. her mind, her life. Why. she had been depressed about nothing. It was the Riviera that had ruined her marriage. Now they were back in Paris, back with friends, with wonderful people who really cared for them. Everything was going to be all right. She'd make it all right. There was nothing that she couldn't do.

"How about the other side?" Mark said.

Garden looked for the spoon she had dropped. "Oh my. yes." she said.

The party now included Vicki's artists. They elbowed each other in a struggle that Garden found terribly funny, trying to get into the car with Vicki. Vicki watched. not saying a word. When three were in the car. she waved a hand at Maupin. The chauffeur pushed the remaining two painters aside and closed the door.

Their faces were so doleful that Garden giggled. "Come on," she said, grabbing their hands. They got into one of the taxis lined up in front of the house. "Follow that car!" Garden yelled at the driver. She was having a glorious time.

They all went to the Jungle, on the Boulevard Montparnasse. It was so crowded that the dance floor could not be seen under the feet of the dancers. Vicki flashed her fingers to say they were a party of sixteen, then counted out sixteen hundred franc notes. The head-waiter cocked his head at two burly men near the door. They followed him and stood by while he tapped shoulders and told people to leave. "Bounced," Vicki laughed. "You see, it doesn't matter a bit that I don't speak French."

They sat down only long enough to order champagne. "Ten francs a bottle," said the artist at Garden's side. "It had better be good. These people are thieves." He lapsed into a scowling silence. Garden left him there and went to dance with David. Sky and Mark pushed their way to the bar to get partners from among the prostitutes posed invitingly at one end. Garden thought it was very funny. The nightclub had a revolving mirrored globe above the dance floor, with colored spotlights playing on it. Pink, blue, yellow dots passed across the faces of all the dancers. Garden looked down at David's white shirtfront, tried to catch the dots.

Mark saw what she was doing. "Change partners," he said abruptly. "Garden, I think I let you have too much coke for a beginner. Come sit down."

"Oh, no, no, no, no. Mark. I'm having such a good time." She wrapped her arms around his neck. "Dance with me. I'm a very good dancer. Ask Miss Ellis." She giggled, moved her feet. "They're playing a tango. Come on, Mark. Ba-de-dum-de-dum-da. Come on."

Mark led her into the dance. "You are a good dancer, Garden. I thought the only thing you could do was the Charleston."

"Pooh! I can do anything, anything at all. I feel wonderful. You taught me how. I love you for teaching me. Kiss me. Kiss me hard."

Her beautiful eyes glimmered under half-closed lids, her lips were pouted for a kiss. Mark's teeth tugged gently at her lower lip, then he pulled away. "Not yet," he said. "Not here."

68

Mark was right, thought Garden when she woke up the next day. No hangover. Her tongue did not feel furry and too big for her mouth, the way it always had in Monte Carlo. "I feel like a new person," she said to the gilt cupids holding the canopy over her head. She rang for her breakfast and planned her day while she waited for it to come. She was going to do herself over, she decided. A new person deserved new everything. She'd start with some new clothes. The pink dress could be thrown away. No, she'd give it to one of the maids. What did Sky call them? Maries. Yes, she'd give the dress to a Marie. And buy what? She could ask Laurie. Laurie knew everything. No. Laurie knew everything about New York, but this was Paris. Fashion capital of the world. The perfect place for a new person to buy new clothes. She giggled. The cocaine had long since worn off, but she was still euphoric.

Vicki. Vicki would know. She'd be glad to help.

Garden was positive that she saw the doorman sneer when she entered Paquin. A small dark-haired woman hurried forward to greet her. Garden felt that she should apologize for her too-long dress and coat. The woman's skirt hem was almost knee-high.

But Garden was much wiser than she had been a few short years before. She knew that sables spoke for themselves. "*Bonjour*," she said. "*Je m'appelle Madame Schuyler Harris.*"

"I have been expecting you, Madame Harris. The Principessa telephoned. I am your vendeuse, Mlle. Raspail."

"You speak excellent English, mademoiselle. That will make things easier for me."

"It is my pleasure to be of service to you, madame. If you will just come with me? The lift is this way. Ordinarily the collection is shown at eleven o'clock. We are delaying until you are ready."

Garden expected to be shown some dresses, some gowns, either on a hanger or modeled. That was what the best dressmakers did in New York. Then, if she liked anything, she would look at fabrics and the dress would be made to her measurements. Paris, she soon learned, was very different.

The vendeuse ushered her into a big room, handed her a program and a pencil, whispered, "I will be in the lobby to meet you after the showing," and scurried away.

The room had an elevated aisle down the center, three tiers of gilt chairs on each side of it, and the angry faces of approximately fifty women who were sitting on the chairs, waiting for the person who was delaying the show. Garden sat in the closest vacant chair.

A woman with gray marcelled hair peeking out from a beaded lace cloche stepped through velvet brocade curtains at the far end of the aisle. Her frock, Garden saw, fit her in an indefinably different way from anything in Garden's experience. The woman took her place behind a lectern to one side of the curtained doorway. "*Bonjour*, good morning. *Bienvenues à Paquin*, welcome to Paquin. *Numéro cent vingt-deux*, one hundred twenty-two. *Après-midi à Longchamps*, 'Afternoon at Longchamps.' "

A mannequin appeared between the curtains in a blue dress trimmed with gold buttons and braid. She walked quickly along the aisle; her legs flashed by Garden's face; at the end she paused, turned, paused, then walked back. In the short time it took her to walk forth and back, she had also removed her jacket, showing that the dress Garden looked at was really a suit. She disappeared through the doorway, and another mannequin took her place. "*Numéro cent vingt-cinq*," said the woman by the door.

Garden looked at her program. What happened to twenty-two, -three, and four? When she looked up again, all she saw was the mannequin's heel disappearing through the curtains.

A young woman sitting next to her touched Garden's wrist with her pencil. "First time?" she said in a hoarse whisper. She was American.

Garden nodded.

"They're racing to get back on schedule. Don't worry. They'll slow down at the end for the hot numbers."

Garden looked at her helpful neighbor and smiled, missing another dress.

"Say, aren't you Garden Harris?"

Several women made hissing, shushing sounds. Garden's neighbor made a gesture of slicing her throat with her finger, then of shooting herself. Garden held her program over her mouth to cover her giggles. She watched the procession of gowns and dresses enthralled by the intricacy of their trimmings and by the fluid movement of the mannequins.

Then the mannequins came out, one, two, three, four, rapidly, one after another, all wearing long gowns of pale green silk. Each gown was different, each elaborately beaded, each a work of art. Together, they were breathtakingly beautiful, a fragile, moving composition of femininity and festivity. Garden joined in the applause with enthusiasm.

Throughout the room women began to gather gloves, purses, and programs. Garden turned to her neighbor. "Yes, I'm Garden Harris. I feel very stupid and rude. I'm afraid I don't remember your name."

"No reason why you should. We've never met. I've seen your picture in the papers. My name's Constance Weatherford, Connie for short."

"Hello, Connie. I do thank you for telling me what was going on."

"You're welcome. . . . Do you mind if I ask you something?"

Garden stiffened slightly. This Connie was probably a reporter. "No, I don't mind."

"What are you doing at Paquin? I mean, somebody like you, why are you interested?"

"Someone arranged for me to come."

"Where else are you going?"

Garden consulted the note in her pocket. "Callot Soeurs and Poiret."

"Well, listen, Garden, whoever made your arrangements is no friend of yours, or else she's a real dummy. All those designers are on their way down. They were great in their day, but the sun is setting. Madame Paquin doesn't even do the designs for this place anymore. She retired four or five years ago."

"Where should I go, then?"

"Depends on what you're looking for. There's Lanvin, Worth, Chanel, Molyneux, Vionnet, even Hermès for some things and Fortuny if you've got all the money in the world. But then, you do, don't you? Sorry; that sounds offensive. I don't mean to be. I mean, a fact is a fact." They were a bottleneck for people trying to get to the exit. Garden put her gloves on, stood up. She looked at her talkative neighbor with an urgent, imploring grimace.

"How do I escape the vendeuse?"

Her new friend laughed. "Look like something smells bad," she said. "That's the way the vendeuses look at most people. Tell her you may be back. May, not will. It'll serve the snob right."

There was a press of bodies toward the door. "Quick," Garden said, "I'm being swept away. Will you meet me downstairs?"

"Sure, I'd love to."

Connie Weatherford explained that she was a typist at the Paris office of *Vogue* magazine. "I was on a tour of Europe last summer. You know the kind of thing, fifteen girls chaperoned by the French teacher. It was my graduation present. I bolted, that's all. I didn't want to leave Paris after three days. I marched in to the *Vogue* office, told them I'd type fast and work cheap, and got a job. My parents were furious, but there wasn't much they could do. So here I am, happy as a bug in a rug. I get to use the *Vogue* credentials to go to the showings on my day off. I guess they figure that makes up for paying me almost nothing. I guess I figure that way, too. I really love fashion. One day I'm going to be a designer."

Garden was intrigued by this daring, independent, ambitious girl. Connie was nineteen, Garden's age, yet she seemed to Garden to be both much older and much younger. She knew so much about some things, like traveling and working and living on her own, and yet she was as gauche and green as a child. She blurted out the first words that came into her head; she exclaimed over commonplace, insignificant things like the comfort of the car and the size of the menu at the Ritz, where Garden took her for lunch. Garden thought it amazing that someone connected with *Vogue* could be so unsophisticated. But she liked her.

"Where are you going this afternoon?" she asked Connie. "Would you come to the other dressmakers with me?"

Connie snickered. "If anybody hears you call the Paris designers 'dressmakers,' Garden, they'll drag you off to the guillotine. These people are 'couturiers,' and their establishments are 'houses of couture.' I don't see why you want to bother with the Soeurs or Poiret. Why don't you go to Chanel? She's my favorite. Everything she does is so modern."

345

"Do you think I could get in?"

Connie laughed so loudly that people turned their heads to look. "Garden, listen. All you have to do is walk by in that coat, and the doorman will practically knock you down and drag you in off the street. There just aren't that many people who can afford four or five hundred dollars for a piece of clothing."

From Connie's tone of voice, Garden concluded that she was talking about a high price. Garden did not know what anything cost. She knew nothing about money. Before her marriage, her mother had given her an occasional dime or quarter to go to the movies or to go to the movies and the ice-cream parlor. As Mrs. Schuyler Harris, she just picked out what she wanted at shops, and it was delivered or put into the car. Miss Trager saw to it that there was always cash in her purse, but Garden seldom used any of it, and she never counted it. Now that she thought of it, five hundred did sound like a lot of dollars, but how could she know? It was, in fact, Connie Weatherford's annual salary, and approximately one third the annual salary of an American working man with wife and family. At a luxury specialty shop on Fifth Avenue, a dress could cost as much as fifty dollars, but that was acknowledged to be outrageously expensive. Garden put the idea of money out of her head. It wasn't very interesting.

"Would you mind going to Chanel with me, Connie? I'd appreciate your help. How do you keep up with it all? Everything moves so fast."

"I'd love to come along. And you'll catch on quick enough. Remember, all the women there are old hands; they know what they're looking for, what to expect. They follow fashion the way some men follow baseball. They know every designer's batting average, and they know a home run when they see it. Then they make a pencil tick next to the number, and that's the one they order."

"Sounds like fun."

"More fun than anything. Let's go."

69

At Chanel, Garden selected four dresses, a suit and an evening gown, known as a *robe de style*. "You know, Garden," said Connie, "you make it hard for a person to like you." She stayed with Garden while she was measured for the dress dummy that would be created in her image and used for the preliminary fittings. Garden was bored and annoyed. In New York, there weren't one third as many measurements. Connie was fascinated. She had never gotten behind the scenes at a couture house before.

Garden requested and got champagne. Connie requested and got to meet Mlle. Chanel herself.

"One of these days I'm going to ask her for a job," said Connie when they were in the car again. "Then I'll get to see the workrooms and the whole design process."

When Garden got home, she was exhausted. As she had done the day before, she took a nap and woke up still tired and out of sorts. She wondered if Vicki would pass around the cocaine again tonight.

The little bowls were on the table when they sat down for dinner. Garden could hardly stand the slow course after course and the seemingly endless wait before Vicki laughed and picked up her little golden spoon.

Garden warned herself that she must not expect the same fantastic sense of well-being that she had experienced the night before. That was too good to be true.

But it was true. She felt it begin even while she was still fighting off the terror of the freezing sensation in her nose. She gasped, looked around the table at everyone, smiled, and announced, "I feel wonderful."

Before they left for the nightclub on the Champs-Élysées, Vicki opened Garden's bag and dropped in a small gold phial. "Now you can keep on feeling wonderful all the time. Just remember: go in the ladies' room to use it."

Cocaine, Garden discovered, had all sorts of beneficial effects. She was never hungry, she had unlimited energy, and she needed almost no sleep. She liked everyone she knew, everyone she met, strangers on the street, everyone. And nothing seemed to upset her. When she spilled coffee on her gown, she didn't care. When her hair color came out too pale, she didn't care. When Sky disappeared from a nightclub with his arm around some woman's waist, she hardly cared at all.

Time didn't seem to matter either. She went to all the couture houses and ordered new, bright, happy clothes for the new, bright, happy Garden. The hours of fittings did not annoy her, nor the wait while the intricate hand seaming and trimming was done. If she couldn't have the *robe de style* for Wednesday, then the Wednesday after that would be fine. Or the Wednesday after that.

Time was elastic. She wasted so little of it in sleep that there was always room in her life for one more thing. And there was so much to do in Paris. There were more than a hundred movie theaters. Ramon Novarro was evilly handsome in *Ben Hur*, John Gilbert smoothly handsome in *The Merry* Widow, Douglas Fairbanks dashingly handsome in *Son of Zorro*, Ronald Colman charmingly handsome in *The Dark Angel*. Valentino was Valentino in *The Eagle*. Charlie Chaplin's *The Gold Rush* made Garden cry. She laughed until she cried at Harold Lloyd and Buster Keaton, shivered at *The Phantom of the Opera*, yawned at the real opera they all went to the week after they saw the movie because no masked phantom appeared.

She blushed at the *Folies-Bergère* when she first saw the bare breasts of the showgirls. After four or five visits she was bored, but the *Folies* was always the first thing new arrivals in Paris wanted to see, so she and Sky were there almost every week with someone fresh in from New York. Garden admired the elaborate, towering headdresses on the showgirls for a while, comparing the problem of balancing them with the logistics of balancing a basket of laundry. But after a while that became boring too.

Boredom was the great enemy. Luckily, there was always a new fad to ward it off. Crossword puzzles crossed the Atlantic from America and became an obsession with everybody overnight.

After breakfast, she and Vicki had another coffee together to compare their solutions to the puzzle in the Paris *Herald-Tribune*. Both of them bought the puzzle-printed camisoles and step-ins that even the best lingerie shops were showing. Then Harold Vanderbilt developed a new kind of bridge game, contract bridge, and everyone took it up. They played for high stakes. Sky and his partner usually won. He said the practice at roulette and baccarat was the reason for his success.

In the spring, they went to the Exposition Internationale des Arts Décoratifs and shared in the wild response that swept Paris and then the whole world. Black became the only color for fashionable women or homes, punctuated with "tango orange." Vicki had all the furniture reupholstered in black satin; Garden made a frantic dash to the Rue de la Paix, ordered gowns in black sequins, black beaded silk, black organza and black linen for the warm weather ahead. She ran into Connie Weatherford and forced her to accept the gift of a shawl just like the one Garden was buying, a silk fantasy of swirling peacock feather eyes, but in greens, yellows, oranges on black, with a twelve-inch fringe of tango orange.

The crowd did not bother to leave Paris when summer came; there was too much to do. The bateaux-mouches went from the Louvre all the way to Saint-Cloud and back. They took musicians with them and turned the slow boat trip into a floating nightclub. Vicki gave a ball under tents in the Jardin des Tuileries, and they moved music and dancing into the Place Vendôme, stopping the traffic, dragging people out of their cars to join in the party.

They thought themselves spectacularly democratic. After a few hours at the Café de la Paix or one of the elegant champagne *clubs de nuit* on the Champs-Élysées, they would drop in on one of the *bals musettes* in Montparnasse. There was no orchestra, only a violin and accordion on a platform built on a pole. Men had to pay a few sous every time they took a partner onto the dance floor. Sky and Mark and the other man paid and danced with the working girls and artists' models. Garden and the other women merrily accepted the invitations of the working men and artists. It was not at all like the Riviera. Here there was no rowdyism, no broken glass. Garden learned the Java, a dance found no place except the *bals musettes*, and taught everyone to do the Charleston. It had not yet reached France. She also talked about Charleston, asking all the painters if they knew anything about Tradd Cooper, her Aunt Elizabeth's son. No one did.

She asked also in the cafés of Montmartre, the old section where the artists had congregated before they moved to Montparnasse. The crowd was often there, at the Moulin Rouge or the Lido. She had no luck about Tradd, but it didn't really matter. The only important thing was to have fun, to be on the go, to be chic, sophisticated, young and beautiful. Laurie Patterson told her she was burning herself out, that she was getting too thin, that she looked twice her age. Garden ignored her.

She knew she looked wonderful, because she felt wonderful, so how else should she look? Everywhere she went, people returned her smiles. And in the clubs, everyone applauded when she did the Charleston. The real Charleston. When the dance floor was crowded, someone always found a table for her to dance on. She liked that best, because then they usually turned a spotlight on her, and she could feel everyone's eyes admiring her and hear the clapping hands and stamping feet and shouts and whistles while she danced and became part of the music.

The attention and the applause filled the emptiness in her that she was trying so hard to run away from. The emptiness that used to be filled by Sky, his love for her and hers for him. Surely she could replace the lost love of one man with the love of rooms full of people. And with the happiness in the little vial that Vicki kept filled for her

In August, Paris was closed. The French went on their annual vacation. The groups led by Sky and Vicki went together to Deauville. The Riviera had siphoned off much of the channel resort's clientele. By Paris standards it was very tame. But there was the elegant casino, horse racing and, for men, the pleasures of the beach where women paraded in their tight black bathing suits, the latest revolution in fashion. Garden was conspicuous on the sands in floppy silk chiffon beach pajamas printed with big orange flowers and a huge white straw hat with orange silk poppies under the brim.

Even when she stayed under her big orange striped beach umbrella, the sun reached her; after a few days she abandoned the beach. She filled the hours with shopping, crossword puzzles and an occasional pick-up bridge game with older women staying at the same hotel. It required more and more trips to the ladies' room with the gold vial to keep her spirits up.

Until the afternoon that she was playing patience in one of the hotel's small lounges off the lobby. She had just laid out the cards and was studying them before making her first move when she felt a hand touch her neck, then a warm mouth. The lips traveled up to her ear. "Now," Mark whispered.

He had loved her from the first moment he saw her. Mark said. Sky was a fool, he said, to neglect her the way he did. A fool and a swine, to flaunt his women in front of her the way he did. He did not appreciate how lucky he was to have a wife who was so sweet, so beautiful, so talented . . . caring . . . exciting . . . sensual . . . soft . . . fragrant . . .

It was different, making love with Mark. He was greedier than Sky, and more demanding. After the first long, slow seduction he was always impatient, once almost ripping her dress when the zipper would not open. And he wanted her all the time. They met daily, when Sky went to swim before lunch, but that was not enough for Mark. He would whisper in her ear when they were dancing at the casino, and she would go to the ladies' room, then slip out a side door and run down to where he was waiting in the striped canvas tent on the beach, a blanket already laid out on the sand. If Sky went off with the English girl who was his newest adventure, Mark would take Garden immediately to his rooms and keep her there until dawn. The danger of discovery was exciting, and her constant awareness that his kisses and his body were unlike the kisses and the body of her husband was guiltily thrilling. But, for Garden, the excitement and thrill were incidental. What mattered was that her love-starved heart was fed, her aching body fulfilled.

They all returned to Paris in September, just in time for the most explosive fad of all, the craze for all things Negro.

La Revue Nègre at the Théâtre des Champs-Élysées was the name of the show, a music hall revue. It was advertised by a poster on every kiosk, a bright, grotesque cartoon of wide white grins in shiny black faces. The gossip was that it would be the hit show of the season, so they got tickets for opening night.

The star of the show was Maud de Forest, and when she sang her smoky blues lament, the audience demanded two encores. They applauded the saxophone solo by Sidney Bechet for over a minute. Then the next act began. A giant black man, naked to the waist, his thick, muscled body gleaming with oil, entered from left rear of the stage. He was holding a young black girl. Her legs were perpendicular to her naked body in a split, and she was upside down, one leg balanced on his shoulder. She held a single pink flamingo feather between her legs. At midstage, the man swung her in a slow cartwheel to the floor. Her hands fell to her sides, and she stood like a statue, a statue of a brown Venus, with a perfection of body that seemed unreal in a human.

The audience went wild. The girl was an unknown nineteen-year-old dancer named Josephine Baker. Within weeks, all Paris was mad for her and for all things Negro. Stylized black faces made of enamel or ebony decorated diamond-studded bracelets and brooches. Department stores sprayed the dummies in their windows black. Pink flamingo-feather fans warred with tango-orange ostrich fans in the best nightclubs. Every orchestra featured a saxophonist and the music for the dance that had traveled the Atlantic with the Revue. At last, France had the Charleston.

Garden's friends were smug. "We've known it for years," they said, showing off in clubs where the French were still doing the easiest steps. "Dance, Garden, dance. Show them. You don't have to be a nigger to be a dancer." And Garden danced. It was the only thing she knew that she could do.

Mark went to America, taking a French mannequin with him.

Sky was hospitalized with a broken jaw; he had tried to take a black girl away from her escort in the Boule Noire, the nightclub that supplied blacks for Parisians to dance with.

David Patterson met Garden at the Ritz bar to tell her that Laurie couldn't get there to keep their date. He took her to dinner, then to the bar of his hotel for a nightcap, then to his room and his bed.

He rented an apartment in the Latin Quarter where they could meet for cocktail rendezvous, called the five-to-seven by the worldly French. Garden bought a black chiffon dress at Molyneux because it was called the *cinq à sept*. She thought it was funny. Given a steady supply of cocaine, she thought everything was funny.

But her hands shook sometimes, and she could not manage the delicate little spoon. She learned to use a short paper soda straw, bought boxes of them from a bar where they were put in crème de menthe frappés.

She fell from a table when she was dancing at the Jungle into the lap of a Spanish friend of an English friend of Vicki's. He welcomed her with a long kiss that everyone at the table applauded, and he held her on his lap for the rest of the evening, filling her champagne glass with one hand while the other moved on her leg beneath her skirt. Garden giggled into his shoulder. The next day, when she met David, everything he said and everything he did was boringly predictable.

Alexa came to Paris with Felix, a suntanned blond Swiss who had been her ski instructor at St. Moritz. She told Garden that she ought to see a doctor. Garden laughed. That night she pretended to trip, and she tumbled into the Swiss's lap. "Sky," she giggled, "will you buy me some skiing lessons?" He stretched across the table and slapped her across the mouth.

It made her nose bleed.

70

"You have a dangerous addiction, Mrs. Harris," said the doctor. "If you do not stop using cocaine, you will die." He gave her a note. "This is the address of an excellent clinic and the name of the doctor who operates it. I suggest you make a reservation there at once."

Garden put the note in her handbag. As she did, she felt for the little gold vial. She had the shakes; she needed a pick-me-up. "Thank you, doctor," she said. "I'll take care of it in the morning."

Sky, Alexa, and Felix were waiting for her outside the door of the Emergency Room. Garden touched the bloodstains on the front of her gown. "I'll have to go change," she said. "Then let's go to Au Pied du Cochon. I'm dying for some onion soup."

* * *

She learned to rinse her nose with a syringe, and it became less sore. She also cut down on her intake of cocaine, but she had such terrible headaches that she couldn't stand it. And it made her depressed, too. That was worse than the headaches. Even when she was high, some things depressed her so much that she had to go into another room and weep. It usually happened when they were at one of the nightclubs with a black singer. They had sprung up like mushrooms. The singer was always applauded loudly, no matter how bad he or she might be. Often, people threw money and flowers on to the stage, whistled, demanded encores.

It was natural that the singer would be pleased, but it offended Garden to see the man or woman racing around the stage picking up the money, bobbing and grinning. It was undignified. Didn't the singer know that the crowd was throwing money the same way it would throw peanuts to a monkey or a biscuit to a performing dog? Didn't the singer hear the comments about "coons" and "niggers" and "jungle bunnies"? Didn't the singer know or care? Didn't the people with her, her husband, their friends, didn't they realize that black people were people, not pets?

She tried to make Sky stop, but he told her she was only squalling because she thought all blacks should still be slaves and should belong to her precious Charleston family. He didn't understand at all. Nor, for that matter, did she understand why it upset her so. It was really none of her business. Her business was to keep busy, to have fun, to be entertaining and attractive and desirable.

She bought new dresses, new gowns, new coats, new lingerie. None of her things fit her anymore. They were all too big. She bought brighter rouge and began to have her nails painted a bright red to match the lipstick that she applied with a lavish hand.

She was coming out of Hermès one day in early February when a man took off his hat and bowed to her. There was something familiar about his caped coat flapping in the cold wind. "Hello," Garden said. "I know I know you, but I'm afraid I can't remember . . ."

"Francis Faber," he said. "We crossed on the *France* together."

"Of course!" Garden giggled. She was feeling exceptionally good. "I remember you. Tell me, Dr. Faber, are you still such a good kisser?"

Faber winced. "I insulted you. I did not intend to. I had hoped that you might have forgotten."

354

"Not for a minute. I cherish the memory. Look, it's freezing, and my car's right here. Can I give you a ride someplace?"

"I'm going to my hotel. It's only a few steps."

"Get in. It's too cold to walk."

In the car, Garden tucked her hand under Faber's arm. "I'm delighted to see you, doctor. You're just the man to explain to me how a lady should react when her husband is having an affair and brings the woman into the house to live. Why don't you buy me a drink and tell me why it's the most natural thing in the world?"

"Really, Mrs. Harris, I don't know what to say." Faber was miserably embarrassed.

"But you must, doctor. You're a doctor. Why don't you tell me that the wife should not let it bother her, that she should amuse herself the same way, that it's the most natural thing in the world."

Faber looked at her, his embarrassment gone, his eyes calculating.

The car stopped in front of his hotel. "Won't you come in for a drink, Mrs. Harris?"

"Please call me Garden. Shall I tell my driver not to wait?"

"Please do."

Faber was in Paris for three weeks. He joined the group of Americans on their rounds of pleasure, watched Garden dance with his eyes blazing. She was even more exciting a bed partner than he had imagined. He could hardly keep his hands off her in public. At the party for the third anniversary of her wedding to Sky, he was so jealous of Sky's careless arm around her waist that he bolted from the room. Garden ran after him, took him into the ballroom/studio and made love to him on the platform where models usually posed.

When Faber left Paris, she continued to use the platform for a couch, with one of Vicki's artists as partner.

Then another.

She posed for a third, nude except for her jewels, then sent the painting to Felix. Alexa burst into her room when she was having breakfast. "What the hell do you think you're doing, Garden?"

"Just what you did to me, Alexa," Garden said coldly. "No hard feelings, I hope."

"You're sick, Garden. And a fool. Felix would never leave me for a druggy like you."

That night Garden dressed with a smile on her face. She added more heavily scented oil to the bath Corinne prepared, and she oiled

355

her arms and legs after she was dry. "No stockings," she said when Corinne held them out. She let Corinne slip her new *robe de style* over her head. It was a waterfall of silver fringe, three shimmering tiers from just above her breasts to just below her knees. Corinne attached the strips of diamonds that Garden had had made to replace the original straps. "That will be all," said Garden.

As soon as Corinne left, Garden got out a straw and the powder box that Vicki kept supplied with cocaine for her. When she was high again, she pulled the dress over her head, took off her underclothes and unbound her breasts. Then she put the dress back on.

Perfume, powder, makeup, a band of diamonds across her forehead, diamond bracelets and rings and a diamond necklace tied around her right leg above the knee. She was ready. She stepped into her silver pumps, wrapped the silver lamé cape around her and held it closed with the hand that clutched her evening bag. It was made of silver bugle beads. It glittered, the rings on the hand holding it flashed. Garden held the cape tighter so that the broad band of white fox that trimmed it would frame her face and caress her cheeks. "Have a good time, Snow White," she said to her reflection in the mirror. It laughed with her. Life was so deliciously funny.

She was a whirlwind of silver when she danced. The others on the floor moved back and she was alone, spotlit, under the revolving mirrored ball. With all eyes on her alone, Garden danced until she was beaded with sweat. Then she ran across to where Felix was sitting with Alexa. She stepped up onto a chair, then the table, and danced with total abandon, shimmering, shaking, twisting, kicking her glittering foot near Felix's head, surrounding him with the musk of her oiled leg, giving him and him alone a glimpse of the flashing diamonds on her thigh.

At the end of the dance she stood, panting, unbound breasts rising and falling, setting the fringe in motion. Felix rose from his chair. "I'll take you home," he said. His voice was guttural.

Garden blew a goodbye kiss to Sky and a flicking salute to Alexa. Then she put her left arm through Felix's and made her exit, dragging her coat behind her, Alexa's trademark, like a matador after a kill.

Corinne was alarmed by the sounds coming from behind the closed door to Garden's bedroom. She went in search of Miss

Trager. "All night it went on, mademoiselle, and now it is louder than ever. It is after eleven. I am afraid Mr. Harris will come home, and I do not know what might occur."

Miss Trager listened, paled. "I will bring the Principessa," she said. "It is her house; she has a right to enter."

Vicki threw open the door and walked in as if she were paying a casual friendly visit. Miss Trager and Corinne peered from the doorway.

Garden had introduced Felix to cocaine. The bed was littered with straws, and their naked sweaty bodies were streaked with white powder. They were both bedecked with Garden's jewels. They scintillated every color in the mirrors that were balanced on the chairs pulled near the bed. The two of them were sprawled side by side, shaking uncontrollably and laughing hysterically.

Garden turned her head to look at her mother-in-law. She laughed even harder, speaking in disconnected gasps. "Hi . . . Vicki . . . this is . . . Felix . . . He's . . . teach . . . ing me to . . . ski."

Vicki laughed with them until she had to hold her sides. Then she left, still laughing, to go to her rooms. Her laughter was a paean of triumph.

Miss Trager followed her. "Why?" she said when they were alone. "I've never asked, Principessa. I've followed all your instructions. But now I need to know that there's a reason for destroying this girl. I'm having a hard time living with myself."

Vicki's stare was cold. "It is of no concern to me, Miss Trager, whether you live with yourself comfortably or not. I told you when I hired you that the job was not one for a weakling. If you're squeamish, get out. Garden no longer knows who's around her and who isn't. And she'll get worse. And then, worse still. It's what I've planned from the first moment I heard her name."

Vicki began to pace back and forth across the fur rugs that lay strewn on the floor of her sitting room. Her arms were folded, hands tucked in her armpits, as if she were holding in the passion that made her voice quiver.

"I'm going to see her destruction, watch every downward step. Why do you think I stayed in Paris all summer, let strangers finish the plans for the villa, order the decoration, hire the servants? Because I do not want to miss one single moment of her degradation,

357

her pain, her suffering. She owes me. She's a Tradd. She'll be losing her mind soon, but I won't send her away. I'll keep her here, put bars on the windows, look in on her every day, ten times a day if I want to. She'll beg me for cocaine, she'll beg me to let her die. She'll pay me back."

Miss Trager was frightened and horrified. "She's your son's wife," she whispered.

"And she'll stay his wife. He doesn't even notice what's happening. I've seen to that. He lost interest as soon as she became ordinary, just like all the women he knew, bobbed hair and all the rest. He thinks she's just a drunken little slut. It's more convenient for him, so he's glad to believe what I tell him. The next time he marries, I'll choose the bride. By then, this one will be dead. Her body must be shattered already; she eats nothing. Next, the mind. Then take away the drug. As my son's wife, she'll stay in my house, in my care."

She looked at Miss Trager. "What about your conscience, Miss Trager? What is your tender sensibility worth to you? Do you want to give up a thousand a month and look for another job? I'll give you an excellent reference . . . Don't you have anything to say?

"Then go back and listen to the merry young lovers. See to it that they have anything they want. I want dear Garden to be happy; she's giving me so much pleasure."

71

Someone helped Garden out of a cab. She looked around her. Everything was blurred. Things were so often blurred lately. "What is this place?" she asked. "Where am I?"

"Place Pigalle, ducks. We're going to the club Josephine Baker just opened, remember? We're going to eat, drink and be merry. Welcome in the New Year. Come along, now, it's only a few steps."

Garden peered at the man who was hurting her arm, pulling her along the street. "Do I know you?"

He threw his head back to laugh. "Only in the biblical sense," he said. "I'm only in Paris for the weekend."

She remembered him then. He was the one who had hurt her so much, the one who said Paris was like Sodom and Gomorrah. No, maybe not. This man was fat. She thought she remembered that the Bible one was very thin. Or was it the Italian one who was so thin? She couldn't remember. It didn't matter anyhow. Nothing mattered.

"Whose friend are you?" They were always somebody's friend. They were always introduced. Only a tramp would go to bed with a man who wasn't properly introduced. She didn't want Sky to think she was a tramp. She wanted him to be proud of her.

"I guess you could say I'm your husband's friend. He's with my wife, you see."

"I see." Garden heard the music coming from a place just ahead. She began to dance in the street. "I love music," she said. She smiled. The beautiful smile that was so rare with her now. "I love to dance, see?" She did a Charleston kick. "Everybody loves me when I dance."

"I can see why." The man put his arms around her. "How about a little Happy New Year kiss? It's almost twelve."

"Why not?" Garden turned her face up and closed her eyes. Her feet and body continued to move with the music.

"Wow. That's some Happy New Year, dearie. Why don't we skip this party and go to my hotel?"

"I thought we'd already been to bed."

"Yes, but that was last night. I was drunk. Let's go now, while I'm still sober."

"No. I want to dance." Garden walked away from him to the door of the nightclub.

The crowd were all waiting eagerly for them to arrive. Sky came forward and led them to the table. "Don't sit down, Garden, come on. There's something you've got to do."

"I want to go to the ladies' room."

"No, no, honey, that can wait. You haven't even had a drink yet. Come on, this is too good." He took her to the edge of the dance floor. In the center of it was Josephine Baker, resplendent in diamonds and a white satin dress hemmed with ostrich plumes. She was showing a portly, overdressed white woman how to do the Charleston.

"That's the gimmick," said Sky. "La Bah-kaire herself teaches the lady customers to dance. We've all been waiting for you, Garden. When she finishes with this old bag, you go out there. Let her show you a step, then do one that's flashier. It'll be a riot."

"I think that's mean."

"Don't be so Sunday-school. She's a big star. She'll have to grin and bear it. It's a sure winner. White girl puts Josephine in her place."

"I won't do it."

"Yes, you will, Garden. You have to. We're all counting on you. I told everybody around us that my wife can outdance Josephine Baker. They didn't believe me. You've got to make me proud of you." Sky kissed the top of her head. "Go on, darling. It's your turn." He gave her a little shove into the spotlights.

Josephine smiled at her. *"Bon soir,"* she said.

"Bon soir, Mademoiselle Baker," said Garden. She walked through the lights until she was very near the exquisite young dancer. "I have to tell you something very fast. I can Charleston like crazy. My husband has bet some people that I can dance better than you."

The black girl looked amused. "Really? Do you think you can?"

Garden was deadly earnest. "Probably," she said.

Josephine laughed. "That'll be the day. Come on, then, let's see what you can do." She waved to the orchestra, which began the familiar song. With an air of sweet patience, she did the basic forward-back, back-forward step of the Charleston.

Garden repeated it, adding a kick at the end.

Josephine did Garden's step, with a double kick.

Garden matched her, plus a double kick to the rear. She grinned at Josephine. Josephine grinned back, raised her eyebrows. "All right," she said. "Let's go!"

The two young women threw themselves into an exuberant duel, both smiling, both enjoying the music, the spotlights, the challenge. They presented a picture that no one who was there ever forgot. The dark-skinned beauty in white versus the blond white beauty wearing black. They were about the same size, danced with about the same style; they were a perfect match.

The orchestra stepped up the beat, and their feet moved so fast that the audience could hardly see them. They threw their arms wide, and their diamonds flashed fire. "Aiyee!" cried Josephine. "Aiyee!" echoed Garden. They were mad with the joy of movement.

The audience was screaming. "*Vive la nègre . . . danse*, Jo . . . go, Garden, go . . . brava la Bah-kaire . . . Gar-den, Gar-den . . . Joséphine . . . Charleston, Garden, Charleston . . ."

There were shouts, and whistles, and a hundred hands clapping to the beat of the music, faster and yet faster. Flowers flew through the air, and the women kicked them where they fell. More flowers, then, and a gold coin, and then money was bouncing all around them, the big French bank notes crumpled into balls to be thrown. One hit Garden's arm, then another struck her shoulder. She looked around, blinded by the lights and confused by the drugs in her body. The air was full of flowers, of wads of paper. There was something, something she had to remember. The music was insistent; she danced as she had not danced in years—freely, happily, unaware of Josephine, unconscious of the cheering and shouting. But things kept hitting her. She had to remember. What was it? It was important.

And then she knew. They were throwing money at her, like biscuits to a good dog. She was not a person, she was a clown, a pet, a toy. She was nothing to anybody.

No. She wouldn't believe it. They loved her. Her friends. The men she couldn't remember. The strangers out there beyond the lights. They thought she was wonderful.

But they were throwing things at her. They were paying her, tipping her, giving her money, not love.

She was exhausted. She could barely get enough breath to stay alive. But the music demanded, and she danced. And her exhausted spirit had no strength to hold on to the delusions she had built. She fought the truth with a frenzy of motion, listening only to the music.

And yet, the truth won. She heard the doctor telling her she was an addict, Alexa calling her a druggy, Connie saying that Vicki was her enemy. She saw the faces of the men she had been with, heard her own manic, drug-intoxicated laughter. Memories pelted her like the money and flowers, and she was filled with a burning shame. Her feet stopped and she stood in the bright spotlight, her soul naked. She wanted to die.

"No!" she cried aloud. "I don't want to. I want to live."

She did not hear the thunderous applause, or see Josephine Baker's outstretched hand. She pushed frantically through the people swarming around her. "Let me go, let me go, let me go."

Her desperation cleared a path for her. She ran into the street without her coat and huddled herself into the corner of a waiting taxi, shouting the address of Vicki's house. She was shivering from cold and shaking from the need for more cocaine.

Suddenly there were loud noises everywhere. Bells, sirens, explosions. Garden twitched, every nerve in her body raw. "What's that?" she cried.

"It's the New Year. It's nineteen twenty-seven. Happy New Year, madame."

Garden could not stop shaking. She had to get home. There was something she had to do. "Quickly," she begged, "please hurry."

"Mrs. Harris!" Bercy was astonished to see her, concerned by her wild appearance.

"Pay the taxi," Garden ordered. "Pay him double. Triple. Tell him happy New Year."

She ran up the great enclosed stone staircase, reaching hand over hand up the bronze rail to her right. Her nerves were screaming by the time she got to her room. She pulled out the drawers of the table by her bed. "I know I put it somewhere," she sobbed aloud. "Please let me find it." She dropped the drawers on the floor and fell to her knees, her shaking hands scrabbling through their contents.

And she found it. I'll just have a little snort, she told herself, and then I'll be in control. It'll be easier to manage. But the truth she had so recently found told her that she would never save herself if she did not do it now.

She crawled into the sitting room. Her legs would no longer support her. It was so far to the telephone. She whimpered, collapsed, pulled herself forward with hands and elbows.

The telephone fell on her arm when she pulled it off the table by its cord. Garden could hear the operator's shrill, distorted voice. Her own voice did not want to work. She moved her head across the rug, scraping her cheek, until her mouth was touching the phone.

"Help me," she whispered. "I need someone to help me."

The operator spoke slowly and clearly to her. "I will help you."

She listened to Garden's weak voice, waited for the long minutes it took her to read the letters that were written on the note. Her mind could not turn them into words.

"I understand," the operator said. "You wait where you are. I will tell you when you must speak again." She opened a new line, spoke, spoke to the person who answered, became more urgent, waited anxiously, then breathed a sigh of relief.

362

"Dr. Matthias, thank you for interrupting your celebration. I am an operator in Paris. A young woman reached me, read me your name and address. No. I correct myself. She could read only the letters. She is very weak, very confused. She may be dying."

"Do you know her name?"

"No, doctor."

"Is she American?"

"Yes, doctor."

"I believe I know who she is. I will speak with her. Do not leave the line, operator. I may need you to call an ambulance for me."

"Mademoiselle," said the operator, "I have the doctor you are calling."

"Is this Mrs. Garden Harris?"

Garden's teeth were chattering. She could hardly make her lips form words. "Will . . . you . . . come? . . . I need . . ."

"I know what you need, my child. Is this Mrs. Harris?"

" . . . Gar . . . den . . ."

"Yes. Good girl, Garden. I will have someone with you in a few minutes. He will give you something for the pain, and he will bring you to me. Be brave a little longer. It will seem a long time, but it will be only a few minutes. You can do it. The hardest part is over."

72

Garden had not been sick for more than six days total in her entire life. She was phenomenally strong and healthy by nature. She needed every fiber of that strength now.

For two weeks she was in hell. An inferno of pain, jagged nerves, hallucinations, strong hands holding her down, soft background voices, firm, unemotional voices telling her that the pain would go away, that she must be brave. She heard the animal screams of a soul in torment, and she was angry. Could she not at least be given some quiet place in which to suffer. The screams assaulted her ears, her nerves. She gathered her strength. She would shout, tell the creature to shut up, to give her some peace. But she could not shout. Dimly she recognized that her mouth was already open, her throat corded with effort, and from a great distance she understood that the screams were her own. "Poor Garden," she wanted to say, but she could not. She was screaming. After the screams came the mewling, and then the racking sobs and then the long, low, continual moans.

And then one day everything was quiet. She heard only the rapid sponge-pressure sounds of rubber-soled feet. A white-wimpled nurse appeared at the side of her bed. She was holding a white bowl. White steam rose from it and wreathed her head. "Would you like some soup, Madame Harris?"

Garden realized that she was ravenously hungry. She stretched out both hands for the bowl.

The nurse smiled. "I'll spoon it for you," she said. Her voice was a gentle singsong.

Garden's strong young body restored itself quickly. She was cadaverously thin and too weak to hold a spoon when the pale beef broth trickled down her throat, but an hour later she was able to lift her head when the spoon neared her mouth, and by evening she was propped upright on her pillows for the fifth feeding. In three days she was sitting in an armchair by the window with a tray-table across her lap, feeding herself raisin-speckled porridge with butter-streaked milk on it. She thought of nothing but food and her appetite for it, and she did nothing but eat and sleep for a week. She had no past and no future, only an instinctual animal drive for survival and health.

"*Bonjour*, Madame Harris. Here is your breakfast. Today you will enjoy an omelet and some cheese with your porridge." Garden looked at her nurse. She could see only her face and hands; the rest of her was covered by her starched white uniform and headdress. She did not look quite human. Garden wanted to ask her name, to make friends. But she was intimidated by the nurse's professional air of power.

"I'd like some coffee," Garden said, "and a cigarette." She watched for a reaction.

"No breakfast, Madame Harris?"

"Of course, breakfast. You know I'm starving. I want that first, then coffee. And a pack of cigarettes."

"Very well."

"She's bitchy and demanding," the nurse reported to her superior. "She's getting well."

"Take her in the wheelchair after breakfast," said the head nurse. "After lunch, start her walking."

Dr. Louis Matthias operated two clinics. There was a large one with a hundred beds in the town of Sierre, in the southern part of Switzerland. It provided the most up-to-date care, at no cost, for the poor of the province, the canton of Valais. Above Sierre, nestled in the Alps in the village of Montana, the second clinic had accommodations for only ten patients. These were the rich, addicted to drugs or alcohol. The fee of a thousand dollars a day supported both clinics.

Dr. Matthias was a genuine humanitarian. He did not despise his rich patients. Their pain was as real as the pain of the sufferers in the other clinic, and he responded to it with equal clear-sighted compassion. He gave them what was good for them and what they needed. If it was not actually injurious, they could also have almost anything they wanted. Dr. Matthias saw no need to punish them. They had punished themselves already with their addictions. His role was to make them well. Or as well as they were capable of being. To achieve that, he prescribed healthful food, clean air and exercise. And saw to it that his prescription was followed.

After breakfast Garden was given a sponge bath. Then she napped until midmorning, when she had a bowl of strong broth. She put the bowl on the table next to her bed and closed her eyes, but before she could doze off, her nurse came in. She was carrying a thick terry-cloth robe and a pair of woolen bootielike slippers. "I'm going to take you on a trip now, Madame Harris. Around the clinic."

Garden looked passively at the clinic's facilities as she was wheeled in and out of rooms, along corridors, and onto a deep, glass-enclosed porch. She saw a few people. One, swimming in the long green-watered pool through wisps of steam; another, a woman, having her hair washed in the modern beauty salon; two men playing chess in front of a bright fire in the library; a group of four playing bridge on the porch. The people did not interest her, nor the facilities. But she was fascinated by the brilliant white landscape outside the glass walls of the porch.

"I'm in Switzerland, aren't I?"

"Yes, madame."

"I remember. I wanted to come here. I love snow. Is that the Alps?" A mountain rose above the clinic, distanced enough so that its crest could be seen, a scree of gray rock striped with untouched white.

"We are in the Alps, yes, madame. That is one mountain."

Garden sighed. "Mountains always surprise me. They're so high." She thought of Wentworth and wondered whether she was happy, then found that she was crying and could not stop. The bridge players did not look up from their game. The nurse wheeled Garden back to her room.

Her tears were a steady seepage rather than an outburst, and they continued while she ate her lunch, while she tottered around her room supported by her nurse, while she slept. When the nurse woke her for dinner, her pillow was soaked, and the sheet and blanket tucked under her chin. She looked dumbly over her tray at the woman in white, kept looking at her while she hungrily forked food into her mouth, her tears salting the food. "I don't know why I'm crying," she said when she finished eating.

"You'll figure it out," said the nurse.

When the tears were all gone, Garden felt hollow, less than alive. She lay in her freshly made, newly tear-soaked bed, inert, waiting for sleep to come. Instead, she felt a deadening sorrow. "Poor Garden," she said to the darkened room. "Poor Garden." And she shook with dry, hopeless sobs.

Self-pity ravaged her for days. It wasn't my fault, she said to herself. About the cocaine, the indiscriminate sexuality, the infidelities of her husband, the futility of her life, the failure of her marriage. She wanted to be left alone, to go over and over the same things in her mind, to build a cocoon of justification and misery.

But her nurse made her walk, made her eat, made her shower, made her submit to having her hair washed and her nails manicured and her body massaged.

And the orgy of self-pity spent itself. On February first Garden looked out her window at the falling snow and felt a desire to go walk in it. She remembered clearly what excitement she had felt in New York the day she first saw snow; she remembered the delicate cold, wet touch of it on her face. It seemed so long ago. Ten times longer than the four years that, in fact, had passed. She was not a girl anymore. She was not even twenty-one, although that was her age. She was tired, soul-tired. But she could still enjoy some things, like the snow. And she was glad to be alive. She rang for the nurse.

"Do I have a coat?" she asked. "And some clothes, some shoes? I'd like to go for a walk in the snow."

The nurse led her to the opposite side of the big chalet that housed the clinic. "This is your room, Madame Harris."

The room Garden had left was small and hospital-like; only the red plaid curtains at the window brightened its white sterility. The new room was very large, with pale yellow walls, a blue carpet, and a blue-and-yellow floral print in the curtains and bedspread. The furniture was massive, clear pine carved with a geometric peasantry design, a tall-backed bed, a wardrobe, and a chest of drawers. The windows were french doors. They led to a balcony, and they had a view of the mountain. Inside the room, a deep-cushioned yellow armchair was near the windows. On the balcony, there was a wooden deck chair with a folded steamer rug laid across one arm. Bright flower paintings hung on the walls, and a flat yellow vase of flowers sat on the bureau in front of a mirror.

The nurse opened the wardrobe. It was full of Garden's clothes. So was the chest of drawers. "Your mother-in-law sent them," said the nurse. "We told her what you would need." Her mouth thinned to a disapproving line. "She also sent your jewel case. It is in the doctor's office, in the safe."

Garden found a small laugh. "I get it. I'm not noisy anymore, so I can move."

The nurse softened from disapproving to prim. "You are on the road to recovery, Madame Harris."

Garden put on a wool suit, wool stockings and fur-lined boots. She had never seen the stockings or boots before, and she thanked Vicki in absentia. Her sable coat was in the wardrobe, and she thanked her own carelessness. She had never had it shortened.

She found her way to the living room, the hall beyond it and the outside door. The snow kissed her face as she walked down the two steps to the path that had been cleared through the snow.

The drifts were as high as her shoulder. Someone had sculpted the ones on each side of the path into a fantasy wall with crenellations centered by urns. The snow that was falling blurred the shapes. Garden started to brush them clear, but her gloves became soaked, so she removed them and put her hands in the coat's pockets.

The path made a complete circumference of the chalet. Garden was surprised at the size of it. She wondered briefly how many other patients there were. She didn't care; she did not intend to have anything to do with them.

The light from the chalet's windows was warm and cheerful-looking. Garden felt safe. She walked slowly, because she was still unsteady, an aftereffect of her addiction. But she walked without tiring. It surprised her that the enforced frequent walks with the nurse could have made her so strong.

After a while, she stopped noticing the action of her legs, and she moved more easily and more quickly. And she thought.

I am getting well. Sometime, in a week or month or whenever, I will have to leave. What do I have to go back to? Sky doesn't love me. All the people I called my friends think of me as some kind of joke, a wind-up dancing doll, wound up on champagne or coke and some applause. I don't have anything. A tear froze on her cheekbone; she rubbed her face against her collar to get rid of it. No more self-pity. That time was past.

The soft touch of the fur was comforting. She turned her head from side to side, caressing her cheeks. Sable's softer than mink, she observed, deeper and more furry than ermine. It doesn't tickle like fox. I should have had this coat shortened. I haven't worn it since I first got to Paris.

She stopped walking. She had just thought of something. I'm very rich, she said to herself. I have every kind of fur, every kind of jewel, everything that anyone could ever want. I live in luxury, waited on hand and foot. It just happened, and I never thought about it. I was so busy learning how to act that I hardly noticed. My God, every woman in the world would like to change places with me. What do I have to feel sorry for myself about?

So my husband doesn't love me. So what? My father didn't love my mother, most of the men I know don't love their wives. I'm no different from them. Except that I am. My mother had to scrimp and ration her rides on the streetcar. Laurie Patterson had to get her thrills out of taking somebody else shopping for the things she couldn't afford to buy herself. I can have any damn thing I want. There's no reason why that shouldn't be enough. I'll make it be enough.

I don't have to do anything I don't want to. Sky doesn't really care whether I go to nightclubs with him and the crowd. I can pick and choose. If it would amuse me to go. if there's something at the movies or the theater that I want to see. then I'll go. And I don't have to spend all my time with those people, either. I'll make some friends of my own. That *Vogue* girl. I liked her. I'll call her up. She'd probably love to go to the theater or out for dinner. There are plenty of places that two ladies can go without needing escorts. Men aren't essential.

Certainly not to me. Not anymore. I never want to feel a hand under my skirt or a body squashing me again. It was disgusting.

She walked again, stepping firmly on the snow, hearing it squeak, holding her face up to the falling snow. She felt strong with resolve. Almost happy. When she got back to her room, she threw her coat on the chair and exchanged her boots for shoes.

She brushed her hair, appalled at the inch-long growth since it had last been bleached. The red streaks look like scalp wounds, she thought. She rang for her nurse.

"I need to have my hair done. Immediately. And I want my jewel case in my room."

That night she dressed for dinner in one of the severe black crepe cocktail dresses she had bought in the fall. She put on makeup and diamonds.

"How elegant you look, Madame Harris," her nurse said. "Would you like to eat in the dining room tonight?"

"No, thank you. I prefer to eat alone."

"Very well." She put Garden's dinner on a round table in the corner. "Did you enjoy your walk, madame?"

"Very much. Tomorrow I want to do some shopping. I have no warm gloves."

"Someone will drive you to the village."

Garden did not say anything. She took her place at the table and began to eat. Why should I try to make friends with a nurse? she thought. She must laugh at all the patients behind their backs. And she's only a servant, after all.

369

73

There was only one shop in the village of Montana, and it was not stocked for the carriage trade. The clinic's driver took Garden farther down the mountain to Crans. It catered more to skiers, a sport that had become popular in recent years among the more intrepid vacationers. Garden had a feeling of holiday. It seemed to her that she must have been in the little white room at the clinic for months.

She found some fur-lined gloves almost at once, but she wanted to extend her outing so she looked through all the other things the shop offered. She bought three heavy sweaters, knit in bright-colored patterns very like the decorations on the furniture in her new room. Then she found a knit cap to match one of the sweaters. It had a frivolous pom-pom of wool in all the sweater's colors. After that she could find nothing else. She did not plan to take up skiing.

She wandered from counter to counter, idly picking up folders and scarves and ski bindings and putting them back where she got them. The store was not at all organized. Behind a box of emergency flares, she came across a bottle of perfume. It had a bright blue bulb atomizer with a heavy tassel at the end. How tacky, thought Garden. I'll bet it smells like Woolworth's five-cent special. She squirted some on her wrist, rubbed it and sniffed. It smelled rather like fresh-cut grass. She couldn't decide whether she liked it or not. Still, there was something very mountainy and Swiss about it. She decided to get some.

She began to spray scent on her neck, below each ear. "Stop!" shouted a man's voice. A hand snatched the perfume from her.

Garden glared at the outraged man. He was no taller than she, and extremely thin, but she was unable to stare him down. "I intend to buy some," she said. Her manner was haughty. "And if you don't want people to sample it, you shouldn't put an atomizer in it."

370

The man looked at the bottle in his hand. "Do you believe for a moment that I would sell this eau de haystack, madame? I beg to correct you. I am merely doing you a service. You were getting perfume on your pearls. It is the worst conceivable crime you could commit. Perfume kills pearls; it destroys their luster."

"Does it really? Thank you for telling me." She turned away from the stranger and pursued her dilatory exploration of the shop.

When there was nothing left to look at, she instructed the proprietor to send his bill to the clinic and to put her parcels in the car. She had not, after all, bought the perfume. She was afraid that she'd always think of it as "eau de haystack."

She was irritated by how tired she felt. Perhaps there would be time for a nap before lunch. She almost stumbled walking to the car.

The man from the shop was in the front seat next to the driver. "Hello again." he said. "I didn't know you were at the clinic too. I walked down, but I need to ride up. I hope you don't mind sharing your car."

"Not at all." She supposed he must be one of the staff.

He corrected the impression at once. "Please permit me to introduce myself. My name is Lucien Vertin. I hold the record for slowest cure in the clinic's history. I've been there since the third of November." He was extremely cheerful.

Garden's blood chilled. That was three months. How long would she have to stay? "How awful," she blurted.

"Not so bad, really. There is generally someone who plays chess. Do you play, madame?"

"No."

"Pity. My current partner is being discharged tomorrow. I suppose I shall have to learn bridge."

"It's not hard. I learned quite easily."

"Will you, perhaps, teach me?"

"No, monsieur. I prefer to stay away from company." Garden pulled her coat more tightly around her.

"I understand. I believe you are mistaken, but I understand. If you change your mind, I will consider it a great favor. I will try to repay it, if you like, by telling you about perfume. That essence was revoltingly bad."

"Indeed? If you will excuse me, monsieur, I'm going to close my eyes. I'm tired."

The driver woke her when they reached the clinic. Vertin had already left the car. Garden thought that was the end of that.

She had never been more mistaken in her life. Vertin virtually haunted her. When she went out for a walk, he caught up with her within twenty paces. When she went out onto her balcony to nap in the sun, she found a note from him on her deck chair. He was always cheerful, and he did not talk a great deal, as he had done in the car. But he was an annoyance. After two days of it, Garden turned on him in a rage. She valued her walks in the snow, and she didn't want to have to stay inside to escape him. "You're deliberately following me," she said. "You don't just happen to take a walk every time I do."

She expected an apology and a retreat. Instead, he smiled and bowed. "But naturally. I lurk, madame. I lay in ambush. And when I see you go out, I am right behind you. I like to look at you. You're so healthy."

Garden was taken aback. Healthy was the last thing she thought of herself as being. She was still excessively thin, and her hands still shook so badly that sometimes she dropped things.

"How can you say that? If I were healthy, I wouldn't be here."

"Ah, but all things are relative, are they not? Look at the others. Leave your room and regard. Look at me, for that matter."

It was true. Lucien Vertin was a ghastly sight. He was peculiar-looking at best, with an enormous beaked nose and receding chin and hairline to match. In addition, his skin color was gray-white, and he shook as if he were palsied. To Garden's ear, accustomed to the French of Paris, his accent was also somehow unhealthy, blurred and missing syllables at the ends of words.

"But I don't want any company. Why won't you leave me alone?"

"Because I am a swine." He looked pleased to have an answer.

Garden laughed. He was comical.

"There," said Vertin. "Is it not more agreeable to laugh than to think about whatever makes you look so sad when you are alone? I am an excellently entertaining companion. Also informative. Do you know the story of William Tell? No? I shall enlighten you. It is such a very Swiss story; it features an apple—which, as we know, is good for you—and it has no humor whatsoever."

Garden gave in. They walked together twice that day.

That evening she even had dinner with him in the dining room.

He was, as he had promised, both entertaining and informative. When she was drifting off to sleep that night she tried to remember the last time she had laughed so freely. She couldn't.

Garden spent three more weeks at the clinic. And in those three weeks Lucien Vertin became the closest friend she had ever had. They were together from morning to night. They even napped together, in deck chairs side by side on her balcony or his. He snored, with a whistle at the end.

They walked together, took outings together, rode the funicular from Crans down to Sierre and back—a perpendicular railway that ran on cogs and teeth straight up the side of the mountain. It terrified Garden, and her terror convulsed Lucien with amusement. He treated her like a child teased her, scolded her, gave her orders. She must breathe more deeply, get more exercise, drink more milk, eat more of the eternally available porridge.

He also encouraged her to talk. She would not discuss the events that had brought her to the clinic, nor did he ever approach that subject. He asked her about her childhood. She told him about the Barony, the Settlement, Reba, Matthew, all their children. He asked her to sing some of the songs they used to sing. She sang "Moses in the Bulrushes," and began to cry. Lucien gave her a handkerchief. While she used it, he sang a French folk song about a little miller and his white duck, slain by a royal prince. It made them both cry. His voice was an untrained rich baritone. He and Garden taught each other their favorite songs and sang them together. She could not remember the last time she had sung.

Lucien persuaded her to swim. The pool was covered by a roof, but there was no outer wall around it. If the day was windy, snow blew in and melted on the edge of it. Garden had looked at the pool one time and decided that she would freeze if she tried it. Lucien nagged. "I do not swim," he said, "but you do. Therefore, you must. It will invigorate you." He watched while Garden approached the green water, bent, put a hand in. The expression on her face delighted him. The water was bath temperature, and briny. It became Garden's favorite activity. She floated or dog-paddled, talking to Lucien. Or listening to him talk.

He was a farmer, he said, but not a farmer of oats or barley. He was a farmer of flowers. Acres of roses, carnations, lilies of the valley, lavender, and yet more roses. He was from a family of perfumers in Grasse. "You see this nose?" he said, stroking the

373

tremendous expanse of it. "It is one of the most valuable noses in France. Some aesthetic types might consider it the smallest bit exaggerated, but in the world of perfume, it is legendary. It is an inherited treasure, this nose. My father has it, his father had it, and his father before him to the sixteenth century. The Vertin nose is the envy of all perfumers. It can create perfumes that speak, that sing, that enchant, that entrance . . . Alas, it seemed that God had granted me this nose to give me a capacity for the cocaine that also surpassed the nose of normal men. But that is happily in the past."

Garden loved to hear Lucien talk about perfume. She had never wondered where it came from or how it was made. The facts were astonishing. A ton of blossoms yields a little over two pounds of essence, Lucien explained, and that is only the beginning. The essences must be blended, the ingredients in varying proportions. At times as many as fifty, a hundred, five hundred attempts must be made before the perfect mix is attained, the perfume that meets the ideal in the mind and nose of the maker.

"I would love to make a perfume for you, Garden. With your name, such a name for a perfume. *Jardin*. Simply that. It would be like you, the way I see you. Complicated. Musk for the deepest, most secret womanliness of you. Some hint of African spice for your childhood. Fresh, light flowers grown in sunshine for your youth. Jasmine for your plantation woods. Roses, always roses, for blushes and girlhood, and violets because of their fragility and because you make me think of them. Perhaps one day I shall make it. If you ever see, in a shop, a perfume of exorbitant expense and exquisite delicacy, and its name is *Jardin*, you will buy the largest size, and you will never wear anything else. Do you swear?"

Garden swore.

"Furthermore, you will wear it as it is meant to be worn." Lucien shook a finger at her. "The way Frenchwomen wear perfume, not the cowardly way you Americans do. A little dab here, a little squirt there. You never lose the smell of soap, you Americans. It makes my nose ache to think of it." He walked along the edge of the pool, an imaginary atomizer in his hands, making small pinching gestures near his chin. "That is an American woman. Now this is a French-woman." He held the make-believe atomizer ahead of him, his hand squeezing, circling as he mime-sprayed. Then he stepped into the area, sniffed, a beatific expression on his face, and pirouetted around. "Ah," he sighed, "I am magnificently covered with tons of flowers now. I am an intoxication to the senses. It is truly a crime that only women can benefit from my genius. In the eighteenth century a man had equal privileges. But then, at Versailles it is said no one ever bathed because the rooms were too cold, so it is likely that even perfume by Vertin did not help."

When Garden left, Lucien kissed her hand. "I shall miss you, Jardin. When I return to my farm I shall think of you, in the sun, in a sea of flowers as far as the eye can reach. You will have millions of freckles, and you will sing many songs, and I shall create a perfume that will make you immortal. *Adieu.*"

74

Miss Trager came to get Garden. She brought Corinne to pack her things. She had hired a limousine in Geneva. Garden felt her old life closing around her, and her throat tightened.

The Principessa and Mr. Harris had agreed, Miss Trager reported, that the best thing to do was to act as if nothing had happened. They had told everyone that Mrs. Harris had gone to a spa in Switzerland to take the waters for a trifling liver complaint. Happily, the reporters had not learned otherwise.

"I see," said Garden. She reminded herself of her resolve to make the best of her life and the privileges it afforded her. She need not care what Vicki and Sky thought or did not think, said or did not say. She would be impervious, separate, unhurtable.

But she felt a heavy ache. Someone had telephoned daily from Paris, her nurse had told her. They wanted to have a regular report on her progress. They were concerned about her. Garden had never asked who the caller was, and she had never called Paris. She wanted to think that Sky was the one.

"I'll stay in my compartment on the trip home from Geneva to

Paris, Miss Trager. Please have my meals served there. I am accustomed to bouillon between meals. I expect not to be disturbed."

Sky met the train. He hugged her close. "Darling, I'm so glad you're home." For a moment Garden thought that her dreams had come true, dreams she had not dared to admit to herself. Then she saw how uneasy he was, and how artificial. "It's good to be back," she said calmly. "Switzerland is so damned clean." She would not be hurt anymore. She had a wall of finest stainless steel.

She went straight to her rooms when they got to the house. Sky trailed along after her, talking nervously about people she knew, who was in town, who had gone away, where they had gone.

"I'm tired after the trip, Sky. I'm going straight to bed. You understand. Why don't you call around and have dinner with some people and go out?"

"Are you sure you won't mind?"

"I'm sure. Maybe tomorrow I'll feel like doing something."

She sipped bouillon and dictated letters to Miss Trager. She had no idea what mail she had received in what she thought of as "the bad times" or whether she had answered it or not. She sent almost identical letters to her mother, Peggy, Wentworth, her Aunt Elizabeth. She had been vacationing in Switzerland, she told them. The Alps were spectacular. It was very cold, but didn't seem so because of the sun and the dry air. Her hotel had a heated pool surrounded by snowbanks carved to look like castle walls. She was well and happy and she sent her love.

The next day she had Miss Trager locate Connie Weatherford at *Vogue*. They met for lunch. "I've been out of touch with things," Garden told her. "I even missed the February collections. What's new? Where should I go first?"

Connie launched into an analysis of the fashion scene that left Garden's head spinning. The girl knew every detail down to the buttons. The only fact Garden could hang on to was that skirts were shorter than ever and that black was still the only color that counted.

"What do you think of this?" Connie said. She stood up and walked back and forth near their table, doing a burlesque parody of a mannequin's hips-forward slouch. She was wearing a black wool knit suit, plainer than anything Garden had ever seen. The skirt was straight, barely covering the knee, and the jacket was almost like a sweater, with narrow sleeves and patch pockets and no trim at all, not even buttons. It was the most austere costume imaginable, except that over the plain white blouse, Connie wore a mass of jewelry—pearls, gold ropes, a tremendous pendant plaque studded with rubies and a gold chain with jade circles joining the links.

"It's stunning," said Garden. Certainly she was stunned.

Connie sat down, tremendously pleased with herself. "Of course the jewelry is all costume," she said, "but that's part of the look. Costume is chic now, provided it's good costume and bold enough. This is the big news. Naturally, Chanel. She's such a genius. The whole idea is to make the clothes look like nothing, plain as can be, pared to the bone. Then overdo the jewels. Day and night. Old Poiret is livid. He's still doing the gussied-up gown. Thousands of hours of hand beading et cetera. Do you know what he said? He said, 'What has Chanel invented? Poverty de luxe.' Isn't that choice? He said women in Chanel clothes look like 'little undernourished telegraph clerks.' "

"He sounds upset. You wear that well, Connie, but I don't know if it's a good look for me."

"You'd be perfect, Garden. You're so gorgeously thin."

Garden touched her gaunt cheeks. "I'm trying to gain weight. I look like a corpse in black. Will Chanel make her styles in colors?"

"Heavens, no. She's showing black in practically everything." Connie got a funny, conspiratorial look on her face. She hitched her chair closer to the table and leaned across it. "I do know of a way," she said in a hushed voice.

She had gained access, she said, to the underground of the fashion business. There was a regular network of spies and double agents, as secret and as risky as any government's intelligence service. Women and men with photographic memories and artists' skills got into the collections with forged credentials, then dashed off to sketch what they had seen. These sketches were worth fortunes to manufacturers of mass-produced dresses. They could have cheap copies in the stores almost before the private clients of the houses received their hand-crafted originals. Even more valuable were the *toiles*, the muslin patterns used in the house to cut the originals. They made it possible to reproduce the original exactly, with the intricacy of each designer's genius intact. Someone behind the scenes at a couture house who had access to the toiles could name her own price.

"She has to earn enough to retire far from Paris, and she had to get it in one season, because she's almost always found out. Although,

377

the word is there's someone at Lanvin who's been black-marketing for years without getting caught." Connie ran her fingers down the front of her jacket. "So that's how you can see me in a Chanel. I met this girl Thelma who's the go-between for some American stores. She knows where to get everything, the fabric that's made especially for the house, the buttons, the works."

Garden found Connie's story intriguing but deplorably dishonest. "I wouldn't feel quite right going to a black-market dealer, Connie. I'd be taking business away from the couturiers. I'm a regular customer."

"Don't be such a tourist, Garden. Some of the most fashionable women in Paris do it. They go to one collection wearing a copy of a different designer, and they pick out the numbers they want somebody to steal for them. I don't know her name, but Thelma does. There's a duchess who is known as one of the best-dressed women in the world, and she doesn't have an original thread on her body. Even her shoes are copies of somebody else's design."

"I don't know. The other way's easier."

"But not nearly as much fun. And you could do your own designing in a way. Like color instead of black."

Why not, Garden thought. It might be amusing. And she had nothing else to do. "All right. I'll have one of those suits made in blue. Do you still have the toile? And a good dressmaker?"

Connie's smile faded. "I've got a super dressmaker, but there are no toiles from Chanel. Her security system is too good or her people are too loyal. Still, the line is so plain, it's easy to do from sketches."

Garden lit a cigarette. She put it in a long holder and felt like Mata Hari. "Then I'll tell you something even you don't know. I've bought a lot of clothes since we met. If you don't have Chanel's toile, you don't have a real copy. She does something with her sleeves that nobody else can do. I don't know what it is, but they let your arms move when other designers' jackets will bind or bunch. I'll tell you what. I want the blue suit. I'll buy one in black and give it to your dressmaker for a toile. She can cut my blue suit, and I don't want to know what happens to it after that."

"Garden, you're a princess."

"No, darling, that's my mother-in-law. She's in the South of France right now, thank God. I've decided that she doesn't like me very much. Too generous to be true."

"I don't understand."

"You're not supposed to. Now, tell me how your life is? Are you still planning to be a designer?"

"But of course, as we say in Paris. That's why getting in on the black market is so exciting. I get to study the toiles and the sketches and everything. I'm learning so much." Connie's face was alight with enthusiasm. Garden envied her so much that her dessert stuck in her throat. She hoped that Connie would get her dream. She forced a swallow.

"I'd better go to Chanel, then, so you'll have some more to study. Why don't you come with me? You can tell *Vogue* you're setting up an interview or something."

"In this suit? They'd attack me with their scissors. I'll take a raincheck, though. It's good to see you, Garden."

"It's good to see you, Connie. I really mean it."

When Garden left Chanel, she walked over to the Place Vendôme. Maybe costume jewelry was chic, but she'd rather have real. She went to Cartier and Van Cleef et Arpels and Boucheron, buying gold chains, beads, pendants and necklaces made of semiprecious stones, pearls and jades. She tried to convince herself that she was very fortunate to be able to do what she was doing.

75

Connie called the next day to set up a time for Garden to meet Thelma. Soon Garden found herself deeply involved in Thelma's netherworld of fashion. She was introduced to black-market bootmakers, glovemakers, hatmakers, and furriers. One of the furriers showed her a design for a cape made with the skins worked in a herringbone pattern. Garden had never seen anything like it; she ordered it in white fox. Connie told Garden proudly that she had done the design, and Garden began to take a more optimistic view of Connie's ambitions.

Thelma loved the intrigue of her chosen profession. She was a chubby young woman from Chicago, with a kewpie-doll face that made her look too innocent to be suspected of so much as taking a towel from a hotel. Her success, she said, was in her natal air. Chicago had so many gangster shoot-outs that she had inhaled bootlegging and treachery from the moment of her birth.

She was fond of complicating things. She gave Garden an elaborate key to a code of her own devising that was based on pages in *The Seven Pillars of Wisdom*. Garden asked Connie where she could buy a copy of the book, and Connie told her not to bother. "Thelma writes notes to everybody warning them not to talk or to write notes. We all throw them in the trash."

Shopping on the black market was much more difficult than shopping on the Rue de la Paix, but Garden didn't mind. It took more time, and time was what she needed to fill. She had too much time, time to think, time to get depressed. And too often her thoughts led her to the box in her dressing table, still three-quarters full of cocaine, and the cure it promised for the bleakness of her spirit. Buying things did not really help. She even ordered a custom-designed automobile from the famous body makers Georges Kellner et Fils. One of the sons helped her choose the fittings: blue velvet for the two down-cushioned armchairs that composed the rear seat, blue flowers for the needlepoint rug made to fit, and blue enamel drawers for the Lalique cigarette box, ashtrays, makeup containers and champagne glasses. The summer slipcovers for the chairs were white with stripes of blue flowers. Garden told Bercy to find her a chauffeur and send him to Kellner for advice on livery to match the car.

And still she was mired in a lethargy that she could not escape. Sky was more attentive than he had been in a long time. He was insistent that Garden have cocktails with him, dinner with him, go to the theater and nightclubs with him. He did not leave her alone, he had no recognized mistress. Garden told herself that she should be happy. But Sky's attention was watchful, not affectionate. She was sure that he was afraid she was going to commit suicide in public or commit some other scandal. She was quiet when they went out. No Charlestons, no flamboyant flirtations. She made no effort to be the center of attention. She was ashamed that it had ever mattered to her.

The only time she was lifted from her dark mood was when she received a letter from Lucien Vertin. The first one arrived in mid-March, after Garden had been home about two weeks. He was discharged, he wrote, and already at work on the perfume that would bear her name. The clinic had been a desert without her. The only companion he could find was a man who not only defeated him at chess but also defeated him in his mightiest accomplishment. The man's nose was bigger than his. Here Lucien drew a cartoon of the man. His nose continued for three pages. Garden laughed. It felt good.

"Would you like to dictate a reply to your French letter, Mrs. Harris?" Miss Trager was exceedingly casual.

Why, she looks at my mail, Garden thought. That's why the envelopes are slit, not so that it's easier for me. "Yes, I would," she said. She remembered that Miss Trager's French was almost nonexistent. She rattled off a sentence to test her. "My umbrella is under the bed of my uncle with his dog, the English terrier," she said in French.

Miss Trager squirmed in her chair, suggested that perhaps Garden would prefer to write her letter in English, finally admitted that she did not understand what Garden had said.

"Don't worry, Miss Trager," said Garden. "I'll write it myself." She sat down that instant and covered page after page with all she could remember of a long poem she had had to memorize when she was in school. "Please mail that for me." she said. "The address is on the letter I got this morning." She wondered if Miss Trager would bother to look words up in a dictionary, and if she did, what she would think about the story of the fox and the crow and the piece of cheese.

She went to a café, drank café au lait and ate brioches while she wrote Lucien a real letter. It took a long time. Garden's French was excellent when she spoke, but she had a difficult time figuring out spelling and accents for the written word. She thanked him for his letter, told him about Miss Trager's perfidy and her language dilemma, and asked him, if he had time, to write her again. "The most slangy words you know, please, and as filthy as possible. I'd like to see Miss Trager sweating over her Larousse."

Lucien complied, with an inventiveness and breadth of vocabulary that staggered Garden. She did not understand half the words herself.

The ones she did understand were scatological, pornographic and, as she wrote Lucien, "of a depravity to make the angels weep."

He wrote two or three letters a week and never repeated himself. At the bottom of each, he added a P.S. with a report on the perfume. By April first there had already been more than forty blends. His nose had rejected them all.

On April first, in Paris, it began to rain. A cold, driving, relentless rain that stripped all the new leaves from the trees and dropped branches on the streets. It never let up, day and night, day after day, until the walls of the great stone house felt clammy inside and all the cupboards had to be treated to prevent mildew. Sky caught a cold, but would not stay in bed. He moved his entire crowd of friends in, and there was no escape from the sounds of records, clicking billiard balls, shuffling cards, dancing feet, popping corks, and loud arguments. The confinement drove everyone slightly mad. And it continued to rain.

Vicki came home and ousted all of Sky's friends to make room for her own. They complained bitterly about the weather. She had rounded them up in the South of France where the sun and flowers were abundant to bring them to Paris where there was not even a green tree. She pooh-poohed their grievances. They should appreciate their good fortune, she said. They were going to be present when the new Picasso was announced. One of her artists had proved to be a genuine talent, and a major gallery was giving him a one-man show. The vernissage, an opening reception for press and invited guests, was scheduled for April sixteenth.

Garden looked at Vicki with undisguised curiosity. She had wondered a great deal about Vicki's openhandedness with the cocaine. Vicki used it herself, Garden knew that, but Vicki couldn't use much or she wouldn't be as healthy as she was. She had kept Garden's powder box full; she must have known how much she was using; had she done it on purpose? Or was she simply unaware of what coke could do? Garden felt it was important for her to know, but she didn't know how to find out.

Her scrutiny made Vicki uncomfortable. After a day of it, she made a point of including Garden in the bridge game she was organizing. "Darling Garden, you be my partner. We'll play against the men and beat them silly. You're looking simply lovely, dear. Doesn't she look lovely, Henry?"

The retired banker dutifully agreed. In truth, Garden did look sternly beautiful. She had been conscientious about her exercise and her meals, and she had gained to almost normal weight. She was wearing a wool jersey dress for warmth. It was loose, with long surplice sleeves and a rope belt tied slackly around the hips. Her hair was a shining helmet, with bangs straight across the forehead. She looked like Joan of Arc. Connie had sent her to Alexandre, the new hairdresser *Vogue* was calling "the greatest in a century." And Connie had designed the dress to go with the haircut. Garden went along with it. She was an advertisement for Connie, and she didn't really care what she looked like.

The next day, she did. A letter from Lucien said that he was coming to Paris on the fifteenth and expected to find her looking like a Rubens or he would refuse to give her the perfume. It had been discovered; the fifty-second blend was *Jardin*.

The fifteenth was only three days away. Garden put her breakfast tray aside and went immediately to the telephone.

"I am as fat as a pig," she said when Lucien was at the other end, "and I shall wear an apple in my mouth so you'll recognize me."

"No. You will wear that grotesque cap you were buying when first I saw you. I insist on it."

Garden laughed. Miss Trager looked up from the note she was making in Garden's appointment book.

"Where are you staying? When will I see you? I have a vernissage the next day, and I want you to come. You can be nasty about the paintings."

"Is the artist Swiss?"

"No. French."

"Then I will not be nasty. Mournful, perhaps, for the loss of the glory of France, but never nasty to a countryman. I am staying at the Crillon. We shall stroll in the Tuileries Gardens and rejoice that there is no snow."

"We shall have a drink in the bar and deplore the rain. Paris is miserable."

"Impossible. Even in the rain, Paris is Paris, and not Switzerland."

"What time shall I meet you?"

"Shall we say four-thirty?"

"We shall. I'm very glad you're coming."

"I also. I determined to come the moment my nose announced that *Jardin* was born. I would have telephoned, but I feared to reach your dragon secretary. Tell me, has she enjoyed my letters?"

"I don't know. I certainly have. You must be a very wicked man."

"Very."

"You've certainly added to my vocabulary."

"Improved it. Your American finishing school French was sadly unfinished."

"But sufficient." Garden stole a look at Miss Trager. Her back had an angry, angular hunched cramp. She couldn't understand a word of the conversation. Garden laughed. "I have been having such fun torturing my dragon, Lucien, that I sent a huge check to my old school. I am forever grateful that Mlle. Bongrand forced French into my thick skull."

"You must give me the address when I see you. I, too, shall send a check. Now, my little corpse, go drink some milk and tell your chef you want some porridge. With flies in it."

"Raisins."

"Winged raisins. Those Swiss never fooled me for a moment. *A bientôt*, Jardin."

"*Au revoir*, Lucien."

"You're in a very good mood today," said Vicki when Garden sat down at the lunch table.

"Yes, I am. I had a call from a very dear friend who's coming to Paris on Tuesday."

"How nice, darling. Someone from Charleston?"

"No, from the clinic."

Sky dropped his fork and knife with a loud clatter. His voice was equally loud and jarring. "Don't think of bringing them here," he said. "I don't want to meet any junkies."

"Lucien!"

"My Garden." Lucien took Garden's hands in his, kissed one, then the other. "Come. Sit. Let me look at your fat, beautiful face. Take off that lunatic cap; I will be asked to vacate my room if I'm seen with you."

Garden did as she was told. "You look well, Lucien." It was a lie.

"I thrive on challenge. I cannot wait another second; I must show you *Jardin*. Here. I have had bath salts made as well." He opened a box on the table and offered Garden a plain glass bottle, a laboratory vial with a ground glass stopper. "Very professional," he said. "I have not yet spoken with the designer for the container. Smell. Smell."

Garden removed the stopper, put the vial under her nose.

"*Imbécile!*" roared Lucien. "On the arm, to become one with the skin, with the oils. You Americans are almost as bad as the Swiss."

Garden rubbed a few drops on her wrist.

"Name of God," Lucien muttered. He took the bottle from her, poured perfume in his hand and spread it the length of her inner arm from wrist to elbow. Fragrance filled the air around her. It was fresh, light, sweet, tender, delicate, and at the same time intensely sensuous. An impossible, contradictory combination.

"Lucien, I believe you now. You are a genius."

"And an artist. Don't forget artist."

"I won't forget. You are an artist. It's the most fantastic perfume in the world. There's nothing like it, nothing. It's everything wonderful, all at once together."

"Like you, Garden. It is you, Jardin."

"Oh Lucien, I've never had such a compliment." She put her hand on his. He covered it with his other hand.

"It is not a compliment, Jardin. Not merely. It is a proposal. I have been unhappy without you. I have no laughter without you, no life. I need your presence to make the day bright. I need you with me."

Garden pulled her hand away. She felt tricked. "I thought you were my friend," she said.

"But so I am. How could I love you if we were not friends? I did not say to myself, this is a woman of great beauty and passion, I will seduce her. I said, this is a girl who should laugh more, I will become her friend. And so I did. It was not in my mind to fall in love. Only after you were gone did I discover that you had left a great darkness where all had been light. Only when I had it no more did I realize what there had been.

"Tell me, Jardin. Speak true. Was it not so for you? Did you not find that you missed the funny little man with the big nose?"

"Yes. Yes, I did. But I missed my friend, Lucien. Not a lover."

"You are wrong, my little Garden. You do not permit yourself to understand. There is no love so true as the love that is not confused by overheated bodies. We love each other. The minds, the souls, the laughter, the foolishnesses, the music. That love comes rarely and never dies. Ask yourself: what do I need in my life to make it complete? If you reply: Lucien, then you must not turn away, or you will be empty your life long.

"Say nothing, not now. You must talk with your heart, not with me. Now we shall drink some of this excellent French wine and talk about my plans for your perfume. Perhaps a figurine for a container. I have always had a secret longing to collect little figures. Those Dresden delicacies, the English pottery, the Chinese dogs, the smallest of the dolls one wins at fairs. What do you think, my flower, of putting your perfume in a miniature Swiss Alp? With a St. Bernard for a stopper?"

Garden laughed, as he had meant her to do. They were able to talk then, as they had always been able to talk. And to laugh. And to share, unmentioned, the isolation the cured addict feels in the face of the normal world.

At six o'clock Lucien said he had to leave. "I have an appointment with a rival nose. We shall get a little bit drunk together; I because I drown my pity for him, he because he must somehow continue to exist with the knowledge that he can never be as great as I.

"Tomorrow, Garden, I will go the vernissage of your third-rate artist. I will meet you in front of the most deplorable of the paintings, a choice which will doubtless be difficult to make. And you will tell me if you have decided to make us both happy. You must talk with your truest self until then. My train leaves tomorrow evening. I have reserved two compartments. I want you to come with me, and I want you to bring nothing. I want to give you a new life. I love you with all the love the world has ever known, my Jardin. Take your perfume and go. And come to me tomorrow."

Garden rode home in her new car. She had just barely time to bathe and change before cocktails, dinner, and another evening of noisy nightclubs. Vicki's guests had driven Sky out for amusement, even though his cold was no better.

Garden was very quiet all evening. No one noticed any difference in her. She was always quiet these days.

But she was different. She was trying very hard to find truth in her inmost self. She was thinking about Lucien, wishing she had a friend to talk to about him. But he was her only friend.

Many miles away, Dr. Matthias was talking to a friend about Lucien. "A tragedy," he was saying, "I could reverse the effects of the cocaine, but nothing can be done about what drove him to the addiction. He is entering the final stages of syphilis. A tragedy."

76

Garden woke up with a feeling that there was something special about the day. Her hand groped amid the clutter on the table by the bed, searching for the bell. What a difference it was to be happy to begin the day.

She was sitting up against the pillows waiting when a Marie brought in her tray. She had remembered what made the day special. Lucien. "*Bonjour*, Marie," she said. What would she say, I wonder, thought Garden, if I said to her "*Bonjour* for the last time, Marie"?

"*Bonjour*, madame," the girl replied. She opened the curtains onto a beautiful, sunny morning. "It is almost like spring today."

It should be, thought Garden. The rain is over, time for a fresh beginning. She inhaled the rich aroma of her coffee as she poured it. She felt sure that it would taste delicious.

There were a lot of letters today. She looked through them quickly. Perhaps there was a note from Lucien. No. Just as well. They had perhaps not been quite discreet enough. Thelma had sent her usual indecipherable scrawl about nothing. A letter from her mother. What did she want now? Garden left it in its envelope. A letter from Miss McBee thanking her for the gift to Ashley Hall. Garden thought fleetingly about the reason behind the donation, and she smiled. Good heavens. Wentworth Wragg had written too. This was certainly a Charleston day.

Miss Trager tapped and entered. "Alexandre telephoned, Mrs. Harris, to confirm your appointment. At ten o'clock, they said. I

told them I would call back. I don't show anything in your book."
Miss Trager had the prim look she always wore when Garden made any changes.

"I should have mentioned it, Miss Trager. Call and reconfirm. I'll be there."

"Are there any other changes, Mrs. Harris? I show a fitting at the furrier, luncheon with Mrs. Patterson, a vernissage at the Galerie Michel, the train to Nice at eight-thirty."

"That's right, Miss Trager. Put the schedule on my dressing table, will you? And tell Corinne to draw my bath. I have to get started."

Garden poured Lucien's bath salts into the tub and sank down in the water until it covered her shoulders. She wanted every pore on her body to exhale the intoxicating scent. "Corinne," she called, "transfer some of the new perfume to a vial. I want to take it to the hairdresser." She'd have them put it in the final rinse. She closed her eyes and breathed deeply through her nostrils. Lucien would recognize it at once; he would know what it meant.

"I'll want the peacock Chanel, Corinne, with the usual jewelry." He liked her best in blue, he said.

"It is nine o'clock, madame."

"I'll be right there." Garden smiled at the careful colorlessness of Corinne's voice. The entire house must be wondering what had gotten her up so early. Well, they'd know tomorrow. And have plenty to gossip about.

The blue silk chemise felt cool on her skin, and Garden realized that she was warm from the racing blood in her veins. She touched Lucien's perfume to her throat and wrists, her inner elbow, knees and between her breasts.

Corinne held the blue skirt for her to step into, then the thin satin blouse with its deep, muted jewel-toned paisley pattern. Garden saw her eyes darken when the blues in the satin framed her throat. Corinne covered her shoulders with the white combing-out jacket, and her eyes regained their usual color. Changeable, Sky had once said, like the sea.

"Bring me all the blue necklaces, Corinne. I think I remember some turquoises."

Garden brushed powder on, then brushed off all but an invisible coating. She could still see the shadows under her eyes. She applied a dusting of blue shadow on the lids, a line of blue in the indentation

388

of the socket, the navy blue mascara. She looked at herself in the brightly lit mirror. Yes, that would almost do. Her face was still too thin, the bones too pronounced, but the eyes were so bright that they distracted attention from the shadows under them and the prominent bones. She applied rouge with an expert touch, and her fatigue disappeared.

Corinne put a tray down in front of her and took away the shoulder robe. Garden put on a long thin gold chain, then a thick twisted gold rope. A shorter rope with a Maltese cross of emeralds, then a chain of oval, faceted sapphires. She tilted her head and squinted. The blues and greens brightened the paisley and were, at the same time, dulled by the dark pattern. It was almost right. A little more blue. She took a length of lapis lazuli scarabs from the tray.

Her fingers found the turquoises. No, these were just beads, not jewels at all. And too blue for turquoises. She couldn't remember buying them. There were no diamond settings, so they couldn't be one of Sky's gifts. She rolled them between her finger and thumb; some memory was trying to surface.

Of course. The plantation and Old Pansy, her tiny black wrinkled hands touching these beads. How funny. Letters from Charleston and now old memories of Charleston. Garden held the beads up to her throat. They looked exotically plain next to the emeralds and sapphires. She removed the lapis scarabs and put on Old Pansy's charm against demons.

Then the turquoises. Yes, they added just the right shock of brightness. She stood and slipped her arms into the jacket of the suit that Corinne held ready. Corinne sprayed perfume in a cloud of mist. Garden walked into it and turned while it settled on her.

"Have Laborde bring the car around. It's quarter of," she said, dropping a rope of pearls over her head.

"The machine is in disrepair, madame. There is a taxi waiting."

Garden put on a sapphire ring with a guard band of emeralds. "Very well. Put some money in my purse, then."

"It is done, madame."

Garden held out her hand for the hat. It was a cloche of peacock feathers. Overlapping iridescent blue-green and deep blue transformed Garden's head into a jewel. She tucked all her hair under it, painted her lips and studied the result while she stepped out of her mules and into the blue crocodile pumps Corinne put onto her feet.

Glitter, riches, chic. She would do. She looked very Parisienne.

Alexandre brightened the gold in her hair, trimmed the expert geometry of the shingled back and the point on her neck, cut her bangs to a side-sweeping fan and changed the squared-off sides to a series of points along her temples and cheeks. Garden was pleased. Next week half the women in Paris would have the same look, or at least an approximation. But for today, it was hers alone. A new look for a new life. And she would not be here to see the copies. She smiled radiantly when she said goodbye.

"A new lover," said the receptionist to the manicurist. "Her beauty was so cold. I never knew she could smile like a girl. It must be a lover."

"Or someone died and left her a fortune," the manicurist suggested. She had lovers aplenty. In her opinion, it would take an inheritance to warrant such happiness.

Garden swung her hat in her hand, enjoying the wintry sun on her burnished hair, ignoring the impropriety of hatlessness. She wished she could walk to her fitting, but her black-market furrier was way out on the edge of the city. She waved the peacock feathers at a cab.

"Driver. Slow down. Isn't that the Flea Market?"

"Yes, madame," said the driver, speeding up to pass a tram.

"I've changed my mind. Stop here." The furrier could wait, Garden thought. Could wait forever, for all she cared. What would she do with a white fox cape on a farm? She wanted something for Lucien, something special. She'd get him a shepherd and shepherdess. Not from an antique dealer, with a proper provenance and no particular charm. This gift must be from the heart, not the checkbook. She would find it herself, somewhere in the teeming warren of stalls and canvas tents of the Flea Market.

She paid the taxi and plunged into the crowd. Everywhere she looked there was color, life, excitement. Two men shouted insults and waved their fists in a fervid bout of bargaining. An Indian woman tried on a motheaten rabbit-fur jacket over her gold-and-red sari. A stallkeeper caught a shoplifting urchin and paddled him with a ruler. Garden felt the energy of the market in her blood. She would find what she was looking for. She knew it.

A table covered with bits of china caught her eye. She went to it, picked up a figurine and held it up to look for a maker's mark. Beyond it she saw a small, dirty painting hanging from the support of the striped awning over the table. For an instant she thought it was a picture of Charleston. This is my Charleston day, all right, she said to herself—I'm seeing things. She put the little figure down on the table and looked more closely.

There was no mistaking it; it was St. Michael's Church. A not-very-exact St. Michael's, but recognizable. The gates to the graveyard were perfect. The style was Impressionist and just a little bit primitive. Garden moved closer and saw that the artist had put palm trees in the graveyard, and black women with baskets full of flowers on their heads were walking under the church's portico. How very funny. She'd buy it and send it to Mr. Christie and Mlle. Bongrand. No French painter could have visited Charleston without their knowing it. Maybe it was signed.

It was. The signature was "Tradd." It had to be Aunt Elizabeth's son.

Garden grabbed the painting and went in search of the proprietor of the stall. He was drinking coffee with a friend at the next booth. He stood when he saw Garden approaching. "Ah, Madame has found something?"

"What can you tell me about this artist?"

"Madame has a most discerning eye. One of the flowers of the Impressionist movement. An intimate of Monet, madame, and he shared a flat with Pissaro, many say a mistress as well."

Garden was too impatient to listen to any more salesmanship. "How much do you want for this painting?"

"I sacrifice myself to honor your beauty. A thousand francs."

Garden reached in her handbag. "Here." She put the painting under her arm and walked away.

"What folly," the seller marveled. "I would have been overjoyed to get fifty."

"Americans," his friend said. "I light candles to the saints with prayers to send me Americans . .. My God, she returns. You must light bonfires."

"Do you have any more paintings by this artist, monsieur?"

"Unhappily, madame, I do not. But I can procure one, I am sure. Even two. If madame will come again tomorrow, or perhaps the following day."

Garden smiled for the first time. Both men blinked, startled. "Then you know someone who has a collection. Take me there. I would like to talk to the owner."

The proprietor thought of the forty-five francs he had paid for the painting. He had no intention of allowing this mad American to meet the owner of the others. There were, he thought, at least eight more. He could almost certainly buy them all for five hundred francs, probably less. "It is impossible, madame."

Garden's smile vanished. She looked at him coldly. "I do not enjoy being taken for a fool, monsieur. I will pay you for an introduction to the collector, but I will not be robbed one painting at a time. I do not have hours to throw away. I ask you for a last time, will you oblige me?"

The dealer clasped his hands, held them out to her, shaking them in supplication. "If only I could, madame, I would be the happiest man in France. It is not in my power."

"You, monsieur, are an imbecile." Garden stalked away.

"Michel," said his friend, "you are the imbecile of imbeciles."

"She will return."

"And I tell you, she will not."

"And I tell you she will."

A man and woman stopped at Michel's stall. "Daddy, look at that precious teapot," said the woman in English.

Michel winked at his friend. "More Americans," he said. "The saints are rewarding me for my blameless life." He approached the pair, smiling. "Marie Antoinette, madame, brewed the tea with her own hands, wearing the costume of a milkmaid . . ."

His friend disappeared into the crowd.

He found Garden on the avenue looking for a taxi. "A thousand pardons, madame," he said. "I know where she can be found, the lady who has the paintings . . ."

77

He led Garden to a tall, narrow house on the rue de Clignancourt. It was not unlike any of a thousand Paris houses: gray stone, green mansard roof, black iron patterned grillwork at the base of the windows, black iron gate backed with glass as a front door and black-garbed concierge visible through the glass, sitting on a low chair in the slate-paved entrance hall.

"The name?" said Garden.

"Lemoine, Hélène," said her guide. Garden gave him a thousand francs. He tugged his cap and hurried away. Garden prepared herself to discover that she was chasing the proverbial wild goose. She rang the bell.

She had a ten-franc note ready for the concierge. Anything larger would make her even more suspicious than concierges were supposed to be. As it was, she had to wait while the concierge took her calling card up to see whether she would be received. Garden had scrawled across the back of the card "a friend of Tradd Cooper."

"You may mount," said the concierge when she returned. Garden entered the iron cage of the elevator without much confidence. The groans and rattles it made carrying the concierge had sounded as if it was about to disintegrate at any moment.

A woman was waiting on the third floor. She watched silently as Garden rose to her level. Then she opened the door of the elevator for her. "*Bonjour, Mademoiselle Harris,*" she said. "I am Hélène Lemoine."

"It is Madame Harris, Madame Lemoine," Garden said. Hélène Lemoine was an eccentric-looking creature. Petite, heavily powdered, her gray hair held in a complicated series of waves and a pompadour by a number of small tortoise-shell combs. She was wearing a black lace floor-length dress with a tall boned collar edged in white. A white lace shawl lay across her shoulders. Her only ornament was a filigreed gold chain with a gold lorgnette at the end of it. She held the lorgnette in a small hand knobby with arthritis and scrutinized Garden slowly from top to bottom.

"It is Mademoiselle Lemoine," she said when she finished. "Follow me."

Garden followed, into another era. The sitting room was crowded with overstuffed furniture, tables with lace cloths covered with bric-a-brac, a piano draped with a silk shawl that was nearly hidden by ranks of photographs in elaborate silver- and gold-colored frames. The windows had fringed velvet draperies over fringed lace curtains. The skirts of the chairs and sofas were fringed, the shawl on the piano was fringed, the lampshades were fringed, and a fringed drape covered the mantel above the bright coal fire that made the room feel like an oven. Paintings and pictures covered the brocaded walls from floor to ceiling. Garden was overwhelmed by the clutter.

"Sit down, madame," said Mlle. Lemoine, "and tell me why you are here."

Garden sat on the edge of a tremendous chair. She held out the painting she had bought. "I was told that you have more paintings by this artist. I would like to buy them."

Her hostess lifted the lorgnette again. "Ah, the little Tradd's church. What a brigand that Michel is. He must have sold the frame at once and left the painting out to become grimed." Her gaze moved to Garden. "Why did you lie, madame? You are too young to have been a friend of this artist. What is your interest?"

"He was a cousin of mine, though I never knew him. His mother is my great-aunt. My maiden name was Tradd."

"It cannot be. I was told that all Tradds have fire-red hair."

Garden was becoming impatient. "My hair has red streaks. I bleach them."

"How very foolish."

"Mademoiselle Lemoine, I am not here to discuss my hair. I want to buy those paintings. I will pay you a very good price." She opened her handbag.

"No, madame," said the Frenchwoman.

Garden could not believe it. "But you sold this one to the man at the Flea Market," she said. "I will pay much more. You do have others, do you not?"

"Yes. I have many others. But there is no need to sell them at this time."

Garden lost her temper. "Look, mademoiselle, I do not have time to play games. You want to push up the price. Very well. I am willing to be pushed. I don't care what they cost; I want them."

Hélène Lemoine nodded. There was a small smile on her face. "Yes, very creditable, that. I can believe that you have part red hair, that you are part Tradd. But the paintings are still not for sale."

Garden was thunderstruck. It was her experience that anything could be bought if the buyer was willing to pay.

"But you must sell them to me," she said. Her temper was gone; she was pleading. "My Aunt Elizabeth came to Paris herself looking for them. She searched everywhere. She's never seen even one. Tradd was her only son, Mademoiselle Lemoine, and she lost him. The paintings are the only thing he left."

Hélène Lemoine picked up a china bell from the table by her side. She rang it with a vigorous wave. "You should have told me that in the beginning, madame. For the little Tradd's mother, it is a different story. We will have coffee and come to terms."

Garden relaxed. Obviously there was no rushing this old lady, and she had hours before she had to meet Lucien. She'd simply stand up Laurie Patterson for lunch. The important thing was to get the paintings. "How many paintings are there, mademoiselle?"

Mlle. Lemoine shrugged. "How can I say? A dozen, twenty, thirty, perhaps. He was not a very good painter, your cousin, but he worked very hard. There is an armoire full of them.

"Ah, here is the coffee. Céleste will pour; my hands are very bad today. Will you take milk, sugar?"

"Both, please."

The maid was almost as old as Mlle. Lemoine, and as fat as her mistress was thin. She gave Garden a cup of café au lait; Hélène Lemoine's she put in a bowl, which could be cradled in two hands. Then she put a footed plate near Garden. It was mounded with macaroons.

"Eat them," said Mlle. Lemoine. "Céleste is an excellent cook. You may leave us now, Céleste; you've had your compliment.

"Tell me about your great-aunt, Madame Harris. The fascinating Bess."

"Elizabeth. She is a remarkable lady. She lost her husband very

395

young, and she had to run a business herself to bring up her children."

"Yes, yes, I know all that. I want to know what she is like now. Is she content? Is she in good health? Is she lonely? Has she married? She is a fascination to me, the only rival I ever had whom I could not surpass."

Mlle. Lemoine made an impatient clucking noise.

"Don't look so incredulous," she said. "Do you believe that because we are now old, it follows that we were never young? We are of an age, Bess and I. She is perhaps a year and some months older, but I am generous. We shared a lover, the charming Harry. Name of God, what charm he had. I was very close to losing my head over him. Naturally, he adored me. But he loved Bess. How I wish I could have known her . . . Drink your coffee. It is too expensive to waste." Mlle. Lemoine lifted her bowl to her lips. Garden obediently lifted her cup. Her mind was reeling. The Frenchwoman's faded blue eyes watched her over the rim of the bowl.

"You are recovering, yes?" she said when her bowl was empty. "Now you can tell me about Bess. That is what Harry called her, and it is how I call her. Is her life satisfying to her? I wish her well."

Garden imagined her great-aunt's life as best she could. "Yes," she said. "I think she is happy."

"Happy? What is that? I asked was her life satisfying. You young people irritate me. The truth is, you do not know how Bess's life seems to her. You have never asked yourself. Your own life, your own satisfaction is all you consider. No doubt that is the reason for your unhappiness."

"But I am not unhappy."

"Of course you are. If you are unaware of it, then you are an idiot. It is blazoned on you for all the world to see."

"How dare you speak to me like that?"

"I dare because I have an interest in you. Not because you are interesting, but because the noble-hearted Bess is your aunt. I am confident that your misery would be a sorrow to her. Also your stupidity. I will help you, if you permit. For her sake."

There was something about the Frenchwoman. Her lack of emotion, perhaps, or her unassailable assurance. "How can you help?" asked Garden.

Mlle. Lemoine's faded eyes looked into Garden's brilliant young ones. "I can make things clear," she said. "Tell me about you."

Garden did not know why, but she believed that it was vital to do exactly what the Frenchwoman said to do. So she talked. She talked about Lucien, the clinic, the "bad times" of cocaine and promiscuity; she talked about Vicki and her houses; she talked about Sky and his women, his airplane, his gambling; she talked about Sky in the beginning, about the yacht and the private jokes and about her fears and her attempts to become part of his world; she talked about losing him.

When she stopped talking, her throat was sore, her mouth dry. She was trembling, exhausted.

"I see," said Mlle. Lemoine. "And now, because your husband no longer loves you, you intend to run away with a man who says that he does."

"He does love me. I know it."

"And what will you do when he ceases to love you? Find another man? Return to the cocaine?"

Garden held her hands up, trying to ward off the Frenchwoman's words. "You are cruel," she cried.

"I am a realist. What you are doing, my child, is looking for yourself in the eyes of another. You must look inside yourself for yourself. Answer me quickly. What do you want?" She all but shouted the question.

Garden was startled into answering without thought. "I want Sky," she said. "I want to have a baby and our own house."

"Ah, a *bonne bourgeoise*. Excellent. We shall have a small lunch, and then we can begin."

Garden was examining the words that had risen spontaneously to her lips. Now that it was said, she recognized the wish as the deepest truth of her heart. And as unattainable, no matter how much she might want it.

"What can we begin?" she said dully.

"Why, to obtain for you that which you want."

"Never. Didn't you hear what I told you? Sky is tired of me. He doesn't love me."

"Paugh! That can easily be remedied."

"Really? Are you sure? How?"

"Patience, patience. I am sure. But we cannot begin on an empty stomach. The liver will rebel."

78

"While we digest," said Hélène Lemoine, "I will tell you about my life. It will give you confidence.

"I was born in Lyons, the sixth child and fourth daughter of a good bourgeois family. It was clear from the beginning that there would be no dowry for me and therefore no marriage. It was intended that I take the veil, enter the convent where I went to school. Unfortunately, I had not the vocation, and I ran away to Paris. To what other place should one run? I had few clothes and less money, and I had to find work. The possibilities were few. It was 1875, and I was fifteen years old. I was well-educated, I could play the piano, sew, and speak German and Italian almost as well as my native tongue. The languages directed my course. I was walking along the Champs-Élysées when I heard a fearful argument. A woman was screaming at another while a man shouted at them both. The women were Italian, the man German.

"I knew it by his words; I did not look at him. I looked only at the women. They were like none I had ever seen. One of them, the one in the carriage—did I say that the man and women were in an open phaeton?—was dressed in satin, in extreme décolletage, with a hat of unsurpassed magnificence of flowers, aigrettes and plumes. She was also as bright as a night sky with diamonds. Most astonishing of all, she was painted on her face. She was hitting the other woman over the head with a parasol, screaming that it was the wrong one.

"The other woman fixed my attention. Her face was bare and her only jewelry a small gold crucifix and, poor creature, she had no hat at all. But her gown was, to my eye, even more beautiful than the satin of the carriage. It was blue moiré silk, with a bustle of a size and a frivolity that I had never seen. Within its folds were raspberry-pink velvet bows. Ah, how I longed to touch them. They looked so richly soft.

"The unfortunate with the exquisite bows was, of course, the maid to the magnificent in the carriage. She had brought a blue parasol, when her mistress was wearing green. As she deserved, she was being dismissed from her position.

"A maid dressed in such a manner! I wanted to be such a one. I hurried to the gentleman, who was in a terrible rage because of the public scene, and I rapidly explained to him, in German, the occasion for it. The woman in the carriage, I told him, was driven to frenzy by the fear that her appearance would bring shame to him. I then ran through the door that stood open behind the maid, located a parasol of the most delicate salmon hue, raced to the street, curtsied, and offered it. In Italian, I asked to be engaged as lady's maid.

"My employer was one of the great *cocottes*, the *grandes horizontales*, they were called. She was an actress of sorts—this is to say, she posed on the stage of the *Folies-Bergère* in very few garments—but primarily she was an enchantress. Her lovers were many, were wealthy and were generous. Or they ceased to be her lovers . . . You gape. Surely you have heard of courtesans before."

Garden had not. She thought Mlle. Lemoine meant prostitutes.

"Diane de Poitiers . . . Madame du Barry . . . Joséphine de Beauharnais, who became Empress of France—hardly prostitutes. The great courtesans were stars, like your cinema stars today, except that they had more talent. They had to, because they were on stage at all times. In public and, more demandingly, in private."

"What was the name of your employer?"

"Giulietta della Vacchia was her name, but it was never used. She was called 'La Divina.' Divine she was to look at, and she had the temperament of one of the more irritable goddesses. Still, she was very generous. It was the nature of the great cocottes. So much was showered on them that they were profligate in spending and in gift giving. La Divina never wore a gown more than once. Then it was mine. I had to wear uniform only when admitting gentlemen to her rooms, and when answering the bell while they were there if she wanted anything.

"You can imagine that I learned a great deal. When I knew as much as I needed to know, I began my own career."

Garden could not believe that the sharp-tongued, bent, gray-haired woman had ever been a courtesan. But she kept her thoughts to herself. It was, at least, a good story.

"You are skeptical," said Hélène Lemoine. "It will pass. I was by this time sixteen years, and I was very pretty. Not beautiful, like La Divina, but my face was very pleasing to the eye, and my body was ravishing, as is so often the case at sixteen. And I had learned, by listening at the door, how to please.

"La Divina was best known for two things: her rubies and the number of suicides she had caused. One gossip columnist dubbed her the Russian Roulette because three Russian noblemen shot themselves in one year on her account."

Garden gasped. "That's terrible."

"It is the Slavic temperament, my dear. And those were the days of great extravagance in everything. In any event, she had one lover, a government official, who was clearly near desperation; despite the attentions he paid her, she would seldom receive him. I knew that she intended to reject him altogether. And in public, so that it would be in all the papers. You see, there had not been a suicide in months, and she was concerned about her reputation."

Garden was appalled. By La Divina and by the casual attitude of Mlle. Lemoine.

"Yes," said the Frenchwoman, "La Divina was brutal. But these men were fools of the greatest magnitude. One does not suicide over a love affair, most particularly when there is no pretense of love. La Divina was like an expensive commodity at auction. No one had to bid, but the presence of other bidders applied pressure to do so.

"I felt rather sorry for poor Étienne, and I also knew that an equal opportunity might not present itself again for some time. I waited for him outside the Jockey Club on a Thursday, my day off. I looked especially lovely in a hooded cape—they are so romantic. And I told him that La Divina had dismissed me because she learned that I was in love with him."

"Were you?"

"Certainly not. Not in love, and not dismissed. If my little game had not worked, I needed my job. However, it did. Étienne offered me a glass of wine, then a dinner, then his protection. I became his mistress that night. I was a virgin. Men are overcome when they are the first. Dear Étienne. We are friends to this day. He can never forget, you see."

"Weren't you sad, Mademoiselle Lemoine? Not being in love, I mean?"

"My dear Garden. I have decided to grant you the 'tu' and my first name, which is Hélène. My dear Garden, had I had a dowry, I would have been married to a man of my father's choosing, and I would have afforded him the same privileges, but with less skill and less reward. Étienne was even more generous to me than he had been to La Divina. He installed me in a charming suite of rooms at an *hôtel privé*, presented me with a carriage, horses, coachmen and footmen and opened an account for me at Worth. He also gave me my first jewels—a pearl dog collar, as we called it, with diamonds pavéed on the supports. I engaged an excellent maid of quite remarkable ugliness, and the hôtel had an adequate chef. It was a very good beginning."

Mlle. Lemoine was visibly nostalgic. Garden warmed to her. How sad it must be to have only memories. She remembered her own marriage. How sad it was for her. She had only memories, too.

"Were you lovers for a very long time?" she asked gently.

"But no. I had my career to make while I was young. Étienne took me out, of course. Being shown off was one of one's duties. And at Maxim's one night, La Divina attacked me. She pulled out a handful of my hair. My reputation was made."

"You became a—what is it—a *grande horizontale?*"

"Briefly. The truth is, I did not have the disposition for it. One had to make scenes, get one's name in the columns, be talked about. It soon became wearing. I am at heart, like you, *bonne bourgeoise*. I prefer a more tranquil existence. So I made myself a *demi-castor.*"

"What is that?"

"A *demi-castor* is a courtesan of smaller ambitions and greater selectivity. She is mistress to only one man at a time, and she serves as hostess to his friends in the home he maintains for her. I was noted for my table. I always insisted on a superb chef, even if it meant fewer maids."

"How long were you someone's mistress?"

"It varied. One had to be vigilant. There was always the risk that the protector would fall in love. And I wanted no suicides. So I would exchange protectors if that seemed about to happen, or if I saw a means to better myself."

"And did you never fall in love, mademoiselle?"

"Hélène."

"Hélène. Was there no danger for you?"

"But naturally. Not that I would fall in love with my protector; my obligation to him demanded better than that. However, I became a protectrice. I bought this flat and used it for a protégé. Usually an artist. There is a studio above. On my day off, Thursday, I always came here. I loved Montmartre. I still do, though the artists have gone."

"What an extraordinary life you have had, Hélène." Garden felt sad and sympathetic.

The elderly Frenchwoman lifted her chin. She looked down her narrow nose at Garden. "Indeed?" she said coldly. "You are thinking, poor Hélène, who had to be displayed like a pet poodle on a leash, poor Hélène who had servants and jewels but no husband, poor Hélène, who sold herself to men. Let me think, also. Poor Garden, who displays herself, poor Garden, who has servants and jewels but no husband, poor Garden who sold herself for love and has exhausted the supply. At no time, poor Garden, did a man willingly let me go. And I could today have any one of the men who knew me as my protector again. So who is to be pitied?

"I am harsh with you, Garden, because you do not learn, you do not think. You must do both if I am to help you . . . Stop that crying, or, at the very least, use a handkerchief. You will make spots on the upholstery." Hélène's voice softened. "Listen to me, my child. I told you that long story so that you will believe that I know about men and about what you call love. I have the knowledge that you need. I will give it to you. If you are willing to pay close attention and to work very hard, I am willing to teach you. You can have your Sky and your baby and your life of *bonne bourgeoise*. Is it your wish to learn?"

"Oh yes, please. I'm sorry if I was rude."

"You were not rude; you were sanctimonious. That is infinitely worse. It is getting late. Should you not be someplace?"

Garden looked at the clock on the mantel. It was after five. The vernissage was half over. Lucien was probably already gone. It did not seem important, except that his feelings would be hurt. She'd write to him tonight.

Tonight. "I'm supposed to go to Antibes tonight," she said. "With my husband and some other people."

"And what will happen if you do not go? Will everyone stay in Paris?"

"No. They'll go without me."

"Very good. Tell your Sky that you must stay, that you must indulge an old woman in conversation in order to gain the paintings of your cousin. Be here tomorrow at eleven, and we shall begin your instruction." Hélène smiled, and Garden could see that she had indeed been very pretty.

"I have done this once before," she said. "It was very enjoyable. My last protector before I retired, he married an enchanting young girl. I did not see him for fully two months. Then he was back, as I expected, with an especially fine set of emeralds and enough flowers for the funeral of a prince. Two months later, the little bride came to me in tears. She was a sweet child, so I took her under my wing. They have six children now. Liane sends me flowers and hot-house grapes every week. She wanted me to be godmother to the firstborn, but I corrected her at once.

"Go away, Garden. Come back tomorrow. I need my rest before dinner. I shall teach you to be totally irresistible."

79

"Let us commence with your assets," said Mlle. Lemoine. "You are extremely beautiful. That is moderately useful. You must remember, however, that your Hollywood films have beautiful young women by the dozen. Beauty is not that rare a commodity. Particularly when it is ordinary. You tell me that you have distinctive hair. Commence instantly allowing it to grow out from the bleach. Wear turbans.

"What else have you? You carry your head and shoulders proudly. That is rare. And it is more instantly observed than a face or a figure. It is your most valuable asset.

"Next is your voice. It does not assail the ear. A difficult quality to attain. You are fortunate.

"And you are well-bred. Convenient. Manners must be drilled

until they become automatic, and that takes a great deal of time. We will be able to omit that.

"That completes your assets, Garden. Everything else about you is a detriment. You are well dressed without chic. Where are the necklaces you were wearing yesterday?"

"At the house. They don't belong with this dress."

"Who told you that? And whoever it was, why did you believe them? I had hopes of you yesterday. Your costume was a copy, and you were wearing a string of beads that was not from Cartier or Van Cleef, like your other jewelry. Today you are dressed by Lanvin, not by Garden Harris.

"Ah, well, the dressing can wait. We must first attack the fundament. Tell me, Garden, have you at any time in your life experienced an education?"

"Of course. I went to a very good school."

"And did you do well in school?"

"I think I did. My grades were not high, but I learned a lot."

"And did you enjoy learning?"

Garden thought about Ashley Hall. She could smell the mixture of chalk dust, ink and floor polish that filled the classrooms. She thought of Miss Emerson and her crisp voice, her demands for full effort, her patience when Garden was trying her hardest but having difficulty, her pleasure when Garden succeeded in understanding. Garden remembered her own pleasure, her sense of accomplishment, the satisfactions of disciplined hard work. "Yes, I enjoyed learning."

"Then why did you stop? Don't try to answer. There is no adequate answer short of death. One must continue to learn or life becomes savorless. And a woman, even more than a man, must be constantly curious, constantly learning. For that is the root of charm. I am curious about you: what do you do, think, believe, love, hate? You tell me. I am interested. I disagree with you, tell you why. You respond, tell me I am wrong. What are we talking about, you and I? We are talking about you, your mind, your interests. Naturally, you find me charming. I am discussing what interests you most, yourself.

"Tell me, Garden, what interests your Sky?"

"Women and drinking."

"Bitterness does not advance us. You do not know. That is what you are really telling me. No wonder you bore him. You do not ask what interests him, and you have nothing that interests you."

Hélène Lemoine stripped Garden's character to the bone, dissecting everything about her, finding it flawed. Then she began the difficult, disciplined work of rebuilding. Garden had lived in Paris for two years without ever walking the fascinating crooked streets or visiting the museums or sitting at a sidewalk café. Until she met Hélène, she had not spoken to a French man or woman, other than to buy something.

Hélène gave her assignments.

Books to read, on the history of Paris, of France. The books had to be bought at the stalls on the quais of the left bank of the Seine, not at a bookstore. And Garden had to talk to the other people strolling, poking through the used books, ask them what they were looking for and what made those books worth reading. Garden learned that books were for pleasure, and that Paris was an endless source of stories and fascination.

Then the assignment was to walk. Through museums, through neighborhoods, along the Seine. Looking. Stopping in the little parks that dotted the city, smelling the growing green things. Reading a newspaper at a café, watching the other people, listening to their conversations. Without being aware of it, Garden learned not to be afraid to be alone, and then to enjoy it.

And always conversation. About what she had read, and what she had thought of it. What she had seen and what she had thought of it. What she had heard, what people she had met, what streets, paintings, churches, parks she had visited. And what she thought of them. Bit by bit, Garden progressed from passive to active, from observation to opinion. She learned to think.

"We talk about nothing but me, Hélène," she said one day. "Where I've been, what I've done, what I thought of it. You're charming me, aren't you?"

Hélène laughed. "Do you not find me the most interesting conversationalist in your experience?" Garden admitted that she did.

"There you have it. And you put it together for yourself. You are making real progress, my dear."

One must be up-to-date, Hélène said firmly. Garden read magazines and newspapers. She learned about Hitler, Houdini, Gertrude Ederle, the Davis Cup, Winnie-the-Pooh, Mussolini, Chiang Kai-shek, Al Capone, Joseph Stalin, Commander Byrd, and Peaches Browning.

And Charles Lindbergh. Garden called for Hélène on Saturday

afternoon at five for the short ride out to Le Bourget Airfield. Like many others in Paris, they had been listening to the radio bulletins since the day before, when the young American took off in the early morning, early afternoon by Paris time. Garden sat up all night by a crystal set, the earphones clamped on her head, listening to the static, trying to tune in any news transmission. She understood, better than most, what it must be like for Lindbergh. She remembered the wind in her face and isolation she had felt when all contact with the world as she knew it was cut, when the earth became a patchwork quilt and houses looked like toys. The image of flying through the night alone, with nothing below but featureless ocean, was vivid and terrifying in her mind; the courage of the young aviator was awesome. She desperately wanted him to be safe, to make it across the long, long thousands of miles. At one in the morning she heard a report that he had left sight of the North American mainland almost an hour earlier. There was no reason for her to listen any longer. But she did. It was, in some way, as if she were helping him.

Miss Trager found her still in her chair, still listening at nine the next morning. She ordered coffee followed by breakfast. When Garden had eaten, Miss Trager shouted at her, penetrating the baffle of the earphones. "Mrs. Harris! There cannot be any report for hours. Mrs. Harris! You must stop this now."

Garden removed the headset, rubbed her sore, tender ears. "You're right, Miss Trager. Or I won't be able to hear when it's time for him to be sighted." She stretched, rubbed the back of her neck. "Oh, I'm stiff. I'm going for a walk."

After she left, Miss Trager wrote her weekly letter to Vicki. "Mrs. Harris continues to be solitary. She reads every night and takes long walks by day. She has not visited the hairdresser again this week." Miss Trager deliberately omitted mention of the changes in Garden, her singing, the liveliness in her eyes and in her step, her air of well-being and her smiles. Let the Principessa think the girl was depressed. Then she'd leave her alone. Miss Trager might take Vicki's money and follow her orders; she didn't have to help her.

Garden walked all the way to the river. By every newsstand, on every corner, there were knots of people talking excitedly about Lindbergh, Lindbergh, Lindbergh. She crossed to the Île de la Cité, walked to Notre Dame. Inside, the cathedral was crowded with people praying for the safety of the young American. Garden joined them for a moment. Why, I haven't been to church for years, she thought. I didn't know I missed it until now. Suddenly she felt a conviction that Lindbergh was all right. And that she was, too.

She ate lunch in a quiet restaurant on the Île St. Louis. Here, too, all the talk was of Lindbergh. After she paid for her meal, she sought out the proprietor behind the bar. "Monsieur, I am an American," she said. "It would be an honor if you would permit me to purchase the wine for all your patrons. I would like to toast Captain Lindbergh."

"*Mais non, madame.* It is a toast we French are proud to make without aid. Allow me to offer a glass to you, as an American." He tapped on a glass to get the attention of everyone in the restaurant, proposed the toast. Men and women stood, raised their glasses, bowed their heads toward Garden and drank. She bowed in return and accepted the salute on behalf of her country, then toasted the hearts of the French people and their generous spirit. She felt immensely proud and happy and loving to all mankind.

"Draw my bath, Corinne, and lay out something comfortable for me to wear. Low-heeled shoes. I'm going out to the airfield. The newspapers predict a landing at seven-thirty this evening."

While the bath was running, Garden telephoned Hélène Lemoine. Yes, said Hélène, she would like to be there when history was made. Garden sent instructions to the kitchen to prepare a picnic basket. She couldn't sit by the radio any longer. She had to be there when Lindbergh completed his flight.

"We shall be very early," said Hélène. "That is good. We shall find a vantage point before the crowd is too heavy. There will certainly be a crowd."

There was, even when they arrived. There were police, too, and soldiers, keeping the crowd contained behind the steel fence on the east side of the field. The police opened the gate for the big car and waved them through, onto the field. "What luck," said Garden. "I wonder how that happened?"

Laborde turned his head. He was grinning. "I took the liberty, madame, of attaching an American flag to the mount of the headlight."

Garden and Hélène whooped. "They believe we are a delegation

407

from the embassy," said Garden. "I'll write a thank-you note to the ambassador."

At seven, the genuine reception committee from the Embassy arrived. The cars were sent to park near Garden's. She lifted a glass of wine in a welcoming salute. Laborde had set up the picnic table and chairs at six-thirty. They wanted to be finished before Lindbergh landed.

"Whew," Garden overheard from the embassy car, "there must be fifty thousand people out in that crowd." She translated the comment for Hélène and Laborde. He was eating with them at Garden's insistence. "After all," she said, "you're the brains in this delegation, Laborde." It delighted her that the other Americans kept looking curiously at her party. It made her feel naughty and clever and even more gala.

The scene was dramatic. To right and left, great beacons of light cut up into the darkening skies. Red and green and white skyrockets climbed and burst into showering colored stars. The excited babble of the crowd could be clearly heard over the hundred yards that separated the cars from the fence. It was seven-thirty.

A caravan of three limousines flying the tricolor bumped across the edge of the field. The French reception delegation had arrived. But Lindbergh had not. Laborde walked over to the nearest French car and talked to the chauffeur. He returned, shaking his head. "We must wait," he said. "The *Spirit of St. Louis* was sighted about an hour ago over Ireland. He will not be here until almost nine."

"Then we'll just have to celebrate in advance," said Garden. "There's only champagne left. Ireland is what counts, he's crossed the ocean. Everything is all right."

After an hour they got into the car. It was dark. Big arc lights went on—one, then two, then a burst of brilliance on all sides of the field, illuminating it brighter than daylight. "He's coming," Garden cried. She jumped out of the car and looked up at the heavens. There were no stars to be seen; they were bleached away by the lights around the landing field.

Then in an instant, the stars were back. Only the searchlights continued to move their beams in slow, lazy circles. The landing field was dark. "What is it?" Garden said. She ran to the nearest automobile, pleading for information.

"I don't know, lady," said an American in the car. "Maybe they were testing the lights."

"What time is it?"

"Quarter past nine."

Garden remembered to say thank you, then she walked slowly back to her car. She would not believe that the English Channel had done what the broad Atlantic could not do.

Hélène patted her hand. "At the most desperate moments, dear Garden, one must face facts. They are the only rocks to hold on to. What facts do we have? The brave captain was seen safely across the ocean. He had large amounts of fuel. He is an experienced pilot. He is late. That is all we know."

"But it is dark, Hélène, and he has no instruments for navigation. It was planned that he would arrive while there was still daylight."

"When it is dark, there are stars. Men navigated by stars long before they devised instruments. Facts, Garden, facts." They waited, silent. At long intervals a single skyrocket flared, then scattered its colors. Laborde spread a lap robe over Hélène's knees; it was getting cold.

The field lights went on. Garden caught her breath. Yes, there was the sound of a motor. They could hear the crowd cheering. The spotlight searched the heavens. "I knew it," Garden said. "I knew he'd make it." Hélène crossed herself, murmuring quiet thanks. "When he lands, we'll get out of the car," said Garden. "I want to see him taxi up and get out. I want to see his face."

The lights went out. "Laborde!" Garden cried.

The chauffeur was already running to the operations building. The groans of the crowd were very loud. Garden held to the facts. And to the certainty she had felt in Notre Dame that afternoon. When Laborde returned, she was able to ask him calmly if he had learned anything.

"It was another plane, madame, not destined to land here. But Captain Lindbergh was seen to cross above Cherbourg at eight-thirty. He is coming."

"What a drama," said Hélène with a chuckle. "I would not have missed it for the world."

"Do you hear it, madame? A motor." Laborde lowered his window.

"Yes, yes, I hear it. Ah, but it's fading."

The field lights and a dozen skyrockets, all at once. Hélène and Garden shielded their eyes. Garden fumbled with the door handle.

"At last," she said. As she opened the door, she heard a roaring, as if the plane were diving at them. Laborde pushed her back inside before she was completely out of the car. Garden looked around.

"Name of God," said Hélène.

The crowd was surging across the field, shouting and cheering. They had pushed down the steel fence, pushed aside the police and soldiers. They were like a tidal wave. Laborde was caught up and swept away with the wave that surrounded the car and passed it to encircle the small silvery airplane that had stopped a hundred and fifty yards in front of them.

"By great good fortune," Hélène said, "I brought along a flask of brandy. Who knows when our driver will return."

"He made it, Hélène, nonstop across the ocean. Look, they're carrying him on their shoulders. Just listen to all the cheering. I want to cheer myself."

"Then do so."

Garden lowered her window. The door was blocked by delirious, yelling men and women. She stuck her head out and joined in. "Lindy! Lindy! Bravo! Bravo!"

When Lindbergh had been hurried away and the exuberant crowd was dispersing, Laborde made his way back to the car. His cap was gone and a sleeve ripped. "Are you all right, Laborde?"

"Extremely well, madame."

A straggling line of top-hatted officials was weaving through the remaining throng, looking almost as much the worse for wear as Laborde. A distinguished gentleman with a slash of ribbon across his chest was jostled into the side of the car. "A thousand pardons," he said, touching the brim of his top hat with white-gloved fingers. Then his eyes widened. "Hélène," he said, "what are you doing here?"

"Simply enjoying myself, Marius. It has been most pleasurable. Now, go on about your ministerial duties. Your colleagues will miss you."

Mlle. Lemoine chuckled gently the whole way home. Garden giggled.

80

"My dear Garden," said Hélène next day, "I was very pleased with you last night. I was pleased with the experience, but even more was I pleased with you. I shall tell you why as soon as you cease to stare out the window. What are you thinking?"

"Oh, about Sky, and how I wish he had been there. He's a flier too, you know. He would have understood, much better than I did, what Lindbergh did, what he must have been thinking and feeling."

Mlle. Lemoine thought it highly unlikely, but she did not say so. She said instead, "Well, he was not there. That is a fact. Another fact is that you involved yourself, you made plans, arrangements; you got yourself there. With me, but that is of no consequence. You did everything necessary. Alone. And you enjoyed yourself; you are happy that you did this thing.

"You were also, from what you tell me, conscious of yourself as an American. This excellent Captain Lindbergh has produced in you, dear Garden, the first glimmers of positive self-consciousness. You have now learned that you are an American, that you have interests, that you have the capacity to pursue those interests, and that the pursuit is worth doing.

"This is the path you must now follow. You must discover who you are. An American. Yes, and what else? You must identify yourself to yourself. We have discussed your life at length, and I will tell you what I have seen. A girl, now a young woman, who has done what she was told to do, done what others did, been carried along by others like the chauffeur by the throng. You have been forever a particle, never a unit. You were your mother's creature, then your husband's, then the plaything for your so-called friends. You saw yourself through the lenses of their wishes and their opinions. Now you must begin to look through your own eyes. You have begun to build a mind, some information, some curiosity. Use

411

it and create for yourself someone you respect, whose company is a pleasure to you. You have made a beginning. Keep on as you are going, but work harder."

Garden nodded, her brow furrowed. "Yes, I understand what you are saying. At least I believe I do. I certainly feel better than I used to. I feel as if I'm doing something with my life, now that I'm learning things and noticing things. I won't ever go back to the way I was, Hélène. It was too empty. But I don't see how getting to know myself is going to get Sky back. When will you teach me how to do that?"

"My child, I told you long ago. That is the easy part. The hardest you have already done. You have turned your attention outside and found it worth doing. Now that you have begun, you will continue. That will render you more interesting.

"It is now the twenty-second of May. Go away. Explore yourself, as you have been exploring Paris and your books. Come back in a month, and if you have done well, we will be ready for your final lesson."

"But Hélène, that will be more than two months, with more to come. You told me that in two months you did everything for the little wife of your protector."

"Ah, but she was French, you see. She had no bad habits to unlearn."

Hélène Lemoine hardly recognized the young woman who appeared at her door a month later. Garden was wearing a plain white blouse and black skirt, and her hair was cropped as short as a boy's. It was a mottle of gold and red.

"*Mon dieu*," breathed Hélène.

"It's horrible, isn't it?" said Garden cheerfully. "Five prostitutes stopped me and offered interesting lesbian practices. I just couldn't stand wearing those turbans any longer."

"When it grows, it will be a conflagration," said Hélène. "If I had had hair like that, I could have become Empress of All the Russias. Or China. Or any kingdom of my choosing. Sit down, my Garden. I see a basket in your hand. What have you brought me?"

"Fraises des bois, Hélène. And out of season. More difficult than hothouse grapes, but then I'm not French."

"You have sharpened your tongue. Be careful how you use it."

"Only to laugh. I have seen many things to laugh at, and I have been very naughty. I've been teasing poor Miss Trager terribly, talking to myself, cutting my hair. She thinks I'm losing my mind."

"And reports as much?"

"How clever of you, Hélène. Yes, I figured that out. I couldn't figure out why the Principessa hates me so, but it's not important. The hatred is a fact, and it has nothing to do with me, except that I have to be on my guard."

"You have learned a great deal. I am pleased. We can proceed. Only, I wish to know why you are dressed like a shop clerk and why you are wearing that object around your neck."

"I'm dressed this way because I've gained weight and none of my clothes fit me. I didn't want to bother to go to the couture; I was too busy. So I stopped a smart-looking girl on the street and asked her where she bought her clothes. She directed me to a shop on the Left Bank."

"And was she also wearing a bone? And a feather?"

Garden laughed, touched her necklace. "This was given to me as a charm against the evil eye. Also those beads I was wearing when we met."

Hélène crossed herself rapidly three times. "Don't worry," said Garden, "I'm also going to church. The American church, and Protestant, but the same God, Hélène."

"It is distinctive, your talisman."

"It's part of my past, part of what shaped me. Don't you want to hear what I've learned about myself?"

"I know it already. Now that you do, let us get on with things. I must earn my strawberries. What have you learned about this Sky of yours, or have you been too busy to think about him?"

"I've realized that he needs novelty, change, movement. He bores easily."

"Ah, you are an excellent pupil, Garden. You must have French ancestry. Have you devised a plan?"

"I couldn't do that alone. I tried to think of new things we would do together, things Sky wouldn't think of, but I didn't do very well. Nightclubs are the same everywhere, so travel isn't really the answer."

"No. Although you are now able to enjoy it. The answer is you, my dear. Now that you are a person, and a person whom you know, you must create a Garden who cannot be known. A Garden who is not like anyone else, who has mystery and passion, and who is always changing. You must play a role."

413

Garden frowned. "My God, Hélène, I've been playing roles all my life. Now that I've finally gotten past that, you're telling me to start all over again. I won't do it."

"You are being obtuse. If you create your role and play it, you are not diluting yourself. It is a skill, like cooking. You are the chef; the role, the soufflé. It is only when you confuse yourself with an egg that you make your life the muddle it used to be. You want this man. You recognize his needs. You have only to answer them, and he is yours."

"It sounds so coldhearted."

"It is. If you are very lucky and very skillful, you will be able so to enchant him that he will devote himself to discovering the Garden behind the mask. Then you can abandon the role."

"So I still have to work a long time."

"You exasperate me. Have you not learned that marriage is the hardest work of all? You do not have Thursdays off."

"Will you help me create this fascinating role—Garden?"

"But what else have I been doing? I have given you the skeleton, the armature of discipline, the tools of awakened senses. The design must be your own. Remember always that it must attract attention, but not notoriety, and that it must be unique. You must be desired by all, accessible to him, but never his possession."

"Will I not see you anymore, then?"

"But naturally you will. I have an interest in you. And I have trained you to be interesting. I look forward to your friendship."

"And will you let me buy Tradd's paintings now?"

Hélène smiled. "You have been good about that situation? You have said nothing to Bess?"

"Nothing. I gave you my word. But I am longing to tell her. It will mean so much to her to have them."

"Then she will have them. All except one. I shall keep my portrait. It is a poor likeness, but I have a forgiving nature. Come. I will show them to you."

The paintings were all landscapes, street scenes for the most part. "They traveled, you see," said Hélène, "and when Tradd began to paint, he painted the scenes he remembered most fondly. Harry took him everywhere. England, Scotland, the rocky islands of the sheep and the sweaters. Then Scandinavia, the Continent, the Mediterranean islands, Greece of course, and North Africa. From Egypt they took a caravan across the desert, I believe, and went to Persia,

Constantinople, Bangkok, Benares. I do not recall all the names. Some places I recognize from the paintings. This must be Russia, there is a turnip dome and all that snow."

Garden looked at the canvases spread across the floor of the big skylighted studio. "They really are quite bad, aren't they?"

"Quite. You have been visiting museums, I see. But he was a dear young man."

"Did he ever try to sell any?"

"Garden, he considered himself an artist. He was not a dilettante."

"Poor Tradd, he must have been terribly disappointed."

"But why? He sold them all. At handsome prices, for the time."

"I don't understand—or do I? You bought them."

"Yes, but he never knew. I have an old friend who has a gallery, a respected gallery. He arranged everything. He even kept them hidden until Tradd left."

"You are a wonderful person, Hélène."

"That is true. I have a small suggestion to make. The complete works are perhaps a bit overwhelming. One begins to notice how much they are all the same. Should we perhaps select three or four for Bess and overlook the existence of the others?"

"I think that would be kind . . . I don't see your portrait."

"I have hung it. There, above the table."

Garden walked over to look at it. "Hélène, this is a nude."

"So it is."

"You posed nude for Tradd?"

"Why not? We were lovers . . . Come now, Garden, you are wearing your ignorant prissy face again. I met Tradd when he was a child, new from Charleston. He was sixteen, but so young that Harry would find amusement for him elsewhere on my Thursdays. After some five months or so, Harry took him away on his travels. It was nine years before I saw either of them again. Harry stopped in Paris on his way to someplace, I forget where. Tradd decided to stay and to paint. He was a man. Twenty-six, I believe. And I was at my peak. I was forty. We made each other very happy."

"On Thursdays."

"On Thursdays."

"What about Harry?"

"Ah, yes. I do not know what became of Harry. He was not well when last I saw him. A broken leg had not mended properly, and he

415

was in great pain. He had heard of a doctor, he said, and he would soon be well. He was lying, I am sure.

"But I do not remember him that way. I think of the Harry who never tired, who never knew pain or sickness. Endless curiosity he had, and such an appetite for life. To be with him was to be more alive, more aware. Colors were brighter, peaches sweeter."

"And he loved Aunt Elizabeth. Why did she let him go, I wonder?"

"Dear Garden, one could not hold Harry. He was quicksilver. And restless. He could not stay still. He wanted to take her with him; he could not remain with her. She did not trust him, or perhaps herself. She would not give up her Charleston."

"But she gave up her son. I find that odd."

"She must have loved him very much, her Tradd. She gave him the greatest experience a young man could ever have—the world, with Harry Fitzpatrick as interpreter. While she was left without either of them. She has a noble heart . . . I could not have done it."

"What was Tradd like, here in Paris? I want to write it all to Aunt Elizabeth."

"Not all, surely. It was the Belle Époque. He was a painter in Montmartre. There was absinthe, the Moulin Rouge, the Place Pigalle, the Can-Can. It was a glory of a time and place for a young man, but not necessarily what a mother would wish to know."

"I think she would."

"Then I shall write to her. You will be too occupied with your creation of the new Garden."

81

Garden spent two more months in Paris alone, preparing herself for her role as wife-courtesan-enigma. With her limitless resources of money and her awakened, growing mind and imagination, she found the work and planning exhilarating.

She enlisted Connie to design clothes for her, Thelma to have things copied, but with variations that Garden wanted. At a time when black was still the shade of fashion, Garden would have only white or colors. The look for women was thin and boyish, slim hips, no bust. Garden was female, and determined to stop hiding it.

She made three colors particularly her own. The sharp blue of old Pansy's beads and the shades of her hair, gold and copper. She went to only one of the fashion houses, the smallest and most distinctive, Fortuny.

Mariano Fortuny was Venetian, a genius inventor as well as architect and designer. He had perfected a method of spinning, tinting and pleating silk that no one was able to match. The pleats were incredibly fine, as many as two dozen to an inch width of fabric, and they never lost their precision. From this pleated silk Fortuny made his Delphos gown, a simple fall of silk over the body, sometimes with a cord tied at the waist, sometimes with a tunic top, almost always trimmed with fragile beads of Venetian colored glass.

Garden consulted the master, let him borrow one bead from Pansy's necklace. He made for her Delphos gowns in blue, in gold, in copper, in white, and in ombrés of shades that only a great artist could create to complement her hair's exotic blend.

She incorporated Pansy's beads into her jewelry, too. She had bracelets and necklaces and brooches redesigned and reset so that a blue bead sat amid diamonds or punctuated pearls. The charm on the knotted string required the skills of Paris's most accomplished jewelers. Cartier assigned three men to work on nothing else. When, after six weeks, the necklace was done, the bone and the feather and the bead were still knotted at the end of a string, but the bone and feather were now encased in thin enamel, colored to re-create them exactly, and the string was made of filaments of gold, twisted together precisely as the cotton threads of the string. It was as flexible as string, and made a knot that held the charms and a knot that held the necklace together at the back of Garden's neck.

Garden spent arduous days searching for the specialist who could deliver the most difficult ingredient for her invented identity. When she was about to give up, he found her. She was in the flower market behind Les Halles at four in the morning, trying to talk to the busy men unloading their trucks, when a young man in a smock shyly asked if she would remove her hat. He was, he told her, a developer of hybrids, in a small way. The streaks of color that he could see in her bangs were the very shades he was trying to cross in a chrysanthemum. If he could just see the proportions of gold and red . . . ?

Garden was fascinated. What were hybrids, she wanted to know. What did it mean, to cross a chrysanthemum. She and the young man had coffee together, and onion soup. Before full daylight arrived, Claude Dupuis was Garden's newest friend. Before the week was out, she made arrangements for a propagation nursery and laboratory for Claude, and he made arrangements for the outstanding plant men all over France to begin intensive cultivation of gardenia plants under lights. Claude applied his passion for detail and experimentation to the problems of bloom dates and rail schedules. Before Garden left Paris at the end of August, he announced triumphantly that she would have what she wanted: four gardenias at the peak of their bloom delivered to her every morning, no matter where she might be.

There was now very little left to be done. Garden went to Alexandre. "I have been told that I resemble a chrysanthemum," she said. "Encourage the resemblance. With regard for the future. I intend to allow my hair to grow."

Then she swallowed her distaste and hired a publicist for Connie. "You may discreetly use me to call attention to Mademoiselle Weatherford's designs," she said. "At one time, I was much in the news."

There was no further reason to wait. Garden was more frightened than she had ever been in her life. What if Hélène was wrong? What if, after all this, Sky still showed no interest in her?

You have to try, she told herself sternly. You can't hide forever, busying yourself with plots and preparations. "Miss Trager," she said, "wire Mr. Harris and the Principessa to expect me on August thirtieth. Tell Corinne to pack. Send the trunks ahead. Make reservations. You and Corinne will go to Antibes direct on the twenty-ninth. Laborde will drive me down. I will arrive the following day."

"Dear Lucien," Garden wrote, "you haven't answered my letters, but I refuse to let that discourage me. As I told you in my second letter, my first one was an inadequate explanation for my not showing up at the vernissage, and I am sorry. I did hope that the second letter, with the fuller explanation, would provoke a response. I hoped you would say that you understood and that we could still be friends. I do believe that's what we are, Lucien, and always were. I do not believe that friendship is so common that one can afford to let it slip away. In my life, it is rare. That is why I refuse to accept your silence. I will be driving down to Antibes and I am going to stop off in Grasse on the way. I'll be there midmorning on the thirtieth. You should be able to smell me forty miles away. I use more *Jardin* than I do water, and I smell delicious all the time. Happily, I found it had entered distribution last week, and I was able to buy the entire supply at my perfumer's before my private stock was exhausted. The glass pyramid container is extremely handsome, I think, and I congratulate your designer. I do, however, miss the dog. I also miss my friend and look forward to seeing him."

A telegram arrived just as Garden was leaving the house to get into the car for the trip. "Do not come," it said. She scribbled a reply and gave it to the delivery boy to send for her. It read, "Too bad. Did not receive your wire."

Lucien was waiting in a darkened room. He was only a shadowy outline. "Dear Garden," he said, "I am very happy that you disobeyed me. I was a miserable coward not to have written you, and I probably would have continued in my cowardice but for your determination.

"No, my dear, don't say anything. Let me say what I could not write to you. I did not attend the vernissage, Jardin. I was in Paris for two purposes, to see you and to see a doctor. I believed a rumor that he could cure my illness. I learned that he could not."

"Lucien. I won't believe it."

"You must, my Garden. I told you that I loved to look at you because you are so healthy. The sound never believe in death, but you must believe. If I were braver, I would turn on a light, show you the face of death. But I am vain. I want you to remember the handsome devil you knew . . . Don't cry, my darling. I intend to make you laugh.

"We had good laughter, and tenderness. You were a richness to me. You remain a richness. And you inspired my greatest achievement. At this very moment, you smell better than any woman on the face of the planet. You were wicked to buy all the perfume, my love. Everywhere, women must be gnashing their teeth in rage. I have made provision for you to be supplied for life with your perfume. You will receive enough for five women, ten. Now you must swear to me that you will stop there. Let some others have a small drop. Swear it."

"I swear."

"Such a trembling little voice. Swear hugely. With a smile. I can hear the difference."

"I swear."

"That's better. I will throw rocks from heaven down on your head if you permit Lucien to be a sorrow to you. I am very much afraid that heaven is full of rocks. I have had a vision, a nightmare. Heaven is radiant, bright, white, a celestial Switzerland. Angels yodel day and night, and everywhere there is porridge and cream. I would greatly prefer hell, but my confessor tells me that I have no chance. I have led such a blameless life.

"Ah, I feel you smile. That is good. I tire now, beloved. You must leave me. I am grateful that you came."

"Lucien?"

"Yes?"

"May I kiss you goodbye?"

"No! That you may not do. You are probably covered with bacteria. I insist on my own germs. Now go. I am sleepy. And be happy. I command it."

When Garden got to her car, she found her chair occupied by a life-sized toy St. Bernard. It had the traditional cask under its chin, this one filled with perfume. She put her arms around its neck and laughed and cried with her cheek resting on its head while the automobile drove between hedges of blooming lavender.

82

Garden shook the tension out of her shoulders and walked across the terrace into the villa. She had timed her arrival for the cocktail hour. She wanted to have people around when she saw Sky. It would help her feel like the actress she had to be.

She heard the familiar sounds of laughter and tinkling ice cubes and followed it to a living room with broad doors open to a terrace. There were only about a dozen people there. She knew none of them except Sky and Vicki.

Garden paused in the frame of the doorway. "Help," she said with a laugh, "I'm parched from travel." When all eyes were on her, she swung the white linen cape from her shoulders and peeled off her white nubbly cotton cloche hat. She shook her head as the hat came off. The bright shaggy petals of her hair fell into place; they repeated the rich hues of the short Delphos gown that brushed and clung to the full smooth curves of her body.

She dropped her cape and hat on a chair. "Don't tell me the well's run dry." She walked to the bar in the corner of the room, seemingly oblivious to the stares of its inhabitants, but very much aware of Vicki's sudden pallor and Sky's bright eyes. She had seen that look often, but always for other women in recent years.

"Darling!" Sky stumbled in his haste to get to the bar. "Let me fix you a drink. You look wonderful."

Garden offered him a cool cheek. "You too, love," she said. Then she left him standing there. "I'll have a vermouth cassis," she called over her shoulder. "Vicki, dear," she said. "I'd swear I was on the Left Bank. The villa is so *décoratif.*" She touched her cheek to Vicki's, on the left, then on the right. And walked away, into the center of the aggressively Art Deco design of the rug. It was a declaration of war.

"How do you do," Garden said to the first stranger, a man who

421

was staring at her full breasts under the thin pleated silk. "My name is Garden. I'm Sky's long-delayed wife." She moved smoothly from one person to the next, shaking hands, then returned to Sky. "Thank you, darling," she said, taking the glass from his hand. She looked into his eyes as if they were alone in the room. "How have you been, Sky? Have you missed me?" There was no pleading in her voice, no invitation. It was a challenge.

The conquest of her husband was absurdly easy. "I'm just not sure how I feel anymore, Sky," she said, and she kept him at arm's length for weeks while he followed her everywhere she went. And she was always going someplace.

She went to the Lérins Islands, an hour's sail from the harbor at Antibes, and visited the dungeon of the Man in the Iron Mask. She went to the twelfth-century castle in Antibes. She went to the strange, sad little shows performed by Isadora Duncan, dancing in cafés while Jean Cocteau read his poetry. She went to the beach every day, wearing the white caftans Connie had designed for her with hoods deep enough to shadow her face from the sun, and always the mysterious glittering gold-and-enamel charm. When the sun went down, she went to the beach again and watched it drop behind the distant peaks of the Maritime Alps, staining their snowy tops with crimson.

And she sat on the dark beach with Sky, talking. The lights of Nice twinkled in a wide curve across the sea, and their cigarettes were like fireflies in the dark. "Tell me what it's like to climb a mountain," Garden said. And "What were the stunts you did with the barnstormers?" And "It must have been lonely, being an only child. Was your nanny very strict?"

The darkness was necessary because it kept Sky from seeing the longing on her face, and the tears when she heard the bewildered unhappiness in his voice. She wanted to take him in her arms, tell him how much she loved him, promise to make up to him for the emptiness in his life that he did not know how to fill.

But she had learned her lessons well. He wanted her, she knew that. And knew that it was not enough to hold him once the wanting was satisfied. He had to learn to love her. Then to trust her. Only then could she be all to him that she wanted to be.

* * *

Vicki took up the gauntlet that Garden had thrown. To Garden's delight, she was clumsy. She called Sky to her side when he was with Garden, asking him for a drink or a light for her cigarette, holding his arm, patting the sofa next to her as a command to sit down. Garden focused her attention on the person nearest her, then, and set out to charm him or her, following Hélène Lemoine's rules. Almost invariably she became genuinely interested in the conversations that she had feigned interest in to begin. "You knew that would happen," she wrote to Hélène. "You are sly as a fox." Hélène answered her note with a single cryptic line in French. "Fools tell all they know and eat neither grapes nor strawberries." Garden left it out for Miss Trager. It would be easy to look up the words in the dictionary and would mean nothing at all to her. Hélène would be proud of her, she was sure. Garden was proud of herself; she felt the strain of acting all the time, but she was confident that she had the strength to sustain her role for as long as necessary.

But after only two weeks, she broke down. She and Sky were having a date, lunch alone together, away from the wedding-cake villa and its incongruous chrome-and-lacquer interior. They were both lighthearted when they got away. "Let's go to Nice and pretend we're English," said Garden.

"What are you talking about, Garden? I never know what you're going to come out with these days."

"You do so know. The English think Nice is their personal discovery. Let's walk along the waterfront, on the Promenade des Anglais. We'll point at the palm trees and the boats and say 'I say' and 'What?' and 'By Jove' and things like that."

"Blimey," said Sky, "what a ripping idea, old thing." Garden grinned. "You look simply smashing, better half," Sky said.

"You're cheating, Sky. We'll run out of English before we get there."

Sky laughed. "Pip, pip," he said, "and tally-ho." The car sped along the coast road.

They Englished the length of the Promenade, amusing themselves with their silliness, and then Sky suggested that they walk over to the Place Masséna. "It's right by the shopping. I'd like to get you a little something, darling."

"But you gave me those beautiful earrings yesterday, Sky."

"That was yesterday."

"You are dear. I'd like lunch first, though. Let's go to the Negresco, and have a Negroni. I've never tasted it. What's in it?"

"I'm not sure. Pink gin, probably. Will you settle for champagne?"

"Only if it's English. We mustn't be inconsistent."

"Then gin it is, but not pink."

"And Salade Niçoise. I feel very local color."

"You do say the silliest things. I love you, you know."

"You do say the sweetest things. Good, here's a table with an umbrella. Let's sit out here and make fun of the American tourists. We English always do that."

"Jolly good." Sky held a chair for her.

The martinis were sharp and cold and delicious. "Not English at all," said Sky, "but I'll drink it. Do you suppose they think we're Americans?"

"Couldn't possibly, old boy." The gin added to the giddiness Garden was feeling. She and Sky had never been so foolish or laughed so much. It was a perfect day.

The salad was a work of art, its ingredients arranged in rings and blocks of color. "It seems a shame to eat it," Garden said, "but I'll force myself. Ummmm. Why is it olives are so much better on the Mediterranean? Here, taste." Sky caught her fingers between his teeth. Garden caught her breath.

She pulled her hand away before it began to tremble. She had to say something quickly. She looked for someone in a funny hat, anything.

"Look, Sky, there's Isadora Duncan. Remember, the dancer we saw. Do you suppose she's going to do a show here tonight? Oh, I guess not. That's hardly Cocteau."

Isadora was holding the arm of a too good-looking, very young man. He led her to a long, low open car and helped her in.

"That's a great-looking auto. I don't recognize it. What do you think? Italian, is it?"

Garden clutched Sky's arm. "No, Sky, stop her. Quick, quick. Don't you see? Around her neck. That long scarf, it's hanging down by the wheel. Don't let that boy drive off. Oh, oh, my God." Garden was standing, her chair knocked over. "Stop!" she screamed. "Stop!"

Then everyone was screaming, and Garden had her hands over her face, rubbing it, trying to erase what she had just seen. She lurched to Sky and fell against him. "I can't bear it. Take me home. Hold me. Oh, Sky, hold me. Don't let go of me, ever."

On the drive to Antibes, she was sick over the side of the car.

"What's wrong with Garden?" said Vicki when they reached the villa. Garden staggered up to her room, weeping. Sky told his mother about the dancer's grotesque death. Vicki rushed to the terrace to tell the group lunching there. Garden stayed in bed all afternoon, shuddering and crying. Sky asked Corinne how she was, but he didn't come in to see her. You're not attractive when you're weak, Garden, she told herself. Remember that. When you need him, you're trouble, a burden, a bore.

She did not break down again, not even when she went down to dinner and found Vicki's friends gathered around a bronze statuette of Isadora Duncan dancing, cymbals in her hands, bare feet arched, draperies floating around her body.

"My dears," Vicki was saying, "I simply tore to the dealer. He hadn't heard yet, and I snatched it for the price he had on it. By now, he must be foaming at the mouth."

After dinner they all went to Eden Roc to dance at the nightclub there. It was crowded with Hollywood actors and actresses. Cap d'Antibes was the smart place to be now for the end of summer.

Garden did not look at them. They looked at her. She alone was pale amid the suntans. She was wearing a white silk Fortuny tunic dress. At her shoulder was a single gardenia pinned with a bar of diamonds that held one off-center blue bead. The bead and her eyes and her hair were shockingly bright against the white of her gown and her immobile, beautiful white face. The photographers turned from the Hollywood stars. That night her legend was born when a copywriter attached a tag to her photograph. "*La Dame aux Gardénias*."

The next day Garden was in control of herself again. She soon regained the ground she had lost with Sky, and soon after that she walked into the water on a moonlit night when they were alone on the dark beach. "It's wonderful," she called, "come swim."

"Garden, you have all your clothes on. You're crazy."

"I don't have them on anymore. Take yours off."

When she and Sky were making love, Garden could not act, play a role, control things. All the passion that surged through her was real, and all the love that she hid under her act was allowed full rein. It was still a miracle, a sharing, a joining of two separates into one complete entity. And for that little time, Sky was hers totally.

But, for him to remain hers, the created Garden had to keep him fascinated. "Let's go someplace," she said when she saw his restlessness begin. "I've never been to London . . . Venice . . . Rome . . . Athens . . . Vienna . . . Copenhagen . . ." She studied guidebooks and histories in secret so that she could arrange for them to happen onto interesting restaurants, cafés, castles, parks, views, and they shared the thrill of discovery. She talked to people and collected the companions that Sky needed to have around him. She wore her gardenias, and her perfume, and she was beautiful, and everyone admired her, and newspapers and magazines idolized her, and Sky was charmed by *La Dame aux Gardénias*.

They traveled for almost a year. And then Sky wanted to stop. At last, it had all come true. He had no need to search for novelty anymore. All that he had ever wanted, he found in Garden.

"Let's settle down, old bean," he said. "Aren't you tired of all the trains and hotel towels?"

"Are you?"

"Sick to death of it. And of all those men panting when you walk by. It's hell having a wife who's famous."

"Let's go home then. Nobody in the States gives a damn."

"Nobody in the States serves champagne. We have to be practical."

"Where, then? You pick."

"Let's go to England. We're very good at being English."

"So we are, old chap. The natives won't suspect a thing. And there's all the good theater in London."

"I was thinking more of something village-y. You know, tweeds and dogs and long walks over the highlands."

"Aye, laddie, in a kilt."

"The moors, then. Would you like that? Just us? Could you stand a steady diet of your husband?"

Garden opened her arms, became herself. "Come here, you loony," she said. "Hold on to me."

83

They decided that Hampstead Heath was just like a moor, with the advantage of London only a few minutes away. "There's Vicki's house in Mayfair," said Sky, "but I think we should have our own, don't you?"

"Oh, yes. Yes, definitely. And not too grand."

Sky agreed. Two days later, Garden found a small box under her pillow. It held a small key. "Not too grand," said the note with it.

The house was Victorian, with a tall iron fence, a rear garden with a carriage house, a fountain and a gazebo, and only eight rooms plus baths, kitchen, pantry and servants' quarters. It seemed very cozy to them. Garden loved the odd nooks and window seats, and the funny tight spiral of the metal stairs in the rear. She laughed every time she looked at the expression of wild terror on the face of the maiden picking flowers in the big stained glass window on the landing of the front staircase. A scorpion must be in one of the flowers, she suggested. Sky said, no, it had to be more frightening than that, probably a note warning her that winter was coming and she had on very thin clothes. Or, said Garden, warning her that Americans were moving into her house. Nonsense, Sky replied, no one could possibly tell.

They bought one big bed and two big armchairs and moved in, camping out, they called it. There was a pub nearby and a small restaurant. Garden waylaid a charwoman going to the house next door and hired her for two hours a day. She left Corinne at the Savoy. Miss Trager had been fired when they began to travel.

They were like children playing house, and they were alone for the first time since they had been married. No servants, no schedules, nothing to do but explore the paths on the Heath and the hearts of each other.

They did not notice the discomfort for almost a week. Even then, they shared the realization that civilized living had its good points, and they laughed at their own foolishness.

"Do you want to pick out things with me?" Garden asked.

"And fight all the time? No, my angel, you do whatever you like. This is your house."

"No, it's ours. You should have some say."

"Then I'll say it. No King Tut, no dragons and no black patent leather." The dining room at the villa was a genuine horror, with shiny black walls and shiny red lacquered furniture, the chairs upholstered in patent leather.

"I think lots of soft, squishy chairs and sofas, and chintz. We English always have chintz."

"Go to it, love. We English gentlemen will find a club to hide out in while you're having the curtains hung."

Garden was soon blissfully busy with auctions, decorators, antique dealers and magazines that advertised the latest developments in appliances. She also went to a very good domestic employment agency. Before long they we : enjoying excellent meals served by an archetypal English butler on a beautiful Hepplewhite table. Sky brought a friend home from his club. Then the friend's wife invited the two of them to dinner. Garden returned the invitation, including the other couple they had met when they went to dinner. By Christmastime they had a circle of friends, young marrieds rather like themselves.

On Christmas Eve they gave a big party. It was a housewarming; they ceremoniously hung the last pair of curtains. And it was Garden's twenty-third birthday. She felt that she had at last reached safe harbor, and that she had finally grown up.

Sky had twenty-three gardenia plants in tubs put in the conservatory off the dining room. And he gave her a complete flatware service with the intertwined initials of their two names engraved on the underside of each piece. "It's not quite complete," he said. "You'll get one more of everything next year, to make it twenty-four." Garden was teary with happiness. It was the first time he had given her something that they would use together. She valued it more than all the extravagant jewels of all the birthdays and anniversaries before.

"*Très bonne bourgeoise*," she murmured. She looked around her at the comfortable big living room and at the not particularly fashionable men and women in it and at her expansively content husband.

Sky was standing by the fireplace, his elbow on the mantel, one heel on the brightly polished brass fender. He was twenty-seven now, but he looked much older. His hair was beginning to recede just a little, and his stomach to expand. Garden's heart turned over with love. He was truly happy with her and with their settled life.

All his old restlessness and need for stimulation were channeled now into his work. He went to the City just like any businessman. He had rented an office, hired a secretary and installed a telephone and a ticker-tape machine. It was almost like the old days in New York, only much better. Then he had played the stock market as a game. Now he treated it seriously, as a profession. He had moved his account from Vicki's ultraconservative money managers to David Patterson's firm, and he was on the telephone with David every day at an hour he reserved for the cable call. He was making money faster than they could possibly spend it, building a fortune that staggered Garden's imagination.

A fortune for their children. It was her Christmas present for Sky. Under the big glittering tree, there was a little square box with his name on it. Inside there was a pair of tiny white wool booties with a note. "To be filled July 15."

84

Tuesday, Oct. 29, 1929

Dearest Hélène,

Your letter was waiting for me when we returned from a weekend's outing in the country. Still looking at houses. Sky is determined to become a squire so that when we have a son, he'll be able to go to Eton. No, I'm not pregnant again, but being a father is such a thrill for Sky that he's looking forward to repeating the experience every year. I remind him that I'd just as soon space things out a little more. Thirty-two hours in labor is not something I'm prepared to do again right away.

Not that it wasn't more than worth it. Baby Helen is a joy beyond anything I could have imagined. She is such a *good* baby. She smiles all the time and gurgles and blows bubbles and does all the perfect baby things. I am mad about her, and Sky is worse. He is thoroughly besotted. She looks so much like him. Brown hair—curly, thank goodness—and brown eyes. She can push up with her arms now, and she holds up her darling round head and smiles as if to say, "Look how strong and clever I am!" Sky says she will certainly be sitting alone by tomorrow and crawling by the day after. I show him the baby book. Helen's doing just what babies all do at four months. Of course, he pays no attention.

I am distressed to hear that your arthritis is giving you such a bad time. No, you didn't say so, but I can read between the lines. Could I persuade you to join us in Cannes for a few weeks? We're planning to spend the winter there. Sky says that Helen must have her walks in the park, and the Heath is pretty bleak and windy come December. That shows you what a Circe the baby is. I wouldn't have believed that Sky would leave the ticker tape for anything. The past week has been nerve-racking, I gather. Big ups and downs and the tape running so late that Sky doesn't get home sometimes until after midnight. We're all right, of course, but a lot of small investors were wiped out. Sky says that you shouldn't buy on margin unless you have enough backing to cover your losses. Yes, I even know what that means. We talk about everything, not just the baby. I am so perfectly, gloriously happy, Hélène, and I owe it all to you. I know you're tired of hearing me say it, but it's true, and I can't say it often enough.

Your namesake is awake, I hear. I must run and snatch some nuzzles before Nanny takes her away to feed and bathe and tuck in again. Let me know about Cannes. The sunshine will be good for all of us, and I am longing for you to meet Sky. He does not know that you are the cause of all our happiness, but I'm sure he will adore you just as much as I do anyhow.

Best love,
Garden.

Garden hastily sealed and stamped the envelope, then hurried away to the nursery to watch Helen's bath. She was splashing the baby's hands in the water, to Helen's delight and Nanny's disapproval, when she heard the heavy front door open and close. One final splash, and she ran to the stairs.

Sky was in the hall, removing his coat. Garden scampered down. "Darling. You're home early. What a wonderful surprise." She held out her arms to him.

Sky turned away. He did not even seem to see her. Garden took hold of his sleeve, tugged. "Darling, what is it? What's happened?"

He looked at the hand on his sleeve, then, slowly, his eyes traveled up her arm to her face. "Garden," he said. "Garden, David Patterson is dead. He shot himself." Sky's lips trembled, crumpled, opened in an oval of fear and pain, and he began to sob.

"Hush, my love, hush. It's all right." She put an arm around his bent shoulders and walked him to a chair. "Sit down, sweetheart. I'll get a brandy." She pushed him gently, and he collapsed into the deep soft cushions. He put his hands across his face and bowed his head. The sounds he made were heartbreaking.

"Here, Sky, drink this." Garden pulled one hand away to take the glass. Sky dropped the other one and looked up at her. His eyes were red and staring, his mouth wet and twisted. "We're finished, Garden, wiped out. I can't tell you how bad it is."

Garden knelt on the floor beside his chair. "Shh, darling, hush now. Drink this. No matter what, we'll be all right. Don't worry. We'll be all right. We have each other and the baby. Nothing else matters."

When all the reckonings were done, it turned out that, in fact, they had very little more than each other and the baby. Like so many other people, Sky had been caught up in the hysterical optimism of the great bull market, and had extended himself to reckless limits. His wealth was so immense that he could have survived the crash, however. Except that, when the market began its precipitous slide, David had dipped into Sky's accounts to cover his own much larger margin calls, as well as Sky's. When there was nothing left for either of them, he killed himself.

They had assets, but there were few buyers for luxury cars, or engraved oyster forks, or Hepplewhite furniture. Garden begged Sky to sell her jewelry and keep the house, but he refused. The prices offered for diamonds were not high enough to help much, anyhow.

"We'll have to accept Vicki's offer," Sky said, "and go live at the villa. We've got enough money to keep Nanny and to do over the rooms for us to live in. Helen won't have to look at patent leather. Hell, darling, we were going to Cannes, why not Antibes? Things are bound to get better soon. Then we'll figure out what to do."

Garden would rather have lived in a tenement. But she saw the fear in his eyes. "I think that's a wonderful idea, darling," she said with enthusiasm. "There are all those orange trees at the villa. The baby will fairly bust with vitamins."

The hardest part for Garden was leaving their friends. She and Sky had led such a footloose life that Garden's only friendships had been short-lived: Connie, Hélène, Lucien, Claude, all intensely concentrated and then behind her. But in London there had been time to build slowly and, she thought, permanently. She had friends who, like herself, had small children and husbands who came home tired from work. She shared their lives, they shared hers. As couples, they dined together, went to the theater, played bridge. Humdrum and comfortable and close. It broke her heart to leave. Sky did not seem to care. He was too despondent to care about anything. Garden did her best to cheer him up, but her own heart was too heavy for her bright good nature to be very convincing. Only the baby was truly untouched by what had happened and genuinely good-humored.

At first it seemed that living with Vicki would not be so bad. She made a tremendous fuss over Helen, buying her dozens of toys and exquisite, impractical little dresses and bonnets. And she insisted on paying for the redecoration of their rooms.

But it soon became evident that the redecoration would be what Vicki thought they should have, and that Helen was supposed to wear nothing other than the clothes Gramma bought and to play with nothing other than the toys Gramma bought. Vicki was paying the piper; she intended to call the tune.

Garden complained to Sky. He said that she was oversensitive, that Vicki was being generous and Garden surly. After that, Garden bit her tongue. Vicki was clever. She praised Garden to the heavens and chipped away at her with small indignities.

She insisted that Garden have a maid, assigned one of the villa's staff who was rude and clumsy. She complimented Garden's tact and seated her at table next to men who got drunk and amorous. She admired Garden's self-reliance and monopolized Sky's time with coquettish pleas for help and advice. Garden's mail went astray, there were no stamps in her desk, there was never a car available for her to use. Her bathroom lacked soap, her shoes were not polished, her books disappeared.

Vicki claimed to have been hit hard by the Crash. She had had to close down all her houses except the ones in New York and Paris. And the villa. But there was no change in her style of living. She kept the villa full of guests, all of whom seemed to be just as rich as ever, gave cocktail and dinner parties, gambled for high stakes at the little casino in Juan les Pins or the big ones in Nice, Cannes and Monte Carlo. She hired the handsomest gigolos for her women friends, and gave dances on the terrace of the villa with an orchestra to play the latest tunes while the gigolos led them in the newest steps. Vicki didn't need a paid partner. She had Sky.

Everywhere she went, Sky and Garden had to go. Vicki provided them with every luxury. Except the luxury of choice. They had no money. They had to eat what was put on their plates. And be grateful. Garden took petty pleasure in not letting her resentment show, in charming Vicki's friends, in being better-looking than any of them in her classic Fortuny gowns, in smiling for the photographers who still found her in public places. She was still *La Dame aux Gardénias* to the press, even though now she wore flowers from the garden on her shoulder or tucked into the French twist of wildly striped hair.

She took major delight in the fact that no matter what Vicki did, Sky's real interest was in little Helen and her development. He watched her budding teeth as if the rest of the world had never had anything but dentures. When she began to crawl, he crawled with her. Her mastery of words for bottle and blanket were, he swore, nothing short of poetry. "Pa-pa" made him strut like a peacock. Garden had told Sky that as long as they had each other and the baby, everything would be all right. In spite of poverty, Vicki's maliciousness, the strain of keeping up a good front of cheerfulness, it was proving to be true. Underneath it all, everything was all right.

Until the spring.

Then Garden noted growing signs of the old restlessness in Sky.

He was drinking more, driving faster, constantly looking for something to do, someplace to go. She talked to him about Helen's most recent accomplishments, and he accused her of being interested only in the baby, not in him. She went to his room, and he pretended to be asleep. She suggested picnics, hikes up the mountains, an apéritif at a sidewalk café. Sky replied that they had done all those things a thousand times, that he despised being in a rut, that he should have killed himself like David Patterson.

Garden was sufficiently alarmed to talk to Vicki and ask her to help. That evening, Vicki announced that she had to go up to Paris for a while. "Schuyler, darling, you will come with me, won't you? A lady needs an escort, and I don't know a soul anymore." She did not invite Garden, but Garden didn't care. She looked forward to being alone, quiet, with time for Helen, for reading and for writing letters. Trying to keep Sky in good spirits was a full-time job.

In the middle of April, Vicki and Sky left. Garden got right to work. They were going to be gone for two weeks, and she had plans for every minute of the time.

She did the difficult things first. A cold, businesslike letter to her mother, explaining for the dozenth time why Sky could no longer send her the monthly check she had come to regard as an obligation on his part. Then carefully worded letters to Connie, Claude, Hélène, Aunt Elizabeth, Wentworth, her friends in London. She had to sound happy without telling any outright lies. It was not easy.

Then she took an entire morning for Peggy. Her sister and Bob were in Cuba now; Peggy was expecting a baby at last. "I'm almost twenty-nine," she had written, "and we always meant to have a houseful, so I'd better get a move on. I'll still be able to work on the action committee for the rights of the sugarcane workers. Can you believe that the landowners . . ." Garden smiled when she read the letter. Peggy never changed.

She wrote her pages of advice on diet and rest while pregnant and added a postscript to Bob urging him to force Peggy to take care of herself. Then she took two of the menservants with her to the storage building to find the boxes of her maternity clothes. Peggy would never get any for herself, she knew, and Sky had refused to consider another baby until their lives straightened out.

Garden sat with the brightly colored dresses spilling out of their boxes around her. She'd only send the lightweight ones. Suddenly she waved the men away. "I'll send for you when I need to move the crates again," she said briskly. "Leave me now."

She held a gaudily striped smock to her breast. "My circus tent," Sky had called her when she wore it. She buried her face in the festive colors and let all the stored-up tears come out.

Facts, she said to herself later. She wiped her face on the smock and folded it neatly. You must hold on to facts like rocks. Hélène taught you that. What are the facts?

She examined the realities of her life. Then she carefully unfolded the smock and cried in it again.

85

When the two-week visit to Paris had stretched to two months, Garden decided to go up herself. Sky was never at the house when she telephoned, and he did not answer her letters. Garden was sure that Vicki was responsible for his silence. He must not be getting her letters or her telephone messages. She couldn't stand it any longer.

She found a pawnshop in Monte Carlo and got enough money for her train ticket in exchange for a ruby and diamond ring that she never had liked. Nanny could be trusted to take care of Helen. She guarded the little girl from contact with all the "foreigners" who were everywhere in France.

Garden arrived in Paris the third week in June. The city was gay with umbrellas at the sidewalk cafés and trees, still fresh green, arching over the palings of the parks. The Seine danced and sparkled under the bright sun. Men were fishing along the quais, and children were running in the Tuileries Gardens with balloons bobbing on strings.

"Madame has made a sufficient sightseeing?" said the taxi driver.

"Yes, thank you." Garden gave him Vicki's address. No matter what she found at the house, it was wonderful to be back in Paris.

*　　*　　*

Sky was on his way out of the house when the taxi pulled to the curb. Garden let out the breath she had unconsciously been holding. He looked well, better than he had since before the crash. Whatever Vicki has done, she vowed, whatever's been going on, I will be nothing but grateful.

Sky saw her, and his face lit up. "Darling, my angel!" he shouted. "How terrific that you're here." He raced across the sidewalk and pulled her out of the cab into a bear hug. Then he kissed her and caught her arm above the elbow. "Come on in. I have to dash, but there's time for a coffee at least." Bercy and a footman went to the cab to pay the fare and get Garden's suitcases.

Garden noted that Sky had not said "time for a drink."

Vicki was in the hall when Sky propelled Garden inside. Her self-control was impeccable. She kissed Garden on each cheek, asked after Helen, offered her coffee or champagne.

Sky interrupted before Garden could answer. "Don't you think it's great, darling? Isn't Vicki the all-time greatest?"

"What, Sky?"

"Ah, come on, Garden. You know. Vicki told you all about it in her letters. I would have written you myself but I've just been so busy."

"I see. Yes, of course. I think it's just great, Sky." Garden looked at Vicki's expressionless face. Her own was equally bland.

Sky squinted at his watch. "Good Lord. See you later, ladies." He dropped quick kisses on their heads and left, shouting that the car had better be waiting.

"What's it all about, Vicki?" Garden said. She kept her voice calm. She remembered her vow.

Vicki lit a cigarette, took a long time fitting it into a holder. When Garden remained quiet, she stopped prolonging the suspense and told her. "Schuyler has gotten interested in horse racing. He's off to Longchamp right now. With Longchamp, Auteuil and Saint-Cloud, he's been fully occupied. He becomes totally absorbed."

Garden was pale. She remembered the way Sky had been about roulette and baccarat. "Are you lending him money, Vicki?"

Vicki laughed. "He's not betting, Garden. He's planning to race, to own horses, maybe to breed them."

"But how? It costs a fortune."

"You're right. 'The Sport of Kings.' I find it rather intriguing myself. If Schuyler's enthusiasm lasts, I'm prepared to back him in a small way.''

"I don't understand."

"One meets such interesting people. Other owners, trainers, jockeys. I think it might be amusing. But I'm not going to get involved myself. I want to see what Sky can do. He spends every day at one track or another, back with the horse people. He's even arranged to go to work at a training stable this summer. Out by Chantilly. If he turns out to have a good eye for a winner, then maybe I'll stake him to a few horses and see how he does.''

Garden was breathless. Sky, working. She had a friend in London whose father was involved with racing. She had heard about the physical labor and rigorous discipline that went into preparing a horse for its first racing season. If Sky could stand it, the work would be the best thing that ever happened to him. She wanted to hug Vicki, to cry, to kiss her hands for what she was doing for Sky. She was giving him the route to self-respect.

"It's very generous of you, Vicki," she said.

"My dear Garden, let's not pretend with each other. You know I never do anything without benefits for me. The truth is, there are no Americans in France anymore worth mentioning. Nobody pops over to Europe to play. I certainly don't want to go back to the States. With the Depression on top of Prohibition, I'd be so gloomy I'd kill myself. Horse racing is chic. The very best people own horses. The Aga Khan, the Rothschilds, all the royals. There aren't that many rich Americans anymore. Nobody sneers at money now. So I'm ready to move up.

"And if I hire a terribly sexy Irish trainer, well, who's to tell me no?''

Garden had to believe her. It sounded just like Vicki's way of operating.

Sky did work on the farm. All summer and all fall. Garden visited him once, found him tanned and mucky and alight with enthusiasm. She came up to Paris in October for the biggest racing event, the Prix de l'Arc de Triomphe, and joined him in the box with the owners of the farm where he had been working. The Comte de Varigny had one of his horses in the race, a horse that Sky had helped prepare.

The Comte also had a niece, Catherine. She was very young and very shy, and she looked at Sky with stars in her eyes.

For a moment Garden thought she saw the full extent of Vicki's planned benefits. But then she heard that Catherine was still in school, that the sisters had only allowed her to leave for the weekend because the horse was a gift from her uncle to her on this Sunday, by coincidence her birthday.

Sky can't even know her, Garden thought. Besides, she's not even pretty, and he acts as if she isn't here at all. He's only interested in the horses.

The Comte's horse, Catherine's horse, did not win. She cried like the baby she was; her uncle bought her an ice cream to make things better.

Garden enjoyed her vacation in Paris. Early autumn was the best possible time for walking, and she revisited all her favorite places. She also saw her friends. Hélène Lemoine seemed to have changed not at all. Claude, unfortunately, had lost his nursery when Garden could no longer subsidize it, but he was content working in the glass houses of the Jardin d'Acclimation in the Bois de Boulogne. Connie was the most remarkable of them all. She now had her own boutique on the Faubourg-St-Honoré, *Choses de Constance*, with dresses of her own design. She took Garden to the Ritz for lunch and bragged engagingly that Thelma was now stealing her toiles. "It would never have happened without *La Dame aux Gardénias*," she said. "I'll be grateful for the rest of my life, Garden."

Garden kissed her friend. "You make me so happy, Connie. I'll be grateful for the rest of mine."

Sky was back home at the villa before Christmas. He had bought a pony for Helen's gift from Santa Claus, and held her on it while he walked her through the groves of fruit trees. He had never looked so well or so happy, not even in the settled days in London.

"I think it's the outdoor life, darling," he said. "I've got a great plan. We'll get a place in Kentucky or upstate New York, near Saratoga. Helen's starting to talk French, and I don't want to have my kid saying things I don't understand. Land's dirt cheap in America now, and so's labor. Vicki's bound to back us. I'm a real whiz at spotting the yearling that's going to make it. What do you say? Can you stand manure on your rugs?"

"I can stand it. We'll have to learn to talk American again. No more tally-ho."

"Giddup, then. Tomorrow, that's what we'll do. We'll teach Helen her first American word."

Garden stopped his chattering by kissing him. She was too happy to talk anymore. She could only express it by making love.

In February they celebrated their eighth anniversary with a dinner at St.-Paul-de-Vence. The next day Sky went back to Chantilly. "Don't cry, girls," he said when he kissed Garden and Helen goodbye.

"I miss you so," Garden said. "When will you be back?"

Sky fidgeted. "I don't know, sweetheart. I've got to get things lined up with Vicki for the deal in the States. I'll run over to Paris first chance I get. I'll call you, don't worry. You just keep teaching Helen to talk American.

"Come on, now. What's Helen got to say to Daddy?"

"Gid-up," said Helen.

"That's my girl!" Sky threw her up in the air. She was still screeching with the thrill of it when he put her in Garden's arms. "I'll miss my train. What has Mummy got to say to Daddy?"

"I love you, Sky."

"And I love you, darling. Giddy-up!"

Garden was lonely at the villa. But she was glad that Vicki had stayed in Paris. And she did not want to risk going up to the city herself. Now, more than ever, it was important to keep out of Vicki's way. Sky might persuade her to set him up with a breeding farm in America, though Garden doubted it. But certainly Vicki would never agree if she thought Garden had anything to do with his wish to leave France.

America. Home. Garden did not dare to think about it. She had not been homesick. She felt as if Paris and London were home more than New York, or even Charleston.

But now that Sky had put the idea in her mind as a possibility, the longing for America was sharp and poignant.

Sky had promised to telephone, to let her know. Garden hardly dared leave the house for fear she would miss the call.

86

She received a letter from Vicki instead. It arrived at the end of March. "Garden: I have talked to Schuyler until I am blue in the face, but he will not see reason. Therefore, I have made the following arrangements. You and Helen and her nanny are booked on the *Roma* leaving Genoa on August 11, arriving New York on August 24. This will save the necessity of traveling across France with the child to sail from Le Havre. Schuyler will sail from Cork on the first date after the Dublin Horse Show and the yearling sales. He will accompany the horses he intends to buy. He may precede you to New York. If not, he will join you there shortly after your arrival. I will inform the staff to have everything prepared for your occupancy.

"It would be absurd to pretend that I am pleased about Schuyler's decision to return to the United States. However, he has always gotten his own way, and it should come as no surprise to me that he has not changed.

"I do not have any particular desire to see you before you leave. I will come to New York for the Christmas holidays. A bank draft will be sent to you for the necessary money for tips on the voyage. A car will meet the ship. Vicki."

Garden danced around the room with Helen in her arms. "We've won, baby. We're going home."

After that it didn't matter that Sky called so seldom, or that he was in such a hurry when he did. It was even all right that he had to miss Helen's second birthday party.

Nanny was the only problem. She refused to go to the United States. "I crossed the Channel for Helen, Mrs. Harris. But I would not cross the ocean, not even for the King himself."

Garden took Helen on her lap. "Do you think you can put up with a mere mother, Miss Harris?"

Helen jumped up and down on Garden's knees. "Gid-up," she begged.

Garden obligingly played horse.

The leisurely crossing was calm and uneventful. Helen immediately became the pet of crew and passengers, and was even invited onto the bridge. Her favorite amusement was playing with the passengers' dogs when they were released from the kennel for their walks. After that, she liked best to be wrapped in a blanket to take her nap in the deck chair next to Garden's. Garden promised her a puppy when they settled in their new home. And, she reminded Helen, there would be lots of ponies.

Helen was not unduly impressed by the Statue of Liberty, but it made Garden's heart bump faster. The skyline of New York excited even the little girl. "Alps," she cried, pointing.

"No, my precious lamb. That's not the Alps. That's home."

The house had not changed at all. Garden introduced Helen to Jennings with grave solemnity. For the first time, she saw Jennings smile. Her rooms were exactly the same. It was a shock for her to realize how many years it had been since she had seen them last.

"What is your name?" she asked the maid who was hovering in the doorway.

"Bridget, ma'am."

Garden managed not to laugh. Sky had called all the New York maids Bridget. "I'll need someone to unpack my cases," she said. "And I'd like to talk to the housekeeper about arrangements for the baby."

"Oh, that's all done, ma'am. I'll show you to her room, if you like."

The nursery was on the next floor up, in the wing of guest rooms. Garden didn't want Helen so far from her. Nor did she like the starched nursemaid who was waiting in the room next to the nursery. "My name is Miss Fisher," she told Garden. "The Select Domestics Agency sent me."

Helen ignored Miss Fisher. She had made a beeline for the low Jenny Lind bed with the stuffed pink bunny on the pillow. *"Bon soir, lapin,"* she said, taking the toy in her arms. She fell asleep at once. Miss Fisher took off Helen's shoes and tucked a quilt around her with an expert touch. Maybe she'll be okay, thought Garden. It's not for long, after all. Just until we know where we're going to be.

She was tired, but too stimulated to sleep. She decided to go for a walk. I should have walked New York, she thought, the way I did Paris and London. I don't really know this city at all.

She walked down Fifth Avenue, loving the noise and hurry of the traffic, astonished by the tall new buildings that had replaced so many of the houses that had been there. She was relieved to see that the Plaza Hotel was still where it had been. It was almost the only thing she recognized. She turned back uptown then. By the time she got to the house, all the kinks of confinement on the ship were gone. She felt relaxed and ready for a nap before dinner.

Vicki was in the living room, drinking champagne. "Will you have some, Garden? I smuggled it in; it's very good."

"No thank you, Vicki." Garden looked around the room.

"Schuyler's not here, Garden. He's not coming. You'd better have a drink. And a chair. You see, Garden, I've won after all."

Garden sat down.

Vicki poured wine into a glass, held it out. Garden shook her head. "Suit yourself," said Vicki. She looked over the rim of her glass. Her eyes were cold. She put her empty glass on a table, lifted the full one.

"Schuyler is divorcing you, Garden. My lawyers have already filed all the papers. As soon as it's final, he will be marrying the little Comtesse de Varigny."

"No!"

"Oh, yes. I have already come to an understanding with her parents. Schuyler will become a partner with her uncle. Catherine is, as you might have noticed, mad about my son. He found it amusing at first, then annoying, then appealing. She's been at Chantilly since she left school in May."

"I don't believe you, Vicki."

"Don't be a fool. Why do you think he married you? Because you were so protected by your Charleston rules and traditions that he could not have you any other way. It gave you a value that his easy conquests did not have. Catherine is chaperoned every waking hour. It provides the same illusion of value. Plus, her uncle has all those horses. Game and set, Garden."

"You're bluffing, Vicki. I've been bluffed before. I recognize it.

Sky loves me. And he loves Helen." Garden was confident. She was even glad to have it out with Vicki at last.

"I don't bluff," Vicki said slowly and distinctly. "I was overconfident once, and you fooled me. I had underestimated you. You got yourself to that clinic, and then somehow you became very clever. I can admit now that you were very good, very smooth, very dangerous. Thank God the stock market crashed." She drained the glass, refilled it.

"I deserve this," she said. "I'm entitled to a celebration. I've had to wait much longer than I expected.

"But I've got you now. With bonuses. You played into my hands with your Lady of the Gardenias routine. The newspapers loved you. Now they'll really go to town over the divorce. There's no better headline than a fallen idol. There is only one legal ground for divorce in New York, Garden. Adultery. I have a half-dozen men who will swear that they, shall we say, enjoyed your favors. A couple of them actually did. Times are hard. Their memories became extremely detailed when they were offered a small fee to cover their expenses to come to New York.

"Naturally, we'll also raise serious doubts about the identity of Helen's father."

"Vicki, you can't! You know that's not true."

"Of course I know it. But I don't want Schuyler to have any lingering fondness for the child. He remembers your wilder days; it was easy to convince him that you continued to have lovers in London."

"He'd never believe that."

"He does."

"I'll go find him. He trusts me. I'll talk to him."

"I hate to see you acting like a fool, Garden. You had made me respect you. Now I'm beginning to think you weren't so much of a challenge after all. Don't you know Schuyler? Don't you understand that when he wants something, that's all that matters? He wants to race horses. He wants the life he sees at Chantilly. He even wants Catherine because she's a part of it. And a total innocent. A virgin, Garden, while you're used merchandise. Give up. You've lost. You've lost big. The papers are being filed now. By tomorrow, or the next day at the latest, your name will be as famous and as filthy as the whore of Babylon. You, my dear, have destroyed yourself, your child, and your whole goddamned family."

443

Vicki lifted her glass. "I salute you, Garden Tradd. You've made me a very happy woman." Her eyes glinted strangely. Her hand held the glass so tightly that the stem broke in two. Vicki drank from the bowl, then threw it on the floor. Her laughter made Garden's blood chill.

She's crazy, Garden thought. She might do anything. She was paralyzed by fear. "Why?" she said, her voice a rasp in her throat.

"I've got my reasons," said Vicki. Her laughter filled the room.

BOOK 6

1931–1935

87

Facts, thought Garden. I must concentrate on facts. If ever in my life I needed a rock to hold on to, this is the time. What are the facts?

Vicki is obsessed. No matter why or by what. The fact is, she is mad with some obsession. Another fact, she means me harm. And Helen.

Fact, important fact. I must get Helen away from here.

Fact. I have almost no money, a few dollars left over after tipping on the ship. Thank God I had dollars and not lire.

Fact. I have no friends in New York.

Fact. I am afraid of her. So afraid that I'm not sure my legs would move if I tried to run.

"You're very quiet, Garden," said Vicki. Her maniacal laughter was now compressed into a gloating smile. "Why don't you cry, beg me to reconsider? I'd like to see that . . . Well? What is it?" Vicki glared at the maid who had tapped on the door.

"There's a Mrs. Pelham on the telephone for you, Principessa."

"I'll take the call in here." Vicki splashed champagne into the unbroken glass. "And send up another bottle." She carried her drink to the desk and lifted the telephone. "Sybil darling," she purred, "how did you ever hear that I was in town? . . . Only yesterday, pet. I'm hardly unpacked."

Garden stared at her mother-in-law. Vicki was incredible. Not a trace of madness remained. She was chatting in her customary high-pitched, artificial, brittle social voice. One would never guess that only seconds ago she had been close to a paroxysm of hatred.

"Southampton?" she was saying. "Heavens no, darling. I closed the house ages ago. It's so depressing in the States. I'm quite the expatriate now. So charming, the French. I spend almost all my time at the château of my dear friend the Count de Varigny." Vicki looked at Garden, then looked away. Garden was immobile.

"That *is* a crisis, Sybil. Too dismal. I know I have her address in my book. Hold on. I'll go get it." Vicki carried her glass with her when she left.

Now's my chance, thought Garden. She'll pick up the phone in her rooms. She might talk for a good while. Garden's mind had been spinning. She knew what she had to do.

She ran to her bedroom. It was crowded with trunks and suitcases, opened but not yet unpacked. Garden went hurriedly through the clothes hanging in the steamer trunks until she found the sailcloth raincoat Connie had made for her. It was designed for her long city walks; pockets of all sizes made it unnecessary to carry a purse and possible to carry purchases of books or whatever without getting them wet. Garden pulled out drawers in the trunks until she found the one that held her Fortuny dresses. It was one of the miracles of Fortuny that his dresses could be wadded into a small bundle and left for any length of time. When they were shaken out, the pleated silk was as fresh and unwrinkled as the day it was made. There were eight bundles, bound with rubber bands. Garden stuffed them into a big pocket.

The seven dollar bills in her purse went into a small one. Compact, lipstick, and comb into another. She looked at the clock. She had spent three minutes. Hurry, her mind said. She opened a big pocket and reached for her jewel case. She'd find a pawnshop open somewhere, buy train tickets to Charleston. She'd go with Helen to the Garden house, to her mother.

The jewel case was empty. Garden wasted a full minute opening the pockets and drawers to make sure. Gone. All her jewels were gone. Even her wedding ring. She had nothing left except the enamel and bead charm on its gold string. It was around her neck.

Garden pulled herself together. She must hurry. The jewels were gone. Fact. She took a gold cigarette case and lighter from her purse. They should be worth something. Then she put on the coat.

The living room was still empty. She could hear the thin scratchy sound of voices coming from the telephone. She ran up the stairs, along the hall, into the nursery. It was empty. Fact, she screamed silently in her mind. Fact, Helen is not here. That's all you know. Don't imagine things. She ran through the halls, opening door after door. All the rooms were empty. Time. How much time had she spent? How much was left? Garden was gasping. Hurry. Hurry.

She ran back through the halls, past the empty rooms. Near the stairs she saw one of the maids. Don't look like anything's wrong, she told herself. She forced her steps to slow to a walk. "Hello," she said. "I was just looking for Helen. I thought I'd take her to the park for a balloon." The maid looked blank. "My little girl," said Garden. "She loves balloons."

"Oh! Yes, Madam. The little girl. She's gone to the park already. Miss Fisher took her."

Garden ran for the stairs, the ones in back, the service stairs where Vicki would never go. The maid stared after her. Rich people certainly were peculiar.

Central Park is so huge, Garden thought. They could be anywhere. Where shall I start to look? She couldn't stay by the house until they came home. Vicki was capable of anything. She might call the police, send footmen to drag her back in. Garden ran through the traffic to the other side of Fifth Avenue. There was a path, an entrance to the park. Maybe Miss Fisher had taken that. There was the Metropolitan Museum. She might have taken Helen there. Garden stood on the sidewalk, overcome with the futility of the odds against her. I can't help it, she thought, I'm going to break down. I'm going to cry. Or scream. Or both.

"Mummy, Mummy, balloon. Balloon for Helen." An imperious tugging at her skirt brought Garden out of her tranced self-control. She stooped down and hugged Helen to her. Her eyes fell on the white shoes and white-stockinged legs of Miss Fisher. Garden stood up, holding Helen's tiny hand.

"Helen had a balloon, Mrs. Harris. She let it go."

"She likes to see it go up, Miss Fisher."

"She cannot have another one. It would teach her to be wasteful."

Miss Fisher was as stiff as the starch in her uniform. Garden prepared to argue with her, then stopped. What are you doing, imbecile, she said to herself. Get away from here. "I'll take Helen, Miss Fisher. We'll go for a walk."

The nurse stepped in front of her. "The Princess told me not to let Helen out of my sight, Mrs. Harris."

"Helen is my daughter."

"I understand that, Mrs. Harris. But I am employed by the Princess. I do what she tells me."

Garden put her face close to Miss Fisher's. "Listen to me carefully, Miss Fisher. I am going to take my child, and you are not going to stop me. If you touch Helen or me, if you dare to try to stop us, I will push you in front of a car." She turned and waved frantically at an empty taxi. She kept watching Miss Fisher while she opened the door and helped Helen to climb in. The nurse shifted uneasily on her feet, intimidated by Garden's blazing eyes and frightening determination.

Garden hopped into the cab and slammed the door. "Drive," she said. "Hurry. Get away from here." The cab started off with a speed that threw her back against the seat. She looked out the rear window. Miss Fisher was waving her arms and running across the street toward the house.

"Where to, lady?" The driver was black. His accent was strange to Garden's ear after the years abroad. And yet it was familiar.

Garden hugged Helen to her. "Harlem, driver," she said. "Take us to Small's Paradise. I have a friend there."

"John Ashley. He's a waiter here. Or was."

"Lady, I done told you. We ain't open yet. Come back around midnight. Everything'll be jumping then."

"No, no, you don't understand. Wait. Please. Don't shut the door." Garden threw out her arm to hold the door open. Her coat swung wide.

The man in the door looked at the charm on her necklace. His hand curled up, with the index and smallest-fingers extended. The sign to ward off the evil eye. "Who is you, lady?" He sounded frightened.

"I'm a friend of John Ashley's. Really I am. From Charleston, from Ashley Barony. I'm in trouble, and I need help. I know he'll help me, if I can just find him."

The man looked uncertainly at the white woman with the overbright eyes and the small white child at her side. Helen began to cry. It was past her suppertime. "Helen hungry," she whimpered.

This was something the man understood. He smiled at the little girl. "Come in," he said to Garden.

Helen sat on Garden's lap eating a chicken leg while John and Garden talked. He had come as soon as his friend telephoned him.

"That sound real bad, Miss Garden," said John. "Sure I know a pawnshop. But if that woman is after you, she going to have folks watching the train station and the bus station all two."

"Maybe I should go to the police. But I don't know what I would say to them."

"Miss Garden, police is mighty partial to rich folks. And you ain't rich no more. You got to get to Charleston. I got a old Model T. Ain't shiny and ain't got a good roof. But it runs. You take that car and this baby and get to your own people. And till you get there, you be real cautious. I seen a lot of strange things since I been working here. Rich white folks think they can do anything they want. Crazy rich white folks, ain't no way of telling what they might want to do."

It was after seven when Garden, following John's directions, entered the new white tiled tunnel from Manhattan to New Jersey. Helen was curled up on the seat beside her, her head in Garden's lap. The white coat was arranged with careful carelessness so that Helen was covered. Garden was freshly powdered, lipsticked, and combed. She had to look as different as possible from a hysterical woman running away with a child. The tolltaker might have been alerted to notice a woman like that.

The tunnel made her very nervous. It ran under the river, a dazzling feat of engineering that Garden did not understand or trust. She imagined that she could feel the weight of the water above her head, and she fought the impulse to speed, to get out of the tunnel, to get away.

The man at the tollbooth leaned down to look closely at her. The tunnel had a strange effect on people, especially women, he thought. And a woman driving by herself with night coming on was strange to start with.

Garden's hands tightened on the wheel. What was he looking at, looking for? She held her breath. If Helen moved, she was done for.

"Going far, lady?"

"What? Oh, no. Just to my sister's house in . . . in . . ." She could not think of the name of anyplace in New Jersey. Behind her, a horn honked. "Well, be careful. The rain last weekend washed a lot of potholes in the road."

"Thank you. I will." In her haste, Garden stripped the gears. Oh God, she thought, he's bound to remember me now. Behind her the tolltaker was shaking his head. In his opinion, women shouldn't be allowed at the wheel of a car.

The long road stretched ahead. We're out, Garden thought. She

451

twisted her head from side to side, shrugged her shoulders. The knots of tension fell away. She turned back the collar of the coat so that Helen would have plenty of air. Facts, she thought. We are out of New York. John lent me twenty dollars for gasoline and emergencies. His friend gave us a bag full of chicken and corn bread. It's only about eight hundred miles to Charleston. Those are good rocks to hold on to.

The car was much rougher to drive than the ones she was used to, and the roads unknown. Garden was glad. She wanted to have to pay attention every minute. She didn't want her mind free to think about Vicki. Or Sky.

Soon the headlights were her only link to the road. Garden's eyes grew tired from squinting against the lights of oncoming cars. As she drove on and on, the cars became fewer. Then lights ahead meant she was approaching a town. She drove slowly through the strange streets, glancing at the illuminated windows of stores and houses. How different everything was from Europe. So spread out, so much wood, so much newness. She drove on. Helen stirred, sat up. "All dark, Mummy."

"Yes, my darling. We're having an adventure."

"Helen hungry."

"Of course you are. I tell you what. We'll have a picnic adventure, how about that?"

Garden turned onto a dirt road and stopped the car. There was a flashlight, John had said. Helen played with it while she ate. She thought the adventure great fun. Garden took the flashlight from her and led her to the side of the road. "This is a picnic bathroom," she told Helen. The woods and fields around them rustled with the movement of the light wind and perhaps the movement of animals unseen in the dark. It added to Garden's feelings of being threatened; she was glad to get back in the car and on the road.

The jolting motion of the car acted like a cradle for Helen. She chattered for a few minutes, then fell asleep again. Garden stared along the path of the headlights. Another town, then another, with streetlights dark. Soon there were only dark shapes of stores and houses and the dark empty road. Garden found a cigarette and lit it.

The sleeping cities were eerie. Baltimore's white steps were like grinning teeth, Washington populated by ghostly white monuments. Garden shivered and touched the charm at her throat. And drove on.

There were occasional lighted windows now in dark farmhouses.

Garden felt as if she had been driving for days, weeks. Her shoulders and arms ached, and her mouth was dry. Richmond: 10 miles. We're in the South, she thought, and she felt better.

The sunrise woke Helen. She sat up and rubbed her eyes. "Helen thirsty," she whined. Garden smoothed the tousled hair from Helen's damp forehead.

"Me too, darling. We'll stop soon."

On the main street of the next town a flashing neon sign competed with the bright dawn. "EATS-EATS-EATS." Garden pulled in to the curb.

A waitress and three men in overalls were talking and laughing across a linoleum-topped counter. They looked at Garden and Helen as if they were creatures from a zoo. Garden was too tired to care. She lifted Helen onto one of the tall circular stools at the counter and collapsed onto the one next to it.

"You look bushed, honey," said the waitress. "Why don't you sit at a table. There's something to lean back on in a booth."

Her kindness made Garden's eyes fill with tears. Oh, Lord, she thought, I'm so tired I'm weak. I can't give out; there's still such a long way to go.

Helen didn't want to leave the stool. She was swiveling from side to side and giggling. Garden put an arm around her waist and carried her, kicking, across the room to a booth. A glass of milk stopped her crying. Coffee and a big breakfast revived Garden.

The car was hot and stuffy when they got back in it. Garden opened the windows. "Now you help Mummy find a gasoline station, Helen," she said, "and then we'll go to Charleston." She felt strong enough for anything now. The breakfast had been just like home, country sausage, biscuits, eggs, hominy and mounds of salted butter. France was a million miles away. Charleston was just down the road.

After an hour, the hot Southern sun made the car an oven. After two, an inferno. The road unwound straight and glaring in front of them, with heat mirages of shimmering water that disappeared when they approached. Helen was restive, then cranky, then miserable. Garden was gripped in a nightmare of bright daylight, gas stations, leaking Dixie cups of ice cream, lukewarm Coca-Cola, and the endless monotony of the flat road, flat fields, flat cloudless horizon. Their clothes stuck to their sticky, sweaty bodies, the air was thick and hot, Garden's eyes dry and scratchy. "How far?" Helen whined, and Garden could not tell her. "What time is it?" she cried, and Garden did not know. She had been driving for an eternity, an eternity in hell.

Helen was asleep, with a thumb in her mouth, when it suddenly darkened and began to rain. Water gushed through holes in the roof and soaked the prickly seats. Garden welcomed it with hoarse, unsteady laughter. Helen woke up and laughed with her. Then they passed out of the rain, and the heat turned the puddles of water on the floor to steam. Garden's legs were trembling from fatigue, her arms two blocks of pain. Helen went back to sleep.

"What's that stuff, Mummy?" Garden had not noticed when Helen stirred. The little girl was kneeling on the seat, pointing out the window. Dear God, thought Garden, I've got to stop. I'm not even conscious anymore. She turned her heavy head to look where Helen was pointing. A few yards from the road there was a stretch of woods. The trees were hung with Spanish moss.

"Oh, darling," she cried. "Oh, Helen, we're in the low country. We're almost home." Her foot pressed the accelerator and she honked the horn in celebration. The next hours were a confused blur. She sang songs, told disjointed stories, stopped at country stores beside the road just to hear people's accents when they directed her to the cooler of Coca-Cola bottles hidden under floating bergs of ice.

Charleston: 5 miles. Garden imagined that she could smell salt water, pluff mud. She was talking to herself now through parched lips, near to hallucination from exhaustion. "Look for a sign for the ferry, Garden, or you'll drive into the river." She laughed wildly at her joke. The air was cooler. The sun was low in the sky. Helen was asleep. Garden nodded.

The Model T lurched, two wheels off the road. Garden jerked, guided the car back onto the pavement. The arrow-straight road was curving. She concentrated all the energy she had left to the task of staying on the road. "Slow down," she told herself, "raise your foot from the pedal." Her hands turned the wheel. Way ahead, there was something in the middle of the pavement. A dog? Deer? She slowed even more.

It was a man. Waving his arms. Telling her to stop. The car coughed, jerked, stuttered and died. Garden's hands felt fused to the steering wheel. She looked through the insect-spattered windshield with dry, dull eyes. What a fool she had been to think that she could escape Vicki, that Vicki wouldn't know where to find her. The man was a state policeman.

88

"Ma'am, you all right, ma'am?" The policeman's wide-brimmed hat filled the window by Garden's head. She looked at his concerned face. Slowly its message reached her brain. He was not an enemy.

"Soldier," said Helen.

"Naw, honey, I'm not a soldier," the man said with a big smile.

"What do you want?" Garden said. It came out as a croak.

"I thought you might need some help, ma'am. Saw your license plates. Folks who see the bridge for the first time get nervous sometimes. Specially this time of day. The sun in their eyes and all. You were kind of weaving on the road."

"Bridge?" Garden tried to think, to remember. There was something she had heard about a bridge. What was it? Why wouldn't her mind work?

The policeman waved his hand, introducing the spectacle ahead. It rose up, up, seemingly sheer as the side of a cliff, narrow as a ribbon, stopping at a peak that looked as if it led to nothing but air and height and falling. "Oh, God," Garden moaned.

"Takes a lot of people that way," the man said. "That's why I'm here. I'll drive your car over for you if you like. We've got a regular system. Do this ten or twelve times a day." He was proudly patient.

"Yes, please," Garden mumbled. She scrambled across to the other side of the seat and held Helen in her lap.

The policeman talked evenly about the engineering marvels of the bridge. It was a well-rehearsed, well-designed, soothing monologue for nervous passengers of cars mounting the roller-coaster slope, then seeing the swooping descent over the crest and the second peak ahead. Garden heard none of it, saw nothing. Her eyes were closed; the lids were hot and swollen, but the darkness and the freedom from driving were balm.

It took more than five minutes for the old car to cover the nearly three-mile length of the bridge. The policeman parked on the side of the street that led from the foot of it. "Here you are, ma'am, little lady."

"Fun," said Helen.

"Thank you very much," said Garden. "I could not have made it."

The man stepped out of the car, touched the rim of his hat. "Glad to be of assistance, ma'am." He turned to go.

Garden sprawled over the seat to reach the window near him. "Officer? Could you please tell me how to get to East Battery?"

The lights were already on in the bayed extension that held the staircase and hallways of Margaret's big house. "Look, Helen, this is Gramma Tradd's. Mummy's mummy. She'll be so excited to see you."

"Helen hungry."

"And there'll be all kinds of good things to eat. Come on, angel." She stumbled along the short path. Her legs didn't want to work.

"Helen thirsty."

"Yes, baby. In a minute." Garden leaned against the wall by the front door. Her knees were buckling. She heard footsteps and forced herself to stand up. She must look a fright, she thought.

Margaret opened the door. Light dazzled Garden's tired eyes. Her mother was just an outline.

"I thought that might be you, Garden," said Margaret. She was crying. "Aren't you satisfied with what you've done already?" She rattled a newspaper before Garden's dazed face. "You can't parade your disgrace into this house. Go away." The door began to close.

"Mama!" Garden cried out. "Mama!" She could not think, the words would not come to speak, to ask what was happening. She could not comprehend anything except that the light from the doorway was being blocked out, that it was gone. She beat her fists on the door. There had to be a mistake. Her mother couldn't shut her out. It was her home. Wasn't it her home?

Helen pulled on her skirt. She was wailing. "Helen tired."

Garden's knees gave out then. She collapsed on the doorstep and took Helen in her arms. What was going to become of them? The shadow cast by the big house felt cool, and Garden was able to cry.

It frightened Helen. She touched Garden's wet cheeks with sticky

456

little fingers. "No," she said. "No. No." Garden took the child's hand in hers.

"Don't be scared, baby. Hush, hush. Mummy will fix everything. We'll be all right." There was no conviction in her tone. Helen cried as if her heart were breaking.

Garden's exhausted body ached, her mind whirled. She had to think. Find a rock, something to hold on to. She cried out in her heart for help. If only Hélène were over here . . . if only this were Paris . . . she'd have someplace to go. She longed for the Frenchwoman's dry, practical paring-down of drama. Then, as if she could hear Hélène's voice, she knew what she would say. Noble-hearted Bess.

"Aunt Elizabeth," Garden mumbled. "Helen, we'll go to Aunt Elizabeth."

Joshua opened the street door wide, the card tray in his hand. "Miz Cooper, she ain't to home," he said formally. Then he saw the forlorn, grimy woman and child on the step. "Lord have mercy," he said, "give me that baby to tote and lean on old Joshua, Miss Garden."

89

"I don't even remember walking through the door," said Garden.

Elizabeth Cooper chuckled. "What you did wasn't what you'd call walking, dear. Poor Joshua was listing like a sinking ship, trying to carry Helen and drag you along at the same time."

"Is she still asleep?"

"Gracious, no. Children are so dreadfully resilient. She's been up for hours, talking Celie to death in the kitchen. She's sure that Celie has a pony hidden in one of the cupboards."

Garden made a small, groaning noise. She didn't want to think about Sky or Vicki or anything else.

"It won't go away." said Elizabeth. "You're going to have to face it."

"Not yet." Garden begged.

"Before the day is over. I have kept last night's newspaper for you, Garden. Make yourself read it. It's ugly, but you have to know what everyone in Charleston has already read."

"It's not true."

"True or not true isn't the issue. You must know. You should also know this. You have a home with me for as long as you need it."

"I can't understand how Mama could have turned me away like that. Aunt Elizabeth. She shut the door in my face. In my face. I can't believe it."

Elizabeth touched Garden's hand. The brief pressure was both an expression of sympathy and a demand for self-control. "You're a grown woman now, Garden. What are you, twenty-five, isn't it? That's too old for kindergarten visions of perfect mothers. Margaret has always placed undue emphasis on society and her place in it. She's basically a very silly, shallow woman and you know it. You have to accept what she is. She'll never be what you would like for her to be."

"But I'm her daughter."

"And you're not what she would like for you to be, either. But she'll never be able to accept the truth. You will, if you work at it. You have a lot of bitter pills waiting to be swallowed, dear. I'm going to leave you now so you can get started."

Garden watched Elizabeth's tall, thin form move to the door. She hated to see her go. She did not want to face what had to be faced. She looked around the room, delaying the moment when she must look inside herself.

She was in one of the third-floor bedrooms. Helen, she knew, had been put in the other bedroom, across the hall from hers. The rooms were obviously not often used. There were several cartons stacked in one corner, and a sewing machine under a dust cover in another. Part utility, part storage room, only rarely guest room. The furniture was old mahogany and well cared for a low post bed and chest-on-chest, small desk and a single, delicate wooden chair, moved from desk to sewing machine at some earlier time. The rug was Chinese, Garden thought, but so worn that the pattern was almost indiscernible. A white candlewick coverlet was folded at the bottom of the bed, and white organdy curtains crisscrossed the windows. The wallpaper was a faded blue-and-white stripe. After the houses she had known and the luxury she had taken for granted, her sanctuary at the Tradd house seemed pitifully shabby.

She wanted to slide down in the bed, nestle into the pillows and find forgetfulness in sleep. But she imagined the disapproval on her great-aunt's severe thin face, and she made herself get up.

Elizabeth had left the newspaper on the desk. Garden picked it up, turned through the pages. Her photograph leaped out at her from the top of page four. It was an old one, from the "bad times." She was blond, wearing a beaded gown with heavy tassels of pearls at the short hem. Her arms were piled with jeweled bracelets, pearl-and-diamond tassel earrings hung from her earlobes, a fox-collared satin cloak was draped across her shoulders. She had a long cigarette holder in one hand, a glass of champagne in another, and a glazed, artificial smile on her face. INTERNATIONAL SET CINDERELLA SUED BY BETRAYED HUSBAND said the headline. Garden sat on the side of the bed.

The article came from one of the wire services. That meant, Garden knew, that it was probably in every paper of any size in every country in the world. It described Sky as "stricken by the shocking revelations" and as a dedicated, hardworking farm manager in an unnamed small town in the French countryside. The implication was that Garden had been living a riotous life of late nights in nightclubs in Paris and casinos in the South of France while her husband, unaware of her activities, was toiling at the noble work of tilling fields.

"It is expected that the trial will disclose evidence of decadence and profligacy unparalleled since the days of the late Roman Empire," the newspaper reported, "and crowds are already lining up in the normally quiet streets around the Court House. Mr. Harris is in seclusion, under a doctor's care. He will be represented by Atherton Wills, noted trial attorney. The whereabouts of Mrs. Harris are not known. Mr. Wills released a simple, moving statement to the press, about the accused adulteress' defense. Her grief-stricken husband has engaged an attorney for her. Even in these lurid circumstances, Mr. Harris' first concern is for his wife's well-being.

"A penniless debutante from the exclusive social world of Charleston, S.C., Mrs. Harris was carried into a life of incomparable luxury by her devoted young husband when they sailed on a honeymoon cruise to the languorous Caribbean on his 185-foot yacht. 'He gave the girl everything she ever asked for, and she asked for everything,' said Mr. Harris' mother, the Princess Victoria Montecatini. The Princess is expected to be a principal witness for the prosecution at the trial.''

Garden crumpled the newspaper into a ball and threw it on the floor. Her first impulse was to fight, to tell her side of the story. Sky's infidelities, Vicki's little bowls of cocaine. She could get witnesses, too. And more of them to tell the truth than Vicki could buy to lie. Fact. She'd still lose.

"My girl," she said aloud, "you danced your way into the trap just as fast as your feet would carry you."

But at least she was in Charleston where people knew her. No matter what the papers said, they knew she wasn't like that. She wasn't a gold digger, a schemer, a nymphomaniac. She had made some mistakes, but everybody makes mistakes. She could count on her friends from school and the choir. Her mother didn't matter. She'd get over it anyhow.

"Mummy?" Helen was huffing and puffing from the climb up the stairs. "Helen ice cream."

Garden looked at her daughter's sturdy little body and healthy pink cheeks. Maybe she had failed as a wife, failed at making Sky happy, at keeping his love. But she was going to be the best mother in the world, she made up her mind to it. Helen would never have a door closed in her face.

"Baby," she said, "we'll have the biggest ice cream, with the most whipped cream and a bright red cherry on top. What do you say to that?"

Helen nodded approvingly.

Garden drove Helen to the drugstore on King Street. The weather was too hot and Helen's legs too short to walk that far. Schwettmann's was infinitely more than a drugstore. It was pleasure palace and social center for Charleston's young people, particularly girls. The left wall had tall wooden display cabinets and glass-topped counters with lighted wells of cosmetics and perfumes. The rear wall had a window to the mysteries of the pharmacy. The center of the store and the rear half of the right wall were the wonderland, with a marble-topped counter, behind it the soda fountain, and small round tables with four chairs each filling the rest of the floor. The tables and chairs had white-painted frames made of wire bent into loops. They were called ice-cream chairs and tables, they screeched on the tiled floor when they moved, and they were in constant use. One could go into Schwettmann's at any time in the day and there would be people one knew to talk to, perhaps to join at a table and have a cherry Coke with. When Garden was at Ashley Hall, a movie followed by a Coke at Schwettmann's was the ultimate in fashionable bliss.

She did not expect now to see anyone she knew. The younger boys and girls were probably monopolizing the chairs. She wanted to go to Schwettmann's because she would feel at home there. And because she wanted Helen to see where Mummy had had her first ice-cream sundae.

The screen door squeaked when she opened it, just as it used to. And the ceiling fans were making their same gentle whirring sounds. Garden looked around. Nothing had changed. It seemed natural to see Wentworth sitting at one of the tables. Two handsome little boys were with her.

"Wentworth!" Garden began to weave her way through the wire forest of chairs. She watched Helen carefully so that she wouldn't run into one. She looked up just in time to see Wentworth put a dollar on the table and hurriedly gather up her gloves and parcels.

Garden stood gaping while Wentworth hurried the boys through the thicket of chairs. They passed within three feet of her. Wentworth did not raise her eyes from the heads of her little boys. "Wentworth?" Garden said quietly.

"Who's that lady, Mama?" said one of the boys in the piercing, carrying voice of childhood.

"Nobody," said his mother.

Garden looked around the half-filled tables. No one met her eyes.

"Helen ice cream."

Garden lifted her chin and walked to the counter. "I'd like a pint of vanilla to take home, please," she said.

"Take this to Celie in the kitchen," she told Helen when they got back to Elizabeth's. She walked slowly into the library, stripping off her gloves. Elizabeth looked up from the book she was reading.

"It's much worse than I thought," said Garden. "What am I going to do, Aunt Elizabeth?"

90

Bit by bit, with Elizabeth's help, Garden started bringing some order into her shattered life. Elizabeth astonished her by offering to buy John's car. She had, she said, been meaning to learn to drive for years. The old Model T would be perfect to learn on because if she wrecked it, it would still look and sound the same after the wreck as before it. "You'll have to teach me, of course," Elizabeth said. Garden was happy to. There was so little she could do for her great-aunt, and Elizabeth was doing so much for her.

"I called on your tedious mother," Elizabeth said one day shortly after Garden's arrival, "and she is going to send you a weekly allowance. She is such a miser, that woman, that she must be black and blue all over from sleeping on a mattress stuffed with gold."

"How nice of her," Garden exclaimed. "Shouldn't I go see her to thank her?"

"Nice, my foot. I told her she had to give you money to live on or else you'd move in with her. There's always a comical side to dreadful situations, Garden."

But Garden was not yet ready to laugh.

"You must use your allowance for Helen," Elizabeth said. "She cannot wear the same frock every day, no matter how nicely it is washed and ironed. And she must have a dah, Garden. It isn't good for you and it isn't good for her that you spend so much time with her. She'll become a tyrant in no time."

Garden protested. "Helen's all I have left, Aunt Elizabeth. And she needs me. Everything's so new to her."

Elizabeth frowned. "You have yourself left, Garden. And you're in danger of losing it if you wrap yourself up in Helen and in self-pity."

Garden exploded. "Goddammit, I'd just as well be back with Vicki. You make decisions for me, you make plans for me, you dole out food and drink, and I'm supposed to kiss your feet and bow down and say thank you ma'am.''

"Believe me, Garden, I will be very happy when you can run your life without my help. I do not relish being a mother again at my age.''

"Then why do it? You can shut your door too, you know. If it's such a pain giving Helen and me house room, why bother?''

"Because, like your friend Mademoiselle Lemoine, I chose to interest myself in you. I care about you, Garden, have cared for a long time. I believe you have good stuff in you. I'm waiting for you to show it.''

Garden stormed off to her room and felt sorry for herself. But a few days later, she took Elizabeth's bracing comments to heart and took her life into her own hands.

She went out to see Reba again, partly for sympathy, she admitted, partly because her first visit, to tell her about John, had been so short.

She found Matthew at home, too, in the middle of the afternoon. He and Reba were sitting on the step to their house, holding hands. The sunlight glistened on thin streaks of gray in Reba's hair. They were going to have to move, they told Garden. The notice had arrived that morning. The Barony was being turned into a retreat, a monastery. The Principessa had given it to the Trappists. The monks, Matthew said sadly, didn't need any workers. They did everything themselves.

But Vicki's not even Catholic, Garden thought. She's not even Christian, as far as I know. She looked at her friends' despondent faces, felt her eyes fill with tears and her throat fill with the bile of frustrated anger. Then she understood the reason for Vicki's generous gift to the Church. It was another blow at Garden, at her family.

"Where will you go?" she asked.

Matthew answered. "'Cross the road, that's all. Seems like all us Ashley folks end up working for Mist' Sam. It ain't so bad, Miss Garden. Pretty near all we friends done gone over there already. But it sad to see the plantation with no Ashley left, black or white.''

Reba released Matthew's hand and stood up. "Let's us drink up that coffee so we don't have to tote it. I'll put the pot on.''

While they were drinking, Reba reminded Garden of her legacy from Old Pansy. "I won't have room for that big old chest of drawers, honey. Can you take it, or do you wants I should bust it up for firewood?"

"Aunt Elizabeth? Where are you?" Garden ran into the dim house, shuttered against the sun. She tripped on the rug, nearly fell, clattered into a table near the wall.

."I'm in the library," Elizabeth called. "Having tea. Come join me if you haven't broken a leg."

Garden laughed. Elizabeth smiled at the sound. Garden was still laughing when she entered the room. "Milk and two lumps, please," she said. "No, make that three lumps. I want to celebrate, and I'm going to need the energy. Aunt Elizabeth, I'm going into business."

"Tell. I'm fascinated."

Garden walked around the room, too excited to sit down. "I went out to see Reba. Remind me to tell you later what that bitch Vicki has done now. Anyhow, Reba reminded me that Old Pansy left me some furniture. A tremendous hulk of a thing, I always used to think it was when I was little. I had a look at it, to see if I wanted to keep it. Wow. It's all covered with about a million years of dirt, but underneath it must be gorgeous. A huge chest-on-chest. The lines are great, and the brasses are original. I learned about all that kind of thing when I was furnishing the house on Hampstead Heath.

"So it came to me like a bolt of lightning. Who still has any money? Vicki's sort. And what do the plantation people and the rich tourists do for amusement? They go to antique shops. If I'm stuck with being so damn famous, I might as well get some good out of it. Nobody will speak to me. I'm disgraced. I'm going to go all the way. Aunt Elizabeth, I'm going into trade.

"People will flock into my antique shop just to get a good look at the Cinderella of the international set. Then I'll browbeat them into buying something. At an outrageous price. With an enormous profit to me.

"Matthew's going to borrow a truck and bring my treasure into town. I'll put it in the carriage house, if that's all right. I can't wait to clean it up and see what I've got.

"Of course I'll need more than just one piece of furniture. But I really did learn a lot in England. I can take stuff on consignment from other dealers, go to auctions, poke in cabins like Reba's. She

464

has a teapot that I'm positive is Chinese export. There's a crack in the lid, but it hardly shows."

Elizabeth coughed gently to signal an interruption. "Boil it in milk," she said. "It'll close the crack right up."

Garden swooped on her great-aunt to hug her. "You're wonderful. Do you think I'm crazy? It's a terrible risk; the odds are all against making a go of it. I'll hock my cigarette case. That'll pay rent on some hole in the wall for a month or two."

Elizabeth laughed. "Yes, my dear, I think you're crazy. And I'm delighted to see it. Thank God for excitement and daring and craziness. Now, about the pawnbroker. I know one that I did a lot of business with in my day . . ."

In response to Elizabeth's phone call the next day, Andrew Anson sent a messenger from the bank. He was accompanied by two armed policemen. Elizabeth signed a receipt for the package while all three men waited on the porch. "I don't know why Andrew didn't just put an ad in the paper. ATTENTION BURGLARS. He was a dear little boy, but being a banker has turned him into an old maid."

She opened the box, and Garden gasped. Not even in Monte Carlo had she ever seen such big diamonds or so many of them. "What is it?" she whispered.

Elizabeth tipped the box and spilled the diamonds onto her desk. "Isn't it awful?" she said with pride. "I always forget how truly revolting it is." She lifted the mass with both hands. It was a necklace, a bib almost, of enormous stones, with a pear-shaped pendant that must have weighed close to thirty carats.

"Dirty, too," said Elizabeth. "We'll have to soak it in some ammonia. Can you imagine, Garden, that my father, who was reputedly a man of fine sensibilities and judgment, bought this for my mother? It is without doubt the most vulgar piece of goods ever made by human hands." She dropped the necklace back on the desk.

"It has," she said, "been the saving of this family, though. My brother, your grandfather, hid it in a hole in a tree trunk when the Yankees were coming. After the War, it was in and out of the pawnbrokers' at least a half-dozen times. It started the fertilizer company, and it bailed me out again and again when I was running it. Now it will start you up in your business."

"But Aunt Elizabeth. I couldn't."

"Of course you could. And you'll have to be a tremendous success and redeem it and give it back to me. It's hideous and all that, but it has great sentimental value for me."

Lowcountry Treasures opened for business on January 6, 1932.

91

Four months passed from the time Garden decided to go into business until the day the shop opened. She was busy every minute of every day in those months, so busy that Thanksgiving, her twenty-sixth birthday and Christmas were hardly more important than any other days.

Most of her crammed schedule was necessary. She had a staggering amount of work to do. But she also made work for herself that was not really required. She needed to stay occupied all the time so that she would not succumb to despair. The divorce trial dragged on through September, to the joy of newspaper circulation managers worldwide. At first, reporters wasted hours in vigils outside Margaret's house, hoping that Garden would appear. Then someone—Elizabeth said sourly that it was probably Margaret, and for money—told them where Garden was living, and her only recourse was to hide behind the shuttered windows and locked gates of Elizabeth's house.

She used the time to study reference books on antique furniture, silver, china, and glass. Within a week she realized that no matter how hard and how long she studied, she would never know enough to be a real expert on any aspect of antiques. She would possibly have given up her plans then, except for a suggestion from Peggy.

Peggy's letter was short and bluntly affectionate. "You sure made a mess of things, Garden. Glad to hear that you're trying to do better now. Get in touch with that man I sold all the Barony stuff to. His name's Benjamin, and he seemed to know his onions. You'll get no sympathy from me about the heat in Charleston. Cuba is one big steam kettle. Bob's due for a transfer soon, and I'm hoping for someplace cool. Even Alaska. Bobby will have trouble adjusting. He's hardly ever had clothes on his fat body. I'm pregnant, due in March, hoping for a girl so I can bring her up to be the first woman President of the U.S. The men have given us such a disaster, there'll have to be a women's party one of these days.''

Garden telephoned George Benjamin. Ah, yes, he remembered Peggy vividly. Yes, he'd be glad to help her sister. Yes, he knew who she was. Certainly, he meant what he said. He'd be happy to help. He'd call on her, if it was inconvenient for her to go out right now.

Mr. Benjamin was a little disappointed in Garden at first. He remembered Peggy with so much admiration and fondness that her sister was a letdown. Garden had none of Peggy's boldness, nor did she have Peggy's buccaneer dash. But she was eager to learn and she was fully aware of her ignorance, two traits appealing to a scholar. By the time they finished their talk, he was quite taken with her.

And he had good news for her. "Do not worry about your lack of knowledge,'' he said. "It can work very much in your favor. Most people who will come into your shop will think they know more than they do. 'Ah, Nelson,' a woman will say to her husband, 'I think that chair is an original Chippendale.' She will then say to you, 'Miss, can you tell me anything about that chair?'

"And you, what will you say? If you are extremely knowledgeable, you will say, 'Madam, that is a late-nineteeth-century Chippendale-style chair clearly from the workshop of one of the New Jersey copyists who made furniture for public dining establishments. I know this is so because of the poorly proportioned rear legs and the weakness of the cross brace.

"But, my dear Garden, you do not know this. You know only that you purchased the chair in a lot at an auction, that you paid nineteen dollars for it, and that you hope to sell it for forty. So you say, *i* cannot tell you very much, madam. As you see, it is mahogany and looks like Chippendale.'

" 'Aha,' thinks the woman. 'This girl is a fool. She doesn't know as much as I do. I will steal this original Chippendale chair from her for a mere fifty dollars.'

"She is happy, you have a handsome profit, and Thomas Chippendale makes one more turn in his grave. You see the value of not being too educated?''

Garden's sides hurt from laughing. Mr. Benjamin smiled benignly. He enjoyed a good audience.

He then spoke seriously about the basic rules she should follow. ''Do not buy anything that you do not like, because you may have it with you for a long time. At the same time, do not become so attached to your merchandise that you are miserable when you sell something. You are in business, and you will only stay in business by selling. The customary markup is fifty percent—that is to say, you should try to double your money. Buy for ten dollars, sell for twenty. However, shoppers are convinced that you can be bargained with. Many of them shop only for the pleasure of bargaining. Therefore you must add on to the price an additional ten percent or thereabouts that you can reluctantly be pressured to discount. Your ten-dollar purchase is now priced by you at twenty-two or twenty-three dollars so that you can ultimately sell it for twenty. Are you following me, Garden?''

''Yes. It seems a terrible waste of time.''

''People often shop exactly for that purpose. They are, in effect, buying your time and attention when they buy a cup and saucer. Often they do not even buy the cup. That is why being in trade has such an odium. You must be pleasant to oafs.

''But you also meet many charming people. It balances out. Now, one final cardinal rule. You must expect to make mistakes, and you must not dwell on them. The broken glass, the fake you thought was real, the auction fever that makes you overbid, these are easily shrugged off. What is most difficult—and it has happened to me—is when you buy, let's say, a pretty little sewing table. You pay fifty dollars for it because you find it enchanting, and you sell it for one hundred. You are amazed. You thought the price too high when you quoted it. You feel lucky and clever. And then you read in a magazine about the genius who found in a small-town store the very table owned by Betsy Ross. And you recognize the illustration. You must, at that moment, force yourself to remember that you made a fifty-dollar profit and that it will pay four months' rent and that it is why you are in business.''

Garden controlled her laughter long enough to say, ''You didn't really sell Betsy Ross's sewing table, did you?''

''No, but it was almost as bad. I will not tell you what it was. I cannot apply my good advice to myself. It still hurts every time I think of it.''

Elizabeth joined them in the drawing room. "I haven't heard such jolly whooping since the time the dentist gave my daughter laughing gas. May I share?''

Garden introduced Mr. Benjamin properly to her great-aunt, then added, "We're doing first names, Aunt Elizabeth, because we're both business people. George is terribly nice. He's making me believe that stupidity is no handicap.''

"Ignorance, Garden. I said ignorance. Stupidity is an insurmountable handicap. Mistress Cooper, I have been coveting every piece in this room. Your house is lovely.''

"Thank you, Mr. Benjamin. I can take no credit for it, I'm afraid. Most of it was just here. I added the lamps, that's about all. I still find electricity a delightful small magic. Has Garden shown you her black elephant?''

"I don't quite understand.''

Elizabeth chuckled. "Then she obviously hasn't shown it to you. She inherited it from an old colored woman at Ashley Barony. It's the biggest, darkest, dirtiest thing I've ever seen in my life, but Garden's convinced it's beautiful somewhere under the grime.''

"Aunt Elizabeth, why did you have to say that? I don't want George to discover that I'm stupid as well as ignorant. I wasn't going to mention it.''

Mr. Benjamin spread his hands. "I don't know what to do now,'' he said. "My curiosity is at fever pitch, but I don't want to embarrass Garden.''

Garden shrugged. "I guess I might as well find out now. If it wouldn't be an imposition.''

George Benjamin stood up. "I'd be delighted to have a look. But remember, if I am not impressed, you must not be too discouraged. There's always the reminder of the Betsy Ross table. I am not infallible by any means.''

Garden opened the door to the carriage house and stood back for George Benjamin and Elizabeth to enter. The big chest of drawers stood in the center of the floor. It was enormous.

Garden wiped her palms on the sides of her skirt. They were sweating from nervousness. In the harsh sunlight that streamed through the door, the piece did look like a black elephant. She felt like a fool.

"My, my," said Mr. Benjamin, very softly.

Garden could think of nothing to say.

Elizabeth stood silently by the door.

Mr. Benjamin walked over to the chest, then walked around it. He took a handkerchief from his pocket and rubbed a circle on the front of one of the drawers. He looked at the greasy black spot on his handkerchief. "My, my," he said again. Garden thought she might scream.

He ran the tips of his fingers down the corners of the chest, along the decorated cornice and across the front where the top section met the bottom. He was muttering to himself. Suddenly he turned on Garden. He looked fierce. "This magnificent piece of furniture is caked with grease," he said.

"It's good? George, is it really good?"

"Barbarism," he said and resumed his examination. He pulled out a drawer and turned it upside down. "Yes, yes, cypress, yes, grooved cross member, dovetail . . . yes, tapering . . . it might be." He pulled out drawer after drawer, giving each the same close scrutiny. He froze like a statue when the next to the last drawer was halfway out. "No, it cannot be," he said.

Garden's spirits fell with a sickening plunge.

Mr. Benjamin removed the drawer and, cradling it in his arms, carried it to the door. He set it on the floor reverently, and took a pair of spectacles out of his breast pocket. Slowly he put them on.

"What is it?" said Elizabeth.

"Quiet!" shouted Mr. Benjamin. He knelt on the dusty floor and bent over the drawer. There was a dirty rectangle of paper in a rear corner. Its corners were curled up. In the center there was what looked like an irregular black spot. Mr. Benjamin put the index fingers of his two hands on two of the paper's corners and flattened them. He did the same with the other two corners. His forehead was shiny with perspiration. He released the paper, and the corners curled again. Mr. Benjamin sat back on his heels and removed his glasses.

"Ladies," he said solemnly, "this is truly a treasure, a genuine contribution to scholarship. Regard that bit of paper. Do not touch it, simply look. It is a cabinetmaker's label.

"It does not look impressive, does it? But it is. It is very impressive indeed, and I will tell you why. In the eighteenth and early nineteenth centuries there were many fine cabinetmakers in the small country this nation then was. They worked in the cities with wealthy populations that could support an expensive way of life—Boston, Philadelphia, Baltimore and Charleston. Philadelphia is today the best.known of the cities in respect to fine furniture making, because so much of it survived in place. Charleston is equally well known to historians, but many, many pieces were destroyed and many more removed during and after the Civil War."

Mr. Benjamin looked lovingly at the drawer. Garden and Elizabeth looked at each other, sharing incomprehension. What was Mr. Benjamin driving at? What was on the paper?

"To a serious collector," he said gently, "it is not enough to guess the provenance of a piece; no matter how beautiful it may be, he wants to know for a certainty who made it. Many pieces bear the label of their maker. Many pieces from Philadelphia. And from Boston and Baltimore. But not Charleston. And why is that? Because labels were attached with glue, and in our humid climate they came off. Or were eaten off by our plentiful insects, some of which have a taste for glue.

"There was until today only one known Charleston piece with a label that was tacked on. Until today."

Garden ran to her great-aunt and hugged her. She would have liked to hug Mr. Benjamin, but, first names or no, she didn't think she should.

"Then it *is* a good piece," she said, with a hint of smugness.

"Is it valuable, Mr. Benjamin?" Elizabeth was remarkably calm.

"Priceless, Mistress Cooper. It should be in a museum."

"Nonsense. It will be the centerpiece of the shop. Garden, you must put a horrendous price on it. Then everything else you have will seem very reasonable."

Mr. Benjamin's shoulders shook, then his entire body. He laughed until Elizabeth and Garden were worried. At last he wiped his streaming eyes, then his spectacles with his dirty handkerchief. "I should retire from business quickly, before Garden opens her shop. First Peggy the negotiator, now Garden the dowser. There is no way to compete. I will send an historian, if I may, to photograph and record this incredible discovery. Not merely a labeled piece—a piece by Thomas Elfe, Charleston's best-known cabinetmaker." He struggled to his feet and replaced the drawer.

"Do not touch anything without me. The cleaning must be precise. I may allow you to help, Garden, since it is yours, but I cannot

471

promise. I can hardly wait to get my hands on it." His finger brushed one of the blackened drawer pulls. "Original brasses. What a day to remember. I must go. I will telephone tomorrow."

Elizabeth saw Mr. Benjamin to the door. "You knew, did you not, Mistress Cooper?" he said quietly.

"That it was labeled? Or what that meant? Not at all. I knew it was valuable. My aunt Julia gave it to the old woman, Pansy, and Julia Ashley never did a cheap thing in her entire life."

"But you professed a contempt for the chest. You must love Garden very much."

"Yes, I do. And I have confidence in her. Unfortunately, she had little of her own. She does now. I am indebt. I to you, Mr. Benjamin."

"It is I who am in debt. All my life I have read about scholarly discoveries. I never dared hope that I would be part of one."

"I'm awfully glad you were, Mr. Benjamin. I would have thrown away that dirty piece of paper because it's so unsightly." Elizabeth smiled wickedly.

Mr. Benjamin shuddered and bowed his farewell. He was speechless.

When he got home, he headed directly for his study without even taking off his hat. He wanted to make some notes, telephone a friend at the museum, relive the excitement of the day. His wife intercepted him in the hall.

"What's she like, George?"

"Dorothy, the most astounding thing has happened. An old colored woman—"

"Later, dear, you can tell me all that later. Right now, tell me about Garden Harris. Was she wearing a lot of jewelry? Did she have on makeup? Was there champagne? Did she look, you know, loose?"

"What on earth are you talking about, Dorothy? There is a signed Elfe. Who cares about diamonds and champagne and foolishness like that?"

Mrs. Benjamin sighed. "I knew you'd miss all the important things, George, but still I had hopes. All right, tell me about the Elfe."

92

"Isn't it wonderful, Aunt Elizabeth? I can't believe it. Isn't George Benjamin super?" Garden was practically dancing.

Elizabeth smiled. "Yes, and yes. Do you realize, Garden, that you have your first asset? Financial asset, I mean. Your good eye is your first asset; it produced the second."

Garden stood stock-still in the center of the floor. "I hadn't thought of that. What a relief. I can always sell the chest if I have to. No matter what, I'll be able to pay you back, redeem the necklace. Why, I'm a real businesswoman." She sat down and looked into space, admiring the visions of the future she saw.

Elizabeth let her dream for a while, then interrupted the reverie. "Now that you're such a success, let's talk about how you're going to live. Wouldn't you like a place of your own, Garden? You must be tired of living in someone else's house."

Garden thought of the brief years on Hampstead Heath when she and Sky had a house of their own. Her euphoria about the Elfe chest faded. "I always wanted a house of my own, Aunt Elizabeth. I had one for a while. It was the happiest time of my life. Things will never be like that again."

"Not the same, no," said Elizabeth, "so there's no point brooding about it. I have a suggestion to make about the future. Let the past alone. The carriage house where your treasure is now would make a nice cottage. There are two rooms upstairs for bedrooms. I've thought several times of fixing it up and renting it, but I never got around to it. We could do it now. Rather, you could. There's that other old building back there, too. It was my office when I had the fertilizer company. All it needs is a good cleaning, and Helen would have a playhouse for rainy days. What do you think?"

"I'd want to pay rent."

"I'd insist on it."

"Let's go look at it right now."

"You go. I've seen it plenty of times. I'm going to have a quiet cup of tea before Helen wakes up from her nap. You should never have taught that child to talk."

It took until the middle of October to get the carriage house cleaned, wired for electricity and outfitted with drains and plumbing. By then the trial was over and Garden was divorced. And the reporters were gone.

"Now I'll start getting things for the house and the shop," she announced. "I can store the shop things in Helen's playhouse." Mr. Benjamin was outraged. The playhouse was the sanctuary for the Elfe chest, and he wouldn't allow anything near it. Every Sunday, when his own shop was closed, Mr. Benjamin spent the day lovingly and patiently removing the layers of dirt and cooking grease with a solution of tepid water, Lux flakes, and turpentine.

"Well, then, I'll find the shop," Garden said. There were plenty of places for rent. The only problem was getting up her nerve to leave the safety of Elizabeth's house and confront the curious stares outside. Garden had deliberately read no more newspapers, but she knew that the trial had made headlines for weeks.

"I'm afraid," she confessed to her great-aunt.

"You'll be afraid forever if you don't face it now."

The real estate agent did his best to be tactful. One after another, he went through the listings, telling Garden that she would not like the property because it was too small . . . too large . . . too dark . . . too bright . . .

"Mr. Smythe, I know there are problems," Garden said. She was very pale. "People don't want me for a tenant, isn't that it?"

"I'm sorry, Mrs. Harris."

"It's not your fault. I understand."

Mr. Smythe felt extremely uncomfortable. Two of the listings were his own property. He wondered if all those stories were true. She certainly was a beauty. And if there was any truth in what the newspapers said . . . Maybe if he rented her his place on Church Street. . . She'd be grateful, and he'd have to go over from time to time to see how she was doing . . . His wife would kill him. "There is one possibility, but the location is not all that good."

* * *

"I've found a place," Garden said when she got home. "It was a stable, and it's filthy beyond imagination, but there's a little brick courtyard in back with a beautiful fig tree. It's on Chalmers Street."

Elizabeth looked at Garden's smiling face. There were tiny lines of strain at the corners of her eyes and nostrils, but the nettle had been grasped, and she had survived. She was out from sanctuary.

In the succeeding weeks the lines deepened as Garden met the realities of her ostracism and notoriety. But she never broke down. She was too busy.

Her favorite activity was the country auction. She would leave before dawn sometimes to drive to towns or farms where there was an auction, getting there in time to look closely at the items to be sold before the auction began. She was very businesslike; she carried a notebook and wrote down the things she wanted to buy and what she was prepared to pay. If the bidding went higher, she stopped, although she often felt angry that anyone else would dare to bid against her.

Sometimes her purchases would not fit into or on top of the Model T. Then on the following day she would borrow the truck from Matthew's friend, pack a lunch and take Helen with her to collect her booty.

She also took Helen along when she "went fishing." She drove then to the clusters of shacks or cabins left near where the great plantations had been. She knocked on doors, asked for a drink of water, and looked around the interior for things that might have strayed from the long-ago great houses to these remainders. The gleanings were rich. There had been so many great houses in the low country. Garden always made friends on these outings. The owners of the pieces were glad to get rid of the "dirty old things" in exchange for money to buy new ones. Often she'd go back and fill up the truck. On the day she found a black-tarnished tall silver urn that was being used as a container for bacon grease, Garden called George Benjamin. "I think I've got something. Will you help me find out what it is?"

He cleaned the bottom and consulted a dictionary of makers' hallmarks. "How do you do it? It's Hester Bateman."

Garden wrote Peggy at once to relay the information she learned from Mr. Benjamin. One of eighteenth-century England's finest silversmiths had been a woman.

Peggy replied that it made perfect sense, and that they were being sent to Iceland. "I said I'd be happy with Alaska. I think this is overdoing it, but the Army's determined to have an airfield."

And then suddenly, after the months of ceaseless scrubbing and hauling and polishing and planning, all at once everything was done. Mr. Benjamin put the final polish on the gleaming wood and brasses of the Elfe chest. Garden swept the last scrap of packing paper out of the shop. Helen packed her doll's clothes in a basket for the move to her new home. Elizabeth put the last bottle of wine from her pre-Prohibition supply in the new electric refrigerator in the carriage house.

"What a wonderful surprise," said Garden when she saw it. "Thank you, Aunt Elizabeth. I'll invite you over for dinner, and we'll open it." She looked at the supplies she had bought for the tiny efficiency kitchen. "America is wonderful. Even I should be able to cook." She had canned soup, Bisquick, peanut butter, apple sauce, and even the latest revolution in modern groceries, sliced bread.

"Queen of all I survey," she murmured, looking at the big room that took up the ground floor of the carriage house. The big arched doors had been replaced by many-paned windows, the earthen floor bricked over, and the bricks waxed to a deep glow. "Good buys" from auctions had supplied the furniture, a pleasant mixture of periods, none of it very valuable, but all of it sturdy. Helen was a very active little girl. Chairs and sofa were slipcovered in blue-and-white mattress ticking, with big extra pillows covered in red-and-white-checked tablecloth fabric. Rag rugs were scattered on the floor.

"It's bright and cozy, Garden," said Elizabeth approvingly.

"And washable and cheap," added Garden. She was very pleased with the results of her efforts. The only expensive thing in the entire room was a large copper cauldron. It was on the hearth next to the fireplace, holding coal for the fire that was burning cheerily. Above the simple pine mantel hung Tradd's painting of St. Michael's, on loan from Elizabeth. There were shelves of books, an Atwater Kent radio, and a blue pottery bowl of apples. What more could a person want? Garden asked herself, and closed her mind to the answer. She had started the fire with a crumpled newspaper containing a long writeup of Sky's marriage to the young Comtesse de Varigny.

That night Garden slept in her own bed in her own room in her own house. She fell asleep repeating Elizabeth's words to herself. "I have lived alone for more than thirty years," Elizabeth had said, "and I have no doubt that it is by far the best way to live."

93

The next day Garden opened Lowcountry Treasures for business.

She was even more pleased with the shop than she was with her new house. The chest-on-chest had the place of honor, on a low platform against the wall, with a velvet rope barrier hung between posts at the corners of the platform. There were five tables of various sizes and designs, each holding a few pieces of silver or porcelain; four armchairs, a pair of camelback loveseats, and a tall bookcase with shelves of china and glass. At the rear of the shop a Queen Anne desk and chair were arranged in front of a window that overlooked the courtyard. Garden's account book, receipt book, and small cashbox were in the drawers of the desk. Not far away was a small potbellied stove with a brass scuttle of coals at its side and copper kettle on top to boil water for tea. She thought it would be a nice added touch of graciousness to offer customers tea while they were waiting for her to wrap up the things they bought. A tray was all prepared with cups and saucers, spoons, tea caddy, biscuit box, teapot, strainer, slop bowl, water pitcher, bowl of lump sugar and tongs. Garden had rearranged everything four times and was upset that she had forgotten to bring napkins from home.

At four o'clock she served tea to George Benjamin. "The door hasn't even opened all day," she said, and began to cry.

Mr. Benjamin patted her shoulder awkwardly. "Dear child, there are many, many days when no one enters my store, and I am on King Street. You must bring a book to read. I have read at least a thousand. As a matter of fact, I am annoyed when someone does come in; it interferes with my reading . . . No, I can see that the thought doesn't appeal to you. Let me see . . .

"I have it. Garden, please don't cry. I know what to do."

Garden looked at him, sniffling but no longer in tears.

"We'll call the newspaper," said Mr. Benjamin.

"The newspaper? I hate the goddam newspaper."

Mr. Benjamin was shocked. He was sixty-four years old and a gentleman. He had never heard a lady use profanity.

Garden glared at him. "How could you even think of such a thing, George? The newspapers hounded me and made my life miserable. I want nothing to do with them."

"Ah, of course. Yes. I understand. But you do not, Garden. Understand. They would not be coming to talk to you. They'd be here to see Thomas Elfe."

Garden considered. "I'm afraid you're being naïve, George. They couldn't resist a gibe at the scarlet woman. Sin sells more papers than scholarship."

"Not if I talk to my good friend who is an editor. I will be immensely clever. I will not tell him what is here until he agrees to my conditions. What do you say, Garden? Chalmers Street is very far from the beaten track."

"Let me think about it."

A week later Garden sent him a note. "Have thought. Will do."

She had had only one person walk in, a man she knew slightly from her debutante days. He had married a girl who was two years ahead of her at Ashley Hall. She smiled particularly brightly because she couldn't remember his name, or his wife's. He smiled also and suggested, in very coarse language, that she must be very lonely and that he would be willing to help her out.

"If you don't leave here at once, I'll hit you with this poker," Garden screamed, arming herself.

"Don't play games with me, honey. I know you must be dying for it." His hand went to his zipper.

Garden thrust the poker into the stove. "Take it out, and I'll burn it off," she promised.

The door closed behind him, and Garden began to shake. She was afraid to be alone anymore. The shop was isolated from the buildings around it and on a street with almost no traffic. Even newspaper publicity was better than fear. She had told Elizabeth, with showy bravado, that she'd have customers come in just to see the infamous Garden Harris. Okay, now she'd tell them where to find her. Just so long as they kept her from being alone and vulnerable, they could stare all they wanted to.

The press coverage was just as George Benjamin had-promised. The shop was photographed, the chest, the open drawer with the Elfe workshop label. Garden was mentioned only once, as "G. Harris, proprietor of Lowcountry Treasures."

The small spring bell over the door rang constantly for days after the article appeared. Most people were just curious to see Garden. "G. Harris" had not kept the public from making the connection with the scandalous trial. They stared and gaped and whispered among themselves. But they also bought things. There were also some people who were genuinely interested in seeing the Elfe chest, and a number of them saw something on display that "would be just perfect in that corner by the door" or "is exactly the color of my curtains." Garden filled an entire page of her account book and watched the classified ads carefully for announcements of auctions. Unfortunately, they were all on Saturday; she had to be in the shop.

By February the rush was over, and the serious buyers began to appear. Representatives of museums, of serious collectors, of the big auction houses in New York. When Garden was asked the price of the chest, she plucked the biggest figure she could think of from the air. "Fifty thousand dollars," she said. A man from Wilmington, Delaware, seemed about ready to take it, and her heart nearly stopped.

She received so many inquiries in the mail that she had a card printed with information about Thomas Elfe and a line drawing of the label and another of the chest, with its dimensions. It cost her twelve dollars to have the cards made, and she raised the price of the piece to seventy-five thousand.

"I use a lot of stamps answering all this mail," she said to George Benjamin as justification. He thought it the funniest thing he had ever heard.

Most of the mail consisted of formal letters on heavy, handsome letterpaper, but some of it was clearly sent by eccentrics. One was simply an account of the chest torn out of the New York *Times*. "How much?" was scrawled across the photograph in green ink.

Garden sent a card to the address on the envelope and threw envelope and newspaper into the trash.

It did not occur to her to turn over the torn paper and read the back. If she had, she would have seen part of the story about the automobile accident that had killed Sky and his new wife. He had been driving too fast for a curve on the Haute Corniche.

94

"Busy day today?" Elizabeth nodded at the steaming basin of water with Garden's feet soaking in it.

"Not busy enough. I really like it better when there are lots of people. No, today was slow but infuriating. I'll tell you about it after the show." Garden's life had evolved into an active, generally pleasant routine. She got up at seven and fixed coffee for herself, hot cereal for herself and Helen. Belva. Helen's dah, came at eight-thirty and took over while Garden bathed and dressed. She was almost accustomed to doing for herself now, but there were times when a button was missing or a blouse not pressed and Garden longed for Corinne and breakfast in bed and leisurely sweet-smelling baths.

At nine Garden went to the shop to sweep and dust before she opened at ten. At two-thirty she hung the Closed for Lunch sign on the door and went to Elizabeth's for Charleston dinner. Back to the shop from three-thirty to six, then home to let Belva go, fix supper for Helen and play with her until her seven o'clock bedtime. After that she fixed her own supper, ate it, cleaned up the kitchen and settled down with coffee and a cigarette. Elizabeth joined her just before eight, and they listened to "Amos and Andy" until eight-fifteen.

They usually talked until nine or so, then Elizabeth went back to her house and Garden had time to read, wash her stockings and underthings, wash her hair, or listen to other shows on the radio. She still marveled at it. What a difference from a few years earlier when she had had only earphones and a crystal set to listen to, waiting for news about Lindbergh.

"Do you want to hear Kate Smith?" said Elizabeth.

"Not especially."

Elizabeth turned off the radio. "They do make me laugh. Kingfish, especially. Now, tell me what infuriated you."

"Oh, it's just Charleston. These people. You know, not one soul that I used to know has been in. All the customers are Navy people or tourists. That's bad enough. But I can't stand being invisible when I walk to the shop and back. People on Meeting Street just look right through me. Today, Lucy Smith sent her maid to ask about the tureen in the window. Her maid! She could have at least telephoned. She wouldn't have had to say who she was. I guess she thought the phone would be contaminated by my voice."

Elizabeth was silent for a long time after Garden's outburst. "There's always a punishment for breaking rules," she said quietly.

"But that's so long ago. I'm different now. And even if I have to be punished, why punish Helen? Belva can't take her to the Battery, or the Post Office park. The other dahs won't let their children play with her. It's vicious. I hate Charleston."

"You have to prove yourself, Garden. You've been here less than six months. In time, people will come around."

"I don't believe it. Why should they? I'll wear a scarlet letter all my life. And Helen, too. It's too awful."

"They'll come around because you're a Charlestonian, and Charleston always takes care of its own. You don't know anything about this place, your home. Your idiot mother never knew anything except that it has a reputation as a highly exclusive society. She thinks the Saint Cecilia is the be-all and end-all of living. She can't tell the difference between symbol and actuality.

"Listen to me, Garden, I'll tell you about Charleston. When the Civil War started—yes, the Civil War, not the War Between the States or the War for Southern Independence or the Late Unpleasantness. When brother fights brother, it's called a civil war. Anyway, in 1861 this city had almost two hundred years of history behind it, and for more than a hundred and fifty of those years Charleston had been the most civilized place on this continent. Opera, art, theater, architecture, gardens, education—we had all the frills and all the essentials. Because we were phenomenally wealthy. If you think the Principessa and her friends have a luxurious way of life, just try to imagine it multiplied by ten. Or twenty. That's what Charleston was. With one crucial difference.

"It was genuinely civilized. Honor and duty and responsibility and consideration and respect and self-respect were all real concerns, not mere words. Noblesse oblige was the other half of privilege.

"Came the war, and the wealth went. But not the civilization. Charleston was small enough for everyone to stick together, to help one another keep up standards to live by. We all knew each other, were related to each other; we were us, and the occupying army was them. I remember those days. My Lord, it was hard.

"But we stuck together, and we made it. Because nobody gave in. Not to poverty, not to fear, not to an easy sell-out of principle for money. Plenty of people must have been frightened, tired, even hungry. But they kept their self-respect and their honor. Because Charleston was all of us, and we did not allow one another to give up.

"We still don't. Times are a lot easier now. The papers and magazines groan about the Depression; it doesn't mean much to us. We've had our own Depression continuously since the end of the Civil War. There's no difference now, except that the cost of things is less, and that's a blessing.

"What you're being punished for, Garden, is that you are a Charlestonian and didn't behave like one. You lost your self-respect. You not only broke the rules of civilized society, you were flagrant about it. I'm not saying that Charlestonians don't drink, don't commit adultery. But they don't rub other people's noses in it. Discretion is not the same as hypocrisy. Discretion is the convention that allows people to be tolerant and to look the other way, not to make judgments. This is a small community. In our different ways, we are all sinners. But we can continue to live together, to take care of one another, as long as we can maintain our ignorance—real or contrived—of each other's sins.

"No one can pretend to be ignorant of yours. Not for a while. The injury you did has to heal. You belong here. These are your people, and they'll fight for you against any outsider. The price you must pay for that unified support is unified disapproval when you have broken the bonds of obligation to civilization.

"I've been lecturing for half the night, it seems. I thought it would be easier for you if you had some understanding of why

482

you're being treated the way you are. Do you understand? Was my long-windedness any help at all?''

Garden shrugged. ''I get it, in the abstract. But on a personal level, it doesn't help. I still hate Charleston.''

''Then I'll just have to hope you get over it. I enjoy having you here. I'd hate for you to leave.''

''Don't worry about that, Aunt Elizabeth. I need to put myself back together before I'd have the nerve to try and make it on my own anyplace without you to help.''

''That's ridiculous, but I'll accept it for now. It serves my purposes. Good night, Garden.''

''Good night . . . say, Aunt Elizabeth, if I keep my nose clean, how soon will I be out of Coventry?''

''I really don't know, Garden. We're all human. I'm sure it would be faster if you weren't so beautiful. Go to bed. It's late.''

Elizabeth's portrait of Charleston did help, because it gave Garden some hope that things would change. She was busy, but not busy enough to block out the truth that she was lonely. Sometimes in the evening the radio would play ''Mood Indigo'' or ''Love Letters in the Sand,'' and she would cry uncontrollably.

But the next morning Helen would say something funny, and then someone would come into the shop and compliment her on a flower arrangement, and Celie would have made red rice for dinner because she knew it was Garden's favorite. And Garden would tell herself that she shouldn't be a crybaby.

On March first, in company with every other mother in America, Garden realized that she had no right to complain about anything. The Lindbergh baby was kidnapped. It was a horror too dreadful to think about and too vivid to ignore.

Once again, everyone was talking about Lindbergh, Lindbergh, Lindbergh. Newspapers, radio, street corners, customers in the shop, the name was on everyone's lips. Garden remembered the jubilation in Paris, and this shocked sympathy was all the more tragic by contrast. He was so young, Charles Lindbergh. She remembered his smile when the crowd at Le Bourget was carrying him on their shoulders. She felt as if, by sharing that place at that time, Lindbergh was in some way a part of her life and she a part of his. His tragedy was her tragedy as well.

She was glad that Helen was not accustomed to going to the park because she did not want her to leave the yard outside the carriage house. She did not even want to go to work. She wanted Helen in her sight every minute of the day and night.

But she had to work, and it saved her. Even though she took the radio with her every day to listen to news bulletins, she could not spend all her time next to it. She had to dust and polish and rearrange things and talk to customers and point out the characteristic Elfe fretwork on the chest and explain the rarity of the label and give directions to the art gallery and Fort Sumter and the Huguenot Church and "a nice place to spend the night." The tourist season was underway.

Garden began to learn that life has to go on, no matter how desperate the conditions. Peggy wrote "It's a boy. Again. Frank. I adore him." It reminded Garden that good things could and did happen.

One day two couples entered the shop, archetypes of the bargain seekers George Benjamin had described. Garden had a wonderful, wicked bit of fun being ignorant about the camelback loveseats, and each couple bought one after agitated whispers between the wives. It was particularly enjoyable because she had met one of the couples before. They had been Vicki's guests in Southampton. And they didn't recognize her.

She began to believe that the past was truly gone, and, by just a little, she missed Sky less and gave up the buried hope that he might come back to her.

And she concentrated on the sudden emptiness of the shop. She'd have to find something to fill up the space the loveseats had taken. She hired a Navy wife to work in the shop on Saturdays and started going to auctions again.

She recognized some faces that she saw again and again, and they recognized hers too. But not the face of the newspaper stories—the face of an antique dealer, like themselves. There was a camaraderie, with congratulations and shared gripes and stories about customers and rumors of an especially good auction coming up soon. Garden could believe that it was possible to build a new life, that she would not be forever known as the "Jazz-baby Cinderella."

When the Lindbergh baby's body was found on May twelfth, Garden's agonized sorrow was for the baby's parents, not for herself. She knew now that Le Bourget and the arrival of the *Spirit of St. Louis* were an important memory, and no more. She was not part of Charles Lindbergh's life; she had her own life, separate and distinct and in her own hands.

She wept, and the weeping was a catharsis. She emerged from the emotional storm with a heart ready to accept the realities of her life. It was a good life. She had a real home, a child she adored, work that she enjoyed, and people who cared about her. She was richer than she had ever been before.

"Do you want to know something nice, Aunt Elizabeth?" Garden said a few days later. "I'm really very happy."

95

It was July fourteenth, Bastille Day, and Garden was singing "La Marseillaise" as she tidied up before closing the shop. It was too hot for anybody to be wandering around shopping, she told herself. It wouldn't make any difference if she closed early today.

The excuse didn't fool her. She knew why she was closing. The next day was Helen's third birthday, and she wanted to get her the Little Orphan Annie doll she had seen advertised in the *News and Courier* that morning. It was too expensive, and she had already bought too many presents for such a little girl, but Helen loved to listen to the radio show. She could sing the opening song, and did, forty times a day. Garden switched from the French national anthem to the radio program's theme song.

> "Who's that little chatterbox?
> The one with pretty auburn locks?
> Who can it be?
> It's Little Orphan Annie . . . "

The bell over the door jingled. Garden put her hand over her mouth, smiling under her fingers. Not very dignified for an antique dealer to be caught singing. "Can I help you?" she said.

There were two men just inside the door. They looked very hot and uncomfortable, in dark suits and hats. Tourists, Garden thought, have to be. All Southern men know to wear white hats and suits in the summertime.

"Are you Mrs. Garden Harris?" said the taller man.

Aha, Garden thought, Yankees after the Elfe. I wonder what museum they're from. "Yes, I am," she said.

"I have a warrant for your arrest."

They were punctilious; one of the men took Garden's keys and locked the door to the shop. But they were none too gentle. They hustled her into a black car that was waiting out front without saying a word in answer to her terrified questions; she had bruises for weeks where their fingers had gripped her upper arms.

There was every reason for them to be harsh in their dealings with her. She was charged with the crime that the whole country considered the most loathsome of all. Kidnapping.

They took her to the city jail on St. Philip Street, a fortresslike stone building with castlelike doors and black-barred windows. Garden tripped on the steps going in because the men were pushing her so fast; she did not fall, because they were gripping her arms so tightly. Her feet pedaled frantically, trying to regain purchase on the floor while they half-dragged her to the tall desk in the entry. On her left, Garden heard a woman's brokenhearted sobbing. The place smelled of disinfectant and fear.

One of her captors spoke. They were the first words Garden had heard since they left the shop. "Federal officers," he said. He flipped open a leather folder containing his badge of identification. Then he took a folded paper from his breast pocket. "Here's the warrant. Will you hold this prisoner while we contact our superiors?"

A thin, tired-looking policeman was sitting behind the desk. He looked at Garden with curiosity. "Sure thing," he said. He poised a pen over the open book in front of him.

"Officer, I don't know what this is all about," Garden cried. "This must be a mistake. Tell these men; I haven't done anything. Please, please help me. They won't talk to me, they've hurt me; I don't understand."

"Shut up, lady," the policeman said. "I'm talking to these officers." He dipped the pen into the inkwell. "What's the charge?"

"It's on the warrant. Kidnapping."

The policeman had two small children. He looked at Garden with disgust and hatred. "Lock her up," he said to someone behind him. While he copied down the information on the warrant, another policeman took Garden to a cell. His fingers pressed the bruised spots where the federal officers had held her.

"You can't do this," Garden screamed. "Let me go. They're crazy. I haven't done anything."

He shoved her into a space six by eight feet and slammed a barred door behind her. The sound echoed loudly. A bolt rasped; Garden stood against the wall that she had stumbled into and trembled all over. She was too frightened to move.

She was still standing there an hour later when a third policeman opened the door. "Come on," he said, "we need your fingerprints." Garden could only stare at him. Her teeth were chattering, her entire body shaking. Her hair had fallen from its smooth twist and was streaming in disarray around her face.

"Say, wait a minute. I've seen you before. I remember that wild hair—Jesus! Did you used to go to Ashley Hall?"

Garden managed to bob her head.

"I was on traffic detail on the corner there. Gosh, lady, do these guys know who you are? Listen, you'd better come with me and sit down someplace while I find out what's going on. Would you like some coffee? Or a Coke? Come on, ma'am. Lean on me. Here, let me help you. I'm going to take you to the captain."

Elizabeth and her lawyer, Logan Henry, took Garden home. As they left the jail, reporters shouted questions at them and photographers jumped in front to take pictures. "Ignore this rabble," said Mr. Henry haughtily. Elizabeth took a more direct and more effective approach; she poked them out of the way with the point of a parasol. Garden moved like a somnambulist, unseeing and unhearing. Elizabeth had pinned up her hair; she held her hand to lead her.

She gave Garden a sleeping draft and tucked her in under a light cotton spread on the sofa in her study. Then she sat with her, still holding her hand, until Garden awoke around midnight.

She began to shake again as soon as she was aware of what had happened. Elizabeth gave her a glass of brandy and made her drink it.

"It's all over, Garden," she said. "Everything's going to be all right."

It was not all over, and there was no real assurance that everything would be all right, but it was what Garden needed to hear. So Elizabeth said it.

The next day Helen's birthday party was a great success. The Orphan Annie doll was not missed at all. Helen tore into her presents with appropriate three-year-old greed and destructiveness. She shouted with joy as each gift emerged from its battered wrappings; she even insisted on wearing the fur parka from "Aunt Peggy, Uncle Bob, Bobby and Frank." Her favorite trophy of the day was the newspaper she had found in the trash can. It had a picture of her mother in it.

"Socialite Arrested" said the caption that Helen could not read. Next to it was another photograph of a figure on a stretcher being loaded into an ambulance. "Mother Collapses."

"Margaret is perfectly all right," Elizabeth had told Garden. "Some fool reporter jumped out of the bushes by her door and shouted at her, and she fainted, that's all. I talked to her doctor."

When all the debris was disposed of and Helen was napping, Garden fell into a chair and kicked off her shoes. " 'Mother Collapses,' " she said.

Elizabeth took the chair opposite hers. "I'm glad you can laugh."

"What else is there to do? I can't shoot myself; it would wake Helen up."

Elizabeth smiled. "Then I would shoot myself, too." She gazed at Garden's tired face. Her eyes were closed, but the twitching lids indicated that she was not resting.

"Logan Henry is older than Methuselah," said Elizabeth in a conversational tone, "but he's the smartest lawyer in Charleston. There's really nothing to worry about, Garden. The hearing on Monday will be private, in Judge Elliott's office. He will dismiss the charges, or whatever the term is, and it will all be over."

Garden opened her eyes. "No, it won't," she said. There was no emotion in her voice. "It will never be over. It was Vicki. You heard what Mr. Henry said. Vicki is the one who notified the FBI that Helen had been kidnapped, that I had done it. She'll never leave me alone. I can't understand why she hates me so much."

Elizabeth started to speak, then stopped. Garden frowned. "What is it, Aunt Elizabeth? What were you going to say? You know something, don't you? What is it, for God's sake?"

Elizabeth sighed. "I'd hoped you'd never need to know, Garden. It's a sad and ugly story.

"Victoria, as I called your mother-in-law, was always spoiled as a child. Oh, yes, I've known her a very long time. Her father was one of my dearest friends. No, I'll change that. Her father was absolutely my single dearest friend. Victoria's mother died when she was about twelve, and her father raised her after that. They lived here in Charleston.

"When she reached the age of crushes, she got a big one on your father. I'm sorry to say that it went much too far. He got her pregnant."

"My father? And Vicki? It's not possible!"

"It's true, though. And worse. Victoria adored her father, and he was killed, shot. By your father. It was a wild fit of temper, the famous Tradd temper. And it was fatal. Victoria was twice-over heartbroken. She had been betrayed and orphaned by a boy she thought she loved. I was at her father's funeral with her. She swore on his grave that she'd get revenge. I didn't pay any attention. She was only a girl.

"I arranged for her to go to some cousins in New York. Later I learned that she had had an abortion."

Garden shook her head. "I could almost feel sorry for her," she said, "if I weren't so afraid of her. I sort of wish you hadn't told me, Aunt Elizabeth."

"I wish there was nothing to tell. I thought, when she approved of your marriage, that maybe I was wrong, that she had put it all behind her. I hoped she'd even grow fond of you. You were so young and defenseless. It wasn't until you arrived here that night last summer that I knew anything was wrong. Your letters were all so cheerful.

"Then came the divorce trial. That should have been vengeance enough for anybody. And no support settlement for you or for Helen. It sounded like the end to me. I can't imagine why she hasn't had enough."

On Monday, they learned the answer. The kidnapping charges were dismissed at once. Garden was unquestionably the child's mother; it was not a case of abduction. But Vicki's lawyer argued eloquently for her good intentions when she made the accusation against Garden. She only wanted the best for Helen, he said. There was no malice toward Garden. The Principessa was distraught with grief over the death of her son. Her granddaughter was the only part of her son she had left.

Outside the judge's chambers, he approached Mr. Henry with an offer. The Principessa would pay Garden a million dollars if she would give Helen to her. If Garden didn't agree, Vicki meant to get Helen some other way.

"My God," said Garden when she and Elizabeth were at last by themselves, "how much more can I stand? Sky is dead. I love him, I'll always love him, and he's dead . . . And Helen is not safe from Vicki, no matter what I do . . . and my mother has had a heart attack or something, all because of me. I've learned one thing. I was feeling so happy—and then the world caved in. Just like the days on Hampstead Heath and then the Crash. I'll never trust happiness again."

96

The weeks before Christmas were very busy at Lowcountry Treasures. George Benjamin had told Garden that she should not hope to show a profit for at least three years, probably longer because of the Depression. But the pages in the account book filled rapidly once Thanksgiving was past. It looked as if maybe she'd even be in the black at the end of the first year in business.

She looked around the shop and mentally patted herself on the back. It was less charming than in the early months, but much more businesslike. No big pieces of furniture to take up space, excepting always the Elfe chest. Now there were many tables, and a full wall of shelves. They held little things at low prices. People still wanted to give gifts, but even in Charleston the Depression was making itself felt. Two dollars was a lot to spend. Twenty was unheard of. At auctions now, Garden looked for acceptable things rather than exceptional ones. It took most of the excitement out of her forays, but she reminded herself that she was working, not amusing herself. And it was paying off. Paula King, the Navy wife who came in on Saturdays, was now coming in every day. She and Garden took turns wrapping the purchases for customers. It was a messy, back-breaking, uncomfortable job. They had put a table in the courtyard with paper, twine, boxes and excelsior. On sunny days the only problem was the wind, but when it was cloudy they had to shorten the shifts because they got so cold.

"How much is this, ma'am?" A naval officer was holding out the Bateman silver urn.

Damn, Garden thought, I'll have to polish off the fingermarks. "That's three hundred dollars," she said pleasantly.

"You've got to be kidding." He turned it around and looked at every angle of the graceful piece.

More fingermarks, thought Garden. "It's by Hester Bateman," she said, still pleasantly.

"Who's that?" He was touching the base now, holding the urn up at arm's length. Garden's professional good humor deserted her.

"If you don't know, you won't want it," she said crossly. She took the urn from his hand and put it back on the shelf. Another customer asked her if a two-dollar teapot was Spode or Wedgwood. Garden smiled stiffly. "I don't believe it's either; it says 'Bavaria' on the underside."

The back door opened and let in a blast of cold air. "Garden. My fingers are blue."

"I'll be right there."

"Well, if it's only Bavarian, I don't want to pay more than a dollar for it." The woman held the teapot up to the light from the window. "I can't even see my fingers through it. All my own china is so fine that you can see your fingers."

Another woman showed Garden a tiny chip on the edge of a crystal vase. "This is damaged," she said.

"Yes, that's why we're selling it so cheap," Garden replied. "It fell from its shelf. It was twelve dollars, and now it's only a dollar and a half. The flowers will cover the chip."

"Hi, John," said Paula to the officer. "Garden, I think it's going to rain."

Garden nodded to the women with the vase and the teapot. "This is Mrs. King," she said, "she'll be glad to answer your questions." She hurried outside to look at the clouds overhead.

At six o'clock she and Paula ushered two "just looking" women out and locked the door.

"What a mess," Paula moaned.

"At least the rain held off. Let's go home before it changes its mind. I'll come in early tomorrow and straighten up."

"I'll try to get in early, too. Say, Garden, I've got a last-to-trade for you."

"What?"

"A last-to-trade. You know, I heard somebody say something nice about you, and I'll tell you. But you have to tell me something nice somebody said about me first."

"Good Lord, Paula. I haven't heard 'last-to-trade' since I was in high school . . . Okay, how's this? Helen said she thought you were prettier than Blondie."

"Out of the mouths of babes. I'll tell Mike he has to start fixing his own sandwiches. Well, I guess that has to count. Here's mine. John Hendrix asked me who you were."

"That's a compliment?"

"You didn't let me tell the rest. He said you were the only really attractive woman he's ever seen in Charleston."

"I think prettier than Blondie is a stronger statement. Who on earth is John Hendrix?"

"Garden, you're so dense sometimes. You were talking to him. The lieutenant commander. With those killingly blue eyes. Don't tell me you didn't notice."

"I noticed he smeared up the Bateman. Come on, Paula. We'll get drenched."

Hurrying home through the first sprinkles of the rain shower, Garden tried to remember what the naval officer had looked like. She drew a blank. It made no difference. A lot of men had told her she was the most attractive woman in Charleston. Not as offensively as the first one, the would-be rapist, but with the same basic intention in mind. The newspapers had branded her promiscuous, and they seemed to think she'd jump at the chance to jump into bed,

She had learned that an icy stare worked just as well as hysterics. Now she used it before the man could make an overture, and she had no trouble.

John Hendrix came into the shop again at the end of January. Garden left her chair by the stove when the door opened. It was a dark, rainy day, and the brick building was cold. She hated to walk to the front.

She didn't recognize him until he said, "I've come to look at the Hester Bateman urn if it's still here."

Then she stared coldly. "It's on the shelf by your head," she said. He took off his gloves, then his hat. Gloves in hat, and hat tucked under arm, he rubbed his hands together.

"Mind if I use your stove? My hands are stiff from cold." He walked past Garden to the rear of the shop.

She minded very much. She minded the thoughts she believed he was having; she minded customers who wanted to look instead of buy; she minded having to polish the silver every time some casual passer-by handled it without appreciating what he was touching.

"That's better," said Commander Hendrix. "Could I just put my hat down here?" He dropped it on the floor by the desk without waiting for an answer.

He walked past Garden again and took the urn from the shelf. "It is pretty," he said. He turned it upside down and looked at the hallmark. "And it is Hester Bateman."

Garden was astounded.

John Hendrix grinned. "I looked her up. I don't know anything about silver, but you were so snippy about it, I figured it was worth learning."

And you came back to check on whether I was lying, thought Garden. "And now that you know, Commander, are you interested in buying the urn?" she said.

"Yes, I am. I'd like to send it to my sister. She's passionate about women's equality. Unfortunately, I can't afford it. I'll write and tell her about Hester, though. It'll add to her arsenal."

Garden was tempted to tell him about Peggy, but Hendrix didn't give her time. He thanked her for her help, replaced the urn, retrieved his hat and was gone before she knew what was happening. Garden shrugged and returned to her warm corner.

The following week Hendrix was back again. It was a typical

493

February day in Charleston, so warm that Garden had both doors propped open. "Hi, there," said Hendrix. "Just came to see Hester. How is she?"

"Still here," said Garden, "and no cheaper, if that's what you want to know." But she was laughing as she insulted him. Spring was too sweet for hostility.

"My sister couldn't believe I knew about a successful woman that she'd never heard of. I scored a gold star in her book."

"It was the same with my sister," said Garden.

They compared stories on sisters, agreed that John's Dorothy and Garden's Peggy were two of a kind. Then Hendrix patted the urn, said "So long, Hester" and left.

The next week he came in again. Garden was talking to a customer. Hendrix looked around the shop and went at once to a small porcelain bowl on the corner of one of the tables. He cupped his hands and held it in them, looking down at the deep blues and reds of the design. When the customer left, he brought it to Garden. "What is this, Mrs. Harris?"

"I don't know," she said. "It's an Imari pattern. That's all I can tell you."

"Well, look, I don't want to be a wiseacre, but I spent a good bit of time in Japan once, and this looks to me like a really old Arita piece, maybe even a Kakiemon. Don't you think so?"

"I don't know what you're talking about."

"You don't?"

"No. Not the foggiest."

"I'll be damned. You knew so much about silver, I just assumed that you knew all about porcelain as well."

Garden shook her head.

"I don't know enough to say for sure," said Hendrix. "The point is, this bowl might be worth a lot more than you've got it marked at. Why don't you get an expert to look at it?"

Garden shook her head again. "I don't know what to make of you, Commander. If I've missed a treasure, why don't you buy it and take advantage of my mistake?"

"I don't want to cheat you."

Garden laughed. "Then you have no business in an antique shop. That's the basis of most people's love for buying in shops like this. They think they're putting something over on the owner."

"What a cynic you are. Do you really believe that?"

"I didn't want to, but I've found it to be true too many times to doubt it."

"That's too bad . . . Well, I'll buy this, then. But I don't think you should let me do it."

Garden wrapped it for him. Very carefully, just in case it was as valuable as he said it was. While she was wrapping, he was talking to Hester.

"How's Peggy doing?" he asked Garden before he left.

"Fine, as far as I know. She doesn't write often. How's Dorothy?"

"Same as Peggy. Thanks for the bowl, Mrs. Harris."

"You're welcome." Garden wished he would stay and talk a little longer. Stop that, she told herself. She called George Benjamin to ask about Japanese porcelain, but he knew very little. "Did you get your markup?" he asked.

"Twice over. I'm pricing for the tourist season now."

"Then don't think about it anymore."

Garden followed his advice. With the tourist season approaching, she was able to buy more interesting and expensive pieces for the shop. And with spring bursting everywhere, she was eager to be out of doors. She persuaded Paula to come in on Wednesdays as well as Saturdays, and she took Helen out every Wednesday for treasure hunts in back-roads cabins. Soon their picnic lunches in the woods were eaten amid the tender white blossoms of wild dogwood and the intoxicating sweetness of jasmine's perfume. She told Helen stories about living on the plantation when she was a little girl and playing in woods just like these. And her heart broke for her little girl's solitary, confined playground in Elizabeth's backyard. If her own friendless existence bothered her, she pushed the thoughts away. She had her work, and Helen, and Elizabeth, and Jack Benny, Fred Allen, Amos and Andy, the Easy Aces and Walter Winchell. She bought another radio to keep in the shop. Then she had daytime companions in Ma Perkins, Helen Trent, and Don McNeill.

And she told herself it made no difference to her whatsoever that John Hendrix had not stopped in the shop for three weeks.

In April, in the busiest part of the tourist season, she got a postcard from him. It was an overly tinted view of Guantánamo Bay, with a message. "Wish Peggy were still here. Things are deadly dull. John Hendrix. P.S. Give Hester my love."

* * *

When the brief tourist season was over, Lowcountry Treasures was picked clean. Garden had even sold four of the tables that she used to display the things that were for sale. All she had left were the vastly overpriced prestige pieces—the Elfe chest and the Bateman urn—and her mistakes, things she should never have bought in the first place and would quite likely never sell. Garden made a sign for the door. CLOSED FOR VACATION.

"I've never seen such a pitiful sight in my life," she told Elizabeth gleefully. "It's like Mother Hubbard's cupboard. I'll have to clean out five or ten auctions before the shop will look decent again. Happy days are definitely here again."

Garden was not alone in her feelings. The new President, Franklin Delano Roosevelt, was inspiring confidence in millions of Americans by his fireside chats and avalanche of programs to fight the Depression.

Garden stretched, feeling her knotted shoulder and neck muscles crackle. "I feel as if six trucks had taken turns running over me. Aunt Elizabeth, I'm going to take a vacation for real."

"You've earned one. You've been working every day for over a year."

"Sixteen months. Lately I've been counting the days. The new stock can wait for a week or even two. It'll have to be the cheap stuff again, and that's so sad to buy when what I really like are the good things. I'll work up some enthusiasm while I'm on vacation. I think I'll rent a cottage at the beach. Helen always loved the beach at Antibes. Just wait till she sees a beach with sand instead of pebbles. She'll go wild. It's too early to swim, so I should be able to get one for a song."

"I don't think you'll want to take Helen. She got some mail today. An invitation to a birthday party."

Garden's outstretched arms dropped. "What? Oh, thank God." She felt like crying, like dancing, like falling on her knees. At last the cruel closed door was opening.

"It's a beginning, Garden, but no more," warned Elizabeth. "Everybody knows that Helen's almost four now. That's when girls and boys start having little parties and playing at each other's houses. She won't be left out. Charleston doesn't judge children. But probably things won't be any different for you. Not for a while."

Garden smiled, her eyes brilliant through happy tears. "It doesn't matter about me. I've got my work. Helen is the important one. When is the party? She'll have to have a new dress. And shoes.''

Elizabeth blinked her own tears away. When she spoke, her voice gave no indication of the pity she felt for her great-niece. "The Primrose Shop is having a big sale," she said. "Also, if you'd like to go to the beach, I have a house at Sullivan's Island. I turned it over to Catherine and her children years ago, but I can still let you use it. They won't need it until summer. Catherine is such a prisoner of routine; it's never occurred to her that she's no longer bound by the schedule of the school year now that her youngest child is practically thirty. I can't understand how I ever had such a half-witted daughter.''

Garden laughed. "Don't rush things, Aunt Elizabeth. Rebecca was in my class at school, remember? We've got almost three years to go before thirty gets us . . . I don't think I'll use your house, though I am grateful you suggested it.''

Elizabeth looked through wise old eyes. "Are you still having trouble with my grandson?"

"No, not trouble. Maine is really terribly nice. He comes in the shop once in a while, that's all. We don't really have very much to talk about, and it's awkward. If he came over to the beach, it might get sticky.''

"He always cared for you, Garden.''

"Hogwash. He had to watch out for me because Papa and Stuart were both dead.''

"So you say. But we both know different. You could do a lot worse than to marry Maine.''

Garden nearly lost her temper. "That's fine advice, coming from you. You never remarried. What makes you think that I can't make it on my own just as well as you did?''

"My goodness, you certainly do need a vacation," said Elizabeth with a chuckle. "You sound like a Tradd through and through.''

97

Garden rented a small cottage on Folly Beach. Folly was on an island west of Charleston, while the more popular Sullivan's Island and the Isle of Palms were east of the city. There was a pavilion on Folly and three restaurants, but she was far down the beach from them and from the crowds they attracted even in the off season.

She put away the groceries she had brought with her, hauled in the sack of coal for the kitchen stove and ice for the icebox, filled the oil lamps, unpacked the books she had been meaning to read, and uncorked the expensive bottle of burgundy she had gotten from a bootlegger with a reputation for importing his wine from France and not somebody's backyard.

While it was breathing, she walked across the wood plank causeway from the house to the top of the sand dunes. Below her was the wide deserted beach and the sparkling ocean. The tide had just turned from high and the waves were tall combers, white-foamed and awesome in their rolling, crashing attack on the sands. A strong breeze tugged at Garden's wide-brimmed hat and fluttered the long, full sleeves of her blouse. She turned her face up to the sun, licked the salt from her lips. "Bliss!" she shouted. She pulled off her hat and threw it up into the air. It planed down onto the beach and rolled like a hoop, sending a dozen sandpipers scattering.

"Come and see me get freckles," she cried and ran down the steps to the sand. It was late afternoon, but in ten minutes she felt the telltale tightness of sunburn across her cheeks and nose. Her skin had not been exposed for fifteen years.

She turned back from her walk then. She didn't want to spend her vacation week groaning and applying ointment to burns. She retraced her steps, putting her feet carefully in the indentations she had made in the sand. She felt like Robinson Crusoe, with the heartening difference of a stocked kitchen and a half-dozen novels. Near the cottage she retrieved her soggy hat from the edge of the water. She'd need it if she intended to go out in daytime.

She began the first novel after dinner. It was *Tobacco Road*, which had created such an outrage in the South that it was almost impossible to find a copy at the bookstore. After a few chapters, Garden understood why. She didn't want to be depressed, and she was long past the capacity to be shocked, so she put it to one side and started to read Lost Horizon. Before long, she was deep in the magic spell of Shangri-La.

When she first became conscious of the music in the distance, she dismissed it as her imagination, a natural accompaniment to the mystic beauties of the story she was reading. Then she realized the music was jazz. She put her book down and went out onto the dark porch to listen. It was very good jazz. Garden was surprised that the pavilion would have such a good musician and that the sound could carry so far.

The tide was low now, and the breakers only a gentle whispering like a brush on a drum behind the syncopated tune from the piano. Garden sat and listened for a long time. She felt that she was in a kind of Shangri-La, with the music and the waves and the limitless star-flecked heavens.

Garden used her vacation time well. Being alone, accountable to no one, with no schedule, was a hedonism she had never dreamed of. The brightening light woke her in the morning and she walked for miles on the hard sand near the water while the sun climbed from the ocean's horizon. She did not need her hat then, and she let her hair stream in the wind.

When she got back to the cottage, she felt cleansed and ravenously hungry. During the heat of the day she stayed on the porch, reading in the sagging hammock or simply remembering and thinking.

She thought a lot about Antibes. The contrasts between that beach and this one were so clearly defined. She missed the servants, she admitted to herself. She missed being rich. She missed the caftans that allowed her to go out in the sun and Connie, who had made them, and the dozens of closets full of clothes and drawers full of delicate, soft silken underthings. The slacks and blouses she had bought for her week at the beach were ordinary to look at and rough against her skin, and she could not forget the many pretty, flowered silk beach pajamas she had owned.

The Atlantic was harsher than the Mediterranean and gray-brown, not azure. The cottage was plain, the bed lumpy, the floors gritty with sand blown in by the wind. Her cooking was primitive at best, and on a coal stove it was not even reliable. She ate burned eggs, raw hamburgers and lots of peanut butter sandwiches.

And she was content. She wrote to Hélène Lemoine and reported that her life was satisfying. She did not take the time to tell much more. Hélène would already have heard about the normal happenings in her life. Elizabeth and Hélène corresponded regularly, Garden knew. Occasionally Elizabeth asked her the meaning of a word that was not in her French-English dictionary.

In the late afternoon Garden walked on the beach again, while the sun slowly faded to a finale of purple-streaked crimson. These were the hours Garden reserved for Sky, for saying goodbye to him. She no longer dissected their years together, wondering what she had done wrong and how she could have kept them together. She had tortured herself that way long enough. Now she tried to see her life and her marriage as if she were watching a play or reading a novel. What she saw was two people who wanted, who needed, opposite lives. Sky had to have novelty, change, excitement. And she longed to be the settled *bonne bourgeoise* that Hélène had recognized at once. No one was at fault, not Sky with his restlessness, not Garden with her attempts to put down roots and to hold him still.

He was gone. Dead. She wept for him, for the ultimate stillness of the grave, his wanderings halted for all time. And she let him go.

At night, the faint music lightened her grief and continued playing in her mind when she fell into deep, refreshing, salt-scented sleep.

When the week ended, she was lightly tanned, heavily freckled across the bridge of her nose, and ready to face the shop, the round of auctions and the wait until Charleston should welcome her home. Her roots were here, and Helen's were too. She had had enough wandering, enough excitement, enough desperate chasing after happiness to last five lifetimes.

"The beach was wonderful," she reported to Elizabeth when she got home. "I didn't see a living soul except an old beachcomber collecting driftwood. I made tracks in the sand just like Crusoe, and I even had a man Friday, although I never saw him. There was somebody else there out of season. He played great piano; it was like a private concert every night."

500

"Of course. I forgot he was going to be there. You had better concerts than you knew, Garden. That was George Gershwin."

"*The* George Gershwin?"

"How many can there be? He's turning DuBose Heyward's play into an opera."

"Your friend DuBose Heyward? From the Poetry Society? That I met here, who was so nice to Peggy? He wrote a play? You never tell me anything."

Elizabeth looked at Garden with a flat stare. "I sent you the book, Garden. DuBose wrote a book first, in 1925. Then Dorothy, his wife, made it into a play. It was on Broadway, a big hit. I'm surprised you didn't hear about it, even in Europe."

Garden couldn't tell her great-aunt that she had been in a cocaine delirium and a drying-out clinic at that time. "I missed it." she said.

"Well, in my opinion you didn't miss all that much. I'm tremendously fond of DuBose, and I admire his poetry. But his novels are all about colored people. This play *Porgy* is really about Goat Sammy, you know, the crippled beggar who pesters people on the corner by City Hall."

Garden remembered the small black man. He had no legs below the knee, she thought, and he sat in a low wheeled cart with a white goat harnessed to it. She had never walked on his side of Broad Street, because it made her feel sad to look at him and mean because she didn't have any money to put in his plate.

"He never pestered anybody, Aunt Elizabeth. And anyway, he's not there anymore. I pass that corner on my way to work every day, and I haven't seen him."

"He's probably got a limousine now that DuBose has made him famous. Imagine writing an opera about Sammy Smalls. Why not Francis Marion or John C. Calhoun? Besides, the goat pestered people. It tried to snatch a bag of cakes right out of my hand . . . What are you snickering about, Garden?"

"I was just remembering Vicki in her artistic period. She was forever inviting artists and writers and composers to visit her at the villa. She tried her damnedest to get to know Hemingway and Picasso and Scott Fitzgerald when they were in Antibes. But she had to settle for third-rate spongers. If she knew George Gershwin was in Charleston, she'd boot the poor monks right off the Barony."

"I wouldn't speak of the devil. He might hear you."

"It's been a year, Aunt Elizabeth. Almost. She'd have done something by now if there was anything to do. I think we're safe."

A week later, Lowcountry Treasures was full of auction plunder and ready to open again. The afternoon it opened, Garden regretted her airy dismissal of menace from Vicki. She cursed herself for a fool. "Yes, I'm Mrs. Garden Harris," she said to the heavy-set, dark-suited man who had just entered. He looked exactly like the men before, from the FBI.

"I'm a detective, Mrs. Harris. We've been looking for you for almost two years." He put his credentials on the table in front of him. Garden could not see his face; it was shadowed by the deep brim of his dark hat. What on earth was he talking about? Vicki knew where to find her. What could she have possibly done two years ago that she was in trouble for now?

"It's about this perfume."

"Perfume? What on earth are you talking about?"

"It couldn't be delivered, you see. Someplace in France. It's French perfume. So the company that makes it hired some outfit in France to find you, and they found out you'd left for the States, so the company hired us—"

"Lucien!" Garden cried.

"Ma'am?"

"An old friend of mine. He promised me I'd have perfume for the rest of my life. Oh, I'm afraid I'm going to cry. No, I'm not, I'm going to sing. In French. About a little white duck."

The detective backed uneasily toward the door. "Er, I have the package in the car," he said.

"I'll come out and get it. Hurry up. I've been waiting for this delivery for two years, after all."

An hour later, Garden looked up at the sound of the bell and saw John Hendrix. He was inhaling deeply. "Smells mighty nice in here," he said. "Did you get my postcard?"

98

"Garden. my dear." said George Benjamin. "why don't you do as I do and close your shop for the summer? There are no customers, only people who want to get indoors for some shade. On Chalmers Street, you don't even have them."

"I have you. George."

"I'm an old pest. I come to sit here in the shade of your fig tree like an Old Testament patriarch and drink your excellent iced tea. I believe I'll bring a clump of mint from my herb garden and plant it over there close to the gutter spout."

"That would be nice." Garden half-closed her eyes, listening to the leaves stirring in the wind and the bells of St. Michael's telling the hour. Four o'clock. Too late for him to come. She couldn't tell George Benjamin that she kept the shop open because John Hendrix came in once or twice a week. She had trouble admitting it to herself.

But it was true. It was because of Hendrix that she had bought the old icebox and got ten pounds of ice every day from the ice wagon. She had bid on the metal outdoor furniture because of him, too. The small courtyard was shadowy and inviting in the summer; now there was someplace to sit with a tall, cool drink. After a month of visits, John no longer pretended to be making sure that the Bateman urn was still there. He walked right in, removing his hat as he entered the door. If there was no one else in the shop, he took off his coat immediately, then breathed a sigh of relief and said hello. "Oasis," he called the courtyard.

The name caught on. "I spent most of the day in the oasis," Garden would say when Elizabeth asked her how business had been. "May I introduce a friend to the oasis?" Verity Emerson asked from time to time.

Garden's former English teacher had showed up quite by accident in June. She had no idea that Garden was back in Charleston. "I've been away for two years," she said. "My father died, and I went home to help my mother sort out the tangle of his affairs. I intended to stay, even started teaching in a school in Lowell. But I found I was homesick for Charleston. Miss McBee said she would be glad to have me back, and here I am."

It was a shock for Garden to realize that it was ten years since Miss Emerson had been her tutor and her heroine. So long, and in so many ways, so short. Somehow Ashley Hall and its orderly, disciplined routines seemed to be part of a past too distant for measurement in time.

Miss Emerson insisted that Garden call her Verity, a step that made Garden stammer at first. But then she realized that her idol was in fact human, and she was able to enjoy the friendship offered her.

Verity Emerson had rented a house on Queen Street, only a block away. About once a week she called to ask for an invitation to the oasis. She always brought little cakes or sandwiches to accompany the tea that Garden served. Occasionally she brought a friend, one of the writers or artists from the colony of talent that lived on Queen Street.

Almost every day Garden had one or more friends to talk to. And, despite George Benjamin's predictions, there were occasional customers. At home Helen chattered incessantly about the doings of all her friends. Belva now took her to the Battery every day to play on the cannon and bandstand and the prickly grass shaded by great live oaks. Helen was a little Charleston child. She called Garden "Mama" now instead of "Mummy" and begged for groundnut cakes and recognized all the street vendors' songs and ran out onto the sidewalk for a free sample whenever the strawberry woman passed by.

When summer was over, and Charlestonians came back from the mountains and the beaches, Garden was invited to rejoin the choir at St. Michael's. "How forgiving and Christian," she said sardonically to Elizabeth, but she was profoundly pleased to be asked. She loved to sing with other voices, she loved the regimen of learning the alto part and blending it with the others, she loved the majesty of the church service and the quiet peace it left in her heart. There were still some people, always women, who snubbed her, delicately looking elsewhere when Garden was around. But many more spoke to her now, casually, as if nothing had ever happened.

"I notice that my mail doesn't include any invitations to birthday parties," Garden said. "I guess I'm on probation." Her smile was wry. And relieved. She had almost begun to feel invisible.

The end of summer also meant that George Benjamin opened his shop again. And Verity Emerson went to work. "Now I can do something about those chairs in the oasis," said John. He was wearing a denim work shirt and pants and carrying a box from which he took a wire brush, paint, paintbrush and several bottles of beer.

"Just tell your customers that I'm the janitor, if they ask," he said with a grin. "The rust on that metal furniture has been driving me crazy all summer. In the Navy, rust is the enemy." He put his beer in the icebox, with a cheerful promise to replace it with something more interesting when the states finished ratifying repeal of Prohibition.

"At least President Roosevelt gave all you drunks beer as soon as he was elected," Garden pointed out.

"That's why we drunks voted for him," John agreed. "The man's a genius." He sat cross-legged on the cobbles and attacked the rust on a chair leg, whistling tunelessly through his teeth.

John Hendrix worked on the furniture throughout the long, mild Charleston autumn. He came in at least once a week, sometimes twice. When there were customers in the shop, he pulled an imaginary forelock and said, "Janitor, ma'am," to Garden as he walked to the back door. She controlled her laughter admirably, even when a young woman said to her companion, "That's odd. He looks just like my Jerry's commanding officer."

The shop was much busier than it had been in the summer, but things were still slow. It was a long time until the Christmas rush. When the shop was empty, Garden went into the courtyard. Her heart always gave a pleasing and frightening lurch when she opened the door and saw John there. He always looked up with a crooked smile that made her heart leap again. Paula was right, Garden had decided a long time ago, his eyes in his tanned face were "killingly blue." They were edged by intriguing deep crow's-feet that became pale lines against his dark skin when he was not squinting or smiling.

They talked comfortably while John worked. Garden told about the previous weekend's auction, what she had bought, what she had wanted but had not bought, what the other dealers had said about business in their stores.

John complained about being on shore duty, stuck at a desk, and told stories of the places he had been when he was on sea duty. He seemed to have been everywhere. His favorite places were Japan and the Mediterranean, he said.

Garden did not mention that she knew the Mediterranean from the shore in a different way from his view from the deck of a ship. By some unspoken agreement, they never talked about themselves. John's stories were all bits of history or descriptions of how a place looked. The only personal note came when he expressed his preferences. As for Garden, she had no acknowledged existence outside of her role as antique dealer. No child, no husband, living or dead, and no past.

The friendship between them was curiously tentative and guarded. Garden told herself that she liked it that way. It made no demands on either of them. It did not force her to think about what she might be feeling. It did not even give her any right to feel anything at all. When she talked to Paula King, she did not mention John's name. And she insisted to herself that she was glad Paula never referred to him either.

Just before Thanksgiving, John put the final coat of paint on the tabletops, and the furniture was done. "You'll be playing Santa's elf starting next week," John said, "but you have to promise me something anyhow."

"What is it? You want me to give you Hester as payment for your labors?"

"Almost. We'll have repeal any day now, and I've got a legal bottle of champagne all lined up. I'll bring it over at closing time the day repeal is announced, and we'll drink it out of Hester."

Garden agreed. Later, she realized that John Hendrix had asked her for their first date.

"Repeal" said the headline on December fifth. Garden was an hour late opening the shop. She went to Condon's Department Store and bought one of the silk dresses they had advertised in the same

506

paper. It was the first dress she had bought since she left Europe, and it cost $2.95.

"It's not Fortuny," she said to the mirror in the fitting room, "but it's new." She rolled up the Delphos dress she had been wearing and put it in her handbag. She had worn it, or one of the other Fortuny gowns, every day for over two years, and they were still as beautiful as ever. But John had seen all of them several times by now. Only the white tunic Delphos had not been shortened. Garden was saving it for the first evening party that she would be invited to. She was confident that it wouldn't be very long now. And she could wait. Life was satisfying.

"This is super," said Garden. She passed the urn to John. He took a swallow.

"Sure is," he said. "The silver polish adds a certain special something." He offered her the urn. Their fingers touched when she took it from him. Garden looked quickly at John's face to see if there was any reaction. "I'm going on leave tomorrow," he said. "I'll have a white Christmas with my family."

99

"Happy birthday, Mama. Can I have another piece of cake?"

"May I," Garden and Elizabeth said in chorus.

"May I have another piece of cake?" said Helen.

"No, you may not," said Garden. "You've had two already. And it's way past your bedtime. Santa Claus won't come if you don't go to sleep."

Helen weighed the certain pleasures of staying up against the tantalizing possibilities of Christmas presents. Her small forehead furrowed and her nose twitched. Then, her mind made up, she kissed Garden and Elizabeth good night and went upstairs to bed.

"Are you going to tuck me in?" The pitiful tiny voice floated down from the top of the stairs.

"I tucked you in. And I read you 'The Night Before Christmas.' And I gave you a glass of water. And I kissed you good night. Then you came down mooching for more cake. Now get into bed and go to sleep or you're going to get nothing but a bag of switches and lumps of coal from Santa Claus." Garden shook her head. "Are they all like this?" she asked Elizabeth.

"Or worse. I found Tradd on the roof when he was about eight. He planned to capture Santa Claus and take all the presents in the sleigh."

"What did you do?"

Elizabeth looked into the fire. After a few moments she said, "Do you know, I can't remember. That's the sad part of being a mother. When your children do or say something the least bit unusual, you're sure you will never forget it. And you almost always do."

Garden put some more coal on the fire. "What am I going to do about Mama, Aunt Elizabeth?"

Elizabeth snorted. "That's the sad part of being a daughter. You may get a mother like yours. Well, she said in her note that she wants to see you and Helen. And it's Christmas. I guess you'll have to go."

"It makes me nervous. She wants something, I know. Every time I got a letter from her after I was married, it was always about something she wanted. I just can't imagine what it could be."

"You'll find out tomorrow. Don't waste time worrying about it now . . . I don't hear any noise from upstairs. Shall we get the presents out?"

Garden hesitated, took a cigarette, lighted it, spoke with an unconvincing casualness.

"Aunt Elizabeth, were you in love with Harry Fitzpatrick?"

"Ah. I wondered when you would ask me about Harry. Yes, I was very much in love with him, what you young people today would call 'madly in love.' There is an element of madness."

"Then why didn't you marry him? Hélène Lemoine told me Harry wanted to marry you."

Elizabeth smiled. It was a very private smile. "Hélène wrote me that she was extremely envious. I believe her, and I understand. I am envious of her because she had a part of Harry that I did not have."

"But why didn't you marry him?"

"Garden, there are always more good reasons not to marry than there are to marry. One was age. Harry was seven years younger than I. I became a grandmother while I knew him. He claimed it made no difference, and he was right, for him. But it made a difference to me. He was so very attractive. There would always be women who wanted him."

Garden was crestfallen. She had never thought of Elizabeth as a coward.

"But the age worry was only an excuse," Elizabeth continued. "In reality, Harry had a rival, and the rival won."

Garden tried to imagine not one, but two suitors. She couldn't, but she did not doubt her great-aunt for a moment. "Who was he?" she asked.

"It wasn't a he, it was me. Me and Charleston together. I had lived through a lot, been frightened, won through. I was my own person. I didn't need to become Harry's wife, or anybody's wife, to be somebody. And I loved Charleston. I still do. I love every brick and cobblestone in it. I love the orderliness of it, the predictability, the dependability. I love knowing that I am part of a world that still values care for others. I love the beauty. In all my travels in Europe, I saw no place more beautiful than Charleston. I love the harbor and the ocean, the marshes and the sharp pine woods. I missed the pluff mud when I was away, and the trees all looked cold to me with no Spanish moss for shawls. Oh, I did the right thing. As much as I loved Harry, and I loved him very much, there has never been a day that I doubted that I did the right thing."

"But you let Tradd go. You sent him away. Charleston was his home, too."

"And it was too small for him. Tradd was confined in Charleston. He had imagination and curiosity, and he wanted to learn. If he hadn't gone away, all the things that are richnesses to me would have pulled him down. Charleston is too easy for some people. It keeps them from testing themselves, making their own way. I expected him to come back, and he was coming back when the ship went down. Charlestonians always come back. Like you, Garden. No place else is home."

Garden looked at her living room, with her furniture, the decorations for Christmas put up by her own hands with help from her little girl. Yes. she felt. I have come home.

"I'll go up and make sure Helen's asleep."

Garden walked quietly down the stairs. "Like a Christmas angel," she whispered. her face soft with love.

There was a muffled pop. Elizabeth proudly displayed a champagne cork wrapped in a napkin. "Now we can have an adult happy birthday," she said. "I've grown to despise cake in my old age."

Garden began to cry. "I . . . I . . . I'm . . . sorry . . ." she sobbed.

Elizabeth poured the wine. "Drink this," she said. "If it doesn't make things better. it will at least make them seem that way."

When Garden was calm. Elizabeth asked her if she wanted to talk about whatever was bothering her.

"It was the champagne." Garden said. "It reminded me of repeal and Hester." She told her great-aunt about buying her first new dress for her first date and the blow when John said he was leaving. "I've missed him so. Every time I go out in the courtyard to wrap packages, I half expect him to be there. But he isn't."

Elizabeth sipped her wine. her wise old eyes on Garden's tear-streaked face. "Do you love him?" she said.

"I must. I couldn't miss him so much if I didn't love him."

Elizabeth put her glass down with a clink. "Nonsense. I expect more sense from you than that, Garden. You've been cut off from the world. You're lonely. You're young and healthy and normal, and you want a man. This John is the only one around. That's not love, it's hunger."

"But it's not like that, Aunt Elizabeth, really. I like being with him, talking to him, watching him work. He's such a perfectionist, and he enjoys doing things so much. Besides, he doesn't treat me the way other men always have; he's not trying to get me into bed."

"Now you've really got me worried. He must be a deviate."

"He is not!"

"How do you know? What do you know about him?"

Garden had to admit that she didn't know anything at all.

"When is he coming back?" Elizabeth demanded.

"New Year's Day."

"Then as soon as you hear from him, you tell him that your old

Aunt Elizabeth wants to meet him. I didn't stop you from one disastrous marriage; I'm not going to stand by quietly this time."

"Aunt Elizabeth, there's no question of marriage. I'll be humiliated if you say anything to him."

"Hah! Garden, you are God's own imbecile. It's always a question of marriage, one way or another. And I won't say anything to him, but he certainly will say a lot to me. I'll see to that." Elizabeth stood up.

"I haven't had such a wholesome fit of rage in years," she said. "I feel twenty years younger. Now where are the presents?"

Garden brought the packages from their hiding place. "What in heaven's name is that?" Elizabeth said when Garden took a baby doll from its box. "It has a hole in its mouth."

"That's for the bottle, see? You fill it with water and the doll drinks it. Then it wets its diaper. It's called a Dy-Dee-Doll."

"How perfectly revolting," said Elizabeth.

"It's the latest thing. Helen's been begging for one. I had to practically knock down some poor lady who was reaching for it. I got the last one Kerrison's had left."

Elizabeth laughed. "You'll regret it before tomorrow's over, much less the weeks to come. What mischief will they think of next? Defecation and vomiting; then it will be just like a real baby."

"Aunt Elizabeth, you talk so awful. I want you to know you don't fool me one little bit." Garden kissed her great-aunt's lined cheek.

Elizabeth patted Garden's hand. "You could at least pretend that I do. It would give me such pleasure. Now, I'm giving Helen a Raggedy Ann. And the storybook. She'll love them. She can pull the hair out of the doll and the pages out of the book."

"Hello, Mama, Merry Christmas. Helen, this is your grandmother; say Merry Christmas to her."

Margaret wrapped Helen and Garden in a tearful hug. "I'm so happy to see you," she sobbed.

Garden extricated them. "Come on, Helen, let's go upstairs. Look how they go round and round, isn't that fun?" She hissed over her shoulder at Margaret, "You'll scare Helen to death carrying on like that, Mama. Stop it."

Margaret followed them, sniffing dolefully.

A big pile of boxes wrapped in bright red and green paper was on a sofa in the drawing room. "The red ones are for Helen," Margaret

511

said, "and the green ones for you, Garden. Helen, do you know your colors? Can you tell red? All those red boxes are yours. You may open them." Helen ran across the big room.

Margaret looked tearfully at Garden. "She's such a beautiful child, I hate myself for the way I've ignored her. Please forgive me, Garden. I know you don't want to see me. Why should you? But I wanted to have my last Christmas with my grandchild and my daughter. There won't be another one for me."

"I don't know what to think," Garden said to Elizabeth that evening. "Mama says she's had three heart attacks and the doctor says the next one will probably be the last. I don't know whether to believe her or not. I hate to be so mean, but there's something about Mama that brings out the worst in me.

"The house was freezing cold, you see. Grates full of ashes. Zanzie has finally given up. After all those years of waiting on Mama hand and foot and doing all the cooking and cleaning in that huge house, she's gone to live with her nephew and his family. I had to rummage in the kitchen and fix her something to eat. She doesn't even know how to open a can."

Elizabeth was intrigued. "Margaret invited you over so that you'd fix dinner? She must be desperate. You could scorch water if you boiled it."

"Aunt Elizabeth, it's not funny. She wants Helen and me to come live with her."

"What did you say?"

"I said no. I'd be crazy inside of two days. But I'll have to find her some help."

"And pay them. Margaret's a notorious miser. I'm amazed she gave you and Helen presents. What were they?"

"Things from the attic. But the wrapping paper was new." Garden started to giggle. "I don't know why I'm laughing," she said, "she's really pathetic." The giggles took her over. She was in a kind of shock. The scene at Margaret's door, when she was turned away, had rushed over her when she stood there again. The effort to control her emotions until she got back home had stretched her taut nerves to their limit. Now she could not stay calm. She could either cry or laugh. She giggled in painful paroxysms until Elizabeth held ammonia under her nose and brought her out of the seizure.

100

Garden couldn't think of any easy way to deliver John Hendrix to Elizabeth as ordered. She worried about it so much that when he appeared in the shop on January second, she blurted it out almost before he finished wishing her a happy New Year.

"I'm having tea with my great-aunt on Saturday, would you like to come?" she said all in one breath. Then she remembered to add the excuse she had dreamed up. "She has some lovely silver. Not Hester Bateman, but you might enjoy seeing it."

"I'd like that very much," John said.

Garden relaxed then. "How was your Christmas?"

"Very white. How was yours?"

"Very red and green. I'm about to have a cup of tea. Will you have one?"

"No thanks, Garden. I've got to get to the base. I'll save my tea thirst for Saturday. I just wanted to drop this off." It was a bottle of champagne. "I thought we could do like the Chinese and celebrate the New Year later than other people."

"I'd like that very much," Garden echoed. She gave him Elizabeth's address.

Elizabeth Cooper was very grand-dowager-behind-the-tea-tray when she received John Hendrix. Garden had never seen her act imposing before, and she wanted to kill her.

In no time at all, Elizabeth extracted from John the information that he was thirty-six years old, had graduated from Annapolis in 1923, was born on a farm in New Hampshire, had three sisters and two brothers, both parents still living, and had never been married.

Elizabeth was deft, but she did not waste time being devious. When she was finished with the inquisition, she smiled at him. "All your own teeth, too, I'll bet."

513

John roared with laughter. "And vaccinated against smallpox," he said. "I even eat Wheaties."

Elizabeth raised her eyebrows in a question.

"That's from a new radio show," Garden explained. "Right after the Lone Ranger. It's called 'Jack Armstrong, the All-American Boy.'"

Elizabeth laughed. Then she engaged John in an intense discussion of world politics that Garden could not follow. She had been too busy with the shop even to read *Time* magazine. She recognized the names Hitler and Mussolini, but Salazar, Dollfuss and Stavisky were all strange to her. It didn't matter. She could tell that Elizabeth and John were enjoying each other.

When they left Elizabeth's, John turned to the back instead of toward the street door. "May I see your house, too?" he said. "I've met one important member of your family; I'd like to meet Helen."

"How did you—"

"Paula King told me. Where you live, that you have a little girl, that you're a widow."

"But I'm not really. I'm divorced."

"Same thing. You're not married."

"What else did Paula tell you?"

"That was all I asked her. I'm not as thorough as your aunt. What a woman. I know how a fish must feel when it's been filleted."

"I'm sorry, John."

"Sorry? I'm not. She's wonderful. I think I'm in love with her. But I could sure use a drink. Are you going to invite me to your house or not?"

A fire was glowing red in the grate. A bowl of red camellias was on the low table in front of the sofa. "You do have a gift for oases, ma'am," John said quietly.

"Well?" said Garden to her great-aunt.

"Grab him," said Elizabeth. "He makes Maine look like a stick."

After that Saturday, Garden saw John Hendrix every Saturday. It became understood that Saturday was their time. He went auctioning with her and responded with dangerous enthusiasm. "Higher," he'd whisper to her, loudly enough to be heard a half block away, when the bidding was spirited. He examined every item for sale with such care that the auctioneer lost some of his creativity in describing things. After a month or so, he brought a magnifying glass for better examination. He had, he said, never had so much fun in all his days. After three months, he knew as much as Garden did. After six, she relied on his judgment whenever she was undecided.

They came home from the auctions to Garden's house for a drink and some time with Helen. John always found something to buy for her playhouse. Garden said he was spoiling her. John said so what; there were very few ladies he knew of who could be spoiled with a ten-cent gift. He always presented it with great ceremony just when Garden was coming downstairs after bathing and changing. Helen began urging them to go out and stop staying around the house. "That little girl will almost certainly grow up to be a brilliant politician," said John. "She's already greedy for bribes."

They went out for supper, usually spaghetti, and then to a movie, unless there was a dance at the officers' club at the base. The theaters changed their bills every week, and there were a lot of movies that they both wanted to see. Soon they decided that they might as well add a Sunday matinee to their schedule. And then it became obviously more sensible for John to have supper at Garden's than to bring her home, then go to the base. He revealed a hidden passion: he loved to cook. Garden concealed one: she hated kitchens.

That was her only deliberate concealment. But she never mentioned anything about her life. They had so much to talk about—the auctions, movies, Helen's spurt of growth, John's latest culinary creation, the antics of customers in the shop. There was really no point in Garden's complaining about the need to visit her mother every weekday at lunchtime or about Margaret's inability to keep a maid or about the drain on Garden's meager resources of money and limited resources of time and energy.

And John, unlike Elizabeth, had no questions about earlier days.

Garden had a question, though. It bothered her more and more. They went to Folly Beach on Labor Day; the weather was oppressively hot—thunderstorm weather, tension-building weather. When the ferris wheel stopped with their car at the top, Garden's fear of heights made her nervous to the point of recklessness. "John," she cried, her voice high and thin, "I've got to know why you never even kiss me good night. Is there something wrong with me? Or with you?"

For an answer, he put his arm around her and kissed her firmly. It was an entirely satisfactory answer to Garden's questions. There was nothing wrong with either of them.

The thunderstorm broke with a fusillade of lightning bolts into the ocean just after they got off the ferris wheel. John grabbed Garden's hand. "Quick, to the car," he shouted through the thunder. "The road will be jammed in five minutes." They were among the first to reach the causeway through the marshes that led toward town.

The heavy rain on the roof was deafening. They could not talk, so they sang "Stormy Weather" all the way home.

John parked the car in front of Elizabeth's house. The rain had slackened, but it was still steady. "This can't keep up too much longer," John said. "Let's have a cigarette and wait for it to ease up before we run in."

Garden put her head on his shoulder and tilted her face up. "Let's play ferris wheel."

John touched her lips with the tip of his finger. "No, Garden, let's not. We're not high school kids. Necking is not for us. If I kiss you, I won't settle for that. I'll want to make love to you. And I don't think that's what you want. You're too fine."

It was what Garden wanted with her entire passionate nature. But she said, "You're right, John," and sat up on her side of the car. She would not, for all the world, tarnish his belief in her.

A month later, that was precisely what she felt she had to do. Garden called John at his office, something she had never done before. "I must talk to you about something," she said. "Can you come to Aunt Elizabeth's this evening?"

"Of course. I can leave right now if you want me to." The metallic edge to Garden's voice was alarming.

"I would be grateful." A click told John that Garden had hung up. He broke all speed limits getting to town.

She was in the library with Elizabeth. When John came in, Elizabeth left. She pressed his hand as she passed him. Her elegant thin face looked like a death's-head. Garden looked as if she were carved from marble. Her eyes stared straight ahead, ringed by bruiselike shadows. They were the only color in her drawn face. John went to Garden, but she held up a hand and stopped him. "Don't," she said. "Sit over there at the desk. Read those clippings."

They were from New York papers, dated October first through

fourteenth. "Trial of the century . . . Boudoir secrets bared . . . Maid tells of Gloria's gay parties . . . Lurid stories . . . Must a woman be 'good' to be a good mother?" read the headlines.

John scanned the articles. "I don't understand," he said. "These stories are about Gloria Vanderbilt. What do you have them for, Garden?"

Garden laughed harshly. "They were a gift. Sent to me from New York. I've been reading about the Hauptmann trial. The Lindbergh kidnapping, you know. I don't know whether the Charleston paper even mentioned this Vanderbilt trial.

"But it will have to mention mine. This is just a preview. I know it. I know who sent those clippings. You see, the Vanderbilt child is being taken from her mother by an aunt who has lots of money. The mother is poor, and she has a bad reputation. That's what's going to happen to Helen. Only it's her grandmother, not an aunt. And my reputation is already in the newspapers' files. They're going to have a wonderful time.

"I have to tell you about myself, John. I'm not what you think I am . . ."

"Garden." He got up and walked toward her.

"No, stop. Let me talk. I've got to tell you. I don't want you to hear it from some reporter. Or read it, with pictures. I owe you the truth."

"Shut up, Garden." John put his hands under her elbows and raised her from the chair.

"No!" Garden tried to free herself, but he put one arm around her waist and held her close. His hand cupped the back of her head and pressed it to his shoulder.

"Listen to me," John said, close to Garden's ear. "There is nothing to tell. I know about the divorce, what the testimony was, what the papers said. And it doesn't matter. You must understand that, Garden. What was true, what was a lie, none of it matters. I'm here. I'm with you. We'll fight your mother-in-law together. She won't win. We won't let her. Hold on to me, Garden. I'll be your wall. They won't get past me to hurt you."

Garden's arms closed around him. "Oh, John," she said. "I'm so sorry for what I did."

"That was a long time ago," he soothed. "It doesn't matter anymore."

"I'm so afraid."

"Hush, now. There's nothing to be afraid of."

"Hold me."

"Yes, yes. I've got you."

"I'm so frightened, John."

"You don't have to be frightened anymore."

Garden's head grew heavy on his shoulder, and her arms slipped down to hang limply by her sides. She had fainted. John carried her to a sofa and laid her down on its cushions. Then he went to find Elizabeth.

"How bad is it?" he asked.

"As bad as anything could possibly be. The grandmother is powerful and ruthless and perhaps insane."

"What's going to happen? What can we do?"

Elizabeth touched John's arm. "All we can do is reassure Garden. She mustn't lose this war of nerves. I don't know what's going to happen. It all depends, I suppose, on what the New York courts do. It's unbelievable that they would take the Vanderbilt child away from her mother, establish a precedent like that. A mother's rights are sacred."

On November 11, the judge in *The Matter of Vanderbilt* ruled against the mother.

101

There were no policemen, no snap-brimmed agents this time. Simply an unimpressive sheet of ordinary paper delivered by a shabby out-of-work schoolteacher happy to earn the three-dollar fee for serving a subpoena.

The shop was crowded with women customers when he came in four days before Christmas, and he was as conspicuous as if he were wearing a neon suit. Garden walked over to him. "I think you're looking for me," she said. "The timing is about what I expected." She was very calm.

She had been very calm from the moment the decision was handed down in the Vanderbilt case. It was as if she had removed herself from life. She continued to work, to play with Helen, to talk, smile, even laugh. But she was at a distance.

"You worry me," Elizabeth told her.

"I'm sorry," Garden said. "I wish you could stop worrying. I'm not really upset anymore. I was foolish to get upset when I got the clippings. I always knew that Vicki would never give up. It doesn't hurt me as much as you think, Aunt Elizabeth. I told you before; I'd learned not to trust happiness."

The subpoena commanded her to "deliver" herself at 9 A.M. on the morning of January 12, 1935, before Judge Gilbert Travers in Room 237 of the County Court House. The handsome old building was at the intersection of Broad and Meeting Streets, diagonally opposite St. Michael's Church. Garden counted the strokes of the steeple's bell while she waited in her place in the courtroom.

Logan Henry had insisted that she be costumed properly, so Elizabeth took Garden shopping. "Your silk uniforms are wonderfully attractive, my dear, and that won't do. Even a middle-aged judge would recognize that there was something special about those pleats and colors. You must be very American." Garden was wearing a gray wool dress. The hem of its pleated skirt was only nine inches above the ground. It had a wide white linen pilgrim collar and white cuffs and small black buttons from the neckline to the hem. Her hat was a simple black felt pillbox. Her gloves were white.

Drat, thought Elizabeth when she met Garden that morning. She's still dazzling; no matter how hard I try, there's no toning down the effect of her hair and eyes. Elizabeth was sitting on one side of Garden at a table facing the judge's bench. Logan Henry was on her other side.

Five lawyers sat with Vicki at a similar table parallel to Garden's. Vicki was dressed in gray also, a bias-cut wool jersey dress that emphasized the youthfulness of her body, with a coat of gray chinchilla. She wore nothing that Elizabeth would call a hat. A lozenge of gray velvet was perched on her blond hair, low on the forehead. It was decorated with long gray-and-white speckled feathers that stuck out behind Vicki's head, above the gray velvet band that circled her crown and held the hat in place. She was also wearing a small smile.

As St. Michael's finished counting the hour, bailiffs opened the

519

double doors to admit witnesses and spectators. Elizabeth thought they sounded like a stampeding herd of wild marsh cattle. She did not turn to look. Nor did Garden, in spite of the shouts from photographers, "This way, Garden . . . come on, Cinderella, give us a million-dollar smile . . ." Logan Henry had brought them into the court by a back way, but there was no longer any way to escape the attentions of the press. They needed new pictures. The ones they had on file had been used up in the pretrial rehashings of the divorce revelations.

"All rise."

Judge Travers entered and seated himself in his tall-backed black leather chair. He looked dyspeptic. He glared at the crowded room from under thick, beetling brows heavily salted with white. His head was bald except for a neat fringe of the same brown and white. "We are here today to listen to testimony about an extremely grave matter: the well-being of a five-year-old child. I will tolerate no interruption, no disturbance, no levity. The bailiffs stand ready to eject any party or parties that do not maintain the decorum appropriate to these proceedings."

He tapped his gavel. "Let us begin."

As if on cue, a flurry of noise broke out in the rear of the courtroom. Judge Travers tapped harder. The noise, a muted rumble of voices, continued. He banged the gavel on its rest, and after a final screech of chair legs on the floor the noise stopped.

"Mr. Selfridge, are you ready?" said the judge. One of Vicki's attorneys rose and bowed.

"Ready, Your Honor."

"Then, if you please . . ."

"Thank you, Your Honor. If Your Honor please, we have here an opportunity to right a most grievous wrong. A wrong done to an innocent child, whose very innocence—the very essence of childhood—is in danger of corruption by the blatant immorality of the very person who should be most concerned with the preservation and protection . . ."

Garden concentrated on the drill of memory that was going on inside her head. She silently recited to herself the long poem she had learned for the declamation exercises her first year at Ashley Hall. She created a screen against the words of the prosecuting attorney, a screen against her surroundings, a screen against what was happening.

If she could just not listen, not look, then she would be able to sit here undisturbed while her life fell into jagged pieces around her.

"That's a damned lie!" came a shout from the rear of the room. Everyone except Garden turned to look.

Judge Travers gaveled for order.

"And you're a damned liar, whoever you are!"

The judge pounded his desk. "Remove that woman," he shouted. There was a scuffle, and then the doors slammed closed. The woman's voice could be heard receding down the hall. Elizabeth leaned across Mr. Henry and shook Garden's arm. She was laughing. "Garden. Garden, pay attention. Garden, Peggy's here."

"Peggy?"

"We'll see her at the dinner recess. She hasn't changed a bit."

Garden's discipline broke for a moment. The thought of seeing her sister was a ray of pure, shining happiness. Then the clouds of reality extinguished it. Peggy would be besieged by reporters too, humiliated, shamed by her sister. Two times two is four, Garden thought desperately, two times three is six, two times four is eight, two times five is . . .

The parade of prosecution witnesses began. Chauffeurs, bartenders, hairdressers, footmen, maids from New York, all testifying to scenes of debauchery they had witnessed. "Old Selfridge is like a chef," a reporter from the New York *Mirror* said to his neighbor, "he's just whetting the appetite with hors d'oeuvres." Garden concentrated on the bubbling and clanking of the radiator under the window. It had a certain regular pattern, a rhythm. She tried to fit songs that she knew to it. A black shouting song almost fit. She touched the outline of Pansy's charm that she was wearing under her dress.

Garden did not see Peggy during the recess for dinner. Logan Henry had arranged for Robertson's Cafeteria to send trays for them to a room in the courthouse. The reporters would be cheated of two appearances that way.

Garden ate methodically, nodding when Mr. Henry spoke to her, thinking of the song Lucien had taught her. What came after *"O, fils du roi, tu es méchant"*? It was good to have to remember something that did not hurt.

In the afternoon, the prosecution introduced more servants, this time from the house in Southampton.

"Mr. Selfridge," said Judge Travers, "how many houses does your client own?"

"Seven, Your Honor."

"And are we going to have the pleasure of meeting every servant from every one of them?" A titter ran through the audience. Vicki's train had brought a dozen of her friends as well as the witnesses who would testify. She had taken four floors at the new Fort Sumter Hotel on the Battery.

"I submitted a list of witnesses, Your Honor," said Manning Selfridge, Esquire. He assumed the position that photographers most liked to capture on film.

"Mr. Selfridge," said Judge Travers wearily, "I am only one man, not a jury. You can fill my head with the testimony you want on record in one twelfth the time necessary in a jury trial. Do I make myself clear?"

"Eminently, Your Honor."

"Excellent. We will adjourn until nine o'clock tomorrow morning. At that time, I will expect to find on my desk a revised list of your witnesses."

"It will be there, Your Honor."

"Fine." Judge Travers tapped the gavel, rising as he did so. "This court is adjourned." The people in the courtroom struggled to get to their feet before he was through the door behind the bench.

Peggy was sitting on the floor in Garden's living room with a baby in her lap; Helen and two little redheaded boys sat near her, entranced by the story she was telling.

"So the huge, horrible policemen grabbed Susan B. Anthony and dragged her away. They were waving great big sticks at her. 'I'll bust your head in,' said the ugliest one. 'I'll spill out your brains. But I'll never, never, never, ever let you vote.'"

"Oh, Peggy," Garden cried, "I'm so glad to see you."

Peggy stood up, dumping the baby onto the floor, and waded through the children to Garden. They hugged each other closely, saying nothing.

"Story! Story!" chanted the little boys.

Peggy kissed Garden's cheek and let her go. "The boys love that story," she said. There was a tremor in her voice. "Bob says it's because they see themselves with truncheons going after the baby. It was so nice of him to let me name her Susan, and he's determined never to let me forget it."

"Is Bob here? Where are you going? Why didn't you write?"

"Bob's over at the Winter Palace, i.e., Mama's house. And we're on our way to Alabama. And I didn't write because the orders were very rush-rush. Bob's going to be with the TVA. That's Tennessee Valley Authority, dummy. Dams, power plants, roads, bridges, moving riverbeds. It's the biggest thing since the Romans decided to build roads. And President Roosevelt wants everything done by yesterday. Bob's so excited he can't see straight. He and Mama are a pair, Garden. He's talking about hydroelectric stuff and she's talking about how expensive her light bill is, and they think they're having a conversation. I had to leave. I was laughing too hard.

"And freezing. After Iceland, too. But she's got one little lump of coal on the fire in a room the size of our whole house on the base. How long has she been such a skinflint? Did she get wiped out in the Crash?"

"Aunt Elizabeth says Mama loved having money so much when she finally got some that she couldn't stand to let go of any. But Aunt Elizabeth doesn't like Mama at all, so I don't know if there's any truth to it. Sky gave her a lot, I do know that. Let's hope she held on to it."

"No, let's hope she lets go of some of it. She has four lovely grandchildren to spend it on."

"I can hardly believe I've never seen your children before. Just look, Peggy. The boys are real Tradds."

"With the temper to prove it. Brutes. Come on. They're dying to meet you. They think you're still rich."

"Peggy! You're terrible."

With the children to talk to and talk about and feed and separate when they fought, Garden was able to keep her mind off her dread of the next day. Peggy referred to the trial only once. "Sticks and stones and all that stuff, you know, Garden. Everything'll be all right, it has to be."

"Sure." Garden lied.

102

The next morning the reporters got what they had come for. Logan Henry was like a jack-in-the-box shouting objections, and Judge Travers ordered the courtroom cleared of spectators midway through the testimony of the first witness, a saxophone player who claimed to have been one of Garden's lovers in Monte Carlo. The other band members had also been her lovers he testified, with graphic detail. The reporters nearly knocked each other down rushing for telephones. They didn't even mind missing the eight self-confessed lovers who testified later.

Garden conjugated irregular verbs and listed the kings of France and their wives and children in her head. Elizabeth was a pale totem.

After the dinner recess, Garden began on the kings of England. She was tangled in the Wars of the Roses when she felt something had changed.

For the first time, she looked up from her gloved hands. Miss Louisa Beaufain was swearing to tell nothing but the truth so help her, God. Miss Louisa was one of the great ladies of Charleston, admired and revered for her rectitude and her dedication to the city's proud traditions. ". . . in your own words, Miss Louisa," said Logan Henry. She turned in the witness chair and looked at Judge Travers.

"Garden Tradd Harris," said Miss Louisa, "is a young woman whom I respect from the bottom of my heart. She is a valuable member of this community; she is a responsible and serious person; she is a devoted and attentive mother. Whatever anyone might claim to be faults on her part, I have no reason to put any credence in the claims. I have always found her to be a young lady of irreproachable ethics and behavior."

Garden leaned close to Logan Henry. "I only met Miss Louisa once in my whole life," she whispered.

"Hush up," said Elizabeth.

"Thank you, Miss Louisa," said Mr. Henry. "Do you care to cross-examine, Mr. Selfridge?"

Mr. Selfridge did not. Logan Henry walked to the witness stand and offered Miss Louisa his arm. Judge Travers stood as she returned to her seat, escorted by Mr. Henry.

Vicki jabbed Selfridge with a manicured finger. "You'd better get on the ball. I warned you about this place."

Mr. Selfridge cross-examined all succeeding defense witnesses, but he was wasting his time, and the time of everyone in the courtroom. The spectators and reporters were allowed back in, and soon the reporters were scribbling new leads for the story of the trial: "Choir director of historic St. Michael's church says Garden an angel. All choir members agree . . . Civil War veteran recalls Garden as a child . . . U.S. Senator comes home to testify for embattled mother . . . kindergarten head rates Garden 'perfect mother' . . ."

The testimony continued for two more days while the throng of reporters grew. Walter Winchell broadcast the highlights of the testimony every day.

"I don't understand," said Garden to her great-aunt, "but I'm so grateful I wish I could kiss every single person there."

"You're a Charlestonian, Garden," Elizabeth said, "and Charleston always takes care of its own. You can write thank-you notes when the trial is over. As a matter of fact, it will be expected of you."

Vicki did not come to the final day of the trial. The judge's decision was not something she wanted to hear. An enterprising Charleston boy waited in the train station for a day and a night and was rewarded by getting a picture of her with his Brownie box camera. "Did you visit your granddaughter, Princess?" he shouted as Vicki boarded her private car. Vicki turned toward him, her face a garish, grotesque mask of cosmetics in the harsh morning light. He sold the photograph to *Newsweek* magazine where it appeared with a story headlined THE SOUTH WILL RISE AGAIN.

"Charleston, South Carolina," the story said, "is an old city known as the site of Fort Sumter, where the Civil War began, and as the home of an aristocracy for whom it has never ended. So exclusive is Charleston society that no one who does not belong to it even knows the names of those who do. But this week, this fabled group sacrificed its cherished privacy to defend one of its children against the attacks of one of New York's most prestigious law firms, acting for the fabulously wealthy Principessa Montecatini, a member in good standing of another exclusive group, New York's Café Society. The South won this war . . ."

Paula King was reading *Newsweek* when Garden came into Lowcountry Treasures. She dropped it on the desk and rushed to hug Garden. "Boy, am I glad to see you," she said. "The place has been jammed every day. There wasn't all that much left after Christmas anyhow, and what there was is gone. I was going to bring in my wedding china that I hate so much and sell it piece by piece . . . Listen to me, I'm babbling like an idiot. Gosh, Garden, I'm awful happy for you, I really am. I couldn't figure why your lawyer turned me down when I offered to be a character witness, but now I know. He had more than the room would hold.

"Say, what are you doing in here today? You were supposed to take a whole week to rest up."

Garden looked around the shop, smiling. "It looks wonderful to me," she said. "All that space just begging for me to go buy things and fill it up. And you look wonderful, too. Mr. Henry told me you had called him. I can't express how much I appreciate it, Paula."

"Don't be silly. What are friends for? Now I want you to go get some rest. You must be wrung out. Come back on Monday."

"But you've been working six days a week."

"I love it. Really. Mike's away on a cruise, and I don't have anything to do with my time."

Garden hugged her friend again. "What luck. I've got so much to do I hardly know where to begin. Let's work out a new schedule."

Garden had written letters to all the people who came forward to help her, but even before she put them in the mail her desk was piled with notes and invitations that had to be answered. Charleston was welcoming her home. All the way home.

She asked Elizabeth for advice. "The truth is," Garden said, "I don't know all those rules you talked to me about. Should I accept everything? Nothing? Only big parties or only small parties or what? I had no idea there was so much going on all the time."

"First rule," Elizabeth said, "party all you like until Ash Wednesday. Then only quiet times with close friends during Lent. Theoretically, without any alcohol at all. That justifies the big

526

cocktail party that the Yacht Club always has on Easter Sunday after church.

"A lot of these invitations are probably for the pre-Lent rush. Let's see. Um-huh, right, yes. See, Garden, people always arrange parties at busy times of the year so that you don't have to say no to one in order to accept another. There are three cocktail parties and a supper party on the second. What you do is stop in at each cocktail party for a half an hour and a half a drink. Then you go to the supper party. Before you sit down to eat, everybody will be there, including all three couples who gave the cocktail parties."

"But why not have just one party in the first place?"

"Because people like to give parties. And go to them. Young people, that is. When I was your age, I loved getting all dressed up and going out. Now I let people come to me. It's one of the privileges of age. Charleston is a wonderful place to be old in. We cherish our monuments, including the living ones; and we very nearly worship our eccentrics. I sometimes feel that I'm letting everyone down because I don't ride a bicycle or shoot pigeons from the attic window."

"The way you drive should be enough."

Elizabeth smiled proudly. "Yes, I am a good driver. Everybody recognizes that old car three blocks away and pulls over to the curb to let me have the street. I consider it very mannerly of them."

"Aunt Elizabeth, I love you very much."

"Well of course you do, Garden. I'm a lovable old humbug." She went through Garden's mail, sorting it in piles, making notes on a calendar. Then she explained basic principles.

Older ladies usually confined their social activities to a regular "at home" day every week or two weeks. People invited to call on these days were on their "visiting list." They might be old or young, male or female.

Younger ladies also had visiting lists, but in their case the list meant that these were people, including the old ladies who were "at home," upon whom the younger lady could call.

Both old and young had other lists, the big-party list and the small-party list. Small parties were for close friends.

"You will build up your lists in no time, Garden. Start right away putting in the names of everyone who wrote inviting you to call. That's the start of your visiting list. Your party lists will evolve as you find out which groups you like and don't like. By now your

527

debutante and school group will have split into other groups. They are all on each other's big-party lists, but not necessarily the small-party one."

"My head is reeling." Garden groaned.

"It's really very simple. You'll get used to it in no time. Now, about these invitations for bridge and to join clubs and serve on committees; I suggest that you telephone, not write. It's more personal. I also suggest that you say you can't accept right now, that you are very busy at work, but that you'll be in touch again soon. Don't lock yourself in with any organization or club until you've gotten to know the people. You might not like them."

"And they might not like me."

"True."

"You weren't supposed to agree, Aunt Elizabeth."

"Have to keep you on your toes. You'll need fancy footwork to be a social butterfly. Or fancy wingwork. Ah, never mind . . . Now, one thing you really do need is an escort. An attractive, unattached woman is a nightmare at parties. The wrong man might try to attach her, like the hostess's husband. Do you want John Hendrix to take you to these parties? The hostess will be delighted if you bring an extra man."

"I'll have to think about it. I've got to think about a lot of things. Everything's so different, now that I don't have to worry about Vicki anymore."

"Her lawyer did say he was going to appeal."

"He had to say that. Mr. Henry had made a fool of him. Even if he does, I can't see how an appeals court could reverse the decision. All the character witnesses for me were such substantial people."

"The bishop didn't come. I'm very cross with him."

"The bishop doesn't know me, Aunt Elizabeth."

"What difference does that make? I could have told him whatever he needed to know."

"Sometimes, Aunt Elizabeth, you really are an old humbug. I think you work at it."

"I amuse myself. Now go ye and do likewise. I'm going to have a rest. And take all your mail. And answer it."

"Yes, ma'am."

And think, said Garden to herself. About the changes in her life. And especially about John.

103

Garden had kept John at a distance after the envelope of clippings arrived. She didn't want him tarred with the scandal she believed was coming. Paula King had told her enough about the Navy for her to understand what damage a scandal could do to John's career. And John had told her enough about himself so that she knew that the Navy was his life and always would be.

"I joined up in the World War, because I wanted to fight for my country," he said. "I figured I'd go back to New Hampshire when it was over and farm rocks, just the way my family had always done. It's a good, hard life, and I would have been perfectly happy if I'd never left. But the sea got to me. The sea and the Navy. Once I'd had a taste of it, anything else was like food without salt. When the war was over, I got an appointment to the Naval Academy, and here I am. An officer and a gentleman by order of Congress, and a swabby in my blood."

John had accepted her statement that she had no time for auctions and movies and spaghetti suppers because of the Christmas rush at the shop. He'd had no alternative but to accept it. And then in December he was called to Newport for a two-month program that he did not describe to Garden. She was irrationally upset that he was not nearby when the trial started. I wouldn't have seen him, she told herself, or even talked to him on the telephone. I wouldn't have gotten him involved at all. But he could have been there, just the same.

Now it was the middle of February, and he was back. He was coming to see her. Garden told herself that she didn't care whether she ever saw him again or not. While she arranged flowers in a bowl on the table the way she knew he admired, put his favorite cheddar cheese out with the crackers that John liked so much, sped upstairs to freshen her makeup and add another spray of perfume.

"Anybody home?"

Garden ran downstairs, and into John's arms.

The evening was like dozens they had had before; John made dinner, a chicken curry that was one of his specialties, then they went to see the newest Marx Brothers movie and John did a Groucho walk from the theater to the car, and then they came back to Garden's and lit the fire and talked.

But this evening, everything was different. They talked about themselves. Garden had no need for reticence, no secrets to hide anymore. John knew the worst about her past now, worse than the worst, if he believed the newspapers.

He had always known, he told her. "That first day I met you, I went directly to the library. I looked up Hester Bateman, and the librarian told me where to find the newspaper files about your wedding and your divorce. I thought all the same goblin thoughts, Garden. Like any other swine of a man when his pants suddenly get tight. I hung around looking for a good time to make a move.

"While I was hanging around, I got to know you a little. Then I realized that you weren't what I thought, what I expected. You were a lot more. Brave and sweet and—all of a sudden—very important to me. I guess it was the freckles that did it. When you quit being so damned perfect, so beautiful it kept you from being real. Then I could fall in love with you."

"And it doesn't make any difference to you, John? About all those things I did, about the bad times?"

"Sure it makes a difference. I'm not going to lie to you, Garden. It makes a difference that you were married, that you loved your husband. It makes a difference that I've known women before you and loved a couple of them. But I honestly believe that it's the same kind of difference for both of us. When a man has sexual experiences, he's called hot-blooded, and it's praise. When a woman does the same thing, she's called promiscuous. That's all wrong."

Garden tried to laugh. "You can sure tell that you've got a women's rights sister," she said. "I guess I'm Victorian. I believe in the double standard. I'll always be ashamed."

"It will fade. What counts is that it's past, over with. I'm not going to tell you about other women, and I'm not going to ask about other men. The only thing that matters is where we go together, starting now. I love you, Garden, and I want you to marry me. Will you? I'll be a good father to Helen. You know I'm crazy about her.''

Garden looked lovingly at his face, so familiar and so dear to her. She touched the white wrinkles from his eyes to his temples and the bump on the bridge of his nose where it had been broken. "I love you, John," she said, "but I can't marry you. Not yet. Not now. A wonderful Frenchwoman I know told me once that being married is the hardest thing in the world, if you do it right. And I'd want to do it right. I guess I'm sort of scared.

"I was twenty-nine in December, and sometimes I feel like I'm only starting to grow up. Will you let me do some more growing, John? Will you be patient, give me some time?"

He ran a finger across the spray of freckles on her upturned face. "Haven't I been? Aren't I the most patient man you ever heard of? I can wait a little longer. How about a new proposal? Will you be my girl?"

Garden sighed and rubbed her head against his shoulder. "I already am," she said.

That spring was a time of exploration and discovery for Garden. She explored and discovered Charleston in its myriad aspects. As she had done in Europe, she walked and she looked. Elizabeth was right, she soon learned. There was no city more beautiful. Time had been gentle with Charleston, fading its pastel pink and blue and yellow and green and sand-colored stucco houses to pale tender tints that refreshed the eye and the soul. In contrast to the delicacy of man's work, nature was bold and excitingly lavish with bright color and stirring scent. Wisteria and jasmine overwhelmed the senses; the translucent fragility of azalea petals belied their gaudy pink and purple shades. The special dark green grass that bore the city's name gave its own perfume to the air after mowing, and the gardenias that bore Garden's name stopped the breath with their sweetness.

Everywhere patterns caught her eye. The herringbone of old brick sidewalks, the geometry of curved tiles in straight overlapping lines on steep-pitched roofs, the little triangular shadows that slept between rounded cobblestones, the swirling precision of the wrought iron in gates, fences, balconies and the rigid grids that covered the storm sewers.

She looked and she saw and she marveled at so much beauty so freely spread in an ever-changing feast for the eye.

And ear. The cries of the vendors, the song of the mockingbirds, the intoxicated hum of bees with a surfeit of nectar, the liquid syllables of the flower women's conversation, the whispering kiss of the harbor's waters against the seawall, and the eternal melody of St. Michael's old bells reminding the old city of its years and its tenacity. Twice had the bells been silent; they were captured by the British when the United States was being born and again by Sherman when the country was split asunder in the Civil War. Broken and scattered by the city's foes, the bells had been reclaimed each time, repaired, recast, rehung. Earthquake and cyclones had swung them in wild dissonance, but they endured. As Charleston endured. And their powerful, sweet sound floated out from the tall white steeple day and night, a grace note of background beauty and serenity to the orderly pattern of lives measured by its strokes exactly as the lives of generations before and generations yet to come.

Nothing changes, thought Garden when she saw the gawky thirteen-year-old girls and boys climbing the steps of South Carolina Hall to Friday-night dancing school.

Nothing changes, she thought, looking up at the magic of Ashley Hall's flying staircase when she went to register Helen for first grade the following fall.

"Nothing changes," she said happily to the boy behind the soda fountain at Schwettmann's when she took Helen in for an ice-cream sundae.

Nothing changes, she thought, except me. She was at the Yacht Club Easter party. The men were all gathered around the bar talking about hunting and fishing; the women were in clusters around the rest of the big room. It was exactly the same as the party that had bored Garden so about ten years before. But now she was part of it, and she was not bored at all.

She was talking with Milly Andrews about what would be the best size for the tables in the children's room at the new public library. Milly was on the committee that had to make the decision, and she wanted to know what the mothers of young children thought.

Patricia Mason passed by; Milly caught her arm to ask her opinion. Garden urged Patricia to agree with her and not Milly. Both Garden and Milly knew, as did everyone else, that Patricia's father had just learned that he was dying of cancer. If she wanted to talk about it,

532

they were there to listen. If she didn't, they were there to remind her that she had friends who cared and who would be with her when she needed them.

Patricia said she thought it was better to have the tables seat six, rather than four. Then she acknowledged a wave from someone across the room. "See you later," she said to Garden and Milly.

Garden's eyes followed her as she moved through the crowd, speaking to everyone. They'll all be there when she needs them, Garden thought, just the way they were all there for me. And will be for Helen. She saw Wentworth and smiled. Helen would have friends like Wentworth, too. They would giggle when they were thirty about things they had done together when they were thirteen. And if they had an argument or an estrangement, they would make it up, too, just as she and Wentworth had done. Her gaze moved on to the bar, found John. He was talking intently with Ed Campbell, so it must be about boats. Ed was building a sailboat in his backyard and could talk about nothing else. Ed was a bore, everyone agreed, but Ed was also the kindest man on earth. Everyone knew it and admired him for it and eventually got interested in the height of the mast and depth of the centerboard on Ed's boat.

John and Ed laughed about something. John's eyes almost disappeared in the network of deep wrinkles. Garden smiled. She had everything a woman could ever want to make her happy. If only she could take a chance, trust her feelings, trust happiness.

"Happy Easter, Mr. Henry," said Milly. Logan Henry's cheeks were very pink. He was celebrating the end of Lent with enthusiasm.

"Happy Easter, Milly, Garden." Garden returned his greeting. "Garden, I'm looking for your mother. Have you seen her?"

"Yes, sir. She's out on the porch."

"Thank you. I'll brave the crowd out there, then. You got my letter all right, did you?" Garden nodded. "I'll keep you up to date. Excuse me, ladies. Must be of service."

Garden heard him muttering "widows" as he left them. "Poor Mr. Henry and his widow clients," she said. "A lawyer's lot is not an easy one."

"Not an old bachelor lawyer anyhow," agreed Milly. It was a standard joke in Charleston that wives urged their husbands to hire Logan Henry as their attorney because he could always be dragooned into escort service for the widow when the time came.

"I wish Mama could browbeat him into marrying her," Garden said. "I feel like he's my father already after all he's done for me." She didn't have to specify what Mr. Henry had done, and no one would ever put it into words. The trial and its ugliness were common knowledge and universally ignored. The same would be true, Garden knew, for the next trial.

Mr. Henry's letter had been about Vicki's appeal. The state Supreme Court had refused to judge the appeal. It had, however, ruled that the first trial contained an error. Judge Travers had not permitted the prosecution to present all its evidence. If Vicki insisted on it, she could have a trial from the beginning; but she couldn't get a reversal of Judge Travers's decision.

Logan Henry did not think the Principessa would go through the whole thing again. If she did, the result would be exactly the same. Charleston takes care of its own.

Mr. Henry passed Garden and Milly again, heading for the exit with a protesting Margaret in tow. "Sorry, Garden," said Milly, "I don't hear wedding bells in Mr. Henry's voice. He's got the right idea, though. It's almost dinnertime. I've got to find Allen."

"And I've got to rescue John from Ed Campbell. Frying pan to fire. We're having dinner with Mama." '

"New cook?" Margaret's servant problems were well known.

"Since Thursday. I'm crossing my fingers."

"There's always Helen's Easter basket. Hard-boiled eggs and chocolate bunnies, if worse comes to worst."

"That was a good dinner," said John. "You've really found a cook worth keeping." He held out his hand for Helen to hold while they crossed the street. On the other side, she ran across White Point Gardens to the cannon and started to climb the pyramid of cemented iron cannonballs.

"One Easter dress destroyed," Garden commented. "The cook won't last. Mama doesn't really care how good the food is or how clean the house is. What she wants is another Zanzie, somebody to take care of her as if she were a baby."

"That's pretty harsh, Garden." He spread his handkerchief on the edge of the bandstand and lifted Garden up to sit on it. "It's too bad you don't get along with your mother. Can't you forgive her for shutting you out?"

"Lord, yes. I've forgotten that. I even feel rather kindly toward her. She's lonely, and she can't stand being fifty this year, and she's terrified of being poor again, so every time she spends a nickel she goes into a decline. It's sad.

"I've thought about her a lot. There was a time when I worshipped her, then a time when I hated her, now she's just somebody I know and feel sorry for and have a duty to. I can't give her what she wants. She wants to be taken care of and adored. That's not possible."

Helen started to howl. John broke into a run. Garden took her time jumping down from the bandstand. She knew that howl. It was rage, not pain. Helen might look like a Harris, but inside she was all Tradd.

The problem, Garden translated for John from Helen's sobs, was that another girl had passed by wearing a dress exactly like Helen's. But with a ribbon sash instead of a belt.

"She has a bad case of fashion jealousy," said Garden. "I guess my little girl is growing up."

John took her hand in his. "I think her mama is, too. Is it about time for me to go down on knees?"

"Not yet. Soon, maybe, but not yet."

104

"Aunt Elizabeth, is it true that Harry Fitzpatrick was your lover?" Garden had been working up her courage for three days to approach her great-aunt. When they were finally together and Helen was definitely asleep, all her prepared, tactful speeches left her mind. She blurted out the question with no preamble.

Elizabeth's mouth twitched. "Does Hélène Lemoine want to know?" she said mildly.

"No. I do. I mean, I want to know how you did it."

Elizabeth laughed. "Six ways from Sunday, and then back again."

Garden's face was bright red.

"I'm sorry, dear, I couldn't resist teasing you. You mean how did we keep our affair secret, don't you?"

Garden nodded. "You know . . . discretion and all that. I can't risk getting talked about. It's too easy to stir up the past, and I couldn't bear it if I got shut out again. But I'm going crazy from wanting John."

Her face took on an earnest, prim expression. "It's not just lust, Aunt Elizabeth. John wants to marry me, and I couldn't possibly make a decision without knowing if we were sexually compatible."

Elizabeth laughed until her eyes were wet. Garden got redder.

When Elizabeth could speak, she asked Garden for a glass of water. She was her usual serene self when she finished it. "Garden, my dear," she said, 'I hope you'll forgive me. But you young people with your Freudian claptrap are really terribly comical. The fact is, you are a young, passionate woman who is sexually attracted to a virile young man. You want to go to bed with him. You may or may not want to marry him, but the two have very little to do with each other.

"I would almost certainly have married Joe if he hadn't been killed, and I never once longed to go to bed with him.

"Harry was a different thing altogether. I wanted to be in his bed day and night. I thought at the time that no one knew anything about it, but of course they must have. Naturally, nothing was ever said to me . . ."

Garden shook Elizabeth's arm. "I can't stand it when you drop these bombshells and go on talking, calm as you please. What Joe? Why were you going to marry somebody you've never even mentioned before?"

"You're so scatterbrained sometimes, Garden. You asked me a question, and I'm trying to answer it. Now let me finish. I had a great advantage when I fell in love with Harry that you don't have. My daughter was already grown and married and out of the house. Tradd was still living at home, but boys are not as perceptive as girls. And I sent him to the beach for the summer. Then Harry could be here.

"That's exactly what we'll do. Not for the summer, she's too young, but I'll take Helen to Sullivan's Island for two weeks.

No—I'll probably regret it, but I'll make that a month. Rebecca and her children will be there, so there'll already be a dah. You can give Belva a vacation. Which do you prefer, July or August?''

Garden hugged her great-aunt until Elizabeth protested that her bones were creaking. "July," she said, "that's sooner. And now stop being so infuriating. I know and you know and I know that you know I know that you do it on purpose, so don't play dotty old lady with me. Who—is—Joe?''

Elizabeth grinned. "It fools most people. Joe was Joe Simmons. I have mentioned him before, you just don't make connections. He was the dearest friend I ever had. He was also your husband's grandfather.''

"Oh. I remember now. But you never said you loved him.''

"I said he was my dearest friend. Of course I loved him. One can recognize love so much better when it starts with friendship instead of sex.''

Garden looked thoughtful. "Lucien said something sort of like that to me.''

"Lucien? Oh yes, the perfume man.''

"He was a very special friend, Aunt Elizabeth.''

"Very special?''

"Very. I almost ran away with him.''

"Why didn't you?''

"I met Hélène that day. She told me I was running from, not running to, and that wasn't good enough.''

Elizabeth nodded. "I think I might take French lessons and go to Paris. I like Hélène so much. I'd like to meet her.''

"Are you serious?''

"Certainly I'm serious. Why not? I've been to Paris before. I doubt that it has moved since then . . . because of my age, is that what you're thinking? Dear Garden, I am only seventy-five. I'll be seventy-five for several more months yet. Yes, I'd better go before my birthday so that Hélène won't crow about being younger. I'll start my lessons next week.''

"Aunt Elizabeth?''

"Yes?''

"Please, will you tell me about Joe?''

"I don't know what you want to hear, Garden. I loved Joe all my life. He was like an older brother to me when I was growing up. I didn't know that he loved me except like a brother until much, much later, after his wife was dead. And I was already involved with Harry by then. Joe loved me more than I deserved, but then love is never just. And in his own way Harry loved me. I was a very lucky woman.

"I sent Harry away, which was right. And I told Joe I couldn't marry him. Then he said he knew I'd change my mind and that he'd wait until I did. He was killed before I had a chance to tell him that he was right, that I'd changed my mind.

"I felt cheated. Worse, I felt that somehow I had cheated Joe. Maybe, if I'd told him earlier, everything would have been different.

"But who can say? And, as time passed, I came to think that, in some horrible way, Joe's death was the best thing that could have happened. There was no way to learn if we would have withstood the pressures of marriage. No way for what we had to be destroyed.

"I ended up with my independence, and that is more important than you understand at your age, and my self-indulgent life, lived the way I want it. As an undeserved extra, I have the memories of two great loves. One where I loved, one where I was loved. They warm me in the rare, cold moments when I feel alone and wonder what might have been . . . Garden, stop that. You cry more than any girl I ever saw."

"I hate to think of you being lonely."

"You thick-headed child. I am never lonely. Once in a great while, I regard my solitude as less than a blessing. That is rare. In general, I have never changed my opinion. A life of one's own is the best possible kind of life."

Garden stepped back and looked at the sign she had lettered. The words weren't centered exactly right, but she decided that it would do. CLOSED FOR VACATION it said. She thought for a minute, then took it out of the window. The tourist season had been very successful, business since then very dull. Paula's Mike was due back from sea duty any day now. Why not? REOPEN AUGUST 1ST she added. She propped the sign on a plate stand in the center of the window, pulled the plug so that the icebox could drain, locked the back door, picked up the gift-wrapped package from her desk and left the shop, locking the front door behind her.

The package contained a present for John It was the Hester Bateman urn. Inside it, decorated with red, white, and blue bows were a toothbrush, a razor and a tube of Burma Shave. The long Fourth of July weekend started tomorrow.

105

"Garden, are you feeling all right? You're not like yourself."

"I'm just fine, John. I don't know what you mean."

"You're so fidgety. It's too hot for you to be scooting around like that. Leave the dishes. They can wait until we get back from the movies."

"Let's not go to the movies, John. There'll be a long line, and I'm not all that crazy about Bing Crosby."

"Good. We'll go see *Mutiny on the Bounty*. Don't tell me you don't like Clark Gable. I know better."

"No. You can see your ships at sea pictures on your own time. I said I don't want to go to the movies at all." Her voice was edgy.

John raised his eyebrows. "I think the heat's getting to you. We'd better go see something. The theater's air-cooled. How about Fred Astaire and Ginger Rogers?"

Garden wanted to hit him. He hadn't noticed the new dress she was wearing, or the candles on all the tables, ready to light as soon as it got dark, or the rinse of perfume in her hair. He hadn't even mentioned the package on the table, asked what it was, who it was for. Nothing was going the way she had planned.

"All right," she said glumly. "We might as well go to the movies."

It was dark when they left the theater, and although the night was breathlessly hot and humid, the darkness gave an illusion of coolness.

Elizabeth's house had no lights on, John commented. Garden told him that Elizabeth had taken Helen to the beach. They stood on the dark piazza. The heavy night air pressed around them, quiet, as if waiting. There was no breeze. It was hard to breathe.

Garden moved slowly, like a sleepwalker, or a swimmer on the floor of the sea. She stepped close to John. "We're all alone," she said simply.

"Garden . . . are you sure you know what you're doing?"

"Oh, yes." Her arms slid around his neck, her body pressed against his.

The long months of restraint, of waiting, of wanting, had built a pressure that exploded when their hungry mouths found each other. They stumbled through the darkness then, stopping only to kiss and touch and break apart again in confused urgency and need for each other and for the sanctuary of Garden's little house.

There was no time to light the carefully placed candles or to open the thoughtfully chilled champagne or to reach the freshly made, turned-down bed. They made love on the floor just inside the open door, with joyous cries of recognition when their bodies joined and burned together in almost instantaneous climax.

They held each other then, silent except for thudding hearts and rapid, mingled breaths while the demanding desire rekindled. Then they loved again, and yet again until the urgent need was satisfied.

John held Garden's face in his hands and kissed her slowly. "Nice soft rug you've got here," he whispered. Garden tightened her arms around his waist, and their bodies shook together in shared laughter at themselves.

Later they lit the candles and opened the champagne and looked at each other as if for the first time, discovering new depths of love at each meeting of their eyes.

"I didn't mean for that to happen," John said.

"I did," said Garden. "Are you sorry?"

"I've never been happier in my life. You?"

"The same."

The month passed in the peculiar telescoping manner of special time removed from, yet enveloped by, time as measured by the world. When they were together, time did not exist, and it surprised them when they found the hours gone. When they were apart, there was only time, crawling minutes that refused to hurry so that they could be together again. John left early every weekday morning to drive to the base, came home as soon as he could after his work was done.

John was staying at Elizabeth's was the story, watching over the house while she was away. Garden took childlike glee in jumping around on the bed that John supposedly was sleeping in, messing it up for Elizabeth's maid to find.

"Do you think we're fooling anybody?" John asked.

Garden giggled and shook her head. "We're being discreet, though," she said. "Obeying the rules."

They did not avoid the world. Garden often stopped in at a friend's house for coffee and conversation in the morning. She and John went to two informal supper parties. They even gave one, with the table outdoors under the big oak tree, hung with Japanese lanterns. Garden wore her white Fortuny.

Everyone brought records; Allen and Milly Andrews lent their electric Victrola for the evening, and after supper they all danced on the small brick terrace. "Cheek to Cheek," "I'm in the Mood for Love," "Moon Over Miami," "What a Difference a Day Makes," "The Very Thought of You," "Blue Moon," "Deep Purple," "I Only Have Eyes for You." It was a perfect time to be in love.

Garden refused to let anything break the spell of the month that Elizabeth gave them. "I'm so grateful," she told Elizabeth when she and John went to the Island on Helen's birthday.

"Gratitude is cosmetic, then," Elizabeth replied. "You look like you shine in the dark. There's a light under your skin."

Garden repeated Elizabeth's words to John when they were driving home. "Radiant," said John. "That's what she meant, and it's what you are. Radiant and gorgeous and beautiful." He glanced at Garden, then looked back at the road; his hands tightened on the wheel. "Radiant is what people say about brides, Garden. You know how I feel."

She tapped his hand with her finger. "Ssh, not now, not today. I'm too happy to think about anything except this minute and how it feels."

"You're going to have to think, Garden. You know from Peggy what life in the service is like. I could get transferred any day."

Garden put her hands over her ears. "I won't listen." She squeaked and moved her hands to cover her eyes. "And I won't look. Tell me when it's over." The Cooper River Bridge was ahead.

*　　*　　*

541

She couldn't cover her ears when Logan Henry talked to her, but she put off thinking about what he said. Mr. Henry was worried. The courts were always recessed for the summer; the temperature climbed to over a hundred inside the courtrooms, and the judges took their vacations. But he had just received notice that the new trial over Helen's custody was scheduled for August 26. It was unprecedented, and the elderly lawyer mistrusted anything that had no precedent.

The end of August was a month away. Garden could think of nothing other than the dwindling store of days left in July. How could the weeks have fled so fast?

John looked over the top of the newspaper at Garden. "There's an announcement of an auction in Summerville on Saturday. Want to go?"

Garden took her attention away from the page of comics. "What? Do you think if I dyed my hair black I'd look like the Dragon Lady?"

"I said, there's a good auction Saturday. And you'd look like something the cat dragged in. Would you like to go?"

Garden thought. John did love auctions so. And she did need things for the shop. On the other hand . . . "I honestly don't know," she said. "It's our last weekend. Helen comes home on Monday, and the shop opens on Wednesday."

She wanted John to say that he'd rather the two of them spent the weekend together, not seeing anyone or going anyplace. Instead, he waited for her to make up her mind.

"Oh, why not?" she said. "Let's go to Summerville." Once she said it, Garden realized that she really would like to go.

They left very early Saturday morning. They'd get there even before the auction room opened, but the drive would be cooler. And maybe they'd stop on the way. Garden hadn't seen Reba and Matthew for a long time, and she wanted John to meet them.

"You take the picnic basket, and I'll run upstairs and get my necklace. I'll be right behind you."

"You look very pretty," John said when Garden got into the car. "Why so gussied up for Summerville?"

"It's not for Summerville, dummy. I like to get gussied up for you. Besides, I always wear my charm when I see Reba. It sort of ties me to the old days. After all, Old Pansy gave it to me."

542

"Who's Old Pansy?"

"Oh, John, I must have told you about Old Pansy. I know I did. About when I lived with Reba when I was little and all."

"I remember Reba, but nothing about anyone with a great name like Old Pansy."

Garden launched into her reminiscenses of the old woman. "So you see," she concluded, "that's how I got the Elfe chest and the charm against plat eye. I know it's foolish to be so superstitious, but I always feel safer when I remember to wear it."

"I think you should wear it all the time."

Garden laughed. "All right, tease me all you want to. I told you, I know it's foolish."

John did not laugh. "I don't think it's foolish at all. In the Far East, there are all kinds of beliefs that Westerners laugh at, and in the modern, progressive West, there are hundreds of superstitions that people mock, but still hold on to. Who's to say what's real and what isn't? If that old woman could heal burns without a blister or a scar, I wouldn't ignore anything else she did."

Garden smiled. "You're loony, but I love you. Reba's going to like you a lot."

Reba did. So did Matthew. So did almost twenty men, women and children who came to their house to see "Miss Garden and her sailor." They were all Ashleys in one degree or another, all part of the Barony, even though they had not lived there for many years.

"I love these people," Garden said as she waved a final goodbye through the window of the moving car. "Reba's my real mother, in my heart. Much more than Mama . . . Gracious, look at the time. Get a move on, sailor."

"Aye, aye, captain."

"I like that. 'Miss Garden and her sailor.' It sounds romantic."

"It sounds like the start of a limerick to me."

They had missed the beginning of the auction, but it made no difference. It was so hot that the auction was held outdoors, and the items to be sold were arranged in a wide circle on the grass around the area where the bidding was going on. There was plenty of time for Garden and John to examine the things that interested them. And to visit the stand set up by the ladies of the Methodist Church where lemonade and pecan pie were for sale.

The merciless sun drove many of the people away. Garden and

John got umbrellas from the car and more lemonade. Thin crowds meant good buys. At three-twenty in the afternoon they were the only ones left. The auctioneer took off his straw hat and mopped his sweat-drenched head and face.

"Sorry, little lady," he said. His voice was hoarse. "I'm afraid I'll have to call it a day."

Garden handed him the glass of lemonade she had saved for him. "No you don't, Mr. Biggers. You've still got two people here. That's all it takes to make an auction."

"Ma'am, you'll put me out of business."

"Pooh. I've seen you sell tarnish for gold plate, Mr. Biggers. Be a good sport, because you're caught this time."

Biggers drank the lemonade and laughed. "Okay. But make it as painless as possible, will you?" He held up a cracked flowered china slop jar and started his spiel, winking at Garden. "Who'll start the bidding on this fine porce-you-laine object of art? Do I hear ten dollars? Five? Two? Come on, ladies and gentlemen, don't insult the owner of this valuable museum-quality piece, a family heirloom from one of the greatest plantations on the Suwanee River . . . What do you want to buy?" asked Biggers.

John brought the things Garden wanted to the platform where Biggers stood. Then they "made the auction." Biggers held up a teapot.

"Five cents," said Garden.

"Six," said John.

"Seven," said Garden.

"Sold," said Biggers.

"What a haul," Garden crowed. The car was packed with booty. She had the real treasures on her lap and around her feet. She and John were dirty, smelly and triumphant. "Let's take them straight to the shop," Garden suggested. "I can't wait to try the samovar in the window. What do you suppose some Russians were doing living in Summerville of all places?"

She was exhausted, but full of energy and excitement and plans. It was good to be working again. The end of their magic month wasn't the end of the world after all.

"Hey, John, you know what? It'll be filthy hot for two months yet. I'll bet we can do the same thing practically every week."

"Garden, you have the soul of a pirate."

"Listen who's talking. Did you or did you not persuade old Biggers to put all those spoons into one lot so that we could buy the whole batch for almost nothing?"

"It was fun, wasn't it? Maybe I'll get a tattoo. Skull and crossbones. Every sailor should have a tattoo."

"Every sailor should have a bath. We stink."

"I'll scrub your back if you'll scrub mine."

"Sold! To the gentleman with the tattoo."

"Why does the phone always ring the minute I get in the tub?" Garden splashed, starting to rise.

"I'll answer it. I'll tell them you'll call back."

John came back into the bathroom a few minutes later, a glass of brandy in his hand. "Drink this, Garden. Your mother's had a heart attack."

Garden waved the glass away. "She's always having heart attacks, don't worry."

"I'm afraid this time it's real. You're to go to the hospital right away. I'll go with you."

106

After that, everything happened so fast that Garden could do nothing except try to keep up with events.

"Your mother is very frightened, Garden," said Dr. Hope, his kind face looking worn from strain. "You'll have to be patient with her. You see, whenever she had those little spells of palpitations and dizziness, she really believed that they were heart attacks, no matter how many times I explained that they weren't much more than wind.

"Now she's met the real thing, felt the real pain. She had an extremely mild attack of angina. She was lucky. But she can't believe me now when I tell her she'll be all right, any more than she could before when I told her there was nothing wrong with her."

Garden couldn't believe him either. "Heart attack" sounded so terrifying. "Will she really be all right?"

"She will be if she doesn't scare herself to death. Literally. She needs to rest, and to eat lightly. Most of all, she needs to be calm. I'm sending her home. The hospital frightens her. I'll give you the names of some good nurses, but it would be better if you took care of her for a few days at least. If she sees a nurse, she'll think she's sick, and she isn't. Not yet."

"What do you mean, 'not yet'?"

"She'll bring on another attack if she keeps fretting about herself. And it might be more serious. Don't go in to see her now; you look too worried. Make whatever arrangements you have to, then come back when you're ready to take her home."

John drove her to her mother's house and helped her get things ready. Despite the sixteen-foot ceilings and the cooling effect of the water beyond the seawall across the street, the air in the big house was oppressive.

"I'm going to put her on the ground floor," Garden said. "We'll never get her up those stairs on a stretcher, and it's cooler down there than anyplace else. The kitchen's there, too. It'll be easier to fetch and carry."

Besides the kitchen, the ground floor contained a living room–dining room combination and four bedrooms. They had been used by the servants of the owners of the house before Margaret. Garden cleaned one of the bedrooms, made up the bed, filled vases with roses John cut from the garden outside, and draped the windows with fern-patterned green and white curtains that she found in the bureau when she cleaned it.

"There," she said. "It looks nice, and it's as cool as anyplace can be. Mama won't like it, but it's the best I can do."

"It's great, Garden. Look, we've got electric fans out at the base. I'll go get one."

"That would be wonderful. Will you bring down the radio from the sitting room, too? I'll help you carry it."

"Leave it. I've got a table model. I'll bring it, too."

"That's wonderful. I'll wash my face and hands and catch a ride with you. If you'll drop me at the hospital, I can ride in the ambulance with Mama."

Margaret looked very small and childlike in the hospital bed. Her

546

face had few lines, and her pale hair did not show the gray in it. It was braided and hung over the breast of her coarse white hospital gown onto the white sheet pulled up almost to her shoulders, covering her arms.

"Hello, Mama," said Garden softly.

Margaret opened her eyes and began to cry.

"Ssh, don't fret. Everything's all right. I've come to take you home."

Margaret tried to hold out her hand, but she was confined by the tucked-in sheet. Garden hurried to the bed and helped her free it. Margaret clutched Garden's wrist. "Don't leave me," she whispered.

"I won't. Don't worry, Mama. I'm right here."

Margaret did not like the room . . . the noise the fan made . . . the soup Garden prepared . . . the nightgown Garden brought from her bedroom . . . the station Garden tuned on the radio . . . the scent of the roses . . . the softness of the pillows . . . the hardness of the pillows . . . the taste of the tea Garden fixed . . . the way she had been neglected in the hospital. . . the way Garden hovered over her . . . the way Garden left her all alone . . .

She fell asleep at eleven that night. Garden smoked a dozen cigarettes while she made notes of what had to be done:

Helen home
Shop open
Hire new cook
Hire new maid
Bring clothes—me, Helen
Oil.fan
Get groceries

She fell asleep at the desk.

Margaret was not an easy convalescent. After breakfast with her mother, Garden put a small porcelain bell on the table near Margaret's bed. "I'm going to make some phone calls and have a bath and then I'll fix you a cup of tea, and we'll plan our lunch. You ring the bell if you need anything before I get back."

Her foot was on the first step when the bell rang.

Margaret had her hand to her heart when Garden entered the room. "I'm sure I felt a funny kind of thump, Garden. You'd better call Dr. Hope."

"All right, Mama. I'll call him before I call anybody else."

"And come right back and tell me what he says."

"All right."

Garden's foot was on the second step when the bell rang again.

"Tell him he'd better come see me. And don't let him talk you around, Garden. He'll try, but don't let him. And before he gets here, help me change my gown and bring me the bedjacket that's on the shelf in my wardrobe in a blue Kerrison's box and help me do something with my hair."

The delicate, sweet tinkle of the bell became a nightmare sound to Garden.

"I'm going to kill myself," she told Elizabeth on the telephone that afternoon. "That's the only way I can think of to keep from killing Mama."

"Marshall Hope is ten kinds of jackass," said Elizabeth. "Call three of those nurses right away and get them working eight-hour shifts. Then telephone your mama's cronies, you know who I mean, the hypochondriac harpies. They'll all come to call. They love to talk about their illnesses. Margaret will be able to lord it over them for once. Betty Ellison's kidney stones used to be the ace of trumps.

"Don't worry about Helen. I'll take her home with me."

By going without sleep and cultivating deafness to the bell and to Margaret's complaints, Garden managed to get the house organized with servants and nurses and groceries and sickroom supplies. She cleaned the living room and fixed a couch for Margaret to lie on while she received guests. She even persuaded the telephone company to install a phone downstairs.

On Tuesday afternoon she looked in on Margaret's gathering of callers, greeted everyone, declined invitations to join them, agreed that her mother was looking wonderfully well and told Margaret that she was going to the shop to get ready for the reopening the following day. Margaret waved a brave, deserted goodbye.

"Helen, you're so beautiful and brown. Give me a nice big hug." Garden closed her eyes and smiled, appreciating the strength of the little arms choking her and the smell of healthy child. "I missed you, my angel."

"I missed you too, Mama. Mama, can I go back to the beach? I only got nine sand dollars, and Billy got eleven."

Garden disentangled herself, thanked Elizabeth for saving her life

548

and ran away to the quiet of Chalmers Street and the work that awaited her.

At the end of a week Garden was haggard. "But I think things really are under control," she told John on the telephone. "I'll get away next Saturday, when Paula's at the shop, no matter what. Mama will hardly notice. She has callers all day. It's only at night that she keeps me hopping . . . Oh no, the nurse won't do. She wants me. She's fired the nurse six times already. Thank God I'm paying her. She just grins at Mama with her store teeth and pays no attention . . . I love you too, and I miss you something terrible. Oh hell, there's the door, and the maid's gone to the store. I'll have to get it."

Garden was astonished to see Logan Henry on the doorstep. She didn't know his duties to his clients included sick calls.

Mr. Henry had come to see her, not Margaret. And he told her that things were not under control at all.

"The trial date has been changed, moved forward. We have only a week to prepare ourselves. It must be deliberate maliciousness. So many of our witnesses are in the mountains or on the Island. They had planned to be here on the twenty-sixth; it will be a major inconvenience for them to rearrange their lives to be here on the tenth."

Garden's alarm was evident. Mr. Henry unbent so far as to pat her shoulder. "They will be here, Garden, never fear."

Then he took away the confidence he had just given. "What worries me is the judge. I don't know him. The reason given is that there is a backlog of cases, and all the judges of this court are away on vacation. But I don't like it. This man is a stranger, a Yankee for all I know. He doesn't know Charleston and Charlestonians the way Travers does. He isn't one of us.

"Still, the testimony is irrefutable on our side. He can't possibly rule any way other than for us. And our case is strengthened by your presence in your mother's house. Nothing could be more correct."

Mr. Henry looked vaguely past Garden to a corner of the room. "Er, that pleasant young Naval officer, it would be just as well if you did not see him until after the trial. Imputations could be made that might sound questionable, even though totally groundless."

"I understand," said Garden. The August afternoon was stifling, but she felt a chill of fear.

107

There was only one reporter at the entrance to the Court House. He was local and very young. Garden thanked God. She was no longer news.

Some of her witnesses were already sitting on the benches in the rear of the courtroom, fanning themselves with palmetto fans. Garden smiled and nodded at them. How lucky she was. St. Michael's started the chimes that preceded the tolling of the hour. She felt the comfort of knowing that she was at home, that she was safe.

And then she saw Vicki, and she knew that she was wrong, that there was no safety, that she was in greater peril than ever before. Vicki was smiling at her, a smile of venomous sweetness. Garden took her seat. Her legs were weak. Only Vicki's expression identified her. The rest of her was disguised. She was all but unrecognizable.

In the seven months since the earlier trial, Vicki had gained at least thirty pounds. She had a cushiony double chin and a soft, stout body. It was enveloped in a matronly dress of navy blue georgette with a lace-edged white collar. Her thick ankles bulged over oxford-type lace-up shoes with a thick, low heel. She wore a plain navy blue straw hat squarely set on her neatly waved gray hair. Her face was bare of all cosmetics, and her only jewelry was a cameo brooch. She looked like a grandmother.

That was how her lawyer introduced her when he made his opening statement to the judge. "This grandmother, Your Honor, has brought suit against the mother of her granddaughter with the greatest reluctance. She bears no animosity towards this lovely young woman, although it is true that Mrs. Harris abducted the child from her grandmother's house and has never so much as sent a photograph or a note about little Helen's state of health to her grandmother. No, I repeat, there is no animosity. Only profound sorrow. Sorrow for her separation from the child she loves so much and concern for her granddaughter's well-being. This grandmother, Your Honor, wants no conflict, no ill will. She is moved by only one heartfelt desire, a desire so powerful that she feels forced into this litigation. That desire is one for which no one can condemn her. She wants the best, the very best, for little Helen.''

Garden looked at Logan Henry. He was busy making notes on a pad that he had taken from his briefcase. His lips were pursed; wrinkles radiated from them throughout the parchmentlike skin of his face. He looked very old and tired and worried.

As the days passed, Mr. Henry progressed from tired to ill to near death.

The trial would have exhausted five men younger and stronger than Logan Henry. The heat was intolerable. Charleston was customarily visited in the summer by afternoon thundershowers that broke the pressure of the heavy humidity and cooled the air, at least temporarily. But day after day went by, with brilliant towering clouds building until their roiling white peaks seemed to touch the top of the sky, and the storm never broke. Heat accumulated in the courtroom, taking all life from the air, and waited there overnight, to be intensified when the next day's sun beat down on the building and radiated from the pavement outside. Each day was a hell, and each additional day an eternity.

But Mr. Henry did not waver. He filled page after page with notes, attended to the testimony of the prosecution witnesses with such concentration that his body quivered, interrupted with objections, cross-examined with an intensity that left the witnesses enraged and distraught.

The witnesses were men and women unused to opposition of any kind, accustomed to deference and adulation. They were eminent experts.

A noted child psychologist talked about the irreversible damage suffered by the child of a working mother.

A prominent educator outlined the advantages of the big, long-established school equipped with the latest, most elaborate facilities.

A famous doctor discussed the tremendous gap in availability of modern skills and technology in big versus small communities.

A curator from the Metropolitan Museum of Art explained the programs for children of members.

A renowned pianist recounted the details of his training in the studios of Carnegie Hall.

A respected teacher, one who had been a mentor of the pianist, described the gentle approach he used with young children.

An instructor from the New York Skating Club painted a word picture of the happy children taking lessons there.

A teacher from the Central Park Riding Academy showed a movie of the children who rode and learned to care for their own ponies under her tutelage.

An internationally known retired ballerina expressed her eagerness to introduce Helen to the joy of dancing.

Their testimony filled two days.

On the third day, Vicki's lawyer introduced evidence in the form of photographs, newspaper clippings and affidavits. Hour after hour the shocking, sordid story of Garden's "bad times" was read into the record. "You see, Your Honor," he concluded with a sad, stern expression, "the shameful history of the child's mother. It is a matter of public record, a shadow never to be erased, a disgrace that will blight little Helen's life as long as she is in the mother's household."

He timed his summation for delivery immediately before the recess for lunch. In the afternoon, clergymen from three New York churches and United States ambassadors to three countries testified to the noble moral character of Victoria Montecatini.

The morning of the fourth day was overcast, promising rain, holding humidity close to the earth. Inside the courtroom a bailiff collapsed from heat prostration. Vicki's lawyer approached the bench and spoke in hushed tones. "Your Honor, it is now my duty to reveal confidential information that would never have been exposed were it not for a grandmother's selfless devotion." One after another, in rapid succession, bankers, accountants and brokers gave evidence of Vicki's assets: mills, shipping companies, a Charleston bank, stocks, bonds, gold bullion, jewels, houses, acreage, automobiles, train, yacht, and in cash, in a numbered Swiss account, eleven million six hundred and eighty-four thousand nine hundred and thirty-two dollars and sixteen cents. Outside, thunder rumbled in the distance, but the rain did not come.

Another accountant gave statistics on the state of small businesses in America in 1935, the annual rate of bankruptcies and the forecast for the antique business in particular. His calculations indicated a probability of failure for Lowcountry Treasures that exceeded ninety percent. Balance sheets, bank statements and account books subpoenaed from Garden showed that she paid herself a salary of one hundred dollars a month, had made a profit of two hundred and eleven dollars in 1934 and had four hundred and two dollars in the bank. A spattering of rain drew all eyes to the window. Then it stopped.

For his final witness, Vicki's lawyer called one of his partners. He read two documents aloud. The first was a will presently in effect in which Vicki disposed of her entire estate to charity. The second was a transfer of all properties to Helen, to be held in irrevocable trust, with her grandmother and legal guardian Victoria Montecatini as administratrix. The second document, said the lawyer, would be signed in the presence of the judge at the moment his client was awarded custody of the beloved grandchild.

He bowed with a flourish to Logan Henry. "We rest our case," he said with a smirk.

Mr. Henry did his best. The character witnesses for Garden took the stand one after another, throughout the rest of Thursday and the better part of Friday. They had left their comfortable homes, given up their vacations, endured the grueling days of insufferable heat— all on her behalf, to help her keep her child. Logan Henry, his voice quavering from strain, led them through their testimony with a deference that paid tribute to them. Garden, until now numb with despair, allowed the tears to fall from her eyes, tears of inexpressible gratitude and admiration and love.

Vicki's lawyer made a show of respect and sympathy for the witnesses' quixotism. He bowed to each and elected to waive cross-examination.

Then he made his closing statement.

"Your Honor, this is a very simple case. There is only one issue to be considered, the best interests of a little girl only six years old. I could talk about all the points raised by the experts who testified in this room. I could be eloquent about the emotions of a mother whose only child was tragically struck down in his youth. I could then describe the abundance of love this lonely woman longs to pour onto the only living creature who matters to her in this world, her grandchild. But those are not the real considerations here. The real consideration is the welfare of little Helen. Shall this innocent child be deprived of a life of the finest care and education . . . shall she be cut off from an inheritance that will guarantee the same privileges for her children and her children's children . . . shall she be denied the love and generosity of her grandmother . . . by a woman who can offer neither security nor a morally fit environment?''

He held his declamatory pose for a moment. Then his outstretched arms fell limply to his sides and his leonine head dropped from its impassioned forward thrust to a brooding slump. Exhausted by the expenditure of emotion, he returned to his chair.

Mr. Henry pushed back his chair with a mood-shattering screech and stood up. His white linen suit was baggy on his angular bones, splotched with his sweat. ''I compliment my learned colleague,'' he said slowly, ''on his eloquent disclaimer of eloquence. I'm too tired and too ordinary to attempt anything like it. I can only say a few plain words about love and money.

''Now, Helen Harris doesn't have much money. Her mother doesn't either. Helen gets two pennies a week to put in the Sunday school collection plate. Her mama ties them in a knot in the corner of Helen's handkerchief.

''But then Helen's just a little girl. She doesn't know about money. She has nine sand dollars that she picked up on the beach with her cousins, and she thinks she's rich.

''Your Honor, I think Helen's right. She is rich. She has just about as many cousins as that lady, her grandmother, has dollars. She has a mother who has loved her since she first felt Helen kick inside her womb and who will keep on loving her no matter what. She has her own room, with a bed for her and a bed for her wet-me-wet doll, and a tricycle and a penny under her pillow every time she loses a tooth. A little girl can't sleep in but one bed at a time or one room at a time or ride more than one tricycle at a time. And the tooth fairy means a lot more to her than a bank account in Switzerland.

''What I guess I'm saying, Your Honor, is that Helen is a happy little girl with everything she wants in life. I don't know of anything richer than that. I don't think she'd be happy at all if she was taken away.

''Her mama works hard. These days, that's no guarantee of success. But Helen's never going to go hungry. She'll always have a roof over her head. She's a little Charleston girl, and in Charleston we take care of our own.

"It seems to me that a whole city full of people caring about you is better security than a bunch of stockholders managing your investments.

"It seems to me that Helen is where she belongs, and she should stay here."

The judge did not react. He had reacted to nothing that had been said or done all week. He looked at the watch he had laid in the desk. "It is four o'clock," he said. He had a nasal twang. "This court will now adjourn. All parties will keep themselves available as of 9 A.M. Monday. The clerk will notify you when to assemble for the decision in this case."

108

"Well? What happened?" Margaret sat up on her couch.

"It's over, but there's no decision yet. We have to go back Monday."

"I can't stand all this. You know that, Garden. Dr. Hope said I wasn't to be upset. My heart is fluttering like a caged bird. I think maybe a tiny sip of iced tea with lemon would soothe my nerves. It's so hot in here."

Garden switched on the electric fan.

"You know that noise disturbs me, Garden. I don't know how you can be so inconsiderate . . . Where are you going?"

"I'm going home, Mama. I'm going to spend the weekend with Helen."

"You can't just go off and leave me like that. You know my condition."

"Mama, you've got a nurse in the next room twenty-four hours a day. Plus a cook and a maid. You'll just have to do without me for two days. I'll be back by eight on Monday."

"Garden! Garden Tradd, you come back here." The sound of Margaret's bell pursued Garden out the door.

She walked through the thick heat to Elizabeth's house. There were no people on the street, and Garden was glad. She couldn't talk to anyone right now, not even to exchange a simple hello. She knew that she was going to be spending her final weekend with her daughter.

Mr. Henry had been brilliant, but he couldn't alter the facts. Helen would have everything with Vicki, whereas she would never have real security with Garden. Sand dollars wouldn't take care of her wants much longer. It was a pretty idea, but blocks of gold were real, not seashells. Garden was surprised the judge hadn't decided right away. Maybe there was a rule that they had to seem to think things over.

I won't cry, she promised herself, and I won't grab hold of Helen and hold her. She hates to be held too long. We'll have an ordinary weekend, nothing special. That's what I want to have as a memory.

Elizabeth was waiting by the door. She touched Garden's cheek with a trembling finger. "Logan Henry called. I know. I'm sorrier than I can say."

"Thank you, Aunt Elizabeth. I'm still numb; it's probably for the best. I'm not going to say anything to Helen. I'm going to try not to act any different."

"I think that's best. John's here. Helen is with him. They're back in your house. I told him."

Helen was sitting on John's lap, talking a blue streak and trying to unpin the ribbons on his chest. Garden knelt down and put her arms around Helen. John held them both in his embrace. He helped Garden make the weekend what she wanted it to be.

When Garden entered her mother's house Monday morning, she heard Margaret telling the nurse she was fired. "That's all right, nurse," Garden said, "you can go. I appreciate everything you've done. I'll take over now."

Garden fixed breakfast for her mother, coffee for herself. She drank two cups, then was agonizingly sick in the sink. She rinsed her mouth with salt and water and was sick again. Margaret's bell rang.

"Stay with me, Garden. Talk to me. I can't stand this waiting."

"I can't either, Mama, but we're both going to have to. It isn't even nine o'clock yet. Listen.'' St. Michael's was ringing the three-quarter hour.

"It's so close in here, I can't breathe.''

Garden felt the same way. It had not rained for ten days. She bathed Margaret's forehead with cologne. Then she went through all the rooms making sure the louvered shutters were closed over the windows to keep the sun out. They were also supposed to keep in the cool air of the night before, but there had been no cool air at night for over a week. As she checked the last window in the drawing room, St. Michael's struck the hour. The phone rang.

"I'm sorry, Mrs. Ellison, but I can't put Mama on the phone. I need to keep the line open. May I ask you a great favor? Would you please telephone all Mama's close friends and beg them for me not to ring up here today. Thank you so much.''

"Who was that, Garden?''

"A wrong number, Mama.''

It was impossible to believe that it could get any hotter or more humid than it already was. But it did. It was oppressive, airless. Garden opened the shutters and looked out at the rosebushes. Their leaves were curled and dry. All the trees in the garden looked parched and spiritless. She drank some water. St. Michael's chimed the quarter hour.

This is unbearable, Garden thought. She looked at the telephone on the table by her side, willing it to ring. A trickle of perspiration ran down her back. She was in the sitting room on the second floor. She could hear her mother downstairs complaining to the maid, Elvira.

Garden's mind began a squirrel-cage circle of worry about money. She had hired the nurses and the servants in a rush, wanting the best for her mother, needing some help for herself. She had paid them, knowing that Margaret would not. How could she continue? The bank balance entered as evidence at the trial was now one fourth that amount. The rent on the shop had to be paid, and Helen's tuition. Money—was there no end to the worry of it?

Money. Inevitably, her mind went back to the trial and the overwhelming weight of Vicki's arguments. She could give Helen every advantage, every luxury. I lost, Garden thought, why can't I accept that? Why do I still have hope? Why doesn't the damn phone ring? A drop of sweat beaded on her right eyebrow, rolled down into her eye. The salt stung.

St. Michael's sounded the half hour.

Which half hour was it? The room was an inferno, so the sun was surely well up. Was it twelve-thirty already? No, couldn't be. She had been here, fretting, for a long time, but not that long. It must be eleven-thirty. She stood up, pulling her skirt from where it had stuck to the chair, glued by perspiration. There was a tall clock, ticking loudly, in the hall. She walked to it. It was nine thirty-two.

Garden tried to read. John had given her the new novel by F. Scott Fitzgerald, *Tender Is the Night*. Garden was caught up in it at once. It was about Antibes. She knew the people Fitzgerald described, she had seen them on that beach, the woman wearing her pearls down her back, the man raking seaweed. How long ago that was, and how distant. That life was like something she had seen in a movie or read in a novel, as she was reading now. That Garden with the blond hair and diamond bracelets had nothing to do with her.

But it did. "Everything you ever saw or thought or did is a part of you," John had told her. "What matters is, what do you do with it now?"

The book fell to her lap. She had read two chapters and could not remember a word she had read.

Maybe the phone was out of order. But if she picked it up to see, then it would give a busy signal when Mr. Henry called her. She held her hand on it, imagining a vibration, a preparation for ringing. When she couldn't bear not knowing any longer, she bent her head close to the telephone and snatched the receiver off the hook. It was not out of order. She hung up at once, went to look at the clock. It was almost ten.

Just as St. Michael's struck the first note of its chime, Margaret's bell sounded.

She wanted Garden to feel her heartbeat. "That can't be normal. I'm sure there's an attack coming."

"There's nothing to worry about, Mama. It's perfectly regular."

"What do you know, Garden? And you sent the nurse away. She could have told in an instant what was wrong. You'll have to call Dr. Hope."

"I can't tie up the phone, Mama. You know I'm waiting for Mr. Henry to call."

"That old fussbudget. You should have had a better lawyer. He has never been really interested in us."

Garden gritted her teeth. "Mama," she said with difficulty, "I am going to go upstairs. If I stay here, I will hit you."

Margaret's chin quivered. "Don't go, Garden. Don't leave me all alone. I'm afraid that my nerves will give out. I'm afraid of the pain."

Garden held her mother's hand and stroked it. "It's all right, Mama. Everything's all right. I tell you what. We'll get you dressed and go into your living room. Then you can teach me that new game you've been playing with your friends until I have to go to court."

The temperature climbed, the fan whirred, the clock in the hall ticked monotonously, the dice rattled, St. Michael's chimed. The minutes moved slowly, slowly. Margaret and Garden played Monopoly.

The phone did not ring.

Elvira brought in dinner. Garden turned her eyes away from the food.

"Go to jail. Go directly to jail . . . Take a walk on the Board-walk . . ."

"Garden, pay attention. You passed Go and didn't take your two hundred dollars."

"Sorry, Mama."

Garden brought a Turkish towel from the bathroom so that they could dry their hands before picking up the dice. "I've never known it to be so heavy," Margaret wheezed. "I can't breathe."

Garden was gasping. Elvira came to the door. "Excuse me, ma'am, but they's thunder. Cele and me, we wants to know could we leave early."

"Yes, of course," said Margaret graciously.

"Mama, wait. I'll have to go out when Mr. Henry calls. You'll need somebody here, and the nurse doesn't come until four."

Elvira twisted her apron in her hands. "The streetcar shoot all kind of spark when they's lightning," she whined.

Garden clenched her slippery, sticky hands into fists. There was a roll of thunder, and Elvira screamed. The telephone pealed shrilly. Garden started, bumping her knee on the table.

"Hello? Hello?"

The line crackled with electricity. She could hardly hear. "Yes?"

she said. "Yes. Could you speak louder, please? Is it you, Mr. Henry?"

She replaced the phone in its cradle. "You and Cele can go, Elvira." She looked at Margaret and tried to smile. "The clerk called Mr. Henry. The judge has decided, but we don't know what. It's so late now that His Honor has set nine tomorrow morning for the time to be in court.

"Whatever it is, at least it's over. We know when we'll know." For some reason, she felt a little better now. She had been trying, by wanting, to influence the judge. She had felt that if it was taking so long for him to decide, then there must be some hope. Now there was really nothing she could do. "It sounds like we're finally going to get some rain," she said. The thunder was closer.

The phone rang. Garden let her mother answer. It was the nurse. She couldn't come in. "It makes no difference," said Margaret. "I don't like her anyhow. You can fix my bed and give me an alcohol rub."

"Yes, Mama."

"Ha. You landed on my property. Let me look at this cardboard thing . . . You owe me thirty-eight dollars."

The game ended at last with Garden bankrupt and Margaret the proprietor of three hotels, all the railroads and both utilities. Just like Vicki and me, thought Garden. She covered her mouth with her hand, afraid of the hysteria trying to escape. "That was fun," said Margaret.

"There might be a breeze," Garden said. "I'll open some shutters." She had to get away from her mother.

The stairs seemed very steep. She pulled her weight up by hauling on the banister rail. The round stairwell felt as if it were bulging from the pressure of the stale, hot air in it.

Garden went out onto the second-floor piazza. The scene before her was ominous, eerie. The sky was a strange color, muddy-looking, yellowish. The air was colored, too, a transparent green-gray. Nothing had a shadow, and edges were preternaturally defined. It was very still. Expectant. The horizon was dark, with quick streaks of heat lightning.

The harbor was like glass, the water flat. It looked as if someone had ironed the water, transformed it into a sheet of dull, gray-brown metal or wool serge.

St. Michael's sounded very near. Dum-dum-de-dum . . . Garden listened, not moving, caught by the inert atmosphere. One . . . two

. . . three . . . four. She strained her ears against the silence, expecting to hear five . . . six . . . seven . . . on and on without stopping, measuring the distortion of the light, the breathlessness, the expectation.

A sharp rattle made her jump. She looked down at the street. On the edge of the sidewalk, a palm tree shifted its fans. A gate squeaked and swung on its hinges. And a hot, harsh gust of wind raked her face. Then everything was still again except for the distant muttering thunder.

She opened windows on both sides of the house, then went downstairs. "Boy, Mama, there's a whopper of a storm coming. I'm going to open everything up. We'll have a breeze in no time."

But it did not come. The weird green air darkened, and dusk was premature. Garden turned on lamps. They added to the blanketing, suffocating heat. Margaret rearranged the Monopoly board for another game.

"Look at that, Mama." The curtains were stirring.

"It's about time," said Margaret. "The heat killed my appetite, and I have to keep my strength up. What are you going to fix for supper?"

Before Garden could answer, the wind came. Not a breeze, but a gust that sent the curtains sailing across the room and knocked over the lamp. Both Margaret and Garden let out screams. It did not subside, but blew steadily, hot and scratchy. Garden set the lamp upright. "Hold on to this. I'll close the shutters."

They banged when Garden released their latches; Garden jerked her hand away just in time. She adjusted the louvers to let the wind through. "It's getting cooler," she said.

Suddenly it was raining; sheets of water roared outside the window, drummed on the earth and pavement, battered the roof.

"At last!" Garden cried. "I'll go upstairs and shut the windows. Thank goodness. Feel that air, Mama, it's like a movie theater."

Garden stood in front of one of the windows on the north side of the house. It seemed a shame to close it; the rain was falling straight down, a curtain of refreshing water. None was coming in. But if the wind came back, it wouldn't take long to soak the rug. She tugged at the sash. The opposite windows were protected by the roof of the piazza; they could stay open. Garden went out onto the porch and felt her skin cooling off. It was glorious. She looked over the porch railing; the rain was so heavy that the house next door was invisible. The ten-day drought was ending with a bang, she thought.

A crash of thunder followed her thought. "With a bang," Garden said aloud, laughing. The tension that had built steadily with the long heat wave was broken. Perhaps her life was broken, too, but she did not have to face that until the next morning. Now she could appreciate the blessing of feeling cool again. She was even hungry. She went downstairs to fix supper.

"Garden, you'd better fill the bathtubs and some pails with tap water."

"Whatever for?"

"This isn't a regular rainstorm; it's a hurricane."

"Oh Mama, you always exaggerate so much."

"Don't get sassy with me. You do what I say."

Garden turned on the faucet in the bathtub. It was easy enough to humor her mother. The water bill was one that Margaret paid herself.

While she was cooking supper, the sound of the rain changed. It was still heavy, but not deafening. It gusted, then subsided. The wind was back.

The lights went out while they were eating. Garden had expected it as soon as the wind started up. She had some candles ready to light. Their flames danced in the drafts of cool air through the louvers. "I always thought it was such an adventure when there was a storm and we had to light candles. Remember on Tradd Street when Wentworth and Lucy were spending the night? We told ghost stories and screamed our heads off." Garden's fingers strayed automatically to the charm at her throat.

"I remember that you got wax all over the floor. Zanzie complained for a week."

There was a comfortable intimacy about sitting with her mother in the small circle of light while the wind and rain threw themselves at the strong old walls of the house. Garden drank her tepid coffee and lit a cigarette from the candle flame.

"Did you turn off the tub?"

"Yes, Mama."

"You'd better check the windows again. I don't want the wallpaper spotted."

"As soon as I finish my cigarette." The intimacy was no longer comfortable.

Garden heard the shutter banging when she was halfway up the stairs. She ran the rest of the way. The candle flickered behind her protecting, cupped palm. It was one of the piazza doors from the drawing room. She ran to stop it before it could shatter a window. Her candle went out.

When she stepped onto the piazza, the wind grabbed her and threw her against the wall of the house, tearing the breath from her mouth. The wind was a whine now, high and insistent, gnawing at the nerves. Garden felt a primitive terror of nature's power. It was still raining, raining on the piazza, into the drawing room. Garden felt it whip her face and body. It was like a million knives. This storm was like none she had ever known. She tried to cover her face, to protect her eyes from the sharp rain, but she could not move her hands. They were flattened against the wall on each side of her body, pinned there by the force of the wind.

Garden tried to turn her head, to escape the insistent whining. Beneath the high sound of the wind, she heard the low, steady, reverberating gong of St. Michael's bells. No, not bells—a single deep bell, ringing, ringing, ringing. She had never heard it before, but she knew what it was. It was the tocsin, the alarm, the warning to the old city to beware, hurricane was coming.

A fan of stiff fronds, a limb from a palm tree, flew at Garden. The jagged, torn end impaled itself in the tossing shutter near her shoulder, and the whipping fronds were flattened across her body. She tried to scream, but she had no breath.

Then, for an instant, she felt the pressure cease. The wind had halted, gathering its strength for a greater assault. Garden pushed away from the wall. Carrying tree limb and shutter with her, she staggered toward the open door. The wind returned, hurling her into the room and across it into a table, which went crashing to the floor.

109

"Garden? Garden, what on earth are you doing? Why didn't you fix that shutter? Why are you sprawled on the floor like that? It's not ladylike." Margaret held up the kerosene lamp in her hand to look at the wreckage. "Good heavens, you're all bloody. I hope I've got some iodine."

"Mama, it's a hurricane."

"Well, I told you that. Get up. We've got a lot to do. You've never been through a real hurricane, but I have. I know what to do. We have to get to work. I'm not about to have my nice rugs ruined."

It seemed to Garden that they worked for a hundred hours. Trimming wicks and filling lamps, rolling up rugs and lifting them onto mantels, piling furniture in corners away from windows, taking down curtains, nailing diagonal braces across the storm shutters that were stored in the attic. Tiny Margaret was a dynamo of energy. She lifted and shoved and pulled with Garden, outstripping her younger, stronger daughter in every way. There was no mention of her heart.

When she was satisfied that everything was done that could be done, Margaret said, "Well. This house has weathered plenty of storms before this one. One more won't bother it. Let's go downstairs and look in the icebox. I'm certainly glad I didn't get one of those newfangled electric refrigerators, like you. With the lights out, all your food's going to spoil."

"Are you hungry?" Garden was appalled. Hunger was too ordinary for a night of tempest.

"Starving. We might as well have something to eat, because we'll be up all night. It's going to be too noisy to sleep. We'll play Monopoly."

The wind was battering at the house, shaking the boarded-up windows, trying to get in. Garden was terrified.

"Don't look like you'd seen a ghost, Garden. Come on. We have to sit it out, that's all. This is just the beginning. It'll get much worse."

Garden didn't believe her. Nothing could be worse than the ferocious attack that the storm was making. She soon learned that Margaret was right. The whining of the wind modulated to a roar that steadily deepened in pitch and heightened in intensity. The hurricane became a beast, ravening, maddened by the thick walls, constantly striking, searching for the weakness that would open a breach. Terrible blows hit the house as flying objects were hurled against it. Garden winced at each one. Then there was an explosion. "Oh, God," Garden cried.

"That was a window. Hurry, Garden, we've got to plug it up." Margaret gathered up the fern-printed curtains that had blown down and ran to the hallway. Garden brought a lantern. Halfway up to the second floor, the rain was pouring in, cascading down the stairs, bearing bits of broken glass with it.

"Help me," Margaret cried. Garden took the curtains from her and stuffed them into the jagged hole with strength born of desperate fear.

"It'll never hold," Margaret said. "We've got to nail something over it. Get the leaf from the kitchen table. I'll hold the plug."

Somehow they managed to wedge the plank in and nail it. But it was shaking, threatening to tear loose, and no number of nails would make any difference.

"Mama, I'm scared," Garden said.

Then Margaret frightened her even more. "I am too," she said.

There was no Monopoly, no sandwich snack, no respite from fear. Mother and daughter huddled together on the floor in the living room, surrounded by a wall of sofas and upholstered chairs, feeling the fragility of their defenses against the relentless pressure of the wind. Their ears popped again and again; they hurt from the hours of listening. The winds tore across the wide harbor and battered themselves against the proud tall houses of Charleston's waterfront. Garden was tortured by thoughts of Helen. "Please, God," she prayed, "let her be all right. Don't let her be too frightened. I'll let her go. I'll be glad. If only she's not hurt, I won't ask for anything else."

It stopped. Everything. The rain. The wind. The noise. In an instant, it was gone. Garden shielded her eyes against a ray of blinding sunlight.

"What happened?" she said. Her voice sounded horribly loud.

Margaret was crying. "Oh, my God, we've made it. The walls did not give. Come on, Garden, we don't have much time. We have to look at the damage."

"I don't understand. Is it over? It's so quiet I want to scream."

"Scream when it starts again. Then I won't hear you. This is the eye, the center of the hurricane. I don't know how long it takes to pass over, but it can't be long. Then it starts again, only stronger."

They ran frantically from room to room, putting buckets under leaks, hammering more nails in the splintered storm shutters, wadding a quilt behind the table leaf over the broken window. They worked especially hard on the room they had used for refuge. Garden threw all the bed pillows and chair cushions down the stairwell, and Margaret piled them inside the rampart they had made, making an inner wall. They opened umbrellas then, to give themselves a roof against flying debris if the storm shutters gave. Quilts covered the umbrellas.

"Get some water in a bottle. We'll get thirsty before it's over." Margaret was decisive again. "Now we'd better get in our hole. There won't be any warning." The bright sunlight seemed to mock them. It made the imminent menace more horrifying.

Just as they arranged the roof of their shelter, a new sound made them stare wildly into each other's faces. It was the knocker on the front door. The everyday normality of it was insanely incongruous, like the sunshine.

"Helen," Garden cried. "Something's happened to Helen." She clawed her way out of the cocoon of pillows and quilts.

Margaret followed her, shouting. "Don't open that door, Garden. If the storm comes, it will be in the house."

But Garden was already sliding the bolts and wrenching at the heavy doorknob.

She blinked at the light that poured in. The sky overhead was a brilliant clear blue with clouds of white sea gulls flying across it, crying in agitation. "You're not even dressed, Garden. I'm not surprised. I thought you'd be afraid to show up, so I came to get you. I want to watch your face. We're due at the courthouse in half an hour." It was Vicki, in her grandmother disguise.

Margaret reached past Garden and jerked Vicki inside. She slammed the door closed and bolted it. "Wait a minute. What do you think you're doing?" Vicki snarled. She tugged at the door bolt.

Margaret hit Vicki's arm with her fist. "You fool. You'll get us all killed."

Vicki threw her off. "You're the fool. Don't you know the storm's over? Open this door and you'll see." She pulled the bolt from its latch.

Garden did not think. All the pain and anger in her heart surged into a backhanded blow that knocked Vicki to the floor. Margaret shot the bolt. And the hurricane struck.

The door bulged inward, but it held. Vicki scrambled away from it on her hands and knees, her mouth open in a scream that could not be heard amid the din of blows on the door. Across the street the weakened seawall was breaking up, and the wind made missiles of its giant rocks.

Vicki followed Margaret and Garden to the protected area they had constructed and squeezed herself in with them. There was no time for personal animosities. The three women leaned on each other, trying to make themselves as small as possible against the storm. The great rocks continued to barrage the house. The walls shook at each impact.

And a new enemy appeared. Water seeped under the heavy front door, the doors to the ground-floor piazza, the door to the kitchen yard. It converged silently on the barricades of pillows and furniture and then inside.

They abandoned the nest of pillows when the water reached their ankles. Still holding on to each other, they stumbled across the hall, past the front door, now groaning against its hinges. At the stairs, they broke free to run. The walls that enclosed the staircase felt as thin as paper to them. Exposed on three sides, the projecting bay was shuddering.

Vicki was the last to get above the patched window. It blew out, sending the table leaf and sodden quilt spiraling in the stairwell. The wind picked up the carpet from the center of the stairs and shredded it.

All around them, they heard the loud explosions of windows breaking. Margaret ran and Garden and Vicki followed.

She led them to the drawing room, the biggest room where they could be farthest away from the vulnerable windows. They crouched in the center of the one windowless wall, in front of the fireplace, with water pouring down the chimney to form puddles around their buttocks and legs. Margaret and Garden pulled the rug down from the mantel as a tent against flying glass, and the three women covered themselves. Then they could only wait.

There was no reality but the hurricane. No time, no place, no discomfort, no cold, hunger, thirst. There was only the savagery of the storm, punctuated by exploding glass. Then the hurricane was inside with them, kept away only by the rug.

After an eternity, the uproar began to abate, but they did not know it. They were deaf to distinctions.

Then Vicki heard the sound of water pouring down the chimney. "Hey!" she said. Margaret and Garden stirred. "Hey, it's slowing down." Vicki pushed at the rug tent, and it fell away from them.

She stretched her cramped limbs. "Christ, I'm stiff as a board," she groaned. She crawled forward, away from the water around the fireplace, and got to her feet. Garden and Margaret followed her movements with dazed eyes. They could see her clearly. There was light through a gaping window, denuded of its glass. Outside the window, rain was falling and wind gusting, no more than a heavy rainstorm.

"It's really over," said Garden. She hugged her mother. "Over. We made it. Helen must have made it, too."

"She damn well better have made it," Vicki said. "I'm taking her home with me tomorrow. My lawyers are positive. I won the trial, you know, Garden. You couldn't have doubted it. It was a sure thing from the beginning."

Garden could not answer.

Vicki walked around the room, smiling at the damage. The walls and ceiling were stained with water, the floors gouged by broken glass, the furniture thrown and broken by the wind that had come through the window.

"I never thought I'd be grateful to a hurricane, but I am," Vicki said. "It infuriated me when Schuyler bought you this house. And then, when I couldn't take it away from you, I was wild.

"But now look. It's ruined. A wreck. What a clean sweep. I'll have Helen, the Tradds will have nothing."

"This house has nothing to do with the Tradds," said Margaret. "It was built by my family, and it is known by my family's name. This is the Garden house."

Vicki stood in the center of the room and flung out her arms. "Some mess to be so proud of, Mrs. Tradd." She threw her head back and laughed. Then her face froze. Her arms stretched upward. "No!" she cried.

Garden looked at the focus of Vicki's gaze. The chandelier was swinging wildly as the tremendous garland of plaster gardenias caved inward, weighted by the water that had flooded the floor above.

Vicki tried to run; her heel caught in a deep cut in the floor. A gardenia hit her shoulder and knocked her off balance and onto the floor.

The avalanche of plaster sounded like the roar of a train. It was sodden, and there was no dust; it buried the beautiful cobweb of crystal that had centered it, and Vicki, under a gray mound of jagged chunks.

Garden and Margaret stared, unbelieving. Then Garden made a small, frightened, mewling sound and propelled herself forward on her cramped legs. She fell, struggled to her hands and knees and crawled to the pile of debris.

"Help me," she begged Margaret; she grabbed a big block of plaster and threw it to one side.

"I hope she suffocates," said Margaret.

Garden dug. The rough edges of the pieces tore her hands.

Then she gagged and fell back.

Vicki's head was exposed. Her gray hair was still in its neat waves, but bits of gray plaster clung to it and marred its freshness. Her eyes were open, staring up at the huge hole in the ceiling. A sliver of crystal glittered in the dim light. It was in the center of the pupil of the left eye. A glaze misted the iris. The flesh on her face sagged from the bones in the final slackness of death.

110

"You'll never guess how I got here," Garden said to Elizabeth. "Ed Campbell was paddling his sailboat along to look at the break in the seawall, and I gave him a shout from the piazza. He came right over and got me. It was better than Venice." She held Helen on her lap, kissing the top of her head every few minutes. Helen was squirming.

"Let her go," said Elizabeth. "You're making her fidget."

Garden set Helen down, watched her scamper away.

"She's not going far," Elizabeth said. "We'll be marooned for some time."

The streets were four feet deep in water. Broken tree limbs formed clogs against houses, and on street-level floors, furniture floated in bobbing motion as boats passed, sending out waves. In Elizabeth's house the ground floor was only fourteen inches underwater. She and Garden were in the drawing room on the second floor. Helen had run to the piazza and was looking down enviously at three twelve-year-old boys floating in inner tubes.

"Things will never get dried out," Garden said. "At Mama's, even the walls are wet. The paper is peeling off all by itself."

"You'll be surprised," Elizabeth said. "Charleston is used to making comebacks. There are already boats with milk and groceries that you can eat without cooking. You just holler down what you want and let down a basket. Would you like a peach?"

Two days later, the streets were steaming as the sun dried the last of the dampness. The whole city hummed with the sound of hammers and brooms; rugs hung over porch rails on every piazza. It was like a fair, with people calling greetings and street vendors crying their wares.

Garden walked along Meeting Street toward Chalmers. She had a mop and a broom across her shoulder, and she was wearing an old smock over her beach slacks. Lowcountry Treasures was at street level, and she expected the worst.

She found it. A stench of mildew and rot flowed from the door when she opened it. The stiff, bloated body of a drowned mouse was on the threshold.

"Ugh," she said. And started to work.

"Excuse me, ma'am. Is this the store that has all the nice slime for sale?"

"John! No, don't come in, everything's filthy. I'm filthy." John ignored her warning, and kissed her thoroughly.

"Now you're filthy, too. You might as well kiss me again." He did not ignore the invitation.

Then he stepped back to look at her. "I've been half crazy worrying about you, you gorgeous creature. I tried the telephone, but half the phones downtown still aren't working. And the road is an unholy mess. But I got to town. Then I went to your mother's and heard what an ungrateful wretch you were to leave her, and then I went to Elizabeth's, and Helen told me how cruel you were not to let her go swimming in the street, and now I've finally found you. You're lucky that I like you so much; you're on everybody else's blacklist."

"Did you hear about what happened?"

"Vicki? Yes. I did shut Helen up long enough to talk with Elizabeth. I don't know what to say. 'I'm sorry' isn't true. 'I'm glad' isn't exactly true either."

"It's over. There's nothing else to say. I'm glad it's over, and I don't think about how or why. I'm so glad to see you. It's been so long." She put her head on his shoulder. "Hugs," she demanded.

"Garden."

"Hugs." John crushed her with a strength that told her something was wrong. There was something despairing about the intensity of his embrace. She freed herself, looked at him. "What is it, John?"

He started to speak, stopped, made a choked exclamation. "Hell!" Then he took a deep breath. "I'm leaving, Garden," he said. "I got my orders three weeks ago, but I couldn't tell you, not with the trial coming up. I'm going to San Diego. I'm getting my first command, a destroyer.

"You know what I want. You know how I feel. I can't play waiting games any longer, Garden. Will you come with me? You've

571

got to decide now. We can be married, then go to California together, all of us, you, me, Helen. It's a great train ride. And a great life. But it has to be now."

Garden shook her head. "I can't decide, just like that. It's not fair to ask me to."

"It's not 'just like that' and you know it, Garden. I've been asking you to decide for a long time."

"But I've got so many things pressuring me, John. I haven't had a chance to recover from the whole Vicki business or Mama's sickness . . ."

"There are always pressures, Garden. I guess I'm another one. Tell me. Is it yes or is it no?"

"I can't think."

"I'll make it simpler. Is it yes? Yes, John, I love you and will marry you. Is it?"

Garden opened her hands, a gesture of helplessness. She didn't speak.

"That's my answer then," said John curtly. "Goodbye, Garden."

"Wait!"

"For what? I don't want to make your life harder, and I don't want our last time together to end up in denunciations. I'm going. It's easier for us both to make it quick."

It's not fair, Garden cried silently. I can't stand it if he goes. But I can't go with him. I can't leave home just when I've found it. John's wrong to force me. He's not even trying to understand. He's bullying me. Well, I won't let him. I won't stand for it.

She attacked the mess in the shop with a burst of angry energy. When the daylight was beginning to fade, she had almost finished. The furniture gleamed with polish; attractive arrangements of glass and porcelain reflected in the finish. The floor was clean, and the window. She sighed and shrugged. It was all she could do for now.

I won't cry, she said to herself. Then she sat at her desk, put her head on her arms and wept.

"Whew, Garden, go bathe right now. You're rank."

"Aunt Elizabeth, I need to talk to you."

"I see. Serious. What is it, dear?"

Garden talked and cried and talked some more, spilling her dilemma into Elizabeth's capable hands and wise heart.

"Garden, what are you asking me? What I would do? You know

572

what I would do, what I did. I kept my life my own. I believe it's the best way to live.

"But if you're asking me what you should do, then you're both impertinent and a fool. You have no right to impose responsibility for your future happiness on me. Nor have you any right to feel sorry for yourself and helpless. You have to make a choice. Count yourself lucky. Most people in this world have to take what life deals them and make the best of it. You have options. Thank God for it. And make your own decision."

Garden's temper flared. "You aren't even trying to understand. You're as bad as John. It's not that simple. I can't just make up my mind for myself. I have to think about Helen. She has friends here, a good life, a future where she'll have a place she belongs. And I have to think about Mama. No matter what there is or isn't between us, I have a responsibility to her. Peggy's gone. I'm the only one . . ."

Elizabeth was laughing.

Garden wanted to strangle her. "What the merry hell is so god-damned funny, may I ask?"

Elizabeth held out her hand. "Come with me," she said.

Garden would not take her hand, but she followed, stamping truculently up the stairs behind her great-aunt. Elizabeth pointed into the room that Garden had slept in when she first returned to Charleston.

Margaret Tradd was sitting in a chair by the bed, a bowl in one hand and a spoon in the other. "Now don't be naughty, or you'll make me cry," she said to the redheaded, red-bearded man in the bed. "Open your mouth, and I'll feed you this nice hominy. You know you love it. I remember when you'd eat yours and mine too."

"That's your uncle," Elizabeth whispered to Garden. "Anson Tradd. Everybody thought he'd been dead for a million years. He ran off, and he's been living at Folly Beach, calling himself John Smith, or something equally original.

"The hurricane destroyed the shack he was living in, and he got a terrific whack on the head. It knocked him so silly that he forgot and gave the Red Cross his real name. They patched him up and took him to the only Tradd in the phone book, your mother. Can you believe it? She brought him here because she couldn't keep him at her house, she said, without a chaperone. At their ages! It's too funny."

Garden looked at her mother. Margaret had a ribbon in her hair and a glow on her face. She looked like a girl in her twenties. Anson

573

Tradd opened his mouth and accepted the spoonful of grits. He looked at Margaret with adoring eyes.

"So you see, Garden," Elizabeth said, "your dear mama has someone to bully who will absolutely eat it up. She doesn't need you at all, except maybe as a bridesmaid. She'll have Anson at the altar before they take the stitches out of his head—Garden, where are you going in such a rush and racket?"

Garden stopped on the stairs and looked up at Elizabeth. "There must be a phone somewhere in this neighborhood that works. I'm going to find it and call my sailor to see if his offer still stands. You're you, and I'm me, Aunt Elizabeth."

Elizabeth smiled. "I could have told you that," she said. "As a matter of fact, I believe I did. . . . Godspeed, my dear."